Zemindar

Zemindar is drawn from personal experience. Valerie Fitzgerald's grandmother lived through the Indian Mutiny. When her soldier father was posted to Lucknow in World War Two, she spent winters in the city and summers on a zemindari. She now lives in Ottawa, Canada.

VALERIE FITZGERALD

Zemindar

HEAD
of
ZEUS

This book is for my father

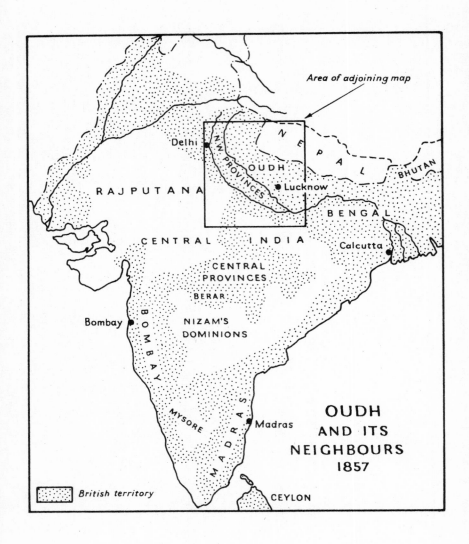

Area of adjoining map

NEPAL

Delhi

N.W. PROVINCES

OUDH

Lucknow

BHUTAN

RAJPUTANA

BENGAL

CENTRAL   INDIA

Calcutta

CENTRAL
PROVINCES

BERAR

Bombay

NIZAM'S
DOMINIONS

BOMBAY

OUDH
AND ITS
NEIGHBOURS
1857

MYSORE

MADRAS

Madras

British territory

CEYLON

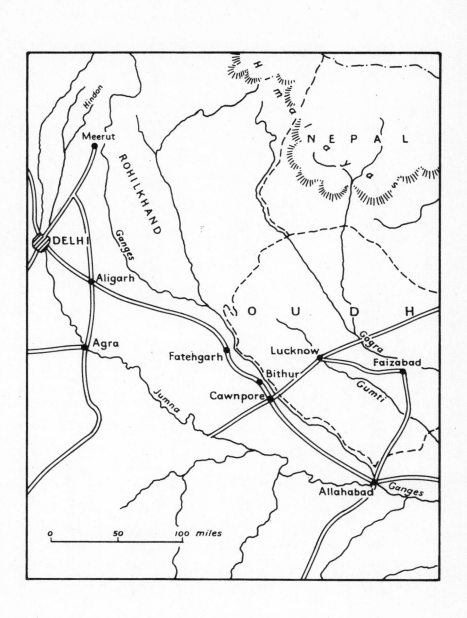

Hindon

Meerut

ROHILKHAND

Ganges

DELHI

Aligarh

H m a l a y a s

NEPAL

O   U   D   H

Agra

Fatehgarh

Lucknow

Gogra

Faizabad

Bithur

Gumti

Cawnpore

Jumna

Allahabad

Ganges

0   50   100 miles

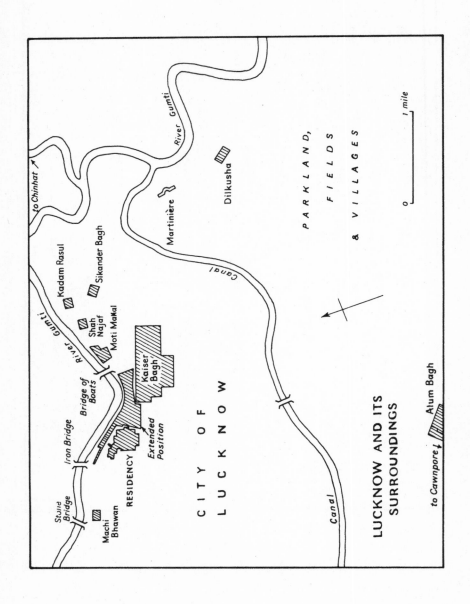

Stone Bridge

Machi Bhawan

Iron Bridge

River Gumti

Bridge of Boats

RESIDENCY

Extended Position

Moti Makal

Shah Najaf

Kadam Rasul

Sikander Bagh

CITY OF LUCKNOW

Kaiser Bagh

Martinière

Dilkusha

River Gumti

to Chinhat

Canal

PARKLAND, FIELDS & VILLAGES

Canal

to Cawnpore ⅓   Alum Bagh

0   1 mile

LUCKNOW AND ITS SURROUNDINGS

BOOK I

LANDFALL

'… all the present time is a point
in eternity. All things are little,
changeable, perishable.'

Marcus Aurelius

CHAPTER 1

'Landfall! ... Miss Hewitt! ... At last we have landfall!'

Mr Roberts waved to me jubilantly as I appeared on deck and walked towards him where he leant on the rail gazing intently at the horizon.

Though it was still very early in the morning, scarcely more than dawn by English standards, it was already hot, and a haze born of the heat sapped the colours of sea and sky and effectively obscured my first and long-awaited glimpse of our destination.

'But where?' I shaded my eyes from the glare of the water and peered in the direction to which my companion pointed. 'I can see nothing. Are you sure?'

'Quite sure. You just missed the look-out's shout from the crow's nest—about a quarter of an hour ago—but I think I caught a glimpse of the coast a moment since. It has disappeared again—no—there it is! Look—that small smudge of darker grey low down near the water? Do you see it?'

'I see something, but surely that cannot be land? It looks as insubstantial as the haze itself.'

'Ah, but it's land for all that! I'm sure of it now—and so is the crew. See them crowding the rails! That is India, Miss Hewitt. India on the horizon!'

Quite spontaneously we turned to each other and shook hands, as though we had something to congratulate ourselves upon. And indeed, looking back on the long journey of more than five months' duration, most of it accomplished in bad weather and all in circumstances of discomfort, perhaps we had.

The Indiaman on which we had embarked from the Pool of London the previous April was old and dirty and still stank of the hides and skins that had formed a previous cargo. For weeks, as we bucketed down the western coast of Africa, every board and beam had squeaked and squealed in an agony of protesting age; and then, when we had rounded the Cape of Good Hope and turned northward again, the great winds of the south-west monsoon had bellied our patched sails to bursting, and, though we had made good time, the vessel, ill-balanced and forced beyond its capacity as it was, vented its rage at the elements on its twelve unhappy passengers. Few of us saw much of the sky between Cape Town and Calcutta, and of those few only two can have been said to have enjoyed the voyage—Mr Roberts and myself.

Not that I was entirely immune to *mal de mer* myself; but I had discovered early on the voyage that I could keep my feet pretty comfortably as long as I was in the fresh air. Thus I had formed the habit of settling my cousin Emily for the day in what scanty comfort her hot and airless cabin could provide, and then taking myself up on deck until the midday meal. Sometimes, indeed, I found it more prudent to miss the meal altogether, but whether because I soon became accustomed to the motion of the ship, or whether because I was constitutionally a better sailor than the others, by the time we were in the foul weather of the Indian Ocean, when all the hatches were battened and the ports shuttered, I was still able to rise, dress and pass the day in the unpleasantly close atmosphere of the saloon rather than in my bed.

Mr Roberts never turned a hair whatever the weather, and so, thrown much together as we were, and over a long period, a forced acquaintance had developed into a genuine friendship.

I dread to think what my state of *ennui* and frustration would have been had someone other than Mr Roberts kept me company over those long weeks. Of the remainder of the passengers, few would have been as pleasant and none as interesting.

There were only two ladies aboard apart from Emily and myself: Mrs Wilkins and her daughter Elvira, both of whom had suffered continuously and severely from sea-sickness. On embarkation they had had with them a ladies' maid, a pathetic little orphan girl named Jepthah. But at Cape Town Jepthah, having endured the rigours of her own and her employers' ill health for several weeks, was granted leave of absence to see the sights, and with commendable resourcefulness had neglected to return to the ship—which, despite the wails, threats and maledictions of the Wilkinses, sailed away without her.

At the time this happened I could afford to be amused at Jepthah's defection and hoped she would be happy in her new environment. But within days I had occasion to wish the young woman had possessed more staying power, for, being the only female aboard capable of helping them, I could not in common charity neglect to assist Mrs Wilkins and her daughter, who were both by this time unable to do anything for themselves. Though they were not as demanding as my cousin Emily, anyone who has had to nurse a bad sailor on a long voyage will realize that my duties were far from pleasant. Even when the weather improved, they remained so debilitated that they could do nothing but lie on their hard cots and try to regain strength with the aid of gruel prepared in the galley by a kind cook and port wine donated by a kind captain. I sat with them for a brief period each evening, but the better I got to know them, the gladder I was that it was Mr Roberts who was my usual companion.

Mrs Wilkins was an 'old India hand' (as she was fond of describing herself) and with the misplaced assurance of the vulgar, took it upon herself to enlighten me as to the customs and character of that country—volubly, enthusiastically and, as I was to discover, inaccurately. For Mrs Wilkins belonged to that class of female, all too frequent among our countrywomen, who can travel the world and spend a lifetime doing it, then return to Surrey or Kent as totally innocent of any enlarging experience, of even their own character, as when they first left the shores of England. The boundaries they set themselves in Bokhara or Bombay are the selfsame with which they guard their nonentity in Bristol or Brighton—children and servants, social *mores* and petty scandals—and their minds remain unopened by rational curiosity and imprisoned by mean suspicion of the people they are (generally) well paid to live among.

Of such was Mrs Wilkins, and her daughter Elvira, anaemic and silly, had small chance of making better use of her opportunities.

Our male co-travellers were no more promising than the Wilkins ladies. There were two army men returning to their regiments, and still showing, despite a year's furlough, the ravages of tertiary ague or other tropical fevers; a couple of young clerks going out to commercial concerns in Calcutta (very brash these, with hair as brightly polished as their patent-leather boots); and two elderly brothers who, after a lifetime in India, had retired to Shoreham-on-Sea, but after one winter had decided to return to the more familiar infelicities of the East. They were reputedly very wealthy and obviously seldom sober.

Small wonder I was grateful for the company of Mr Roberts.

Mr Roberts was a middle-aged widower with two daughters safely married in England. By avocation he was an indigo factor, though he had started life as a 'writer' in the service of the East India Company, and his work took him all over the north-eastern regions of India, following the course of the great River Ganges and its tributaries. From his conversation I learned that as well as buying indigo crops, both raw and processed, from established planters, a part of his time was spent in promoting new plantations in untried areas and advising on the cultivation of this plant, which provides the blue dye used to colour the uniforms of our navy and those of most of the navies of the world, including Russia and America.

He was a quiet man with gentle ways, very self-contained, of medium build and neat appearance. When I knew him better, for all his quietness I found he could talk well on the subjects which interested him and discovered also that he was possessed of a wealth of knowledge about India and a depth of sympathy for its people that astonished me. Ignorant as I was of everything pertaining to the sub-continent, innocent—when I left England—of any but the haziest generalizatons of what I would find at the end of the voyage, Mr Roberts took me in hand, and as we huddled in our mackinaws on the gale-swept deck or took our lonely meals in the heaving cabin while the lantern swung violently above our heads, he educated me with tact and humour and that enthusiasm which comes of real affection for one's subject. By the time the morning dawned when land was at last in sight, I had accumulated a fair knowledge of the geography of India, more than a mere inkling of its complex history, and a great desire to learn for myself something of its diverse and gifted people.

There was little to distract me from Mr Roberts's teaching. He was the type of man who carries a small library with him wherever he goes, and when I was not actually talking to him, I was reading one or other of the numerous volumes he was pleased to lend me. Of course, for a time, part of my day was occupied by the Wilkinses and always I had to listen for the tinkle of Emily's little silver bell summoning me to do some service for her, which, with a little more hardihood, she could as well have done for herself. But on the whole I was free to apply myself to my studies of Mr Roberts's books and listen to his conversation, and, because I knew that otherwise I would have spent too much time thinking of Charles, I was grateful for both diversions.

By the time we neared the coast of India, I had become accustomed to the sight of Emily and Charles together. It was no longer necessary for me to avoid his nearness for fear of betraying myself, and if I still hung on the sound of his voice or allowed my eye to linger a little too long on his face, it was but seldom, and I prided myself that no one seeing us together could have guessed the true nature of my feelings for my cousin's husband—least of all Charles himself.

Not that I could delude myself that my love for him had dissipated, let alone disappeared. At night, as I waited for sleep, it was still impossible for me to stifle my memories of the time, not so long ago, when I had known myself to be the magnet that drew him to Mount Bellew. Who knows, perhaps in those early days his interest in me, his apparent regard for me, were genuine? But then Emily came back from the holiday she had been spending with relatives in Bournemouth. Emily was seventeen and beautiful and gay, and so sure of her ability to charm that it was taken for granted that Charles would fall in love with her.

And he had.

I think he was bewitched by her the very first time he saw her, when she was wearing a muslin gown sprigged with small cherries and tied with cherry-coloured ribbons, sitting in a hammock slung between the two great spreading cedars on the Mount Bellew lawn. One small foot in its bronze boot tiptoed the grass and kept the hammock swinging, and on her lap she held a blue bowl of polished red apples. I had recognized Charles's step coming towards us over the grey flags of the terrace, and my heart had leapt, knowing he was searching for me. Instead he had found Emily.

All I had to be grateful for in the weeks that followed was the fact that I had never betrayed my feelings—either to Charles or my relatives. It was a bitter time for me. Within two months Charles and Emily were engaged, and within six had married. My aunt, reluctant to see her adored only daughter leave home, had tried to delay matters. My uncle, however, aware of Emily's 'giddiness', and perhaps knowing that if she remained at home she would become even more spoilt by her mother and brothers, had declared the match a capital one and furthered it by every means.

As it happened, that circumspection for which I had been so grateful, that reluctance to reveal my feelings even to those nearest me, was my undoing.

Charles's mother, the redoubtable Mrs Flood of Dissham Manor, suddenly decreed that the wedding journey should take the happy couple not to Paris, the Rhine or Italy, but to India. There were several reasons for this decision. To begin with, Charles had recently taken up a position in the firm of Hewitt, Flood & Hewitt, Importers and Agents, of which my uncle was a Director, as had been the late Mr Flood, Charles's father. Both families concurred that the young man would benefit from a closer knowledge of the country with which most of the firm's business was conducted. 'A great experience; a *necessary* experience!' my uncle had declared. 'Why, it will give the lad a head start over every other young feller in the City. If he plays his cards right, he could even end up on the Board of Directors of the Company itself.'

Mrs Flood also had another reason, which I believe was more cogent than her son's career in Hewitt, Flood & Hewitt. She had a son by a previous marriage, a man much older than Charles, who was resident in India. We knew little of this gentleman and, according to Charles, that little was as much as he knew himself, for he had never met his half-brother. It was known, however, that he was a wealthy man, in possession of large estates in Oudh, unmarried and therefore inevitably, in Mrs Flood's mind, in need of an heir. And being Mrs Flood, she did not trouble to disguise the fact that she very much hoped, as in this instance she could not command, that her elder son would see fit to make her younger son that heir. Once thought of, the matter was settled as far as she was concerned, but I had my doubts. After all, the elder son would not be so old that marriage could be entirely precluded, but it was no business of mine, so I said nothing.

My Aunt Hewitt, however, had a great deal to say about the whole enterprise. She was against the idea of Emily even visiting India, but, when she found that her daughter might even have to live in India, her agitation was great.

'Not at all a likely contingency,' my uncle reassured her. 'There was something "off" about that whole business, don't you remember? Never did get to the bottom of it, but some quarrel about the guardianship of the boy and so on when the first husband died, and

Maud was never allowed to have the lad at Dissham. French blood somewhere!' he concluded as though this explained all.

Uncomforted, Emily's mother continued to protest. Emily was scarcely eighteen; she had seldom left home and then only for the houses of her relatives; it was unthinkable that she should be required to make a long voyage to a barbarous and unhealthy country on her own. Besides, Emily was impractical, untried. Aunt Hewitt even went so far as to admit that her daughter was headstrong and wilful.

At last, when all other arguments had failed, my uncle suggested a 'companion'. Somewhat soothed, my aunt immediately advertised, and a succession of respectable females was interviewed. A sensible widow, who had spent some years in India, was engaged, and preparations for the wedding went ahead. Then, just three weeks before the young Floods were due to embark, the widow sent her regrets; she would be unable to accompany the couple as her health had suffered a sudden deterioration and her doctors forbade it. My aunt took to her room and had the vapours for an entire afternoon; my uncle fumed; and Emily rejoiced openly at the defection of the lady whom she had already dubbed 'the Gorgon'.

Then they thought of me, Laura Hewitt, and wondered why I had not been considered earlier. At twenty-four years of age I could be counted upon to have some common sense and decorum, I was fond of Emily and knew her ways, and had I not done some travelling myself, coming all the way from Genoa, alone, when I was just Emily's age? Above all, Emily would not object to having me with her.

I had protested with all sincerity against being made part of the wedding journey, but as the true reasons for my reluctance could not be divulged, those that I gave lacked urgency. Moreover, though I foresaw the suffering that constant proximity to Charles could mean for me, though I realized the dissimulation and pretended lack of feeling might prove too much for me, yet beneath and beyond my fears and anxieties I discovered a bittersweet joy in knowing that I would be near him. No wonder my arguments against going were not forceful enough to deflect my relatives from sending me. So, with much haste, I too was fitted out and prepared for a long absence from home.

Towards the end of the voyage, as we sailed north-east in the Indian Ocean, Charles took to joining Mr Roberts and myself as we promenaded the deck each fine morning. Emily, finding the heat too much for her and fearing for her complexion, spent most of her time in her cabin or the sparsely furnished saloon, garnering criticisms of her fellow travellers. While he was ill, Charles had paid no thought to how I was passing my time, but now that he was up and about, I found he seemed to resent the pleasure I found in Mr Roberts's company. I could see no reason for this resentment; he knew nothing detrimental of my friend. But I learned to dread his appearance as our comfortable conversations *à deux* necessarily came to an end, and what followed too often became mere argument between Charles and Mr Roberts in which I would take no part. I could not hide from myself that Charles, speaking out of ignorance and prejudice, had no right to engage in dispute about things Indian with a man as well-informed and just of mind as my friend. The trend of Mr Roberts's mind was to inform—not to contend—and often I was embarrassed into silence by the forbearance of the one and the unthinking arrogance of the other. Mr Roberts, typically, saw into my mind and tried to ease it.

'You must not be so sensitive, Miss Hewitt,' he said, watching Charles stride away in a pet after a particularly silly argument about caste, a matter about which Charles conceivably knew less than I did, which was next to nothing.

'Mr Flood is mistaken, but entitled to his opinion, after all.'

'Not when it is based on prejudice alone,' I disagreed.

'Then why did you not tell him so?'

'Because I thought you would,' I answered.

'Oh, no! My dear Miss Hewitt, I am far too old to tell a young man he doesn't know what he is talking about. He is bound to find it out in due course, and more or less painfully no doubt.'

'I admire your self-control,' I said unhappily, not caring to see my idol's feet of clay so obviously apparent.

'You must not mind when men disagree; they do it all the time, and generally are the better for it.'

'But ... but he made himself look a fool!' I burst out.

Mr Roberts laughed. 'Ah, yes, that's the barb! And you think that some of the foolishness must attach itself to you? Isn't that it? But, Miss Hewitt, none of us is responsible for our relations, even less our relations by marriage. You must not expect them to behave as you would, understand the things in which you are interested—merely because you are connected with them. That is beyond the capacity of human nature, and the family, as you must know by now, is the field most likely to give rise to contention and … er … embarrassment.'

We left it at that. Mr Roberts was in many ways a wise man, but not where the young female heart was concerned.

At breakfast on that steamy August morning when we first sighted land, all the passengers took their places at the table except the two old 'Bengal civilians', who never appeared before midday. All knew by then that landfall had been achieved, and an air of relieved cheerfulness pervaded the party. Even the salt beef, ship's biscuits and dried apricots went down more easily now that we had the prospect of fresh vegetables and good meat so near.

'Oh, Miss Hewitt,' said Elvira Wilkins as she sprinkled sugar on to her apricots, 'what a treat I can promise you when you taste your first mango! It is quite the queen of fruits.'

'Not better than the peach, surely?' objected Emily, who was inclined to resent the imputation that anything could be superior that was not English.

'Oh, vastly, I assure you!' said Elvira innocently. 'It combines something of the peach and the plum while being quite unlike either. There is no describing it—except in superlatives.' I watched her curiously as she ladled her apricots into her mouth. Like many thin and bloodless people, she had a hearty appetite, and spent a large part of her time, now that she was recovered from the sea-sickness, thinking and talking about food. I was about to say I looked forward to my first experience of this exotic fruit, when Elvira's mother broke in.

'Now don't believe a word of it. Nasty things mangoes are; resinous at one end and apt to give you the runs!'

'Mama!' expostulated Elvira, blushing to the roots of her thin hair, while the two young clerks giggled, the military men looked pained and Emily pretended not to have heard.

'Well now, and so they do, as everyone well knows! What's more, you eat too much of 'em and you get dreadful sores, big as florins, all up your legs. It happened to me, and I have the scars still!'

For a horrid moment I was afraid Mrs Wilkins was going to display these mementos of intemperate mango eating, but Mr Roberts came to the rescue.

19

'Well, what about lychees, Mrs Wilkins? Do you care for them?'

'They look right pretty growing, that I'll allow. Like huge bunches of cherries with hard, knobbly skins.'

'How curious,' said Emily. 'What are they like inside?'

'Eyeballs!' grunted Mrs Wilkins, and everyone laughed. Yet it transpired that, when peeled, this fruit did resemble the human eyeball, but bore a large brown stone at its centre.

Then everyone who had been to India before came forward with their own experiences of various gustatory delights, from which it was but a short step to our being warned of how to deal with all the evils prevalent in the country, from pests to the plague, and since disaster is so much more dramatic a possibility for general conversation than food, I rose from the table with my head full of half-credible stories of snakes lying coiled in shoes, scorpions lurking in the folds of a dress, mad dogs rushing through city streets, heat that killed hundreds, rain that washed away whole towns, and noseless lepers begging at every corner.

But, despite these horrors, we were assured that no luxury known to our Western world was unobtainable in India provided one had the money to pay for it, and the country itself produced all manner of refinements to living unknown in England. The interest and anticipation aroused in me by Mr Roberts's scholarly accounts of the country were now whetted by the more trivial reports of our fellow travellers, so that it was with some impatience that I watched, all through that day, the coastline grow gradually nearer.

By nightfall we could see the winking lights of coastal villages and, when we had dined, the night being fine, we sat on deck watching the pinpoints of gold advance and recede mysteriously under the stars as we skirted the convolutions of the land.

Black water, silver crested, lapped languidly against the aged timbers of the hull; above us furled canvas told us we were standing out in the roads until daylight, and the scream of gulls, diving into the bilge in search of gullish delights, spoke more eloquently than maps or instruments, or even those distant anonymous lights, of land ahead. We were all relaxed and content, and even Charles and Mr Roberts puffed their cigars together in amity.

'I think I am correct in believing that you do not intend to remain long in Calcutta, Mr Flood,' said Mr Roberts after a time, probably more in order to make conversation than from any real interest in our movements.

'No longer than we can help,' Charles answered. 'I have some business to attend to, but as soon as that is accomplished we shall move on up-country. Lucknow is our first destination.'

'Ah! A magnificent city, sir. And in the cold weather a very pleasant one. You have friends there, no doubt?'

'My wife has a cousin—Army, y'know—with whom we intend to spend some time. But I also have some family business to attend to in Oudh. In fact I hope to make the acquaintance of a relative, a half-brother, whom I have never met. He lives some distance outside Lucknow, I believe.'

'Also in the Army?'

'No, he's not in the Army. Nor in the civil administration. As a matter of fact I hardly know what he does do, except that it is something connected with land—farming and so on, no doubt. We know very little of him, and I suspect he knows even less of me. His mother is my mother, but on the death of her first husband she left India and the boy, who was about four years old, was given over to his paternal grandparents for rearing. My mother has not seen him since. So now, more to please her than myself, as we are going as far as Lucknow, I intend to make myself known to my brother. He is … er … now what is the term? Oh, yes! He calls himself a *zemindar*. Whatever that may be!'

'Indeed—a *zemindar*? Most interesting!' There was a note of genuine interest in Mr Roberts's voice.

'I suppose I must seem very ignorant, Mr Roberts,' Charles continued after a moment's hesitation, 'but what exactly is a *zemindar*? The term has been much bandied about in my family, but no one has ever given me a satisfactory definition of it.'

'Oh, it is quite simple really. The word is really two words—*zemin* and *dar*—and means, literally, a holder or guardian of land. *Zemindari* is a system of direct taxation, land tenure and kindred matters instituted by the Moguls (who, as you no doubt know, conquered India about three hundred years ago) and much in use in the northern parts of India to this day. As Muslims, the Moguls found it expedient to appoint their co-religionists as viceroys or governors over their Hindu subjects, and these in turn appointed other minor officials, subdividing their own duties in return for suitable reimbursement from the men they appointed. The *zemindar* was given the right to raise rents and taxes for the state, and in return was allowed the hereditary right to a—generally—large tract of land, as well as other privileges.' Mr Roberts, who enjoyed imparting information, regarded his glowing cigar tip for a moment as he marshalled his sentences.

'A thoroughly feudal system it is, with overlord, landlord and fief. In the course of time, as you may imagine, such tax-collectors became wealthy and powerful men, for so long as the Treasury at Delhi received the stipulated amount, no one cared how much extra the *zemindar* squeezed out of the peasants for his own pocket. Many of those who have taken to themselves the title of Rajah or Nawab today are in fact no more than *zemindars*. Naturally, this system has always been very open to abuse. Graft, sir, and corruption, are the great evils of India, and, as you can no doubt envisage, a system based on personal integrity and probity cannot help but fail in such a society.'

'No doubt, no doubt!' Charles answered somewhat impatiently. 'But my brother is no Muslim. How is it that he is, or rather calls himself a *zemindar*?'

'Well, perhaps he—though more likely his father before him—bought the right to levy the taxes in a certain district and administer the land. This would have been sufficient to give him title to the land. Or he may have acquired the rights and title in quite a different fashion. Fifty years ago, when the whole country was rife with internecine warfare, many strange things took place. Much money and more land changed hands, shall we say, dubiously. Or perhaps your half-brother was asked to take over the district legitimately, because of the absenteeism or other dereliction of the former owner. I have known this to happen in my own time, but not, of course, in Oudh, which has so recently been annexed by the British. But ... however he might have come by his estate, you can take my word for it that on his own acres your brother, Mr Flood, is a very great man!'

'You astonish me. I believe he is a wealthy man, of course. My mother, naturally enough, does not speak much of her previous marriage or her brief time in India, but I had, nevertheless, got the impression that the family into which she had married was somehow not ... well, not quite *comme il faut*, if you understand me. For instance my half-brother was sent to school not in England, nor even in Scotland, though his name is Scottish, but in France!'

'But, Mr Flood, there is really nothing against receiving an education in France. The French are a most cultivated people.'

'Just so—but it's deuced queer all the same, don't you agree?'

Mr Roberts merely smiled to himself, reflecting no doubt on the stubborn insularity of the average English gentleman.

'So! A *zemindari* estate in Oudh,' he mused aloud. 'I have no doubt that you will find your half-brother's mode of life most interesting. It is very unlike the life we more mundane and humdrum mortals must live in this country, you'll find. Much grander; often downright luxurious, indeed. They enjoy a sense of spaciousness, of almost total freedom in their everyday existence, much envied by the military and mercantile element tied to the routine of office or parade ground. You will of course visit your relative on his estate?'

'Really can't be sure, sir. My mother wrote to inform him of our intended visit, but no reply had arrived by the time we left home. He probably thinks we will be a nuisance. But I shall have to try to see him for my mother's sake. Then, if he wishes, he can leave us to our own devices, and I am sure we will do very well without him. Taking into account his family's total disregard of my mother over all these years, I will ask no favours from any Erskine, even though he is my mother's son.'

Mr Roberts looked up suddenly.

'Erskine?' he queried. 'Your half-brother would not by any chance be Mr Oliver Erskine—of Hassanganj?'

'Why, yes, he is,' agreed Charles. 'Do you know him then?'

'Not personally. But we have corresponded, and I am to meet him this coming winter. He has recently begun the cultivation of indigo and I have been able to assist him with advice. His name, however, is well known in northern India, even outside Oudh.'

'Ah! Then perhaps you can tell me more about him. What manner of man is he, Mr Roberts?'

'As I say, I do not know him personally.' I thought Mr Roberts spoke guardedly. 'I believe—that is, I have heard—that he is a man of most marked character and attainment. Perhaps, well, a trifle eccentric. But a most able man, most able. He has made quite a reputation for himself

23

within the Kingdom of Oudh ... as an administrator!' he added hurriedly.

I felt certain that Mr Roberts could have told us a good deal more regarding Mr Erskine, but Emily, becoming bored with a conversation in which she could take no part, insisted that we should all sing part-songs to while away the rest of the evening, and so my curiosity had perforce to remain unsatisfied for the time.

CHAPTER 2

I had hoped to be up on deck early the following morning to observe our entry into the broad mouth of the River Hooghly, upon which the city of Calcutta stands, but instead spent the time between waking and breakfast gophering the frilled sleeves and hem of the muslin dress that Emily had decided was the only garment she could wear for the disembarkation. I thought the dress was unsuitable for the occasion, but Mrs Wilkins had told Emily that the arrival of any ship from 'Home' was a social event in Calcutta, and that all the European residents would be at the quayside to watch the new arrivals, even if they had no excuse for greeting them, so nothing would content Emily but to appear in a gown more suited to a garden party than travel. Lacking a maid, and Emily being unhandy with a gophering iron, the tedious task of freshening the yards of frilled muslin fell to me. However, even in my tiny cabin I realized when we had left the open sea, since there was so great a difference between the manner in which the timbers of the ship had creaked and strained and the whole vessel laboured in meeting the surge of the ocean, and the calm of our progress once we were in fresh waters.

I hurried through my breakfast and then flew up on deck, tying the strings of my large straw hat as I went in a way that would surely have shocked my Aunt Hewitt, who said that no lady ever appeared in public before making sure that every button and bow was precisely fastened. But I was not thinking of my aunt's dictums on deportment at that moment.

We were sailing, very slowly, up a river that at first sight seemed more an inland sea since it was so wide the banks were scarcely discernible. It was very hot and the sunlight, diffused by haze, was reflected back from a great shimmering sheet of almost motionless brown water, upon which a few native craft bobbed with their nets trailing behind them. Here and there a marshy island raised itself a few feet above the water, or a mud-bank fingered a trail of ripples on the water. I was disappointed that no more was visible, but felt too restless to return to the saloon or my cabin. So, in spite of the heat, I decided to spend the morning in the shade of the bulkhead where a bench had been placed for the passengers' comfort.

I had my sewing with me, but, though I made an attempt to work, I soon put it away and sat with idle hands, watching the banks close in as we progressed upstream. Soon I could see indications of the native life: temples with white onion domes, villages of mud huts thatched with palm leaves clustering at the water's edge, and miles of drying fishing nets. Palms and bamboos were all I recognized of the vegetation, but sometimes I caught tantalizing glimpses of flowering trees and shrubs. As the morning wore on, we passed more small craft of every description, from dug-out canoes plied by native fishermen to quite elaborate vessels bearing Europeans to work or pleasure; these generally hailed us joyfully in passing. I pitied Emily, whose fair complexion kept her below decks during most of the daylight hours, and for the first time saw some advantage in having an unfashionably dark skin which no amount of sun could damage.

We were close enough to the shore to observe a road running through groves of trees and along which travelled a diversity of traffic, when a sudden curious noise, between a blast and a wail, made me start and caused Mr Roberts, who had just joined me, to laugh at my discomfiture.

'Don't be alarmed. It's only a conch—a large shell which is held to the lips, so'—he cupped his hands against his mouth—'and blown into. Probably some holy man in that little temple there honouring his patron deity.'

'Then I hope for the sake of the deity's eardrums he doesn't often get honoured,' I said, making room for Mr Roberts beside me.

'That is one of the most typical sounds of India,' he said. 'That and the sound of dogs barking in the villages at night. When I am at Home, I can never get accustomed to the absolute quiet of the English night, particularly in the country. For so many years I have been used to the ceaseless rumble and murmur of Indian nights, the dogs, the squeak of unoiled cartwheels—people here generally travel by night, you see— the crickets, the hoot of the nightjars, and in the rains the deep croaking of the toads. All the sounds that spell familiarity to me.'

He paused reflectively, and then went on: 'But I expect you will find it all very disturbing at first; it is so unlike anything you have been used to. I do hope you are going to enjoy your stay in India.'

'I am sure I shall, Mr Roberts, thanks largely to your kindness in sharing with me your knowledge of the country. Besides, I am very adaptable. It has always seemed to me to be a waste of time not to make the best of what comes one's way.'

'An estimable philosophy, Miss Hewitt. I have often admired your gift of contentment—rather a rare quality in young ladies.'

'Thank you, Mr Roberts—but whatever strengths there are in my character, I owe to my father. He was a very remarkable man, and I was not the only one to find him so. Though he has been dead seven years, I still find myself calling to mind his most original maxims. He used to call them his "entirely un-English maxims!"'

'Such as?'

'Oh, well, there was one he was very fond of, by which indeed he guided his life, and which has landed me in no end of difficulty from time to time: "Caution should always give way before curiosity."'

'Ah!'

Mr Roberts was a little disconcerted, so I hurried on. 'He was an artist, you see, every inch an artist, though never a successful one and not even a very good one. He was a dilettante, I suppose. Very, very unlike the uncle with whom I have made my home since his death—Emily's father. He couldn't bear England, always said it was too cold, climatically, intellectually, spiritually, to support human life! So we lived in Italy, outside Genoa, and after my mother died, when I was very young, he married an Italian lady. I have learnt to love England, but Italy is still the home of my heart.'

'You have achieved quite an odyssey in your young life, then. All the way from Genoa to Calcutta. Or rather, I should say Lucknow, as I take it you will accompany your relatives up-country?'

'Certainly. I am looking forward to it. There is a large English community in Lucknow, is there not? But in spite of that it is an Indian city?'

'Very much Indian—not at all like Calcutta, as you will find. Calcutta, though it has of course a large native population, is in essence a European city, and a very new one as these things are counted in India. The architecture, the plan of the city and so on are all European in concept, with certain modifications, due to the climate of course. But Lucknow is all Indian. The buildings are imposing, enormous— romantic, I suppose. Its architecture is a somewhat debased form of Mogul, and since it was until so recently an independent kingdom, British influence has not yet made any impact on the city itself. It has, like other native kingdoms, had a Company connection for many years, but the majority of Europeans are either on the Resident's staff or in the Army, and the Army people live in their own cantonments, some distance from the city proper.'

'Good. I am glad to hear that.'

'Why?'

'Because I want to see the real India—the Indian India.'

'As to that—well, you will have an excellent opportunity if you visit Mr Erskine on his estate. And, after all, your cousin's husband intends to make his half-brother's acquaintance, so what could be more natural than a visit to his estate?'

I should have remained silent. One should not discuss one's connections with even the kindest of acquaintances, but something— perhaps the novelty of the scene, which impelled a strange feeling of being somehow 'out of myself'—prompted me to try and discover more of this enigmatic half-brother of Charles's.

'There is a great deal more to be known of Mr Erskine than you divulged to Charles last night, is there not, Mr Roberts?'

Now I am not coquettish by nature or acquirement, but I confess to trying to sound a trifle pert when asking this question. I must have succeeded, for Mr Roberts showed no sign of annoyance but merely smiled in a conspiratorial fashion.

'A great deal more, my dear young lady,' he agreed, 'but you must not expect me to divulge it to you!'

'Oh!' Naturally enough, I was left with the impression that what there was to divulge was less than flattering, so I could not leave it there. I thought of attempting the sort of pout that Emily was so good at when disappointed, but realizing that this would make me plainer than usual, smiled instead.

'May I ask you some questions then?'

'Fire away!' he replied, confident that I would discover nothing of interest in this fashion.

'You know Mr Erskine only by hearsay?'

'That is correct.'

'Do many people know of him then?'

'In certain circles.'

'He is influential?'

'Again—in certain circles!'

'He cannot be a young man.'

'From where I stand he appears so.'

'And yet he cannot be old, either?'

'From where you stand he would probably appear so!'

'He is rich?'

'Unbelievably!'

'Popular?'

'Hardly!'

'Is he, Mr Roberts ... is he a rogue?'

'Now that would depend on your definition of the word.'

'*Touché!*' I laughed, and gave up.

We were silent for a while and in the stillness I again became aware of the heat.

'But now, to return to the subject of Lucknow, and to your desire to see the "real" India, I must confess that I wish your visit could have taken place at a happier time.'

'But what is wrong with the present?'

'Nothing. For the moment. It is the immediate future that I fear. I am uneasy at the idea of any party of young and—you must pardon me—ignorant Westerners venturing so far into the hinterland these days.'

'Will you tell me the reason?'

'I don't believe I have one. Merely an intuition backed by experience.' He paused, with his hands in the pockets of his white alpaca jacket and his eyes on the dully glistening water. 'But I think I have lived in this country long enough to have learnt to trust my instincts, and a sort of sixth sense tells me that we can expect trouble of some sort in the near future.'

'But you must have been given some cause to think so?'

'You must not allow me to alarm you, Miss Hewitt. Remember that I am not an Army man, nor yet in the employ of the Company. But for all that I have a very wide experience of the country and a fairly sound appreciation of its people. India has been my home since I was sixteen, and I speak and write more than one of its languages. My work, as you know, requires me to travel much, and over the past two years I have heard many things that caused me uneasiness—not great things, mind you, apparently the official mind finds them entirely too trivial for notice. But I have become aware of a restlessness—almost something of perturbation in the mind of the ordinary man that was not there, and this I swear, five years ago. The atmosphere of the country has changed.'

His face was serious and his eyes sombre as he spoke.

'I cannot pretend to understand this, but I know it is so, and I fear that in the months I have been away matters may have disimproved— particularly where you are going. The Kingdom of Oudh.'

'Because of the annexation?'

'Precisely.'

We had heard before leaving home that Lord Dalhousie, the Governor General, after repeated warnings to the Nawab Wajid Ali Shah of Oudh to mend his profligate and extravagant ways or lose his throne, had at length implemented his threats, deposed the Nawab, and annexed the kingdom. 'A good thing too—and high time!' I remembered my uncle commenting. 'Damned feller is demented!'

But that was all I had heard, and if there had been discussion about the rights and wrongs of this seemingly high-handed action they certainly did not take place in our immediate circle. Mr Roberts himself had enlightened me considerably as to the system of government obtaining in India, both the British territories and the independent native kingdoms, and how it was that the East India Company, 'a parcel of penny-catching traders' as he called them, had come to be the effective rulers of the whole vast country. So I knew that the British presence in Oudh was of over a century's standing, and that the influence of the Company had over the years, and due to the increasing decadence of the Nawabs, extended into the administration and government of the kingdom, as indeed had happened in several other territories. But such was still my ignorance, it had not occurred to me that the annexation might cause trouble.

'The natives are then averse to the measure?' I asked.

'Naturally!' Mr Roberts said drily. 'For many reasons, but perhaps for none that are immediately apparent to the Westerner's outlook. Shortly before we sailed, Miss Hewitt, I received a communication via the overland route, informing me of conditions in the newly annexed state. Within a month of the Nawab's leaving Lucknow, my correspondent was able to discern a marked and expressed dissatisfaction among that section of the population upon which we British most depend—the Army. Perhaps you do not know that for many years past more than two-thirds of the Company's native soldiery—sepoys we call them—a corruption of the Persian word *Sipahi*—have been recruited from the State of Oudh. The men of Oudh have flocked to the Company's banner in such numbers that it is scarcely too much to say that mercenary militarism is the main industry of the kingdom, as it is certainly the most profitable. Hardly a family in Oudh but does not receive a few rupees a month from one of its members serving in the Army, and when these men retire they take their pensions back to their villages.'

Mr Roberts rose to his feet and stood with his back to the rail and his hands on his lapels, a stance that could not fail to command attention.

'One of the chief incentives for this enthusiasm to serve the Company—the Government, that is—was that since the middle of the last century there has been a British Resident at the court of Lucknow, the deposed Nawab's court, you understand. This functionary, in addition to his duties of watching the interests of the Company's trading affairs in the kingdom, was in charge of all matters pertaining to those citizens of Oudh who had enlisted in the Company's Army—and of their families at home. These men were thus peculiarly privileged, particularly in matters involving the native law. You will not see the force of this until you understand that a love of litigation is inherent in the Indian character, amounting almost to a passion. At the same time the native courts of law are notoriously corrupt. When you put together these two facts, you will begin to see the advantages of serving with the Company and thus assuring oneself of the offices of the British Resident as advocate and arbiter.'

'Yes, I think I begin to understand. But then what has gone wrong? Is the kingdom not in a happier condition now that all alike enjoy a juster government?'

'It is not as simple as that. As you realize, the people are now subject to a system of laws which is more just, but it is the fact that the law is uniform and common to all that is causing the dissatisfaction among the sepoys. Two-thirds of our native Army, so my correspondent informed me, are now disgruntled. Corruption, after all, cannot be done away with by the stroke of a pen. When these men were far from their homes for long periods, they could be sure that their land, their interests—for instance their rights of inheritance, should a father die—would be protected by the very special and necessary privileges of their position in the Company's Army. Now the Company is in control, and theoretically such privileges and safeguards should no longer be necessary, but human nature being what it is, and the mills of statecraft grinding almost as slowly as those of God, the sepoys are in a worse case than ever before, and no longer have the hope of redress through a greater power.'

'You think then that the trouble you anticipate will come from the Army?'

'I do not know what to think. But I fear that if I am right, then that is where the trouble will start. In the Army. Trouble there has always been in this country. Drought, famine, disease—these are everyday happenings. Also tribal jealousies and religious fanaticism. These we have been able to meet and deal with in the past with the help of the Army. But if the Army itself is the cause of the trouble, then, Miss Hewitt, may God help us all.'

'I see,' I said thoughtfully. 'But then, surely, have you not forgotten that we have our own troops here as well—British troops?'

'No, I have not forgotten. I am remembering only too well that there are some 35,000 Queen's troops scattered all over this huge country in small and isolated pockets. There are more than 300,000 native sepoys, and when the sepoy fights, he has the incentive of fighting for his own rights, his own little patch of soil—his own country. If, that is, he fights at all.'

I got up and walked over to the rail, and as I went my shadow was short and very black on the soap-stoned planks of the deck. Watching the river flow past in oily brown eddies, and hearing, as I had so often heard over the last many weeks, the creak and rasp of the ship's timbering, the slap of canvas against the booms, the shouts of sailors, and now the monotonous chant of the leadsman crying the fathoms, I felt a little chill of foreboding run up my spine, and thought with longing of the calm security of Mount Bellew. Would I ever know enough of this great brooding land stretched below its flat, dun-coloured sky to feel safe and at home in it?

Mr Roberts must have seen the apprehension in my face.

'Alas, I fear I have alarmed you,' he said contritely.

'I asked for reasons.'

'We can still hope that my anxiety is unfounded. Certainly you will find many brave gentlemen in Calcutta who will tell you so.' He smiled ruefully. 'I am known to be somewhat pessimistic in my approach to most things, somewhat too cautious by nature. A "croaker" in fact. I must hope for all our sakes that in this case my denigrators are right. And there are a great many enjoyable things for you to look forward to, both in Calcutta and up-country. You will find among us Anglo-Indians a spirit of kindliness and hospitality. Most of us have had to spend enough time in our own company to learn the value of society, and you will be quite overwhelmed with invitations and entertainments. I have no doubt Mr Flood has provided himself with useful introductions, but if I can be of any service, please believe I am at your disposal.'

I expressed my sincere thanks and the hope that we would often meet in Calcutta—he had already made known his intention of waiting upon us as soon as we had settled in. As I turned to leave him, he said, with a twinkle in his eye, 'I'm afraid you did not discover very much more about Mr Erskine, so in case it will further your conjecturings, I must tell you that he is one of the few who would agree with my prognosis of the state of the country, and he, Miss Hewitt, has forgotten more about India than I will learn in a lifetime.'

'But I thought you had never met him?' I pointed out somewhat tartly.

'It is not necessary to meet Mr Erskine to know his views. He, like me, has many detractors in Calcutta.' And, with a polite bow, the provoking man left me.

CHAPTER 3

After luncheon, while Emily rested in the saloon, I went down to the cabins and completed the packing of our effects in readiness for disembarkation. Several trunks already stood in the companionway outside our doors, but I had still to empty drawers and cupboards of all those small things that cannot easily be dispensed with until the last moment. The furniture in the cabins—cupboards, tallboys and beds— was our own, purchased in a ship's chandlers for use on the voyage as is customary, but it was unlovely stuff, and one of the ship's officers had told us we could dispose of it at a fair profit at the usual auction of such effects held soon after a ship put into port. The inhabitants of Calcutta, so the officer informed us, more wealthy than particular, were always anxious to buy anything that could be said to have been 'brought out from Home'. In any case, we did not expect ever to make such a long voyage again, since Mr Roberts (who had himself used the service on his journey to England) advised us to return by the overland route through the Red Sea and thence from Alexandria to Constantinople by dray which took no more than two months if one used the East India Company's new fleet of steam packets plying between Bombay and Suez.

I had left the door of my cabin ajar while I packed, in order to catch the least movement of air, and as I was looking around for almost the last time, making sure I had forgotten nothing and with a feeling oddly akin to nostalgia, Elvira Wilkins sidled in and asked in her apologetic, breathless way if I would mind going to her mama for a moment, since she wished to thank me for my kindness during the voyage. This was the last thing I wanted, but of course I had to comply.

Mrs Wilkins, dressed in a gown of purple satin, and with a dolman of the same satin trimmed with jet beads and bugles hung carefully on a chair beside her, was sitting bolt upright on her bed, cooling her fat red face with a palm-leaf fan. Her hair, freshly dyed in henna, was of a startling orange, and Elvira had arranged it in almost the latest style— for a young girl. Elvira herself, though I guessed she was several years older than me, wore a gown of limp white muslin with blue bows at the hemline and forget-me-nots round the neck. Her sparse straw-coloured hair was screwed into a mass of small curls, but the damp heat was already destroying the effect of the tongs.

The purple dolman was removed and I was asked to take a seat on the chair, facing Mrs Wilkins.

'You must forgive me for asking you to come in here,' she commenced. 'I know I am intruding on your time, but Elvira and me wanted to thank you special for all you have done for us, and we thought it would be better done in private.'

I made polite noises and hoped I did not look as uncomfortable as I felt.

'You have been very good to my poor Elvira and me, Miss Hewitt, in spite of not caring for us,' she added almost shyly, and then as I made to deny this assertion, held up her hand and silenced me, laughing good-naturedly. 'No, no! No apologies! We are all what the good Lord made us! You are what you are, we are what we are, and I don't suppose the Almighty ever intended us to be bosom friends. We don't deny, Elvira and me, that we would like to be counted as your friends, but we can well see that maybe you would wish otherwise. Now if the Major, my husband, had been with us, maybe you would have thought higher of us. He's a proper gentleman, my husband, with book-learning at his fingertips just like you and that Mr Roberts. He can talk about politics and that just like the best of 'em, even if he did start life in the Band. Brains, you see! That's what he has—brains! And it's brains that makes the difference in life, even more than birth and money. As he always says to me, "What's the use of a high place in life to a man who hasn't the sense to make use of it?" '

'Oh, absolutely!' I murmured. 'I certainly wish I could have met Major Wilkins.'

'Well, perhaps you will, perhaps you will. I heard Mr Flood say that you was all hoping to be in Lucknow by the cold weather, and, if that's so, then perhaps we shall see you, as the Major is stationed for the moment not far outside the city, and no doubt we will have to be in Lucknow for some of the coldweather functions y'know—*levées* and banquets and that, that has to be attended by anyone in the Major's position. When a man has to make his way, he can't afford to neglect such engagements, however much he prefers his own hearth and home, and the Major is a real home bird—and I don't mind telling you that I believe in putting myself out to keep things cosy for him, just like when we was first married.'

'Oh, I'm sure you do!'

'Yes, but that's not what I wanted to tell you about, Miss Hewitt, and you must be thinking me just a gossiping old woman wasting your time. Maybe you'll laugh when you hear what I *do* want to say, but, though Elvira and me have been poorly all this long voyage almost, we still have eyes in our heads. Now I know that your fine relations will do all they can for you, Miss Hewitt, but Elvira and me has talked about things and come to a certain conclusion. We see that you are a young, single lady come to a strange and often cruel land. You have no way of knowing how things will turn out for you while you are here. Of course you have no intention of separating from your relatives, we know, and we hope they are as kind to you as you deserve, which no doubt they are, but there's all kinds of sicknesses and misadventures out here, Miss Hewitt, which you wouldn't hardly credit. Why, I've known as many fine young men and women cut off in the flower of their days as would fill a fat book. God forbid that this should happen to any of you, but it might, Miss Hewitt, it might. And this isn't a country in which any young lady should be left alone, which is why Elvira and me want you to know that you can count on us, and the Major of course, for any sort of help you might ever need. *Any* sort of help!'

Here Mrs Wilkins heaved herself forward, and seized my hand.

'You are a real Christian young woman, Miss Hewitt, and just between the three of us, Elvira and me doesn't think a great deal of that hoity-toity young cousin of yours, who uses you like a lady's maid and orders you about just because she has a husband, and money too, no doubt, and you haven't! Yes, of course you must deny it, dearie, and that's only proper seeing as how she is your cousin, but I can see otherwise. Now I'm not saying anything, mind, not suggesting nothing, but if it so happened that some time you wanted to go home without her, maybe, or she fell ill and died say, and you couldn't properly stay alone with the young gentleman, or if anything happened to make you need more money than you had, well then I want you to remember Gwendoline Wilkins.'

Embarrassment and chagrin fought for precedence in my mind as Mrs Wilkins's pudgy moist hand clasped mine tenderly, and her boot-button eyes regarded me earnestly from under the fringe of orange curls. I had thought all my secrets so safely kept, and yet somehow this coarse, kind and acute woman had discovered them. A change had indeed taken place in Emily since her marriage; I had observed it with some surprise at first—are we not all surprised to see the people we love grow up and grow away from us? Emily had always been petted and spoiled and I had never thought twice of her habit of 'ordering me around', as Mrs Wilkins had put it. In the early days at Mount Bellew I had complied with her petty dictations as the rest of the family had, and now it was habit. Less easy to forgive were the condescending airs she had assumed towards me since becoming a wife, her sometimes deliberate lack of consideration when requiring some service from me, and a tone of voice nicely blended to convey contempt and irritation. I had put it down to the headiness of her new state in life, not wishing to think her capable of considering me inferior because I was dependent, but during the voyage it had become increasingly clear that, whatever my status might have been when I left home, my position in my cousin's household was likely to become that of a superior domestic rather than a favoured friend. If I allowed it to! There had been times when I was genuinely hurt by her attitude; when I wished I had not allowed myself to be overruled by my relatives, and that I had persevered in my intention of obtaining a post as governess in some genteel household.

'I am sure you are most kind,' I said, somewhat stiffly, 'but I assure you I am not in want of any material aid, nor can I imagine any circumstance which would make me so.'

'Aye, I'm sure you can't, m'dear, but then you haven't seen as much of life or of India as I have. Now'—and she dismissed the matter of Emily from her mind—'I have something I want to show you, just so that you don't think my promise of help is another polite nothing. I have a little hoard of my own, which I can do with as I please without taking the bread out of my family's mouth. Be sure the door is shut fast, Ellie!'

Elvira turned the key in the lock, and stood with her back to the door and her arms crossed over her flat bosom, like a soldier on guard.

Mrs Wilkins lowered her voice to a whisper.

'I have a fortune in my garter,' she breathed.

For a moment I wondered whether her protracted suffering from sea-sickness had unhinged her mind, and could only look on in silence as she began to draw up her purple skirts until she had exposed to my view one stout leg clothed in a white cotton stocking and fastened just below the knee by a wide black garter.

She unclasped this band and held it out for my inspection.

'Go on, look at it!' she urged.

I examined the garter. It was made of black satin bordered with lace, and was unexceptional enough. I surmised that Elvira had embroidered her mama's initials on it, and turning it over discovered the inside was quilted with the same pink silk used in the monogram.

'Yes, that's it, that's it,' chuckled Mrs Wilkins. 'On the inside.'

I ran my finger round the quilting, and, as I was beginning to suspect, my touch discovered a series of hard lumps, and on a closer inspection found that some of these were large enough to be visible to the eye. I handed the thing back, unable to repress a smile at Mrs Wilkins's patent triumph.

'Eighteen pearls in there,' she whispered as she refastened the garter below her knee. 'And four diamonds; an emerald like a pigeon's egg, and seven fine rubies! A small fortune for anyone, and a big one for me! My husband took 'em off a dead man on a battlefield—sewn all over his jacket they was, and the emerald in his turban. Oh, no! Don't look like that'—as I shrank back—'it all happened so long ago, before we was even married in fact, when the Regiment was fighting in one of the states, it was. You've no need to worry about the man who wore 'em. He was quite dead. There used to be two more pearls, but one I sold to get passage money when my first baby died, and one to get weddin' clothes for my Ellie, but the marriage never did happen.'

'I am so sorry,' I said to Elvira.

'Yes, tragic it was!' continued her mother with the complacent enjoyment that the mention of disaster produces in certain women. 'A beautiful man 'e was too! Charlie was his name, with a flowing golden beard almost down to his waist. 'E died!'

'Shot?' I hazarded politely, my mind still wandering on jewel-strewn battlefields.

'Cholera!' volunteered Elvira in a subdued voice.

'Yes! Dead as mutton six hours after 'e took it! But don't mind that now. What I want you to remember is this, dearie, that if ever you are in trouble or want for anything that money can buy, you have only to write to Gwendoline Wilkins! There's not many as would have done as much as you have for as little cause, Miss Hewitt. Well do I remember that port-wine jelly that you made for us down in the hot galley when the whole ship was bucking like a bee-stung horse. Settled a treat on my stomach did that jelly, even if it was a mite too wet, the first thing in days that did, and only due to your goodness. Now that's not the sort of thing that can be repaid with money, not any amount of money, but things being as they are, us coming out of different boxes like, my little nest egg is all that we have to offer you, so, believe me, it's yours for the asking. The jewels will be safe enough there,' and she patted her leg chuckling, 'for I'm a saving sort of woman, can't abide waste, whatever my other faults may be. I'll not squander 'em, so they'll be ready for you when you want 'em.'

It was difficult to know what to say. I was overwhelmed by shame at the arrogance and lack of feeling that had allowed me to jeer—only in my own mind, I was relieved to realize—at these two warm and genuine women, whose lack of education and social finesse were so amply compensated by honesty and generosity. I did the only thing possible under the circumstances. I bent down and kissed Mrs Wilkins's patchouli-scented cheek, and then, turning, did the same to Elvira.

'Our address,' gulped Elvira, dabbing at her eyes and handing me an envelope. 'It's the regimental headquarters, and will find us wherever they send Papa.'

'Thank you. I don't know what else to say, but thank you! I do sincerely hope we will meet again, and I shall certainly always remember your kind offer.'

I backed towards the door, and left the cabin with Mrs Wilkins's last words following me: 'You deserve well, Miss Hewitt. God grant you only good!'

CHAPTER 4

It was late afternoon when we eventually got ashore. The port of Calcutta was thronged with vessels and we dropped anchor in midstream among a multitude of ships from every nation: big three-masters from Holland, Portugal and distant China and a British man-o'-war towered over a jostling crowd of skiffs, bumboats, fishing-smacks and out-riggered canoes. We were all packed and ready to disembark long before the small boats came alongside to take us off, and crowded the rails inspecting the river traffic, marvelling at the opium ships, the tall tea-clippers, the neat small steam packets that were now used for coastal trade, and most of all at a large American vessel, ungainly and ugly, which Mr Roberts said was propelled by means of a steam-engine on its upper deck.

Despite our readiness and my impatience, we were the last of the passengers to leave the ship, Charles having decided to wait until a large tender that the Captain had ordered came to take us and our baggage ashore together, so that we would not have to await our possessions' arrival on the dockside.

I was sorry to see the last of Mr Roberts, and hoped that he would indeed call on us as promised. The Wilkins ladies went ashore with the washed-out soldiers, Mrs Wilkins waving a pink-and-purple-striped parasol until they were obscured by the hull of another ship.

In spite of the bustle on deck as sailors readied the hatches for the unloading of cargo, and officers with lading bills passed busily too and fro making calculations with stubs of pencil and hailing each other for information, I felt curiously lonely and lost standing at the rail for the last time as the shadows grew long and the swift dusk descended. Our time aboard had been a little lifetime in itself, distinct from everything that had gone before and from everything that would follow. Soon it would have no more importance—as the promises of Mr Roberts and the Wilkinses would perhaps have no more importance. At that moment I doubted that we would ever see each other again. The tide of daily life would soon wash over the small indentations left by their personalities upon ours and ours upon theirs; in a matter of months we would find it difficult to remember their names, impossible to recall their faces and would have forgotten, most probably, even those things that most irritated and annoyed us in each other, and that had sometimes assumed such disproportionate significance during the confinement of the long voyage.

Emily, however, knew no such sentiments. She was assured, now that we had the tender to ourselves, of making her arrival in Calcutta a moment of some glory, and was concerned only with the set of her gown over her hoops and keeping her bonnet close over her ears so that her hair would not be disarranged. The Captain himself helped us into the tender and waved us away with every appearance of cordiality, a small attention much appreciated by Emily. I did not look back as we were carried through the shipping to shore.

We were met on the dock by Mr and Mrs Chalmers, a middle-aged couple, both stout, florid and smartly dressed, with whom we were to reside while in the city. Mr Chalmers was a business associate of my Uncle Hewitt's (and therefore of Charles's) and, while he and Charles remained behind to see to the conveyance of our baggage, Emily and I accompanied Mrs Chalmers to her carriage through a crowd of Calcutta citizens come to see the new arrivals, all dressed in their best, some promenading along the dirty dock, some seated in open carriages, but all alike unashamedly interested in the appearance of Emily and my less resplendent self. So much so, indeed, that I was grateful to be on my way at last, seated beside Mrs Chalmers on one seat, while Emily spread her skirts out elegantly on the other and rested one white-gloved hand on the knob of her long parasol with a truly patrician droop of the wrist.

However I soon forgot her nonsensical airs. The carriage was an open landau which enabled me to take in something of the city and its life as we passed through it, and I found myself pleased and surprised by the generally sophisticated appearance of it all. The streets were broad and clean and lined by fine trees, many of them in flower, while the houses, each set in its own large garden, were well-proportioned and imposing, though naturally of a very different style to anything known at home. It was the hour of the evening promenade and the residents were out riding or driving, many of the ladies elegantly dressed, and many of the men in fine military uniforms, with good horses under them and native grooms running at their horses' tails.

'I think we shall do very well in India,' said Emily with some condescension, looking around her with deceptive coolness. 'Only think how pleasant it will be when we have our own carriage and drive out with Charles beside us on a fine mount and a little black boy running along behind him!'

'Very pleasant—except for the little black boy,' I answered drily.

'Oh la, Miss Hewitt,' said Mrs Chalmers, 'don't waste pity on the boys! Believe me, they are much more content to run at a horse's heels and earn a good wage than remain in their homes and starve!'

I said no more as I was still conscious of my ignorance of the country, but I noticed few natives in the part of the city through which we drove who gave any sign of poverty. They appeared self-respecting and well-mannered, pursuing their own avocations quietly and without any interest in their white fellow citizens. When I observed as much to Mrs Chalmers, saying I had thought to have seen many more of the native population on the streets, she told me that the Indians generally were not allowed on the streets during the promenade hours—only the rich 'and they are nothing but merchants and money-lenders and such', she added contemptuously, 'though of course since the Nawab of Oudh took a house in Chowringhee and brought all his relations and friends with him, there have been a lot more of them around than there used to be in these parts.' She sniffed disapprovingly.

'The Nawab of Oudh?' said Emily. 'Does he live in Calcutta too?'

'Yes indeed, and no credit to the city either! Came here after he was deposed, y'know, and lives in such style *and* at Government expense, that you'd never believe it! Mr Chalmers says he doesn't know what the Governor General is about in allowing him to live in the greatest luxury, with all his family and his servants and officials about him, and even a menagerie, of which they say he is excessively fond—lions and tigers and so on—when all the world knows he is the most worthless creature living and well deserved to be knocked off his *gadhi.*'

'*Gadhi?*'

'Throne! Mr Chalmers says if poor Lord Dalhousie were still here, the Nawab would soon be cut down to size, but Lord Canning, the new man, y'know, is altogether a different sort of character. Too good. Too tolerant. It's just as well the country is as peaceful and quiet as it is at the moment, Mr Chalmers says, because otherwise there's no telling what might happen. As it is all Lord Canning has to do is to continue on the lines laid down by Lord Dalhousie, and long may it continue to be so.'

'Oh, but poor creature! It must be terrible for a man who has been a king suddenly to find himself a no one,' commiserated Emily. 'Whatever did he do that was so dreadful?'

'Well, it wasn't only this Nawab. Oh, no! It was his father too, and his grandfather and I don't know how many others before them. They were all a bad lot. Drink, don't you see, and opium and extravagance and … debauchery. Of *every* kind! Why, this one even went through the streets of his own city playing his drums like a common *tamasawallah*—a strolling showman I suppose you would say—with all the population looking on, and never gave a thought to the running of his kingdom, which has fallen into the most dire state as a result of his neglect, so that now the Government has had to step in and take it over entirely to put things to right. And after all that, the Nawab is allowed to bring his menagerie to Calcutta with him!'

Mrs Chalmers sniffed in great dudgeon, and I thought I could detect even in her sniff an echo of the denunciations of her husband. I wondered idly whether I would ever be capable of taking on a man's opinions merely because he was my husband? Perhaps, if he were very sensible and his opinions were really the expression of my own mind. But on the whole it was as well that I stood in small danger of matrimony.

'Well, I suppose he's very terrible as you say, but I had hoped that when we were in Lucknow we might see him, meet him perhaps too,' said Emily. 'But I suppose he sees no one now, and as he is not a king any longer it wouldn't signify much anyway.'

'Oh, kings are two-a-penny in this country,' answered Mrs Chalmers, 'and if you take my advice you will have nothing to do with any of 'em. Nasty, grabbing, vicious people on the whole, and I'd sooner put my feet under the mahogany of an English gentleman any time.'

'I expect you are right. But it would have been nice to have told people at home that we had called on a king,' said Emily with regret.

The Chalmerses' house was set by the river, and its lawns and gardens led right down to the water. It was a typical *bungala khoti* or

Bengal house—a term which we English with our flair for etymological adaptation have turned into 'bungalow'—a building of great height and extent, but comprising only one storey. A deep verandah surrounded it, and the rooms were dark, cavernous and bare, at least to eyes accustomed to the amount of ornament and bric-à-brac fashionable in recent years. The bedchamber to which I was conducted was the largest room I had ever seen, let alone occupied. Three tall doors led on to the verandah, and from it opened a dressing-room and a bathroom furnished with a tin bath and an enormous earthenware container full of cold water. This was full of mosquito larvae and other insects drawn up with the water from the well, something which caused Emily only a little more uneasiness than the prevalent Indian custom of taking a bath every day. She was sure so much subjection to tepid water would be bad for her health and complexion.

We were each supplied with an *ayah,* a sort of lady's maid, while Charles found himself waited upon by a neatly turbanned and fiercely-moustachioed bearer. Thus amply were our creature comforts supplied by the hospitable Chalmers, and within a few days I had become accustomed to such strange matters as sleeping under a mosquito net, rising at dawn to walk along the river and returning to drink tea and eat fruit on the verandah, spending the greater part of the day in the dark and shuttered house to escape the heat, emerging only in the cool evenings to sit on a brick platform in the garden and watch the sudden and colourful sunsets.

Very thoughtfully the Chalmers had decided to allow the young Floods a few days' rest before introducing them into the local society. Mr Chalmers would not even hear of Charles accompanying him to his office, which was the only justification we had for being in Calcutta, for at least a week. And certainly, once we had settled ourselves in our comfortable quarters, all three of us became aware of a sudden tiredness and lack of energy. No doubt the heat, the humidity and the change from the sea air all contributed to our inertia. But in a couple of days we were ourselves again and Emily began to fret at what she termed 'this odious inactivity'. I must admit that I was almost equally irked by our inability to get out of the house and grounds and take a look at our new surroundings. It was, according to Mrs Chalmers, quite unheard of for an English lady to walk the roads, even in this residential area, unaccompanied—indeed, to walk at all. 'This climate,' she said, 'precludes exercise for ladies during the hot weather.' We did take a decorous stroll along the riverbank before *chota hazri* at dawn, but after that the long hot day lay before us bereft of interest or occupation. On the second evening Mrs Chalmers asked whether we would care for an airing in the landau, but with such obvious lack of encouragement that even the impetuous Emily did not take up the offer. 'Well, perhaps it is better not,' she said with relief, 'the horses suffer as much as we humans in this heat, poor things, and if we go out after dark when it is coolest there are the insects, y'know, and anyway nothing can be seen!'

Mrs Chalmers spent a large part of the day dressed in a loose wrapper, lying on a *chaise-longue* reading novels and writing endless 'chits' to her friends, which were then conveyed to their destinations by one of the many servants. The house appeared to run itself. I never saw her plan a menu, make a laundry-list or so much as enter the kitchen quarters. I could not help recalling the active, useful life my aunt led in Mount Bellew, her intimate interest in every facet of housekeeping, her concern for each member of her household, and her many charities in the village. I had no doubt at all as to which mode of life I would prefer. I was able to fill my time quite adequately with needle-work and sorting the clothing which had accompanied us in our big trunks but which we had not needed on the voyage, but soon discovered that any mending, washing or ironing, even of delicate laces, was not my duty but that of the *ayahs*, the washerman or the tailor who sat cross-legged on the floor of the back verandah. It was pleasant to discover in my trunk a hoard of half a dozen books, all old favourites, for apart from Mrs Chalmers's novels (which came from a lending library) the meagre bookshelves contained only works on accountancy, the principle and practice of commerce and the horse.

Emily's interests and habits did not serve her well in solitude. Within a few days she was privately rebellious and openly glum. 'Wretched woman,' she said unkindly of her hostess, 'can't she see we're bored and miserable? Couldn't she even have a little dinner party so that we would see some new faces? She's the laziest thing! Can you imagine Mama in a wrapper at *noon*!'

'It's the climate, Emily,' I said placatingly. 'People have to adapt to the climate.'

'Well, I shan't! Not if it means I spend my days alone in a great gloomy house and my nights sweating under a mosquito net from nine o'clock onwards. Never!' Then she turned to her husband. 'Charles, why can't we move out of here to a hotel, or better still rent a house of our own, just a small house? I remember Mrs Wilkins saying such things were very cheap in the hot weather because so many people are in the hills—and it would be much better for all of us.'

'Because, firstly, it would be impolite; secondly, it would not be good policy, and thirdly, it would still be expensive!' her spouse replied firmly. 'However, I believe I will hire a carriage of some sort. We have a real need of one, and I believe Mr Chalmers would be pleased that his own horses are spared extra effort in this heat.'

'Well, that will be better than nothing. But I do think we should have a house of our own too. Oh, Charles! Do let's take a house ... please!'

'No house,' he replied.

Emily said nothing but set her lips and regarded Charles through narrowed eyes in a manner which I recognized as boding trouble. I had realized very soon after we set sail that the marriage of the young Floods was likely to be a tempestuous one. Emily was wilful and Charles strong-willed. There were many points on which they disagreed, and, though Charles did attempt to reason matters out with his wife, even to coerce her into agreement, he had soon shown that he had no intention of giving way to her poutings and temper, a fact which at first had surprised Emily and then enraged her. Later that day, at *tiffin*, it was obvious from their faces that they had had a quarrel, but it was not until the evening, as I sat on the verandah alone, the Chalmerses having gone out to dine—with many apologies to us, it was a long-standing engagement which they could not break—that Charles told me of my part in it. Emily, in time-honoured female fashion, had pleaded a headache and remained in her room, and I was sitting happily enough in the warm, scented darkness, watching the stars come out, when Charles joined me. His face was still set and angry, and as soon as he sat down he called to one of the eternally hovering servants to bring him a brandy and water.

'Nothing I can do is right any more,' he said after a short silence, taking a gulp of the liquor. 'Nor you either, apparently!'

'I'm becoming used to that,' I returned with equanimity, 'and she will very soon forgive you.' I was curious to know in what way *I* had erred, but thought it better not to add fuel to the flames by enquiring.

'She gets more difficult to deal with every day, Laura. I thought I knew her inside out when we married, but I swear I had no idea she could be so … so contrary, and stubborn and … well, foolish as she is being at the moment!'

I said nothing.

'It's this matter of the house she wants, if you please. We are only going to be here for a couple of months, but she's furious because I won't hear of it. Says I'm mean and parsimonious and threatens to write and tell her father I'm misusing her dowry! Now I ask you! How can I misuse it when I can't even touch it? And she knows I can't. The old man has tied everything up so carefully that I might as well have married a pauper. I probably would have been better off if I had,' he added, attempting to joke.

'Perhaps you have not really explained the matter to her,' I suggested. 'She has no way of knowing what such things really cost, after all. She has never had to deal with money, and even since she married she has had no opportunity to learn.'

'But I have tried to explain to her as reasonably as I know how! I told her that, though things are cheaper out here than they would be at home, it was still foolish to throw away money just so that she can make a splash in Calcutta. She wants to give her own parties, dinners—balls too for all I know, and we have yet to meet a soul in the place. She thinks it her duty to entertain for *me*, she says. I owe it to my "position"! And the Chalmerses apparently aren't half good enough in their style of living for my lady.'

'And what did you say to that?'

'That I didn't have a position in Calcutta and didn't want one. I said too, and this of course was wrong, I acknowledge, that I was only out here as a superior sort of errand-boy, that neither her father nor anyone else had ever allowed me any responsibility in the business when I was at home, and that everyone here would realize it as soon as I opened my mouth. Which is true, you know! I'm the most junior member of the firm, and that only because my father was on the Board. Of course I know that I was very lucky to have this opportunity to come out here and see how things are at first hand; it will give me a real advantage, so they all say, but after all we owe it to my mother, not her father, that we are here. She's footing the bills. And I'd like to see her face if I wrote home for further funds because we'd had to take a house of our own for a miserable six or eight weeks.'

I could see his point but I held my peace and he remained silent for a while, glowering into his glass and thinking of his wrongs.

'Wish to God I'd never entered the firm!' he mumbled eventually. 'I always wanted the Army, but after my father died, Mama decided she couldn't afford a commission in the Guards, and she couldn't see me in anything less. I have no aptitude for commerce,' he confessed with some embarrassment, 'and it bores me. I'm already looking forward to the time when I can retire quietly to Dissham and ride a bit and shoot a bit and manage my tenants. But Emily is always throwing her father and brothers up at me—what astute business men they are and how young they were when they started to make money and so on. It's not even as though we were poor and I had to make do with a salary!'

The mention of poverty made me smile rather sadly to myself. No, indeed—these young people would never be poor! Not as I was poor at any rate. My father, though certainly never profligate, had never shown, either, any very economical bent. His inheritance, as the younger son of a very 'sound' family, should have been sufficient for him to live on in modest comfort. But he had had many friends less fortunate than he, and many interests that seemed to consume as much of his money as his time; so between generosity and enthusiasm he managed to go through a very large part of his patrimony. On his death his widow inherited what remained of his money, while I was despatched to my Uncle Hewitt in Sussex with the minute income that was all the lawyers had managed to salvage of my own mother's marriage portion. It was some time before I could forgive my father his improvidence, much as I had loved him, and I still had daily cause for gratitude that my uncle and aunt were the civilized and magnanimous people they were. They had provided me with all I needed; a great deal more than I had ever had in Italy. And when I had agreed to accompany Emily to India, my uncle had insisted that I receive an adequate imbursement, although I had pleaded that all I wished was a chance to show my gratitude. 'You must consider it a gift—to a much-loved daughter,' my aunt had insisted, 'certainly not as a *salary,* dear, as though we were the sort of relatives who would allow you to put yourself out to work!'

She had smiled as she spoke, but Emily, who had heard the remark, laughed acidly and said to me, 'So, you're a paid companion now, are you? And I shall make you feel your position—just as people do in books! How I shall enjoy it!' I had thought she was joking at the time, but her behaviour towards me over the last few months had often made me remember her words.

Musing in this fashion, I did not realize that Charles was speaking again, and pulled myself together abruptly to hear him say, '… and she is convinced that, unless we make a proper splash in the social whirlpool and spend a vast amount of money in order to get invited to the Governor General's assemblies and so forth, her father will consider that I have failed him and will not further my career. I ask you! Did you ever hear such nonsense? She forgets that, if my mother had not been anxious for us to meet Oliver Erskine, our wedding trip would have been a month in Paris. And now—well, now she chooses to see me as a sort of … of ambassador, no less, from Hewitt, Flood & Hewitt to India. All she talks of is my "position" and her "position" and what people here will "expect" of us. But I can't make her see reason. She's just … just childish! Absurd! As though all there is to marriage is a house of one's own and servants and a carriage and a calling list as long as your arm. But she'll have to learn. And it looks as though I'll have to teach her!'

'Yes,' I concurred heartily. 'But leave me out of these lovers' quarrels!'

'Lovers!' he exclaimed, rising suddenly from his chair and going to look out on the dark and aromatic garden with averted face. There was an odd note of bitterness in his voice. I had the impression that he was about to speak again, but after a pause he returned to his chair and said in his normal voice, 'Yes, I'll have to do something about it. She's lying on her bed now like a baby, pouting and crying and saying that if she had known how disagreeable it was to be married, she would have stayed a spinster like you.'

'Oho,' I chuckled, 'that convinces me that she is really angry! She has never envied me my lot before.'

'No. But she thinks now her father sent you out with us to "keep her in her place", if you please. Says everyone at home always treated her like a child and you continue to now she's married. She even hinted that you and I are in league in this matter of the house—that you realize that it would be your "duty"—mark the word—to act as housekeeper and that you wouldn't care for that since it would make you look "inferior". I tell you, Laura, I cannot understand the way her mind works.'

'I believe I am beginning to,' I answered. 'She is just trying her strength—with you, with the world, with me. I felt from the beginning that she resented me travelling with you, and I certainly don't blame her. At sea I had more than a hint of it in her manner, and things she said and the way she said them. It seems to me that she can only feel secure in her place by putting me in mine. But cheer up, Charles. I have no intention of allowing myself to be ill-used by Emily or anyone else. We must both remember that she is very young, after all, and rather spoilt, and has had too much change too suddenly.'

'Perhaps,' he said, again in that bitter tone of voice, 'perhaps she has not had enough change.'

'What do you mean?' I asked, puzzled.

'Oh, nothing. Just words.'

We sat in silence for a time, the tip of his cigar glowing intermittently in the darkness. I felt his nearness acutely, and felt too that there was more he wished to say, that he was debating within himself as to whether to make some disclosure to me. I realized that my love for him, and my sensitivity to his needs, enabled me to guess this. I did not fight the knowledge; it was enough that I could hide it.

'I must be patient,' he said at length. 'But when I remember how sweet-natured and, well, biddable she was at first! It was what made me fall in love with her even more than her beauty. Her sweet temperament. But, as you say, she is very young, and I must just go on being … patient.' Once again I knew that 'patient' was not the word that conveyed his true meaning.

Emily sweet-natured and biddable? Truly, love is blind!

I had a swift mental image of the young virago with whom I had so often had to deal from the time she was ten years old: fists clenched, foot stamping, face red with fury until she had her way. We had given in to her too often, that was the real trouble. Neither her four older brothers nor her parents had ever been able to withstand her rages, and even I, though generally impervious to her avowals of everlasting hatred, sometimes found it simpler to walk away and let her pursue her temper to exhaustion. Now Charles was reaping the fruits of our combined weakness and good nature. Poor Charles! Convention inhibited me from disillusioning him as to the true character of his bride, but I had a premonition that he was not going to enjoy the discoveries of the next few months.

And then he put out his hand in the darkness and covered mine as it lay quietly on my knee. 'Dear Laura,' he said gently. 'A rock of strength, good sense and serenity in the turmoils of our silly troubles. Where would we be without you?' Then he left me.

I remained alone on the verandah for a long time afterwards, remembering all the many occasions on which my 'good sense' had been my downfall.

CHAPTER 5

Charles must have decided that night that the only way to distract Emily from her present discontents was to give her something else to think about. Accordingly, on the following day a servant was dispatched to the city to hire a landau as much like the Chalmerses' as possible. He himself, with the aid of Mr Chalmers and a native groom, chose the horses, and that evening we took a drive along Garden Reach. The following day, despite Mrs Chalmers's opinion that they had not allowed themselves sufficient time to recover from the voyage, he took Emily calling.

Emily had been in a twitter about what she should wear since waking, and had changed her gown three times before satisfying herself, but even so it was very early when they set off, Emily in dove-grey silk and a large straw hat, and Charles very neat in his new tropical kit of cream alpaca.

I was delighted to know that I was not to accompany them—though I had an idea my absence was a concession made by Charles to Emily's bad humour—and settled down comfortably to my needlework with Mrs Chalmers on the dark cool verandah until the gathering heat should drive us indoors. Looking through an arch from the gloom of the verandah to the garden bright with zinnias, cockscomb and cannas against the pearl-pure morning sky, I got the impression of looking at a picture in a heavy frame. Several gardeners, wearing only loincloths, squatted on their haunches and scratched apathetically at the flowerbeds. Various tradesmen, carrying on their heads flat, round baskets of fruit and vegetables, came and went to the kitchen quarters. And a Chinese merchant entertained us with a display of silks and laces, embroidered linen and jade figurines, all produced from a finely woven basket-pack and then replaced with beautiful precision and great good humour, although we had made no purchase. The garden was patronized by all manner of birds, some dull, some most beautifully coloured. All were noisy; one or two had a recognizable song but in the main they chattered, clucked and squawked, and as the heat increased they fell still, all but one group of drab, untidy little things (known, Mrs Chalmers told me, as *Sath Bhai* or Seven Sisters) who continued to quarrel and scream at each other in an hysterical fashion all the hours of the day.

By ten o'clock the sky was leaden and lowering and we had just determined to retire to the comfort of the *punkah*-cooled drawing-room when, heralded by a tremendous peal of thunder, the rain came. It was the first true monsoon downpour I had experienced, and after the first few moments, when I was almost alarmed, I found myself enjoying it. Never had I imagined anything like the vehemence of that sheeting, pouring, clamorous rain! The storms at sea had been violent, often frightening, but now the heavens literally split and a solid wall of water descended, driving us, in a matter of seconds, into the house. I stood at a door and watched, while Mrs Chalmers, shouting to make herself heard above the din, begged me not to be alarmed: it was 'only the monsoons'. Soon the garden had become a muddy brown lake, every pathway and patch of lawn awash in inches of water, every plant battered to the earth and every tree lashed and writhing beneath the onslaught.

The gardeners ran for shelter as the first huge drops hit the ground throwing up a spray of dust like miniature cannonballs, and the noisy family of Seven Sisters hopped on to the verandah for shelter, where they remained fluffing out their bedraggled feathers in an aggrieved manner and grumbling to each other about their situation.

Then in something less than an hour the rain abated and ceased almost as suddenly as it had started. I put on my rubber overshoes and went out into the garden to view the damage, convinced that everything must have been washed into the river. The poor bright flowers hung their heads in muddy shame, but the water was running off the paths and beds as I watched, led away by a complex system of little canals leading down to the river. Birds, revived by the deluge, had begun to twitter in the dripping trees; the gardeners came back to work impassively at the tasks they had so suddenly abandoned. And then the sun came out from behind a great bank of cloud, and with it the heat returned and made the wet earth steam like a boiling kettle and caused a dozen flowering shrubs and trees to release their perfumes which, mingling with the scent of damp, warm earth and scythed grass, delighted my senses. I splashed about, helping the zinnias to unload their burden of raindrops and, thus, with muddy skirts and wet hands, was discovered by Mr Roberts, who, true to his promise, and despite my doubts, had come to call.

'How nice!' I called, as his coachman unbuttoned the water-proof apron of his light gig. 'How very nice of you to remember us.'

'Could you doubt that I would, Miss Hewitt?' He waited for me to cross the soaked lawn and then took my hand with every appearance of pleasure.

'No, not really. But in this weather—and I am sorry that my cousins are themselves out calling and so you will have to do with only me.'

'How nice!' he said, echoing my words, and we went indoors.

Mrs Chalmers had retired to her sitting-room and her novels, but she had to be informed of my visitor. Mr Roberts took out a card, bent down the top left-hand corner, and placed it on the silver salver with which the Chalmerses' chief bearer had approached him. Much sooner than I had expected (since she had to dress), Mrs Chalmers was with us and I made the introductions. Her reception of Mr Roberts, though polite, was hardly cordial, but I put her coldness down to annoyance at having a caller at such an unseemly hour and having to don her gown so hastily. I tried to mend matters with Mr Roberts by showing a too-gushing interest in his doings, hanging on his every word as he talked of Calcutta and what we should see and do while residing in the capital. We confined ourselves to small-talk, but as he was preparing to leave, he said, 'By the way, you will be interested to know that I found a communication from Mr Erskine awaiting me when I arrived.'

'Well, that is more than Charles has done!' I said. 'We have received no word from him yet.'

'No doubt you will—in Mr Erskine's own time,' he added with a twinkle. 'He has invited me—summoned me, rather—to inspect his indigo plantation this coming winter.'

'And will you go?'

'Certainly. Few can afford to refuse an invitation from Mr Erskine.'

'And which Erskine would that be, Mr Roberts?' Mrs Chalmers asked curiously.

'Of Oudh,' replied my friend. 'Is there any other?'

'Oh, not Oliver Erskine? My gracious, fancy being invited to his place! I almost envy you, truly I do.' For a moment she lost her distant manner. 'Why, the Erskines live almost like rajahs or nawabs, they say, though come to think of it the old lady is dead, is she not? She must have been a great age too.'

'Yes, she has been dead some years, I believe. Mr Erskine has recently taken up the cultivation of indigo and I have been advising him on the matter over the last couple of years. Hence the invitation.'

'And Mr Flood is also acquainted with him?' Mrs Chalmers turned to me.

'He is Mr Erskine's half-brother, but they have never met. Charles hopes to get to know him when we go up to Lucknow.'

'But how extraordinary. Never to have met—and Oliver Erskine, of all people!'

'You know him then?'

'Oh, no, certainly not! But all Calcutta knows *of* Oliver Erskine, I assure you, Miss Hewitt. Why, I can remember myself, in the old days of course, seeing old Mrs Erskine in her magnificent carriage, with matched greys and a whole horde of postillions, outriders, grooms and even guards, all in expensive livery, driving on the *maidan*. They used to come down to Calcutta every year to shop, and there wasn't a tradesman in the place who had eyes for anyone else when the Erskines were in town. They always entertained the Governor General, as though they were the superior, you know. And often stayed at Government House too. She was a beautiful woman, French, y'know, and her husband treated her like a queen. They say Oliver did too, after the old man died. My—to think that the Floods are connected!'

'Charles's mother is Mr Erskine's mother.'

'My!'

This intelligence was too much for Mrs Chalmers, who relapsed into round-eyed silence, thus allowing Mr Roberts to take his leave.

He had not been long gone, and I was casting about in my mind for a suitable manner in which to again broach the subject of Mr Erskine to Mrs Chalmers, for I was sure she would be much more informative about this intriguing gentleman than Mr Roberts had been, when Emily and Charles returned from their visiting, very satisfied with their first glimpse of Calcutta society. Emily had lost the peaked and pouting expression she had worn for several days, and Charles was also happier.

'Only think,' exclaimed Emily as we sat down to *tiffin*, a meal of far too many highly flavoured courses to be enjoyed in such heat, 'Calcutta lacks nothing that can make life pleasant: good shops and balls, a theatre, a racecourse and everything! Why, they have even opened a proper picture gallery! It will be very like London. I told Mrs Grimsby how skilled you were with your paints, Laura, and she promises to take us all to Thacker and Spink's gallery as soon as she has returned our call. And we are to dine tomorrow night with the Frasers and take you (which was *very* kind), and I believe Mr Roberts is to be there too which will make it pleasant for you.'

'It seems that everyone here knows everyone else, certainly,' observed Charles. 'Calcutta is a very close-knit society.'

'Oh, wait until you get up-country for that!' laughed Mrs Chalmers. 'I assure you we are quite strangers to each other here compared to the smaller stations. When you live in a small community, the first thing you learn is the impossibility of keeping anything to yourself, for however discreet you might be, your servants will undo all by gossiping away with your neighbours' servants about everything that passes in your house. And never delude yourself that they don't understand you. They pick up every word, believe me!'

'Then we must be very decorous,' announced Emily firmly.

'Or very uncaring,' I suggested jokingly, but was taken up sternly by Mr Chalmers.

'Indeed, Miss Hewitt,' he said, fixing me with his bulging pale-blue eyes, 'not one of us can afford to be uncaring here in India. You have to realize something of the awesome task we have: to bring the civilization of our country and, above all, the comfort of our faith, to these poor heathens wallowing in their evil and ignorance. You must always remember that our lives must present a pattern of Christian decorum and prudence, in public and in private. We have a duty to show the natives the advantages derived from piety and the exercise of the Christian virtues of sobriety, truthfulness and thrift, to say nothing of diligence. After all, my dear young lady, it was the exercise of these virtues that gave us India, so surely it is now our privilege to give India these virtues?'

'I had understood that conquest rather than Christianity brought us India,' I demurred mildly.

'And could we have conquered without Christianity—the fortitude, the strength, it brings us?'

Privately, I was convinced we could have, but it seemed unwise to press the point.

'We have all recently been made to see how much rests in our own hands by our most excellent Archdeacon Carter, Miss Hewitt. Calcutta has quite reformed since he came to us, I assure you. Mr Chalmers and I sit under him twice each Sunday, in the cold weather, of course, and I cannot tell you how beautifully he speaks. Such noble sentiments, so inspiring! And all he says so true. We really must do all we can to bring these poor Hindus to the fold of Christ!'

Mrs Chalmers heaved a sigh and wiped a moustache of curry from her upper lip. 'Not that it is always *easy* to present a correct appearance, mind. This heat, y'know, the general inclemency of the climate, and now that so many more women are coming out, women without the fortitude of my generation (if you young ladies will pardon my saying so), standards have begun to deteriorate rather than improve! You'll never credit it,' she added *sotto voce* to me, 'but I have heard of ladies—women, rather—who let themselves go to the point that they receive morning callers while wearing no stockings!'

I failed to see the connection between this startling revelation and the message Christ left his Apostles, but fortunately Charles just then spoke, and I was spared the necessity of comment.

'One of the gentlemen we met this morning,' he said, 'a Colonel Thorpe, I believe, talked a good deal of the unrest in Oudh. He appears to expect trouble and rather alarmed me with his opinions, since we intend to spend a time in Lucknow as you know. Do you think there is anything in it, Mr Chalmers?'

'Certainly not. Nothing to it!' Mr Chalmers practically erupted with annoyance. 'We have had rumours of war and insurrection here in Bengal too, y'know. Only recently a mutiny, a piddling little affair of course, was quelled in Barrackpore—and very successfully too, I may add. Some matter of discontented sepoys trying to take things into their own hands. We made an example of them, I can tell you! But no, sir, no sensible man gives a hearing to these stories that go the rounds. One has to talk of *something*. That is all it amounts to. The country is more secure, more stable than it has ever been. The people quite devoted to us, quite devoted! And so they should be.'

'I am glad to hear you say so. Colonel Thorpe also mentioned the sepoys—I believe a large number of them come from Oudh, do they not?—and hinted that all was not well in their ranks, particularly since this business of annexation.'

Here I broke in: 'Why, Mr Roberts was telling me just the same thing! The gentleman who was here this morning.' I turned to Mrs Chalmers.

'Roberts? Not Henry Roberts? Jute and sugar?'

'And indigo,' I agreed brightly, while Emily and Charles, who had not yet heard of my caller, looked up in surprise and Mrs Chalmers nodded her head with something like sorrow.

'Hm. An alarmist if ever there was one,' Mr Chalmers observed gruffly.

'Indeed, and is that so?' Charles's tone showed satisfaction. 'He travelled out with us and seemed most well-informed, but of course we are not in a positon to judge the accuracy of his views.'

'Well-informed?' Mr Chalmers now looked definitely sour. 'Well, I suppose so. In some sense. Reads and all that, y'know. Has theories about politics and the rights of man. We need no politics out here; we have enough troubles without *that*! What we need out here is a firm hand. But people like Roberts can't be made to see that. Always talking— and writing, mind you. Damned fellow prints articles in the newspapers— about the awakening of the Indian mind, the necessity for justice and seeing the native's point of view. Tosh! The chap's a Radical! A Liberal!'

Here Mr Chalmers subsided into his meal, first bellowing to one of the *khitmagars* to bring him more rice and be pretty damned quick about it.

Not for the first time I wished that someone had persuaded me in my impressionable years that young females should learn to hold their tongues. Not content with having brought one hornet's nest about my head, I had actually invited a second. I should have realized from Mrs Chalmers's manner to Mr Roberts that morning that he, poor man, was somehow *persona non grata* with the house of Chalmers. And yet I had dragged him into the conversation.

'I am relieved to have your opinion,' Charles was saying. 'I must certainly visit Lucknow; I promised my mother to do as much, but if I felt there was really trouble on the way I would leave my wife and Miss Hewitt in Calcutta naturally.'

'No need for that,' assured Mr Chalmers. 'None at all. Fine place, Lucknow, most enjoyable to visit, so long as you keep out of the native quarter. Never could understand these people who had to make much of the wretched Nawab and his relatives though. Of course you wouldn't be drawn into all that now that he's been deposed and lives down here.'

'No indeed. We intend to stay with Emily's cousin and her husband. He is in the Army.'

'Oh, Will,' exclaimed Mrs Chalmers to her husband, 'I knew there was something I had to tell you! Just fancy, but I heard this morning from that Mr Roberts of all people that our young Mr Flood is half-brother to no less a person than Mr Oliver Erskine. You remember the Erskines? From Oudh?'

'That so?' Mr Chalmers was obviously impressed, but turned to Charles for confirmation of the intelligence.

'Yes, that is true. But I am not yet acquainted with my brother.'

'I see,' said Mr Chalmers, who obviously did not.

'I hope to meet him when we reach Lucknow of course, and perhaps visit him on his estate for a short time before going on to Delhi. However, though my mother has informed him of our visit to India, we have as yet received no letter from him, much less an invitation.'

'And *that* doesn't surprise me,' Mr Chalmers said, between bites on a large and luscious mango. 'A very ... er ... eccentric gentleman, Mr Erskine, so they tell me. Not much given to company. Now, when his grandfather was alive, that huge place of theirs was always full of people. Capital shooting parties, tiger-hunts, expeditions into the *terai* to round up elephant—everyone tried to cadge an Erskine invitation. And great parties and balls and *levées,* even though it was next door to nowhere and halfway back again! Remember 'em well, the old people, I mean. Always made a splash when they came to Calcutta to shop each year, my wife will tell you that, a real splash! But this young feller's a different story, so I hear. Three generations after all! They all go to seed a bit after a time, get too fond of the black fellers, y'know ... to say nothing of the black ladies, ha! ha!'

Mrs Chalmers clucked and said 'Will!' reprovingly.

'Oh, sorry, sorry! But it's true, m'dear, as you very well know. Look around you today, after all. How many of the old guard are there, people like Skinner and Hearsey, Wheeler—oh, dozens more—who have got themselves fixed up with a local lady, one way or the other?

And it's always the ones who have been out here too long, or whose fathers were here, y'know. Now that won't do. Won't do at all.'

Charles, after a quizzical glance at me, said, 'Well then, I must hope I reach my poor expatriated brother in time. Perhaps I can persuade him to return to the land of his fathers and so save himself!'

'Oh, laugh if you will, young feller. Laugh away. But mark my words, your Mr Erskine will have some surprises in store for you!'

CHAPTER 6

In the weeks that followed, during which we got to know Calcutta and its life, I often had cause to doubt Mrs Chalmers's confident assertion that the place was 'quite reformed'.

It is true that Sundays were observed with due care, almost everyone of any standing attending one or both of the services at St James's Cathedral. But privately I questioned whether this was not due more to social usage and a desire to do the acceptable thing than to any religious conviction. However, I could not criticize, as I was happy enough to fall in with the local custom myself—though I was not by inclination pious. My father had been something of a free-thinker, and my mind had early been impressed with the desirability of question and analysis—a facet of my character which I took care to conceal, my aunt having pointed out to me its unfortunate unmaidenliness. I could not alter the critical bent of my mind, but I did learn to disguise it, having learnt that my aunt was correct in thinking men deplored fault-finding and self-confident women—not to mention intelligent ones.

The congregation at the Cathedral was large, and whatever the heat and humidity, dressed to the top of its bent. Enormous *punkahs* swayed ceaselessly above us, their squeaks and sighings sometimes drowning the preacher's voice but doing little to cool the red faces above tight uniform collars or beneath elaborate bonnets. All perspired freely and great was the mopping of faces and necks that ensued as we sang the familiar hymns, and great indeed the relief when at last the final 'Amen' sounded and we were free to pour outdoors, mount our carriages and take the evening air on the *maidan*.

This ceremonial attendance on Sundays, however, was all I discerned of Calcutta's moral regeneration. Having listened to a twenty-minute exhortation to love our brethren (sermons being restricted to this length by order of the Governor General), most of us saw nothing inconsistent, on issuing from the Cathedral, in verbally belabouring the unfortunate coachman who had had the temerity to snatch a nap on the plush upholstered carriage seat.

For the rest of the week, and despite the heat, the monsoons and the absence of a large proportion of the female population in the hills, Calcutta seemed bent on only gaiety—even dissipation. Or perhaps it was because we were newcomers, and therefore represented novelty, that we were so hectically entertained. Whatever the reason, as soon as we had started to leave our cards, hardly an evening passed without the carriage driving up to the front porch to carry us to some dinner, private ball or other festivity, and in a very short time Emily had a calling list that at home would have done honour to a duchess.

I had expected that in my undistinguished position as travelling companion to my married cousin my entrances into society would be restricted. But such was not the case: due to the prevailing hot-weather famine in females, I was invited almost everywhere with Mr and Mrs Flood. This did not quite please young Mrs Flood, nor indeed myself, as my wardrobe was far from extensive and I did not wish to spend my money on expensive gowns. I was rescued from this dilemma by Mrs Chalmers who, seeing my difficulty, introduced me to the custom of having one's clothes made by a native tailor or *derzi*. All I had to do, then, was buy a length of material, find a plate in a magazine illustrating a suitable gown, and, lo and behold, within a couple of days I would find myself wearing its absolute replica, and at a very small cost to myself. This miracle was performed by a gnome of a man, brown, bent and wizened with steel spectacles at the end of his nose, who, with one end of the material clasped firmly between his great toe and the next, cut and stitched and fitted one piece of fabric to another with all the easy expertise of a Bond Street mantua-maker. I had to keep his ministrations secret, for Mrs Chalmers told me it was considered *infra dig* to admit to *derzi*-made clothes. Everyone had them, of course, but vowed they came from Paris or London.

Emily and Charles enjoyed every aspect of their new life. Each day Charles accompanied Mr Chalmers to the offices of Hewitt, Flood & Hewitt, where he put in the required number of working hours—and very short hours they were in comparison to those in London— returning with Mr Chalmers at *tiffin*-time, with only the prospect of the afternoon sleep and the evening's gaieties before him. Although he considered himself of little importance in the firm, as the representative of a rich and influential concern he was shown almost obsequious consideration, and to my disappointment began to take it seriously. Emily soon became everyone's 'dear little Mrs Flood', was petted and fêted outrageously, and her airs and affections became more marked. This, together with Charles's new hint of pomposity, sometimes made me wonder with apprehension what effect the country was having on my own character, and I rejoiced that in fact I had little enough to turn my head.

For I was rather less impressed with the company we now kept than were my cousins. What ladies there were in Calcutta seemed curiously lacking in interesting qualities; all their energies were directed towards preparing for the next festivity or recovering from the last. They had no work to do in their own homes, seldom had children to care for, took no interest in the country around them and did not even trouble to learn the native language.

The gentlemen were hardly more stimulating as companions. They talked almost exclusively of guns and horses, and I began to see why so many ladies needed iced champagne at parties to keep their spirits up. No doubt these gentlemen made admirable soldiers, excellent administrators and notable business men, but in a drawing-room they were, not to put too fine a point on it mere bores. After the first few evenings, when novelty had lent everything distinction, I began to dread the appearance of the carriage. So I was always pleased to find my sensible friend Mr Roberts making one of the company, as he never drank to excess and was prepared to talk to me rationally, despite my sex. He it was who, early in our Calcutta days, suggested that I study Urdu, the polite form of Hindustani, which is the *lingua franca* of Northern India (rather than Bengali) and took the trouble to find me a suitable tutor.

The household on the whole were inclined to view my lessons with disapproval. 'You can't be *singular*, Laura,' as Emily put it, while Mr Chalmers, who was suspicious of any form of mental activity in women, said loftily, 'Lots of young women like to try this sort of thing when they first come out. Doesn't really signify at all—they never stick it. Too difficult, y'know.'

It was certainly difficult, but that remark made me more than ever determined to 'stick it'. The language was very strange to my unaccustomed ears, but with diligence and determination I began to make some progress. My tutor or *munshi*, a little old man with exquisite manners and endless patience, arrived each morning at seven, and, having sharpened a fistful of bamboo pens, shaken up his horn of ink and spread out a sheet of porous native paper before us, would commence the lesson by chanting the Urdu alphabet, swaying his body from the waist in unison with the beat of the chant. Mr Roberts never again came to the Chalmerses' house, but often sent me simple books and primers to assist me with my studies and when we met helped me with my pronunciation.

One morning, as we sat at breakfast on the verandah—the three of us were alone as Mrs Chalmers always slept late and Mr Chalmers had his breakfast in his dressing-room—a packet of badly printed pamphlets was delivered to me by a *chaprassi* wearing Mr Roberts's monogram upon his jacket. As I opened it, Emily remarked, 'I declare you have made quite a conquest there, Laura,' indicating the booklets and indirectly Mr Roberts. Her expression as she spoke was sneering, and I felt my cheeks flush with annoyance. Mr Roberts was old enough to be my father, still devoted to the memory of his dead wife and nothing more than a kindly and considerate friend. I raised my eyes very slowly and gave Emily a long, cool look to convey my annoyance, but she merely tossed her head at me and laughed. I decided to hold my tongue.

Charles, who was immersed in a two-month-old copy of the London *Times* that had arrived the day before, had caught his wife's remark and looked up to say, 'That was surely unnecessary, Emily, and in very bad taste.'

'Oh, I'm sure you think so!' she replied haughtily. 'And no doubt you know just how Laura feels, but can you be so sure of Mr Roberts's feelings too?'

'Emily! How can you suggest such a thing!'

'But why ever not? *I* think nothing could be more suitable. Of course he is a little old, but after all, Laura, you're not so young any more either. I see no harm in his making sheep's eyes at you, and you must admit he does.'

'I admit no such thing,' I answered icily, 'and I have had enough of this silly conversation.'

'Oh yes, of course, I am sure you have. Enough of "silly" Emily's "silly" conversation!' she mimicked in parody of my tone. 'But let me tell you that "silly" Emily has eyes in her head and can put two and two together as well as any. When I remember all the time you spent alone with Mr Roberts on the ship, why, you have given him every excuse to think you reciprocate his regard. And as I have said,' she added spitefully, 'I think it would be a perfectly suitable match. I can't see what you are fussing about just because I mention it.'

'Emily, that's enough. I'll hear no more of this nonsense.'

Charles got to his feet and stood glaring down at his wife in a manner that betokened, even to me, the injured party, a quite undue annoyance. Emily set her lips, lifted her chin and stared back at him defiantly.

'How dare you speak to me like that, Charles Flood?' she asked angrily, after a moment. 'I am not a child. I am a married woman!'

'Then why don't you behave like one?'

'Why don't you treat me like one?'

I knew suddenly that both were oblivious of my presence. As they glared at one another across the table, I saw in their faces a total absorption in their own thoughts—angry, injuring thoughts, thoughts to whose existence I should not have been privy, as I should never have heard their words.

'What do you mean by that?' Charles asked, very quietly, when the silence had grown desperate.

'Just what I say!' Emily almost shouted, though now her chin was quivering. 'I will not be treated like a senseless child any longer. Not by you, nor Laura, nor anyone else. I am a married woman, and I will have the con … consideration due to me.'

Another uneasy silence followed; then Charles grated between clenched teeth, 'As you will then, Emily. As you will. I see I have been mistaken. But I have learnt something from my mistake. Let it be as you will then, Emily—from now on!'

I could see that these words had a far deeper significance for Emily than they bore for me. She flushed and bit her lip to control the quivering of her chin, but continued to stare at her husband with eyes that, though now tear-filled, remained hostile. In white-faced silence Charles picked up his paper, buttoned his alpaca jacket and reached for his hat which hung on the antlers of a deer's stuffed head on the verandah wall. Then, without another word, he turned and walked with bowed head to where the carriage stood ready to take him to his morning's work at Hewitt, Flood & Hewitt's offices.

The day that followed was an uncomfortable one in every sense. No rain fell, and the sticky heat mounted hour by long uneasy hour, filling the big, dark house with a silent oppression of acute discomfort. Emily went to her room and cried, and when I followed her, hoping to make my peace, refused to be comforted. She lay on her high white bed sobbing hysterically and between sobs accused me of 'unfeelingness', Charles of 'hatefulness' and herself of stupidity for having ever married such a man. Realizing anew that her trouble of mind bore little relation to my brief annoyance at her remarks regarding Mr Roberts and myself, I withdrew and left her alone to her tantrum. There was more here than met the eye, or than I was willing to discover.

Tiffin was a very quiet meal, due as much to the heat, which sapped all alike of energy, as to the ill humour of some of those present. But by dinner, which was always taken early by English standards, Emily appeared to have recovered her spirits, and came to the table very becomingly dressed in a gown of pink gauze trimmed with silver leaves. As usual, we were to spend the evening in company, and I knew from her choice of this favourite gown that Emily had made up her mind to forget her woes and enjoy herself. I was truly relieved, and in my relief managed to enjoy myself rather more than usual. Charles remained aloof in his manner towards his wife and spent all his time in the card room, at a particularly noisy table where brandy goblets were more in evidence than cards. I seldom touched liquor myself, and to the best of my knowledge Emily had never had anything stronger than lemonade in her life. But that night I saw her accept a glass of champagne from the hands of one of the adoring young men who somehow contrived to get themselves invited wherever young Mrs Flood was expected. I felt no great surprise at seeing Emily take champagne; after the morning's passage of arms, I construed it as merely a gesture of independence and hoped she would not get a headache. The wine must have agreed with her. She laughed, danced and flirted all through the evening with the greatest verve and, when at last we were in the carriage driving home, recounted her triumphs in a way well calculated to irritate her silent spouse, who sat upright in his corner and vouchsafed never a word.

I went to my bed glad that the trying day was over. But sleep eluded me. The heat was unbearable, and the slight breeze that swept inland from the sea and stirred the mosquito net so desultorily was as warm and comfortless as the stale air in the room. My skin burned at the touch of the sheets, and my nightgown was soon drenched with sweat. Neither was there any way in which I could improve my situation, for the *punkah* swayed regularly above my head and every door and window stood wide open; even the inner doors, as is usual in Indian bungalows, were louvred from top to bottom to allow free passage to any wind that stirred. In the thick darkness of the night dogs barked, jackals yelped, and the watchman struck the quarters on his gong, then cleared his throat and shouted to let the world know he was awake: '*Ko hai? Ko hai? Q'abr dar*!' (Anyone there? Have a care!)

I tossed and turned and tried to find the best position in the bed to catch the draught of the *punkah*. And then, above the drone of the mosquitoes and the noises of the Indian night, I became aware of the sound of voices in the room occupied by Emily and Charles across the wide corridor from mine. Those tall louvred doors shut out as little sound as they did air, but I had never before heard more than the low murmur of voices from that room. Now I realized, as I shook myself loose of my dozing, the voices were raised in anger, or I could not have heard them so clearly. The morning's quarrel was continuing then. I shrugged mentally and berated Emily for being such a self-willed little fool. But I was not much concerned; there had been other quarrels. I was, however, glad that the raised voices would not be audible to the Chalmerses, who slept at the other end of the house. I turned over in my bed and once again tried to settle to sleep, but odd words and phrases, dulled but distinguishable, came to me through the doors.

'Why did you not...' That was Charles.

Then Emily, '... you never have listened ...'

'... but at the start you were not ...'—Charles again.

Then Emily, 'No, no, even then I ...'

'... and so now I am never to ...'

'... as though there is nothing else ...'

Then Charles again, '... my need, Emily ...'

Then Emily, quite loudly and shrilly: 'I don't care; I do not care! ... You are ...' Her voice was suddenly stifled, as though she had put her hand over her mouth, and then broke out again, in a scream, a shrill scream: 'No ... no ... no, Charles! I won't let you! Don't touch me! No-o-o!' At this I shot up in bed. It could not be true! Surely Charles could never strike her?

Then suddenly all was quiet again. I found I was shivering despite the heat, and with the awareness of my shaking limbs came too awareness of what I had really heard. With flaming cheeks I buried my face in the hot pillows, pulling them up around my ears so that I should hear no more. For hours, it seemed, I struggled there with my imagination, with my memories and with my own long-dead hopes, until at last, hot, exhausted and distressed, I gave way to tears and wept for Emily, for Charles, and most of all myself.

But how could I guess then that the unwilling loving of that night would result in such tragedy for us all? That it would bring life—and death—and turn the tides of all our days towards a sea of events that finally engulfed a nation?

CHAPTER 7

A couple of days later Mr Roberts was included in a party made up to view the works in Messrs Thacker & Spink's picture gallery. This was a new acquisition and provided the inhabitants of Calcutta with opportunity for much spite and malicious laughter, as most of the artists exhibiting were amateurs from amongst themselves, and many of the subjects of the portraits were also personalities of the place.

The gallery consisted of two or three large rooms above a shop. The wall space was occupied with a diverse collection of works in every style and medium—the portrait in oils predominating, followed in number by what were obviously ladies' watercolours, indeterminate, conventional things, too much like what I myself was able to produce.

Mr Roberts and I, as usual, found ourselves in company as we paced along the walls. I had determined not to be disconcerted by his particularity, but to treat him in just the same manner as I had before my cousin's foolish remarks, but, despite this resolution, I was very conscious of the company's eyes upon us and thought I discerned the odd knowing look pass between some of our acquaintance. Probably this was only my imagination, and since Mr Roberts appeared unconscious of anything unusual I pulled myself together and concentrated on the pictures.

Few of them were competent, let alone admirable, but all had been loaned freely by the artists or owners in order to get the gallery off to a good start, so I felt that the ruder comments and louder shouts of laughter could have been suppressed. I was disappointed to discover no single example of Indian art, though there were several portraits of Indian gentlemen, magnificent in jewels and plumed turbans, which Mr Roberts said were probably painted by itinerant Italian artists in the earlier years of the century.

'What a pity there is nothing of native work,' I said to my companion. 'I have heard that the Rajput manner is very interesting, and had hoped to see some here.'

'Ah, no, I fear not. The best of that is seen in private houses and the palaces of the great. I do not admire it greatly myself; the want of perspective makes it unlovely to the Western eye. But,' he added with the justice that I so much liked in him, 'it is certainly lively, and the colours are most intense and jewel-like. No doubt you will find an opportunity to view some of it in Oudh. Lucknow is reputed to be a treasure house of such things—or at least it was in the days of the Nawabs.'

Mr Roberts moved on a few steps, but I remained to look at a pleasant water-colour of mountains and a lake, unoriginal but well executed, and was startled by his sudden urgent call to come and look, for he believed he had found something that would interest me.

This was a portrait, almost life-sized, of a young man.

The subject posed against a bleak landscape of solid rocks and uncompromising trees, with, in the distance, a building that one guessed was a fort or castle of some sort. He stood erect, his right hand on his hip, and on his left a chained and hooded falcon, and gazed straight down at the viewer. It was obvious at first glance that the portrait was the work of two different artists, the body having been done by a very unaccomplished apprentice. The stance of the figure was stiff, the limbs appearing to be riveted to the trunk like those of a puppet, and the whole covered by clothing that bore no sign of wear—no wrinkles, not a hint of the contours of the limbs beneath, no indication of movement.

But, by some touch of genius or happy flash of insight, the artist who had painted it had brought to vivid and assertive life the strongly featured face. It was a long face, the forehead high, the chin strong and markedly cleft, the mouth wide and unsmiling but at the same time not wholly stern. A beaked nose stood out beneath dark brows, shadowing eyes that were heavy-lidded, narrow and hazel in colour, and that drew the viewer's eyes as a magnet draws a pin, so full of life were they, so charged with the expression of their owner's character. The man might have been any age between twenty-five and thirty, though I inclined towards the older limit.

We regarded the portrait for some moments in silence, I, at any rate, ignoring the lifeless body and endeavouring from a study of the complex face to form some assessment of the man's personality, and wondering how it came about that two such differently endowed hands had come to work on the same subject. No doubt it was this point that Mr Roberts considered would interest me, but I knew a little of the system of apprentice painters in portraiture and was not as surprised as he had been.

'A most interesting face, is it not?' murmured Mr Roberts, keeping his eyes fixed upon it.

'Very,' I agreed, 'but I cannot think I would like the man.'

'Is that so?' Mr Roberts's voice told me he was smiling. 'You have come to your conclusion very quickly. What is it that you do not like in him?'

'Perhaps his arrogance. Look at the way the head is set on the shoulders. Stiff-necked and proud.'

'That could be a fault in the painting.'

'Yes, but see, it is in his eyes too, and in the cut of the nostrils.'

'Hm. What else do you see in the eyes?'

'Intelligence—wouldn't you agree?'

'Certainly.'

'And … and humour, I think. The mouth bears that out—see the faint quirk at the end of the lips? But I feel it must be a most sardonic humour. Look at these long lines coming down by the side of the nose past the lips.'

'Smile lines, perhaps?'

'It would be a cruel smile that left such marking on a face in repose.'

'Or it could be a wide one? What else?'

I considered for a moment. 'Imagination. That breadth of forehead, you know. And he has great strength of character. That is a despot's nose.'

'Yes, there I must agree with you. But do you see no sign of any gentler characteristic? Sensitivity perhaps?'

'Well, there is a hint of delicacy in the moulding of the lips, but I think it has long since been overlaid by assertiveness.'

'Generosity?'

'Certainly nothing of the contrary! There is no hint of meanness or smallness of mind that I can detect.'

'No indeed, no pettiness there. I remember, Miss Hewitt, once telling you that he would be accounted a great man in his own acres, and now, looking at his face, I am inclined to think his greatness lies not wholly in his possessions.'

Mr Roberts pointed, with a small air of triumph, to lettering, dark against dark foliage, which I had not before noticed. I bent forward, and following his finger read:

OE ... HASSANGANJ ... 1848

'This is the gentleman in whom you displayed so much interest on board ship, Miss Hewitt. Mr Oliver Erskine!'

'Mr Erskine? But how can you be so sure? You told me you had never seen him, and the initials may stand for many other names, even the artist's.'

'True,' agreed my companion imperturbably, 'but not in conjunction with "Hassanganj". That is the name of Erskine's estate, and that,' he pointed at the fort-like building in the background, 'that is the house at Hassanganj. It is quite famous, I assure you.'

'But how extraordinary.'

I looked with a new and livelier interest at the face, and the more I examined it the more enigmatical it became. All I had read in it before was still there, but the more I studied, the more I found my curiosity aroused. Perhaps the novelty of masculine features entirely clean-shaven added something to my puzzlement. It was rare indeed to meet a gentleman quite unbewhiskered, and I was not sure I liked the effect. At all events, my first feeling of antipathy remained.

'We had better introduce Charles to his brother,' I said at length, and signalled to attract his attention. He and Emily were together, but Emily had chosen to lean upon the arm of one Lieutenant Charlton, a most devoted admirer, rather than upon her husband's. They took their time in coming, but as they approached the picture to which Mr Roberts and I had again bent our attention, Emily said, 'Oh, who is that *ugly* fellow!' and shuddered in exaggerated distaste.

He was certainly singular but he had many other qualities as well, and I could have cheerfully shaken Emily as she chattered on about his great 'hooked' nose, and the unfashionable cut of his coat.

Mr Roberts allowed her to run on, and then said mildly, 'I am sorry that you have so poor an opinion of the gentleman's physiognomy. You will probably be much in his company before long as he is your husband's near relative—Mr Erskine.'

'Mercy!' My cousin clutched Lieutenant Charlton's arm and made as if to swoon, and I had to grit my teeth to remain silent. This ridiculous response to trivialities was one of her new affectations that I most disliked.

Then all had to be explained anew. Charles was properly impressed, wondered how the portrait had come to Calcutta, who had commissioned it, and whether it was a true likeness or not. We all, save Emily, gave our findings as to the gentleman's character, and at the end Charles and I had something of an altercation, he professing to see in the face much that was powerful, even noble, and I failing to find too much to admire.

'It is a fine manly face,' he declared.

'Excellently executed,' I demurred.

'True. But no painter could invent an expression of such strength and marked intelligence.'

'Portraitists are notoriously flattering in their approach,' I pointed out. 'Their living depends on it.'

'You can hardly consider that portrait flattering, Laura. As Emily has said, my brother is far from handsome.'

'And I should say he is too conceited to want to be thought otherwise. If my guess is right, he would sooner be considered dominant and self-confident than handsome, and in that case the artist very likely played up the qualities his sitter fancies in himself. Flattery can take many forms.'

'Well,' and Charles smiled, 'I can see that you are not to be influenced, and perhaps we shall soon have an opportunity to find out which of us is right.'

'But is it not curious how little similarity there is between the two of you? Neither in colouring nor in feature is there anything to suggest a relationship between you.'

'Perhaps, when we get to know each other, some affinities of character, at least, will become apparent.'

As we turned away, Emily took a last look and declared, 'Well, no one will make me think much of his looks, and what is more I am sure I shall be afraid of him.'

Mr Roberts laughed, and turning to me said that that was the best joke of the day. The others had walked on, so I was left to ask him what he meant.

'It must be a most misleading portrait after all, Miss Hewitt. No wonder Erskine parted with it,' and he laughed again. 'You see, in our little party the ladies and gentlemen have reversed the usual pattern of opinion regarding Mr Erskine. Mr Flood and I have found that we can like and admire him, while you and Mrs Flood have both expressed a marked antipathy. But from all I have heard—and it is of course mere hearsay—it is the men who commonly criticize Mr Erskine, while the ladies find him quite irresistible!'

Well, I thought to myself, there is no accounting for tastes, but I knew that I would have no difficulty at all in resisting Mr Erskine.

We were now more than halfway through the month of September. Abruptly the daily monsoon downpours ceased and the 'rains' (as the locals termed the annual three-month deluge) had ended for the year. The heat and the humidity both abated, and we began to turn our thoughts to plans for our journey upcountry. Captain and Mrs Avery, with whom we were to stay while in Lucknow, would have to be informed of the date of our arrival. Emily had received no less than three letters from Wallace Avery, communicating his pleasure at entertaining his wife's relatives in his 'humble' home.

But still no word arrived from Mr Oliver Erskine. 'Well, we shall just have to plan without taking him into account,' Charles said firmly, though I knew that he would hardly dare to face his mother if he had to return home without visiting his brother. There had been several letters from her, too, but none of them mentioned any communication from her elder son, though each one exhorted Charles to make every effort to meet him.

Charles reckoned that he would have the 'hang' of methods of business in Calcutta by the middle of October. So, tentatively, we planned to leave Calcutta then, spend the intervening weeks until Christmas with the Averys in Lucknow and then, in the cool, clear month of January, make our way to Delhi where further introductions from Hewitt, Flood & Hewitt awaited us—though these were merely social, no business being conducted by the firm in the old Mogul capital. In March we would take the overland route home and be back in England by the end of April, just a year after we left it. However, if Oliver Erskine did extend an invitation, our itinerary would have to change. Everything would be delayed, and as the overland route in the middle of the hot weather was said to be very trying, we might then spend a few months in one of the hill stations, delaying our departure until September. Privately, and though I was almost sure I would dislike having much to do with Mr Erskine (his ill-manners in regard to his brother only buttressed the opinion I had formed on seeing his portrait), I very much hoped that our time in India would be extended. I wished to see as much as possible, and not least the great Himalaya mountains. Fortunately I knew that at the back of Charles's mind was the intention of making any visit to Hassanganj as long as possible, for he was not unaffected by his mother's hope of his inheriting the Erskine properties, though he would never admit it.

Emily took very little part in our discussions and planning. She seemed to have lost interest in everything; where once it had seemed that she found her chiefest joy in contradicting me and thwarting Charles, now she acted as though she had no part in any of our plans. She adopted Mrs Chalmers's habit of remaining in a muslin wrapper until midday, retired again to her room immediately after *tiffin*, and only at night, particularly when we were to be in company with some of her young admirers, did she display any sort of animation. And then she displayed too much, flirting with all comers, and pointedly ignoring her husband, who, instead of remonstrating with her on her behaviour, seemed relieved to be free of her presence. I did not like this turn of events, but there was nothing I could do, and neither of the young people ever mentioned their discontent with each other to me.

At the beginning of October Emily finally attained her dearest objective: an invitation to Government House. She and Charles attended a small but very grand ball, were presented to Lord Canning, the Governor General, hobnobbed with other titled heads and important personages and were for once in agreement in being very well satisfied with their evening of grandeur. The following morning they left the required cards of appreciation in person and, that done, there was nothing else in Calcutta to turn our minds from our forthcoming journey to Lucknow.

CHAPTER 8

I like change, I like travel; and nothing lifts my spirits sooner than the prospect of new places to be seen and new people to be met. So it was with great anticipation that I set out on the next stage of our journey.

India's first stretch of railway line had recently been opened from Calcutta, and we were accompanied to the railway station by a throng of friends and well-wishers, most of them, I fancy, more taken with the novelty of such a departure than any real concern for us; but in all it was a cheerful, noisy occasion unclouded by those griefs and regrets customary at partings. I would certainly miss Mr Roberts, of course, and was much touched by his presence on the station and by the large packet of books that he put into my hands by way of a farewell gift.

'I hope very much that we will meet again, Miss Hewitt,' he said, pressing my hand in farewell. 'You have been like one of my own daughters to me, and I shall miss your company. But who knows? Perhaps I will see you again quite soon. I am usually in Lucknow sometime during the cold months, and now that Oudh is opening up perhaps I shall have more frequent opportunities of seeking out my friends.'

'And don't forget—you have been summoned to Hassanganj,' I laughed, trying to withdraw my hand before Emily observed Mr Roberts's tender clasp and sorrowful face.

'Ah yes, but that entails a separate journey. However, I do hope you will manage to see the place. That's the real India for you, Miss Hewitt. Now let me know if there is any way in which I can be of service. Please! You have my address?'

I said I had, and at last managed to withdraw my hand and climb the steps up to the carriage, but as I leant out of the window to wave, I wondered for a second whether Emily could possibly have been right regarding Mr Roberts. Standing there on the crowded platform, in his neat alpaca suit with his hat in his hand and his hand on his breast, he looked quite mournful as the train drew away.

Dust flooded in on us as we began to move, and by the end of the journey we were as black as coal miners, our eyes red with hot cinders and our hair gritty with ash. However, all our friends had contributed something towards our comfort, and the carriage was so full of fruit, boxes of sweets, bottled chickens and tinned tongues that there was scarcely room for us, and I was ungrateful enough to wonder what was to be done with all this provender when we had to transfer to *dak-gharis* at the end of the brief stretch of line. A zinc bathtub, packed with ice and sawdust and containing bottled soda water and half a dozen bottles of moselle, was a wonderful help in allaying our discomfort and in passing the time.

My recollections of the rest of the journey, when we debouched from the train and took to the road, are not pleasant. Over a week we spent jolting over rutted, unpaved roads, in a sort of wooden box on wheels, ill-sprung and fitted with hard seats specifically designed to leave no bone in the body unbruised. We travelled by night, resting, or trying to rest, by day, in a succession of dingy *dak*-bungalows, eating badly cooked food in dirty rooms crawling with insects and loud with the hum of mosquitoes, sleeping on hard beds under tattered netting, and waking, unrested, to another long night of dust, heat and fatigue. Often we were delayed because we could get no change of horses; the Eurasian in charge of the *dak* would explain volubly that military men and the servants of the Company had priority on the half-starved, broken-winded beasts available. It was not until the third day's travelling that we discovered that a judicious bribe could be counted on to transfer the priority to ourselves. Thereafter we got along more quickly, if no more comfortably, while Emily bewailed our lack of official status and the fact that we had no travelling carriage of our own, and Charles inveighed against the prevailing corruption of the populace.

Our Calcutta servants accompanied us in another *ghari*—the two *ayahs*, Charles's bearer and a water-carrier who, as soon as we halted in the compound of a *dak*-bungalow for the day, set about heating water for our baths, while the bearer made up beds with our own linen and the *ayahs* washed and pressed our clothes.

Just a few months before I would have considered so many attendants unnecessary, but then I had not known the impossibility of getting an

Indian servant to perform anything but his own explicit and restricted duties, nor had I seen the veritable retinues of factotums that accompanied 'old India hands' on even the briefest of peregrinations. And having sampled the *dak*-bungalow food, we soon regretted turning down Mrs Chalmers's suggestion that we should bring along our own cook as well.

But eventually the journey came to an end, and we found ourselves approaching Lucknow very early on a cool, fresh morning. There had been a shower of rain during the night, so the air was clear and the pale sky luminous in the rays of the rising sun as we drove through country that, though not heavily cultivated, bore every mark of fertility. I was impressed especially by the magnificence of the trees: grand groves of ancient mangoes whose dark foliage shone in the soft light, massive peepuls and long avenues of towering jarmins or feathery sheeshums broke up the stretching plain most pleasingly, lending the whole scene a parklike aspect. Early as it was, the villagers were already astir. Bullock carts, their drivers muffled in cotton sheets, lumbered along rough tracks leading off the road; wells, worked by yoked oxen ambling eternally in a small circle, had begun to creak, and men and women padded silently to their work in the fields, accompanied by long, pale, early-morning shadows.

In a state of high excitement at having reached our destination, we hung out of the windows exclaiming at all we saw when, all at once, a stronger ray of light glinted on a gilded spire as we topped an incline, and there below us lay the domes, the towers and minarets of the city, seeming from that distance and in that clear yet quiet light like a vision of the Arabian Nights.

We knew that the city of Lucknow was more than thirty miles in circumference; that it contained a million and a half souls; that it was said to combine the qualities of Paris, London and Constantinople. But not all these statistical statements had prepared us for the sheer extent of the place. We seemed to be advancing towards an ocean of rooftops, but had only time to exclaim when the view was once again concealed by the contours of the country, and we were forced to master our impatience for a nearer acquaintance.

Within the hour we were driving through the tree-lined roads of the suburb devoted to the Army's quarters—the Mariaon Cantonment. On either side of the road neat European bungalows, very similar to each other with their deep pillared verandahs, stood in large gardens well provided with flowers and blossoming shrubs. Ladies and gentlemen were out for their morning rides; children walked hand-in-hand with their *ayahs,* followed by liveried *chaprassis*; dog-boys exercised their wellfed charges, and everything proclaimed security and comfortable familiarity to such an extent that I could not help thinking that Mr Chalmers had probably been right in considering Mr Roberts an alarmist.

Wallace Avery was a Captain in the 13th Native Infantry, a Company as opposed to a Queen's regiment. His wife Connie was the daughter of Mrs Hewitt's sister, and therefore first cousin to Emily, but no relation of mine. I had never met them and Emily herself remembered them only dimly from a long-ago leave when she was a small girl.

Wallace was a short, corpulent man in his forties, with a balding head, a very red face, prominent eyes and a loud voice. Nothing could have been more cordial than his welcome of our party as we alighted, dusty and travel-stained, on the gravel sweep before his bungalow, while a horde of servants and coolies swarmed over the *gharis* to unload our boxes, all yelling as though some alarming crisis had overtaken them, while dogs barked, a parrot on the verandah squawked and somewhere a child cried to add to the hubbub.

He kissed Emily enthusiastically, slapped Charles on the back, wrung my hand so that it hurt, and at the same time gave orders to the servants, roared imprecations at the *ghari* drivers who couldn't control their horses in the confusion, and called for his wife to come and greet us.

'Good to see you. Very good. Not a bad journey, eh? How was the railway train? No, damn you!' (to a coolie) 'Take it down by the straps, not the handle. Can't trust these blighters to use their heads even in a simple matter like handling a trunk. Now—you're tired, I'm sure, but bear up, we'll have you all snug in no time. Ours is a humble home—not like Mount Bellew, ha! ha!—but you are very welcome, very welcome. Connie! Confound the woman! What is keeping her? Always late, Connie. Her only fault. Come in, come in! Co-o-n-nie!'

And so in an atmosphere of the utmost confusion we entered the bungalow just as Connie, unmoved by the uproar, issued on to the verandah to greet us.

She was a tall woman, several inches taller than her husband, and thin to emaciation. It would be kind to say that her hair was auburn, or Titian-tinted, or even red. But not true. It was just plain ginger, faded and lustreless, and straggled out from under her cap in kinky waves. Her complexion was very pale, almost white indeed, and pale blue eyes gazed out apathetically from under sandy brows. She presented us each with a limp hand, murmured that she was pleased to see us, and without further preamble showed us to our rooms and then left us.

'Isn't she odd?' whispered Emily, poking her head in at my door a few moments after our hostess had disappeared. 'What do you suppose is the matter with her?'

'The climate,' I whispered back. 'She has probably had too much of it.'

'Poor thing. Of course she has lost lots of children too.' The Averys had lost five children in India, and the only surviving one, a little boy of three, was extremely delicate. 'But all the same, she really is queer.'

I could not disagree, and as I tidied myself for breakfast, wondered with some misgivings how Emily would assort with her cousin.

Breakfast, as is very usual in India, turned out to be a social occasion, several of the Averys' friends and neighbours having been invited to meet the new arrivals and hear the latest reports of Calcutta and England. The table was set on the side verandah, an extraordinary number of courses were produced, all poorly cooked and carelessly served, and Mrs Avery's sole contribution to the entertainment was to feed the parrot, a large grey bird chained to an iron perch just behind her chair, and to exhort us all to listen as the bird, with a morsel in one horny claw, bobbed its head and said either 'Thank you, dear,' or 'Good girl, Connie, good girl.'

'And now let's get acquainted,' said the lady next to me with determination, when we had all laughed dutifully at the bird for the third time. 'I'm sure you haven't taken in Connie's introductions, so let me say that I am Kate Barry, and that nice kind-looking man up there with the white hair is my husband George. We live on the next road, just a few minutes away, and have known the Averys for years and years. And you are …?'

'Laura Hewitt, Emily Flood's cousin.'

'How do y'do, m'dear. And so this is your first time in India? Yes, you didn't need to tell me. There is something about the complexion of you girls straight out from Home. One can always tell. "Newcomer, Kate," said I to myself the moment I clapped eyes on you, and do y'know, m'dear, I rather wish I was in your shoes. I've been in India now over thirty years, and I've loved every minute of every year—not like some I know,' she said with a wink in Connie's direction. 'Yes, I believe I envy you. I'd like to be starting out all over again, just as you are now. There's no place like this heathen country, if you can stand the climate, that is. Now me, I've only once had a summer in the hills. Couldn't abide all the silly gossiping females, y'know! I like the men, so I stay in the plains and look after 'em when their wives go to Simla or Mussoorie to preserve their complexions.'

Here she took off her rather battered black bonnet and fanned her face, grinning cheerfully at the company and disregarding Emily's horrified expression at this breach of decorum.

'It's a great comfort being old and ugly,' she went on. 'You see, no one suspects me of flirting with their men, and so I can love the dear things as much as ever I want to. George, my husband, y'know, well, he finds me a bit overpowering and takes every opportunity of getting out of the station on exercises and manoeuvres and what not; but that still leaves me with plenty of fine lads around me, and that's what I like. Never know a dull moment!'

She slapped me on the knee, and roared with laughter—probably at my expression which, I am sure, betrayed surprise.

Mrs Barry wore stout black boots (the other ladies were in the lightest of slippers) and a rusty black dress whose skirt was quite four inches above the ground. Her hair was snow-white, abundant and soft-looking, and framed a brown face as weather-beaten as a mariner's, from among the multitudinous wrinkles of which a pair of very bright periwinkle-blue eyes looked out benignly with a sort of unsurprised innocence.

The others looked towards us when she laughed, smiling themselves, as her laughter was infectious.

'Now, now, Kate. Don't shock Miss Hewitt too much on her first morning in Lucknow. Remember she is not used to you yet.'

'Away with you, Wallace. I couldn't shock a fly and well you know it,' she retorted. 'Besides, as I always say, if a grown female over the age of sixteen can be shocked by any other female, she's better off dead. Not that I'm worried about Miss Hewitt here. I imagine it would take a deal to shock her, for all her quiet looks. I've just been giving her some of my life story and telling her that India is God's own country, if you know how to take it.'

'Oh, Kate, you are always saying that,' wailed Connie Avery, momentarily diverted from her parrot. 'But you can't really think so. I declare I don't know why I am still alive, I hate it so, and what with all we have to put up with here, the horrid heat and the boils and the cholera and the dust and the white ants and the snakes and the servants, why, we might just as well be dead. Really, Miss Hewitt, if it hadn't come about that we have at last managed to save some money so that I can go home with little Johnny soon, I declare I *would* be dead!'

'Nonsense, Connie,' retorted Mrs Barry firmly. 'You are always dejected in the mornings. You'll feel much better by *tiffin* time.'

Connie gave up the unequal battle and returned unenthusiastically to her meal, and I was glad that Wallace, in an effort to distract the company's attention from his wife's outburst, had launched into some story about his little son. Then I heard Mrs Barry's next question.

'Have you come out to be married, m'dear?' she asked frankly, licking butter off her fingers.

'No! Oh, no! I have just come to keep my cousin Emily company, look after her a little. She is very young, and her parents wished it.'

'Ah, well, that's a good beginning but I daresay you will get married. Can't see a good-looking, sensible girl like you remaining single very long with all these men around. Absolutely anyone can get married in India, if they want to—and, after all, who doesn't? It's one of the charms of the place, d'you see? But I hope you will be staying in Lucknow and not hurrying off again right away?'

'No. At least I don't think so. We plan to be here until Christmas at least.'

'Well, that will be nice for the rest of us. Lots of jolly things going on here in the winter, y'know. Balls and picnics and shoots and what not. Have you ever been on a shoot, Miss Hewitt?'

I said that I had not.

'Then I must show you the ropes. Don't fancy tiger shoots myself, though I go on them, y'know; can't bear to see those beautiful beasts shot, sometimes trampled by the elephants too, and ending up on someone's drawing-room floor. Much better leave them where God intended them to be—in the jungle. But I like duck shoots. Generally go with George, though he hates me to, since I won't let him shoot more than we and our friends can eat. Thinks I'm a contrary old divil because I don't like waste, and what does shooting three or four hundred duck before breakfast mean if it don't mean waste? But mark my words, when you have a husband—just learn to put up with all his foolishness and go wherever he goes. That's the only way you can keep a man out here. I've still got mine, though he's been struggling to escape for years, and only because all this time I have worked with him, played with him, marched with him, got sick with him—we took the smallpox together, back in '43—shot with him, ridden with him ... and even drunk with him,' she ended with triumph.

It was much cooler than it had been in Calcutta, and the air was dry and pleasant. On the coarse grass of the lawn a hoopoe strutted, head bowed in concentration, intent on a worm; then it made a sudden dart, expanded its crest like a lady flicking open a fan, and gobbled its prey in one greedy mouthful. A gardener squatted by a flowerbed planting out seedlings with m eticulous precision, and little Johnny Avery trotted down the shade-dappled driveway hand-in-hand with his stout, white-clad *ayah*.

'Oh, look! There's Johnny going for his walk. Ta-ta, Johnny,' said his mother ineffectually, as the child was too far off to hear, and waved her table napkin at his retreating back.

A silence fell as everyone, rather foolishly, turned to watch the child go; then Kate turned to Wallace and said, 'By the way, Wallace, didn't you tell me a short time ago that Mr Flood was acquainted with Oliver Erskine?'

'Hm?' Wallace was watching his wife with a sad expression in his protruberant eyes. 'Hm? Oh, yes, Erskine. Yes, of course, he is Charles's half-brother, I believe.'

'Half-brother? Bless me. I didn't know he had such a relative alive.'

'My brother and I are not at all acquainted, ma'am,' said Charles in a rather stuffy tone. I guessed he would have preferred not to discuss his family with a lady who took off her bonnet at the table, laughed so loudly and wore such short skirts, but there was no escape for him.

'The divil you ain't,' said Mrs Barry and regarded him with curiosity more than surprise.

'I hope to rectify that now.' It amused me to hear a note of apology creep into his voice under Mrs Barry's direct gaze. 'We were brought up in entirely different circumstances and until now have had no opportunity of meeting each other. Making myself known to him is in part the reason for our visit to Lucknow, though so far he has displayed deuced little interest in our movements.'

Then curiosity got the better of Charles's sense of fitness: 'You have met him perhaps, ma'am?'

'Met him? I should say I have. I used to know him well—when he was a lad, y'know, in the days when his grandmother was alive. His grandmother and I were very good friends. She was a fine woman, and I have seen Oliver occasionally since her death. I'm very fond of him,' and she looked round the table with something like defiance. 'He's a difficult divil, mind, and I'm not surprised on the whole that he has taken little notice of you. You'll be his mother's son then?' Charles nodded. 'Hm. There was that trouble with the Nawab, of course,' muttered Mrs Barry, no doubt thinking she was addressing only herself but in fact informing the whole table, and then went on aloud: 'It's not his way to write letters. I remember the trouble his grandparents had with him when he was at school in France. Does he know you are here?'

'He was informed by my mother of our plans some months ago, and I have also written to him recently, from Calcutta.'

'Then he'll turn up in due course, but only when it suits him.'

I was congratulating myself on my accurate estimate of Mr Erskine's character, for obviously a man who showed so little consideration for his relatives was both arrogant and conceited, when Emily broke in: 'We saw a portrait of him in Calcutta. He looks very terrifying, I must say. Is he really so very ... plain?'

'Oh, yes. Plain as a pikestaff. But a man for all that!' Mrs Barry wagged her white head, chuckled and began to peel an orange.

'You are speaking of Mr Erskine of Hassanganj?' The question was put by a Captain Fanning, a blond young man with silly pale eyes and an ingratiating expression.

'Is there another?' Mrs Barry chuckled again.

'I have met him too, on a couple of occasions. Nothing personal, of course, but I did speak to him.' And Captain Fanning looked round the table with an air of pride so obvious that Charles, not always sensitive in such matters, asked with amusement, 'Is speech with my brother an accolade then?'

'Well—you know ...' began Captain Fanning, but another gentleman, an elderly major by the name of Dearden who sat at my right, grunted into his luxuriant grey whiskers and said crossly, 'Accolade indeed! Chap's a bounder!'

'Oh, come now, Dearden.' Wallace glanced apologetically at Charles. 'We none of us know him personally. His views are a bit, well—unorthodox, but that's not enough to make him a bounder.'

Major Dearden bit his moustache and looked as though he would like to disagree; Captain Fanning goggled, and Charles flushed a little. Mrs Barry looked expectantly from face to face, seeming to know that the matter would not rest there.

'The fact is, y'know, you'll realize it sooner or later, and I suppose it's better coming from me'—Wallace's tone was conciliatory—'but Erskine is very much his own man. No respecter of convention or, I might add, of other people, or so they say, which naturally does not make for popularity, particularly out here where we are all so dependent upon each other. He's not often seen in Lucknow, though everyone knows of him of course, and because of his wealth, I suppose, all manner of odd stories have got around about him. He don't entertain, y'see. If he would even do that much, people would forgive him a lot. But apart from a couple of big shoots each winter for the local planter-*wallahs* near him, he does nothing to show an interest in the rest of us. Just keeps to his estate, which they say he runs as a sort of private kingdom, and they say too that he wears Indian kit, and has a ... well, has generally gone native, though I myself don't believe it, mind. However, there can be no doubt that he knows the native mind and speaks the *baht* like one of 'em. And of course there's the house— 'straordinary place, enormous, and fabulous inside, of course. Everybody dying to have a look in.'

'I used to know it quite well once,' said Mrs Barry, not without satisfaction. 'George and I often went there for the shooting in the winter.'

'Did you really?' Emily was clearly intrigued. 'What is it like then?'

'Oh, very grand, very grand. Not a bit what one would expect on the very edge of India. Oliver's grandmother was an artistic woman, you see, something of a connoisseur, and, well, with all that money, she could afford to buy the best. But of course that was years ago. Termites have probably got at it now. Things need so much lookin' after in this country.'

'And does he truly wear native garments?' Emily pursued.

'Not to my knowledge, but I certainly wouldn't put it past him.'

'How singular.' Emily's tone spoke her disapproval.

'Well now, as to the native clothing,' interpolated George Barry in his soft, slow voice, 'when I first came out here, thirty odd years ago, it was the custom for everyone to get into pyjamas and a muslin shirt as soon as they were out of uniform. Damned sensible too, if you ask me. Much cooler than trousers and jackets and starched collars. Can't think why the custom was given up.'

'Can't you? Well, I'll tell you, George.' Major Dearden spoke with marked irritation. 'Because we've learnt that we have to put a distance between the native and ourselves. Doesn't do to let them think we are taking on their ways. No, sir! They must take on ours! And they are doing so, they are doing so! Ten years ago you wouldn't have seen a native in English kit. Now they are all adopting it, and a damned funny, dressed-up lot of beggars they look too. But it's better that way than the other. We lose dignity, "face" as they say in China, when we adopt the native customs.'

'Well, perhaps you're right,' agreed Major Barry without acrimony. 'But all the same, can't see what good it does for a man to be more uncomfortable than he need be. And it doesn't seem to me that the Indian is anxious to learn the more important things we have to teach. We've made no significant difference to their way of thinking, after all, to their religions, caste, their ideas on marriage, for instance.'

'We have abolished *suttee*,' reminded Major Dearden with heat.

'True,' agreed George Barry imperturbably.

'And done away with *thugee*.'

'True again. But nevertheless, if I asked my bearer, Kulu, to take a sip out of my glass, he would sooner die than agree.'

'Pshaw! It's a filthy business this caste. Degrading and abominable!'

'But inescapable nevertheless. For myself, I am not too happy about all this Bible-reading and praying that is going on now-adays. I think it makes for ill-feeling and misunderstanding. When I was a young man, we had our own ideas about such matters and allowed the Indian to have his. It was better so.'

'You'll soon be saying, as I believe your Mr Erskine says,' Major Dearden turned to Charles as he spoke, 'that there is no real difference between the teachings of Christ and ... and ... of Buddha!'

'But then he does know what Buddha taught,' pointed out Kate Barry wickedly, but Major Dearden preferred not to take the point.

'Erskine may be considered an extremist by some,' said Major Barry quietly, 'but I would agree with him in thinking that we should have some respect, some consideration, for the native—that we should know more about the Indian's beliefs and customs. As you say, Dearden, we have the responsibility for this country, and surely a good part of any responsibility is understanding.'

'Understanding is one thing! Pandering to the debased and disgusting habits of these heathens is something else.' Major Dearden was becoming heated. He glared at George Barry, summoning up his reserves, and we were all grateful to Captain Fanning, who suddenly broke in on a lighter note.

'By the way,' he said, 'talking about caste and all that, have you heard the latest from the lines? Some joker is putting it about that the widows of the men who died in the Crimea are to be sent out here by the Queen and forcibly married to the sepoys. To break their caste, don't you see, and ensure their loyalty to the *Raj*. Laughed till I cried when I heard that one. How do they manage to think them up? I ask you—the widows of the Crimea of all people!'

Even Major Dearden smiled.

'One thing's true though,' he said. 'This new General Service Order that's just come out, making it obligatory for new recruits to go overseas if necessary—that's going to cause trouble. Mark my words. I suppose it's due to this business looming up in Persia, but whatever the cause, the *Baba-log* aren't going to like it! No, sir!'

'Why not?' asked Emily unexpectedly. 'What can be wrong with that? If they are in the Army, surely they must expect to go overseas sometimes, just as our men do?'

'They have not been required to so far,' explained Major Dearden. 'Crossing the ocean, you see, the "Black Water" as they call it, breaks caste, Mrs Flood, like drinking from an untouchable's cup. And when a man's caste is broken, he is not only degraded in this life, but damned in the next. Until, that is, the gods and the holy, men have been propitiated with suitable offerings, ritual ablutions and I don't know what else. A lot of childish nonsense, Mrs Flood, but something that you at least will not have to bother your pretty head about.'

'It's strange though,' said George Barry thoughtfully, playing with a pepperpot, 'this wave of anxiety about caste. It's commonly thought that Canning took Dalhousie's place in order to Christianise the country, and that the overland route has been opened up so that more and more women will come out, increase the white population and so undermine Hinduism. A variation, I suppose, of the Crimean widow theme. If they harp on it long enough, I suppose it could mean trouble of some sort.'

'Yes. Yes, indeed.' Captain Fanning nodded eagerly at the assembly, proud of having something to contribute. 'And that's another thing. Mr Erskine believes there is trouble on the way all right. I heard him say so. We were at a big *levée* together after a tiger shoot in the *terai*. He wasn't speaking to me, mind you, but I overheard him say so to another chap—a civilian. He spoke in Urdu or Hindustani or something, and translated what he had said. A proverb it was, I expect.'

'And what was the proverb?' asked Charles.

'Oh … something about "He who grabs the rice gets his hand burned." '

'Scarcely original,' sneered Major Dearden.

'But pretty apt all the same,' countered George Barry.

CHAPTER 9

Calcutta had been our initiation into the life of the British in India: a city rich, powerful and self-important, which, despite its distinctive situation and character, its particular advantages and its peculiar drawbacks, remained in essence a Western city placed fortuitously in the Orient. Its lack of antiquity, its architecture and its arrangement all bore witness to its European origin. Our time there had been interesting and on the whole enjoyable, but I hoped that life in an up-country station would prove more foreign and more exotic than that of the great busy seaport, and had persuaded myself that once away from the circles of governmental and mercantile interest, we would come to grips with the real India—the India of the Indians.

In this hope I was largely disappointed.

Life in Lucknow, I discovered, though certainly different to life in Calcutta, was not unlike that lived in any English cathedral city or large market town: enclosed, narrow and sufficient to itself. Here, however, instead of the churchly gossip of the Close that makes for entertainment in Norwich or Wells, the prevailing topics of conversation were the minor misdemeanours of regimental officers, the blunders of the civil authorities, petty scandals, and only occasionally the eccentricities of the natives. We were involved now in a small society (often I found myself castigating it as an infantile one), tightly knit and seldom broached by outside interests. Far from 'Home', but retaining punctiliously, often foolishly, the standards of 'Home'; a society, though no doubt basically well-meaning, consciously, even proudly ignorant of the wider world in which it existed—buttressing its insularity with childish snobberies, and reft, even in itself, by sharp and acrimonious factions.

Physically it was a pleasant world: a world of pretty bungalows in well-kept gardens, of high green hedges and cool avenues of trees. Its tempo was slow, relaxed and regular. Early parade for the men, followed by an hour or so in office or barracks, while the ladies paid or received calls. After *tiffin*, a sleep to combat the afternoon heat; then a drive or ride to one of the many parks or palaces, or perhaps a gathering at the bandstand, where a military band rendered the favourite airs of the day and one met friends and gossiped. Then home to dinner, followed by cards, music or perhaps an entertainment at one of the messes.

Within a week I had discovered that even in so small a community there were three distinct parties or social levels. First there were the officers and families of the British (or Queen's) regiments; then there were the officers and families of the Native (or Company) regiments; and quite apart from these, as well as somewhat superior in the social scale to both, were the officials of the Resident's staff, who kept a haughty finger on the social pulse and sometimes deigned to share the others' entertainments. In addition there were various tradesmen and professional men living in the city itself—English, Jewish and Armenian—who were *of* the British but not often among them.

Of the vast Indian population that lapped the outskirts of cantonments, with all its diversity and complexity, its ancient culture and its cruel wrongs, I knew nothing, and it seemed I never would know anything. Our closed circle of whites lived in a world apart, touched at its fringes only by the anonymous, unfathomable lives of servants and sepoys. My own sole contact with the natives was through my Urdu lessons, for George Barry had procured me the services of one of the regimental *munshis,* and here, as in Calcutta, my devotion to my early-morning lessons was regarded with indulgent contempt.

'Oh, I wouldn't have one of them near me, let alone sitting at the same table; it's all I can do to give the servants their orders,' shuddered Connie Avery when my lessons started, quite forgetting the long-suffering *ayah* who combed her hair, put on her stockings and buttoned up her boots.

But, in truth, the orders Connie gave her servants were inadequate to ensure the smooth running of her household. She was negligent and uncaring in all her ways; her home was a place of physical discomfort and constant emotional upheavals, and I soon learnt to forgive Wallace Avery his almost nightly absences from his own dinner table.

He was a good-tempered, shallow and gregarious man, and since his wife either could not or would not entertain his friends in his own home, he went to theirs. Connie seemed not to care. She was seldom visible between meals and disappeared almost immediately they were eaten, a habit that was disconcerting to Emily and myself, as we were thus left entirely to our own devices; had it not been for Mrs Barry, we would have led a very dull existence. Fortunately, Kate decided to take us under her wing, and while Charles accompanied Wallace to the various regimental messes for card-nights and billiard parties, she drew us into her circle of friends, who were just then busily rehearsing for the Christmas theatricals. Emily was found a part in the play, but I expressed my preference for behind-the-scenes activities and was put to work on the costumes.

I was more than a little worried about Emily's health, and was glad to see some return to her old spirits in her joyful participation in the theatricals. The climate of Lucknow was much more clement than that of Calcutta, but ever since our arrival in Oudh Emily had appeared lethargic and had quite lost the girlish rosiness of her complexion. She was no thinner than usual, but her face was drawn, and she had developed a propensity for nodding off to sleep in the most unusual circumstances. Most significant, to me, was the docility with which she accepted the restrictions and discomforts of the Avery household. She had found plenty to complain of even in the Chalmerses' comparatively luxurious style of life because it did not quite suit her, but here, where I knew that matters must have pleased her a great deal less, she accepted all in disdainful silence. Naturally, many were the acid comments she made on poor Connie's appearance and peculiar notions of hospitality, but she bore the charred beef, the undarned sheets and the lackadaisacal ministrations of the servants without criticism, appearing not to notice them. And when we drove out in the evenings in a smart carriage that Charles had bought soon after our arrival from an officer who had been transferred to another station, she would sit quietly beside me for an hour on end, only her eyes moving without interest over the unfamiliar but often beautiful landscape.

Relations between herself and Charles were still strained. They had little to say to each other, in public at any rate, and Emily seemed relieved rather than otherwise that Charles spent so much time away from her in Wallace's company.

It must have been about a month after our arrival in Lucknow that Emily complained one morning of feeling ill. I made her stay in bed, and, haunted as I was by the tales of drastic illness and sudden death that made up a large part of Anglo-Indian conversation, was very relieved when she announced at *tiffin* that she had recovered, and ate an adequate meal. This happened again the next day, and the next, and it was not until the fourth morning, when Mrs Barry had dropped in to enquire after the invalid, that the simple explanation of her sickness was borne in on me.

I had taken Kate to see Emily, who, pale and wretched, lay on her bed recovering from a violent attack of nausea. Kate sat down beside her, took her hand, ran an appraising eye over her features, and then chuckled in a most unsympathetic manner.

'Well, by all the saints. And have you really no inkling of what ails you, m'dear?'

Emily shook her head and moaned, 'No. But I feel so wretched you have no idea.'

'No,' Kate agreed cheerfully. 'Can't say I have—but I have a pretty good notion of what is wrong with you just the same.'

'What is it?' I asked, my anxieties to the fore.

Kate looked at me with twinkling eyes. 'You're a fine one to be put in charge of your young cousin, I must say. Why, my dear, I'll lay a button to a barrel of beer that this young woman is about to become a mother.'

'What?'

'What else?'

'Emily ...?'

Emily opened her eyes wide and regarded Mrs Barry with horror.

'What did you say? Me? I'm going to have a baby?'

'That's my guess anyway. The symptoms are all there. And why not? Fine young girl like you, I'm surprised you haven't started before this.'

Emily let this sink in, her face stiff with anguish, as her mind recalled all the giggling, half-shamed gossip of the servant girls at Mount Bellew, and possibly of her own young friends.

'It's not true,' she said at last in a whisper. 'It can't be! I won't! I don't want any baby. Not now and not ever! Oh, Mrs Barry, you are joking, aren't you? Wha ... how can I have a baby ... here? It's nonsense. It must be nonsense.'

There was no mistaking the complete unbelief in that wide, shocked gaze.

Mrs Barry stopped smiling and stroked Emily's hand soothingly. 'Well now, there's no sense in taking on about it, m'dear. If it's to be, it's to be, and you will have to make the best of it. Maybe I am wrong after all, and the doctor will soon put us right. Anyway, you'll feel much better shortly, and then you won't mind so much if it is a baby.'

She left the room to ask Connie to send in some tea, and I sat down on the bed and tried to find something to say. Emily was now in tears.

'Oh, Laura! Please say it's not true. Say it can't be a baby. I don't want a baby, Laura. I tell you I don't want it—I won't have it!' she wailed, hiding her face in the pillow.

'Well, maybe it isn't,' I tried to comfort her. 'We can't be sure. But it will be all right if it is, Emmie, almost all women have babies—even out here—and this sickness of yours will pass quite soon just as Mrs Barry says.'

'But it's not that, Laura. You just don't understand. I don't know how it ...' But the rest of the sentence was drowned in sobs. I patted her shoulder and tried not to realize that the baby would be Charles's child too.

'I won't, I won't! Oh, it's all too horrible! Laura, pray that it's something else. I think I would sooner have the cholera!' She was pounding the pillow with her clenched fist, and the sobs gave place to a paroxysm of weeping. I feared hysteria, so I took her by the shoulders and shook her.

'Emmie! Emmie, control yourself!' I said harshly. 'This is no way for you to behave.'

'Oh, yes, it is!' she answered shrilly. 'If ... if you knew what I know now, and what I have ... the horrid things I've had to do ... Oh, Laura, I hate him for it! It's all Charles's fault, isn't it? If he hadn't made me behave so ... so disgustingly—if he had just left me alone! But he never would, even though he said once he'd never touch me again and I thought he meant it. But it's horrid and I hate night time because of it. And now it's made me have a baby and I hate the thought of that too, and of Charles and of everything. Laura, Laura, how could he? He knew I ... I wasn't like that ... that I never wanted to ... to, you know? Oh, Laura!'

She heaved herself up and threw herself into my arms, burying her face in my neck as she had been used to when she was a little girl and her brothers' teasing had been too much for her.

'Oh Emmie, Emmie!' was all I could say as she sobbed, her face damp against my neck.

'But Emmie, you love Charles,' I ventured after a time. 'You married him. You must not think like that.'

'No, it isn't true. Not any more. I thought I loved him, Laura, but then I didn't know about … about what he would want to do to me. Nobody ever told me about that! I've tried to be brave and bear my trouble on my own, but he knows I don't love him—not as he wants me to. And then you see, he doesn't love me either. Not really! He never seems to notice me really, you know. He doesn't care about what I think, or what I want, or what I am inside—you know what I mean? It's not me that is important to him, only that I *am* his. That's what makes it all so … so disgusting. That's what makes me hate him, that he can go on with … it, and all the time it might just as well be someone else. If he would only make me feel, well—special!'

She detached herself from me and buried her face again in the pillows.

She would be just nineteen when she became a mother, but my mother and hers had both been younger. Had they, I wondered, felt as she did? Had they, too, rebelled at the responsibilities consequent upon marriage, the duties of that state? Or was it true that Emily no longer loved her husband, had perhaps never loved him? Was it not only too probable that she had mistaken a girlish infatuation, the flattery of being sought by a personable young man, for love?

I turned my mind away from such dangerous channels, knowing in my inmost heart that I found some twisted satisfaction in realizing that she had never been capable of giving Charles what I would so willingly have given him myself. To assuage my guilt, I stroked the tangled masses of her golden hair, murmuring endearments, trying to encourage her to pull herself together.

I did not hear Connie enter the room and was startled when she spoke.

'Poor Emily,' she sighed. 'Poor Emily, I guessed it was a baby, but nothing I say signifies, you know, so I kept it to myself. Only I was always ill too, so I know, and just like you, just in the mornings. Poor Emily.'

She stood at the foot of the bed, a tall wraith-like figure, her ginger locks straggling round her face, and the hem of her dress dipping unevenly where the hoops beneath the skirt were broken or bent.

'I hope it won't die, poor little thing. Mine would die so, you know, though I tried so hard to keep them.' She dabbed her eyes with a ball of grey handkerchief, and hiccoughed politely behind her hand.

'Tell you what, though,' she went on. 'You should get Charles to take you home right away. You've money enough, you see; you don't have to go on and on waiting until you have saved up the passage money. And then perhaps it won't die. If I had been in England, I would have had six children—not only Johnny—four boys and two girls.'

She hiccoughed again, while Emily and I watched in silence as she swayed gently on her feet, twisting her handkerchief in her fingers. Seeing us watching her, she put out a hand to the footboard of the bed to steady herself, then continued unperturbed: 'It's the climate, y'know, that kills them. That and the dysentery. And they put them in such tiny little coffins, white ones, with silk inside—but they cost almost as much as the big ones, Wally says. Wally says it's more economical for them to die grown up, but I expect he was joking. He has to think about money such a lot, poor fellow, and still we never have any. My medicine too, I suppose, but I can't do without it, though Wally says when I get to England I will have to learn to do without it because there'll be no one to buy it for me, and it's not delicate for ladies to buy it for themselves.' She frowned to herself, looking suspiciously from my face to Emily's.

'Do you never buy it?' she asked peremptorily.

Belatedly, I was beginning to understand why our hostess had to spend so much of her time in her own room, but Emily, who had never seen an inebriated woman before (neither had I if it came to that), was watching her aghast. 'What does she mean?' she whispered to me, her recent trouble for the moment forgotten.

'Hush,' I whispered back, for Mrs Avery was waiting for a reply.

'Have you really never bought it then?' she asked again angrily.

'Bought what, Connie?' I asked, standing up.

'Why, gin, of course. That's my medicine, you know. Gin with quinine in it. The doctor made me take it years ago—for the ague—and it's done wonders for me. I ... I sometimes think I would really die if I didn't have it, only not with the quinine of course. I don't need that any more because I don't often get the ague now, but the gin is very strengthening. And when you've been out here as long as I have, you need something to strengthen you and make you forget the bad things. Of course sometimes ... sometimes it makes me confused, and then

Wally is apt to get angry and shout at me in front of the *ayah*. And that makes me cry always, so when he goes away I have to take a little glass to get my strength back. But he says I won't be able to have it in England because he won't be there to buy it for me.'

Suddenly she slumped down on the bed, her feet planted wide apart on the frayed drugget, and regarded her broken and unpolished slippers with great concentration. I believe she had quite forgotten us.

'You won't need it in England,' I suggested hesitantly. 'You'll be happy in England, and Johnny will grow strong and well and so will you.'

'Yes,' she agreed politely. 'Perhaps. And then, you see, I'll have servants in England, proper ones in aprons and caps, and I haven't told Wally this—oh! You mustn't tell him either, promise?' I promised hurriedly, wanting to induce her to leave the room, 'But, you see, if I have proper servants, I can always make them buy it. That would be quite unex … unex … all right, and no one could object. If I have any money, of course,' she added in sudden dejection.

'Of course you'll have some money,' I said mendaciously. 'Wally will make sure of that when he sees how much you need your medicine.'

'I don't know.' She sighed deeply. 'There are so many other things that Wally has to buy. And then soon there will be Johnny's schooling and Wally says he doesn't know how he is going to manage that along with everything else. It's very hard, isn't it? I wish I were like Emily and didn't have to think so much of money; it must be nice to …' Her mind wandered away and she lapsed into silence, again examining her slippers.

This then was the explanation of many things that had puzzled me in the Avery household: from the carelessness in domestic arrangements, the impudence of the servants, to the aura of peppermint that accompanied all Connie's movements. It explained, too, the relief and frequency with which Wallace left his home, and the shabbiness not only of the furnishings but of Connie's attire as well.

I went to her, and put my hand on her shoulder. 'Connie, I think Emily would like to sleep a little now. Shall we leave her?'

She looked up, blinking her pale eyes in puzzlement, then got to her feet and stalked out of the room without a word.

Emily pulled the coverlet up to her and turned her face away from me. Then she put out her hand and reached for mine, without looking at me.

'I'm sorry, Laura.' Her voice was muffled and I could tell that she was still close to tears. 'I meant what I said, you know. It's not only because I'm sick. I suppose I am very wicked to feel as I do, but it's no use pretending. Please help me, Laura, even if you don't understand. Please help me!'

'Of course I will.' I pressed the small hand in mine. 'Of course I will, Emmie. That's what I'm here for after all, aren't I? We'll see it through together, Emmie, and in the end everything will work out more happily. You'll see.'

She shook her head but said nothing, and after a moment I went out and left her alone.

CHAPTER 10

During the next few days I became aware of a gradual shifting in the bias of my personal relationships, first with Emily and Charles, and then, to a lesser extent, with Wallace and Connie Avery. In recognizing the change that was taking place, and endeavouring to appreciate the reasons, I felt a development in my own struggle towards maturity.

Regarding Emily, I felt guilt as well as a renewal of the old affection and indulgence; guilt not on account of my own feelings for her husband, but because I had failed her in not guessing something of what her distress had been during her first months of marriage. Remembering the resentment I had felt at her seeming condescension and arrogant little airs, the irritation induced in me by her silly affectations, I could not altogether blame myself for my blindness, but all the same I should have realized there was more behind these annoyances than a childish desire to exert her new-found importance. It was, in fact, her feeling of helplessness, her lack of proper self-esteem, that had found a vent in her attitude towards me—not unjustifiable pride. Somehow Charles had bereft her of importance in her own mind, and in treating me as she had done she was only trying to redress the balance of her shaken self-confidence. Poor Emily—and indeed, poor Charles, for he too must have suffered from her unwillingness and lack of affection. Honesty prevailing, I had to admit that, so far, I had been aligned sympathetically with Charles and against Emily, though I had taken great care that neither should be aware of this. Now I too had a balance to redress, in justice to Emily. I found myself relieved to realize that Charles no longer had the power to upset my judgements—either of him, of his wife, or of anything else. That, at least, was a step in the right direction.

Where Wallace and Connie were concerned, my mind was easier, since I had not presumed to judge either on so short an acquaintance.

Having got to the root of the trouble in the house, however, I went out of my way to be helpful to Connie, and, seeing this, Wallace was embarrassingly grateful and was soon discussing his wife's trouble with a frankness that could only be considered complimentary. His devotion to the poor creature was real and deep, and he taught me to see her through his eyes—as an unhappy woman once capable of love, still worthy of love, but whom now no love could really reach. Left to myself, I might have condemned her as a drunkard and left her to her own devices, but Wallace's confidence in my concern for her made that concern real, and I was soon enmeshed in the toils of the Averys' domestic problems as I was in those of the Floods, but in a more practical fashion.

Disorder and slovenliness were ever my chiefest hates, and the Avery bungalow was notable for both. My Aunt Hewitt often remarked that I had a 'managing temperament', and because of this ingrained and perhaps meddling habit of setting things to rights around me, I began to give Connie some assistance in her household affairs. As she was more than willing to relinquish the reins of her household, I soon found myself ordering meals, supervising the laying of the table, doing the flowers, suggesting new dishes to the cook and generally superintending the housework. I was glad to have something to do, and found the necessity to communicate with the servants excellent for my study of their language. Wallace was openly grateful for the improved condition of his home, Connie happily, if vaguely, acquiescent, and Emily and Charles relieved to sit down to meals that were both wholesome and edible. For a time I had occasion to be complacent about the order I had brought into other people's lives.

Occupied as I thus was with affairs which I had chosen to make my own, I gave small thought to anything but the people and problems most immediate to me. But one morning late in November, a morning of pure, pale skies and glancing sunlight, of dove call in the garden and the scent of freshly watered flowerbeds under the restless shade of the neems, I set out with Mrs Barry, Charles and Wallace on an expedition to the bazaar, where Charles intended to buy a length of silk as a gift for his mother. Such an expedition was something of a novelty even to Kate Barry, as the ladies of the cantonments preferred to shop on their own verandahs, the local tradesmen being willing to transport their wares any distance for the inspection of their customers.

I had received several warnings against visiting the native city; disease was rampant, I was told, and the more nervous ladies hinted at other evils as well, so I was doubly pleased at being included in the expedition and at having Mrs Barry's company. Because of Emily's condition, now verified by the doctor, Charles had decided against her accompanying us. Surprisingly, she had made no protest. I was relieved, as her curiosity was small and I knew she would have tired of the sights and wished to return home long before I was satisfied with my impressions. Wallace and Charles were on horseback, and Mrs Barry and I rode in the Averys' rather battered buggy. We had settled ourselves and were about to move off, when the postboy ran up to Wallace with two or three letters.

'Bills, nothing but bills,' Wallace said cheerfully as he looked through them. 'Oh, and here's one that looks more interesting for you, Charles.' He pocketed his own mail, and we waited while Charles tore through the seal on a thick white cover and read the letter it contained.

'Well!' he exclaimed. 'If it isn't my long-lost brother, at last!'

'From Oliver Erskine?' called Emily from the verandah where she was waiting to see us off.

'No less.'

'What does he say? Oh, Charles, do tell me, you can't leave me in suspense all morning.'

'It's no more than a note, my dear, and forwarded from Calcutta too, I see. It congratulates me on my marriage, and trusts that he will see us in the near future. He will, he says "make it his pleasurable duty" to visit us in Lucknow. No invitation to Hassanganj, of course, nor any indication of when he will be here. Still it's something, I suppose.' Charles laughed and thrust the letter into his pocket. 'Scarcely an affectionate and concerned brother, but at least we are in communication.'

Kate Barry was a comfortable person to be with. I had discovered that one question, judiciously phrased, could open up the floodgates of her experience and leave me free to listen, almost without comment, for an hour at a stretch. I decided that this ride was just the occasion for some questions regarding Mr Erskine, and, as I had hoped, Kate knew none of Mr Roberts's reticence in discussing him.

'Is it long since you last saw Mr Erskine?' I enquired decorously as we passed through the Avery gate.

'Oh, let me think. Now I believe it would have been some time in the spring.'

'This last spring?' I asked, surprised, as I somehow had the impression that Mr Erskine had not been seen in Lucknow for years.

'Yes, March, I believe. He was with Henry Cussens, down at the Constantia Lake one evening, and I had a few words with him. He comes into Lucknow every two or three months, y'know, on business. Banking, ordering supplies, that sort of thing. Occasionally he looks us up, but he never stays more than a couple of days, and it must be a couple of years now since he even had a meal with us. Of course we are old fogies to him, but he seems to enjoy talking about his grandmother and the old days, and he knows that I am fond of him, and don't care a button about his reputation either.'

'His reputation?' I ventured disingenuously.

'Oh, yes, m'dear. He has—or rather had, for nobody knows how he conducts himself nowadays—but he *had* a terrible reputation! Earned it too, I must confess, contrary divil that he is. But he was much younger then, of course. Very wild. Headstrong and uncaring, y'know. Divil a bit he minded what anyone said of him.'

Kate sat back more comfortably against the worn padding of her seat, and I held my breath, praying that her attention would not be deflected from this interesting subject. I need not have worried; she was merely settling herself for a nice gossip.

'Yes,' she went on, 'very wild. That was after his grandmother's death of course. He was just feeling his oats, I expect. But for a time there was quite a succession of—well, dubious young females who visited him as guests. Of course he was all alone in Hassanganj at that time, so people jumped to conclusions. The right ones too, I have no doubt. There was a young French actress, I remember, and another girl who was supposed to be an opera singer, though where even Oliver Erskine could have found an opera singer in Oudh is beyond me. Oh, and several other less colourful ones. They never lasted long, and then they'd be seen all dressed up, with their bandboxes and trunks neatly roped, waiting in the hotel here to be taken back to wherever they had come from. Of course the local ladies were outraged; you can just imagine it, my dear, now that you know us. Before that, all the mamas with eligible daughters in the station were for ever inviting him to stay with them, or angling for invitations to Hassanganj for themselves. But once the lady friends started, he was dropped like a hot brick. Not that he cared a fig, I'm sure. The crop of insipid young misses we raise out here are certainly not for his culling! For one thing, he's a very intelligent man. Far too intelligent to shut himself up for life, way out there in Hassanganj, with some empty-headed girl who'd lose her bloom by twenty. Not he!

'I always say, or rather I *think,* for George would be scandalized if I *said* it, that he found an excellent solution to his problem in his succession of frivolous young ladies. They did him no harm, and I can't believe he did them any. In fact they probably made a pretty good thing out of his generosity for—well, favours received. And he really did us no harm either, never brought them into society or tried to foist them on to us as relatives, or anything like that. Very proper about it all he was, in his own way. But the fact remains that he worked at earning himself a reputation for being "fast", and, whatever the current state of his morals, "fast" he has remained to Lucknow. And more particularly to Mariaon. But, however, there has been no talk of that sort of thing for years. Now his crime is that his opinions, on annexation and this *talukhdari* settlement thing—handing over the land to the peasants— and so on, are extreme. The folk here think he has too much sympathy with the natives. Perhaps he has, indeed, and who could blame him? He's spent his life among 'em in a way that none of the rest of us have. And he won't hold his tongue, y'see. He will say what he thinks, and, since what he thinks is seldom in agreement with what we think, every time he opens his mouth he adds fuel to the flames. If you see what I mean.'

'Yes. Yes, I do,' I laughed, 'and I must say your account of the gentleman leaves me quite intrigued to meet him. But for Heaven's sake don't breathe a word of any of this to Charles or I never shall. Charles would throw a fit and hustle us back to England immediately.'

'And would he so? Well, I suppose he would have to think of Emily's feelings. But I'm glad you're too sensible to be shocked. This sort of thing happens everywhere, y'know; and as I say, Oliver conducted his little *amours* in a far more gentlemanly fashion than many I could mention. And then, of course, he's settled down a lot in recent years. The thing that really bothers people with him, though, is that he can't be ignored. Too rich, y'see, and too influential in his own way. The "Authorities" still continue to invite him to our jollifications—not that he often deigns to attend—and, well, it is impossible to cut a man who is introduced to you by the Resident or your C.O. or someone like that. So they content themselves with backbiting and resurrecting the old scandals.'

'You mentioned once that there was some trouble surrounding Mr Erskine's relations with his mother. I know Mrs Flood, and it does seem strange to me that anyone as dominating and possessive as she is should have had so little to do with the upbringing of her first child.'

'Ah yes, indeed, there was a tremendous row soon after Oliver's father's death, when Oliver was just a mite, you know. It was the talk of Lucknow for a while, though none of us ever knew what had really happened. His mother ... now what was her name?'

'Maud,' I supplied.

'Of course. Well, Maud had never got on too well with the elder Erskines and as soon as opportunity offered after her mourning, came into Lucknow to spend some time with a married friend whose husband, an Italian y'know, was one of the many rather dubious foreigners who clustered around the Nawab of the time. This man, an out-and-out adventurer, my dear, managed to persuade the silly woman that with his help the Nawab could be influenced into revoking, or at least curtailing, old Adam Erskine's ownership of Hassanganj, and could then arrange matters so that she, Maud that is, would stand to gain much more from the estate than a widowed daughter-in-law could otherwise expect.

'Theoretically, I believe, something of the sort might have been possible, as places like Hassanganj were sometimes conferred by deed-of-gift, and a sufficiently unscrupulous donor, or his successor, could arrange the reversion of the gift to himself. However, Ghazi-ud-din Haider, the Nawab of the time, was one of the more worthy incumbents of the throne.'

Kate paused to open her parasol and settle herself more comfortably, then went on.

'No doubt he was tempted briefly, for if he transferred Hassanganj from Adam Erskine to Maud, as Oliver's guardian, he could demand a much larger percentage of the revenues. But Maud and her friends had not taken into account *izat*, the stringent but admirable Mohammedan code of honour. Ghazi-uddin refused to go against his predecessor's wishes, and so nothing came of the wretched Italian's machinations.

Except the scandal. When Maud got back to Hassanganj she found that news of the affair had preceded her and she was no longer welcome. Of course no one knows what took place, but the upshot was that she was somehow persuaded to leave Oliver in his grandparents' guardianship and take herself off to England—no doubt with a handsome annuity. And Oliver, so I believe, had no communication with his mother until the lawyers informed her of old Mrs Erskine's death.'

'Strange,' I mused, more to myself than to Kate. 'From the way Mrs Flood talked, I'd have thought that nothing but distance ever separated them. I had come to the conclusion that she had not seen him as a child because her second husband raised objections. How easily we can be misled about our acquaintance.' And particularly when they want to mislead us, I added silently, with a vivid recollection of the small, cunning eyes in Mrs Flood's fat face.

A month before, we had exclaimed with wonder at the extent and magnificence of Lucknow—the City of Palaces—lying open to our astonished gaze in the forgiving light of dawn, but the drives we had taken through the parks and gardens around the city, passing many large and imposing mansions hardly less than palaces, had prepared me for some disappointment in the city itself. Now, as we made our way from the shady avenues of Mariaon Cantonment into its teeming heart, I was to discover that Lucknow's glory lay all in the past.

The great structures, the mosques, palaces and temples, whose spires had so beguiled us from a distance, were beautiful now only to eyes able to see them as they must have been, to minds capable of appreciating the artistic vision and architectural mastery that had built them; for as one approached them, the delicate proportions, the elegant strength of design, the strangely beautiful embellishments of plaster, gilt and paint, all faded before an overpowering awareness of dirt, decay and human distress. The massive piles thrust their gilded minarets and airy cupolas out of a noisome sea of crowded tenements, rickety shops, ramshackle shanty dwellings cut through by unpaved alleyways and labyrinthine lanes, the whole seething with the continual crush and movement of a vast and poverty-ridden populace.

That human life should be sustained, *could* be sustained, in such conditions horrified me. Never had I seen men and women so ragged, so filthy and so shameless.

Fetid streets, lined with crazily constructed open-fronted booths, and strewn with decaying vegetable matter and accumulations of ancient ordure nauseous to both nose and eyes, were crowded with shabby, shoving, shouting humanity. Among the bare feet of their elders, naked children slipped in search of anything edible in the debris; mangy dogs, stark-ribbed and yellow-eyed, snapped apathetically at the flies or snarled at the children who crawled too near; great white sacred bulls, with fat humps swaying and dewlaps flapping, nuzzled the gutters, secure in the knowledge that even in this Mohammedan city no hand could be turned against them. Here a couple of goats were tethered to a bedstead on which an old man lay crouched in sleep; there a sheep was slaughtered under the delighted gaze of a covey of pot-bellied children, who leapt back laughing as the arc of blood from the stretched throat soaked them. A caravan of camels, bell-hung and belching, fought for space with three lumbering elephants who swept the open shops of sweetmeats as they passed, and a cavalcade of seedy horses bearing a variety of evil-looking men, black-moustachioed and heavily armed, forced its rearing, neighing way through the throng. Holy men, the 'Sky Born', dressed as their mothers had borne them, long locks matted with ashes, foreheads marked with the ubiquitous symbol of Shiva, sat cross-legged and withdrawn among the cabbage leaves and horse-droppings, and every corner harboured a beggar exhibiting his sores or waving the stumps of his limbs, while importuning and imprecating the passers-by with an equal, hopeless violence.

And over all, enclosing all, accentuating the disgusted be-wilderment that filled me as my eyes roved the scene, was the noise—that sheer shell of sound that seems indivisible from humanity in India: shouting and hoarse cries, the wail of infants, the screams of children at unlikely games, vendors crying their wares, temple bells and beggars' bells and the bells of camels and the deep 'dong-dong' bells of elephants, dogs yelping, donkeys braying, horses neighing.

'Well, Laura? And is it still like the Arabian Nights?' Kate Barry enquired, as the buggy inched forward into the throng.

For some moments I could only shake my head. 'No, not at all,' I then said. 'It's horrible. Terrible, Kate. How can they exist in such conditions?'

'I've often wondered that myself. Perhaps because they have never known anything better, for themselves at least, poor divils.' She brushed the flies away from her face. 'But it's a pity you did not see it a few years ago; then you would have found it rather more like your idea of an Eastern city. There was still the poverty, the disease and the smells. But there was magnificence and pageantry too! All the swells, the princes and *talukhdars*, sometimes the Nawab himself, riding through the streets on jewelled horses and with great retinues of servants, slaves and soldiers all dressed like Aladdin, with scimitars in their sashes and egret plumes on their turbans. The elephants had silver *howdahs* on their backs in those days, and the horses were magnificent, prouder than the men who rode them. And then there would be the royal ladies in silken palanquins, strings of 'em, guarded like jewels, on their way to say their prayers at the mosque. But they have all gone now, poor things, or if they are here, they stay at home in their crumbling palaces. They are nobodies now, y'see, and I expect they feel it just as we should.'

It was difficult to reconcile this picture of past splendours with what I saw around me.

'I thought annexation was supposed to better the lot of the people,' I said, 'but what has been done to help these poor creatures?'

'It will take time,' Kate answered tranquilly. 'And at least now they are not forced off their own streets when the royal household wishes to take the air. The Nawab always feared assassination, y'know, and quite rightly. But there was pomp then, and display, and believe it or not, the people enjoyed it, although they had no part in it. Then we pushed the Nawab off his *gadhi*, so now all that is left is ... this!'

'But cannot something... surely something *must* be done to help them?'

I just then caught sight of a woman in a tattered *sari* with a tiny bone-thin child clasped in her arms. The child's head was lolling back against her arm, and its whole face was a mass of putrefying sores, around and over which crawled a legion of contentedly buzzing flies. The mother made no effort even to brush them aside, but gazed at us dully, with the apathy of long suffering, and mutely extended her open palm for alms. I fumbled in my reticule, but the buggy pushed past her before I could extract a coin, and there were so many other comparable ills around me that with a sigh I replaced it.

'To help them? Who knows but that we will in time. If we have time!'

I would have asked Kate to explain herself, but we had now reached our destination, the principal shopping street, and the driver drew up for us to alight.

I was relieved to see that here the crowd had thinned somewhat, and that the street was markedly broader than those we had already traversed. It was scarcely a salubrious thoroughfare, but the shops were richer and better stocked, though on examination their contents proved disappointing. There were the inevitable booths of the *halwais*, or sweetmeat sellers, spread with copper trays laden with sticky masses all covered with flies; some silversmiths and goldsmiths, the proprietors sitting crosslegged almost on the street, but oblivious of the crowds as they bent intently over their work of weighing, assaying and chastening the precious metals; a number of shops displaying slippers or the small embroidered caps typical of the kingdom, and several emporia of silks, muslins and other fine fabrics. To the largest and finest of these latter we made our way.

The cool darkness of the shop was welcome after the glare and smells of the street, and I looked around me with interest. Bales of gorgeously coloured stuffs, glowing softly in the dim interior, rose from floor to ceiling on three sides of the room; the fourth side lay open to the street and protected from it only by a narrow verandah edged by a wooden rail. A fine carpet covered the floor, and at the far end of the shop, upon a raised dais covered with white sheeting, sat the proprietor with his back against a cylindrical cotton bolster. He was a Hindu, and by the look of him a very prosperous tradesman, well-oiled and acceptably fat, with a fine belly swelling beneath his *dhoti* and white muslin tunic, and a small flat turban on his head. Beside him on the dais an incense coil in a silver holder smouldered beneath a hovering cloudlet of fragrant blue smoke. He rose as we entered, touching his forehead in that gesture it was so difficult not to think subservient, clapped his hands to summon his assistants, and when we were all accommodated on chairs, resumed his cross-legged seat.

Mrs Barry was an old customer; they exchanged remarks in Hindustani, and, having understood what was required, he directed his underlings to unroll his choicest wares for Charles's inspection. Peacock blues and acid yellows, dusky rose and rippling turquoise, satins and silks, cut-velvets and embossed brocades soon lay in gorgeous disarray on the carpet, while the shopman expatiated on the glories of his stock, and Mrs Barry cut down his prices in two languages, both salted, I have no doubt, by her caustic Irish tongue. I watched for a while, amused by the repartee, the emphatic gestures and the comically despairing expression on the shining dark face of the proprietor, but as Kate had taken over the task of advising Charles, and the bargaining looked like being a lengthy process, I wandered over to the verandah to watch the street.

The crowd, though hardly less squalid than on the other streets, was continuously fascinating, and there were here on the Hazrat Ganj not a few people of more prosperous appearance. Or rather I should say not a few men, for one did not see the women of the upper classes unveiled and in public. The poor females whom I watched gliding through the crowds, children straddled on their hips, or haggling over a handful of parched gram from the baskets of the lowest sort of street vendor, were of the most depressed castes and income, poor sexless creatures in ragged clothing, worn-faced and avid-eyed.

However, the ladies of the city were present, even though unseen, passing along in their closely curtained litters or palanquins, and accompanied often by servants. One of these palanquins had come to rest before the shop adjoining that in which I stood. It must have been a silversmith's, for a female servant who wore a *burqha* covering her from top to toe made frequent sorties between the shop and the palanquin with the sort of small wooden boxes I had noticed were used to hold the trinkets produced by these craftsmen. The curtains of the palanquin would open a fraction, a jewelled hand, nails tipped with henna, would take the box and then withdraw, and the two women, one within and one without, would discuss the merits of each article. Then the hand would appear again, the box would change hands and the servant would return to the shop for a further selection. A fine fierce-looking man, tall and well dressed with a long black beard, wearing a sword and carrying a matchlock, stood behind the palanquin, so I presumed the lady it enclosed was someone of consequence. The curtains of the palanquin were of some heavy material, richly embroidered and reasonably clean, and as I watched idly from my vantage point, I was amused to see a small brown face with bright enquiring eyes appear between the folds at the bottom end of the equipage. The lady had brought her child out with her for an airing. The child caught my eye as I watched, and its face broke into a charming smile. I smiled back and nodded my head in what I hoped was a reassuring manner. It smiled again and parted the curtains a little more so that its small shoulders, clad in peach-coloured brocade, were also visible. Then, in a gesture which must be common to the populations of the world, the boy put one small finger to his lips, enjoining silence, and in a trice was out of the curtains and standing between the shafts of the palanquin, looking excitedly around him. For a moment no one missed the child: the warlike guard was leaning on his matchlock watching the bargaining; the bearers had withdrawn to the shady side of the street; the mother and her maid were engrossed in their transactions—and the child was free.

At that instant a commotion broke out further up the street. There were cries and shouts of alarm. I saw the crowd break up and part, as everyone made for the sides of the road, those behind pushing those in front up shaky steps and on to verandahs such as I stood on; and then I heard the sound of hoofbeats and almost simultaneously the first of a string of horses appeared, careering madly—eyes rolling, heads tossing, hooves flailing—towards me. My attention had been deflected from the child, and when I again looked for him he had disappeared. For a second I thought he must have climbed back to his mother, being alarmed by the noise, but then I caught a glimpse of peach brocade between the bodies of the people packed beneath me, and the next instant the child was standing, laughing, in the middle of the road.

There was a sort of long, despairing sigh from the crowd, a wail of anguish from the burly guard, and then he and I leapt together towards the child. I was a little nearer, the crowd around me rather thinner, and I reached him first. Sweeping him into my arms without stopping, I rushed headlong on across the street, aware only of the horses rushing upon me, of a cloud of dust choking me, and then I and the bundle I carried had fallen among the feet of the people on the far side of the street. Dark hands raised me, set the child on its feet and brushed the dust from my clothing. Brown faces peered anxiously into mine, and a babel of voices, congratulatory and exclamatory, arose around me. The guard knelt at my feet, his forehead touching my shoes, his big hands joining palms together before his face. When he looked up I saw tears rolling down into his beard, and he did so only to reiterate his thanks and then touched and retouched his forehead to my feet again.

I found this manner of expressing gratitude embarrassing, though I knew it was the custom of the people, and was truly glad to be rescued by the appearance of my party, none of whom had known that anything untoward had happened until summoned by the wails of the Averys' coachman, who thought I must undoubtedly be dead. Then what a questioning ensued! I was still a little shaken, so Kate turned to the guard, who now clasped the little boy, and spoke to him in Hindustani. The good man must have given an exaggerated account of the matter; it was certainly lengthy and much interrupted by various members of the crowd breaking in to give their amendments, the whole accompanied by a great deal of dramatic gesturing. I felt foolish, now that all was over, and gladly assented to cutting short the shopping in order to remove myself from the curious gaze of so many strangers. The guard helped me into the carriage, making a last obeisance as he did so, and, once seated, I shook the hand of the little boy, who, to his credit, had not even whimpered from the moment I had snatched him up. Only the mother of the child, though she must have known by now what had happened, remained silent, enclosed in her dark palanquin. I could not help but wonder, as we moved away, at the strength of a system that could produce such absolute conformity even in a time of crisis. I know that had I been the mother and the boy my son, I would have broken my *purdah* without a moment's hesitation.

We returned home, and I would soon have forgotten my trifling adventure, but for a sequel that took place that evening, and that was to bear strange repercussions into my future life.

We had formed the habit of gathering together in company to pass the hour before the early dinner, and on that day were sitting on the lawn before the house enjoying the wintry sunshine. The flowerbeds had received their last watering, the grass had been newly scythed, and one of the gardeners, plying a twig broom, had brushed the yellow dust of the driveway into a neat herringbone pattern. Darkness was still an hour or more away but the first of the fruit bats had already flapped on leathern wings across the sky and a young moon showed silver in the evening's pale gold. Conversation had flagged, all of us enjoying the peace too much to mar it with talk. Only Wallace fidgeted in his chair and appeared, as usual, preoccupied and anxious to be away. Connie was absent.

Suddenly there was a stir at the gate and, to our surprise, a cavalcade of five or six horsemen turned in to the drive and trotted up to the house, halting at the pillared porch.

Wallace crossed the lawn to investigate and returned accompanied by a figure of just such oriental splendour as I had once imagined all Indian gentlemen would present. This was a man, short and broad and full-bearded, whose deliberate, stately walk and self-contained survey of the company in which he found himself indicated clearly a habit of authority. His dress, though simple, was rich; snowy breeches and a loose shirt of embroidered muslin were covered by a long open coat of multicoloured brocade. Slippers of black velvet embroidered in gold curled up at the toes to end in golden tassels, and on his head he wore a flat turban, whose precise pink folds were embellished by a fine ruby. Jewels shone too on his hands and in his ears, and a curved dagger in a gem-encrusted scabbard was thrust through the gathered satin of his cummerbund. Behind him paced a servant carrying a large round tray covered with a cloth.

It was obvious that Wallace was at a loss with his unexpected guest, but he ushered him in to our circle of chairs with rather excessive cordiality and said, 'May I introduce Mr Wajid Khan, the Talukhdar of Nayanagar. I believe he has something of importance to say to you, Laura. This is Miss Hewitt, sir,' and he indicated me to the newcomer.

The gentleman bowed politely to the company, then approached me and with his hands joined made a deeper bow.

'Miss Hewitt, madam. My pleasure to meet you is extreme.'

He bowed again while I wondered whether I should extend my hand, rise, or remain seated.

'I have come, madam,' he went on before I had resolved my perplexity, 'to offer you the most heartfelt thanks of myself, my wife and all my family for the great service you have this morning performed for us in the Hazrat Ganj.'

'Oh, the little boy!' I exclaimed, beginning to understand.

'My son. My servants have told me of your great bravery and the extreme promptness with which you acted on his behalf, to rescue him from those murderous horses.' He spoke English with ease but his accent was sing-song and he over-accentuated most of his consonants.

'I have no words sufficient for my gratitude, madam,' and he put his right hand on his brocaded breast, 'but my heart will never be ceasing to remember your act. You have truly been the saviour of my house. I have many children, and other sons, yes, also. But many have died. This boy is my eldest male child and very precious therefore. He is, as you may say, the apple of my heart, so now it is fitting that I, and with me all my household, place myself at your feet.'

To my horror this most dignified personage then went down on his knees and would have put his forehead on my shoes, but that I drew back my feet and jumping up very hastily, so that his turban got knocked slightly askew, I took him by the hands and drew him upright again, exclaiming, 'Oh, please, sir! You have nothing to thank me for. What I did, any other person aware of your boy's danger would have done, I do assure you.' He allowed me to raise him and, since I was slightly aghast at what I had done, thinking he might construe as rudeness what was in fact merely embarrassment, I was relieved to see a twinkle in his fine brown eyes and a slight smile part his whiskers.

'You are more than modest, madam,' he assured me as I dropped his plump hands, 'but I see I have a little upset you and I ask your pardon. Our ways are sometimes not the same. But now, if you will allow me, my wife has asked me to convey her great gratitude to you also, and begs that you will accept some small offering in token of the thanks which she can never adequately express.'

He summoned the retainer who accompanied him, who came forward holding out his burden at arm's length.

'Regrettably it is only some few poor sweetmeats,' Wajid Khan said, taking the tray. 'It is known that English ladies would find difficulty in accepting gifts of value, but my wife has asked me to assure you very thoroughly that, were it not for this, she would have sent you the finest of all the jewels obtainable in Lucknow.'

I knew a moment of acute annoyance at the supposed finer feelings of my countrywomen, while Wajid Khan placed the tray in my hands, with another deep bow. The tray was so heavy I almost dropped it, so I sat down again hastily and, placing it on my knees, removed the covering. It was of heavy silver, finely chased, and built up upon it was a series of cones, squares and pyramids comprised of every imaginable type of sugary delicacy known to Indian cookery.

I exclaimed with delight, then remembered to beg Wajid Khan to be seated. He lowered himself cautiously into a basket chair, sitting awkwardly with his stout legs in their tight white breeches set wide apart, his beringed fingers clasping the chair arms, while, smiling, he watched us all examine his gift.

Emily helped herself to crystallized pumpkin and Wally took a coiled golden *jellabi* at my insistence, but the donor himself would not be tempted.

In the very centre of the tray, placed upon a pile of puffed sugar macaroons, was a small covered basket made of delicate silver filigree. I took it to contain some especially rare delicacy, and picked it up to open it.

In a second our new friend had extracted himself from his chair and was beside me, taking the pretty thing from my fingers before I could raise the lid.

'This,' he said, 'is my own thank-offering to you, Miss Hewitt, and it is maybe best that I explain for you its significance. See ...' He flicked open the lid. 'It is a little bracelet. Not a jewel, you understand—not even a trinket. Itself, it is worthless, but in my part of the country it is a token, a symbol, of the obligations of true brotherhood. It is called a *rakhri*. There is, you will understand, a proper festival for the presenting of these bracelets, but though the festival is past for this year, nevertheless the purpose of the giving is the same, whatever the month, and as I can give you nothing of value to betoken my gratitude and esteem, I am hoping that you will permit me to offer you the undying service of myself and all my family with this unworthy toy.'

The bracelet he held out to me was a charming little object, a row of floss silk rosettes in vivid jewel colours, each one backed by a medallion of silver filigree and strung together on a slender rope of gold and silver thread intertwined. More gold and silver gleamed among the ruby, emerald, sapphire and amber silk, and in the centre of each rosette was a tiny flower of seed pearls.

'Oh, how pretty!' I exclaimed, as he held it up and the others crowded round to see.

'Pretty, yes,' agreed Wajid Khan judiciously, 'but not only that, I am hoping. Perhaps, for who can tell these matters, perhaps one day you will find it also useful. This poor trifle, this *rakhri*, when I have fastened it upon your wrist I will have performed the small ceremony of *rakhri-band* and tied myself and all my family and my resources to you for ever. It will mean, then, that if ever you are requiring help in grave matter or small, I am bound immediately to drop at once my own affairs and do all in my powers to help you ... as if you were truly my sister and I your brother. And if we are far apart, even to the ends of the earth, and you send me this little *rakhri* by speedy messengers in

113

token of distresses you may be undergoing presently, I must immediately hasten to your side.'

'What a very touching custom, Mr Khan. You do me a great honour.'

'I am glad that you are approving. It is also a very old custom, most ancient, and many stories are told in Indian history of the use of the *rakhri* to summon assistance from some king or hero. It is said, for instance, that when the island kingdom of Chitor, many years ago now, was besieged and in foulest peril, the beautiful queen of that kingdom sent a *rakhri* to the great Emperor Akbar himself. Even before immediately he set out to help her with all his armies and his elephants, and it was no fault of his doing that, when he arrived, he found every Rajput warrior slain upon the battlefield and all the ladies of the court dead upon one great funeral pyre. No, indeed. Akbar had done what he could, for such is the power of the *rakhri* in our custom.'

'How interesting, and again, how very touching.'

'I am permitted then ...?'

He hesitated, looking anxiously into my face; then glanced at Charles and Wallace as if to ask their permission. I expect it was difficult for him to realize that English unmarried females are able to make up their own minds in such matters.

'Why, certainly you are permitted, Mr Khan,' I hastened to assure him before Charles could say a word. 'I am most honoured.' And I held out my wrist. Wajid Khan put the glinting gossamer around it and secured the fastening with care. Then he patted my hand in a fatherly fashion and sighed with satisfaction.

'Thank you. Thank you,' he beamed. 'Now I can return to my wife and tell her all with utmost pleasure. But you understand ... it is not a joke, no? By this *rakhri-band* I have obliged myself to you in seriousness.'

'Yes. I understand, sir, and I thank you. I will keep my *rakhri* most carefully all my life and always remember the donor with great kindness.'

He searched my face as I spoke and, then, satisfied that I was in earnest, made a deep *salaam* to me again, bowed to the others present and took his leave. Wally pressed him to stay for some refreshment, and I would have enjoyed learning more of him, his family and way of life but, his errand done, nothing would keep him.

'Well, really, Laura!' expostulated Emily as the little procession disappeared through the gate in the fast falling dusk. 'You do have the oddest adventures. First Mrs Wilkins on the ship'—I had given Emily a truncated account of my last meeting with the Wilkins ladies—'and now this. I declare, all India appears anxious to offer you help, and I never in my life met anyone less in need of it.'

'Long may it continue, if it always takes as pleasant a form as this,' I replied, as I stretched out my left arm to admire the bracelet, while with my right I helped myself to a sweet oozing rosewater. 'Though, come to think of it, it would really have been more satisfactory if Mrs Wilkins had given me her garter too, in earnest of her goodwill, as Mr Khan has given me the *rakhri.*'

'Mother has always said you are too impetuous,' grumbled my cousin in reply. 'Some day you will find yourself in trouble for not taking thought before rushing into things as you do.'

'Then all I have to do is summon Wajid Khan to my side,' I reminded her blithely. Emily had not liked my being the centre of attention; Wajid Khan had scarcely deigned to glance her way. So now I merely cocked an eyebrow and licked my fingers provokingly. But inwardly I was as amused as she was irritated by the very diverse persons anxious to lend me their aid, and the odd similarity of the objects that represented their desire—a black satin garter and a floss silk bracelet.

CHAPTER 11

The year drew towards its close. By the end of November it was cold enough to enjoy the log fires that were lit each evening in the drawing-room, the mosquito nets were taken down, and when I went to bed I was glad of the stone hotwater jar I found between the sheets. There was an autumnal feel in the air, a hint of sadness in the scent of burning leaves and in the slanted, low rays of a sun that had forgotten its zenith. Horses now were blanketed at nightfall, and the spoilt cantonment dogs waddled down the roads in woolly coats knitted by their mistresses.

But still the gardens bloomed, not now with the hard hot-weather zinnia and cockscomb, but with familiar English favourites—heliotrope, babies' breath, love-in-the-mist, London pride and sweet william—all spilling their delicate scent over carpets of pansies, nasturtiums and violets. The cantonment ladies were back from the hills, pink-cheeked and plump, in marked contrast to those unfortunates like Connie Avery who had not been able to leave the plains.

'I used to go every year,' Connie explained one day. 'To Simla, you know. Wally said it was much better to go there than to Mussoorie because Simla is a fashionable place. I had a very good *derzi* there who used to make us all pretty clothes, the babies and me, and a dear little bungalow looking right across the valleys to the snows. Oh, how I did enjoy it all—the smart people and the nice tea-shops and the cool air! But everything has got so much more expensive that I haven't been up for three years now. Wally's mess bills are so much higher since he has been promoted; and we can't do without things here as one could at home. People would notice, y'know, if we didn't have the buggy and the horses and so on, though I'm sure I get little enough pleasure out of them. What's to be seen when we do drive out but a lot of people we see every day anyway, and a heap of shabby old palaces? But still, staying down here has been worth it because Wally says he's quite sure we will have enough money for Johnny and me to go home in the spring. He can't come with us, of course, but he'll follow in a year or two. I don't like to leave him, but Johnny must...' And her voice trailed away in the manner to which I had by now become accustomed.

Although she was still pale and unhappy in the mornings, Emily was improving in health and spirits. She must have been ashamed of her outburst on the day Kate Barry told her the probable cause of her ill-health, because she never again mentioned her unhappiness to me. However, understanding what I could not but believe were her true feelings regarding her marriage and the baby, I now became aware of many indications of the tensions, covert but unmistakable, that existed between Charles and herself. Sometimes I would surprise a look of dejection on Charles's face, an expression of ill-concealed irritation on Emily's when he was near, that saddened me for both their sakes and, let me be truthful, for my own. I could no longer admit, even to myself, that I was 'in love' with Charles as I had been when we left home. If, in my case, familiarity did not breed contempt, it had to a great extent soothed the sentimental anguish of a few months ago. I retained the deepest affection for Charles, a true wish for his happiness, but the tumult of bittersweet passion which I had had to contend with in the early weeks of his marriage was now quite allayed.

But still, sometimes when I was tired, and the weight of loneliness seemed to crush me, I would acknowledge that had things been otherwise I could indeed have loved him; and so, seeing his love for Emily unreturned, I suffered for him. He had developed during our months in India. He was quieter and more contained. The well-shaped lips beneath his moustache were compressed now in a way that revealed resignation as much as firmness, and the expression in his fine blue eyes was often too long-suffering for a man of his years; particularly when they rested, as often happened, on his gay little wife flirting outrageously with one or other of the young officers who flocked to her banner here in Lucknow just as their counterparts had done in Calcutta.

At home in Mount Bellew it had been the custom for me to brush Emily's long fair hair at bedtime, while she sipped a glass of hot milk and we gossiped over the doings of the day. Necessarily, this little ceremony had lapsed during the first months of my cousin's marriage, but now, with Charles so often out late playing cards or billiards with Wallace and his friends, we had again fallen into the habit. It soothed and comforted Emily, I believe, to revert to this childish pattern, even though childhood was behind her, and it was she who now came into my room with her brush, and as I stroked the tangles into shining order, we would reminisce about our family or dissect (not always kindly) our Indian acquaintances.

One night she bounced into my room, flung off her slippers and sat down cross-legged on my bed, turning her back towards me and holding out her brush in a peremptory manner, quite like the Emily I remembered in Mount Bellew.

'Old *cats*!' she spat out, as I took the brush. 'Nasty, illnatured, mean old cats!'

'Oh? Who are?'

'All of them! All those dreary women Connie and I were drinking tea with this evening.' They had been to a ladies party at the house of Wallace's commanding officer. 'They talked of nothing but babies. Having babies and bringing up babies, and babies being ill and babies dying and who was about to have a baby. You'd think there was nothing else in the world to interest a woman.'

'Oh, poor Em,' I comforted. 'But still, that doesn't make them ill-natured or mean—just limited.'

'Yes, but... but somehow they have already discovered that I, that I am ...'

'I see: that you are going to have a baby?'

'Yes. I can't think where they can have heard it, because I certainly haven't breathed a word and I'm sure Kate wouldn't have either. But there you are, they know!'

'Connie, I expect. You know how good she is at saying the wrong thing.'

'Yes, of course. I never thought of Connie—drat her! She just sat there grinning, with her nose all pink at the end, and hiccoughed into her handkerchief. I felt so mortified, Laura, I can't tell you. What my mother would say if she knew about Connie! All the other women just ignored her; even when she let her cup and saucer slip off her lap. Mrs Sandes just raised her hand for a servant to clear up the mess and went on talking as though nothing had happened, and poor Connie was so apologetic and nearly in tears. And they all looked at me—pityingly— as though Connie was my responsibility. As if I can do anything about her.'

'And that's what upset you?'

'Oh, no! That just made me cross. But one of the old ... the old *besoms*, who sat near me, a fat woman with snuff on the bodice of her dress and under her nose, would insist on squeezing my hand and saying things like, er, "Poor little dear. So far from home, and so young and all your good times coming to an end so early. Poor, poor little dear." Ugh! I could have screamed. And then they all turned and looked at me, measuringly you know, wondering how ... how far along I was, and trying to make out whether it showed yet. It was quite horrid, and the worst of it was that I knew I was blushing.'

'*I* should have been there. I would have looked right back at them in a way that would have made them mind their own business.'

'Yes, I'm sure you would have. You can do that sort of thing so well. But then the fat snuffy one said, and I swear she was gloating, Laura: "What a pity that your dancing days will be over before the Residency ball," and when I looked at her—blankly, you know—she went on about it not being "seemly" to dance when it was generally known that one was having a baby—not "delicate", she said. So I turned away very haughtily and talked to someone else. But is it true, Laura? Will I really not be able to dance at the ball?'

'Heavens, I don't know! I'd never have given it a thought, and if you are feeling well enough I don't see why you shouldn't. But I suppose people might talk, especially in a place like this where everybody knows everybody else's business. It's too bad.'

'Well, if I can't dance, I'm not going and that's that. I'm not going to be stuck in a corner with all the old crows, fed on ices, and forgotten for the rest of the time. I won't do it!'

'Now don't get fussed. The ball is only a little more than a week away, so I expect we'll be able to manage it. The word will have got around, certainly, but so long as Charles doesn't think about the propriety of the matter and forbid you to dance, there is nothing anyone can do to stop you. And I don't believe anyone would be foolish enough to mention the subject to him afterwards, no matter how much they chatter among themselves. We must just contrive somehow that he doesn't think about it beforehand, for if he does, I believe he might keep you from dancing; he is rather a "proper" fellow, after all, isn't he?'

'Sometimes,' his wife rejoined sourly. 'But they know everything about us. All of them. All about my father, and Charles's partnership and the Company in Calcutta. Wouldn't be a bit surprised if they even knew just how much our income is, which is more than I do myself. And of course they know all about Oliver Erskine.'

'Oh, do they?' And with a memory of the strange face in the portrait in Calcutta, and my conversation with Kate Barry, I went on, 'What did they have to say about him?'

'Just the usual things. When were we going out to Hassanganj, and how long was it since Charles had met him and so on. They were quite put out that I couldn't tell them more than they knew themselves, but went on about his being so rich, and his grand house and his horses, and what a recluse he was. That's how they put it, though of course they meant he was unsociable. And I couldn't even say we would be visiting Hassanganj, which was very awkward for me, as having come all this way we really should have had an invitation from the wretched man, and not getting one looks so, well, pointed, doesn't it? I do wish Charles would forget about him and take us on to Delhi directly. I think I've seen enough of India now, and with this wretched brat on the way, I want to get home to Mother and Mount Bellew. But there was something about him, Laura, that I fancy Charles doesn't know and wouldn't like to know.' She swung round and faced me so suddenly that I drew the brush across her forehead and nose. 'Ouch! Mildred Myers, she's the very fat one with rabbits' teeth, you know? Married to that foxy-faced Myers with ginger whiskers who tried to hold my hand under the tablecloth at the Greshams' dinner ...'

'He did what?'

'Oh yes, lots of them do, you know. I used to think being married would put a stop to all that, but it hasn't, not that it is of any consequence, but anyway Mildred told me, *sotto voce* of course, and out of sheer spite too, I'm sure, that he has a terrible reputation with women.'

'Naturally. That is only to be expected. If people don't know anything good about a man, they will certainly invent something bad,' I said disingenuously, having in mind my conversation with Kate Barry on the way to the bazaar.

'I don't think it can be only that,' Emily said dubiously.

'I'm sure it is. He has probably put quite a parcel of doting mamas into a temper by not marrying their daughters, with the result that they are happy to believe he must be unprincipled. It follows.'

'Oh, but it's not girls, that is it's not girls like *us* that he is supposed to be interested in. It's native girls. "The browner the belles, the better he likes 'em." That's how that odious Myers woman put it anyway.'

'Well, I'm sure he is not the first, even if there is anything in it, and it would be wrong to judge him before we have even set eyes on him whatever the gossip,' I said as prosaically as I could, for I was rather startled by this intelligence. We were then just at the time when to acknowledge an Indian wife or mistress was to invite the wrath of the authorities and the contumely of one's peers; a generation earlier such associations were part and parcel of Indian life; later, though they still occurred, they were never mentioned. But at that time, although many eminent men had taken to themselves Indian wives, a floodtide of decorous middle-class opinion, brought out by the dim, prim wives and daughters of officers and civil servants making increasing use of the overland route, was beginning to sway judgement of such matters from tolerance towards outrage. I was sufficiently of my time, as a young woman, to share something of that outrage.

'But, Laura, it would be awful if it were true, for then we certainly couldn't go to Hassanganj.'

'We haven't been invited yet, my dear Em, and you've just said you wished Charles would forget all about going there. But if we *are* invited, there's nothing to prevent us going, surely? Mr Erskine is not likely to flaunt his inamorata in public, is he?'

'I don't have the slightest idea what one does and does not do with inamoratas, but I do know that Charles would never permit it.'

'Well then, we must hope to discover that these tales are nothing more than malicious rumour.' And I added to myself, as I confessed to a growing curiosity about Mr Erskine and his palace in the wilderness, 'Or at least hope that the rumours never reach Charles's ears.'

The ball at which Emily had been advised not to dance was the official opening of what, for want of a better word, I must describe as the 'Season'. It served to announce the advent of the cold-weather gaieties as well as to welcome back to the station the ladies who had been to the Hills for the summer, and had for some time been the topic most in the minds of those who were fortunate enough to be invited. I had reconciled myself to being overlooked, for when Charles and Emily paid their official call on the Resident, I had not been asked to accompany them, Emily having been in one of her more intractable moods that day. However, Charles had asked for one of my cards to leave on Mr Coverly Jackson's tray, and whether due to his thoughtfulness or Kate Barry's influence, I was surprised and pleased when an invitation arrived for me as well as the others in the house.

For days past the cantonment ladies had given little thought to anything but what they should wear for the ball. On every back verandah in Mariaon *derzis* squatted behind screens, stitching, ripping and altering gowns with dexterous haste, and liveried servants trotted from house to bazaar to house with snippets of silk, lace and ribbon for matching and comment. Emily had a lavish and expensive trousseau to choose from, so the question of what she should wear occupied both our minds for some time. At length she decided that nothing would do but her best blue taffeta, and even this was not quite as elaborate a toilette as she wanted so a *derzi* was put to work making a new tulle overskirt and train, and the basque was trimmed anew with part of her wedding lace. I was to wear the coral-pink silk that became my dark complexion best. Emily would have preferred to see me in white muslin and forget-me-nots like Elvira Wilkins on account of my spinster state, but my choice was made as much by necessity as taste, for my wardrobe, although enhanced by the Calcutta *derzi*, was still modest, and my resources too slender to warrant sartorial extravagance. In any event, as I reminded myself, I was a 'companion', and therefore required to look every day of my twenty-four years. But on that evening in early December when the ball took place, I found it difficult to think either of my inferior position or my advanced age. Perhaps the more benign climate, perhaps the smaller circle of acquaintances, lent this event more interest than any of the probably grander affairs I had attended in Calcutta, but I found myself anticipating the hour of our departure with some fervour.

On my advice Emily banished from her mind the stringent dictates of her elderly acquaintance regarding dancing when expecting a child, and, since the days passed with no mention of the matter from Charles, her spirits soared and she threw herself into her preparations with excited zest. No one was to be allowed to outshine her at this ball. Every detail of her toilette was agonized over until she was satisfied it could not be improved. I tried her hair in a dozen different styles before she could choose which suited her best and would do most justice to the little diadem of pearls with matching earbobs and bracelet which had been her father's wedding gift. She wasted an afternoon and half the blooms in the garden making up and then discarding posies in various colours and combinations of flowers; and, so that she could dance every dance with comfort, she wore her new dancing slippers about the house for three whole days. I rejoiced to see her once again her giddy, self-absorbed but endearing self, and only wished her mood could outlast the ball.

At last the great day dawned, and I watched the sky anxiously since nothing would content Emily but accompanying Charles to the ball in a high curricle. This equipage was unsuitable for the use of ladies in ball gowns, but Emily had her mind made up. If it had rained, she would have had to use the Avery buggy along with Connie and myself, and our ride would have been made miserable by grumbles about the cramped conditions, the dust and the sagging springs of the upholstery. Fortunately the weather remained fine and clear, though there was a chill in the air, and, as we bowled along the avenues of Mariaon, the first star appeared in a milky pink sky while the sun had yet to dip behind the dark foliage of the mangoes. Six o'clock seemed a strangely early hour for the commencement of a ball (especially as I learnt on good authority that we could not expect to be home before four in the morning) but there were advantages in setting off by daylight: we were enabled to glimpse the finery of our friends as they drove past us or we caught up with them. Soon we were part of a stream of carriages, gigs and landaus all making in the same direction; young officers on horseback called cheerfully to each other or saluted the ladies in the carriages as they galloped by, each of them with a *syce* running at his horse's heels carrying a cudgel and a lantern to guard and guide his *sahib* home.

Of course it was not the Cantonment Residency to which we were bound, but the City Residency across the River Goomti—more often called the Baillie Guard.

In the middle of the last century, the first Resident appointed by the East India Company to further its trade with the Kingdom of Oudh had sited his house (with a consideration to prudence as well as prospect) on a bluff overlooking the Goomti, which formed the highest part of the surrounding country and gave him, as well as a fine view, the possibility of self-defence in time of trouble. Over the decades, as the position of Resident had grown in importance and power, other houses and bungalows, warehouses, barracks, a church, a gaol and a hospital had been built within the Resident's compound, forming a self-contained community. At one time the compound was probably fortified and walled, but the walls had long since disintegrated or been built over, the only stretch remaining being that flanking the main gate or Baillie Guard, from which the little complex now took its popular name. As the buggy slowed to a snail's pace in the press of traffic and we drove up the sloping roadway and under the arch of the Baillie Guard, I looked about me with no small interest and curiosity.

At first glance I would have guessed myself to be in some Italian resort, for the buildings around me, simple structures washed in white or pastel pink, with jalousied windows and pillared porticoes, were much like those I recalled from my childhood home outside Genoa. Set in smooth lawns dotted with bright flowerbeds and shaded by massive mohurs, peepuls and neems, the lesser buildings clustered, but not too closely, around the Residency itself, a truly impressive pile three storeys high and boasting a fine hexagonal tower, from the summit of which, as it was not yet sundown, fluttered limply the red, white and blue of the Union Jack. Beyond this building, the lawns fell away to the riverbank, while on looking back as the carriage advanced to deposit us at the entrance, I glimpsed again the great domes and golden minarets of the city, thronging, it seemed, almost to the Baillie Guard itself.

The place was *en fête*, from the drugget laid down on the steps to save the ladies' delicate slippers, to the Chinese lanterns hanging in the trees and the horde of chattering, liveried servants clustered about the entrance to watch the arrivals.

Immediately in front of us, Charles, who was driving the curricle himself, swept up to the entrance with something of a flourish, and in so doing managed to lock his off wheel in the wheel of another gig that was just about to drive away. There was a moment's impasse as both drivers endeavoured to disengage their vehicles. Connie, grateful for the delay, fumbled in her reticule and took out a small flask, from which she took a couple of eager gulps behind a delicately raised hand. 'Just to steady me, y'know,' she said without embarrassment as I caught her eye. Meanwhile the driver of the other gig had jumped down and, while

Charles kept his horse in check, put his shoulder to his own wheel and, clenching both hands around the rim of Charles's wheel, exerted his strength in two directions at once, thus, little by little, freeing the two vehicles. When they once again stood independently on the gravel, he straightened his back, wiped the sweat from his forehead, rubbed his palms on the seat of his pants, and then, very deliberately, walked round the horses' heads to face Charles.

He was the oddest little figure of a man I had ever laid eyes on, perhaps in his late twenties, standing no more than five feet in his long yellow boots. His legs were bowed as a jockey's, though his livery and tall hat indicated he was a coachman or groom. Long arms depended from shoulders that were disproportionately broad, and the head beneath the hat was a large one. His face was long and thin, and his eyes, small, black and as bright as boot buttons, were set so far towards his ears that I felt he could not possibly view any object with the two of them at once. He had a small flat nose, and his mouth was looselipped and wide; when he smiled he revealed a double row of large and glistening teeth as faultlessly regular as those of a healthy colt. He was smiling now. For a moment he inspected Charles, his equipage and his wife with dispassionate interest. Then, with his hands deep in his breeches pockets, he spoke: 'You didn't ought to 'ave done that, guv, really you didn't. Now I sees you 'ave your lady with you, so I'll say no more on this occasion. Very embarrassing it would be—for you! But mark this: if you can't handle your ribbons better nor that, you 'as no business driving a high-wheeler—most perticular on a crowded occasion like this. Not safe you aren't. Think what would 'ave 'appened to your lady 'ere, upended in a crowd of blackies.'

'Sir!' fumed Charles, jumping down from his seat, and doubling his fists aggressively.

The little man held up one hand commandingly: 'Now! Now! No offence meant. Just givin' some kindly advice, see. Stick to a perambulator and you'll be all right, guv,' and with a jaunty salute in Emily's direction, their rescuer stalked back to his own vehicle, mounted and swept off in superb style, leaving a chagrined Charles to stare after him, not sure whether to laugh or swear.

There had been a few smiles and sniggers from the crowd of *syces* and coachmen near the entrance, and as we went up the steps Emily was almost tearful with mortification.

'Oh, I'll never feel the same again,' she whispered. 'Fancy anyone employing a ruffian like that—capable of speaking to a gentleman as he did to Charles. The … the villain!'

'And he looked so like a horse himself, don't you think?' put in Connie with unaccustomed accuracy, while Wallace exhorted Emily not to give the matter another thought: the fellow was just a lout getting a cheap laugh from the natives.

'He hadn't a leg to stand on. It was as much his fault as mine,' put in Charles with something less than truth, 'but I certainly couldn't bandy words with a groom, so I had to let him get away with it. Most unfortunate.' And he ran a finger under his high white stock. Thus was masculine honour saved and, the business of the evening once begun, our discomfiture was soon forgotten.

CHAPTER 12

The reception rooms were already filled with people when, after leaving our cloaks in an upstairs room, we rejoined the men, made our curtseys and shook hands with our host the Chief Commissioner (as the Resident was called after annexation), Mr Coverly Jackson. His manner towards his guests bordered on the disdainful, but since there were several couples behind us, we did not bother him with our conversation too long, and were soon free to find our own enjoyment.

It was truly a most elegant occasion. The rooms were large and light, with long windows and high ceilings, the furnishings rich and comfortable. Fine polished floors, gleaming mahogany and mellow satin-wood, old silver and brocaded hangings were reflected in long mirrors set to catch the light of splendid chandeliers and countless candelabra, and everywhere there were flowers, massed on tables and sideboards, banked in pyramids in the corners of the rooms, and festooning the daïs on which the band was seated. Music was provided by the bandsmen of three separate regiments in turn, and I wondered if I were alone in my astonishment at how well our old airs were rendered by dusky musicians who knew nothing of the Western tonic sol-fa and had never read a note of music in their lives.

'Oh, how very delightful it all is,' sighed Connie. 'I declare it makes me feel quite young again to hear the music and see all the pretty gowns.' And her pale eyes came nearer to sparkling than I had ever seen them. Poor Connie, she had chosen to wear a dress of pale yellow muslin, rather limp and *démodé*, which did less than justice to her colouring. But Wallace was very smart and military in his tight blue pantaloons and jacket of blue faced with grey and silver.

Dancing was already in progress as we wandered through the bright rooms in search of friends. The ladies, bell-hooped and crinolined, swam beneath the chandeliers in a tide of satin, silk and sarsenet of every hue, and the gentlemen, in tight pea jackets faced with flashing scarlet, yellow or silver, chests be-medalled, whiskers curled, served only to rival their partners in splendour, while here and there a lone civilian in sober black pointed a contrast.

We were soon joined by Kate and George Barry, Kate, as always in a high-necked, long-sleeved gown of black, her only concession to the occasion being low black slippers in place of her usual high button-boots. 'Why, Emily,' she exclaimed with her customary frankness, 'you are certainly the loveliest young thing here. A very vision! Laura, just look at how the heads are turning in our direction, though goodness knows, you look so charming yourself tonight I declare half the admiration at least must be for you.' We laughed, but there was no doubt that Emily was attracting a good deal of notice, something of which that young lady was delightedly aware. The tallest and most graceful female in our party, the pale blue of her gown enhanced the deep blue of her eyes. Her cheeks were flushed with excitement (and a judicious pinch or two in the cloakroom) making her delicate skin whiter than ever.

I must confess to some complacency regarding my own appearance. The Fates did not bless me with beauty, and I am of too short a stature ever to aspire to true elegance. But my figure was neat and shapely, my coral gown suited my complexion and fitted me excellently, and I knew that few women in the room could match my head of hair, my only outstanding feature, which was long and heavy and glistened with the same dark but ruddy glow as a newly cobbed chestnut. Owning no suitable jewellery, my only ornaments were a corsage of fresh, deep-coral japonica from Kate's garden, and a matching wreath in my hair. A glimpse of myself in a cheval glass left me content with my overall appearance, and it was with a light heart that I surrendered my programme and its small gold pencil to Captain Fanning, who was the first to claim a dance. I would have preferred not to be the first of the party on the floor but, having no reason to refuse the gentleman other than a desire not to upset Emily, I allowed myself to be led away.

Captain Fanning was hardly a conquest. He was a goodnatured ninny, who thought I must be flattered by his opinion that I was the most 'fetching spin' in the Station that winter. His manner, however, was so guileless that I made an effort to appear as pleased as he thought

I should be. As a dancer he was erratic, but he was a great gossip and, before returning to my party, I had learned that our host, Mr Jackson, was the most ill-tempered and contentious man in India and that no one could serve under him and survive for more than six months, except for Mr Gubbins, the Financial Commissioner, and he only because he was Mr Jackson's match. 'Fight like a couple of toms on a roof,' remarked my informant. 'Old Buggins is all bounce and blow and too conceited to admit that he's anyone's subordinate, so he has Jackson hopping like a flea on a hot brick.' He pointed Mr Gubbins out to me, a portly man dancing with measured deliberation, and wearing on his round red face that expression of patriarchal but brittle benevolence that can only be achieved by the pompous.

I returned to my place in good humour. But in my absence something had gone awry. Emily, whom I had expected to be dancing, was seated on a sofa against the wall, with Kate Barry next to her and Charles standing stiffly, almost at attention, beside them.

'What's the matter?' I asked, as Captain Fanning handed me to a chair. 'Why ever aren't you up and dancing?'

Captain Fanning bowed and took himself off for further conquests, as Kate answered drily, 'Charles feels it would not be the thing for Emily to dance tonight.' Charles himself said nothing, but Emily looked at me with eyes swimming in tears.

'Oh surely, Charles,' I protested too hastily, 'there can be nothing amiss with Emily dancing—at least with you.'

'And if she dances with me, can she refuse to dance with any other man?' he pointed out shortly, but with truth.

'But ...' I began, but he silenced me.

'We have already been over the matter, Laura, and Emily knows my wishes.'

I was quite sure she had not known them when we set out, or she would sooner have stayed at home. As it was, her position was ridiculous: the prettiest girl in the room sitting like a wall-flower guarded by an obviously ill-tempered husband.

'We do not intend to stay long,' Charles went on, as though to mitigate the sentence he had imposed. 'Directly after supper we shall return home, but you, of course, can come back later with the Averys.'

'Thank you,' I said coldly. 'And in the meantime may I suggest that it might improve matters for all of us if we moved to one of the side rooms where there are light refreshments. We can at least seem to be happily employed—eating!'

So we moved. Charles provided us with ices, and then, when Connie and Wallace joined us, suggested to Wallace a saunter through the cardrooms; they made their way out through the crowd, and we four females were left to our own devices, with the tantalising strains of a waltz audible over the chatter and laughter. Having danced once with his wife, Wallace was now intent upon the tables, and I knew we would not be able to count on much male company for the rest of the evening, which now loomed ahead as a desert of frustration and boredom. I had not the heart to dance myself when poor Emily was forbidden the pleasure. Two or three other ladies came to speak to us after a time, and while they occupied Emily and Connie with small talk—they were tactful and did not ask why Emily was not dancing—I had a quiet word with Kate.

'What happened?' I asked.

'Och, woman dear, very little.' And she shrugged her shoulders expressively, speaking behind her fan. 'I told Charles to be a man and take his wife on to the floor, and he just said that Emily would not think of dancing at the moment. That was how he put it. Poor Emily, she looked quite stricken. I thought she would flare up and object. I know I would have, and she looked as though she would like to, but Charles bent down and whispered something and, well, that was that! Never heard such nonsense in my life. After all, the infant is still a secret, isn't it?'

'Not any more apparently. Emily was told recently by Mrs Barnum that it would be "indelicate" for her to dance tonight, so I expect all Mariaon knows about it. But we had both hoped that Charles ... well, that Charles would not think about the matter as Mrs Barnum had.'

'Indelicate is it, then? Pooh! Old women's nonsense and nothing more! The girl is as fit as a fiddle, young and lovely and dying to dance, and to my mind that husband of hers is a sight too fond of the proprieties.'

I had to agree, and caught myself reflecting on how much my own ideas regarding Charles, and many other things, had changed over the last several months. A short time ago Charles's dictum on any subject under the sun had been my law, but now here I was allowing him to be criticized, joining in that criticism, without a thought. I was glad to recognize my return to common sense, and at the same time reluctant to admit to it completely, so I said as primly as was in me, 'He would be wrong not to consider his wife's reputation, surely?'

'Maybe,' agreed Kate without enthusiasm, 'but he forgets that she is a very young girl as well as his wife, and I declare that music is making even my old foot tap as briskly as a castanet. No, it's cruel he is to the child. Downright cruel!'

'Oh, look!' Connie broke into our private confabulation. 'Here's a whole tray of champagne. I declare I could do with something to freshen my spirits a little. Wally and Charles are so naughty to leave us all alone; we'll just have to signal for some ourselves.' And she stood up and waved her moth-eaten ostrich fan at the resplendent scarlet-and-gold minion who bore the tray. The champagne was iced and entirely delectable at that unhappy moment. Even Emily cheered up as she sipped it, and we all became more animated, despite the horrid dearth of male company. I felt, wrongly, no doubt, that every eye was upon our curious little knot of ill-assorted women, and that everyone wondered why we were not taking a more active part in the jollifications, so that when at last the men rejoined us to take us into supper, I was so relieved I almost forgave them their neglect.

Our absence from the dance floor had meant that my programme remained unfilled, and I was chagrined at the prospect of going into supper without a supporting male arm. But luck was with me. Captain Fanning, seeing me unattached as we crossed the lawn to the Banqueting Hall where the supper was laid, joyfully demanded the honour of waiting upon me. His relief in finding a lady unbooked for the supper dance to escort was equalled only by mine in being escorted.

The Banqueting Hall comprised the lower portion of a long, arcaded building of two storeys, the upper floor, so Captain Fanning informed me, being guest rooms for important visitors. The long chamber was crowded to suffocation, and almost as we entered we lost sight of the others in our party, but Captain Fanning, fired by the unexpected clemency of the Fates in providing him with a partner, pushed and shoved a way for us through the throng, and found me, to his own obvious surprise, a very pleasant seat beside one of the windows giving on to the wide verandah. The window was open, and the soft night air, laden with the scent of trampled grass, damp earth, night-blooming flowers and the musky smell of the river, was grateful to my flushed cheeks and exacerbated temper.

What a fiasco the whole affair had proved! I was so sure I would enjoy this ball, and yet I had danced only once. I was almost in a mood to indulge in sententious reflections on the vanity of life, so when Captain Fanning left to fetch me something to eat, I was glad of the resulting solitude which would allow me to compose myself. I leant my head against the window frame and, opening my fan, looked out to the brightly lit windows of the Residency across the lawn, and beyond it to the indigo sky set now with stars and a sickle moon.

Behind me the babble of conversation and laughter, the clink of glasses and cutlery, faded as I turned my head and attention away and became engrossed in my own discontented musings. But after a short interval my mind was brought suddenly back to the present by the sound of two male voices talking desultorily in the semi-gloom of the verandah just outside my field of vision.

'... nothing of much significance in its own right, but put the lot together and I believe we have an indication of what is in the native mind.'

A deep, pleasant voice this, speaking in a tone of decision. I began to listen consciously.

'Hm. We are aware of something like it here too, among the men. A sense of unease more than anything else. Not troublesome, but disturbing, at least to those of us to whom the *Baba-log* are capable of normal, human reactions.'

This second voice was precise in diction and pitched in a higher key than the other. It was not hard to guess it belonged to a military man.

'To my way of thinking, it is only a matter of time before the whole situation boils over,' said the deep voice.

'You croak like a raven.'

'Perhaps, but that is what I believe, and I also believe that we don't have much time. Anything could start it off. All that is needed is a focal point, some cause common to the lot of them.'

'Nothing can be common to all in this country.'

'What about a grievance?' the first man asked thoughtfully. 'And, good God, I'd have thought they had enough of those already. Every section of the population in this province has enough of the sort of grievance that should send a government toppling; that would in a European country.'

'Oh, come now, my dear chap, surely that's a little extreme? A certain amount of disaffection due to annexation is inevitable. But what alternative was there, after all?'

'It's a lot more than "disaffection". Annexation was an injustice to every man in the kingdom, one way or the other. In the *mofussil* the *talukhdars* are virtually dispossessed or labouring under crippling difficulties. Damn it all, it's not only their prerogatives but their livelihood that that fool Thomason with his reforms and his notions on equitable settlement would take from them. And the villager is no better off for the dubious privilege of now owning his own land—the revenue bands see to that. With their guns and flaming torches, their methods of extortion are a damn sight worse than any *talukhdar*'s, and they give no protection in return, as the *talukhdars* did. Truth is, they go in fear of their lives from the city magistrates themselves. And here in the city—well, you can see for yourself—the people are crawling with poverty, and not only the lower, helpless castes and classes either. We have exiled their fool of a king and yes, I know, I know, he was corrupt and dissolute and had been given ample warning of the measures that would be taken against him. But who amongst his people believed that we had the right to dispossess him, however he behaved? But what has happened to his family, his retainers, his army, his squads of useless officials? They are still there, in that city below us, begging their bread because Lord Dalhousie omitted to realize that they too are human. They still have to live somewhere, to eat sometimes, but Lord Dalhousie forgot them, as the populace among whom they drag out their miserable existence cannot forget them, or ignore their indignities, or overlook the contemptuous manner in which they have been jettisoned!'

'True, unfortunately true,' agreed the soldier. 'It was a most ill-advised move.'

'Ill-advised! Criminal folly! Short-sighted stupidity!' I liked the vehemence of the deep voice.

'And, my God, what have they done with Wajid Ali's army? Disbanded some to swell the want in the villages, and enlisted the rest in our own ranks!'

'Surely that at least was constructive?'

'Surely!' The voice now was heavy with sarcasm. 'It's always possible to serve two masters, and in military matters no doubt desirable. Not a year ago those sepoys out there were lounging about the Hazrat Ganj, out of elbow, unpaid, but nevertheless part of the forces of their rightful king. They are not going to forget that when trouble comes; they will be in no two minds as to where their loyalties lie. But we, we British—almost, Cussens, I am impelled to say *you* British—expect those loyalties, the loyalties of a lifetime, to be overlaid by an extra shilling a month, which, I am told, is all they get in the way of benefit from us.'

'Well—yes. I must admit your point.' The military voice was a hint impatient. 'But damn it all, man, it's not as though these things aren't realized in Calcutta.'

'If they were realized, why were they permitted?'

'I feel you take too gloomy a view of the whole situation.'

'Easy enough to feel *that* living here in your smug little world of perfunctory parades, balls and tea-drinkings with the ladies. Things are otherwise where I am, Cussens; I cannot overlook the obvious.'

'What brought you in anyway? You don't often honour us with your presence.'

'Oh, you could call it a family matter. But I had ignored so many invitations that I felt I had better make an obeisance to Mammon in the form of our revered Chief Commissioner.'

'Damn fellow is going shortly, so rumour has it.'

'Thank God for small mercies, eh?'

'Precisely.' And the two men laughed together in a manner which indicated a long and comfortable acquaintance. There was a pause in the conversation.

Presently, as I waited unashamedly to hear more, the deep voice came from another angle. The man must have moved over to a further window, and from what followed was standing looking in at the supper room.

'Come here a moment, Cussens. Look, and tell me what you see.'

There was the creak of a cane chair and a pause as 'Cussens' made his way over to the window.

'See? Why, a very jolly occasion, surely. People enjoying themselves, all that.'

'And I see emotion.'

'Don't know what you're driving at, old man. Know you don't care for the ladies yourself, but surely men have a right to have their wives and daughters with them?'

'Every right. No doubt about that, unfortunately. It's the consequences of that right that I am thinking of. If there is going to be any form of trouble, and you and I are both agreed that trouble of some sort must come, those females in there are going to complicate matters no end. When men kill men, it's merely war. But when men kill women, well—it becomes martyrdom, massacre and mayhem, and everything gets out of proportion.'

'Oh, come now. I cannot let you away with that. I agree that the province is unquiet and there may be trouble of some sort, but really that's a very different thing to expecting war, or any sort of organized violence. That I do not expect, and I cannot have you running off with the idea that I do.'

'Well, I must hope that you are right and I am wrong. But mark my words, if things do develop in the direction I believe they are going, all those white doll-faces in there, with their ridiculous garments and absurd airs, are going to be no joke. Deuce take it, don't you see you have too many of 'em?'

'As a matter of fact, none of them are "mine",' the soldier said acidly.

'What does that matter, when it is *you* who will pay the piper for them anyway?'

'I believe, my dear chap, that you are more worried on your own behalf than on mine! Now what you should do is settle yourself up with a nice young girl while you are in Lucknow, and then I'll wager I'd hear no more nonsense from you about there being too many of our females with us!'

'Cussens, Cussens, don't you know me yet? And to think that you and I have run the gauntlet of matrimony successfully, neck and neck, for so many years ...'

'Ah, but I thank heavens I'm too old, but you ...' And they moved away chuckling amicably together so that I could hear no more.

But I was left with a vivid recollection of Mr Roberts and his explanation of the uneasy state of Oudh. He, too, according to Mr Chalmers, had 'croaked like a raven', and when Captain Fanning returned to me with two laden plates, I found it difficult to keep my mind on what he was saying as I tried to remember exactly what Mr Roberts had told me. The man with the deep voice had echoed most faithfully his general sentiments, of that I had no doubt, and a small chill of fear ran up the back of my neck as I recalled the words: 'When men kill women ... it's martyrdom, massacre and mayhem!'

CHAPTER 13

When we had eaten, the Barrys, the Floods, Captain Fanning and I
sauntered for a while through the Residency gardens to refresh ourselves
after the hot and overcrowded supper room. As we paused to admire
the pale moonlight on the river, or exchange a few words with
acquaintances, I kept a sharp lookout for two gentlemen who would
match my mysterious voices on the verandah. The trees were hung with
coloured lanterns, small saucer lamps outlined arches and window-
frames of the buildings, and these, together with the moonlight, made
it possible to remark features even at some distance, but no group we
approached included the sort of masculine forms I could imagine
speaking in the voices I had so unscrupulously overheard.

Emily was extraordinarily subdued and Charles, though I knew
how well he must be aware of her mood, made no effort to draw his
wife into the general conversation. Kate and I worked hard to rouse her
to some enjoyment of the scene, but she answered us in monosyllables,
and averted her head whenever Charles raised his voice. In such
company it was difficult to find protracted enjoyment even in the very
real beauties of the night: the still sheen on the scimitar-curve of the
river, broad and scarcely rippling below us; the magnificent Indian sky
overcrowded with stars; and, not far away, the buildings of the city, a
mass of tumbled cubes, domes, cylinders and pyramids, untidy as a
child's neglected building blocks, a turmoil of dense, dark forms
against the violet night. I was relieved when at length we turned indoors
so that Emily and Charles could make their adieux before leaving. As
Charles had suggested, I was to follow later with the Averys.

There were fewer couples dancing now, and we had no difficulty in
making our way through the rooms in search of Mr Jackson and Mr
and Mrs Gubbins, but, not finding them, Charles decided to look
through the smaller rooms where cards and billiards were available,

and left us. Captain Fanning, having understood that I did not care to dance while Emily only looked on, departed, after many expressions of undying devotion, to seek further prey, and the rest of us grouped ourselves near an archway where we could watch the dancing without being too conspicuous ourselves. Just off the room in which we stood was a smaller apartment, empty at this hour of all but two or three tired yet vigilant servants.

I did not like the look of Emily. She was too quiet altogether, though her foot was tapping, not in time to the music but in anger, and her lips were compressed almost painfully in her set, withdrawn face. I could see rebellion building by the moment, so was unsurprised when suddenly she flicked shut her fan and announced, 'I am going to dance! I don't care what Charles says, or what anyone else says, I am not going home without a dance. Just one. If I let him dictate to me now, he will bully me all the rest of my life!'

'He doesn't mean to dictate, Emily,' I began, in what I hoped was the voice of sweet reason. 'He's only concerned with your good.'

'Well then, he should want to see me happy,' she snapped. Indignation made her speak louder than her wont; two or three officers, speaking to a soberly coated civilian with his back towards us, looked round curiously, then turned hastily away again as they saw I was aware of their interest.

'Absolutely,' agreed Kate. 'And d'you know, I think we have here the perfect place for you to take a private caper, and Charles, with any luck at all, need know nothing about it. Look; there's plenty of space in there, a good floor and not a soul in sight. George Barry—to your duty!' And taking each by an arm she led them into the small deserted room, then came back to me smiling delightedly.

'I had my heart set on seeing that girl dance this evening,' she said. 'Now just cross your fingers that Charles doesn't get back before the music stops.' I crossed my fingers purposefully. Knowing that if Charles were to discover his wife's crime I would certainly be held a party to it, I wished him very fervently away; but nothing that night was to induce the Fates to favour us. Emily, enchanting in her pale blue, restored to good nature in George's arms, had taken no more than a couple of turns around the room, when I found Charles beside me, taking in the scene with a wrathful eye. Kate raised her eyebrows at me, and I prepared for the storm.

137

'What is this?' he asked unnecessarily.

'My doing entirely, Charles,' Kate broke in with a rueful sigh. 'No one is going to see the child dancing in there, and if they do, it's only with my old George. What possible harm can there be in that? Now, do be sensible and let Emily enjoy herself in peace. Come away from that door. I declare you are positively *glowering*!'

She drew him out of Emily's sight.

'I did not wish to spoil her enjoyment,' Charles said stiffly, 'but she knows what my views are, and I cannot think, Mrs Barry, that you acted rightly in inciting her to go against them.'

'Come now, Charles Flood,' Kate chuckled, undismayed by his tone, 'I'm far too old a warhorse to be put in my place by a bit of a lad like you. Now you listen to me ... you must learn to bend to that wife of yours occasionally, or you'll find yourself in a peck of trouble, and that's a promise. She's no more than a child, and you've behaved like a disagreeable old gaoler all evening. Don't take the matter so seriously, for heaven's sake! Now, you let her have a good romp in there, and then take her home—and no scolding mind, or you'll undo all the good I have done.' And while Charles looked dignified disagreement, she turned away from him to watch the dancing in the other room.

He turned to me.

'I am surprised that you should have allowed it, Laura,' he said, more in sorrow than in anger.

'Oh, Charles, do be sensible! I didn't allow it, I could see it coming all evening. Emily was determined to get her way, and you have Kate to thank that she is getting it so inconspicuously.' He looked puzzled for a moment, as though he wanted to say more about my laxness, but then thought better of it.

'Would you ever have thought that Emily could become so contrary—become such a wrong-headed little ... vixen?'

'Yes, indeed,' I said in a reassuring way. 'She gave every indication of it even as a child. And you mustn't forget her condition. It makes the best of women difficult.'

'But this ... this is beyond all bounds! She has deliberately flouted my known wishes.'

'And not for the last time either, Charles. She has wishes of her own, remember. I really do think you are making too much of the whole matter.'

'But, Laura, surely you cannot justify...'

I know not how he completed the sentence.

The sound of a deep voice, heard already that night but now directly behind me, arrested my attention as completely as if I had never heard another.

'Kate? Kate Barry? Is it you ... in this diabolical maelstrom of gaiety? I had thought you possessed of more sense!'

Kate's reply was delayed by surprise. I heard a gasp, then a hesitant footstep on the marble flag, then an exclamation of assured recognition.

'Oliver! Oliver Erskine! It's really you?'

Somehow, I had known all along that it must be.

Forgetting Charles, I turned round in time to see the black-coated civilian who had been talking to the officers bend down to kiss Kate Barry, both of whose hands he held in his own, and, as he straightened up, my eyes were held for a moment by the curious hazel eyes that had so intrigued me in the portrait in Calcutta.

The face had matured. The lines around the sardonic mouth had deepened, and the furrows across the broad forehead were more marked; the finely moulded lips were compressed more firmly together now, and the whole face must have thinned down, for the high arched nose was more obvious than in the portrait. The eyes, however, under the heavy dark brows, were the same, but even more speaking and charged with expression. He was of rather more than average height, but lightly built, and his figure gave an impression, not of force, as did his features, but of energy and disciplined power. He seemed to me to be near his fortieth year.

'Why, Oliver, you wretched boy! No one has seen hide nor hair of you for I don't know how long, and then you just turn up like this at the most opportune moment imaginable.' Kate laughed in delight as he looked down at her.

'Come now, Kate, when was I ever opportune?'

'Never, it's the moment! Come here.' And she led him to where Charles and I stood looking on.

'Now!' Kate stood between Charles and his brother, regarding both with huge enjoyment. 'This is quite an historic moment. Can you guess what I am about to do, Oliver?'

'Certainly not,' with a humorous emphasis and a glance half of apology for Kate's high spirits towards us.

'I thought not. Well then, I am going to introduce you to your brother, Mr Charles Flood!'

'The deuce you are!' And Mr Erskine turned his full attention on Charles, who was as startled by this intelligence as he, though how Charles could have failed to see the resemblance to the portrait was beyond me.

'Well, how d'ye do, Charles? I am in Lucknow this week expressly to make myself known to you. But it is pleasant to be introduced by so old a friend as Mrs Barry. This is certainly something of an occasion as she promised.' And he shook Charles warmly by the hand. He then bowed towards me. 'And the lady is no doubt your wife? Emily, I think?'

The hazel eyes narrowed a little as his glance flicked over me in a manner which I was just experienced enough to recognize as appraisal, though his attitude was all courtesy.

'No, oh, no!' I thought Charles spoke in quite unwarrantable confusion, but before he could say more Emily and George were fortunately with us, Emily wreathed in smiles and George perspiring freely.

'The most heavenly waltz I've ever danced, Charles, and I don't... oh!'

She stopped and looked at the newcomer; her memory of the portrait was stronger than Charles's, for after a moment's hesitation she put out her hand and said, 'Why, this is your brother, Charles. Mr Erskine.'

'Yes, dear. Oliver, allow me to present my wife, Emily.'

'Allow me to congratulate you, Charles,' said Mr Erskine, as he took Emily's hand.

'And this,' Charles continued, 'is Emily's cousin, Miss Hewitt. Miss Laura Hewitt.'

'I see. Then I was mistaken,' said Mr Erskine as he bowed to me. 'I am so sorry.'

The words meant nothing in themselves, but there was something in the tone that made me glance up sharply as I rose from my curtsey. He could have meant that he was sorry he had made a small social blunder. Or that he was sorry I was not married to Charles. Or that he was sorry Emily was. I inclined to the last interpretation. Mr Erskine's eyes, it seemed to me, had rested just a little too long on Emily, in interest possibly and certainly in admiration, and for the purely feminine reason of disliking a snub, even an imagined one, I felt my antipathy towards the man in the portrait thoroughly justified.

'But now tell us, Oliver,' said Kate, 'how have we managed to miss each other all evening? Where have you been hiding yourself that we haven't seen you?'

'Well, dancing isn't one of my favourite pastimes, and I suppose we have missed each other because I have spent most of the evening playing cards with a couple of bachelor cronies who, like me, and unlike Charles, have no charming wife to consider. I had just determined to take my leave when I caught sight of you here.'

'Well, you certainly can't leave now, can you? You must stay and become acquainted with your relatives. Really, I cannot remember ever having been present at such a dramatic occasion, but the two of you just stand there coolly and say how d'ye do! What provokingly unsentimental things men are, ain't they, Laura?'

'Not at all,' Mr Erskine assured us all. 'I am floored by the surprise, and I have no doubt that you, Charles, are the same. But now, surely this is a meeting that calls for some special celebration. Join me in a bumper at the expense of the benevolent Mr Jackson, won't you?'

He summoned one of the servants still hovering in the background with a tray of glasses. We helped ourselves, and Mr Erskine proposed a toast: 'To a newly united family,' he said, and to me the note of mockery in his voice was patent. However, we all drank dutifully while he surveyed us over the rim of his glass, with one eyebrow cocked. I in turn surveyed him, but surreptitiously, buttressing my distrust of him by observing that he was indeed as 'ugly' as Emily had once pronounced him.

'I intended to call on you in Mariaon in the morning—you remember you gave me your address when you wrote from Calcutta. You are comfortably placed?'

'Exceedingly,' said Charles shortly—and untruthfully.

'We are staying with my cousin Wallace Avery and his wife,' added Emily, at last finding her tongue. She had been watching her new relative like a bird mesmerized by a snake, and I remembered that she had said she would be terrified of him. Not that he seemed very terrible now. On the contrary, he was putting himself out to be amiable. It was Charles who was sullen and unapproachable, though whether because of his wife's stolen dance, or his brother's lack of urgency in making himself known, it would be hard to say.

'I am glad you are comfortable,' Mr Erskine assured Emily. 'Will you be staying long in Lucknow?'

'Our plans are still ... uncertain,' returned Charles, although the question had been asked of Emily.

'Well, I hope that you will have time to visit me in Hassanganj before you return to England. You cannot return to Mother without doing that much at least; she tells me that she wishes to hear at first hand just how the old place is doing, and I will be pleased to have you whenever you are free. We cannot let this opportunity pass without getting to know each other, now can we?'

Charles looked glumly into his glass, while Emily assured his brother that of course they would be delighted. They had heard so much of Hassanganj ... they were looking forward to it.

'And now, speaking of getting to know each other,' Mr Erskine put down his glass, 'may I have the pleasure of this dance, Emily? You cannot object to your brother addressing your wife so familiarly even on so short an acquaintance, can you, Charles?'

'Of course not. But my wife is not dancing.'

'Indeed? I thought I observed her waltzing very gracefully with George here as I approached your party?'

'But ...' began Charles, but Emily broke in: 'Oh, pay no attention! Charles and I have had a little tiff. He is ... jealous!' She laughed. 'But indeed, I should be most happy to dance, and since you are so close a relative I am sure he can have no objection.' And the wretched girl took his arm.

Mr Erskine had the grace to look nonplussed, but could do nothing but lead Emily onto the floor of the public ballroom, whither she had determinedly turned. They were soon lost to sight among the gyration of the dancers. At last she had really got her way.

'Oh, Lud! Now what on earth possessed her to behave in such a manner towards you, Charles?' said Kate as they disappeared. 'I declare the chit needs a spanking. That was too much!'

'It is of no consequence.' Charles threw himself on to a sofa and folded his arms across his chest.

'You must expect such things when you are married to a girl as pretty and high-spirited as Emily,' George said comfortingly. 'Why, I remember Kate at the same age, and the dance she led me in those days.'

'Away with you!' returned his spouse. 'I was never a beauty. But after all, though she has been a little rude to Charles, there is surely no harm in her dancing.'

'I sincerely hope not, madam,' said Charles wrathfully, 'but as I see it, not only is my wife's reputation for common decency at stake, but she is risking it in the company of a man who, from all I hear, has a thoroughly bad reputation himself!'

So that, then, was what had made Charles's reception of his brother less than warm: the masculine gossip of the mess rooms.

'Oh, Charles, Charles! You are wrong to judge Oliver Erskine by the envious tattling of cantonments.' Kate's wrinkled face was red with annoyance and she tugged at the high, boned lace at her neck to relieve her irritation. 'It is true that ... that at one time ... and a long time ago it was, mark you, he had a ... a reputation for entertaining the wrong type of young woman. But there's not a lady here, nor a husband, mark you, who could accuse him of any lack of courtesy, discretion or dignity in the way he has always treated ... well, his own class of woman! Never has there been a hint of anything that could sully the name of gentleman. What you have heard in the messes here—a great deal of it anyway—is the ill-natured hyperbole of less well-positioned men, anxious and eager to belittle a strong and independent character. Nothing more. Absolutely nothing more!'

'That's true enough, Charles,' George put in, in his slow, soft voice. 'Never a hint of ill behaviour with the ladies of Lucknow, and a good deal of the rest, to my mind at any rate, merely the ill-natured doing-down of men a lot less fortunate, and less worthy than he is.'

'Perhaps. But the name he has earned for himself remains, whatever the lapse of time or the extenuating circumstances. I cannot approve of my wife dancing with him under these conditions.'

'It looks to me as though you have little option,' exclaimed Kate tartly, and then more softly, 'Och now! Look at the pair of them will you, boy? Isn't it patent and obvious that the girl is enjoying herself... and he too, by the look of him.'

'No doubt!' Charles agreed, glowering at the dancers. 'But yet his neglect and ill manners regarding Emily and myself, ever since we arrived in India, has been most apparent. I cannot see why I should be expected to give him the benefit of the doubt. As far as I am concerned, the less I see of him the better!' And Charles turned away with every appearance of having dismissed the subject from his mind for ever.

In spite of my own aversion to Mr Erskine, my heart sank at Charles's words and manner. There would be no hope now of our seeing Hassanganj and the 'real' India. And perversely, because Charles had condemned his brother without a hearing, I began to think more kindly of him myself.

When the dance ended, Charles got up from his sofa and immediately commanded his wife to collect her cloak while he had his carriage called. I went upstairs with Emily to help her find her things and to repair the depredations of the evening on my own appearance and learnt without astonishment that my young cousin was quite captivated by Mr Erskine.

'He really is the most charming man after all,' she declared, as soon as we were alone in the bedroom whose bed was covered with cloaks, wraps and gay, gauze scarves. 'So polite and well-bred. He doesn't dance very well—stiff, you know—but he said I was the first woman he had danced with in years, so I had to forgive him that.'

'I hope you made a better impression on him during the dance than you did before it,' I said sternly.

'Oh, that.' Emily giggled. 'I was delighted to pay Charles back in his own coin. And Mr Erskine of course never mentioned it, so why should I worry?'

'It wasn't right of you, nevertheless. Charles is in a fearful temper, and will surely scold you all the way home.'

'Well, let him! I don't care a fig if he does. I've done what I wanted to, just once, and I'm ready to pay for it,' she answered defiantly, and then, in a plaintive voice, 'If he wouldn't always try to stop me doing the things I like doing. If, even, he wouldn't always try to make me do the things I don't like doing. But, don't you see, we are always running against each other ... because ... because we don't think alike! He's such a ... such a curmudgeon now, Laura, really he is.' And in spite of myself, I smiled.

She was silent for a moment, regarding her pretty face in the candle-lit looking glass, but not apparently seeing it.

'But Mr Erskine—Oliver, I suppose I should call him—you couldn't call him really *ugly*, could you, Laura?'

'I could!'

'No! Not *ugly*. Certainly not handsome either. Arresting! That's it! I think he has a most arresting face, and I shall tell Charles so directly we are alone.'

I was very glad I was not to accompany them home. The journey, I felt, was going to be an unquiet one.

CHAPTER 14

I remained with the Barrys for the rest of the evening, and now that I was free to do so, accepted every invitation to dance. A knot of young officers had gathered round Kate and George when I returned to the ballroom—they were a popular pair in cantonments—so I had no want of partners. Mr Erskine hovered in the background, but I had no further conversation with him until, towards the end of the evening, he too asked me to dance. I was surprised; he had seemed quite content to stand talking with one or two of the older members of the party, and I had not supposed my charms would be sufficient to lure him on to the floor. The departure of Charles and Emily had relieved my mind and spirits, I had begun to enjoy myself, and was determined that not even a dance with Mr Erskine would stop me doing so. I accepted his hand with a good grace and walked on to the floor humming the refrain of the music.

To begin with, he was very solemn and silent. As Emily had said, he was an unpractised dancer, so perhaps he was concentrating on the music and his feet. Usually I find it easy to fall in with a companion's desire for silence, but Mr Erskine kept his eyes on my face with a sort of frank, unsmiling curiosity that embarrassed me, and I was casting about in my mind for a subject to discuss that was not too trivial when he broke the silence himself, and in the most banal way imaginable.

'And what is it that brings Miss Hewitt to India?' he asked in a tone dangerously near to condescension.

This was a question which I had long become tired of answering, particularly since most people who put it had already answered it to their own satisfaction. The only valid reason for an unattached female, a 'spin', to visit India was matrimony.

'I am in a sense *in loco parentis* to my cousin Emily,' I replied shortly, and then, desiring to get everything said as soon as possible, and at the same time acquit myself of the charge of husband-hunting, went on hurriedly, 'In fact I am her companion, her *paid* companion. She is very young, as you see, and still a little giddy, and her parents did not want her to come out here for so long on her own.'

'Hm. Very commendable of her parents no doubt, but, surely, coming out here with her husband cannot really be considered coming out here on "her own"? Or am I too optimistic in my views of the married state? Is ... er ... "companionship" between man and wife really as impossible as your remarks, and indeed your presence here, would lead one to believe?'

'I think you choose to misunderstand me, Mr Erskine,' I countered coldly.

'Oh, not at all, not at all! I honestly think it most commendable of Emily's parents to have such concern for their daughter's well-being— even after she had left the nest, as the saying goes—and more especially as her husband appears to have little control over her, a fact of which her parents are no doubt aware.'

'Oh, no, you must not think that Emily always goes against Charles's wishes as she did tonight. There were peculiar circumstances involved and, as I say, she is still a little giddy.'

'Ah!' I did not like his tone of voice. 'So that is all there was to it. Well, it was not hard to guess that they had had a quarrel. But now tell me, Miss Hewitt, is it your duty to smooth the path of matrimonial bliss and keep the peace when it is threatened by Emily's er ... giddiness? Is that a part of a "paid companion's" duties?'

'Of course not! It is none of my business! None at all.' But he must have known I was lying, for when I looked up at him he was smiling and I was irritated to discover he had a very pleasant smile.

We looked at each other measuringly for half a turn of the room— he smiling, I wary, and then he shook his head and said, 'Poor Miss Hewitt. I hardly know which of you two is more to be pitied, for never have I met two young ladies less suited to offer each other companionship.'

'We were brought up together in the same house,' I answered with redoubled stiffness, 'and are very fond of each other. Emily is like a sister to me.'

Unconvinced, he merely laughed and shook his head, and I felt my cheeks flush with annoyance. I knew what he meant, of course, but it was unkind of him to remark on how little alike Emily and I were. I knew too well my own deficiencies of appearance and character not to guess where his preference would lie, and for a moment, very irrationally, I wished that I had Emily's grace, beauty and gaiety, or even something approaching them. Not that I wished to charm him. Quite the contrary, I thought to myself, remembering that ambiguous 'I am so sorry' when he was introduced to Emily as Charles's wife. But when I looked up again, he was still smiling that unusually pleasant smile, so that I felt called upon to smile in feturn.

'That's better!' he said, taking a firmer grip of my waist as we whirled down the room. 'I see you are a thinker. But now, you haven't the face for dissimulation, and since we will probably be much in each other's company and I don't like "missishness", let us dispense with the more ridiculous conventions.'

'I am not miss-ish!' I denied indignantly.

'Agreed, so don't try to appear so. Now, tell me, how do you really come to be in your unenviable position? Necessity?'

For a moment I debated how to meet this unexpected and sudden frankness, but the smile held no derision.

'Dire,' I said, and hung my head pathetically. 'I am an orphan and penniless.'

'Then you are exonerated,' he chuckled. 'I thought it might be lack of judgement, or a desire to improve your mind, or to see India.'

'Oh, but I do—want to see India, I mean. Only we haven't managed it so far.'

'And how is that?'

'Well, of course we have seen some of the country, but not what I would like to see.'

'And what is that?'

'Indian India, if I can put it like that. And the people themselves. I'd like to know more of them than we can do, living in cantonments and big towns. I'd like to see how they live, know what they believe in and think about; I'd like to be able to read their literature; learn about their history; look at their art; hear their music. Understand them, I suppose. Oh, I know, I know!' But I would not look at him, realizing that his smile would now be one of long-suffering condescension, like the smiles of so many 'old India hands' whom I had encountered, and to whom I had unwisely unburdened myself. 'I know that my naïveté is past believing. I know enough of things out here now to understand that I have small chance of coming closer to the country than we have done. As it is, I am even laughed at for my Urdu lessons; yet if I were to spend a year in France and neglect the chance to learn the language, my friends would think me criminally negligent, would they not?'

'Indubitably. And so you take Urdu lessons, do you?'

'Young *men* are expected to,' I answered defensively, 'but young women who do are considered peculiar.'

'Exceedingly!'

I looked up, ready to fight, but found him regarding me seriously and with some interest.

'You don't laugh?'

'Why should I? I wish there were more like you. A great many more like you! As it is our ladies—and somehow, though my eyes and experience both belie the fact, I get the impression that all white women in India must necessarily be "ladies"—since they have started coming out in large numbers, have helped to bring about this strange situation of isolation that you have noticed. Even when I was young, things were different. It was possible then for the two races to meet and mingle with mutual respect and enjoyment, as indeed it is today when men are pursuing men's work.'

'Why should the ladies' presence so have influenced matters?'

'Many reasons. Women are more attached to unimportant details. More dependent on the support of familiarity and accepted usage. They have brought their habits, customs and prejudices with them, instead of leaving them at home where they belong and have a place. They have, very largely, refused to bend, to accommodate themselves to the situation here—and they have made their menfolk do the same.'

'I feel you impute too much to my sex. I cannot think we have so much influence.'

'No? Well, look around you, Miss Hewitt! Look at all these charming creatures whirling round us in their silks and satins and ... well, whatever else it is you ladies make your gowns of! Look at yourself, Miss Hewitt, in that mirror over there ...' He paused in the waltz and we stood swaying together, while I did as he said and glanced at our combined reflection in the long, gilt-framed glass. I found nothing to object to in the picture we made: he tall, immaculately dressed in black; I short (but not too short, I assured myself) and looking very nearly my best, with a flush of exercise in my cheeks, my eyes bright and my expression animated. Perhaps my partner caught the flash of self-approbation in my glance, for as he led me into the dance again and I looked up at him for enlightenment, there was more than a hint of mockery in his amber eyes, though he continued to smile.

'Well—I have looked,' I said coldly.

'And I agree, we made a splendid picture.' And he tightened his grip on my waist, threw back his head and laughed. I wanted to be annoyed; but it was not the sort of laugh one can hear without joining in, and, loath though I was to admit it, I had been a little obvious. So I laughed too.

'But what was it you expected me to see?' I asked, when the laughter had subsided.

'See! Why, the extraordinary unsuitability of your apparel! Oh, not only you, Miss Hewitt; indeed, allow me to assure you in all seriousness that nothing could be more pleasing than the vision you make at the moment. But if you will try to see yourself, yourselves rather, for I do not wish to seem personal, in these great billows of skirt, with bared shoulders, arms and … er, feet unapparent to all but the clairvoyant, and then remember where you are.'

'What difference can the fact that we are now in India make to the way we dress? English ladies dress the same the world over.'

'Exactly, and devilish uncomfortable they are as a result! Here in India, a country of extreme heat and often unexpected cold, where one is ankle-deep in dust for three-quarters of the year and knee-deep in mud for the rest of it, the English lady retains her floor-length skirts and her dozen or so petticoats. She constricts her waist in whalebone, whatever the heat, and then cannot understand why she is prone to fainting attacks and even apoplexy. She bares her shoulders and arms to make a feast for every insect in reach, and then cannot understand why she suffers so frequently from the various fevers of the country. She makes absolutely no concession to changes in climate or activity or to her own necessary comfort, and yet still has the energy to weep over the countless head-stones in all our sad little cemeteries that provide ample evidence of the fact that the English lady can pretty well count on being dry bones by thirty if she remains in India!'

'A gloomy picture indeed, sir.'

'A just one.'

'What would you have us do, apart from staying in England, that is?' I enquired sweetly, with the phrases he had used earlier in the evening—'white doll-faces', 'too many of 'em', 'emotion' and 'trouble'—very present in my mind.

'Do? Why, adapt a little! Modify your mode of dress so that you can keep cool when it is hot and warm when it is cold. Why is that so impossible, after all? Deuced if I can see that the Indian female garb lacks attraction, grace or beauty—and it's sensible and comfortable into the bargain. But can you pretend that our ladies would ever adopt it? No, of course not! In clothing, as in everything else, the English lady is restricted in her notion of what is acceptable and has managed to force those same restrictions on her men. And you say the female sex has no influence!'

'You have almost persuaded me to the contrary opinion, Mr Erskine. However, I am still unwilling to believe that the lack of social intercourse, of friendliness and … and sharing of interests and experience which I notice is all the fault of us women.'

'Oh, not at all! The men they send out here are a pretty sorry lot on the whole too!'

'It is something that your strictures are so justly distributed between the sexes.'

'Why shouldn't they be? Women have no corner on stupidity.'

'Thank you,' I commented drily, and again we both laughed.

If Mr Erskine was in the habit of talking as freely and as forcefully to all his acquaintance as he had done to one unknown young woman, then it was no wonder he was unpopular with his compatriots in cantonments. Yet I had to admit to myself that I enjoyed his frankness, however little I could agree with his opinions.

'But now, as to your seeing something of the "real" India, I think I can promise you a nearer glimpse when you come to Hassanganj. Naturally a "paid companion" must accompany her employer?'

'I expect so, and indeed I shall look forward to it, if Charles permits the visit.'

'Permits? A strange word to use in connection with an invitation?'

I could have pinched myself for my clumsiness.

'Has my brother already decided not to develop our connection then?'

151

'Oh, no, certainly nothing like that! I only meant that I have no idea what his intentions may be, and as you say, I must do as he bids.'

'Must you? Then I must see that he "permits".'

He was looking at me again with an expression that was part derisive and part puzzled, though I could not account for the puzzlement until he spoke, after a pause.

'The docility of your words is in marked contrast, Miss Hewitt, to the obvious independence of your bearing, and I believe of your mind. What a very uncomfortable life you must lead! I wonder what is the real reason for your leading it?'

'We have already discussed the matter,' I said firmly. Those amber eyes were too penetrating to be comfortable. 'May we return to the subject of Hassanganj? I would like to know more about it.'

'Ha!' he exclaimed, quite undeceived. 'Hassanganj? I don't know what I can tell you about it, except that it is my home and has been the home of my family for three generations. There is a funny old house, and a garden and park and the things that go with them. I am too used to it all to be able to see it objectively or give you a sufficient picture of it, I believe. I like the way I live, but it wouldn't suit many. I am of a solitary turn of mind and for me the great attraction of the place is that we are a day's journey from the nearest white face, so I do not have many visitors. Apart from that—well, I have my work. I own a fair-sized slice of India, and it takes all I have to give in the way of time and energy to keep it going, and … well, that's about all I can think of.' He paused and I saw that he was searching his mind for some detail that would communicate his life to me. 'I don't suppose you will care for it, even if young Charles does "permit" the visit. But perhaps some of your curiosity regarding the "real" India will be satisfied. It is at least *that*!'

'I am sure I shall find it intriguing.'

'You think so?' And again I found those penetrating eyes regarding me with concentration. 'Yes, I believe you very well might. Well, we shall have to see. Not that you are going to like all that you find in India, Miss Hewitt. It is a cruel country, a cruel and a heartbreaking country. But perhaps you will find the strength to withstand it, as all of us who love it have to learn to withstand it.'

The music had stopped. For a moment we stood at the end of the room furthest from the Barrys, as the floor cleared and the dancers made their way back to their seats. It was then that I was recognized by Mrs Wilkins—once more in purple satin, but now very *décolleté* and befeathered—who uttered a little shriek as I caught her eye, then bore down on us accompanied by a large round officer, who, judging by her proprietorial grasp of his arm, must be 'the Major'.

'My dear Miss Laura, how nice!' she exclaimed, grasping my hand. 'We was hoping to see you here tonight. This is the hubby, and he knows all about you.'

I introduced them hurriedly to Mr Erskine, who had drawn back as they approached me. Mrs Wilkins gushed her delight at meeting him, then turned back to me.

'I was just saying to the Major when we was dressing, "I wonder if those Floods and Miss Laura will be there. My, how I would like her to know you!" And now here you are. And looking so well. Wait till I tell my Elvira! She's not here, poor thing; the invitation was just for the Major and me, and she was so mortified at being left at home. But not quite comfortless, I'm pleased to say, not quite comfortless! A very nice young man she has now—an ensign in the 71st—and they have, made up a little party at home. But she'll be that disappointed not to have seen you. Quite took by you, my Elvira was, on that nasty ship, and so she should be with all your kindness to us. My! When I remember the state we were in until you came and helped us, will I ever forget it! And your cousin? Is she well, and her husband?'

'Very, thank you, but they decided to leave early.'

'Oh, well, that's a pity! I'd love to stay and talk, and let the Major get to know you better, dearie, but I'm that hot and thirsty, and we will be keeping you from your friends, I have no doubt, so we must leave you now. We go back to our station tomorrow, so I cannot even hope to see you soon, as the saying goes, but now that I know you are in Lucknow, I'll write and maybe you can come out to us for a few days—to get to know the Major and let Ellie see you.'

'That would be delightful,' I lied.

Then Mrs Wilkins leant towards me and whispered behind the purple feathers of her fan, 'My! You're a true heartbreaker in that pink. I always knew you'd be a stunner in a pretty dress; too conservative you are, y'know, as a general rule, but tonight you're lovely, dear! And I think I can guess why.' She giggled and winked in the direction of Mr Erskine, who was being polite to her husband; then with more assurances of her affection, she pulled that gentleman away in search of sustenance.

So I was looking 'lovely' on account of Mr Erskine! I wished there were someone with whom I could share the joke.

I had not given a thought to the Averys since we had all gone in to supper together, nor had I caught a glimpse of them since. But, as Mr Erskine took me back to my seat, I began to wonder where they could be, and hoped they had not forgotten that they were to take me home in their carriage. On looking at my watch, I found it was after three o'clock in the morning. The band still played, but raggedly, without the zest of the earlier hours. A few young people still danced, but many more sat around the room in tired silence, the men easing their feet in their tight boots, the women hiding yawns behind their fans. The flowers had drooped in the heat of the long evening; empty glasses and ice cream dishes cluttered the tabletops, and candles guttered dismally before flickering out in a spiral of smelly smoke. Groups of scarlet-clad servants stood hopefully near the doors, anxious to summon the remaining guests' carriages.

I had hardly sat down when Connie, trailing her sad yellow muslin and with her ginger hair all over her face, appeared in a doorway clutching a glass, peered round the room, swaying, and then, spying us, made her way unsteadily across the floor. One of the gentlemen got up hurriedly and offered her his chair—just in time. Connie's legs gave way under her and she flopped down, shrieking with laughter and waving her glass at the ceiling: 'Ish been a lovely parshy,' she informed us, while the champagne she had spilt ran down the side of her face unheeded. 'Oh, shush a lovely parshy.'

The glass dropped from her hand, her head sank forward on her bosom and she was asleep before any of us had done more than gasp.

'Wally!' snapped Kate, getting to her feet. 'George, go and find Wally! We must get her home. It's too bad that the servants should see her in this condition.'

George hurried off, and I picked up the smashed glass and wiped Connie's face with my handkerchief, horribly conscious all the time of the black bulk of Mr Erskine in the background. Connie was no responsibility of mine, but I was living in her house and for some reason that I could not explain to myself, I was ashamed that Mr Erskine, of all people, should see my hostess in such a condition.

George was an age finding Wally. Meanwhile, for us who were left with Connie, the embarrassment grew more acute as her snores grew louder, interspersed with hiccoughs and the agitated movements of her hands and feet. One by one the gentlemen who had formed the party around the Barrys made some excuse and took themselves off, so that by the time George returned, only Kate and myself kept watch over the unfortunate woman—Kate, myself and Mr Erskine. Too much of a gentle man to leave us alone, he had seated himself in a chair vacated by one of the others, crossed his long black legs, and proceeded to make light of the whole business.

'Bless you, Oliver,' said Kate, voicing my sentiments exactly, as the last of our cavaliers drifted away and Mr Erskine sat on, thus publicly giving us his support. 'We have forgotten her all evening and we should have known what would happen. What can Wally be thinking of to allow her to become like this?'

'What indeed? But if her husband is the stout, florid man with the loud laugh and the loud voice, then I can tell you he is thinking of making money at cards. Or was when I looked around the rooms some time ago. He seemed settled for the night at that time.'

'I'm sure he was!' said Kate. 'That would be Wally all right. Oh, thank heaven! Here he is now.'

Wallace bent over his wife, at once ashamed and concerned, and tried to bring her to her senses. But she was past rousing. He slapped her hands and pinched her cheeks, imploring her to 'wake up'. Poor Connie merely responded by taking a wild swing at his head and commanding him in slurred tones to go away. Every eye in the room was upon us, and my mortification mounted, the more so as Wallace himself was far from sober and used a voice to rouse his wife that could have been heard across the river. Eventually, all methods of resuscitation having failed, Wallace and George between them half carried, half dragged Connie from the ballroom, and only the servants at the doorway had the decency not to smile as they passed.

'I had better fetch my wrap,' I said to Kate. 'I hope Wallace has not forgotten that I am going home with them.'

'No, no, my dear, you must come with us. I do not like the thought of you driving with them now. Why, Wallace is in hardly a better way than Connie!'

'I don't care for the idea much myself, but Wallace may need my help with Connie when we reach the house.'

'Then he must manage without it! Indeed, I will not allow you to travel with them. You have had enough embarrassment for one evening.'

'But ...'

'If I may intrude?'

For the moment we had both forgotten Mr Erskine's silent but attentive presence. 'I would be delighted to take Miss Hewitt home, Kate. I have to pass Mariaon as I am putting up with Major Cussens, and if she will direct me, I can have her home in no time.'

'Oh, no, I really couldn't allow it. I...'

'But I insist. You cannot go with the Averys, Miss Hewitt, even if they have remembered that you are expecting to, which seems unlikely, and there is plenty of room for you in my carriage. I will be waiting for you at the door when you have collected your cloak.'

Thus it was that in a short time I found myself beside Mr Erskine in his high, light gig. He handled the reins himself, and behind us on the step stood the odd little man with the high hat with whom Charles had had a passage of arms on our arrival at the ball—such aeons ago. He stood at the horse's head as Mr Erskine handed me up, and did not recognize me. But I could not be mistaken and I smiled as I realized that Charles would certainly consider him one more point in the disfavour of his employer.

The fatigue, of which I had been conscious before Connie's appearance, had vanished in the ensuing agitation, and I felt sufficiently grateful to Mr Erskine for his consideration of Kate and myself to put myself out to be pleasant.

'It was very kind of you to remain with us when George went to fetch Captain Avery, Mr Erskine. It was an unpleasant moment for both of us, particularly Mrs Barry, who had no reason to be involved.'

'Don't worry about Kate,' he answered. 'That poor woman was not the first drunkard she has had to deal with. Not by a long chalk. But you, Miss Hewitt, what reason had you to be involved?'

'Mrs Avery is my hostess. I could scarcely have deserted her, could I?'

'Hmph! And does this sort of thing happen often—in the Avery *ménage*, I mean?'

'No! Well—that is, not so badly! But poor Connie—well, the truth is she acquired the habit of drinking gin when she was ill at one time, her doctor advised it, and now she can't break herself of it.'

'I see.'

I could tell he was smiling, though I could not see his face. It was a dark night now: the young moon had long since descended and the myriad stars were dimmed by great galleons of silvery-grey cloud hurrying before a chill wind that made me glad I had borrowed Emily's sealskin cape.

'My relatives appear to have brought you to a rather unfortunate household, Miss Hewitt. A wife too fond of the bottle and a husband too fond of the cards. It must be an education for you. Tell me, what does my brother Charles think of it?'

'I don't believe he realizes Mrs Avery's weakness. And since he spends a good deal of time with Captain Avery, I presume he does not object to gambling,' I answered primly.

'Do you?'

'It is no business of mine.'

'Of course, I was forgetting. A "paid companion" must just put up with her lot, I suppose? But don't tell me that the delectable Emily is as unconcerned? Surely she is shocked by her hostess's partiality for gin?'

'Yes, she is—and I am very glad she did not see Connie tonight. It would have distressed her.'

'Of course.'

He drove in silence for a time, sitting forward, relaxed, with his elbows on his knees, and the reins gathered in one hand. I sat very erect and uncomfortably close to him on the narrow seat, so that the skirt of my dress overspread one of his knees. I am not by nature shy, but he made me feel awkwardly aware of myself, and I examined the profile of his face, with its high-arched nose, with some resentment. Remembering the snatch of conversation I had heard from the Banqueting Hall window, I was not surprised, now that I knew him, that he had managed to 'run the gauntlet of matrimony' so successfully. He was a disquieting creature.

'How long are you to have the dubious pleasure of sharing the Avery roof, Miss Hewitt?' he asked after a time.

'I'm not sure. I think it was to have been for a couple of months, and then it was planned that we should move on to Delhi and Agra and go up to the hills for the summer.'

'So Hassanganj was not included in the itinerary?'

'How could it be—since Hassanganj issued no invitation?'

'Curious, that—when I have been told in a long and disingenuous letter from my mother that Charles's main reason for visiting India was to see Hassanganj! I took it to be a matter of course. But you speak as if your plans have now been changed. Is this because of Mrs Avery's—er—indisposition?'

'No, not at all! But I think we will have to remain in Lucknow longer than we had thought—at least until we can go up to the hills in April. You see, Emily ...' And I trailed off, realizing suddenly that I had brought up a matter not generally discussed between the sexes at first acquaintance.

'I see, Emily is to become a mother! How inconvenient for you all, and how remarkable that no one should have foreseen such a contingency when you set out. But that's by the way. All the same, and in spite of my mother's hints of suitable fraternal affection, I got the impression tonight that my brother Charles has decided to disapprove of me. There is no real reason why he shouldn't, particularly if he has a ready ear for local gossip.'

This was true, though I could not admit it, and so, not knowing what to say, I said nothing. There was a moment's silence and then Mr Erskine chuckled and looked at me. 'Thank you, Miss Hewitt,' he grinned, 'I always appreciate frankness. But I will have to make him alter his opinion of me if you are to see the "real" India, will I not? And I believe that, whatever the drawbacks of my way of life in Hassanganj, you would all be more happily placed in my house than you are in the Averys' at the moment. I see that I must do what I can to ingratiate myself with my brother.'

Then you must start with his wife, I thought to myself.

Mr Erskine raised his voice and called over his shoulder to the little man on the postillion's step, whom, I suddenly realized must have overheard all that was said: 'What do you say to that, Tod? How are you going to like having our masculine fastness invaded by the ladies?'

'Not above 'alf, Guv'nor,' replied the little man in a strong Cockney accent, and very forcefully.

'No, I'm sure you won't. But still we must make the best of it, I suppose.'

'Thank you,' I said with dignity, but Mr Erskine just laughed again and a voice came through the hood, hopefully, 'The ladies won't like it.

Too lonely, like. All them blackies and no dancing! Won't do, guv'nor—leastways not for young ladies. Not for more'n a couple o' weeks at the most.'

'Perhaps you're right, Tod. Perhaps you're right. We will have to wait and see.'

CHAPTER 15

The day that followed the ball was a trying one for all of us.

Emily and Charles were still on bad terms, a fact communicated to the rest of us by a certain defiant impertinence in Emily's manner and a silent sulkiness in Charles's. Connie remained unseen in her room all day, and Wallace, when he appeared at *tiffin*, was pale, abstracted and quieter than I had ever known him. He had quite forgotten that I was to have come home with him and Connie after the ball, and the Floods were too immersed in their marital wrangle to give the matter a thought, so I said nothing about my ride in Mr Erskine's gig, nor did I mention Connie's unfortunate exhibition at the end of the night. In fact it was not a day that favoured conversation, and was spent for the most part in exhausted, self-absorbed quiet, while four members of the household licked their respective wounds, and I tried to keep out of the way of all of them.

After dinner, the evening being fine and mild, we took our tea on the verandah. Emily had chosen to wear one of her most becoming gowns, a muslin printed with a scattering of small green leaves and trimmed with green ribbons and pleated silk. Settling herself in a large cane chair, with a small worktable before her and a piece of needlework (of many years' standing) in her hands, she composed herself into a beguiling picture of industrious femininity. Nor was it difficult to guess who was to be charmed by this gracious tableau; every time the clop of hooves approached the gate, she looked up expectantly, and each time they continued along the road without turning in, she returned to her embroidery with ill-concealed disappointment. I thought it unlikely that Mr Erskine would stir himself sufficiently to call so soon after the ball, but could say nothing to allay her vexation. When, therefore, a familiar equipage did turn in at the gate as the *khitmagar* was clearing away the cups, I was more surprised than Emily.

The strange little Cockney was driving, and on the step that he had occupied the night before there now stood a huge Pathan dressed in baggy white pyjamas, long white shirt, crimson velvet waistcoat crossed by loaded bandoliers of cartridges, and with a fan of starched and pleated muslin surmounting his high white turban. He had a fine black beard and his moustachios were waxed and curled back fiercely towards his nose. In his cummerbund was stuck a *tulwar*, a curved, broad-bladed sword. When the gig came to a halt, he hopped down from the step and opened the door for his master with a flourish.

Charles, who had recognized his brother's driver, got to his feet with an exclamation of annoyance, Wallace remained in his chair for a moment goggling incredulously at the vehicle and its occupants, so it was left to Emily—Connie was still invisible—to welcome Mr Erskine, which she did very prettily indeed. He did not stay long because he was on his way to another engagement in the city, but it was arranged that he should dine with us on the following night and, said Wallace, 'We'll finish the evening with a quiet game or two. We are expecting some other friends, good chaps all of them, and I am sure you cannot object to a little flutter, sir. Be a change for you after your quiet life in the *mofussil*.'

Mr Erskine bowed his acquiescence, but without enthusiasm, and left soon after.

It was the first I had heard of the 'other friends' who were expected to dine, but it was kind of Wallace to wish to entertain Mr Erskine in form, even though I realized I would have the bulk of the work in arranging the meal. I hoped that Mr Erskine would not find the cards too tedious, but at least Emily and I would be spared the trouble of having to make conversation with a total stranger all evening—not, I recollected, that he was difficult to talk to. The friends whom Wallace had in mind were Captain Fanning and two other officers of his own regiment, with whom he and Charles spent most of their evenings. At my suggestion, a note was also despatched hurriedly to the Barrys requesting their presence on the grounds of their previous acquaintance with the guest of honour.

All were delighted to accept, so the next morning was a busy one as I ordered the meal for eleven people, looked out and hastily mended an assortment of tired linen, and superintended a thorough cleaning of the reception rooms. Emily contented herself with arranging the flowers, and Connie, recovered now as much as she ever would be, drifted about commenting without rancour on my management of what were really her affairs. 'You *are* clever to make it all look so nice, Laura,' she said, fingering the edge of her best tablecloth which I had presumed to use. 'I don't know how you get them to work so hard—the servants, y'know. They'll never do a thing I tell them to.'

'I'm delighted to be of some help to you, Connie, and I'm glad it all suits you. It is so good of you and Wallace to want to make Mr Erskine feel welcome.'

'Oh, it's not me, Laura. It's all Wally's idea. He's so fond of entertaining, but I'm not often well enough to put my mind to it. And then he is so fond of cards too. I expect they'll start playing directly after the port, and so Mr Erskine won't object if I go to bed, will he?'

'No, I'm sure he won't,' I assured her, relieved to know her plan. 'He knows you are a little—er—delicate.'

'That's good,' she returned complacently, and went away to get dressed.

The dinner party went well. Mr Erskine, accompanied by his oddly assorted retainers, arrived promptly and we sat down to the meal at half-past four. Connie smiled silently on the company from one end of the table, and Wallace did the honours boisterously from the other. The cook had excelled himself; the shabby appointments were as clean and neat as hands could make them; the silver was eked out by sundry sauceboats and *entrée* dishes borrowed from the Barrys—a common practice in India—and two of the Barrys' servants helped to serve at the table. With the assistance of a respectable wine, tongues were loosened and tempers relaxed, and when the ladies left the room I could congratulate myself that my efforts on behalf of Charles and his brother had been successful.

Despite Connie's optimistic prognostications, the gentlemen joined us in the drawing-room when they had finished their port, and at Kate's suggestion Emily was asked to sing. I accompanied her on Connie's piano, one of the few Avery possessions still in almost pristine condition, and Captain Fanning gallantly turned the pages. Emily's voice was light and sweet and had been excellently trained for ballads and the sentimental songs well within its capacity. She stood composedly, her fan clasped loosely in her hands, with the lamplight glowing gently on the rose of her dress and her golden hair, and sang without affectation—simply and with an enjoyment in singing that induced enjoyment in others. I can remember reflecting that perhaps it was at just such a moment, as she sang just such a song and made just such a graceful picture, that Charles had first fallen in love with her, in that faraway drawing-room at Mount Bellew. Air followed air, everyone requesting their own favourites, and when at last Emily herself cried a halt to the concert, I was not surprised to see Mr Erskine's eyes fixed on my cousin with an expression of most marked approval. Immediately Emily had sat down, Wallace, who had been fidgety for some time, suggested that the gentlemen should withdraw to the dining-room where the tables had been set up. Our guests were not all eager to play, Mr Erskine less so than any, but as Charles seconded Wallace's motion with enthusiasm, they had little option. Connie then seized the opportunity to retire to her room and her 'night-cap', and Kate, Emily and I were left to entertain ourselves for the rest of the evening.

At eleven o'clock the Barrys and Captains Jennings and Hunt made their departure. Wallace saw them off with many protestations against their leaving so early, and then with a hurried goodnight to us disappeared again into the dining-room, where I caught a glimpse of Charles, Mr Erskine and Captain Fanning lounging at ease in their chairs, with a couple of decanters between them and a cloud of cigar smoke mantling the lamp. Obviously, there was no point in Emily or I waiting up to say goodnight.

Usually I was the first up and about in the Avery household, but for little Johnny, who was also an early riser and spent the hours before his walk and breakfast sitting on his *ayah*'s lap on the verandah while she recounted endless and involved stories to him in Hindustani. Often I joined them, for the stories were told in infant terms, using a vocabulary that I found just within my grasp, and the *ayah*, a good-natured creature, was always prepared to stop and repeat what I did not understand, while Johnny, cradled like a little potentate in her vast white muslin lap, sucked his thumb and regarded me with his big eyes.

On that particular morning, I had just settled myself in a patch of sunlight to listen to the *ayah*'s tale when, to the surprise of us all, we were joined by Wallace Avery.

'I didn't think you would be up so early after the party,' I said. 'Have you an early parade?'

'No—no parade.'

'Don't tell me you haven't been to bed yet? I must say I did not hear your guests leave, but then I sleep so soundly.' I had intended the remark as a joke, but as I spoke realized that Wallace certainly had not been to bed. The crumpled clothes were those he had worn the night before, but now his collar and cravat were both unfastened, and there was a wine stain down the front of his shirt. Neither had he shaved nor brushed his hair. His face was white and drawn, and the expression in his protruberant blue eyes was one of utmost misery.

'No, I have not been to bed,' he said, and sitting down on a sagging cane chair near mine, buried his face in his hands.

'Wallace, are you ill? Is anything the matter?'

'Not ill,' he muttered through his hands. 'But, God, I wish I were dead!'

'Wallace!'

'Well, I do, and that's the plain truth. Finally—I have finally—managed to run myself into the muck. Right down, Laura, and there is no escape for me. I am ruined! Ruined!'

'But how …?'

'A long story. Oh, a long story indeed. Why should I bother you with it? You can probably guess most of it anyway.'

'But—ruined! Surely it cannot be as bad as that. You are very tired … and depressed for the moment … but things will look better when you are rested.'

He shook his head in his, hands, then looked up at me and, seeing both the *ayah* and Johnny regarding him with open amazement, he swore at the woman and ordered her to take herself off. She got to her feet, picked up Johnny and vanished round the side of the house.

'I was trying to help matters. I know, that's what everyone says when they do this sort of thing, and I've always laughed at the man who expected to be believed. But really, I was trying to pull things together again. Give myself one last chance. Was sure my luck must eventually turn, d'you know?'

'No, not really, Wallace. Do you mean you have lost too much at cards? Is that it?'

'Too much! Good God, I've lost all I have! All I ever shall have.'

'Last night?' I was aghast.

'Last night was just the final touch. But a very final one. What's the good of trying to explain? I have nobody to blame but myself, but what's a chap to do when he has no income of his own? No one can live on the sort of salary the Army gives me. Not decently anyway. And Connie …'

'Yes, I know that Connie … that Connie must be a burden to you—and a great worry!'

'That's how it all started, I suppose. Not that I'm blaming poor sweet Con! Wouldn't dream of doing that, y'know. But it helped all right. I began to get into debt very early. Everyone does out here, but most men have some sort of expectations—their Pa's can be counted on to die before things get too bad—that sort of thing. I had no hope of anything coming to me from *my* Pa! He's a country clergyman—or was. Died last year. Anyway, I managed to straighten things out pretty well, to begin with. Kept control. Until Con started to … to drink. After that there was never really any hope. I'd win a bit and put it aside; I've never played because I enjoyed it, d'you see. Never! Only because it was the one way I could hope to make a bit on the side. Some hope, too! I'd manage to keep what I'd won, for a couple of months sometimes, but then the tradesmen would turn up saying their bills were unpaid. I'd storm and fume and then it would come out that Connie had frittered away all the housekeeping and her pin-money. So my winnings would go. And in desperation I'd start playing again. I've spent seven years trying to get together enough to send her home, but it was doctors and medicines and having to send her to the hills to get over the babies, and then the funerals. Oh God, what a mess! What a damned awful mess!'

He lifted his head and stroked his moustache nervously with his short fat fingers.

'Then I managed to get a loan once, when I was pretty badly down. A fairly substantial loan. From a *bunnia*—a moneylender.'

'Oh, Wallace!'

'Yes, not a wise step, I agree. But at the time I thought it was the only thing to do. No other way out, y'know. Owed a chap money and he was going home, lucky devil. He had to have it, of course, so I went to a *bunnia*. Since then … well, Laura, I hope you know nothing of how *bunnias* operate, but you may have heard enough of their methods to guess that I have never been out of their hands since. Never will be now! I wouldn't mind that so much, but I had kept a sum clear—for nearly a year I've been hoarding it—to use when Connie and the boy go home in the spring. But now, well, I'll be forced to use it to pay off the *bunnia*'s interest. Can't hope ever to do much about the capital, of course, but after last night and the night of the ball I'm properly skinned!'

'Connie won't be able to go home?'

'Not now, no.'

I had the tact to remain silent. Poor Wallace was well aware of what the failure of this last hope would mean to his wife.

The world was awakening. Sunshine, the clear pale sunshine of India's winter, flooded the garden and jewelled the arched spray from the gardener's waterbag as he sprinkled the beds. The scent of woodsmoke from the cook's newly lighted range and of damp earth from the flowerbeds filled the air. A string of fat mules harnessed to ammunition carts clipped past the gate, their harness jingling cheerfully. A small detachment of sepoys marched briskly down the dappled yellow dust of the road, and the milkman came up the drive leading his buffalo, which would be milked in the back yard under the watchful eye of the *ayah* who ensured no adulteration of the milk took place between the animal and the jug.

'Is there no one in your family who could help?' I ventured hopefully.

'No one, even if I had the gall to ask 'em. No—I'll just have to face facts.'

He paused, then broke into a bitter laugh. 'Oh, heavens! And I thought I was so clever to ask Erskine round for a game. I lost—well, pretty heavily the other night at the Residency, you see. Enough to make me sit up and think, d'you know, and when Erskine arrived I considered him a gift from the gods. Rich man. No gambler. Not even much interested in cards. What could be easier?'

'You lost to Mr Erskine?'

'And to the others, but most to him, damn him! It wasn't my night. Not my night at all. Yes, most to Erskine. Blast him, he plays like a professional, and luck favoured him all through the evening—couldn't do a thing wrong.'

'What a pity it was him. If it had been Charles, I am sure he would have overlooked …'

'No, Laura! Never! That is impossible—gaming debts are debts of honour.'

'Oh, what nonsense you men talk. Surely Connie's well-being, and little Johnny's, are more important than this nonsense about honour? However, since it is not Charles ...'

'Well, there you are. There is nothing to be done. Nothing!' He sighed deeply. 'This will be the end of my career—in the regiment. Not that I'd mind that particularly, if there were any hope of getting myself out of the *bunnia*'s clutches. I've been warned already a couple of times, when my affairs came to the attention of the Colonel. Old Hande is a stickler for the proprieties: very God-fearing, reads his Bible every morning, that sort of thing, y'know, and wants his officers to do the same. Never touched a card in his life. Nor a drink. Holds prayer meetings for the sepoys—not that they like that, mind you—but he's not going to be understanding about this mess. And then, of course, there's poor Con! Everyone knows what happened to her at the ball. I expect I'll be rusticated; sent off to some hole in the *mofussil* to think over my sins and recoup my finances.'

'But how ... why should Colonel Hande or anyone else know how much you have lost, or how much you owe these *bunnia* people?'

'He'll be told by the *bunnia*, if I don't come up with what's due. And I can't. Then Hande will come down on me like a ton of bricks, and that's when I will have to part with Connie's passage money. It just about covers the interest I owe the swine. But even if I could get Connie home, I couldn't support her there. Don't you see, Laura? Not only have I nothing to fall back on, but every penny I earn is gone before I have earned it!'

'I see. I had not realized that it was as bad as that.'

All day Wallace's confession weighed on my mind to such an extent that I was barely capable of returning a civil reply when addressed. Charles and Emily, naturally, knew nothing of the matter, and were more concerned with wondering when they would next see Mr Erskine. Charles's opinion of his brother had improved markedly, and at dinner he took it upon himself to chaff Wallace on his losing to both Oliver Erskine and himself, saying that he looked forward to another profitable evening before Mr Erskine left Lucknow. I winced inwardly, but Wallace bore it well, though after dinner, instead of going off to the mess with

Charles as usual, he came into the drawing-room and asked Emily to sing for him. After one ballad, he got up and went into the garden, where he remained pacing the gravel drive until bedtime. I could guess the unhappy nature of his thoughts, and though I pitied him, I pitied Connie even more. She was very cheerful that evening, and sufficiently sober to show an interest in the cost of lodgings, food and clothes at home, plying Emily and myself with questions, and interpreting our information as confirmation that her long-held dreams could now come true.

'Oh, it's going to be so wonderful,' she exclaimed with an enthusiasm rare in her. 'With things as cheap as they seem to be just now, Johnny and I will be able to manage excellently. Perhaps we could even take a little house, all to ourselves, near the sea—in Brighton. I must tell Wally that that is what I'd really like best. He is so good to me, he always considers my preferences first, and if we can afford it … . Just a little house, a small one, with a bay window looking towards the sea. Good sea air is just what Johnny needs, the doctor says.'

I considered telling Charles of Wallace's predicament; he was so generous and good-hearted I felt sure he would help. Even if the amount he had won from Wallace was insignificant, he was not a poor man and could certainly loan, or give, Wallace the amount for Connie's passage. But I could not speak to him without asking Wallace's permission to divulge his affairs, and even as I thought of this scheme, I knew that Wallace would veto it. He was a foolish man, and a reckless one, but he still had his pride, misplaced though it might be. If only Connie could be got to England. That was the most important thing. Once there, I was sure that a discreet letter to my Uncle Hewitt would bring forth some solution to keeping her there, at least for a couple of years. But I retired without approaching a solution to the problem.

Generally I sleep quickly and soundly, but that night I tossed and turned for hours before my eyelids finally closed—and some time later wakened suddenly, knowing just what I must do.

The plan that had suggested itself to my sleeping brain filled me with apprehension when I examined it in daylight. I shrank at putting it into practice, but the more I considered, the more I felt sure that it was the only thing possible. I knew, also, that I would not rest until I had forced myself to do what lay within my power to help Connie and little Johnny. If I failed no one need ever know that I had tried. Mr Erskine had struck me as a man who could keep his own counsel.

After *tiffin*, I slipped out of the quiet house and sent the gardener to the servants' quarters to have the horse harnessed and the carriage brought to the front. The man was obviously surprised, the afternoon hours being sacred to sleep, but the household knew I had not yet succumbed to the habit, and if my absence was noted, I would think of some excuse, such as wishing to borrow a tatting pattern from Kate Berry, who often abstained from the afternoon nap. Any surprise caused at the Averys' by my untimely drive did not bother me nearly as much as that I could anticipate at my destination. Mr Erskine was staying at Major Cussens's bungalow. I gave the driver the direction, sat back, and determined not to think of the impropriety of an unaccompanied lady visiting a bachelor's residence at two o'clock in the afternoon.

We met no other vehicles on the short drive. A slight wind soughed through the heavy foliage of the avenues, but otherwise everything was still, everyone asleep. Arrived at the bungalow, a servant, who had been dozing on the verandah, got to his feet hastily and showed me into the drawing-room, then disappeared to summon Erskine *sahib*. Imagining that Mr Erskine, like the rest of the population at this hour, was recumbent on his bed, I sat down to wait in the comfortless, white-washed room, devoid of all those unnecessary niceties that transform a house into a home. Every ugly bit of furniture, arranged mathematically round the walls, spoke a bachelor's house, and moreover a military bachelor's. I smiled to myself, remembering the precise clipped accent that I had overheard on the Banqueting Hall verandah. Evidently Major Cussens was all of a piece.

'Miss Hewitt, this is a surprise! Is something wrong?'

Mr Erskine had come in behind me, and in my confusion, I rose to meet him instead of remaining seated in a contained and ladylike fashion. His expression was amused more than surprised, but I would not stop to wonder why he should find my call funny. I had a very good idea.

'No—well, that is yes,' I began, as he gestured me to my seat again. 'You must forgive me coming here so unexpectedly, and without … without any invitation.'

'Not at all. You are always most welcome. I am sure Major Cussens would echo my sentiments, but he is away for a couple of days. Manoeuvres.'

'Oh!' Worse and worse.

'Well?' He sat down and gave me his whole attention.

'I don't quite know how to begin. I have never done this sort of thing before, you see, and ... and nobody knows that I have come, so I hope you will respect my confidence. I mean ...'

'Yes?'

'Well, I have come to ask your help. I realize it is very presumptuous of me, and of course you are quite free to refuse, but the matter is urgent and I ...'

'Yes?'

Drat the man. Why couldn't he make an effort to get me over the hurdle of explanation?

As if he had heard my thoughts, Mr Erskine went on, 'And you have no one else to turn to?'

'No, if I had ...'

'You certainly would not come to me. I see!'

'No, that's not right either. I'm afraid you are the only person in a position to help.'

'I am flattered. But before we go any further, you can trust my discretion absolutely.'

'Thank you. I felt sure I could.'

We both lapsed into silence, and I twiddled my reticule in my lap while I cast around for the right words. It would never do for him to think that Wallace had sent me. I must remember that.

'Mr Erskine, you will remember that you brought me home from the Residency ball in your carriage the other night?'

'Naturally. And because of that, you need my help? Surely my estimable brother cannot consider that your reputation was endangered by the drive? Kate and George Barry were just behind us, if you remember, and Toddy-Bob was with us.'

'Oh, no! Of course it is no such thing!'

'I am relieved to hear it.'

'Please don't joke. This is a serious matter, but it has nothing to do with me—not directly, that is. I mentioned the drive because we had talked about Captain and Mrs Avery, and I wondered whether you remembered. That's all.'

'Ah! I think I begin to see. Go on.'

'Well, it is the Averys I have come about. Or rather about poor Connie and the little boy. Mr Erskine, I know I should not do this,

170

particularly on so short an acquaintance, but may I ask how much money you won from Captain Avery the other night?'

'Oh, you may ask. I won't answer until I know why you have to know.'

'I want to know because if ... if it is a large sum, I am going to ask you, no, to beg you, to give—or loan—it back to Captain Avery.'

'Are you, by God!'

'Yes, Mr Erskine, I am. Oh, I know all about debts of honour and the other rubbish that men go on about, and I'm not concerned with such things. But I am very concerned about Mrs Avery and her son, who will both, I'm afraid, be in a very bad state if they don't manage to get to England soon, and Captain Avery, you see, has lost so much money gambling that he will not now be able to afford to send them home ... unless ...'

'Unless Mr Erskine comes to their rescue.'

I met his eyes in silence. He got up and took a thoughtful turn around the room, with his hands in his pockets, while I watched him anxiously. Then he stood looking down at me. The smile had left his face.

'I won't insult you by suggesting that Captain Avery has sent you.'

I drew myself up, saying nothing.

'No,' he said, 'of course not. Even Avery wouldn't be that big a fool. So I am to believe that it is your concern for his wife and child—solely?'

'Yes, it is—solely. Is that so hard to believe?' I stood up and faced him. This was even harder than I had anticipated, but I was becoming angry.

'You are a very wealthy man, Mr Erskine. All the world, or at any event all Lucknow, knows that. I do not know how much you won from Captain Avery, and you won't tell me, but whatever the sum, it cannot have the same significance for you that it has for him. If you had lost it, you wouldn't have thought of the matter again, but Captain Avery ...'

'This concern is very touching, Miss Hewitt. But if Captain Avery cannot afford to lose, he cannot afford to play.'

'I know that, and believe me, I have small sympathy for him. I am not doing this to save him from himself, Mr Erskine, but that money might be the saving of his wife and child, who have done nothing to deserve their ill fortune. Mrs Avery—well, you saw her the other night.

171

You know what is wrong with her. But she has lost five children, Mr Erskine, and the remaining little boy is very delicate. His only hope is to be taken home to England.'

'Why have you not applied to Charles for help? He too won money from Avery.'

'I thought of it. But Charles does not know the state of the Avery finances, and I would have to ask Captain Avery's permission to tell Charles. You must see that would be useless.'

'Oh, I do. But then why did you not think it necessary to ask Avery's permission to tell me? Surely it is rather—er, dubious to enlighten a total stranger of the man's affairs?'

'I'm afraid so. Very dubious—but you have promised me your silence. I know Charles did not win a large sum. He would certainly help Wallace, but it would be with his own funds, and Wallace would not allow that. I don't know why he shouldn't. *I* would in his place, especially thinking of Connie and Johnny. But he wouldn't. Perhaps, as a man, you may understand. But I thought if you ... if you had won sufficient to pay for the two passages, I ... well, I could return it to Wallace myself. As though it had come from me. Do you see? Then he need never know that you had anything to do with it at all.'

'And you think he would take a loan from you when he would not take it from Charles?'

'I could persuade him to, I know I could. I have seen how desperate he is—when he told me how he stood after the dinner party. I could persuade him that it was in absolute confidence, and only on account of his wife and child. He would take it from me.'

'Hm! I see. I think we had better sit down, Miss Hewitt.'

We did so, as he continued to regard me with unblinking solemnity. My anger had given way to nervousness again. He looked so hard, so lacking in sympathy, that I began to wonder whether my suggestion was unethical as well as unorthodox. Men had such peculiar ideas about money and gambling and such things, and I had never given them much thought.

He leant back in his chair and crossed his legs.

'Now, Miss Hewitt, let me assure myself that I understand you. You wish me to give you the money that I won from Captain Avery so that you can return it to him. Is that right?'

I nodded.

'Captain Avery is to be persuaded that it is a loan, or gift, directly from you, no mention being made of me. Is that right?'

Again I nodded.

'I see. So you won't allow me even due thanks for my magnanimous gesture—supposing, of course, I agree to make it?'

'Oh, but you will have my most earnest gratitude, Mr Erskine. I know it cannot signify to you whether you have Captain Avery's.'

'But it will signify to me to have yours?'

'Of course not! You know I did not mean it like that!' I felt my cheeks grow warm with confusion. The bare, uncomfortable room vibrated with his suspicion and my hostility, as we stared at each other across an absurd little island of frayed coconut-matting. Then Mr Erskine relieved the tension by throwing back his head and laughing.

'You must excuse me, Miss Hewitt,' he said, controlling himself with difficulty. 'I have never before been engaged in such an interview, and to be frank I do not know the rules of the game.'

'Neither do I,' I admitted. His laughter was disconcerting, but I preferred it to his frown. 'But why need there be any rules? I am merely asking—no, suggesting—an act of kindness, of compassion.'

'Yes. That is how you see it, no doubt.' He passed a well-shaped hand over his hair and shrugged his shoulders in a Gallic fashion. 'How can I make you see it as I do? Oh, you're right, I'm not bothered about the money itself. Nor even the principle of the thing. I quite agree with you that the code which rules these matters is largely ridiculous; I would not be bound by it. But there are other factors, which perhaps you have not taken into account. Can you be sure, for instance, that the money would be used for the purpose you have in mind? Are you sure that the sum would not be dissipated in settling other, smaller but more pressing debts before that unfortunate woman can be got aboard a ship? Have you any notion, Miss Hewitt, of the manner in which gamblers manage their day-to-day affairs: robbing Peter to pay Paul, and then when Peter comes importunate, robbing Paul to pay Peter and so on and so on until everything is so inextricably knotted and snarled that there is no unravelling it this side of death? For instance, Miss Hewitt, I'll wager that Avery has reached his present state of desperation because he is being blackmailed by some *bunnia* or *bunnias* from whom he has borrowed money over the years. They don't want the principal back. That's the last thing they want. But they are threatening in some way to get the interest paid, and that interest, Miss Hewitt, will probably be somewhere very near the original sum that was borrowed. Do you understand what that involves?'

'Yes. Captain Avery has already told me that that is the case and that he can never hope to be clear of debt. I tell you again, Mr Erskine, I hold no brief for him. If he alone were involved, I would think it only just for him to suffer some inconvenience as a result of his own stupidity and rashness. But ...'

'I know. His wife and child. All very touching.'

'Your cynicism is uncalled for!' I spoke sharply, and the edge in my voice caused Mr Erskine to draw his brows together again. But I would say what I had to. 'Captain Avery has told me that he never played for money because he enjoyed it, but to try and eke out his rather meagre salary. And I believe him! He did it for the best, and he is truly concerned for Connie and his son, more so than most men would be who found themselves with a drunken wife on their hands. Don't you see? It is her drinking, and her inability to run her home properly, that has brought him to his present state. But he does not hold it against her, as most husbands would do. He loves her dearly in spite of everything. He has destroyed himself on her behalf!'

For a moment Mr Erskine continued to frown at me, while I met his eyes squarely. Then he shook his head in pity.

'No, no, Miss Hewitt, that won't do! I've knocked around too long not to recognize a born gambler when I see one. Captain Avery's explanation was tailored to his audience, I assure you. Oh,' as I attempted to contradict him, 'I do not pretend to know how he feels about his wife; no doubt he is as devoted as you say. But I think it more likely that she took to gin to allay her loneliness as a gambler's wife, than that he took to gambling because she drank. I've seen many such situations in my time, Miss Hewitt. You can do nothing to mend matters, believe me. And you might well make them worse by meddling.'

'Then you will not...'

'No, I will not!'

I looked down at my hands lying quietly on my lap. I had at least done what I could. But it was small comfort. My sense of defeat was augmented by the knowledge which had grown on me during the interview that I had made a fool of myself in attempting to move such a man as Mr Erskine. He was as hard and unfeeling as the Rock of

Gibraltar, and all that was left for me was to retreat with what dignity I could muster.

I got up. Mr Erskine, too, rose to his feet.

'One moment,' he said, looking down at me with gravity in his eyes, but a half-smile on his lips. 'Had anything been sufficient to make me return my winnings to Avery, it would have been your intercession for him. You are a woman of spirit, Miss Hewitt, even if perhaps just a little too impetuous.'

'So I begin to think,' I agreed coldly.

'You should not have come here this afternoon,' he went on. 'Not that I do not appreciate your visit; quite the contrary! But this is a bachelor establishment, something which perhaps you did not realize, as, perhaps, you also did not realize that so long as I am part of it, in the eyes of all the decorous ladies of cantonments, it is a very dubious bachelor establishment.'

'Your concern is unnecessary,' I informed him stiffly. 'My action was entirely innocent, and I am persuaded that my reputation cannot suffer, as a consequence, in the eyes of those few people whom I respect.'

'A woman of spirit indeed! Allow me to hope that you will not be met by any of the more rigid mamas of Mariaon as you drive out of Major Cussens's drive—alone! I would not like to see you cowed by gossip. But if you will accept a word of advice: the next time you stand in need of my assistance, it would be wiser to send over a chit, and I promise to attend you with all celerity.'

'Mr Erskine, I know well enough that I have made a meddling fool of myself, but really it is too bad of you to rub it in. I will not bother you again. You may depend upon that. And allow me to remind you that I did not come here on my own behalf in the first place.'

He was smiling broadly again, and in spite of my wrath I caught myself wondering why a man with such an unpleasant character should be gifted with such a pleasant smile.

'I believe you are seldom in need of help on your own behalf. More's the pity. It would be quite an experience to see you cast down! But allow me to say that I am delighted our acquaintance is to be prolonged. Your addition to my brother's party is going to make a difference to my enjoyment. No little difference!'

'I will go now,' I muttered and made for the door.

'Please, a moment more!' His hand on my arm detained me, and I had to pause. 'I have not yet finished. This, Miss Hewitt, is the reason why I could not return Captain Avery's losses, even at your request.' He took out a leather pocketbook, and extracted a half sheet of notepaper which he handed me.

I was not so simple as to believe that any cash had changed hands after the game at the Averys' bungalow. I had imagined such transactions were naturally covered by cheques. The slip of paper Mr Erskine gave me, however, was a simple IOU signed by Wallace Avery with a great flourish under the two names. The amount, so I now saw, was amply sufficient to send his wife and son home to England. I looked at it for a moment in some puzzlement; why had Mr Erskine decided to show it to me at all? The matter was finished.

'Well, I see there would have been enough for the passages. Not that it matters now.'

'You see nothing else?'

'I don't understand ...'

'The date, Miss Hewitt.'

The IOU was postdated six months hence.

'But I thought ...'

'Yes, Miss Hewitt. My winnings were purely hypothetical.'

'But, a debt of honour; he said it was a debt of honour!'

'And no doubt he meant it. Of course he would not fob off the men with whom he plays regularly in such a manner. Perhaps he hoped, still hopes, that somehow he will have recouped himself sufficiently to meet this document when I present it in six months' time. He explained when he wrote it that he was a little—er—embarrassed. Actually, I could have refused to take it. But I was his guest; I realized before I played that the man was a gambler; and, in any event, as you have said yourself, the sum is of no great importance to me. So I let it pass. Now perhaps you understand?'

'Yes, yes, I do understand, Mr Erskine!' Anger nearly choked me as I spoke. 'And I also understand that you have been playing a despicable game of cat-and-mouse with me ever since I arrived here!'

'What?' He was genuinely surprised.

'Yes—a game of cat-and-mouse! You have allowed me to humiliate myself; you have added to that humiliation, you have delighted to see me make a fool of myself. And all the time you had that paper in your pocket. Why did you not show it to me when you knew why I had come? I would have left immediately, and we would both have been saved this wretched interview!'

He had drawn back as I turned on him wrathfully, and was watching me with an expression of quizzical incredulity. After a moment's pause, during which he seemed to be debating how best to counter my accusation, he smiled and said, 'But why should I do that? It would have deprived me of your company.'

This flippancy merely augmented my anger, and I swept out of the room.

The driver of the buggy was dozing on his seat, so I had to open the door myself, and as I wrestled with the rusty handle Mr Erskine followed me and, unclasping my hand from the metal, opened the door for me. I ignored the hand he offered and climbed quickly into the vehicle. He slammed the door, signalled to the driver to be off, and we clattered out of the porch.

I inclined my head very slightly as we went.

'*Au revoir*, Miss Hewitt,' he laughed, waving after us. 'Till we meet again!'

CHAPTER 16

The noble certainty in right-doing that had upheld me when I left the
Avery bungalow had all ebbed away when I returned. I was abased in
my own eyes; felt less than the ant and smaller than the atom. My
behaviour had been callow and foolish in the extreme. I had acted too
hastily, too rashly, too unthinkingly. Moreover—and this was the most
cruel knowledge of all—I had exhibited my lack of common sense to
Mr Erskine. I had earned his derision. And he, I now felt, had thoroughly
earned my pronounced dislike. For if I had been hasty, I had also been
concerned; if I had been rash, I had also shown some courage; and if I
had been unthinking, I had not been unfeeling.

But he! He had been cold, cynical and calculating. To have known all
the time that I was on a fool's errand, and to have allowed me to show my
hand and demonstrate my ignorance of men as he had done, was
unpardonable. It was something no true gentleman—no one like Charles,
for instance—would ever have been capable of. Remembering Mr
Erskine's iniquities was a bulwark against recalling my own shortcomings,
so by the time I got home I had worked myself into a towering temper
and a very thorough detestation of the man I had left. I wished with all
my strength that somehow I could avoid meeting him again, but this, of
course, was a forlorn hope. Charles's initial disapproval of his brother
had dissipated over the last few days and I had small reason to doubt that
we would visit Mr Erskine at Hassanganj as soon as an invitation was
tendered. In this belief I was right, the promptings of Charles's good
nature being reinforced by two other and important factors.

The first was a letter which Charles had received that day from his
mother, written a mere two months before. After two cross-hatched
pages of news about Dissham, Mount Bellew, relatives and friends in
England, Mrs Flood had turned her attention to her son's affairs in
India.

I had met Mrs Flood on several occasions and been intimidated by her on all of them. She was one of those large, slow, dictatorial women who plough their way successfully through life, and the lives of those around them, helped only by an immense and unshakeable belief in their own infallibility. Unhampered by intelligence, imagination or sensitivity, ignorant of all such imponderables as the rights or feelings of others, she had managed to bend the world to her will by her sheer incapacity to entertain another's point of view. It was said that she had once been a beauty. Perhaps. But she had run to fat, and now her heavy features gave indication of nothing other than determined selfishness. I had often wondered how such a woman had produced a son like Charles. That she was the mother of Oliver Erskine was in no way astonishing to me.

In her letter she was naturally delighted to know that our voyage had reached a safe conclusion, and hoped that we would all enjoy our stay in Calcutta. However, she exhorted Charles, it would be a mistake to linger in the capital too long. It was Charles's first duty to make the acquaintance, gain the friendship and win the confidence of his brother in Hassanganj. Then followed a eulogy on the extent, importance and wealth of Mr Erskine's possessions—with the emphasis on the wealth. She had always regretted not having the opportunity of visiting Hassanganj and seeing her eldest son again: fate and her second husband had both proved intransigent. But now Charles must take the opportunity of securing to himself some at least of those material benefits that his father had been unable to provide. Oliver was unmarried and showed no inclination for marriage. Charles must therefore realize that as Oliver's nearest relative, he was also his most likely heir. Charles was to give due consideration to this fact and do all in his power to cement the natural ties of blood by subordinating his own inclinations to his brother's, studying his brother's wishes, and insinuating himself thoroughly into his brother's mind and heart.

She remained, as ever, her dear boy's fondest mama.

Letters from home were always read aloud, which was unfortunate in this case. By the time he reached the close poor Charles was red with embarrassment at his parent's vulgarity, and I was grateful that only Emily and I were present.

The second factor that militated against my heartfelt desire never to see Mr Erskine again was an interview between Wallace and his commanding officer that took place the morning after my unfortunate visit to Major Cussens's bungalow.

Wallace was late getting home for *tiffin*, and I knew as soon as he entered the dining-room that what he most feared had overtaken him. He had been 'carpeted' by Colonel Hande. Naturally we were not told the details of the painful meeting, but its general direction could be guessed at, by me at least, and its outcome could not be hidden. I conjectured that Colonel Hande, aghast at what had been brought to his attention regarding the Averys' debts and the altogether unfortunate tenor of their affairs, had had no option but to order Wallace to take up one of the civilian administrative posts now being filled by Army officers. The annexation of Oudh earlier in the year, with all the concomitant responsibilities of such a step, had proved too much for the Company's Civil Service to manage, and in order to bridge the gap between the creation of new posts and the recruitment of new staff, the Army had been asked to second officers to act as civil administrators in many areas. I could not help wondering how adequate an administrator a man with only military training would make, but in Wallace's case, at least, it was a godsend. As he told me later, the alternative Colonel Hande had offered was retirement from the regiment, and as Wallace was a 'Black' or Native Service officer, such a step carried no hope of repatriation. Nor would it have been easy for him to obtain any other employment in India.

The household was thrown into turmoil by this intelligence; only I had been in any way prepared for it, and even I had not looked to lose the roof from over my head.

Wallace told us of Colonel Hande's decision as we sat at *tiffin*. Perhaps he found it easier to break the news to Connie with others present, and in order to get the worst over first, he commenced by saying, 'Well, Con, old dear, Hande wants me to go into the *mofussil*, do a wretched job for the civils who ain't up to it! Interestin' and all that. Bit of a pat on the back, really. Only trouble is, we'll have to put off your little jaunt to England for another few months. There'll be expenses in the movin', setting ourselves up in the next place. All that to think of. Money's going to be a little short again for a time.'

He was white-faced, and his hands trembled as he raised his fork to his mouth. He did not look at his wife as he spoke.

'Put off England? Again?' Connie put down her implements and stared at her husband. 'Oh no, Wally! Not again! Please not!' She was always pale, but suddenly the red rims around her eyes seemed more pronounced, and her flaccid under-lip trembled as she spoke.

'I'm afraid so, my love. Just for a few months, that's all. I'll have things straightened out in no time, but initially—well, you've been through it, old lady, you know how much it costs just movin' the baggage.' He attempted cheerfulness.

'Oh, Wally! Oh, Wally!' And without another word Connie got up from the table and rushed to her room.

Wallace glanced at us miserably, all the ebullience, the silly optimism, drained from his expression, and then carefully and manfully told us of his interview, even mentioning his debts, but not of course their extent, nor how he had acquired them.

'Damned decent of old Hande, really. He's giving me a chance to fill the old moneybags again. Once we're settled, the living will be cheaper, I dare say, and I'll soon be able to get myself out of this little mess. Too bad about Con. She'll feel it for a while. But things will look up pretty soon, and the country air will be pretty near as good for little Johnny as the sea air would've been. I'm sure of that.'

'But, Wallace, she was counting on it so. The disappointment must be terrible. And even in the country, Johnny is going to have to face the heat. Isn't there any way you can manage to send them home?' Emily meant well, but gave small comfort to poor Wallace.

'Not just at the moment, no. But as I say, in a few months I'll see them safe on a ship. Take them down to Calcutta myself, and we'll have a bit of a well-earned holiday together before she sails. It'll be just the thing for us both—much better all round than the present plan!'

But he was not really persuaded of this fact, though he tried to assure us that he was. I saw Charles watching him with compassion and was not surprised when he said, with a hint of embarrassment himself, 'If money is the only problem, Wallace, will you not allow Emily and myself to help? It would give us the greatest pleasure. You could look on it as a very small return for all your hospitality.'

I knew a fleeting hope, and saw it reflected for a second in Wallace's face, but immediately he renounced it.

'Good of you, old man. Very good! But no—of course it's not only the money. Get that together in no time, as I have said. But once she thinks of it, Connie will realize that she would be unhappy leaving me to settle down alone in a new station. Make her miserable not to know how I'm living, people I meet—all that sort of female business, you know. She'll want to fix up the house, sort out the servants, put in a few seeds and shrubs and so on. You know what women are! It's only a postponement, and in the long run it'll turn out for the best. She'll see that herself soon. Just a little emotional for the moment is my Con. But it won't take long for her to see it's for the best!'

'Please remember—if you should change your mind, the offer still holds, and as we are family after all, you must not hesitate to approach me. Any time. Any time at all.'

'Thank you. Very good of you, and I can't say how sorry I am that this should have happened while you were our guests. Would never have suggested you coming up-country if I had not felt we would be left in peace here for a while. 'Course, things are rather at sixes and sevens in the *mofussil*, and I'm not the only one to be banished from Lucknow, ha, ha! No, sir! Two or three others too: men who sling the lingo, y'know, as I do, worse luck. Just as well though that you aren't entirely dependent on us. You had intended to visit Erskine in Hassanganj, hadn't you? Everything falls into place, you see, and it's only the suddenness of the thing that has upset Con.'

Connie forbore to appear at dinner, and directly after we had eaten, Wallace went out alone.

Charles, Emily and I sat in the shabby drawing-room and considered our predicament at length. Emily's condition, of course, was uppermost in our minds, and the expectation of her confinement in early May had already thrown awry the plans we had made in Calcutta. Several alternatives, however, remained open to us. We could return to England immediately by the overland route, but in view of Emily's condition, this was not a favoured possibility. We could return to Calcutta and await her confinement there. Or we could go to Delhi for a few months and then up to the hills where the baby could be born in the healthful, pine-scented air and coolness.

Kate Barry and I had both worked hard persuading Emily that it was perfectly possible to bear a baby successfully in India, and now, seeing my cousin's tranquil acceptance of this fact, I wished we had been less zealous, for the alternative most likely to be adopted and the one most favoured by Emily herself, was a protracted stay in Hassanganj.

'Of course, we would have to be back here … in time,' she said eagerly.

'Or better still, go up to one of the hill stations straight from Hassanganj,' I put in quickly.

'Either alternative would mean our going to Hassanganj first, and we have so far received only the most perfunctory of invitations,' Charles objected correctly.

'Oh, but it *was* an invitation, Charles!' Emily pleaded.

'No doubt, of a sort. But he has hardly been cordial … or truly welcoming, or even very interested in us. No, Emily, we will have to have something more explicit before we can take ourselves to Hassanganj. After all, as things are now, it will mean a visit of several months. And there is no saying he would welcome us for so long a stay.'

Emily's face fell, and I knew she was thinking spitefully of the baby that had ruined all her plans.

'Anyway,' Charles continued, 'we have no idea what life is like in the *mofussil*, as they term it. You'll probably find it deadly flat and boring.'

'And what do you think Lucknow has been, with never being able to ride or be seen dancing, or doing any of the things I would like to do?'

Emily pouted and Charles scowled, and they would soon have been engaged in one of their frequent arguments, but the door opened and Mr Erskine was announced, come to bring just that explicit invitation that was needed to confound my hopes and ensure a further acquaintance with him.

Emily and Charles between them gave Mr Erskine a rather confused account of Wallace's 'transfer', which he heard with a straight face and every indication of sympathy, while I gave my entire attention to my needlework.

'So, you see, your invitation could not come at a better time, and we will be so happy to be with you,' Emily laughed delightedly, looking sideways at her spouse. 'Charles is so anxious to see the place, and his mother will be delighted to know her two sons are together at last!'

'My privilege,' said Mr Erskine gallantly. 'I hope you will not be disappointed. I am not a sociable man, and anyway there are few Europeans in the district—none within calling distance. But perhaps we can arrange a small party at Christmas time, if you would care for it. For the rest, well—I am kept fairly busy on the estate, but you must consider the place your home while you are in India, and come and go just as you like.'

'I declare, I am quite excited by the prospect of it all,' Emily said. 'We have heard so much of Hassanganj and your house and so on, and I have been so curious to see it all, and then we have been so worried as to what was best to do, with poor Wallace being called away from Lucknow, so it is so nice to know we have somewhere to go—and not among strangers either, which I was not looking forward to—just now!'

Mr Erskine affected not to understand the last allusion when Emily stopped hurriedly, but her face flushed all the same. He turned to Charles and promised him the best shooting in Oudh 'if he cared for such things', and soon they were deep in duck, partridge and quail and then on to crocodile, leopard and tiger. His relatives, one on either side of him, hung on his every word in a most flattering manner, and I sat at a distance, intent on my needlework, inwardly bewailing my fate and wishing Mr Erskine in Hades.

He had risen to leave when his attention turned to me. He was waiting for his hat and cape when his eye fell on me in my corner and he turned to Charles in well-simulated confusion: 'But forgive me! I have been most remiss in making no mention of Miss Hewitt. I hope it is understood that I am expecting her company as well as yours?'

'Oh, certainly,' Emily assured him, 'Laura is part of the family! We wouldn't dream of leaving her out of anything. Why, Laura manages us both, and I don't know where we'd be without her help.'

'I can imagine it,' Mr Erskine answered, looking me full in the face. 'I am sure you are a most admirable companion to everyone, Miss Hewitt, and I look forward to making a brief acquaintance into a lasting friendship. You will be most welcome at Hassanganj.'

I bowed as graciously as I could, and as, quite unnecessarily, he had extended his hand, I had to give him mine. When I withdrew it I found myself clasping a slip of paper. I did not have to examine it to know what it was. Wallace would have one worry the less. But in six months' time, who could know how many others he would have acquired in its place?

On the following morning we were joined at breakfast by Kate Barry who informed us that she too had received a call from Mr Erskine—and an invitation.

'Oh, I know I am very wicked to repeat things, but sure and I must tell you what happened! Poor Oliver! He's distraught, quite distraught I tell you, at the idea of having you girls with him in Hassanganj! "I could manage a regiment of males and not give 'em a second thought," says he, "but two proper young Englishwomen. Kate, I don't even know what sort of things they like to eat. Bath Olivers! That's it; all young English females have to eat Bath Olivers at frequent intervals, isn't that so, Kate? And there must be other things—but I don't know what they are. And tea, Kate. I never drink the stuff myself, but I must get in a case of tea. There must be dozens of other things that I should have and don't have. Scented soap. And ... oh, God, what have I let myself in for? I can't manage on my own, Kate. Come with them, please! George shall join us at Christmas, and we'll have some capital shooting. Tell him that, and he'll let you come. Just come for a couple of weeks or a couple of months or however long you care to—just a couple of days if necessary. But come and see that things are as they should be in Hassanganj. It's so long since there's been a woman there, Kate!" "True enough, my lad," I says to him, tapping him on his waistcoat, "and even longer since there's been a *lady*," which took not a feather out of him, mind you! So there you are, my dears. I'm coming to Hassanganj with you—just as soon as you're ready to go. George is charmed at getting rid of me and my long tongue for a while, and I, I can think of nothing better than a Christmas in Hassanganj after all this long time. And what's more, I am to come laden with Bath Olivers and tea and scented soaps and anything else the heart of young females can desire!'

Nothing could have suited me better than to have Kate with us in Hassanganj. My feelings regarding the visit were acutely ambivalent. On the one hand I detested the idea of accepting the hospitality of a man I liked as little as I did Mr Erskine, but on the other hand there was the lure of experiencing India with a closeness and familiarity that would be denied me elsewhere. Kate, cheerful, forthright, shrewd Kate, would provide that neutral and uninvolved presence so necessary to the success of any family party, and would, moreover, be an admirable guide and mentor in the strange life ahead of us.

It was Charles, of course, who suggested we should remain on in Lucknow to help the Averys with their packing and other arrangements. Emily would have left for Hassanganj the day after Mr Erskine's visit, and I was glad for Connie's sake that Charles managed to restrain his own enthusiasm, as I was able to be of some assistance to her before the move. She spent most of the ensuing fortnight in bed or in tears, and poor Wallace was hardly more capable of seeing to his affairs than was his wife. The unhappiness of his parents communicated itself to little Johnny, who whined and sniffed his way among the gathering trunks and chests, bewildered and lost in an adult world gone suddenly awry.

Wallace had been posted to a station about forty miles north of Lucknow. 'I shall be in total command,' he told Connie, with a brief return of his old optimistic blustering. 'You'll be first lady of the station, old girl. That'll be something, won't it? You won't half like being the *Burra-mem* of an entire station!' Later we learnt that there were only two other white men in the station, and a mere handful of soldiers and police. But one finds one's comfort where one must.

I made an opportunity of speaking to Wallace regarding Charles's offer of help, imploring him to reconsider his refusal. He shook his head, sighed and said, 'Perhaps—perhaps, Laura, if only the cost of the passages were involved. But don't you see, I cannot afford to keep up a home for them in England and another for myself here. Even one establishment, as things are now, is going to be a struggle. So what would you have me do? Explain everything to Charles and ask another man to support my wife and child? Indefinitely? No, Laura, that I cannot do. I have some pride! And who knows, things may yet take a turn for the better. They might!'

I said no more. Shortly before we left I gave him the IOU he had signed for Mr Erskine, with an ingenious story of how it had been returned as Mr Erskine did not care to win so much money from his host. The story did not fool even me, but he appeared to accept it and did not question me further. His mind by then was on other things.

We stayed to the very end, and only when the dilapidated buggy had disappeared through the familiar white-washed gate-posts, did we turn our attention to our own journey. Charles had resold the carriage he had bought on our arrival. Mr Erskine had sent his own heavy travelling carriage to convey us to Hassanganj and with it Toddy-Bob, the little Cockney, and eight mounted guards, all uniformed and carrying muskets and looking not very much different from the normal sepoy, except for a certain lack of attention to such details as brass buttons and buckles.

As we drove down the curved driveway for the last time, we passed a bullock cart laden with Avery baggage on the top of which was strapped the parrot's bell-shaped cage, carefully covered with a pillowslip. Poor old Polly, what next for you, I wondered as we went by, and from the depths of his covers the bird replied in raucous tones, 'Good girl, Connie! Goo-oo-ood girl!'

Lucknow and its life were behind us.

BOOK II

HASSANGANJ

'How plain does it appear that
there is not another condition of
life so well suited for
philosophizing as this in which
thou now happenest to be.'
Marcus Aurelius

CHAPTER 1

Our approach to Hassanganj was made on a clear evening in mid-December. Smoke rising from stubble fields, the scent of burning leaves and an underlying sharpness in the air told of autumn, but otherwise the gentle luminosity of the fading sky and the pastel colouring of a temperate west recalled more a spring in England than the approach of the brief Indian winter.

The road from Lucknow had been appalling, rutted and seamed, and if not inches deep in mud then equally thick in fine white dust, so that our progress had been both uncomfortable and slow. We had spent two nights in *dak*-bungalows as dirty and infested with insects as those we had encountered during our journey up-country from Calcutta, and were now near the end of our third full day of travel. Mr Erskine had meant well by sending us his coach, but we soon realized that we would have made better time in the light *dak-gharis* of that previous journey. Rain had fallen each night, and several times our heavy vehicle had got stuck in miry watercourses or sunk axle-deep in dirt roads that had suddenly turned to swamps. The country was more thickly wooded as we moved north towards the mountains; the heavily cultivated landscape of the first day gave way to long stretches of dark forest or close-cropped grazing land. The crops looked good, but the villages were often rundown and neglected, and twice in the second day we had passed small homesteads burnt to the ground—pathetic remains of some poor peasant's lifelong work. Hanging like a monkey from the postillion's perch behind us, Toddy-Bob had poked his head in at the window on each occasion to inform us cheerfully: 'Rohilla raiders around!'

'Raiders?' Emily was apprehensive.

'Yes'm. Big blokes. Six-footers. Rohilkand. Next province. Very fierce! Bastards!' Toddy's natural ease of expression was syncopated by the jerking of the coach.

'No need to worry,' Kate reassured us. 'Probably is the work of Rohillas, but since the kingdom was annexed, they have only descended on this part of the country in small bands. There was a time when they were a real menace; they can still be a nuisance, but it is unlikely that Oliver would have allowed us to travel with so small a company had there been anything much to fear.'

'So our martial escort was sent along for more than effect?'

'Sure and aren't they a part of the Hassanganj *rissal*? The Erskines' private army, woman dear. It used to number several hundred, in the old days, and very necessary it must have been, too. I dare say Oliver has done away with all but a few score now—just enough to see his rents reach the bank in safety—and escort his newfound relatives to Hassanganj. Very well trained and disciplined they are, or were when old Mrs Erskine was still alive and George and I used to visit her.'

'Good God, a private army! Whatever next?' exclaimed Charles with disapproval.

'Och, but as I say, there's no need to worry in these days. 'Tis a relic of past glories; no more.'

I hoped Kate was right, but my mind was not lightened by observing the number of mud forts, walled and moated, which reared up from the fields of sugar cane, gram and millet. Many were now merely ruins, but whatever their condition, they hinted too strongly of a country accustomed to war and unrest, and I observed as much to Kate.

'There's never been peace, what we would call peace, in these parts. Not since anyone can remember, anyway. The last few Nawabs have been rather less than estimable in character, or even strong. While they luxuriated in their palaces in Lucknow, the villagers, poor divils, were subjected to every sort of extortion, bullying and knavery—from their own landlords, the *talukhdars*, y'know, and from the Nawab's tax-gatherers and from these Rohilla raiders. Why, I can remember only a few years ago all these little forts you see in the fields were surrounded by great thickets of bamboo. Bamboo made an excellent stockade: musket bullets just ricocheted off the canes, doing no harm, d'you see, and most rent and tax collection, to say nothing of the "perks" demanded by the Rohillas, were extracted at gunpoint. Our last Resident, John Sleeman, had the bamboo razed in an effort to make the *talukhdars* less willing to resist the Nawab's men, but the little wars and skirmishes continued all the same.'

'And Mr Erskine engaged in them?' I asked.

'Lord love you, yes! What else was the man to do—when it was necessary? Not that it has been necessary too often since Oliver took over. Rumour has it that he entered into some sort of concordat with the Rohillas. Even took a number of 'em into his *rissal*, so they say, by way of good faith. But I'm sure there have been times, even quite recently, when he had to put up a fight to maintain his boundaries, protect his water, that sort of thing, y'know.'

Kate, apparently, saw nothing peculiar in the thought of an English gentleman, in this enlightened age, doing battle for his lands like some medieval warrior baron, but her casual explanation had brought a new dimension to our visit to Hassanganj.

'Mind you,' she continued, unaware of the effect her words had on her hearers, 'he'd have more sense than to fiddle with his dues to the Nawab, and the Nawab's people would know better than to interfere with him, so there'd be no trouble in that direction. But the *talukhdars* around him, and the big *zemindars*, well, naturally they'd resent a white man having his possessions and position, and 'tis *they* no doubt who gave him most bother—when they were able. They've been dispossessed themselves, though, now—this man Thomason, the Chief Settlement Officer, thinks the land should belong outright to the tenants, d'you see—so they'll be having troubles enough for the moment without turning on Hassanganj.'

'But how extraordinary,' Emily breathed, her blue eyes wide with wonder.

'Thoroughly primitive!' Charles averred belittlingly.

'Och, no doubt of that! But 'twould be folly, Charles, to judge matters out here by the same yardstick you use at home. Not only conditions are different, remember, but the people. Their expectations, their requirements. Most of all their necessities. I think you will find it to the Erskines' credit that all down the years they have respected the people's own necessities—not the necessities the government at Home feel the people ought to have!'

I could see that Emily was greatly taken by this unexpected aspect of Mr Erskine's existence in Hassanganj. For myself, I tended to agree with Charles that force of arms was a lamentably primitive way of settling differences, but held my peace, knowing that an Emily subject to romantic excitement was easier to deal with than an Emily suffering from imaginary fears. Small wonder, though, that Mr Erskine had developed so authoritative a manner, brought up as he had been in a private kingdom capable of making private wars. It was an explanation, I told myself, even if not a justification of his autocratic manner.

Late on that third afternoon of our journey, Toddy-Bob told us that we had crossed the boundary and were now in Hassanganj. I had understood that we were approaching the 'hills'—the Himalaya mountains—but there was no sign of them, and hardly an incline had broken the monotony of the countryside we traversed that day, which had been as flat as a tabletop, interrupted only by *topes* of ancient mangoes or the deep gashed banks of a seasonal watercourse. We were all weary, bored and consequently dozing, when Toddy hung into the window and announced, 'Nearly there—the house!' and pointed to a smudge of deep pink just visible among dark trees in the distance.

At once we began to settle our appearances, hampered by close quarters and the movement of the carriage. I patted my hair smooth and replaced my bonnet. As I raised my eyes, something on the skyline, glimpsed through the dusty window, caught my attention.

'Those clouds on the horizon are remarkably still, aren't they?' I asked Kate. 'They look almost solid.'

Kate glanced out of the window.

'Clouds!' she smiled, 'Those are no clouds. The snows are out to greet us.'

'The hills!' I exclaimed, trying to clean the window with the palm of a dirty glove to see better.

As I looked the ethereal forms took on substance before my eyes. Streamers of pale cloud, low in the sky, shifted swiftly and for a moment allowed me a glimpse against the fading blue of the purple flanks of the foothills, crowned by the snowy serrations of the great peaks behind them, and at their feet a line of dark forest. Then the vision was gone again, leaving only the intermittent hint of icy pinnacles apparent in the shredding clouds.

'The Himalayas!'

'No less,' Kate confirmed. 'The *terai*—that forest at the base of the foothills—is only half-a-day's ride from Hassanganj, but the snows themselves, of course, are a weary way from anywhere. We'll have a great view of them all the same; better than if we were closer. Early morning and sunset, that's when they appear, like haughty princesses out for a brief airing, then gone again, leaving only the memory of their shining splendour. Och, but they are a beautiful sight.'

I strained my eyes and willed the hills to reappear, but the 'princesses' would not relent and, as I settled back in my seat, I found we were passing through tall wrought-iron gates flanked by a small lodge and attended by two men dressed in the same livery as those who accompanied us. The house was approached by a long avenue of jarmin trees winding through what was obviously a large and splendidly maintained park. But for the downhanging tails of monkeys busy with the jarmin fruit and the eruption of a flight of screaming parrots from the trees, we could have been approaching a gentleman's residence in any county of England. Deer nibbled the grass among the long evening shadows and peacocks dragged furled tails in haughty isolation as we bowled past groves, plantations and well-fenced paddocks. Then, rounding a corner, the avenue came to an end, and the house rose suddenly before us, visible in all its eccentric size across a wide expanse of grass.

'Good heavens!' exclaimed Charles, voicing my sentiments exactly.

'What … what is it?' wondered Emily, after a moment's shocked silence.

'Well may you ask!' laughed Kate.

Sheer size was the first amazed impression. The place was vast. And then the bewildered eye moved from feature to feature, searching among the embellishments for the enlightenment of a plan. It found none. Turrets and cone-topped towers, castellations and battlements, lancet windows, arrow slits and mullioned casements, wrought-iron roof ridges and decorated gableends, flying buttresses and gargoyled gutters all jostled each other in energetic incongruity, obscuring any original design the edifice might once have boasted. Torrential rains, great heat and sudden frosts had weathered the pinkish stucco to an appearance of age, and the lower walls were covered thickly with climbing plants. The sinking sun touched the myriad windows and turned the panes to gold, and from a dozen decorated chimneys white woodsmoke unfurled into the evening air.

Enormous, eccentric, the unexpected appearance of this mansion in the middle of the Indian plain was electrifying, and Kate was still chuckling her appreciation of our astonishment as we drew up at last beneath a pillared portico. A small, fat native, his livery emblazoned with the Greek diphthong OE, as were those of our guards and the doors of the coach we had travelled in, sprang up as we halted and struck a mallet on a bronze gong hanging on a tripod in the portico. His warning, though a mark of courtesy, was unnecessary, for our host was already standing at the top of the steps leading on to the verandah, with behind him at least a dozen servants in the now-familiar livery.

'A great man in his own acres,' Mr Roberts had once said, and while I waited for the carriage steps to be put to the door I sat back quietly to observe Mr Erskine's demeanour in his own domain. He stood with his hands behind his back and watched the preparations. Only when the steps were in position and the door open did he come forward to assist Emily. Then he was all that was most affable and welcoming, but that small moment of aloofness, while he waited for his myrmidons to set the scene, served once again to confirm me in my opinion of his arrogance.

Mr Erskine kissed Emily dutifully, Kate affectionately and bowed correctly over my hand. 'You are very welcome, Miss Hewitt,' he said, raising his head to meet my eyes. 'India awaits your closer acquaintance.' There was a gleam of humour in his eyes which did not leave me quite comfortable. But if he had not forgotten my chagrin in Major Cussens's bungalow, it appeared that he had also remembered my aspirations at the ball. My smile was warmer than I had intended it to be.

Inside as out, we felt minimized by the size of the house. Beyond the glass doors, which stood open for our welcoming, stretched a wide corridor so long one could only guess it ended. But whereas the external aspect of the house suggested nothing so much as the fantasies of an opium-eater, its interior was fitted out with every indication of taste that wealth and a refined eye could provide. Rich hangings, fine old furniture, silken carpets, exquisite lamps all indicated an elegantly cultivated mind, although they were, for the most part, of a style that has become outmoded during the rule of our present Queen. The corridor, it is true, was hung with so many stuffed heads of wild beasts and mounted antlers that Emily gasped as she entered, and I, my attention caught by the bared fangs of a tiger's snarl, was hardly aware of the white skull of an elephant that hung in the vestibule immediately above a carved chest of Chinese ebony. But in the morning room, where wine awaited the dusty travellers, an Aubusson carpet reflected the moulding of the ceiling, and the goblets from which we drank were of fine Venetian crystal.

So much I was able to take in during the few moments spent in conversation with our host before we were shown to our rooms.

In my bedroom, a large apartment on the first floor with doors leading on to an upper verandah, I found an *ayah* pouring a bath for me before a blazing log fire. Her name, she said, was Bhujni. She had one wall eye and was badly scarred by smallpox, but seemed a cheerful creature and was spotlessly clean. As she moved about the room, unpacking my dressing-case and arranging my few toilet articles on the dressing-table, many glass bangles jangled on her wrists and with every movement she exuded a pleasant smell of freshly starched muslin and the coconut-oil with which she glossed her hair to the appearance of satin.

A bullock-wagon laden with our trunks and bandboxes had left Lucknow a few days before. Now I found my gowns, all neatly pressed, hanging in the wardrobes, my linen freshly starched, and my lace laundered, gently bleached in sour milk, and then stiffened just sufficiently in sugar and water. Bhujni, beaming a black-toothed smile, was delighted by my appreciation of her efforts, but shocked when I put her out of the room while I took my bath. I allowed her to button up my gown, however, and help me with my hair. As soon as I was ready, I descended again, impatient to see more of the extraordinary mansion.

At the bottom of the broad staircase I hesitated, wondering which of the many doors would lead to the drawing-room, but almost immediately a servant appeared from nowhere on noiseless bare feet and opened the appropriate door.

The length of the room and the height of the ceiling only confirmed my first impression of the size of everything in Hassanganj. At each end of the room fires blazed, but only one of the three chandeliers was alight—that nearest to where I entered. I stood for a moment taking in the main features—the fine marble mantels, the long doors draped in velvet, the polished floor scattered with glowing Persian rugs—and was immediately attracted by two portraits, one of a man of middle age, the other of a young woman in a high-waisted gown of white muslin, which hung to either side of the mantel mirror.

I stepped nearer to examine them, guessing they must be the likenesses of Mr Erskine's grandparents. I had a vivid recollection of the last time I had examined a portrait—in Calcutta—and looked to find in the masculine features before me now some hint of resemblance to that other. I was disappointed.

The elder Mr Erskine had been a man of middle height, stockily built and, by the time the portrait was painted, inclined to corpulence. His round face was ruddy with good health and no doubt good living. He was dressed in the fashion of the time, with a high stock, white cravat and frilled shirt. His eyes were dark and gleamed with humour as much as intelligence. I had the impression that he was rather uncomfortable in his silken waistcoat, and that the cocked eyebrow and wry smile were directed as much at himself as at the world in which he found himself. I knew at once that I would have liked him both for his character and for his company.

I crossed before the fire to look at the companion painting. How difficult it was to believe that anyone so young, so graceful, so beautiful, should live on and become a grandmother—perhaps arthritic, fat and cross, as grandmothers sometimes are. The girl could not have been more than eighteen at the time she sat for the portrait. She was all simplicity, purity and innocence, from the soft white folds of her gown to the short, artlessly perfect curls of her well-shaped head. The curls were of bright, dark gold and framed a face heart-shaped and delicate. Her eyes, too, were of bright, dark gold. Her grandson's eyes.

'Her name was Danielle. She was my grandmother.'

Mr Erskine's voice came from immediately behind me, and I spun round alarmed.

'I surprised you. I'm sorry. You were absorbed in the portrait.'

'I ... I thought I was alone,' I said foolishly, made awkward by his presence.

'I was as surprised to find you here. I understood that ladies' *toilettes* were protracted affairs. I came in to look around, see that everything is as it should be. It's a long time since we have entertained ladies at Hassanganj. I hope that all is comfortable for you upstairs?'

'Thank you—my bedroom is beautiful, but I wish you had not put yourself to the expense of employing an *ayah* on my behalf. I have not yet become used to such a luxury, and could easily have shared Emily's.'

'An *ayah?*' I knew from his tone that he had had no hand in the matter, but he recovered himself in a second. 'Oh, yes, well, don't worry about that. My grandmother had a whole assortment of them, and I daresay they are delighted to have something to do again. They have lived on the estate, eating their heads off in idleness, ever since she died. They are married to other servants, you see, and one could not very well turn them away, could one?'

He moved away from me and took a brisk walk around the lighted portion of the room, examining everything as he passed. 'Tell me,' he said over his shoulder, 'is anything lacking? Anything that you ladies are accustomed to and do not see here? Do you need more light for—well—er, needlework, that sort of thing?'

I had to laugh. 'No indeed,' I assured him. 'It is a lovely room and a great deal more comfortable than anything we have been accustomed to in Lucknow.'

'Ah, yes. The unfortunate Averys.' He paused in his peregrination and faced me. The mention of the Averys had heightened my colour, and, knowing it, I raised my chin defiantly as I met Mr Erskine's regard. 'I would have helped, you know,' he said unexpectedly, 'if I had thought my help could do any good. But it wouldn't. You must know that now.' It was a statement more than a question, and before I could reply, his attention had again turned to the room. 'I suppose it is all very old-fashioned now,' he said, looking around him critically. 'It is just as my grandmother left it. I never use it when I am on my own. I stick to the library and the dining-room. This place is too large for one man, so I ignore all but the rooms I need to use. I have not been in here for months.'

It was, as he said, old-fashioned, but the light, straight-legged tables, the fine bow-fronted chests, the simplicity of the chairs and sofas, the many long mirrors and, most of all, the absence of those bobble-trimmed velvet covers and cushions, bamboo what-nots, knick-knacks and china flowers which I had become accustomed to in Mount Bellew, gave the room an airy spaciousness well suited to the climate of the country. Ornaments there were, of course, what seemed to my ignorant eye to be a fine collection of Chinese porcelain and jade, but housed neatly in a succession of cabinets around the room.

'It is a beautiful room,' I repeated, and went on boldly, hoping to avert any further mention of Lucknow. 'In fact, if you will forgive my saying so, all this magnificence—your house, your style of living—is so little what I expected to find so far from civilization, that I almost believe I am dreaming.'

'Hmph!' Mr Erskine glowered at me from under his heavy brows, and muttered more to himself than to me, though obviously I was meant to hear him, 'So "civilization" is confined to the white nations.' Then in a normal tone he went on, 'It's not unusual. Hassanganj is a modest place compared to some of the planters' houses in Bengal, for instance. You know, the old "nabobs' " places? I expect you have heard of them.'

'Are you a "nabob" then?'

'Good heavens, no.' He laughed. 'I believe the race is extinct. But perhaps my grandfather was in his day. I have certainly never thought of him as such—but perhaps he was.'

'It's not only all this,' I gestured at the chandeliers and the cabinets of jade, 'that surprises me. But the house has a settled air, if I can put it like that, as though its inhabitants never intended to leave it. An atmosphere quite different to any of the other houses I have visited in India, and which were obviously only temporary homes, however comfortable. Your grandfather must have intended to spend his life here when he built it?'

'Certainly. And he intended his descendants to do the same—which, as you see, we are doing.'

'He was founding a dynasty?'

'I believe he wanted to. But I am all that is left. Conditions in his day, you see, were very different to those that obtain out here now. When a man came out to India sixty or seventy years ago, it was with the knowledge that he would spend his life in the country. Some few, having made their money—or "shaken the pagoda tree" as they put it—went home to England to die. Most preferred to stay or had to stay; most also had Indian wives or—er—responsibilities. It is only since travel became easier, this new overland route and so on, in fact I would say that it is only since English women began coming out in large numbers, that men have begun to think of India as a career rather than a life. For me, however, things have not changed. Hassanganj is my home, my work and my future. I was born here; I hope to die here. I want no other life.'

Mr Erskine was not the first man I had met who was truly committed to the land of his adoption. I had known officers in the Army and met civilians who felt as he did; who had given all their enthusiasm, all their loyalty, to the men who served under them or the districts they administered. But he was the first known to me who was continuing such a tradition; the others were initiating it. I was intrigued.

Once again I realized that, despite his somewhat forbidding appearance, Mr Erskine was a remarkably easy man to talk to, and though I was reluctant to admit as much to myself, I enjoyed talking to him. Attired in the black broadcloth evening dress in which I had first seen him at the Residency ball, he sat now, incongruously, in a small gilt chair, his long black legs stretched out before him and crossed comfortably at the ankles. His white stock accentuated the weather-burnt olive of his complexion; the lamplight fell on the thick brown hair, bleached to straw colour on top by many Indian summers, and exaggerated the arch of his nose. His strange gold eyes, Danielle's eyes, shadowed by black lashes, regarded the toe of his boot while he talked, or met mine sometimes with a gaze that was at once direct and enquiring.

'Ah! So here is another crime to be laid on the overburdened head of the Englishwoman. She has the temerity to distract her man from India,' I said slyly, recalling previous opinions he had expressed regarding my countrywomen.

'But of course! They would not be out here if they thought they had to spend the remainder of their lives in India. Would you?'

'I only came out on a short visit.'

'True—but could you contemplate spending the rest of your days out here—happily?'

'I do not know enough of India yet, or of my own mind regarding India, to answer that question honestly.'

He uncrossed his legs and sat up in his chair.

'I believe you could.'

'Thank you! I am sure that is a compliment.'

'Certainly it is a compliment. But I have a notion that you and India will do very well together.'

I laughed, though he was serious. 'Only time could tell,' I said, 'and I see no possibility of my remaining in India for more than a few months at most.'

'Hmph!' he snorted, and let the matter drop.

Shortly afterwards the others joined us, and then, at the behest of a gong in the corridor, we went into the dining-room.

Dinner was the usual succession of many courses to which I was now accustomed, but the room in which we ate, and the plate, china and glass, were a great deal grander than any to which we were used.

Behind each chair stood a servant in livery and, though a plethora of servants was a commonplace in India, these were so well-trained and silent that they awed me. It was impossible that any one man should need so many, particularly since I had a suspicion that Mr Erskine's own tastes were simple. But perhaps these men, like the *ayahs*, had also been eating their heads off in idleness and were glad to return to their old duties.

Mr Erskine was an attentive and considerate host and did his best to maintain a general conversation, but it was uphill work. Emily was rendered solemnly silent by her surroundings, while Charles used a voice that was a little too loud in order to stress his self-assurance. I found myself suddenly very tired, and longed for my bed. Only Kate, dressed in her old black satin gown with the high neck, long sleeves and skimpy skirt, seemed at ease in her opulent circumstances and talked comfortably about the 'old days'.

We retired early, all of us wearied by the conflicting impressions of our journey and its end, but when I went to Emily's room to say goodnight, I found her seated at an *escritoire* already writing to her mother.

'Not that she'll believe the half of what I have to tell her,' she said, putting away her paper. 'Who would have thought that Mrs Flood could ever leave all this and be able to settle down in that poky little place in Dissham.' I made no reply, remembering the time, not so long ago, when the 'poky little place in Dissham' had been the acme of perfection in Emily's eyes. 'And really, Laura, I cannot think why people in Lucknow, and even Charles, for a time anyway, should think so badly of Mr Erskine—Oliver, I mean. I expect it is just because he is so rich. They are jealous of him. For really, he has been everything that is considerate to us, has he not?'

'Let us hope that he continues as he has begun,' I replied.

'You are determined not to like him.'

'Not at all. I merely require something other than material wealth to like. If I find he has it—well then, I shall be happy to like him.'

'You are as wrong-headed as Charles is, in a different way. I know Charles is jealous,' she announced with satisfaction. 'Of course he'll never admit as much, but all ... well, all this ... and the park and the servants and everything, are turning him green with envy. I can tell.'

'Admiration, perhaps. Envy, no!' I said with decision.

'Well, have it your own way. It don't affect my opinion and you never will hear a word against him anyway. But I *like* Oliver, even if he is too rich, as Charles says, and I don't agree with Charles that the way he lives is vulgar and ostentatious. In fact I think it is all quite charming, and I think Oliver is charming too—a most charming man!'

'Charming' was the last word I would have applied to Mr Erskine, but I was too glad to know that Emily was temporarily in accord with her situation to contradict her.

For the rest—well, we would see.

CHAPTER 2

Emily's instant acceptance of all that Hassanganj offered was so complete that for a time I believe she was truly happy. Nor was it merely the luxurious yet eminently comfortable mode of life that appealed to her, making up for the dreary discomforts of the Avery bungalow and the uncongenial company of the Chalmers in Calcutta. Here she was surrounded, as she felt she should be, by beautiful things and the evidence of wealth; but here also she was met with an almost deferential consideration from her host, which restored to her a great deal of her lost self-consequence. For reasons known only to himself, Mr Erskine set out to study my cousin's wishes, anticipate her needs and fulfil her every expectation.

It started on the very first morning, when at breakfast Emily found the silver tea service laid before her place, which was, naturally, to the right of Mr Erskine's place at the head of the table.

'It would please me, Emily,' he said courteously, as we sat down, 'if you would play the chatelaine in this bachelor household.' So Emily, with great satisfaction, had poured the tea. For all but Mr Erskine himself. He preferred Turkish coffee, and this he poured for himself, from a small copper jug kept warm on a spirit lamp before him.

That was the beginning. Later in the morning, as he showed us round his gardens, Emily was often applied to for comment and advice and asked to express her own preferences in the matter of fruit and vegetables to be brought into the house each day by the gardener. Within a week, Mr Erskine had asked her to oversee the running of the house while we stayed at Hassanganj. 'The *abdar* and table servants were trained by my grandmother,' he said by way of explanation. 'They assure me they recollect very well what is required when visitors are present, but I would be more easy in my mind if you directed them personally. Times change, after all, and there must be many things lacking for your comfort in the way I have lived all these years.'

Emily was given the keys to the storerooms and pantries by a stony-faced *abdar*, or butler, and thereafter, accompanied by Kate as interpreter, took herself to old Mrs Erskine's *daftar* each morning to make out menus, supervise the weighing of food stuffs and give the cook and butler their orders for the day.

I did not care to think of what the servants made of this interference, but no outbursts of òbjection took place, so I supposed that Kate's tact and Oliver's authority between them smoothed such small difficulties as my cousin's ignorance might otherwise have produced. In any event, Emily was content and good-natured, bustling about the great house in a black sateen apron, examining the contents of all the closets and cupboards, making inventories of the silver, and sorting piles of yellowed Irish linen for mending and bleaching. Christmas was nearly upon us, too, and there was to be a house party. The old servants, excited by this promise of a return to the busily hospitable days of the *Burra-mem*, scoured, polished and cleaned, and in the kitchens the cook and his assistants set to work with a will on old receipts for puddings, pies, smoked tongues and spiced beef, almost forgotten for ten long years.

I must confess that I was a trifle piqued at first by Emily's being considered more competent to run a house than me. I was the practical one, after all, and even at the Averys it had been I who had brought what comfort and convenience was possible into the ordering of the house. But this resentment was slight and did not last long once I realized that, for the first time since leaving Mount Bellew, the major part of each day was all my own, to use precisely as I chose. Or rather—all but two hours in the morning.

On the second afternoon of our stay, as we three ladies sat on the lawn drinking our tea—dinner at Hassanganj was taken very late, and to span the void between *tiffin* and the main meal we had tea and cakes at four o'clock, a custom that apparently Danielle had instituted and which we were happy to follow—Mr Erskine appeared in the company of a tall pompous-looking native dressed in European clothing and wearing shoes.

'Miss Hewitt,' began my host without preamble, 'this is my head *babu* from the factory, Benarsi Das. He has agreed at my request to further your Urdu studies and will spend the hours between nine and eleven with you each morning. You may use the library if you choose. He has orders to procure any books, primers and so on that you may need. Mr Das's knowledge of English is excellent, but we both think it best that absolutely no English be spoken during your lessons. You will learn Urdu as small children do—by speaking it.'

For a moment I was struck dumb by this high-handed disposal of my time and interest, and my immediate reaction was a point-blank refusal, followed as quickly by a return to common sense. I did after all want to learn the language and had meant to ask Mr Erskine to find me a tutor. Surely the fact that he had anticipated that request need not obviate the desire? But his manner! Why could he not have approached me before making the arrangement with Mr Das? I saw a knowing twinkle in Kate's eyes as she watched me struggle with myself, so I bowed politely to Mr Das and expressed myself delighted with the plan. If my tone was rather colder than usual, Mr Erskine remained unaware of it.

'Good! That's settled then! Nine o'clock tomorrow morning.' And turning on his heel he strode off with Mr Das behind him.

'How considerate he is,' said Emily. 'So thoughtful of all our wishes. But how did he know that you took Urdu lessons, Laura? You must have told him.'

'I did—in Lucknow.'

'Oh, I see. But how good of him to remember it. Not many men would do as much, would they, Laura?'

'I suppose not.'

Thereafter Mr Das appeared promptly at nine, and for two hours I struggled like a six-year-old to master the rudiments of grammar without recourse to my own tongue. The letters of the Urdu alphabet, unlike the English, change their form depending on which letters precede or follow them. This results in a vast number of characters and character combinations, making the casting of typeface, and consequently the printing of any material, extremely expensive. All the books I used were, therefore, hand-written, copied out on the crude local paper by village scribes. Often I had difficulty deciphering the calligraphy, and would remain at Mr Erskine's desk in the library until he himself came in shortly before *tiffin* time. On one such occasion my host found me very near to tears of frustration since I could make no sense of an entire paragraph of elementary prose.

'Let me see,' he commanded in his brusque fashion, and took the booklet from my hand, scanning the lines with a quick eye.

'Deplorably copied,' he said, 'but I see your trouble. The dots are misplaced—see, here on the *jeem* and again here on the *ray*. Naturally you could make nothing of it. Now try again.'

I did better once he had pointed out the errors, and he listened judiciously as I spelt out the words.

'Hm. Now give me the page. I will copy it out for you to use tomorrow—and come to me at once when you find yourself in difficulties.' He produced a bamboo pen from a drawer and in a few moments had made a clear and precise copy of the whole vexatious page. Thoroughly worn out by my efforts, I sat and watched him as, with the bleached locks of his hair falling over his forehead, he bent to his work, his supple brown hand sketching the convoluted characters with practised ease. Was he really thoughtful and considerate, I wondered, as Emily often declared, or was there some ulterior motive to his interest? The man was a puzzle, a thorough puzzle, and one which, for the moment, I was too tired to think about.

However, even though my mornings had been thus summarily disposed of by Mr Erskine, I still had the long afternoons to myself and had soon become acquainted with the house and its environs, and my sketchbook filled rapidly with views of the extraordinary edifice from all angles and with details of its odder architectural features. Many were the tranquil hours I spent in the English garden, blooming at this Christmas season with many familiar favourites—sweet peas and heliotrope, phlox, larkspur and love-in-the-mist—in an arbour ariot with roses. The hedges, though not of box, were neatly clipped, the walks between the borders smoothly scythed, and an English lime shed its fragrance on the Indian air. I much preferred this simple, homely scene to the Italian garden on the other side of the house, which was walled and formal, with gravelled paths, stone urns and seats and few flowers, but sang with small cascades and streams kept flowing by means of a waterwheel worked by the usual bullocks plodding in a never-ending circle outside the walls. Behind the house lay the kitchen garden, its paths hedged by the spiky fronds of pineapples, its beds luxuriant with every imaginable vegetable and soft fruit. This was flanked by the orchard, where guavas and custard-apples grew happily alongside apples, pears and lychees, and loquats mingled foliage with plums and cherries.

Beyond these areas again were the stables, barns and coach houses which together with the servants' quarters and elephant houses formed a small village of their own. In addition, I was to discover as time went on that this village included workshops for carpenters, wheelwrights, blacksmiths and tinsmiths engaged on work for the indigo factory and the estate, and that Hassanganj was almost totally self-sufficient where both supplies and services were concerned.

So much I discovered during my first few days, though the world beyond the high mud wall of the park remained a mystery. It was enough, at that time, for me to wander through the gardens and park in the mellow sun of the winter's afternoons and reflect on the man who had conceived the idea of Hassanganj and then brought it to fruition over many years and with much toil. Everything about the place spoke of the energy, intelligence and inventiveness of old Adam Erskine. Often, as we sat in the long drawing-room before dinner, I would glance up at his portrait and think, 'I know now why you were so uncomfortable in your finery. You had too many things going on in your mind, too many plans and ideas, ever to be happy dressed up like a dandy in a ladies' drawing-room. I can see you better, Mr Erskine, tough as a navvy, your unremarkable face shining with health and good spirits, clad in sensible clothes, working out your active, productive destiny here in this strange land with the utmost satisfaction. I believe, Mr Erskine, that you lived and died that rare, rare thing—a happy man!' And the ruddy face with the cocked eyebrow seemed to smile a little more broadly.

Of all our party, Charles seemed the least content with Hassanganj. Comfort is the easiest thing in the world to become accustomed to, so he had soon given up muttering about the 'vulgar luxury' of our surroundings. Mr Erskine provided him with a horse, a groom and a *shikari* or gun-boy, and he spent a large part of each day shooting. But this could not occupy his entire time, and when in the house he was bored and often ill-tempered. One afternoon I realized why. He was not seeing enough of his brother; not being given an opportunity to know him better or to take his interests to heart as his mother had exhorted him to do.

'I say, Oliver,' he said one day at *tiffin*, 'would it be possible for me to accompany you sometimes when you ride on your rounds to the villages and the factory and so on? Be deuced pleased to have something to do, and see how you manage things out here.'

Mr Erskine regarded his brother silently for a moment, leaning back comfortably in his chair.

'Why?'

Charles flushed at the tone of the question.

'As I said, I would like to know how you go about administering this place, what sort of problems you face, how you contrive to solve them, and so on. Your system here must be very different to anything I'm accustomed to at home.'

'No doubt!'

'For instance—the factory. I've never even seen indigo grown, let alone processed. Could I not have a look around the factory to begin with?'

'Certainly—if you wish it. Benarsi Das will take you over tomorrow, after Miss Hewitt's lesson.'

'I ... I didn't mean just a *guided* tour. Is there not anything useful I could do—to assist you, I mean?'

'Scarcely, my dear Charles! I use only the language of the country— or rather the languages. I believe I am right in assuming that you are not acquainted with Urdu, nor interested enough to learn it, as Miss Hewitt here is?'

'Oh! I thought perhaps—well—what about accounting?'

'Also done entirely in Urdu.'

'I see.'

Charles returned to his plate with a crestfallen air.

'However,' Mr Erskine continued after a pause, 'when I am visiting any point of interest, you may certainly accompany me. My rounds at the moment are purely routine. Dull. But in the New Year I will be going up to the saw-mills and collecting outlying rents. You may find those expeditions entertaining, and are welcome to come along. Provided you are prepared to ride thirty or forty miles a day and don't mind sleeping in a tent in the cold. And it will be cold, I can promise you!'

And that was the best that Charles could do for himself on that occasion. Privately, I felt that he would not pursue the matter further, but would content himself with early-morning rides in the vicinity of the park.

Almost as though he had read my thoughts, Mr Erskine turned to me and asked, 'Do you ride?'

'Yes, I am fond of riding,' I replied.

'Well, what would you say to taking a ride each morning with Charles and myself?'

'I think I would enjoy it very much,' I answered truthfully.

'Good! There will be a horse ready for you tomorrow morning at seven o'clock sharp.'

The next morning I donned my long-unused habit and was waiting when the men came downstairs. I knew I looked well—perhaps as well as I ever could with my lack of height. The habit was a deep ruby-coloured cloth, cut simply but well. The tight bodice, mannish collar and close-fitting sleeves, together with the straight lines of the sweeping skirt, lent my form a proportion which it normally lacked. I felt elegant and feminine, and the undisguised approval in Charles's eyes brought a flush of needed colour to my cheeks.

'You look charming!' he said, though he had seen me thus dressed a hundred times at home.

Mr Erskine said nothing, but smiled. Then his eyes turned on Charles for a moment, reflectively.

My mount, a fine roan mare, stood waiting for us in the porch with the other horses. There was a mounting block but, before I could make use of it, Charles had clasped his hands for my foot. I hesitated, remembering that perceptive glance turning from me to Charles, but then accepted his help and swung to the saddle.

'Good! Quite good!' said Mr Erskine, standing back to survey my hands. 'I think you will manage her all right, but she is a trifle fresh, so don't use the whip.'

I nodded and he mounted his great bay gelding with the sort of casual ease that could only come of a lifetime's acquaintance with horses. Charles, I had to admit, rode well—but consciously. Mr Erskine rode superbly.

'We'll skirt the village this morning,' said Mr Erskine as we clattered out of the porch with Toddy-Bob, inevitably, bringing up the rear of the little cavalcade. 'That mare doesn't care for pi-dogs and naked babies playing in the dust. We'll keep to the fields.'

He kept me beside him as we rode down the long jarmin avenue, then edged around the sprawling mud huts of the village and took a track that led us past the vats, tanks and peopled activity of the indigo factory, where the coolies were already at work stamping rhythmically and remorselessly at the shaggy fronds to separate the juices from the fibre of the evil-smelling plant.

The morning was delectably fresh and pure. Shreds of mist still clung about the hollows, and dew glinted on the furry silver leaves of the young gram. Even the faded flowers of the lantana bushes looked less played-out and dusty than usual.

Then, as the village and factory dropped behind us, the mountains reared up to the north, a great dramatic background to the humble but lovely scene. The mustard was in bloom—acres of it, miles of it, stretching all around us, yellow as a canary, pale and bright in the pale bright sunshine, scenting the air with honeyed sweetness, a carpet of light reaching up to the dark line of the forest, the mountains and the soft blue of the early sky. And against that pure sky the snow peaks gleamed in morning glory. Here and there *topes* of sombre mangoes stood knee-deep among the fragrant gold, or a line of feathery sheeshums shimmered delicately along a watercourse. Smoke rose from distant villages smudging the blue. In the sugar cane, partridge called, and quails. A dog yelped far away; a flight of emerald parrots screamed across the blue, and a waterwheel squeaked shrilly as its owner yelled his bullocks into greater activity on seeing the approach of the *zemindar*.

'Oh, it's beautiful!' I exclaimed, as we drew up to take in the scene. 'So tranquil. So calm. Such fresh purity of colour—and the scent!'

'The best time of year here,' said Mr Erskine. 'Doesn't last long either, so make the most of it.'

'And this is still all Hassanganj?' Charles asked. 'All this that we see?'

'All of it, right up to the forest there. Plus a lot to the south that you cannot see, of course.'

He dismounted and led his horse up a little rise where a tumbled wall under a thorn tree provided a slight eminence from which we could better view the entire prospect. Charles and I followed his example.

'By Jove,' exclaimed Charles admiringly, as he took off his hat and sat down on the wall. 'It's splendid. Your grandfather certainly picked a good position, Oliver.'

'Yet this is not the land he chose, and when he came here it looked very different to what it does today. Have you heard the story of how he came by Hassanganj? Did my mother ever mention it to you?'

'Only that it was a reward for some service he had done the Nawab of the time. Is that so?'

'Yes. He was a young writer with the Company then. They had sent him up from Calcutta to do some job or other for the Resident in Lucknow, and in the course of his peregrinations around the city he came by some information of great interest to the Nawab—a plot to kill that gentleman in fact. The plot was foiled, my grandfather received the Resident's commendation, and Mohammedan punctilio being what it is, the Nawab, Asaf-ad-Doula, felt called upon to make a handsome gesture of gratitude. In the first flush of his relief at being alive, he made old Adam a gift of a hunting lodge that stood where the house now stands, and, as the story goes, as much land as could be covered by the ball of my grandfather's thumb on an inch-scale map. At the last moment, however, as my grandfather was placing his thumb on the map, the Nawab's natural rapacity proved too much for him. He jogged old Adam's arm, with the result that his thumb, instead of landing squarely on the cultivated lands to the south of the lodge, covered mostly the fringe of the forest and the scrublands that led up to it. All this!'

'But this is not scrubland,' I said.

'Not now—but it was then. My grandfather realized he had been cheated and that there was no redress. Being a young man of some character, he decided to make the most of the gift the gods had deposited in his lap, and set to work. He left the Company, and with only his wits and the dubious support of the Nawab, came out here to work his land. Over the years he pushed back the forest, irrigated the scrubland to bear crops and put in rough roads. Then from the next province, which was suffering a famine, he brought in settlers, laid out villages and apportioned his reclaimed land. He experimented with crops and stock and, as his revenues began to flow in, started to build the house. It was just a bungalow, quite a small place, to begin with. However, when he met the girl who was to become his wife, he was so overcome by her acceptance of him that he determined she should live in a palace. The result of that determination is the house as it now is.' Mr Erskine laughed.

'And so they lived happily ever after!' I ended the story.

'As a matter of fact I believe they did, for all the unsuitability of the match. He was an unconnected and impecunious young man, at least when he arrived in India; she came from one of the great French families, ruined by the Revolution and the Napoleonic wars, but none the less aristocratic for that. I have sometimes wondered what she saw in him—a strange colonial gentleman from the other side of the earth.'

'Vision. Imagination. Determination. Very attractive qualities in a man. But she must have had intelligence and perception herself to recognize those qualities in him. Perhaps that was why the match was successful.'

'No doubt,' he said, giving me a glance at once approving and surprised.

'And so that is how the old gentleman became a *talukhdar*?' said Charles.

'No, a *zemindar*,' his brother corrected him.

'But are they not the same thing?'

'Sometimes in effect. In fact, very different. A *zemindar* owns the land he works and administers, which may be only a few acres or a tract several times as large as Hassanganj. A *taluka*, on the other hand, is, well, a principality, or perhaps more correctly a barony—much in the way that feudal England was divided into baronies. The land itself belongs—too often only theoretically—to the village communities, but these communities are administered by, protected by, usually bullied by a *talukhdar*, or baron, appointed by the Nawab. Or were. As you probably know, the whole system of *talukhdari* has been suppressed since the annexation of the kingdom. I believe the measure to be a grave mistake but, for the moment at least, it is a *fait accompli*.'

'But why is it a mistake? From all that I have heard, the *talukhdars* seem to have been a corrupt lot … robber barons, if barons at all.'

Mr Erskine shrugged.

'They knew what was expected of them from their people, and on the whole gave them what they wanted. Certainly their methods would not stand the scrutiny of modern Western democracy, but then neither would the demands made upon them. They were unscrupulous, extortionate and warlike; but the people they ruled were ignorant, importunate and badly in need of defence. The *talukhdars* at least gave them that and a sense of cohesion. Our government has chosen to defend the rights of the individual, forgetting that the individual himself is more concerned with the rights of the clan, for that is what we have to deal with in Oudh, a system of ancient and closely knit clans, be they Rajput, Mussalman or what you will. We are imposing on the kingdom a most unwelcome and unwise fragmentation, and I fear will before long be made to pay for our mistake.'

'But how?' asked Charles, as he and I both remembered many discussions on 'trouble' yet to come, I with Mr Roberts on the ship, and both of us on various occasions in Calcutta.

Our host shrugged again. 'This is India. The "hows" are as problematical as the "whys". But—cause and effect. Mistakes must always be paid for, one way or another. Meanwhile the aristocracy of the kingdom, who are almost the only people of any education, whatever their virtues or lack of them, are dispossessed of their hereditary rights, their incomes and their quite legitimate pride of position. And we have made for ourselves three or four hundred most potent enemies.'

'And how will the suppression of this system affect you?' asked Charles in some anxiety.

'In no way. I cannot be dispossessed of Hassanganj, except by death and if I leave no heir. As I have said, a *zemindar* owns the land he administers; the right of tenure is different to that of a *talukhdar*.'

'And then of course, you are an Englishman,' concluded Charles, unwisely wise.

'My rents are paid to me as a *zemindar*, not as an Englishman!' There was annoyance in his tone. 'And I see my duties to my tenants as those of a *zemindar*, not an Englishman. It is my legitimate right to the land that is important; not my race. Were I blue, green or brindle, or my place of origin Holland or Hohenlohe, my rights would remain the same, and my responsibilities.'

'I see that, but surely, Oliver, as an Englishman you must ...'

'Try harder. Not expect more. From anyone!'

'Well!' said Charles. And again, thoughtfully: 'Well!'

'It cannot be too difficult,' I put in, to conciliate the one and silence the other. 'It cannot be too difficult to "try harder" out here in these beautiful surroundings. I am sure you consider yourself a lucky man, Mr Erskine.'

'I do. But as to the beauty, wait until June. Everything's dry then, brown, the fields bone hard under the blistering heat. There's a wind that blows up every day, straight from the hobs of hell, filled with hot dust that cuts the eyes out of you. There's drought, to some extent, every second year. The cattle die, and then the people. Later the monsoon comes, the rivers overflow their banks and wash the fields away and the houses; and the floods and the famine are followed inevitably by disease. Sometimes ...' He rose, went to his gelding and tightened the girth. 'Sometimes one wonders what the point is of trying at all. Let alone harder.' He straightened up and turned to face me, one hand on the saddle.

'And yet you do.'

'Hm, do I?' The amber eyes met mine with uncommon seriousness. 'I suppose, on the whole, I do. But I have come to that time in life when one begins to wonder how much of what one does is truly voluntary, really effortful. How much only the force of habit. I don't know. All I do know is that ...' He paused and looked away from me, kicking at the dewy grass with one foot. Then he raised his head, and his gaze ranged over the serene and lovely scene before us. 'This is to me, in good days and bad, Miss Hewitt, "*jan se aziz*". Is your Urdu up to interpreting the phrase?'

'Well, *jan* is life, I believe?'

'Correct.'

'... And *aziz* is ... oh! something like "sweet", is it not? But as a phrase it means nothing to me.'

'Yes, sweetness, more in the sense of an endearment. An approximation of the phrase in English would be "dearer than life". Or "sweeter than life", if you will.'

'And that is how you regard this land?'

'I do. White Englishman that I may be!' He laughed, almost in embarrassment at this self-revelation, then swung to the saddle and gestured to us to do the same.

My mare had behaved excellently, responding to the bit like a lady, sometimes dancing sideways at some fancied alarm but obedient to my hands on the reins. I mounted her with greater confidence than on the first occasion, and allowed her to canter down the track a little ahead of the men, who were content enough to drop behind and discuss some matter pertaining to the shooting of duck. I felt invigorated by the exercise and the morning air and rode on casually, trying to etch indelibly on my memory the beauty of my surroundings, while I mused, with some mystification, on the character and odd convictions of my host. I decided I liked the phrase '*jan se aziz*', and the way in which he had said it as he looked with patent love over his honeyed land. I had glimpsed a more amiable side of Mr Erskine than his usual manner ever indicated, and was obscurely gratified that he had allowed me to see it.

Suddenly a plover, flattened in a rut of the track before us, rose with a great crack of wings and a spurt of dust. The mare, after one startled backward dance, took the bit between her teeth and raced for the hills.

It was pure luck that I was not unseated by that first agitated step. As it was, finding myself still in the saddle, I clung on grimly and inelegantly, and allowed her her head, knowing there was nothing I could do to halt her and hoping against hope that no pothole would bring her down. After some minutes of flateared, nose-raised speed, when she felt no attempt to pull her in, she tossed her head, her ears rose, and I knew the character of her stretch-legged run had changed from one impelled by alarm to one of enjoyment. Very gently I pulled on the reins. She snorted, continued on for a moment, then responded. She was no longer a runaway but a thoroughly happy horse. At that, my alarm over, I found myself sharing her enjoyment and, bending low on her neck, steadying but not checking her, I gave myself up to a brief period of ecstasy while the yellow fields flashed past and the scented air whipped my cheeks. She slowed of her own accord, and too soon for me. I patted her neck, murmuring my thanks, and drew her into a walk.

Mr Erskine was close behind me; he had tried to shout instructions to me as we raced, and reached us as I pulled in the mare.

For a moment he said nothing. His nostrils were distended and his breathing a little quick, but his hands were folded quietly on the pommel and only the gelding's heaving flanks told of the effort of the chase.

I straightened my hat with hands which were not quite as steady as I wished, and drew in a few long breaths.

'Are you all right?'

'Quite, thank you,' I assured him politely. I guessed there was a lot more he could have said and admired his restraint. 'I let her have her head and she changed her mind about bolting.'

'Indeed! You know a lot about horses—for a "paid companion".'

'Enough to keep right side up at a gallop.'

His face broke into the curiously pleasant smile.

'My congratulations. Any other woman I know would have been off at the start of that. I believe you enjoyed it.'

'Yes, I did. But I'm afraid it was only luck that she didn't unseat me in the first instant. The rest was … quite pleasurable!'

'Laura, Laura! My God! Are you all right, my dear?' Charles leapt off his mount and ran to my side.

'Of course! Quite all right.'

He grabbed my hand and looked up at me with a face full of concern; because Mr Erskine was witness to his emotion, it embarrassed me. I pulled my hand away.

'Really, Charles, it was nothing. I was more exhilarated than alarmed.'

'That beast is far too uncertain to carry a lady, Oliver, and you should have realized it. Laura might have taken a toss and injured herself. Seriously.'

'I warned Miss Hewitt that Pyari was a trifle fresh. Besides, she managed the mare excellently. I have just been complimenting her on the fact.'

'As it happened, yes. But Laura is my responsibility out here, and I must insist that she does not ride that mare again.'

'Perhaps that should rest with Miss Hewitt. It seems to me she must have formed some affinity with Pyari. Perhaps she would not like another animal. What do you say?' He turned to me.

It would have been simpler to give way to Charles, but if I had acquiesced too readily to him, Mr Erskine, I suspected, might put the wrong interpretation on the fact. As he had given me a choice, I decided to take it, and besides I had liked his lack of fuss as much as his compliment on my handling of the mare.

'If Mr Erskine will trust me with her, I think I would prefer to continue riding Pyari, now that we know each other.'

I addressed Charles but looked at Mr Erskine. His lips twitched, but he nodded gravely and said, 'Good. I believe you have her measure now, and I am sure I can trust her with you.'

Charles looked from his brother to me, and gave in unwillingly.

'On your head be it then, Oliver,' he muttered furiously as he remounted, 'but God help you if any harm comes to Laura!'

Mr Erskine made no reply but I could not allow myself to hope he had not heard.

I spent the rest of the ride back to the house endeavouring to soothe Charles's feelings and minimize the terrors of the morning.

Our host, riding very erect yet very relaxed ahead of us, was largely silent.

CHAPTER 3

Happily for me, the household's interest in my adventure, much exaggerated by Charles, was of short duration, for that same evening saw the arrival of George Barry with all the news of Lucknow, which already seemed so far away to me that I had difficulty in matching the names he mentioned to the appropriate faces. The following morning brought the remainder of the Christmas house party: a Mr McCracken and his son Lewis, and a Mr Baird, all planters and neighbours of Mr Erskine, who visited Hassanganj each Christmas. Mr Erskine seemed notably lacking in female friends.

The gentlemen spent the greater part of the holiday slaughtering wildlife and reminiscing about previous slaughters. Each morning saw them set off at dawn to shoot duck, deer or pheasant, or make, perhaps, a longer expedition into the *terai* where tiger were to be found, though as Mr Erskine would not countenance elephant being used in the pursuit of tiger, none were actually shot. And if the day had proved disappointing, the planters and Charles were always willing to forego the comforts of the drawing-room at night in order to hunt 'muggars', a sort of blunt-nosed alligator, with the help of brush-fires built upon the river bank to lure the unsuspecting creatures to their end.

Nor were we ladies neglected; Mr Erskine arranged a series of little expeditions for us, and almost every evening an entertainment took place on the lawn before the front portico. Once a dancing bear, heralded by the enraged yelping of every dog in the vicinity, padded up the driveway with its master and performed an agonized travesty of a dance. It was muzzled and secured by a heavy chain, but its simple presence alarmed Emily into near hysterics. So it was sent away, limping on the poor cut pads of its paws. More successful were two small monkeys, one dressed in a shred of red cotton skirt, one in a braided waistcoat, that performed their tired little tricks with eyes, wary and sad, fixed vigilantly on their trainer's cruel face.

'Oh, aren't they sweet!' said Emily, not seeing the fear.

'Do you think so?' From Mr Erskine's tone of voice I gathered he shared my distaste at seeing animals so unnaturally treated. 'These people travel the length and breadth of India. The monkeys are supposed to be enacting an old drama about a king and queen, Maror Khan and Jahoorin. Their act and their names never change, no matter where you find them.'

'They are so clever. Such appealing little faces,' went on Emily. 'May we pet them?'

'You may not!' said Mr Erskine with decision. 'A monkey bite is a very poisonous and unpleasant thing.'

Emily pouted, but did not persist.

Then there were pigeons, and parrots with rosy heads, who fired tiny guns, drew miniature carts in harness, or fluttered through flaming hoops. There were stick dancers, and tumblers and a snake charmer— all accompanied, as had been the bear and the monkeys, by the curious, double-sided drum, waisted in the middle, which is sounded by means of pebbles attached to strings, which with a flick of the player's wrist fly rhythmically from side to side of the drum. This instrument, like the tale of Maror Khan and Jahoorin, is age-old and country-wide, and the sound of its high, frenetic note in the twilight can mean only one thing—the approach of itinerant entertainers. Every dog in India loathes that high-pitched note with a personal and venomous loathing.

On Christmas Day itself no shoot took place. Charles, who sometimes had moods of piety, was upset that there was no way we could attend a church service, so had asked if he could read the Collects and Lessons of the day to the assembled party after breakfast. Oliver had seemed nonplussed by the request, but had the forbearance to answer loud 'Amens' when necessary, and Charles was obviously pleased with his idea and its accomplishment. Afterwards we exchanged gifts, and then gathered on the verandah under the portico to watch the arrival of the *dholli* procession.

'They come, like the Wise Men, bearing gifts,' explained Oliver in answer to Emily's question as to the nature of the procession. 'A damn-fool idea, seeing that few of them can afford it, but it's the custom. *Dustoori*! And when a thing is *dustoori*, there is nothing that can be done about it—not by me, not by the Government, not by God Almighty!'

So they came, the peasants, the shopkeepers, the scribes and the members of the village *panchayats* from all over the Hassanganj estate, the delegation from each village led by its headman, and the whole procession headed by a band of musicians in worn-out uniforms playing cracked brass instruments and drums.

The house servants, gorgeous in scarlet and white, crowded the verandah behind us to watch the fun, and on the lawn had gathered the gardeners, the grasscutters and watercarriers, the stableboys, grooms and craftsmen, and the women and children from the servants' quarters, all dressed in new quilted cotton coats, their Christmas box.

Mr Erskine stationed himself at the top of the steps, and the ceremony commenced when the senior headman placed around his neck an elaborate and beautiful *har* or garland of gold and silver thread set with brilliants. Then, as each man brought forward his gift, Mr Erskine bowed and touched it with his right hand, after which it was placed at his feet. Immediately, the *abdar* and his assistants bore the gift away to the back of the verandah, where I saw with astonishment that it was examined carefully, then taken apart or dismantled by Toddy-Bob and Ishmial working in concert. Baskets of fruit, trays of nuts and figs, pyramids of sweetmeats, small round boxes of muscat grapes packed in blue cotton wool, all suffered the same fate and were immediately dismembered or split over a succession of waiting trays.

'Why ever are they doing that?' I whispered to Kate. 'Oh, look! That beautifully arranged tray of sweets is ruined,' as Toddy-Bob dexterously reversed a brass platter of *jellabis* on to a large meat plate.

'Bribes!' answered Kate. 'He must show he is incorruptible by examining everything that is offered. Sometimes they put money, gold coins like sovereigns or gold mohurs, among the fruit, or cook jewels into the sweets. If anything is found, Oliver has to denounce the donor immediately—to teach the culprit as well as the others a lesson. See, they are even shredding the cotton-wool from the grape boxes.'

Three goats and two sheep were now lined up on the verandah, and even these were not immune from suspicion. Four swift hands went all over their coats, and their nostrils, ears and mouths were examined to make sure no diamond had been fastened to the skin with sealing wax.

Some of the gifts were valuable in themselves—to my eye at least. There were Kashmir shawls, lengths of brocade, boxes inlaid with ivory, gold-embroidered slippers and a handsome ebony elephant mounted on its own small table. As the procession passed through the portico, its members subsided on the lawn outside to await the ritual giving of *baksheesh*, only the headmen and elders remaining near Mr Erskine to introduce a relative, explain away an inadequate gift or ask a favour on the strength of a handsome one. The procession numbered several hundred, and by the time the last gift had been placed at Mr Erskine's feet all the various cacophonies of a major bazaar had broken out on the staid lawns of Hassanganj, accompanied unceasingly by the band which appeared to know but one tune, which, after giving the matter some attention, I realized was the customary exhortation to the Christian God to save the British Queen. Mr Erskine bore it all with patience and, still wearing the gold and silver garland, walked among the people handing out coins to the adults and sweets to the children, laughing, talking and listening with the accomplishment of a politician.

When at last he joined us in the drawing-room, he flung himself down in a chair and called for a brandy and water.

'Thank God, that's that for another year!' he exclaimed as he sipped his drink gratefully. 'At least I have been spared the marigolds. Can't stand the smell of the things.' I had noticed that all the humbler garlands of marigolds had been placed over his head, then removed by the donor and put at his feet, no doubt so as not to dim the radiance of the splendid *har*. Now Mr Erskine removed the shining garland with its heart-shaped pendant, and sat looking at it for a moment. 'Fine workmanship. Must have cost a fortune. What damn fools they are! They cannot really afford to bring me anything. Not the honest ones anyway, and the *bunnias* bring the least they can, now that they know I will not accept bribes.' He turned the thing over in his hands as he spoke, then suddenly got to his feet, crossed the room to where I was sitting and placed it around my neck. 'There, Laura, you have it. It's too good to give to the servants, and I have a cupboard full of them as it is.'

'But surely you should not give it away,' I expostulated. 'Hasn't it some sort of significance—a meaning?'

'Yes. It can mean anything that the occasion requires—welcome, farewell, good luck, thanks—anything you will. Take it. I want you to have it.'

I thanked him.

'And let us say that its significance this time is ... er ... companionship.' He smiled. 'And it would please me if you would mark the event by not calling me "Mr Erskine" any longer.'

He had begun to call me 'Laura' shortly after our arrival in Hassanganj, but I had hesitated to address him with a like informality. Everyone laughed, and the *har* passed from hand to hand to be admired. Mr Erskine then called for Toddy-Bob and instructed him to bring in the Kashmir shawls with which he had been presented, and asked each of us ladies to choose one for herself. Kate decided on a pale green with multicoloured embroidery; after much indecision, Emily finally chose a pink with a design of blue and white; and I took a white one patterned in deep rose pink—a shawl such as I had never dreamed I would possess.

Of course, we had to try them on. I wrapped mine around me and went to a mirror to admire the effect. Holding a fold of the soft stuff against my cheek, I glanced into the glass and there encountered Charles's eyes as he stood behind me, watching me preen myself. I had been smiling, but his expression sobered me instantly, and I dropped my hand to my side. So we stood, gazing at each other in the mirror for a long moment, in a silent communion more eloquent than words. I shuddered. Someone was walking over my grave, as children say. And there, deeper in the reflection, other eyes met mine. Oliver Erskine's golden, mocking eyes. I blushed and turned quickly away, but not before I had caught the smile on his face and observed him cock an eyebrow at my confused image.

I was assiduous in avoiding both brothers for the rest of that Christmas Day.

There was no ride for me on the following morning. The men had left the house at dawn to shoot duck. After breakfast, Emily and Kate being busy with their domestic duties, I wandered listlessly into the park to try to sort out my confused and conflicting emotions.

I could no longer hope that my feeling for Charles remained my secret; and it was pointless to ignore the fact that it was, in some measure, reciprocated. That all-revealing meeting of eyes in the looking-glass the day before had served only to confirm what I had for some time suspected. On the voyage out and during our first weeks in India I had managed to assure myself that Charles could know nothing of my regard for him. I had managed also to believe that custom and familiarity would be the best cure for my unhappy heart. How many times had I scolded myself for entertaining a misguided infatuation due only to my ignorance of the world, to the fact that I had known so few personable young men, and that my lonely position made me peculiarly susceptible to kindness? How often had I accused myself of folly in permitting myself to believe that my gratitude, liking and respect were love? Perhaps if I had been given no opportunity to guess that Charles also was not wholly indifferent to me, my feeling for him, whatever it was, might have matured to warm affection and nothing more. But there had been too many other hints of his interest lately, as in the anxiety he had evinced when my horse bolted, and expressed in his anger at Mr Erskine's more casual reaction to the mishap. There had been glances, words left unsaid, and a hand extended in anticipation of a need—those small things that are sufficient to let one human being know another cares. So, aware now in my heart that Charles could have been as happy with me as I with him, that both were denied an equal delight, my unhappiness was sudden and great. My confusion and my guilt were acute.

How had it come to pass that we should all be so miserable, when less than a year ago everything had seemed set fair for tranquillity and contentment? I knew what had made Emily marry Charles. But what had made Charles marry Emily? And, having done so, how had his affections so soon been deflected to me? We had all been wrong, all made mistakes through silliness, selfishness or inexperience, but only I had been culpable. For, disguise it as I might, I knew I had always loved Charles, and I had been wrong, grossly wrong, to accompany him and his bride to India, whatever the strength of the family pressures that brought that event about. After all, no one would have forced me to leave Mount Bellew. If the worst had come to the worst, I could have divulged the true nature of my feelings to my kind aunt, and have been spared my present misery. But I had lacked the strength to do this, and the inclination. I had allowed myself to be persuaded because I could not bear the thought of Charles's absence. Now his presence was the torment. Had his marriage been happy, I could have borne my pain with a better grace. But poor Emily, in revealing her unhappiness, had unbared his.

Wandering on through the sunny park I tried to analyse my mind and my motives, and realized with absolute clarity that the most disturbing memory of all was the amused and knowing expression in Oliver Erskine's eyes as I turned away from the mirror.

So, striving to escape the turmoil of my thoughts, I walked further from the house than any of my previous expeditions had taken me. The eccentric towers of Hassanganj were distant among the trees. Feeling warm and thirsty, I looked around for some pleasant spot in which to rest myself before returning.

Before me was what I took to be a shady grove of trees, but approaching nearer I found that it was in fact a banyan, one of those strange Indian trees that drops tendrils from its spreading branches, which on touching the ground take root and form new trees, separate but conjoined with the parent bole by common branches. Increasing in this manner, horizontally as well as vertically, one seed may in time produce a forest of stalwart trunks and heavy foliage. But this banyan was even stranger. Here most of the dependant suckers had been cut away, leaving only a dozen or so young boles growing at the perimeter of a circle around the original trunk. Other tendrils had but just taken root, or hung loosely, rootlets touching the ground, from the tips of branches, and it was clear that the ultimate objective was to form an umbrella-like tent of foliage with the main bole at the centre and the lesser ones forming supports for the walls. For walls there were to be. One section, rather more than half the circle, had already been enclosed with bamboo trellises, up which clambered a variety of creepers and climbing plants. Within this bosky shelter was a pool on which floated the flat green pads of waterlilies, and around this flourished a profusion of ferns and every kind of shade-loving lily. Best of all, beside the pool stood a white iron bench.

I sat down gratefully, relishing the cool damp air of the place, the musty smell of wet earth and rotting leaves, and the pungent scent of a dozen large white lilies glowing in the semi-gloom by the seat. When it was complete—in a generation? In two?—what an elysium this would be, wrought half by God and half by man, cool, refreshing and beautiful. Had Old Adam thought of it, I wondered? Or Danielle?

For some time I sat in the fernery thinking my sad thoughts, but seduced from them frequently by the charm and originality of my surroundings. As at length I rose to leave, my eye was caught by a small figure walking composedly along the path I had traversed. I got up and followed. Hearing me approach, the child turned and eyed me in silence. Very solemn she was, but quite unafraid. Her diminutive white pyjamas were topped by a shirt of blue satin, and a wisp of veiling hung over one shoulder. Her hair was a lustrous brown with reddish tints, her complexion fair and smooth, and the *kohl*-ringed eyes that regarded me so seriously were as soft and dark as the centre of a pansy.

'Good morning,' I said, and then, greatly daring, essayed a few words of Hindustani. '*Nam? Kya nam hai?*'

She looked at me without replying for a moment, I think weighing me up, then lisped, 'Yasmina.'

This was the limit of our conversation, but she took my proffered hand and set off with me contentedly. I was glad to have her company to deflect my thoughts from Charles, Emily and myself. Perhaps she was lost, and I wondered who her parents were and how she had managed to escape them. Her features were too delicate, and her clothing too luxurious for her to be a servant's child. Occasionally she said something in her own language, gesturing at the peacocks on the grass or the squirrels frisking their tails from the trees, and when I responded in my own tongue, she regarded me from under her level brows with faint disapproval. I gained the impression that I was wanting in manners to pursue my own course in this way, and wished my Urdu lessons had been more productive of small talk with three-year-olds.

Eventually, as we neared the house, she was rescued and identified by Toddy-Bob.

'Wandered off she has from her mother,' he said, picking her up and putting her astride his shoulders. 'She's always doin' that, ain't you, love?' He said something in her own tongue and she clapped both small hands to her cheeks and went off into peals of laughter. Toddy-Bob grinned his equine grin and winked at me. 'Real rum 'un this—nothin' won't keep her where she belongs. You'll get used to seeing her around the place, but see she keeps out of the Guv'nor's way. 'E can't abide nippers! There, I think I 'ear 'im now, so I'll away with 'Er 'Ighness! Mornin', miss,' and Toddy touched his high hat to which the child was now clinging and disappeared around the house.

As I went inside, I reflected on the natural duplicity of my host. He 'couldn't abide nippers', but no one could have guessed it from seeing him among his tenants' children the previous day. There was no fathoming the man. If only I could be as sure that he had not fathomed me!

CHAPTER 4

The festivities, decorous and largely masculine in character as they were, continued well into the new year of 1857. On New Year's Eve we sat up late to see the young year in, but it was a dull party. The gentlemen, who would have been much happier gaming and drinking on their own, were polite enough to consider the ladies' want of company and insisted on remaining in the drawing-room, yawning their heads off and counting the hours until they could decently escape, having quaffed the necessary champagne and sung the customary 'Auld Lang Syne'. The elder Mr McCracken and Mr Baird sat together, talking of indigo, soil and the unreliability of the natives, and made no attempt to promote the enjoyment of the party. Young Lewis McCracken hovered at Emily's side with adoring eyes, as he had been doing since his arrival. Kate, Emily and I did our best to relieve the tedium, but no wiles of ours could really rival the delights of cards and brandy in a room thick with tobacco smoke. Mr Erskine seemed particularly conscious of the dismal character of the evening and passed among his guests with the decanter more often than was quite necessary. At one point he did manage to bring a little animation into the gathering by suggesting that Emily should sing.

'Come, Emily,' he said, taking her by the hand and leading her to the fine old instrument in a corner of the room, 'I remember what a charming little concert you gave us in Lucknow one evening. Laura, you will accompany Emily for us, will you not?'

I thought of that evening as I crossed the room and sat down at the piano; the evening of poor Wallace's downfall. And I remembered, too, the evident appreciation with which Mr Erskine had watched my cousin.

He lifted the lid of the piano and whisked his handkerchief along the keys, while Emily looked through some yellowed sheet music in a cabinet nearby. 'Probably dusty,' he said. 'Hasn't been used for I don't know how many years.'

I ran my fingers down the keys, expecting the instrument to be out of tune, but what was my astonishment when no single note sounded. I tried again, laughing, but only produced a series of clicks from the old ivories, as Emily watched, her mouth open with astonishment.

'It hasn't been touched or tuned for fifteen years,' said Oliver with chagrin, as he lifted the top and investigated. 'White ants!' he announced in a moment to the others who had crowded round to watch. 'White ants, blast 'em!' And he showed us that the hammers and felts, the whole interior of the instrument, had been reduced to a fine white powder, and all that remained intact was the rosewood case and the ivory keys.

'It's my fault,' said our host as we resumed our places. 'It never occurred to me to tell the servants to clean around inside occasionally. They have kept it polished, I suppose, but wouldn't dream of opening up the lid. I'm sorry, Emily—Laura. We would all have enjoyed some music. Does it not, after all, soothe the savage beast?'

'What a pity!' Emily said, running her hand over the piano. 'Such a beautiful instrument. I had meant to practise a little each day once the holidays were over. If you had not minded, that is, Oliver? My piano is one of the things I have missed most since coming to India. Never mind. It can't be helped, I suppose. But I do hope you can have that lovely instrument rebuilt?'

'Oh, don't fret, Emily,' Charles put in impatiently. 'I don't believe you have given a thought to your piano since leaving home; you certainly never wanted to practise in Lucknow on the Avery piano!'

'I have more time here, and more inclination than I had in Lucknow. But, as I say, it does not matter, and I am *not* fretting!'

I gave the matter no more thought, and I am sure neither did Emily. But a week later an upright piano arrived at Hassanganj, wrapped in sacking and transported on a bullock-cart, with Toddy-Bob riding beside it. I had not seen him around the place for some days, but knew he often went into Lucknow to make purchases and attend to minor business matters for Oliver. The old instrument was removed and the new put in its place, while Emily, Kate and I exclaimed and wondered.

'How often have I said he is the kindest man alive?' Emily demanded as, directed by Toddy-Bob, the instrument was set on its castors and given a quick polish by one of the servants. 'Really, there is nothing he will not do to make us comfortable and happy. Oh, Charles, will you look here! Oliver has brought in another piano for Laura and me. Isn't that good of him? Where is he? I must thank him right away, and before I play a note!'

Oliver, as it happened, was just behind her spouse. Emily rushed up to him and throwing her arms around him, kissed him on the cheek, very much, I must confess, as she was in the habit of kissing her father or brothers when they had won her approval. But Mr Erskine promptly clasped her round the waist and kissed her back—with every indication of enjoyment.

'My dear Emily,' he smiled, looking directly at Charles, 'if a piano can guarantee me a kiss like this, why, you shall have a new piano every day!'

'Oh, Oliver, you are a dear! So thoughtful of us all. Thank you again.'

'Dashed good of you, Oliver,' Charles said, 'but really, it was not necessary to make such a large expenditure on our behalf. Emily will have her own piano at Dissham to look forward to. She could have done without for a few weeks without any harm.'

I could see that Charles was annoyed, and believed it was more on account of the kiss than the gift. Mr Erskine was also aware of the stuffiness in his brother's tone, and its cause. 'Not at all,' he said politely, 'it is my pleasure.' There was an emphasis on the last word that could not be missed.

Emily sat down and tried the instrument for tone. Then she played a couple of the schoolgirl pieces she remembered, followed by a few ballads which we all sang with her, all that is, except Mr Erskine who had withdrawn to the verandah with his cheroot. While the singing continued, I walked quietly out to the verandah myself. Dusk was falling and it was chilly; soon the gong would send us to our rooms to change for dinner.

'Will you allow me to thank you for your kindness to Emily?' I enquired, very respectfully. Our relationship was now on a more familiar, if not a more friendly footing, but I was still uncertain of him. He might be irritated that I had disturbed his peace, for I realized he was a man who needed to be much alone.

He bowed deprecatingly, watching me with eyes narrowed against the smoke of his cheroot. 'Why should you thank me?' he said, but not unkindly. 'The gift was for Emily, and she has already thanked me very suitably.'

'Yes, of course. But Emily is really fond of her music, and I am grateful for anything that makes her happy.'

'Are you, indeed?' There was no mistaking the caustic note in his voice, and I vividly remembered catching his knowing eyes in the mirror on Christmas Day. I could feel my cheeks growing hot with vexation, and was glad that the dusk would hide this fact from him.

'Emily is my cousin as well as my charge. We are almost like sisters; I owe everything I have or am to her parents. It's true I am paid—and I need the money. But I came out here at her parents' request; I would have come out with her anyway, and...'

'I am sure you would,' he put in quietly, his eyes never leaving my face.

I hesitated, knowing what he meant, then went on icily, 'I merely wanted you to know that I appreciate what you have done for her—not only in this matter of the piano, but the other things as well. It was most thoughtful of you to give her something to do in the house, to keep her employed. She hasn't many resouces, and the house takes her mind off ...'

'Off her unhappy situation?'

'I did not say that. But ... well, naturally she is anxious about the ... the baby, being so far away from home, you know.'

'Naturally.'

'Yes, she ... she is not happy—about the baby,' I ended lamely.

'You dumbfound me! I thought all women were happy about all babies.'

I could not tell whether he was serious since I would not look him in the face.

'Not Emily—at the moment, anyway.'

'Poor Emily!'

'Yes. It is sad, though I suppose you are joking.'

'And you thought I knew all this, and suggested that Emily should employ herself in my domestic matters to keep her mind off her unhappy state?'

'No—not that. I was just glad that she had something to do. How could you know that she did not want the baby?'

'How indeed?' He turned and threw away the butt of the cheroot. 'However, I could see that she was not—well, shall we say "content".

My reason for wanting to keep her busy was both simpler and less noble than the one you ascribe to me. First, I believed a woman would know best what women need to keep them comfortable. In which I was correct, it seems. And secondly, my grandmother always said "An idle woman is a mischievous woman" and my bachelor state has given me an aversion to troublesome females. I thought it best to forestall any likely annoyance by keeping my young relative fully occupied. So you see, it was for my ease of mind and not hers that I asked her to keep the housekeeping keys. I took it for granted, of course, that your—er—companionable duties would be sufficient to keep you on the path of virtue.'

I preferred not to make a reply, but when I looked up found him regarding me with his usual quizzical smile.

'And you, Laura?' he asked, after a moment. 'Are you happy here? I have not had time yet to show you much of the "real India" that you were so anxious to know. Perhaps what you have seen of it already—the few villages we have passed through—has been enough to turn you against knowing more?'

'Not at all. I have found everything most interesting. I just wish I could understand things better, that I knew the origins of so much that is strange and unfamiliar.'

'Well, once my guests have departed, I will make a point of showing you more. And Charles, of course. We mustn't forget Charles's thirst for information, must we? Though I fancy his motives are less admirable than yours.' He chuckled, though whether at my discomfiture or his own thoughts would have been hard to say. But I was very relieved to hear Emily calling me into the drawing-room, thus enabling me to retreat in good order.

The McCrackens and Mr Baird left Hassanganj the day after the piano was delivered, and George Barry went back to Lucknow shortly thereafter. Kate was to remain on until George came back to collect her at the beginning of March, an arrangement that suited both since George was expecting to be away on manoeuvres for a considerable part of the winter, and Kate declared that she would be much happier in Hassanganj than alone in her dark little bungalow in Mariaon.

Our days settled down into a quiet, regular and fairly productive routine. Each morning Oliver, Charles and I rode together for an hour or so. Then, having breakfasted, Emily and Kate settled down to some housewifely chore, while the men set off on their various pursuits and I studied Urdu with Benarsi Das. *Tiffin* brought us together again briefly, and afterwards, while the young Floods rested and Kate defiantly snored, I often went out to sketch or write letters in the banyan fernery which had become a favourite haunt of mine. Sometimes, however, Oliver called me into his office to check accounts with him, or to copy out inventories or orders for articles he needed from England. I was always summoned, never requested. 'You've a good clear fist,' he had commented approvingly the first day, 'much more legible than mine.'

So I carried out the tasks he set me, always bearing in mind that 'An idle woman is a mischievous woman' and endeavouring by my industry to prove my virtue. But soon I became interested in what I began to learn in helping my host with these small matters. I knew Mr Erskine to be a man of both energy and industry, but hitherto had only hazarded a guess at how he actually employed his days. Now I caught glimpses of a timetable that included the management of the indigo plantation and factory, of sal timber stands and saw-mills, and of his own home farm. In addition, there were the dozen or so villages on the estate that had to be visited often and regularly by their *sirkar*. There was continual work to be done on the system of rough roadways that criss-crossed the estate and on the canals that connected the two rivers and irrigated some thousands of acres of fields and pasture land. There were wells to be bored, walls to be built and avenues of trees to be planted to keep the shallow alluvial soil from eroding during the monsoons. Then there was the *kutcheri* or court, over which Mr Erskine presided twice a week, and where he was empowered to try and decide all cases involving land disputes and crop settlements, the thieving of water and the breaching of walls, the non-payment of taxes or rent, and such family matters as overdue payment for a bride, or which son should inherit the plough when his father died. Little by little I discovered that my host was an able accountant, a decisive and impartial magistrate, a competent architect, an efficient engineer and an excellent draughtsman.

I learnt to respect him. More, I learnt to admire the many admirable qualities which were apparent in his administration of Hassanganj. Yet I found it difficult to like him. He was too lacking in that frankness, that amiability, that open-hearted enthusiasm which I admired in Charles and that I had come to consider indispensable to true manliness.

Mr Erskine was generally curt and always reserved; he made it too plain that he cared little for the good regard of others. And his calm assumption of constant and consistent rightness would have been laughable had it not been so irritating.

On one score, however, he earned my sincere gratitude. He gave me the freedom of his library.

The only real hardship India had inflicted on me was the general dearth of reading matter; even the local newspapers were a week old before we saw them, while the English journals might be anything up to four months out of date. One evening Mr Erskine remarked the sigh with which I finally closed the book I was reading, the last of the small stock I had managed to purchase in Lucknow, and sat for a moment with folded hands and a discontented expression, gazing into the fire.

'Out of reading matter?' he enquired politely.

'Absolutely—until the next time the papers come from Lucknow.'

'Can you find nothing to suit you in the library?'

'I have not felt free to use it. The door is always shut, except when I am having my Urdu lesson.'

'Yes, I spend a lot of time there and prefer privacy when I am reading. But the door is not locked. You are perfectly at liberty to enter and help yourself to any volume that takes your interest. I hope you will do so.'

I lost no time in fulfilling his hope: picking up a lamp, I immediately made my way down the long corridor to the library. Thereafter I spent many happy hours browsing among the shelves, either alone or in the silent, unregarding presence of my host hunched over some book at his desk. I often thought with gratitude of the man (Old Adam, as his grandson irreverently called him) who, two days' journey from the nearest city and nearly a thousand miles from a port, had built up this fine collection of works in four languages fifty years before. Here were the great Latin classics and the Greek; all my English favourites and a wealth of literature in French, laid in, I had no doubt, to allay the tedium for his adored Danielle.

Oliver himself had added to the collection, not only with more modern works in English and French, but with Persian poetry, history and drama. I used to sit in the long dim room, when all the servants had gone to their quarters and the great house stirred gently in the afternoon somnolence, and think of the man who had built it and formed this library as its heart. For of that I was sure. These books, though they were bound in fine half-calf and bore his monogram—the Greek AE—on their spines, had been acquired individually to read and ponder over with loving concentration. This was no selection bought in bulk from a bookseller—even a discerning one. No page remained uncut, no book but bore somewhere a neat marginal comment in a fine sloping hand, the hallmark of the previous century's 'writer' in the East India Company. What an unusual person he must have been, combining the roles of man of action, visionary and scholar.

Across the hall the gunroom contained his collection of firearms: old, odd-looking flintlocks, blunderbusses, muskets and pistols, the walls decorated with spears, daggers and ancient unwieldy swords. The hall itself was darkened by a forest of horns and stuffed heads aglow with yellow glass eyes—trophies of the time when Old Adam had first cleared and planted his land: buffalo, *nilghai, gurul*, wild boar, and deer with long horns, short horns, straight horns and curly horns, while over the chest near the door hung the polished skull of his first working elephant, Begum. It was customary for visitors to stroke the big white skull when they entered, much as Papists, so I had been told, stroke the statue of Michelangelo's *Pietà* in Rome.

Before the bow window of the library, in the position of honour as it were, stood Old Adam's vast leather chair and, beside it, the ornate *hookah* or hubble-bubble he had been wont to smoke while sitting in it. I could imagine him, with the long hose of the pipe wound round his comfortable form, the silver mouthpiece between his lips, a liveried *hookah-burdwar* ready at his side to recharge the bowl with tobacco and rosewater, taking his ease in the evening of his days and reflecting (I hoped contentedly) on what he had accomplished. I was fond of Old Adam.

Our life was quiet and pleasant as day followed day and a mild sun set the shadows dancing languidly on the spreading lawns. Beyond the park bounds, the stir and murmur of the crowded village, and beyond that again the great plain of India, still mysterious, still scarcely known to me despite my curiosity and desire to know it. We had few callers; the distances were too great, the roads too bad and our neighbours too few. Occasionally a couple of planters or an official of some sort would stop at Hassanganj for the night on the way to Lucknow or back to some remote station. All were entertained with scrupulous courtesy—some of them indeed seemed in the habit of using the place as a posting stage—but were never pressed to lengthen their stay into a social visit. Our only excitement was the mail from England which Toddy-Bob conveyed back from Lucknow at irregular intervals.

And then, on a Sunday morning early in February, Mr Roberts arrived. He had come to Hassanganj to negotiate for the present season's indigo, but we had not been informed of his impending arrival.

'What a pleasure that my business with Mr Erskine should serve to bring our paths together again,' he said, bowing over my hand in his staid way.

'You are acquainted then?' asked Oliver.

'We are indeed,' I answered. 'Mr Roberts was most kind to me on the ship coming out. I count him a friend.'

'Thank you, Miss Hewitt, and your presence on the voyage was one of its few pleasures for me.'

'Indeed?' said Oliver coolly, leading the way into the house.

I knew that Mr Roberts had never before visited Hassanganj and I saw his eyes turn wonderingly about him as he made his way through the rooms. He remained closeted with Oliver for most of the day, and our host must have approved of his method of doing business, for that night, instead of retiring to the library at ten o'clock as he usually did, he remained in the drawing-room until we went to bed, talking amicably with his guest, who was indeed such a sensible man that his conversation was always a pleasure. Charles and Emily were almost as pleased as I to see a familiar face, and we all indulged in reminiscences of the voyage and our companions. Mr Roberts told us that Major Wilkins, with his wife and Elvira, was now stationed at one of the newly instituted posts only about thirty miles from us. The Major was now a very great man indeed, so Mr Roberts said with a smile, and Mrs Wilkins's purple had taken on a quite imperial lustre.

'And do you remember a talk we once had, Mr Roberts?' I said when there was a lull. 'On the ship? You felt we were not wise to make a protracted stay in the Kingdom of Oudh in these unquiet times?'

'I do,' he nodded, smiling.

'But now look around you and confess that we could not be more comfortable or better placed anywhere in India.'

'Without doubt, Miss Hewitt,' he agreed. 'The amenities of Hassanganj are admired and envied throughout the country. But if you will forgive me pointing it out, it was the general state of unrest in the province that worried me on your account; I had no doubt that you would be entirely happy in Hassanganj itself.'

'That's true,' I acknowledged, 'I was only teasing. But surely the state of the country is peaceful enough to reassure you now?'

Mr Roberts fidgeted in his chair and looked briefly from Emily to Mr Erskine, who was regarding him intently over his cigar. Perhaps it was indicative that Mr Erskine smoked wherever and whenever he pleased, whether or not ladies were present.

'I wish I could agree with you, Miss Hewitt,' went on Mr Roberts. 'But there have been one or two ... well, incidents ... recently that seem to me to point to a gathering storm; the latest being the burning of the telegraph office at Barrackpore last month. This itself was merely the result of another disquieting incident, but no doubt you have heard the story before. I know how swiftly news travels in the *mofussil* of India, so you may very likely know more of the matter than I do.'

'You refer, I suppose, to this matter of the Enfield cartridge?' Oliver spoke without surprise, though the rest of us had heard nothing of this or the burning of the telegraph house. No doubt it had been reported in the papers but, if so, not in such a manner as to cause us concern.

'Yes. It is a matter which is causing uneasiness—in certain quarters, that is.'

'And I can guess the quarters,' added Oliver grimly.

'What exactly happened?' asked Charles.

'Well, word has got around, apparently through a *lascar* working in the munitions factory at Dum-Dum, that the cartridges, a new type for the Enfield rifle, are greased with lard and cow's fat, and, since the cap of the bullet requires to be torn off with the teeth, this would mean defilement to both Mohammedans and Hindus, the cow being sacred to the Hindu, and the Mohammedans regarding the pig as unclean.'

'You are very explicitly informed, Mr Erskine,' said Mr Roberts. 'I must congratulate you.'

'As you say, news travels fast in the *mofussil*,' replied Oliver dourly, not liking the note of surprise in his guest's voice. 'So repercussions have already started?' He rose and walked over to the fire, where he began to fiddle with one of the lustres on the mantle.

'But,' said Charles, 'surely this is nothing more than a rumour, a device to cause trouble? There can be no truth in it. The authorities, after all, must have some knowledge of native customs and prejudices?'

'One must hope so; though British history in India has not been marked by intelligence or insight!' Oliver turned and gave his brother a long, cool look.

'Yes, it may indeed be merely a device for causing trouble, Mr Flood, as you say. All the same, there are other matters cropping up almost daily that, to my mind, indicate a lack of confidence among the people, or more explicitly among the sepoys. As Miss Hewitt remembers, this is no new impression that I hold. I have, as you might say, been scenting trouble on the wind for some considerable time. Now I believe this new order requiring sepoys to go overseas has crystallized matters, and it seems to me the trouble is coming to a head. There are too many variations on the same theme—the theme that the British wish to break caste, to Christianize, to totally subjugate, to annihilate the native beliefs and customs. To us here in this room, all such rumours are ridiculous, laughable. But you know what the native is when he gets an idea in his head!'

'Perhaps the real trouble lies in the fact that only when the native entertains a wrong idea are we interested in what is in his head,' said Oliver.

'And then of course, it is 1857.'

Everyone turned and looked at Kate, who had volunteered this seemingly irrelevant remark.

'Indeed it is, Mrs Barry. Indeed it is!' Mr Roberts nodded in mysterious agreement.

'But what has that got to do with it?' enquired Emily.

'Have you ever heard of the Battle of Plassey?' asked Oliver.

'Well—no, I don't think so. Should I have?'

'Oh!' I broke in. 'Clive! I remember that much. My uncle required me to read Macaulay to improve my vocabulary as a girl!'

'Quite. Clive. 1757. The natives hold a belief that British rule will end one hundred years after that battle, which, as I hope your mathematics have informed you, Emily, brings us to 1857. An interesting point perhaps, Mrs Barry.'

'Good gracious! Do you mean there might be some sort of war?' enquired Emily incredulously.

'Insurrection, I believe, would be more correct as a term.'

'Good gracious!' she repeated. 'Oh, Charles, perhaps it is just as well that we are to return home soon, after all.'

'Oh, come now, Emily,' returned her spouse impatiently. 'There is no possibility of any sort of trouble that would concern Europeans. These people have been quarrelling among themselves for hundreds of years, and I expect they will continue to do so—but we have the Army and ... and ... there can be no cause for alarm on your part.'

'I do hope so. Oh, I do hope you are right. I shouldn't like to be cut off here with a war going on. We would just have to go home sooner.'

'Nonsense, Emily. Out of the question.'

'Your husband is right, Mrs Flood,' soothed Mr Roberts tactfully. 'There is no cause for you to be alarmed, whatever happens, and nowhere in India would you be safer than in Hassanganj.'

Emily allowed herself to be reassured, but I caught a glance laden with meaning pass between Mr Roberts and his host.

CHAPTER 5

Mr Roberts stayed for a couple of days, and then rode off to some other indigo plantation. On the morning following his departure, Oliver and I rode out alone. Charles had overslept and Oliver Erskine waited for no man. I did not anticipate much pleasure from his unalloyed company as, lacking Charles's usual service, I mounted from the block and cantered off after him, with Ishmial, Mr Erskine's impressive Pathan retainer, close behind me. Often on these morning rides Mr Erskine was entirely silent, immersed in his own thoughts, and then I would line my mount with Charles's and we would contrive, happily enough, to ignore our taciturn host. But this morning he was in an expansive mood.

'I have something special to show you today,' he smiled as I caught up with him. 'A little bit of the "real India". Something for you to write up in your journal,' he added slyly, knowing that I did not like references to my schoolgirl habit of keeping a diary. I tried to write something in it each day, and also made small watercolour sketches and drawings which I pasted in to illustrate my entries. A little sketch book and a pencil always travelled in my pocket, and he had often seen me pause to catch a quick impression of morning light striking on an old wall, an unusual temple or a giant anthill rearing out of the earth like an antique castle.

'Today is the official opening of spring—the day the Lord Krishna's feet touched the earth and made it bloom. We call it *Basunta* in these parts. Do you see that bush, with the little yellow flower? That is the *basant*, the herald of spring, and yellow is the colour of spring. Wait a moment, you must wear some!' He bent down to the bush from his saddle and plucked some of the flowers. They were like buttercups and had a sweet honeyed scent. I pinned them to the bodice of my habit, and Mr Erskine, in a moment of gaiety, thrust a single bloom into his lapel.

'There now, we are both suitably attired!' he exclaimed with satisfaction as we rode on, he very upright in his saddle, his left hand at his waist, the right loosely clasping the reins between lean brown fingers. 'And,' he went on, smiling, 'since it is a fine morning, and springtime, let us try to forget the unfortunate absence of Charles and endeavour to promote some friendship between ourselves. Or at least— companionship. Is that too much to ask?'

'Certainly not! But I am not aware that we need to "promote" any friendship.'

'The devil you ain't! Then you must have a cold notion of friendship if you consider your manner towards me has been friendly!'

'I am sorry you think so,' I said and went on, unwisely, 'In what have I erred?'

'In avoiding me with an enthusiasm and consistency quite remarkable, to begin with. Then in accepting my small overtures to understanding ... er ... for instance, the services of Benarsi Das ... my library ... small things like that ... and then allowing the flower of friendship to wither on the twig untended.'

His manner was light, and I was not alarmed by the banter.

'I believe I have expressed my gratitude with all sincerity, for those and many other favours!'

'And with the most eminent propriety!'

'How else should I behave towards you then? With impropriety?'

'A thousand times yes, if it will make you a little warmer to deal with!'

'Now I know you are joking.' And I laughed, anxious to deflect the conversation into easier channels.

'No, I am not joking. I am puzzled. For two months or thereabouts, oh "woman dear", as Kate calls you, I have tried in my rough, masculine way to indicate that, contrary to your obvious belief, I am a human being, that I recognize you as a human being and that I believe the two of us could reach an enjoyable understanding of each other. That at least was the first impression I formed, at the Residency ball and later. And I had hoped that your stay in Hassanganj would be productive of something more than the correct attitudes and meaningless platitudes which are all that you have ever vouchsafed me. I had thought ... I had truly thought ... for a time, that is, that we two could have found some ... some, er ... meeting of true minds!'

He still spoke jestingly, but there was a hint of something—was it bitterness or resentment?—behind his words, that made me realize suddenly that he was profoundly serious.

I rode on for a moment in silence, Pyari carrying me forward, so that when I spoke again it was over my shoulder.

'You confuse me,' I said at last. 'I don't know what to say except that I have never wished to be hurtful, or in any way unfriendly towards you.' I paused, but felt him listening intently, so went on with a rush. 'But it is true—I find you a most ... a most difficult man to know!'

'Yet I am a simple man—if you would see me as such.'

'No,' I said decidedly, 'not simple at all! You are reserved. And so often silent yourself. And I have had no wish to break into your ... well, your privacy.'

'But you do not find it difficult to talk to me...?'

'On the contrary!'

Again there was silence, only the clop of the horses' hooves in the dust and the creak of saddlery breaking the morning hush.

'This barrier. I am puzzled by it, I admit. A little piqued perhaps. I generally get my way with people—yet you ... you have formed an opinion of me—an adverse opinion, I believe—that nothing I can do or say will alter. Admit it now, you are prejudiced against me? Or no, do not make yourself vulnerable by any such foolish admission. It is the sort of mistake one remembers in the future. But remember that I realize it, and that I will not be content to remain the stranger, at arm's length always, that you wish me to. Sooner an enemy any time!'

'That is mere hyperbole,' I said coldly, 'and allow me to say that you misjudge me and my motives. I regret that you find my character and my manner cold and unfriendly. Such was never my intention. But I am as I am. I cannot guess what else you would have me be!'

The gelding now paced beside Pyari, and I glanced up to find Oliver's golden eyes regarding me with a gaze that was both wry and rueful.

'That's only too obvious,' he said, but *sotto voce*, so that I could not be sure of what I had heard. Then, surprisingly, he threw back his head and laughed in the golden sunlight so that the nervous Pyari danced in the track, flattened her ears and snorted in alarm.

'Whoa! Whoa, girl!' he chuckled, quieting the mare with a pat on the neck. 'Very well then, Miss Hewitt, we shall call a truce. For the moment. Forgive my clumsy handling of a delicate matter. Intimacy—er, of the mind, of course—cannot be forced. You are right to resent my trying. But, at least, when I enter the library don't grab the first book you see and withdraw. Fortunately I know that you do not read Latin, or I might have been shocked by seeing you depart in a hurry clutching a copy of the *Saturnalia*!'

For a moment I was nonplussed. It was true that I generally made a rapid exit from the library if he was in it, but I did not realize I had been so obvious. Then the humour of the situation struck me ... for my father had owned the *Saturnalia* in translation. I too threw back my head and laughed, and magically the tension that had arisen between us was dispelled.

We rode on together then, very amicably, and my companion told me some of the legends of Krishna and stories from the *Ramayana*, and said we were approaching the village where his grandfather had begun his work of settlement sixty years before. The ride would be a long one this morning, so at about the time we usually breakfasted we dismounted in a grove and Ishmial produced from his saddlebag a neatly packed parcel of sandwiches and fruit and a flask of brandy and water. The latter I refused, promising myself a drink when we should reach the village. We were sitting silently in the shade on the tumbled remains of an old wall while Oliver smoked a cigar, when a little procession of children approached us, so gay, so charming, that I stood up in delight, eager to miss nothing of the picture they made. There were perhaps a score of them, none of them more than ten or twelve years of age, all dressed in yellow and carrying garlands and bouquets of the yellow *basant* flower. Two or three had small drums on strings around their necks, others played on bamboo flutes and the rest tapped short wooden staves together in time to the drums. They were singing and dancing as they came, and the swirling *sari* skirts and *dhotis* around dusty feet, the primitive instruments, and the joyous childish faces alight with laughter immediately put me in mind of Donatello's cherubic choir. They took no notice of us, but, absorbed in their high nasal chant, swayed through the trees and disappeared from view, only the sound of their voices remaining to assure me I had not witnessed some brief faerie visitation.

'Oh, what a pretty sight, Oliver! They looked so fresh and happy. What were they doing?'

'They are going to visit the shrine of some favourite village deity here in the grove, and lay their flowers and other offerings at the foot of the peepul tree he inhabits. They couldn't have timed it better, could they? That's another little bit of the "real India" that I am glad you have seen. Those children are bred to dirt, disease and grinding poverty but, as you see, India has gifts for everyone who will take them. We like to consider their beliefs mere ignorant superstition, but those beliefs are enough to produce music, laughter and respite from the fields on a day like this, and what god can do more? This evening everyone will eat well, probably for the first time since the last festival. There will be more dancing and music, and perhaps storytelling and wrestling in the village square, and their fathers will get drunk and beget them brothers and sisters on wives for once not too tired to be more than acquiescent. They will make the most of their day, I promise you. Then tomorrow they will put away their yellow finery, sweep their courtyards clean of dead flowers and return again to the intractable fields and their pinched bellies. But they always have another holy day to look forward to!'

The village, when we reached it, was also *en fête*, the yellow *basant* burgeoning on every lintel and arch, while women in buttercup *saris* squatted at their doors readying the celebration meal and men slept luxuriously late on string cots in the sunshine or wandered in groups towards the grog shop. We were now at the edge of a tongue of heavy forest that to the south merged into the *terai*, but the morning was very warm and still and a dusty haze hid the foothills. I foun d myself thirsty and rather tired, which, perhaps, was why I was not much impressed by the first fruits of Old Adam's labours. Here, said Oliver, was where he had made his first camp, living in a tent while he directed the clearing of the jungle, the cutting of tracks and waterways, and the building of the first huts. Whatever his pioneer plans for it, the village now was the usual collection of flat-roofed mud huts, intersected by unpaved alleys—crowded, dirty and smelly. Only the ephemeral gilding of the bright spring flower lent the place a brief beauty.

We rode slowly through the village, stopped often by the inhabitants, who grasped this opportunity to lay a complaint or ask a favour of the *sirkar*, or who, perhaps, were merely curious to look at the unaccustomed white woman with him. Oliver bore himself with a sort of good-humoured assurance, bandying words with passers-by, attentive to supplicants, reassuring to an aged crone who held his horse by the bridle while she poured out her story, but on the whole unmoved—(as was apparent from the resigned disappointment of the faces we left)—by these extemporary pleas for preference. Our objective was a temple tank which Oliver was sure would interest me but, as we rode through the untidy outskirts, I averted my eyes hurriedly from a lean-to thatch shelter built on to one of the huts, where I had seen a bundle of filthy rags stir at the unfamiliar sound of horses' hooves. It was a leper, put out to die by his family in a crude shelter less weathertight than their cow-byre. There he would lie in all weathers, shunned by all comfort, slowly putrefying to a merciful death. Once a day scraps of food would be placed a little distance from him, not to be approached until the bearer was safely out of sight. I had seen other such bundles of rags in other villages, but the sight was not less harrowing on familiarity.

India, Oliver had said, has gifts for all who will take them. Would this end be the gift singled out for one of those happy, singing children in the grove? I shuddered at the thought, and so reflecting on the monstrous and too manifest injustices of fate, the small octagonal pool with its shallow steps leading down into the water failed to move me to much appreciation. Certainly it was very lovely with its white onion-domed temple and a clump of palms beside it. But the water was green with scum, and the resident holy man had long locks matted with ashes and surveyed us with an avaricious eye as we walked past.

'Sitting there praying and raking in the people's food and their poor *annas* when you should be up and out doing some good!' I thought to myself. The bundle of rags, as a leper, was denied even the help of the holy man's prayers.

Oliver had not noticed my preoccupation. He was speaking: '… and much predates the village of course, probably by hundreds of years. No one now can remember the people who built the pool or the ruined fort back there in the forest. It is the last vestige of some old, old jungle culture, or perhaps the culture was here even before the jungle.'

Then, as having circled the pool I stood ready to mount Pyari again, he said with some annoyance, 'Well, and what has gone wrong now? Is it not worthy of your pencil after all? I have kept it in mind to bring you here for weeks and now you turn away as though such things can be seen every day!'

'I'm sorry.' I shook my head and tried to look apologetic. 'I am not in the mood to draw now. But the pool is beautiful, really it is, and I am very grateful that you brought me here. But... but it was that poor leper. I cannot think of my silly sketching when I remember him and what he must be going through. He is a human being!'

The annoyance faded from his face. 'Yes, well, that too is India, I am afraid, Laura. The inescapable India. There are a score of lepers in every village, hundreds in the bazaars. There's no cure, and the natives have long realized that isolating them is the only way to protect themselves from contagion.'

'But it's so cruel ... so barbarous!'

'Undoubtedly. But some things one must accept.'

'Not without protest, without some effort to rectify things, surely?'

'What would you have me do; take him back to Hassanganj and house him with the servants? At least here he is with his own. And they care for him, in their fashion. Come now, it's getting late. Perhaps we can return here another day, if you wish to.'

I was unconvinced, but mounted and followed him dejectedly as we left the village. I was displeased with myself for my own lack of enthusiasm about the pool. Had he not said he had kept it in mind for me for weeks? Was this not another of those overtures to friendship which he had made and I had—to his mind—rejected? It was strange, but his clumsy, even abortive, efforts to break through what seemed to him to be my reserve, had done much to warm my mind towards him. Perhaps because for the first time he had shown a little weakness, a chink in the armour of assurance which repelled me. Now, I found I was unhappy at having disappointed him. For the very first time I discovered myself wishing to please him. But I had lost the opportunity.

The track narrowed as we entered the forest. We were not returning the way we had come, so I hoped we were taking a short cut home since, having forgotten to beg a drink in the village, I was now very thirsty and not a little fatigued. It was nearly noon and, though by no means hot, the temperature here at the edge of the steamy *terai* was warm enough to have stilled the sounds of birds and the chattering of the monkeys. All that could be heard was the dull clop of our hooves in the thick, sun-dappled dust, and an occasional stir in the dry undergrowth as jungle fowl made for cover.

All three of us must have heard the chant simultaneously: low, rhythmic, somehow oppressive in its half-heard insistence.

'*Jai Ramji Jai! Jai Ramji Jai! Jai Ramji Jai!*'

Oliver, leading as usual, held up his hand to halt us.

'A moment,' he said in English, and then spoke in Hindustani to Ishmial. Ishmial paused before replying, listening to the chant grow slowly louder, and when he spoke his voice was emphatic. What he said escaped me, but Oliver nodded his head in agreement.

'It's a funeral procession,' he explained. 'They must be taking the body down to a *ghat* on the river. We must leave the track clear for them, there is probably quite a crowd.'

As he spoke he wheeled his horse off the track through some undergrowth, holding back the boughs for us to pass, and we found ourselves in a small clearing large enough for all and at the same time almost invisible from the track. He swung down from the saddle and stood with his arm across the gelding's neck.

'Would they make trouble if they found us in their way?' I asked.

'They would disregard us entirely—behave as though we didn't exist.'

'Then why this concealment?'

'Merely a question of manners. The track is narrow, and people usually prefer to pursue their burial rites with some dignity. Also I have to think of Ishmial; at times like this, well, religious differences can be exacerbated and lead to insult. Not likely, but possible.' He was matter-of-fact.

'But would we ...' I began, but Oliver held his finger to his lips for silence.

The chant, that strangely disquieting yet unexcited repetition of four small syllables, was very near.

I had not dismounted, and found I had a reasonable view of the track through the foliage, and therefore of the procession as it began to pass. A party of men came into view, walking in twos and threes, all chanting—grunting, under compulsion to mouth the words, and beating their breasts with clenched fists in time to the chant. The body, wrapped in red cotton, was borne past on a string bed, pathetic but anonymous. Then more men, a score or more, shoulders touching, fists thumping, feet scuffling, faces set, and at the very last a girl, hardly more than a child, was half led, half carried across my range of vision. The poor young wife, I thought. For a second she seemed to look straight at me through the bushes, her head being thrown back as she was pulled along, her veil dragging in the dust. Her eyes held no expression—mere nothingness. Perhaps, I told myself, she was dazed with shock and grief.

As the girl passed, Oliver drew himself up quickly and took a step forward. I realized that he too must have seen her, and before I could analyse the strange expression on his face, he had pushed through the underbrush to watch the tail of the funeral disappear down the track, which forked in two a little further on. The chanting had died to an ominous drone before he came back, and I saw his face was white under the honey-coloured tan.

'They have not gone to the river, they have turned into the forest!' he said grimly as he mounted. Ishmial, aloft on his horse, seemed to understand, although Oliver had spoken in English. He uttered an imprecation and spat vehemently into the dust.

'*Suttee*,' he hissed, his eyes on Oliver's.

'What?' I felt the colour drain from my face as the word entered my comprehension. 'But it can't be; it's been illegal for years.'

Oliver merely regarded me with something like distaste.

'*Suttee hai! Sahib, suttee hai*!' Ishmial reiterated with excitement, as though he, like me, felt Oliver had missed the point. Oliver sat still in the saddle, his eyes narrowed, gazing into nothing.

'Blast!' he said. 'God damn and blast 'em all!'

'You must do something!' I said frantically. 'Oliver, you must stop them! You can't just sit there and let it happen. At least speak to them, reason with them, threaten them with the law! She was only a child!'

'Threaten them!' His features were twisted with derision as he looked at me. 'There were more than half a hundred men in that procession. To have been in it at all they were half a hundred fanatics. Moreover, they were well primed with *bhang*. They appeared quiet— far too quiet—but one word from me, or anyone not connected with them, would rouse them to a drug-induced fury which would have the lot of us torn limb from limb in seconds!'

'But how can you know? Surely you are going to make some attempt ...'

'I know! I know too damned well! So does Ishmial there; ask him if you don't believe me!'

'Yes, *Mem-sahib*!' said Ishmial, nodding in agreement and speaking in Hindustani for all that he seemed to comprehend so much in English.

'It is very bad, very bad men, but we alone can do nothing—nothing! Very bad!'

'What I cannot understand,' Oliver mused more to himself than to me, 'is their boldness in having the woman with them in broad daylight. It's generally done at night and in secrecy.'

'You mean it happens often; they burn the widows even though it's been against the law so long?'

'Not often, but it happens all right. These forest people are a law unto themselves more often than not. Still, I don't like the open contempt of the authorities. It can only mean that for some reason they feel safe in doing now what they would never have attempted before.'

'And so they are, if you really intend to do nothing!'

'No, I'm doing nothing! You must suit yourself!' He spurred the gelding through the bushes and was some way up the track by the time we emerged from the clearing.

It was a horrible ride back to Hassanganj in the full afternoon heat.

Among a multitude of conflicting sensations, my predominant feelings were of horror and aversion—a total aversion to the people among whom I found myself, their customs, their beliefs, and to the country itself. The contrasts of India were too brutal: its hidden aspects, when at length discovered, too repugnant; the ideas behind its acts too cruel. I could not attempt to reconcile the many facets of its existence, and no doubt I was silly to try. Contrasts exist everywhere, wealth and poverty, labour and idleness, squalor and beauty, but in India the conjunction was too extreme, too unexpected and ... too apparent. Here no decent veils of convention were pulled across the open sores of life. I felt, overwhelmingly, a sickening hatred of India.

Jogging along, head bowed, eyes down, hands clasped on the pommel, regardless of where Pyari took me, I tried to exorcize the pain in my mind by reliving that little moment in time when the girl had appeared to look into my eyes. I strove to recall how she had been dressed. Had her head been covered, her clothes clean, her face pretty? But my memory brought forward only an impression of youth, and the lifeless gaze of dark eyes in a dark face. Had she known what lay before her? Had she acquiesced to it? Was it possible that she had gloried in it, as, it is said, the women of Chitor gloried in their terrible death? My imagination dragged me with the girl to her end: the heaped pyre by some small tributary stream, the leaping flames in the forest dusk, the two forms—one dead and inert, one alive and struggling—consumed equally but in what dreadful inequality of suffering.

At last the shade of the portico told me we had reached the house, and Oliver, dismounted, was waiting for me.

'It would be better not to mention what we have seen to Emily,' he said in a low voice as I drew up and he came forward to help me dismount. I nodded silently, not looking at him and not surprised to find that he too was now a part of my revulsion against India. As his hands touched mine to free the reins, an insistent ringing in my ears reached a crescendo. I thrust his hand away and practically tumbled to the ground.

'Don't!' I cried with my hands to my ears. 'Don't! Don't! Oh, don't.' And then I fainted.

CHAPTER 6

I had eaten little that morning and drunk nothing; the ride had been long and hot, and my emotions had been most savagely harrowed. So my body took revenge, and I fainted.

I returned to consciousness in my own room, dark, cool and familiar, and lay for a moment savouring the sense of well-being my presence there brought me, but even as I struggled to open my eyes I knew there was something I must not think of, and fought against recollection.

Kate sat beside my bed, waving a palm-leaf fan. Something damp, cold and smelling of vinegar lay on my brow. I raised my hand to remove it, and in that moment the full memory of the condemned girl's eyes leapt at me. My hand dropped back on to the sheet and I began to cry weakly, shamed, fearful and full of helpless pity.

'There now, woman dear,' said Kate, taking the cloth from my forehead and wringing it out in a basin before replacing it. 'You'll soon feel better when you've had a bite to eat. You've had a dreadful experience, and what is really bothering you is that you could do nothing about it, isn't that it?'

I nodded, surprised to find that anyone else could resolve my feelings so easily and accurately.

'Well, m'dear, that is always the hardest part of life, and the one thing we must learn to bear.'

I watched her in silence, grateful for the kind lined face with its bright eyes so unsurprised by evil. I wished I was old, really old, and experienced past shock.

'Sure, and do we not all know the heartbreak of seeing others' suffering and having no way of easing it? 'Tis the Man Upstairs Himself, and only Him, who knows the way of it, and the why of it. But maybe it will ease your mind a bit to talk of it, when you've had a rest and a sup. Wait now while I run downstairs and see what I can find to tempt you.'

'I couldn't eat anything at all,' I gasped through tears and sudden shivering.

'Och, you'll manage a little clear soup no doubt when it's put before you. Lie quiet, there's someone else here to mind you while I'm gone.'

She patted my hands, wiped the tears from my face and beckoned to someone out of my sight. Then her black buttoned boots took her briskly to the door.

A figure came slowly towards the bed. Had I been capable of thought, I would have expected Emily, or perhaps Bhujni, my *ayah*, but in my confused condition I was hardly surprised when Oliver Erskine came to the bedside and sat down in the chair Kate had vacated.

'Better now?' he asked quietly.

I nodded, wondering without interest what had brought him to my bedside—anxiety, kindness or guilt? He could not be feeling proud of his part in the morning's drama. What was it he had said about the leper? 'There are some things one must accept.' What an easy, trouble-free idea to go through life with. He probably didn't care a button about the wretched girl hauled to the flames; that too was something one must accept. Was it cynicism? Or gross insensitivity? Or merely a dedication to his own ease of mind that made him so impervious to the claims of his own kind?

He had been sitting silently beside me for some time when I turned my aching head towards him, trying to get my eyes to focus on his face.

'I believe you've had a touch of the sun to add to everything else,' he remarked coolly. 'That damn fool headgear you wear. You need something with a bigger brim!'

It was a silly hat, but, with its curling frond of ruby feathers, a very smart one, and I clung to it, since Charles once said it suited me.

I narrowed my eyes and his face became clearer. The effort required made me see it as though for the first time. Why did he appear so different? It was the same face, yet not the same. He began to speak, but I ignored his words and went over the features slowly and carefully: the brown hair bleached where the sun caught it, the broad forehead and prominently arched nose (a little crooked it was too), the wide mouth, the cleft chin, the hazel eyes that were amber sometimes, sometimes gold, narrow below heavy lids fringed with straight black lashes. The same face but, I now realized, a different expression. A pleasant, open expression, I saw with surprise. It was as though the active principle that forged meaning in the eyes and twisted the lips into smiles or sneers lay passive for once: as though he had for a moment dropped the mask he chose to wear and allowed himself to be seen undefended by self-consciousness.

He stopped talking when he found I was not listening, and allowed me to scrutinize his face with equanimity.

'Well?' he said at length, unsmiling. 'Satisfied?'

His words pulled me up. I was embarrassed that he should have witnessed my undisguised curiosity.

'I'm sorry,' I whispered, looking away. 'I've never seen you so ... so, well ... *kind* before.'

'Am I such a monster then?' And he smiled.

'No, not...' I began, but explanation was too much of an effort. I closed my eyes and lay still, wishing he would go away and leave me in peace. Only a short while before I had felt I hated him, yet now here he was taking some sort of interest in my welfare and I could think of him as kind. Why didn't the confusing creature remove himself? I kept my eyes shut, but he stayed.

After a time, when I could hear him fidgeting in his chair, probably debating whether to stay or go, he said, 'Laura, are you awake? If you are, there are some things I feel you ought to know, as soon as possible. They'll help you to feel better. Will you listen to me while I talk? Will you pay attention? You need not open your eyes; I know what a sun headache is like.'

So naturally I immediately opened my eyes.

'What else must I know? You have already told me there are things I must accept,' I pointed out with bitterness.

'There are several things about what happened this morning that are not at all as you think them to be now. I know that you will not sleep or rest—tonight or for many a night—while your imagination is allowed to fuel itself on ignorance. That is why Kate asked me to speak to you. She knows a great deal about such matters, about India and Indian ways and how they strike a young woman from England, and she can probably understand your feelings better than you do yourself at the moment.'

I shook my head on the pillow and the damp cloth fell away.

'But ... but that poor girl, and all those horrible men hauling her away to her death!' And I began to cry again. He took both my hands in his and held them, saying nothing. 'If only I hadn't seen it. Nothing is so bad when you only hear about it. Oliver, why ... why didn't you help?'

'I'm not God Almighty, and I told you why at the time!' There was a note of asperity in his voice.

'But ... but to just *allow* it to happen like that! I ...'

'Yes! But now look, Laura, and don't turn away your head; listen to me! You are not one of those hysterical females who can duck the darker side of life by having the vapours. You've got to face things.' And he gave my hands a shake, as he would the reins of his horse when he was impatient to get on.

'First—now hear me!—that girl was in no condition to suffer. She had no idea what was happening to her, and if she had she would probably have gone anyway. She had been filled up with *bhang*—you know what that is? A drug—ever since her husband died. She was unconscious, or at any rate unknowing, when you saw her, and would be unconscious when they strapped her to the pyre.' I shuddered at the dreadful image conjured by his words. 'Yes! I know I'm being brutal, but if I'm not you'll go on lacerating yourself with visions of how you would feel if you were to be burnt alive, and believe me there is no reality in your visions. Quite apart from the fact that the girl knew nothing of what was happening to her, these people are reared to other expectations than ours. A widow who is "*suttee*" is assured of a better life in her next incarnation, and when you know something of their lives here, you'll sympathize with the lengths they'll go to to improve their lot in the next.'

'You cannot be defending it?'

'Good God, no! *Suttee*, and many things like it, must be seen to be evil before we stand a chance of helping these poor devils, really helping them. But you must see their point of view too. For them *suttee* is no barbarous ritual of senseless cruelty, as it appears to you. It is a religious function, solemn, holy, admirable, sanctioned by centuries of usage. And, let's not forget, often necessary economically! Here'—in another voice—'blow your nose!'

He released my hands and gave me his own pocket handkerchief. I mopped up my tears while he went on: 'In the old days the widows used

253

to go to the pyre singing, and it is said that their state of exaltation was such that they died without a pang. Well, none of us can know about that, and now times have changed. The practice is continued here and there, and not infrequently among these jungle folk to the north who have very little contact with anyone outside their own villages. They have remained primitives, and we with our Western ideas have never got close enough to them to make any impression. And that is the whole point of what I am saying; you cannot equate that girl and yourself. She would react to nothing as you would, not even pain. I am not denigrating her humanity. I will not insult you by trying to convince you she would not be capable of pain, of all sorts of pain and mental and physical suffering, because she is primitive. But what you must realize is that both the causes and the effects in her life would be totally different to anything in yours, believe me!'

He paused and sighed, and I caught him looking at me speculatively, wondering whether I understood.

'You thought me heartless this morning, didn't you?'

'And aren't you?'

'Perhaps. The truth is I wasn't so much concerned with the wretched drugged girl. I knew I could not help her. I was wondering what influence is at work that makes ignorant, backward people like that take the law into their own hands so brazenly. Why they should suddenly feel so immune from the law, even though it is almost impossible to enforce it among them. There is something behind it all, and I am not sure what it is.' His eyes became abstracted as he tried again to work the matter out in his mind.

'And you very much dislike not being sure—of anything!' I remarked acidly. 'What a strange man you are. You can worry about the remote implications and yet not give a fig for the suffering individual.'

'That is not quite just,' he decided, having considered my words. 'It would be unwise for me to care too much for the individual. That's not my job. I have over thirty thousand individuals on this estate, Laura, and that means that every day—no, every hour—some tragedy is in the making or takes place that, if I were to give adequate attention to it, might require months or years of my time to ameliorate. I do not like the sights that meet my eyes as I ride through the villages: the potbellied, half-starved babies, the disease everywhere, the children deliberately crippled for begging purposes, the little girls sold into the temples, the

... and the other things,' he added lamely, so that I knew he would have said more had he not realized he was talking to a female. 'But all I can do at this stage is try to provide some small positive good, rather than combat a large negative evil, over which I can never hope to win.'

'I don't think I am condemning you,' I said, realizing not without satisfaction that I had managed to puncture his usual ironic self-assurance. He was actually explaining himself to me. 'I don't know enough about you or your work to condemn. I know that I could never act, or think, in the way you do, no matter how long I lived out here. I could not disregard the evil under my feet.'

He came back to the bed and stood looking down at me with his hands in his breeches' pockets.

'I believe you couldn't. But then you are a woman.'

'Why have you told me all this, Oliver?' I asked.

'Isn't it obvious? I didn't want you to suffer. Unnecessarily. You have too much sense to allow yourself to agonize over imaginary miseries once you know the facts. So I have given you the facts.'

'Thank you. It's true, I do feel easier in my mind now. About the girl, I mean. And I ... I suppose you really had no option this morning. But ... but too many things had happened too quickly, all seeming to contradict each other, and I could make nothing of them, nor of my own state of mind.'

'Good! And now I'll tell you something else. Ishmial has already ridden to Lucknow with a report of the morning's incident. He thinks he knows the village the funeral party came from, and I believe he is right. It is a hamlet, way off any track, and the people are unusually backward and intractable even for that region. They are not the responsibility of Hassanganj, but I have had trouble with them before when they have raided my villages for stock and ... er ... women. That sort of thing. If anything can be proved, and I'm by no means sure that it can, then, eventually, justice of a sort, your sort, will be done. That is as much as I can do. I realize of course that it is not enough in your eyes.'

'My views are of small importance,' I whispered. My head was aching abominably. He made no rejoinder, but the mask was back on his face. 'Oh, Oliver, we will never see anything from the same angle. But thank you for trying to help me. It was good of you.'

'A pleasure,' he muttered. 'Well, I had better go now and let you rest. Drink all the water you can. I hope you will feel better very soon.' For a moment he looked as though there was something more he wanted to say. Then he shrugged his shoulders and walked out of the room. I was glad he had gone. He posed too many problems that I had not the energy to grapple with.

A few moments later Kate came back with a servant bearing a tray. I wanted no food, but forced myself to swallow a few mouthfuls. When I had finished, I asked Kate what on earth had made her persuade Oliver Erskine to come and talk to me. 'He told me nothing you couldn't have, Kate, and he is such an upsetting person when one isn't feeling well. We nearly quarrelled and I know I annoyed him.'

'But I didn't persuade him, m'dear! It was he who suggested explaining matters to you. He was very worried about you.'

She left me then, and I drifted off to sleep with Bhujni fanning my head. Why should Oliver, of all people, have been worried about me, I thought as I fell asleep.

CHAPTER 7

Emily was told that I was suffering from a touch of the sun, and though I guessed Charles knew the facts of that troubled ride, I did not care to mention it to him. In a couple of days I had quite recovered, but for some time thereafter I did not accompany the men on their daily exercise, preferring to remain within the park and garden, so I saw even less than usual of my host.

Emily, Kate and I were now busy making baby clothes, and spent a great part of each morning on the verandah, sewing tiny dresses and petticoats, jackets and bonnets. One day, towards the end of February, as we were so employed, I looked up to see Oliver approaching across the lawn, carrying a bundle of checked calico in his hand. Charles was with him, and both men seemed in a great hurry.

'Ishmial! Ishmial!' Oliver roared as he reached the house. 'Come here—*juldi*!' And he subsided on the verandah step almost at my feet, while Charles, mopping his red face, sat down on a chair. We all stopped work, wondering what was to come. It was unusual to see Oliver about the house in mid-morning.

'Phew,' gasped Charles. 'Haven't enjoyed a chase so much in years, but he was the slipperiest little beggar you ever saw!'

'Who was? What has happened?' asked Emily.

'A little boy—up a tree.'

'You chased a little boy up a tree?'

'But he got away all the same—agile as a monkey!'

'What on earth are you talking about?' Kate put down her work. 'Oliver, will you kindly explain?'

Oliver had been sitting with his head in his hands smiling to himself over what was obviously an enjoyable recollection. Charles looked put out at not being applied to himself, but allowed his brother to continue the tale.

'Well,' began Oliver, chuckling, 'we were walking along the road leading to the factory from the village when I saw something move in one of the old neem trees. Now, you know how I cherish my trees.'

Indeed we did. Most of the trees on the estate had been planted by Old Adam, but each year Oliver put in others to compensate for the depredations of the villagers, who, being perennially short of fuel, thought nothing of cutting down the timber designed to save their soil from wind and water, to warm themselves and cook their food. Only a little less heinous in the eyes of Oliver was their practice of denuding trees of foliage to make fodder, and I had myself seen him suddenly tear away on his horse to make an example of some poor little wretch who was up a tree chopping off small branches to drag home for the family goat.

'So,' he continued, 'we immediately ran forward to catch the culprit. Charles was up the tree in a trice, while I stayed at the bottom waiting for the thief to descend, but damn me if he didn't run along to the end of a long branch, drop to the ground and disappear while we were still trying to believe our eyes. A spirited morsel. What's more, he had not been cutting the leaves off; there was no sign of a chopper or any damage. But we did find this.' He picked up the bundle and showed it to us, 'And I am ready to swear that the lad was the son of the *thanadar* of Nairainganj and that he had a good reason for wanting to keep out of my sight.'

He opened the bundle while he spoke, revealing a pile of *chapattis*, the flat, round, unleavened bread of the natives.

'That's too bad of you, Oliver,' scolded Kate. 'Now the poor fellow will be without his midday meal, or perhaps he was taking it to his father, and his mother will beat him for losing it.'

'I think he'll be in trouble all right, but not for that reason. Ishmial!' he yelled again. 'Where the devil is he?'

Just then Ishmial, summoned by other servants who had heard their master's call, came running down the verandah.

'Good! Now we shall see,' said Oliver as Ishmial came to an apologetic halt beside him. He gestured towards the *chapattis* and asked Ishmial a series of questions in Hindustani. Ishmial picked up the bundle and examined its contents with interest, nodding from time to time as Oliver spoke. He pointed to something in the middle of one of the flat cakes as he turned them over, then replaced the lot in the rag with an air of accomplishment.

'So, I was right!' Oliver tied up the bundle and handed it over to Ishmial, who departed carrying it.

'About the boy?' suggested Emily hopefully; we were all now thoroughly mystified by Oliver's manner.

'No—oh, yes, I think I know the lad—but I'm right about these *chapattis*. Ishmial has come to me twice lately saying that *chapattis* are moving around the country in a mysterious fashion, carried from village to village with some sort of instructions to keep their movement going. And the headman of Mylapore came to me only yesterday, asking whether he should comply with the instructions or ignore them. I just wanted to make sure these were the same as the others, and it is Ishmial's opinion that they are. There was a scrap of goat's meat cooked into one of them.'

'What is it all about?' I asked.

'I don't know—yet. It's a puzzle. They may have some religious significance, I suppose. But no one to whom they have been brought seems to know anything more of their origin or purpose than I do.'

'Well,' said Charles, rising, 'the chase was the thing this morning, whatever the cause of the *chapattis*. Never saw a boy run so quickly in my life before. Like greased lightning!'

So the matter was forgotten, soon overlaid in our attention by the appearance of Toddy-Bob with a bundle of letters he had collected in Lucknow. I received one from Wallace Avery that morning, I remember. Apart from a scrawled note at Christmas time, we had heard nothing from Connie, but I had not supposed she would prove an active correspondent. Wallace had written several times to me or Emily, the letters bearing the imprint of his facile, faintly pompous personality as clearly as his florid face. It was difficult to know just how much of what he said was to be believed, but Emily and Charles were glad to know that their cousins had settled in happily to their new station, that their bungalow was an improvement on the one they had occupied in Lucknow, and that little Johnny was much improved in health this winter. 'I very much hope,' he ended, 'that quite soon my Dear Old Lady and our boy will be on the good old briny on their way Home. Financial affairs in the house of Avery are looking up very well, and so I allow myself to hope that I will soon be able to afford their little trip!' But I did not allow myself to hope in his hope, and, as often before, wondered whether I should not, even now, reveal the whole unhappy affair to Charles and ask for his intercession on Connie's behalf. How gladly he would have helped; I was sure of that. And yet, and yet, it was not my business to reveal the affairs of Wallace to any third party; that much I had learnt the hard way! So I said nothing.

A few days later George Barry arrived to collect his wife and take part in the final great duck shoot of the season, bringing with him Major Henry Cussens, the 'Cussens' whom I had overheard talking with Oliver so long ago it seemed now on the Banqueting Hall verandah on the night of the Residency ball. His appearance at Hassanganj revived the feelings of chagrin and outraged pride that I had experienced that afternoon I visited his bungalow in Mariaon Cantonment; but only momentarily. I knew enough of Mr Erskine now to believe that, whatever his faults, indiscretion was not among them. Major Cussens, I was sure, knew nothing of that visit or its reason. He was a pleasantly mannered, quiet man, with a soldier's direct and simple view of life, and very soon I began to like him. It was restful to enjoy masculine companionship free of those undercurrents of too happy or too unhappy memory, embarrassment, regret or suspicion that marred my relationship with both Charles and Mr Erskine.

Invitations to the shoot had been despatched to various planters and officials in the vicinity of Hassanganj, and on this occasion the ladies were to partake of a picnic breakfast with the gentlemen when the latter had finished their sport.

The *jheel*, or swamp, whose denizens were to be decimated, was still in a state of almost primeval innocence, seldom having been disturbed by a shot and then only at long intervals. It amounted almost to a bird sanctuary, and I did not like the thought of the havoc which a dozen guns would wreak among duck so confident of their security as to be almost hand-tame. But, as Henry Cussens told me, it was for just such a massacre that the *jheel* was so jealously protected.

The ladies were to join the sportsmen at a reasonable hour for the picnic, but I was awake when our host, Charles, George and Major Cussens set off just before dawn and, slipping on a wrap, I went out on to my balcony above to watch them depart.

It was unexpectedly cold with the bone-biting cold of the Indian plain. Though there was yet no colour in the east, the sky had lightened and the few stars visible among the clouds were pale. The hour was the stillest and most silent of the twenty-four, the earth and all its creatures seeming to hold breath in anticipation of the sun's coming. No dog barked in the villages; no cattle lowed; no bird so much as rustled a feather; no wind stirred a leaf. Only the sky changed shade from grey to grey as cloud banked silently on cloud then scudded on, and the great sweep of the plain, featureless, motionless, soundless, spread away to merge into an invisible horizon.

In the deep quiet, small noises made by men and horses were muted. Hoof clinked against stone dully, voices were low, movements almost stealthy. Guns were apportioned to their bearers, ammunition pouches slung around shoulders, girths adjusted in almost total silence, so that, looking on from above, I could have thought I watched a shadow play. Figures were indistinct. Form merged with form and horse with man in the shadowed cold. I strained my eyes for Charles but recognized only Oliver, and he only by his bearing: the quick, decisive walk to his horse, the erect seat in the saddle, one hand on his hip, the ever-present hint of controlled impatience. I was irritated that it should have been he who stood out so clearly, but as I returned to my bed I admitted to myself that he usually did. He dominated any group he found himself in, but I had to acquit him of the charge of doing so consciously. It was his ingrained authority, a calm certainty of his own pre-eminence, and a self-confidence that exceeded conceit, which so singled him out for attention, and annoyed me quite irrationally.

When we ladies arrived at the *jheel* some hours later, the morning was still cold and lowering. 'A dandy day for the duck,' as Kate remarked. The sun was well up but lost in a sky as grey and flat as the pewter water below it. There was a sharp breeze now, and I was glad of my heavy cloak as we settled ourselves under a tree to wait while the breakfast was prepared and the men came in from the hides. The best of the sport was over, but shots still rang out in the morning calm, raising great flights of duck to skim against the clouds for a few moments, then alight again with a crackle of wings and a froth of spray in some other corner of the marsh.

'Stupid things!' observed Emily sourly—she did not care for early rising. 'You'd think they'd have the sense to keep on flying instead of wheeling back to the same place they've left.'

'If they had that much sense, there'd be no duck shooting, m'dear,' said Kate blandly. 'And then think of the misery of all our men!'

A covey of young boys from the nearest village, naked but for loincloths, retrieved the birds from the water as they fell. Shivering but cheerfully purposeful, they waded out into the cold, dirty water, and brought the still-fluttering birds ashore, where, with one dextrous turn of the wrist, the duck were dispatched, then thrown on to a heap of their fellows by the water's edge.

By ones and twos the men began to come in, some on foot, some rowing across the silver-speckled grey in dugout canoes: a couple of Army officers from a small station south of Hassanganj, the newly appointed Inspector of Police and his assistant, and the two McCrackens and Mr Baird who had spent Christmas with us. I wondered at the enthusiasm for slaughtering defenceless birds that could bring these men long distances at such an early hour, and then remembered that a Hassanganj shoot was considered an experience worth having even by the most discriminating *shikaris*. And certainly Oliver knew well how to cater to the creature comforts of his guests.

For some time, appetizing odours had issued from the grove of trees where the cook had established his headquarters, and when most of the party had gathered we made our way to the dining-room, another pleasant grove where a tablecloth had been laid over a tarpaulin and cushions ranged around it for seats. The same battery of servants who would have waited on us at Hassanganj served us now in the companionable babel of the Indian outdoors, while a troupe of inquisitive monkeys worked their way lower in the trees to watch us with many shrilled alarms from the young and grunts of irritation from the old until they were close enough for Emily to exclaim over the 'dear expression' on the face of one of the babies clinging to its mother's back. Small parrots, vivid green but for a band of red around the neck, shrieked and chattered in the higher branches, and small grey squirrels, with three black stripes on their backs, scolded all present impartially as they skittered up and down the rough trunks with the speed and grace of dragonflies.

The menu was more varied than we were used to at this early hour. Pilau and chicken curry, lamb cutlets and baked potatoes, cold beef, venison and salads, bread, hot scones and marmalade, tea and coffee. 'No bacon,' whispered Kate to me. 'The *Talukhdar* is a Mohammedan, d'you see.'

Although it was only ten in the morning, the long ride and the novelty of our situation had given me an appetite and I had no difficulty in disposing of most that was put before me, finding time as I ate to wonder at the ingenuity of the cook, who, from what I could see, had produced all this over a stove made of three flat stones fed with charcoal and dried cowpats.

The last to forsake their sport were Oliver himself and the *Talukhdar* of Nayanagar, who had shared a hide, the *Talukhdar* being the guest of honour and, so rumour averred, the worst shot. As they entered the grove, Oliver looking like a brigand in thigh-length boots and an extraordinary corduroy jacket patched with leather on the shoulder where his gun rested, with a bandolier slung around his chest and a battered felt hat on his head, I caught my breath in astonished recognition of his companion. For the plump dark gentleman, very conservatively dressed in European style, was one whom I had last seen clothed in full Oriental splendour: my friend Wajid Khan.

'I have already the pleasure of knowing Miss Hewitt,' he said, beaming, as Oliver commenced the introductions. 'And the honour! Indeed I may say we are in a sense related!' And he shook my hand with enthusiasm.

'Indeed? How is that?' Oliver motioned Mr Khan to a cushion on one side of me and seated himself on the other, giving me a keen glance as he did so. I fear I must have flushed, for I wanted no recital of my 'heroic' deed in the Lucknow bazaar in the present society.

'Can it be that you have not heard of what Miss Hewitt did for my son—how she saved his life?'

'Never a word! I must prevail upon you to tell me now, Wajid.'

'Oh, it caused a stir, I assure you, Oliver,' put in Emily from across the cloth. 'She was quite the heroine—for a few days—were you not, Laura?'

'It was nothing,' I said, blushing now with anger at Emily's jibing tone. 'I'll tell you some other time, but now let us hear what sport you and the *Talukhdar* have enjoyed!'

But it was useless. Oliver ignored me, as he had Emily, and Wajid Khan, chuckling at my discomfiture, told his story, while I fiddled with my cup and Oliver chewed on a chop bone in a suitably brigandish fashion.

'Hmph!' was his comment as his guest finished. 'Very interesting! And may I say how delighted I am that you should be … er … connected, Laura, to my old friend and neighbour, Wajid here. We have known each other since boyhood, and I can think of no one who would more faithfully serve you should the need arise.'

While Mr Khan showed the palms of his chubby hands and shook his head in silent self-depreciation, Oliver threw the chop bone over his shoulder, and with it dismissed my escapade as a subject for conversation.

'And now, Wajid, tell me something. What is the significance of these *chapattis* that are going round the villages in such a mysterious manner at the moment? You must know about them. Everyone knows of them and yet knows nothing about them.'

Awkwardly placed as I was to watch Mr Khan's face, I could see very distinctly the well-kept hands, lying on his broadcloth-covered knee, strain together convulsively as Oliver spoke. The question went unanswered for a moment. Mr Camp the policeman, who was sitting on the further side of Mr Khan, looked up with sudden interest.

'I ... I do not know the significance,' said Mr Khan after an appreciable pause. 'I have seen nothing of them, but yes, I too have heard that some such matters as passing *chapattis*, some say also goat's flesh, from village to village, is spoken of.'

'Always five of 'em in my district,' put in Mr Camp. 'I believe some instructions are given with them in the passing, but what I do not know.'

'I know.' Oliver spoke conclusively. 'He who receives them must bake five more, then take the new ones to the boundaries of his village, where he must deliver them to the watchman of the next, with instructions to do the same in his turn.'

'Curious,' said Mr Camp.

'Perhaps,' suggested Wajid Khan, 'it is nothing more than the transference of some omen, some charm. This I have known before. Ignorant peoples will do such things without even knowing why!'

'Yes, that's possible all right,' agreed Oliver, 'but this time there seems to me something purposeful behind it. It is all too thorough, too organized, to be the work of some *sadhu* sitting under a peepul tree in Benares. It is more as though it's a trial of some sort—perhaps a competition?'

'Like Pass the Thimble?' I volunteered. 'Who can get rid of them quickest, you mean?'

'Possibly. But to what end, God knows!'

'I have heard of a similar thing in the olden days, when men wished to measure the time taken to pass a message—in wars and troubled times and so on,' said Mr Khan.

'Have you?' Oliver looked up from his pilau and curry. 'Yes, that might explain it. It might be an excellent method of ensuring the quick passage of information—a warning perhaps. Provided you could count on there being no interruption to the service, that is.'

'I had come across them before I left Dacca,' said Camp. 'So the practice is widespread already. Was talking to a feller from the Punjab at one of the *dak*-bungalows on the way up, and he knew all about 'em too.'

'Yes,' said Oliver. 'Yes, very widespread, and they are travelling irrespective of religion or caste, in itself a strange thing.'

'I cannot know,' said Wajid Khan, still clasping and unclasping his fingers. 'We have too much trouble these days; let us hope that this passing of *chapattis* does not bring more. But often these strange things that happen in the villages do bring us trouble. I do not know.'

'There is an incantation that goes with them,' Oliver went on thoughtfully. ' "From the East to the West. From the North to the South." Just that. Have you heard of that too, Wajid?'

'I have heard. But what can be the meaning of such words?'

'A signal? A warning? A preparation, perhaps?'

'And perhaps nothing of those sorts. That also is possible,' countered Mr Khan.

That night, when the last of the guests had departed and we were thinking of our beds, the question of the mysterious *chapattis* again came up. The shooting party had remained to dine with us, so Oliver had not bade us goodnight and left us early as he usually did, but had played the host most cordially all evening, and then rejoined us in the drawing-room after seeing his guests depart, each with his entourage of groom, lantern carriers and bodyguard. A band of *dacoits*, those murdering robbers of the Indian countryside, were active in the region, so the stalwart retainers, with loaded shotguns in their saddle-holsters, performed more than a merely picturesque function, and the gentlemen, with the exception of Wajid Khan, had made no secret of the relief with which they buckled on their pistol belts as they left.

'Hmph!' grunted Oliver as he took his place with his back to the fire, monopolizing the warmth in that peculiarly selfish way men have. 'I don't care for mystery. And I'm mystified!'

'What about?' asked Henry Cussens without much interest, stifling a yawn.

'Our friend the *Talukhdar* of Nayanagar, Laura's esteemed relation.' He smiled at me.

'And what has he done to mystify you?'

'That is what I wonder. Also, how much does he really know?'

'Ah, this business of the peregrinating *chapattis*.'

'Precisely!'

'I think he knows more than he pretends to,' I volunteered.

'Oh, and what makes you think that?' Oliver's tone of voice was interrogative, not derisive, but Major Cussens's brows went up in amusement as I spoke.

'I was sitting beside him when you mentioned the *chapattis* this morning. I could not see his face, but saw him suddenly clasp his fingers together, almost in alarm, it seemed to me.'

'Yes, I saw it too. And we have come to the same conclusion. What I would like to know is not only what he is hiding, but why he is hiding it.'

'I thought you knew him well.'

'As well as an Indian will ever allow an *Angrezi* to know him. Which isn't much to go by! One of his estates borders mine to the south. When we were lads, we used to go hawking together, shooting, hunting *muggar* in the rivers—all the normal things boys do together. His father was the principal thorn in my grandfather's flesh in those days, a murdering, marauding, unscrupulous old *badmash* if ever there was one, but never an enemy, understand! Poor nervous, timorous Wajid must have been a severe disappointment to the old rogue.'

'When did you first come across the *chapattis*?' asked Henry Cussens.

'A couple of weeks ago—from Ishmial. Then one of my headmen told me he had received some with instructions to pass them on, and asked me what he should do about them.'

'What did you say to that?'

'Told him to follow the instructions—pass them on!'

'Surely that was unwise,' protested the Major. 'You don't know what they mean. As you said yourself this morning, they could be a warning, a threat, perhaps even an incitement of some sort. Surely you should have told the man to destroy them.'

'That would have been useless. Even if he had obeyed me, there are countless others who would not. As it is, I learnt the words that accompany them, and have the assurance of any more information if and when the man comes by it.'

'Yes, it's a strange thing. Very strange,' said George Barry in his slow, deep voice. 'They are travelling about in the native lines too, y'know. If, as Wajid suggested, it is a method of relating distance to time, then perhaps they have discovered a most efficient posting system, for use in some future emergency?'

'Yes. But I believe Henry was nearer it when he mentioned a warning, or even an incitement.'

'And how have you deduced that?' Cussens was amused, perhaps even a little patronizing, a fact marked by Oliver.

'Because I am forced to live in the world I find myself in,' he returned with irritation. 'I hear things; I see things; sometimes I learn certain facts. I try to relate these, all these unrelated, or seemingly unrelated things, to reality—not to my own preconceived opinions. I know I cannot expect you to agree with my deductions, Henry. As one of Her Majesty's officers, you find a great deal of what I believe is going on at the moment too absurd to be taken seriously, I know. But I also know that you have become aware, during these last few months, of a change in attitude among even your own sepoys.'

'That's to be expected,' Major Cussens returned equably. 'Of course there is some dissatisfaction with the consequences of annexation, the suspension of privileges and so on. But that is understandable under the circumstances. Things will shake down in due course, as they have elsewhere. Just give 'em time.'

'What makes you so confident that time is ours to give?' Oliver asked, then continued: 'And the sepoy is not the only discontented man in India at the moment. Do you think the *talukhdars*, the men like Wajid Khan, are happy at their loss of power, privilege and income? That they can see our handling of their affairs as anything else but arbitrary, overriding and unjust? Most of all unjust! One of them, in particular, is a gentleman not to be trifled with, and I believe he has recently been on a long journey.'

'The Maulvi of Fyzabad?' put in George Barry.

'Yes. Aman-Ullah, Maulvi of Fyzabad.'

'A troublemaker, a fanatic, a bazaar lawyer—nothing more!' said Cussens contemptuously.

'He is a troublemaker. And perhaps a fanatic. But he is many things beside, some of them admirable, make no mistake. He is clever, unscrupulous, courageous; and, above all, a born leader. He is rebellious with his lot and has good reason to be.'

'And what has he to do with this business of the *chapattis*?'

'My guess is, perhaps everything. He is an intelligent and complex man. This seemingly mysterious passing up and down the country of a handful of unleavened bread, coming from who-knows-where, going who-knows-where, this is the sort of thing which Aman-Ullah would promote to bring disquiet to the ignorant mind. Perhaps the bread has some actual and decipherable significance for a few people in the know. More probably it is simply a method of fomenting suspicion, doubt, fear—a sort of sowing of the wind. We are agreed, are we not, that Wajid Khan knows more than he was prepared to tell us? Well, perhaps it is not without significance that one of his several estates adjoins that of the Maulvi outside Fyzabad!'

'You think Wajid Khan …?' I left my surmise unfinished.

'I'm not in a position to think anything about him, but I'll wager he could explain a lot of inexplicable happenings, if he cared to. He is a conventional, a most circumspect man, not fond of playing with fire. If he knows what is going on, I think it more than likely that every other landowner in the kingdom has the same information.'

'A conspiracy?' suggested George, without astonishment.

'Let us say an expectation.'

'Inflammatory nonsense, old boy!' said Major Cussens with decision. 'You have lived too long alone among these *wallahs* out here. You've lost your sense of proportion. Need a break—at Home!'

My day had started with the sight of dim figures below me riding away, unidentified, into the darkness. It ended in the same way.

I had formed the habit of opening my window when the night was fine and spending a few moments in the fresh air on my balcony before retiring. That night the great panorama of the snows was visible, the overcast sky of the morning had cleared, and a young sickle moon threw a timid glow over the splendid silver peaks. As I stood and admired them, wishing, as always, for a nearer view, three figures emerged from the darkness below me: Oliver Erskine, Major Cussens and a small native wrapped in a cotton sheet that glimmered in the light of a lantern he carried. Oliver and Cussens were talking in their normal voices but, because of the distance, I could not make out all they said. A few phrases came to me, however, as, making no secret of my presence, I leant over the balustrade.

'... surely unnecessary! But if you feel you must...' said Major Cussens.

'Better soon than late, better late than never perhaps. It can do no harm for them to be aware. Old Buggins is a bounder, but he relies on me in this part of the country. Now he must make of it what he will. I have done my part.'

'It will go into one of the endless reports he is preparing for Lawrence, and be forgotten!'

'Probably, but that is his affair, not mine.'

Just then Toddy-Bob appeared, mounted and leading another horse by the rein. Oliver passed a package of some sort to the small, white-clad native, who sprang up to the saddle of the spare horse with surprising agility and, after a few words from Oliver, touched his bare heels to the horse's flanks and moved away with Toddy-Bob behind him.

'... reliable?' asked Major Cussens, as he and Oliver turned away.

'Absolutely and unquestionably,' replied Oliver with decision.

'Well—a long day, and a good one,' he grunted. 'I'm for my bed. You?'

'Better things!'

They laughed together in the comradely fashion that I had first heard at the Residency ball. I seemed fated to eavesdrop on their conversations, I thought to myself with amusement. Perhaps it was that reflection that sent a fleeting memory of the content of that first overheard conversation through my head. What was it Oliver Erskine had said that night? Something about women—yes, 'But when women are killed, it is massacre, murder and mayhem!'

The two men chatted together for a few moments longer, then Major Cussens slapped Oliver on the shoulder and entered the verandah below me. Oliver looked after him for a moment, then turned and set off briskly across the garden towards the park. I watched his quick, easy stride with something like admiration. But surely he had had sufficient exercise for one day without taking a bedtime stroll?

CHAPTER 8

The Barrys and Major Cussens returned to Lucknow a couple of days later. The men preferred to ride, so Kate sat alone in the carriage but for the produce of Hassanganj that she was taking with her; it filled the well of the carriage and ranged along the opposite seat, vegetables and fruit and the roots of shrubs she had admired, rounds of spiced Hunter's Beef from the Hassanganj kitchen, duck, quail and partridge (bound to be 'well-hung' by the time they were eaten) and the skin of a spotted deer, still hard and rather smelly, that Charles had shot and presented to her for her bedroom floor. Her high boots rested on a netted bag full of pineapples, and her bright blue eyes were tearful as she bade us goodbye. 'Come back to Lucknow—soon!' she said to me. 'George and I don't like all this talk of trouble, and this place is too isolated if anything should happen, woman dear. And Emily, she should be nearer to civilization at a time like this. Sure, and don't I know I'm a worrying old woman, and don't I know that you couldn't be in better hands than Oliver's, but really now, George and I will be anxious till you get back to the city and we can keep an eye on you ourselves.' I nodded, but had no opportunity to reassure her, for Emily crowded into the window frame to give her a final kiss in her turn.

The big house was very quiet and dull when they had gone, and I found myself nervous of being left alone all day with Charles and Emily. Kate's presence had provided a bulwark for us all against too great, too painful perhaps, an intimacy. Even on those rare occasions when Charles and I had found ourselves alone together, we had listened unconsciously for the quick tap of her boot-heels, or the hurried appearance of her black-bonneted, uncrinolined form round the corner of the house. Her presence acted, I suppose, like a beneficent conscience; she expected only the best from us all, and so we gave it. Now there would be nothing to control the irritation and ill-humour produced by frustration, misunderstandings, old grudges and even the lack of physical well-being. Emily grew heavier by the day and by the day more crossly conscious of her bulk and clumsiness; without the patient Kate to forestall her wants and run her errands, I knew I would be most tried by her fretfulness and lack of consideration. Now that we were alone, I could foresee an Emily less good-natured, less apparently contented than she had been since our arrival in Hassanganj. I had often wondered at this unusual mood of hers. 'Och, but of course she's content,' Kate had said when I mentioned it to her. 'Isn't she carrying a child then, and isn't that enough to make any woman content?' But I knew otherwise. The few outbursts of temper Emily had allowed herself had always been connected in some way with the unwanted child.

Yet she was uninterested in a return to Lucknow or our contemplated journey to the hills. It was enough for her, for the present, to bustle about the house in her apron, rattling the enormous bunch of keys, and at the end of a well-planned meal to earn the commendation of our host.

'Dissham will seem very small and ... well, unimportant after all this, won't it, Laura?' she observed one morning as we sat sewing on the verandah.

'I don't think so. Dissham is real. This is just a rather exotic interlude, for all of us. It will be pleasant to look back on, of course.'

'Perhaps it won't be only an interlude—for Charles and me, anyway.'

'If you are thinking of old Mrs Flood's hopes for Charles and Hassanganj, I should forget about it. It doesn't look to me as though Oliver has any intention of sharing his inheritance with anyone.'

'But he will have to think of the future. He's not young, even now, and he can't last for ever. It's not likely that he will marry now, specially as he spends so much time out here in the *mofussil* and doesn't seem to care for the companionship of ladies, anyway ... even though he is always so considerate of us.'

'There's still time for him to change his mind about many things. He can't be much more than forty.'

'Oh, he's only thirty-six—Charles knows. But what does age matter when he lives as he does?'

'Well, perhaps. But don't count on it,' I muttered. 'Many a woman has married a plainer face for the sake of a smaller fortune, remember!'

'How many women would be willing to spend their lives out here, without neighbours, or society, or ... anything?'

'Well, I wouldn't say it's without anything,' I countered judiciously. 'A wife might change his tastes, though I think it unlikely, and anyway, look at you, you seem to be quite content out here?'

'Yes.' She thought about it for a moment. 'Yes, I am. I hadn't thought of that, and of course if one were married to him ...'

'Heaven preserve the woman!' I said laughingly.

'Why do you still dislike him?'

'I don't! Honestly! There are things about him, some things, that I positively admire. I don't dislike him—now. He's admirable in some ways. Impossible in others!'

'Very like you, in fact,' she announced, unexpectedly, with an elderly sniff. 'Perhaps that is why you find him so difficult to get on with. You know you can't pull the wool over his eyes.'

'Emily Flood!' I was as much surprised as indignant. 'That's very nearly an insult. There is absolutely no similarity of character between Mr Erskine and myself.'

'But there is—or anyway I think there is. You both always think you are right, only you, Laura, are not as often right as he is, and you are both always, well, active and energetic—and full of opinions—though he is not as free with them as you are. But he has them, and sometimes when you are expressing some of yours, he looks at you as though he knows exactly what you are going to say. And finds it amusing too!'

'Indeed! I have never observed it.'

'Now don't take offence, for goodness sake! You still tend to treat me as a child, and I'm not. I ... I've done things, experienced things, and feelings, that you know nothing about, and when I show you I am not a child any longer, you get annoyed. And that's something too: I expect I've always found it so easy to like, really like, Oliver because he has always treated me as ... well as a woman. And I *am*!'

'Oh Lord!' I said inelegantly.

For a while we were silent, each occupied with her own thoughts.

The morning was warm and still. Rajah, the patriarch of the peacocks, stretched his neck, uttered his ugly cry and then set off in pursuit of one of his hens pecking peacefully further away on the lawn. A couple of hoopoes, disturbed by his impetuous progress, hopped a couple of feet into the air and returned to earth with their crests fanned out in alarm. A dove called in the neem trees edging the lawn, and the axle of a Persian well creaked and squealed monotonously.

'What does Charles think of his chances here in Hassanganj?' I asked curiously.

'Oh, Charles! Of course he sees it as inevitable—because he wants it. Especially now that he is accompanying Oliver on his visits to the villages and so on. Haven't you noticed how he tries to talk knowledgeably about things he comes across—and makes such a fool of himself? Perhaps if he made his interest in the estate a little less obvious, or anyway the reason for his interest, he'd have a better chance. But I expect Oliver is really laughing up his sleeve at him all the time. It humiliates me so. Charles is so ... unintelligent about things!'

'But do you think he would really like to live out here, for good, I mean? How would he like the life and the work, if he knew there was no alternative?'

'I don't know. He doesn't talk to me much about it. I expect he'd be happy enough so long as Oliver was around to ... well, show him the ropes ... hold his hand, more or less. But I can't imagine him out here running this huge place on his own. Can you?'

'I believe it would suit him better than your father's business.'

'Undoubtedly. But could he manage it?'

'Perhaps you underestimate him?'

'Oh, you've always seen more in Charles than there really is!'

'Perhaps you don't see enough?'

'I've seen more than enough! Believe me, I've seen much more than enough!' And with that Emily bundled up her sewing, got to her feet with an effort, and went inside as hurriedly as her condition would permit.

It was towards the end of March that Oliver announced he would be away from Hassanganj for three days collecting rents in outlying villages and inspecting the progress of a new road he was building.

'Would you care to come, Charles?' he asked. 'We'll be roughing it, of course. Hard riding all day, hard sleeping all night. No comforts and no company but mine.'

'By Jove, I'd like nothing better! A chance to really get to grips with things,' answered Charles with a show of enthusiasm that I suddenly saw was a little too patent.

'Good!' said Oliver, one eyebrow twitching very slightly. 'Bring the minimum—but don't forget your gun. It will be your job to supply the stewpot at night. And be ready to leave at six.'

'Tomorrow? It's nearly eleven now!'

'Tomorrow! Your preparations should not take long.'

I got up early to pour the tea for the men's *chota hazri*, and was just in time to watch the departure of the camping equipment, laden on two bullock-carts and accompanied by the usual retinue of *chaprassis*, gun-bearers, cooks, bearers, water-carriers and grass-cutters.

Toddy-Bob had checked the gear twice over: tents, folding beds, chairs and tables, crockery, cutlery and cookware, big storm lanterns, guns and ammunition, bedding rolls, pitchers and bowls, and (for Oliver) a small, three-drawer military chest to serve as dresser, desk and strong-box.

An elaborate idea of 'no comforts' I thought to myself as the carts lumbered away.

There still remained a dozen men in the Hassanganj livery, mounted, armed and with swords in their belts, waiting for Oliver and Charles to set off. They were the bodyguard and would accompany Oliver, the newly collected rents, and Ishmial (who carried the money) wherever they went—a disquieting reminder to me of Rohilla raiders, *dacoits* and the uncertain temper of the times. Toddy-Bob, to his evident disgust, was to remain behind and take charge of the ladies' comfort.

'If there is anything you need, just let Tod know,' instructed Oliver as he swung to the saddle. 'And, by the way, later in the morning he will deliver a little surprise to Emily, a governess cart I came across in the coachhouse the other day. It's being cleaned up and painted, and Tod has found a pony for it. Just something to pass the time, while Charles is away.' And he looked directly at me in a manner I did not like.

'How nice! She'll be delighted. Have a good journey,' I said coldly, and went indoors without bothering to wave them away.

That was the first really hot morning of the summer. Emily and I tried to sew on the verandah as usual, but our palms got sticky with sweat and the thread so tangled and the material so grubby that we soon gave it up. While Kate had been with us, we had sometimes taken our work out to the fernery, but the heat brought out snakes and Oliver warned that such damp and shady spots were especially attractive to the horrid creatures. Characteristically, he had not warned us against using the fernery; only told us what to expect if we did. So we had stopped going there.

The governess cart was duly delivered and Emily was duly pleased.

'Beast's too big for it really, ma'am. Ought to 'ave one of them little Shetlers, the shaggy ones, but they don't do so good out 'ere—too 'ot!' said Toddy-Bob as we examined the neat little white-painted equipage.

'Oh, not at all! She's a dear little mare. She'll do just perfectly. Bring it around this evening, Toddy. I'll try it then. It's too hot to be out just now.'

'Yes'm,' said Toddy without emotion, and led the mare away.

'He couldn't be more thoughtful and kind,' Emily said softly, a faraway expression in her eyes. 'He must have realized walking has become too much of an effort for me now, especially in the heat. He said nothing, just did something. That's so like him!'

After that, each morning after breakfast and again in the late afternoon Emily took a drive in her new toy. She named the mare Olive. I looked forward to my host's expression on his learning this.

The following three days were difficult ones for me, thrown together with Emily and alone with her in the vast, silent house. Apart from Mount Bellew and our family, there was almost no topic of conversation we could touch on that did not endanger the inner comfort of one or the other. The heat exhausted Emily and she slept a lot, while I wandered between the verandah and the library looking for a book that would keep my mind engaged. It was not boredom I suffered from so much as restlessness, a thorough dissatisfaction with my own company, an unformed but insistent need for something I could not name. It was a mood new to me. I put it down to the heat and the silence in the house, and did my best not to give in to it, but I was relieved when the afternoon of the third day at last arrived.

When we had taken our tea, Emily went off in her governess cart with Toddy-Bob walking sedately beside her. I fetched my sketching block and pencils and set out to walk to a distant part of the park where stood a fine group of trees which I wanted to 'catch' wearing their long evening shadows.

My way led me behind the house, past the stables and servants' quarters and to the east of the walled vegetable garden. Here the park opened out and, because of its comparative distance from the house, was rather more unkept than other parts of the grounds. I had not often come this way before—other reaches afforded pleasanter prospects and easier walking—but had once observed a tall building just visible among the trees that formed the boundary of the park. I had mentioned it to Oliver, asking him what it was. 'That,' he had answered briefly, 'oh, that's all that is left of the old hunting lodge, the Nawab's hunting lodge. Probably used it as a watchtower, though they might have kept their hawks in it.'

Now, glimpsing it in the distance, I decided to have a closer look at the place and then return to my trees, by which time the light would be just what I needed. To my left, as I walked on through the unscythed grass, stood the icehouses in their grove of sheltering shade trees. Actually they were three deep pits, thickly thatched, where ice, formed in shallow earthenware saucers during the cold months of the year, was stored for use in the hot weather. It was an ingenious and remarkably efficient system, and I thought admiringly of the Moguls, those slant-eyed sons of the high plateaux of Central Asia, who relieved the rigours of the land they conquered by planting gardens where the play of water rivalled the beauty of the flowers, and devised this method of cooling the sherbet they were so fond of drinking. Now, more than two hundred years later, when the *abdar* poured our wine from a frosted, napkin-wrapped bottle, we never paused to comment.

As I sauntered past the hive-like structures, a small figure detached itself from the trees and came boldly towards me. It was little Yasmina, whom I was now accustomed to meeting in the park, though never in the gardens. She was a sociable mite and, though communication was limited, we had managed to establish a sort of friendship. She took my free hand and together we wandered on towards the tall building. She was in the habit of talking when with me, and I enjoyed listening to her and trying to make out what she was saying. Now, as we approached our objective, I was surprised to hear her repeat several times, in a proprietorial tone, the words '*Mehra ghar*,' or 'My house,' and I wondered what fanciful playworld she lived in that made this curious edifice seem desirable as a home.

The structure, I now saw, was a hexagonal tower, gracefully proportioned and built of the same pinkish sandstone as Hassanganj. It was, however, of a much earlier date, and the suggestion of strength and dignity in its lines made me think it a remnant of those old Mogul times I had so recently recalled. The window apertures were filled with delicate stone trelliswork, and from their positioning I surmised the building contained three floors. I had expected a ruin, but it was in reasonably good repair; from where we stood no door was visible, but Yasmina, tugging impatiently at my hand, led me round the base of the tower to an entrance, and then I found that it was indeed her home. Chattering in delighted excitement, she led me up a couple of shallow steps into a room doubly dark in contrast to the mellow late sunlight we had just abandoned.

I stood still for a moment while my eyes adjusted to the dimness. The room was stone-paved and bare of furniture; only a few copper pots, burnished to a rosy glow, hung on one wall and stood piled in a corner.

An elderly woman squatted on the floor before an iron brazier preparing the evening meal. The rhythmic slap of her palms shaping the dough into *chapattis* ceased abruptly as she looked up and saw me against the light of the doorway.

'*Baba*!' she exclaimed, scrambling to her feet and dropping the dough into a pan. 'Aie! Aie! Yasmina!'

I thought she was going to strike the child, but Yasmina faced her squarely, not flinching. I almost laughed at the defiance implicit in every line of her small body, though I could understand that the woman had probably been anxious for her errant charge, and relief had been expressed, as it often is, in wrath.

'*Thik hai*,' I said, glad that my Hindustani was at least adequate to this elementary reassurance. But the woman could not agree with me that things were now 'All right', for she began to wring her hands and called out: '*Mem—Mem hai!*' in a high, disturbed voice.

I had guessed from Yasmina's manner that the woman was not her mother and now, as I wondered why my presence should cause such consternation, a figure glided swiftly down the unrailed stone staircase that followed the curve of the walls to the upper storeys, paused for a moment, and then came towards me. Yasmina dropped my hand and went to the newcomer. '*Merha Ma*' she announced proudly by way of introduction.

Her mother was about my age, but small, slim and graceful. She was dressed in the baggy pyjamas and shirt of Mohammedan womanhood, and her glistening black hair hung down her back in a long braid finished with cotton tassels. From a small face, whose features were delicate and regular, enormous velvet eyes, very like Yasmina's, gazed at me with an expression so full of malevolence that instinctively I stepped back towards the open door.

It was like a slap in the face.

'What is it?' I asked in bewilderment, as she stood and looked at me with unveiled hatred, and the other woman continued to mutter and wring her hands so that the glass bangles on her wrists jangled. 'What is it? I have only brought Yasmina back to you!' And I gestured towards the child.

At this her mother picked the child up and thrust her into the servant's arms, as if to save her from some awful danger. Then she turned on me, and what she said I could not know, but a torrent of words fell from her lips and she clasped her fists as though she would indeed like to strike me.

Quite bewildered by this unduly warm reception, I shrugged my shoulders and was about to leave them to whatever mistaken impressions they laboured under, when a voice rang out from the upper room.

It spoke in Hindustani, but the tone conveyed very adequately the sense of the words: 'What the devil is that infernal din about?'

His appearance on the stairs a second later was hardly necessary to make known to me the presence of Oliver Erskine.

For a moment we regarded each other in silence. The women too fell quiet and Yasmina hushed her crying.

Then I understood.

I felt the blood mounting to my face, and in a maelstrom of embarrassment and chagrin, I turned and fled into the evening sunlight. As I stumbled down the steps, my sketchbook dropped from under my arm, but I would not pause to retrieve it and, gathering up my skirts, I ran.

CHAPTER 9

Safe in my room, I locked the door and threw myself face down on the high brass bedstead. I had to produce some order in the tumult of my mind before I could face my relatives or Oliver Erskine. I had to determine what course to take, what attitude to adopt, how to conduct myself now that I was party to this secret side of Mr Erskine's life. I had also to face the fact that I was more shocked, indeed alarmed, by my discovery than any young woman of four-and-twenty had the right to be. After all, such 'arrangements', as I knew from Kate, were not uncommon in India. Or elsewhere, for that matter, I reminded myself honestly. Happily Mount Bellew never knew it, but after my mother's death, a succession of plump and pretty young 'aunts' resided in our rambling Genoese villa, invited, so Father said, to make 'us' comfortable; and had not our Italian neighbours danced at my father's wedding just three months before the birth of my short-lived little half-brother? I, of all people, had no right to behave like an outraged schoolgirl.

But what was I to do? Tell Charles of my discovery and ask him to take us away? How could I? It was too delicate a matter to broach with a gentleman, and there was also a hint of tale-telling that I did not like. And if I told him and he did decide to leave, it would be the end of all his hopes (imaginary though they might be) of inheriting Hassanganj. There was also the indubitable fact that men take a much more lenient view of such matters than women. He might even refuse to believe my suspicions regarding his brother. Not that it was a mere suspicion in my mind. I had discovered Oliver Erskine practically in the arms of his native mistress, and he must now know that I realized all the implications of his presence in that secluded tower with the beautiful Mohammedan girl and Yasmina. Recalling the expression on his face as he had looked down at me in the dim room, I blushed anew. No shame! No embarrassment! Merely irritation followed by a look of quizzical enquiry, and I was almost sure I heard him laugh as I ran down the steps and the sketchbook fell from my hand.

Then again, if I were to divulge my knowledge to Charles and he decided not to leave Hassanganj my position would be doubly difficult. Better to hold my tongue. Much better.

My windows overlooked the back of the house and below me now I could hear the minor babel of noise that always breaks out when a group of Indians are engaged in a common task. They must be unloading the bullock-carts, I thought, and putting away the camping equipment. Charles must have returned earlier with Oliver, or had Mr Erskine, starved for the embrace of his paramour after only three days' absence, hastened back alone? This thought was not one I chose to entertain, so again I turned my mind to my own problems: what now should be my attitude to my host when next I met him?

I would have liked to show outrage; enjoyed being indignant. But common sense indicated that if I could not disclose the matter to my relatives any marked change in my manner towards Mr Erskine would need explanation. In any case, I was sure that he himself would be quite unperturbed by my disapproval. Lying hot and sticky in the unlit room, I devised furious schemes for his discomfiture; only after some time spent in this fruitless pursuit did I ask myself why it was so necessary for me to wound him? Because he had hurt me? I discarded the suggestion. He was in no position to hurt me. I cared nothing for him and had known of his reputation with women before ever I had met him. Because he had embarrassed me, then? Yes, that was it! He had embarrassed me and I had not even managed to disconcert him!

To find I was still capable of honesty with myself restored me to a measure of equanimity. The crux of the matter lay in the ridiculous fashion in which I had bolted out of the tower—like a scared rabbit—and I still could not think of any less precipitate alternative. One does not attempt small-talk on such occasions. However, I acknowledged to myself that I was ashamed of my undignified retreat, annoyed that my embarrassment had been so obvious, and above all angry that any man's behaviour could make me look a fool even in my own eyes. But such, I assured myself sternly, was the case. Now it behoved me to recover my self-respect by showing Oliver Erskine that I possessed sufficient *sang froid* to behave as though nothing untoward had happened!

So, after much inner turmoil, I came to the simple determination to act towards him as I had always done, with, of course, private and stringent reservations regarding his character.

I unlocked my door, and allowed Bhunjni to summon the *bhisti* with my bathwater. By the time the gong sounded for dinner, I was refreshed and ready for the rigours of the evening.

The others were already seated when I slipped into my chair at the long candlelit table, and I was conscious that, despite my resolution, I found it hard to meet the eyes of my host. Not that he suffered from a similar inhibition; he was giving Emily an account of the tour, while Charles, sunburnt and obviously tired, added a word of explanation from time to time. A fire, Mr Erskine said, had destroyed a prime stand of sal trees at his northern boundary; Rohilla raiders, he suspected. A gang of *dacoits* had murdered a *bunnia* in one of his villages and cut off the noses of his womenfolk, but since the man was a notorious moneylender, he had probably deserved his death. The eastern canal banks had been breached and water stolen by a neighbouring *zemindar*, and this last was the only matter which he was inclined to take seriously. He would have to place guards along the canal since, with the hot weather upon us, his villagers could not afford to lose their water.

'So on the whole it was a successful tour?' Emily congratulated him, using the matronly tone usual to her when sitting at the head of the Hassanganj table.

'If success is measuring the extent of one's misfortunes.'

'But surely it is as well to know the worst, and there is nothing you cannot deal with after all?'

'As to that, I am not so sure!'

'Come now, Oliver,' put in Charles. 'What is there you cannot put to rights on this estate? From what I've seen, your powers are almost absolute, as are your resources and your knowledge!'

'I can only smooth the smaller difficulties, believe me. I am impotent to deal with my real enemies. I cannot avert a famine, or stop the smallpox. I cannot outlaw cholera or do away with poverty.' He spoke morosely, crumbling a slice of bread in his thin brown fingers. 'But above and beyond these perennial disasters, I believe we are on the edge of another, a new one, and while I was away I had news of something that may well push us over the brink.'

'Is it this trouble among the natives that everyone is discussing?'

'Not so much the natives, Emily, as the native sepoys, and, since few families in my villages are not in some way dependent upon the earnings of the sepoys, I fear that we will be affected by any trouble coming.'

'Is it those strange *chapattis* again?'

'No, or not directly anyway. It's this business of the new cartridges. You already know about them. I did not realize until this week how generally known the story is, nor how seriously it has been taken by the sepoys.'

He fell silent and abstractedly balanced a knife on the edge of a glass.

'As a race,' he continued quietly, 'we seem to be curiously intent on devising our own downfall in India.'

'Everyone makes mistakes!' objected Charles impatiently.

'Yes, everyone makes mistakes, and the wise learn from them. The British in India have not done so. Look—no, please listen to me for a moment'—as Charles broke in again. 'In less than ten years the Company has acquired territories in India equal to more than three times the area of England—by conquest, by chicanery, and latterly by annexation. Oh, of course it was always necessary! Aggrandizement, whether personal or national, can always be justified by necessity, can it not? We tell ourselves complacently that the provinces and principalities we have so acquired are now better administered, more justly ruled, more productively employed than they ever were under their native rulers. This is probably true. I hold no brief for the general run of native princelings and petty rajahs but, whatever their deficiencies, they belonged to the people, were of the people in a way no Company official or Resident can ever hope to be. In deposing these rulers we have not only created a vast discontent among the plain people, but among those we have dethroned are some who will be anxious and able to act as leaders when trouble comes. All that has been needed has been the spark to set the tinder blazing. And I think now we have provided just this spark—in this incident of the cartridges!'

He paused again. Emily was all attention, but Charles played with his salt in boredom as we waited for the next course.

'The irony is that the cartridges themselves have been withdrawn and I am told that only a limited number were issued, let alone used by the sepoys. None the less the damage has been done. I believe that we have managed to supply the aggrieved people of this country with the one thing that can unify them against us—an injury that affects all castes and creeds to the same extent and will inflame them equally. When one remembers the diversity of beliefs and loyalties existing in India, this is in itself quite an achievement. Almost, one might say, an inspiration!'

'You have just said the Army are the ones concerned,' pointed out Charles, 'and now you are talking of the whole country.'

'It has started in the Army and so far is confined to the Army. But will it stop there?'

'What do you expect to happen?' asked Charles resignedly. I could see it was not a subject that interested him much.

'I have no idea. I am only convinced that the trouble is more far-reaching, goes much deeper, than the authorities are yet prepared to admit. I would go so far as to say that matters are coming to a head. And rapidly. A secondary purpose of my tour was to try to estimate the temper of the people and to judge the reliability of certain, well... rumours and reports that have come to my ears. I have not been reassured by what I have discovered.'

Charles was no longer bored.

'Are we—the Europeans, I mean—going to be implicated, would you say?'

'Naturally!'

'But then—why, there's Emily to be thought of! She must run no risks.'

'I don't believe we need fear for our personal safety out here. Unless, of course, matters take a more dramatic turn than I foresee, or the authorities in Calcutta bungle things again.'

'But really, Oliver, if there is any risk at all, I cannot allow Emily to remain here. It would be criminal. I don't want to play the coward, but perhaps we would be wise to leave while the going is good.'

'Go Home you mean?'

'Of course.'

'By ship? With a woman far gone in pregnancy? And in this heat?'

Charles paled beneath the sunburn and Emily blushed. Though long evident to every eye, her impending motherhood had never been mentioned openly, let alone before an unmarried male. I believe I was the only member of the party to retain my normal complexion, for even Oliver was flushed with irritation and wine.

'I suppose you are right,' Charles admitted grudgingly. 'But then what are we to do?'

'Stay here for the present and see how the wind blows.'

'We had intended to return to Lucknow in a fortnight's time. These roads are so execrable, it would be foolish to delay here after that. Emily's ... condition makes it imperative for us to remove to Lucknow very shortly.'

'If trouble comes, Lucknow will be its focus! Not only because it was the seat of the Nawabs of Oudh but because of the military concentrated in and around it. I would advise you to stay on here for as long as possible.'

'But. Emily must have a doctor and a good midwife. My wife is not a barbarian that she should give birth to her first child unattended.'

'A lot of women have to! But that's beside the point. If I am not being too brutal, Emily, may I ask when the event is expected?'

'The end of May,' Emily replied in a small voice.

'I see.' Oliver was thoughtful. 'It gets very hot here by the end of April, as it does in Lucknow. Would you not consider going directly to the hills?'

'But the journey?'

'Yes, the journey will be longer, but if you make it by palanquin, and by easy stages, it should not be any more trying than travelling to Lucknow by carriage. You will like my little bungalow in Mussoorie, Emily, and the town can provide all the facilities you need.'

'Charles?'

Emily looked at her husband, who remained dubious.

'We will have to talk it over,' he replied. 'It is not something we can decide on here and now.'

'Very well. If you decide to go, I will make all necessary arrangements and see that you are adequately accompanied.'

Oliver had the sense not to press his suggestion, but I was certain it would be accepted, once Charles had had time to adjust to the idea.

Emily and I rose to leave the men to their port. The *abdar* opened the door for us but, as I was about to walk through, Oliver got up and detained me.

'You dropped this,' he said, 'and I am sure you would not want to lose it.' With the disarming smile that I had learnt to distrust he handed me my small sketchbook. As I took it, not knowing what to say or how to avoid the amusement in his eyes, something fluttered out from among the leaves and fell to my feet. I stooped quickly to retrieve it, thinking the paper was some sketch or letter of my own, but found instead a sheet of badly made native paper printed on both sides—in Urdu on one, and Hindi on the other.

I looked at it in puzzlement, then gave it to Oliver. 'This must be yours.'

'Oh, yes.' He took it from me, and turned it over in his hands. 'I had it in my pocket, along with your book, and it must have slipped between the pages. I found several of them during the course of my tour; the work of the esteemed Maulvi of Fyzabad, who is at the moment busily employed in distributing them around the country. Can you read it?'

I glanced at the smudged curlicues of the Urdu script and shook my head. 'I wish I could, but my vocabulary is not up to that. What is it?'

'An invitation,' he answered laconically, putting the paper in his pocket. 'To rebellion!'

I was glad that Emily had already walked on into the drawing-room.

CHAPTER 10

Later that same night I sat alone in the long drawing-room turning over the events of the day. I believe I felt rather smug. No one could deny that I had made a startling, even upsetting, discovery regarding Mr Erskine, yet after my initial panic-stricken escape from the old tower, I had managed to conduct myself so that neither Emily or Charles had any suspicion that I was in an unusual state of mind. In handing me my sketchbook after dinner, Mr Erskine had certainly reduced me to confusion for a moment, probably deliberately, but I had recovered myself pretty smartly.

He had bade us goodnight at his usual hour, and I had watched him leave the room with an inward smile at the innocence of my cousins who still believed he was going to his library to study Persian poetry. Emily and Charles had retired early: Charles was visibly fatigued after his three days in the open and Emily wanted to talk over with him Oliver's suggestion regarding going to Mussoorie rather than to Lucknow.

Left alone, I tried to keep my mind on the book I was reading, a travel tale by a Frenchman named Chevenet. I had chosen it out of perversity, since Oliver, who was in the library at the time, had motioned me away from the works in French, indicating that I would find easier entertainment among the volumes in my own tongue. He had been quite right; the book, besides being in French, was tedious, about an India long gone and never very real. Of course I had not allowed myself to be advised, though now I was prepared to admit I was happy to be at the end of it. Satisfied that I knew enough of the contents to answer any suspicious inquisition my host might put me through, I shut it with relief and decided to find something more congenial to take with me to my bed.

Picking up the lamp from the table beside me, I made my way down the long corridor to the library. The big house was very quiet and only a couple of sleepy servants remained, dozing on their haunches outside the dining-room, waiting to extinguish the lights in the drawing-room when I had retired. I felt guilty at keeping them up, and quickened my pace. The lamp I carried created grotesque shadows among the horns and heads above me, glanced off glassy eyes and revealed for a second as I passed them old, dim portraits and time-darkened landscapes of far-away places. Emily and Charles were probably asleep, and Mr Erskine was no doubt in the old tower. I felt so sure of this deduction that I did not bother to knock, but turned the doorknob and entered my host's sanctum with an easy step.

I stopped abruptly.

Lamplight glimmered at the far end of the room, its inadequate glow merely enhancing the gloom around it.

'Now what the devil do you want?' asked Mr Erskine sharply, straightening up from where he had been bending over a figure recumbent on a long leather-covered couch. 'You have the damndest way of walking in where you are not wanted!'

Appalled at what I might now have discovered—was it possible he would bring his mistress into the house?—I was for a moment dumb.

'I ... I'm sorry, Oliver,' I mumbled, backing out of the door. 'I had no idea you would be here. I just came to change my book, but I can do it in the morning.'

'No,' he said curtly, 'now that you are here, you can help. Women are supposed to be good at this sort of thing. Shut that damned door and bring the lamp with you.'

I shut the door and put the book on a table, then approached the sofa towards which Oliver had again turned his attention. He had taken off his coat and his shirtsleeves were rolled up to the elbow.

'I was just about to start on him myself, but your hands are probably gentler than mine. We have to clean up this leg.'

In the darkness behind the sofa, I discerned the short figure of Toddy-Bob. He came forward to take my lamp, and I glimpsed a face unfamiliarly pale.

'This fool has a girl's stomach for blood,' Oliver commented drily. 'Not that this is a pleasant sight. Do you think you can manage?'

Toddy held up the lamp and revealed a figure, small, shrivelled and quite unconscious, stretched out on the sofa. Though I had never seen the man at close quarters something convinced me that this was the companion of Toddy-Bob's midnight and unexplained departure on the night of the duck shoot. The dark face had a ghastly greenish tinge; his eyes were closed and his mouth open, the lips drawn back over yellowed teeth. He wore a dirty loincloth and nothing else. His right leg was a mass of blood from thigh to ankle.

Oliver watched me closely as I examined the little man; he probably expected me to be as nauseated as Toddy.

'Warm water!' I commanded before I could think better of it. 'And a sheet, a clean sheet.'

'We have them here.'

I put part of the sheet under the bloody limb, tore up the rest and set to work to clean away the blood. It was congealed and difficult to move. I was relieved that the man was unconscious and therefore oblivious to pain. As I worked, I began to see that the whole leg was marked with a series of cuts, forming a sort of trelliswork of diamond shapes on the dark skin. Oliver knelt beside me, handing me clean swabs and wringing out the soiled ones in water.

'This is extraordinary,' I said, after we had worked in silence for some time. 'What could have caused such injuries, they are almost regular? And look how one runs into another all the way up.'

'It's kite string, miss,' said Toddy in a depressed voice. 'Very vicious way of doin' a body a injury! Very vicious!'

'Kite string? But that couldn't possibly cut a man to this extent?'

'The string used for fighting kites does,' said Oliver quietly. 'This is a favoured method of repaying a score around here. Painful, but not necessarily fatal. The string, they call it *manja*, is waxed, then drawn through powdered glass. The glass adheres to the string and, when the kites are in flight, the object is to cut down your opponent's with your own.'

'But how did this happen?'

'I imagine he was knocked unconscious and then the *manja* was wrapped around his leg in the manner you have observed. Usually they do both legs; sometimes the arms as well and tie the hands together. When the victim comes round, he tries to struggle free and each movement, because of the way the damned stuff is wound, tightens the knots, making the string bite into the flesh. The glass rubs off into the wounds, and the resulting sensation is not to be recommended. Fortunately Ungud's enemies appear to have been interrupted before they could finish the job. Or perhaps they only wanted to warn him of

what might happen in the future. I don't know. The *thanadar* of
Shahnagar brought him here; he had managed to crawl to a track.'

'But why did they do it to him, whoever they were? Could it have
been *dacoits*?'

'Perhaps. And the why I have yet to discover. Perhaps a family feud,
a debt, even because of a woman, I suppose. Or maybe because
someone disapproves of his association with Hassanganj. He is an
Army pensioner, but I have employed him for some time as a messenger.
He's a good man and I don't want him crippled ...'

'I have nearly finished, as you can see, though if there is glass in
these cuts, it is going to be difficult to get them to heal. Now it ought
to be bandaged, but first have you some sort of salve or ointment?'

'There are dozens of pots and jars in the still room. Come and see
if you can find anything suitable. My grandmother put them up a long
time ago, so God knows what good they are.'

We returned to the library with a pot marked, euphemistically
enough, 'Soothing Unguent'. It smelt clean and pleasant and, since I
found nothing more specific, all I could do was apply it and hope for
the best. As I worked my fingers gently over the poor lacerated flesh,
the man stirred, moaned and then opened his eyes.

'Good, he's coming round. Toddy, the brandy!'

Toddy-Bob came forward with a glass and Oliver held up the man's
head and poured a little brandy between his teeth. Then he laid him
carefully back on the cushions. 'He'll do now,' he said with satisfaction,
'but we must keep him still while that leg heals. Food, Toddy! See what
they can produce in the kitchen. And hot milk.'

'There, that's done!' I sat back on my heels and surveyed my
handiwork. The leg was now loosely bandaged, and only a few small
spots of blood oozed through the linen. 'Can you get him to a doctor?'

'If it's necessary. But he won't like it.'

'I'd be happier if he had professional attention. That glass ...'

'Well, let's wait a couple of days and see how he gets on. He'll be a
damned sight more frightened of a doctor than of the pain, and they
have extraordinary powers of recuperation.'

'*Sahib*.' A faint whisper from the sofa drew our attention and Oliver
bent over while Ungud spoke a few words in his own tongue.

'He wants me to thank you,' he said, turning to me. 'He says the
Angrezi mem has given him healing and he will be quite well in a few

days.' Oliver got to his feet. 'The curious thing is that if he has made up his mind to recover, he will do it. He'll not need a doctor, you'll see!'

'I hope not, but you'll have to watch for fever.'

'Come,' said Oliver. 'We can leave him to Toddy and Ishmial now. They'll find quarters for him when he is rested.' He picked up the lamp and preceded me out of the room.

'I'm going to have a nightcap. Join me!' he ordered, and as we passed the two sleepy house servants, he commanded that decanters and glasses be brought into the drawing-room. When they had arrived, he poured out two brandies and, though I seldom touched spirits, I accepted mine gladly.

'*I* must thank you, too, Laura,' he said, standing and sipping his drink while I thankfully took a seat. His voice was serious as his eyes met mine, and all at once I was overcome by embarrassment at my memory of the afternoon. Perhaps he realized it; his lips twitched, but he was considerate enough to walk away from me to the empty fireplace.

'Nonsense. There was nothing else I could do.'

'You could have fainted. I gather young ladies make a practice of it in … unpleasant situations. How did you know so well what to do?'

'Common sense, and I have lived in a large family where cuts and scrapes were frequent.'

'It didn't … offend you?'

'Offend me? Oh, you mean … Of course not! His blood is the same colour as mine, even if his skin is not. What an absurd suggestion!'

'Yes,' he agreed thoughtfully, and sat down on one of the little gilt chairs that fitted him so inadequately. 'And yet, would Emily have come forward as readily?'

'Emily would not have known what to do. She has never had to consider other people's misfortunes or minor injuries.'

'And you have?'

'I am older than she is. I have a different temperament. Different expectations and duties.'

'You have indeed. Forgive me if I say it, but you are a very uncommon young woman. You meet life, instead of running away from it. I believe you actually enjoy meeting it, even in head-on collision. As this afternoon.'

I was left speechless by the man's sheer barefaced effrontery.

'Oh, you bolted of course. The only way out for you, after all. But I don't believe you were nearly as shocked as you should have been. You met me at dinner with remarkable composure.'

'No other course was open to me!'

'Perhaps not. Yet I half expected you to take Charles into your confidence.'

'I considered doing so,' I muttered, angry with myself for prolonging the conversation, 'but it is no concern of mine, and ... and I believe the others would have been upset.'

'Very likely,' he agreed. 'My brother might even have taken some regrettable step like leaving Hassanganj in protest. And certainly, as far as Charles and his somewhat optimistic expectations go, that would be unfortunate.'

I said nothing.

'If outraged convention impelled him to leave Hassanganj, you see, he could hardly hope to be made my heir. Now could he?'

'What makes you think he hopes that?'

'Oh, come! My mother's letters do more than merely hint at the desirability of such an outcome. Besides, bridal journeys more usually confine themselves to the beauties of the Italian lakes or the Rhenish castles. And neither Charles nor Emily are subject to—er—shall we say, intellectual curiosity. They could both exist quite happily without a closer knowledge of India. But India held the bait. So to India they came!'

'You are a cynic!'

'No, a realist.'

'But if you know all this, or suspect it, why do you keep us here? Why don't you send them—and me—packing? And you've always been so pointedly considerate of Emily?'

'Why should I send them packing, as you so dramatically put it? I'm not bothered about how much they fool themselves; their rather juvenile hopes do me no wrong. And as to Emily—well, I suppose I am sorry for her.'

'Why should you be sorry for Emily? She has everything!'

'No, my dear, you think so because she has everything you fancy you want. Not the same at all.'

His narrowed amber eyes met mine for a long, cool second, but I would not be drawn.

'Oh, of course I know she can be a little termagant. She *is* to you often enough, and I greatly enjoy the sight of you struggling to control your tongue and preserve the impression of cousinly loving kindness which you value so much. She's spoilt, over-indulged. She hasn't the brains of a wren, and God knows, I'd hate to have to live with her for the rest of my days, even more than Charles does!'

'Charles does not …!' I broke in unwisely.

'Oh, but he does! And as I say, I can't blame him. But she is unhappy … and defenceless. Perhaps I'm sentimental, more sentimental than you will credit, but I think the Emilys of this world should be protected a little—helped. If she could, would Emily not find some other way to assert her rights than in using you spitefully? Besides, it takes very little to make a woman like her feel important and necessary, but Charles apparently is not capable of that little. A notable lack of gallantry. And of common sense!'

'It is not for us to apportion the blame.'

'Oho! How righteous we do sound! But you're right, I suppose. She's a child and he's a schoolboy. They should have left marriage to men and women. As it is, they'll always find someone else to pull their chestnuts out of the fire, someone else they can blame, someone else they can turn to for … comfort. It will be enough that the world considers them a "lovely young couple". They'll play up to the idea as best they can and in the end believe it themselves. Their grandchildren will be convinced they were always a most devoted pair, yet they won't have exchanged an idea, or a tender word in forty years.'

'What an odious picture of marriage.'

'Isn't it?' he agreed virtuously. 'And yet a very common one.'

'I hope you are wrong.'

I should have got up and left then.

Oliver rose and strolled back to the fireplace, glass in hand.

'Laura?' He turned and faced me but kept his eyes on his glass as he twirled it thoughtfully between his fingers. 'I have been watching you while you have been here, more than you know. I have learnt how ill-equipped you are to play second fiddle to anyone, least of all Emily. I admire the way in which you try to do your duty, whatever your true feelings are for her and her husband. I see that you have courage; that you are practical and sceptical and yet at the same time a little prone to romance. I enjoy the dogged, ridiculously confident way you manage

293

the storms in your teacup of life. And I like the instinct that enables you to swallow the unpleasant facts of existence, get what nourishment you can from them, and spit out the rest. The one thing I cannot admire, cannot understand, is how you can continue to fool yourself that ... that you love Charles!'

I stood up swiftly.

'I cannot help what you think—however wrongly. I do not need to hear your thoughts!' And I would have opened the door but that he reached it before me.

'Come now, you do not need to deny it to me. You cannot! Oh, I know it's hopeless, that no one has ever yet been argued out of a wrongheaded passion, myself included. But I'm not censorious, Laura. If he was worth a damn, I'd probably help you to get him! But why cannot you see? You've too much sense to love a soft yellow moustache and nice blue eyes indefinitely. Think now, just think of how atrociously dull he'll be in ten years' time. Charles reached his zenith when he became head boy of his school. He'll never do better, never want more. He'll not learn new interests, never entertain a new idea, never question the validity of his old ones. The world turns round the worthy, dull, dutiful, unimaginative men like Charles, but God help the women who do, and you, Laura, could not put up with it for very long. Charles will never develop, Laura. He'll only grow old.'

'What makes you think you have the right to talk to me like this? To impute what you do, and about your own brother? And what flight of fancy leads you to suppose that I will encourage you by discussing it? It is very late. Will you please allow me to leave the room.'

He did not move from the door, and his eyes watched me with a disinterested yet earnest enquiry, as one might view a familiar but unexamined object in a microscope—desiring knowledge yet hoping for no surprise.

'I suppose I cannot expect you to agree with me—yet. But tell me just one thing. What do you intend to do with your life? Are you content to go on dancing attendance on Emily for ever, because it is the only way you can be near Charles? Is that what you want?'

'My future can be of no possible concern to you. Will you please open that door!'

He shrugged, sighed, moved aside and opened the door.

His face wore an expression of mingled impatience and resignation. As I made to leave the room, he stopped me once again.

'Before you go, Laura, I ask you most earnestly; use all the influence you have on getting Charles and Emily to leave here as soon as possible. There is trouble coming. That you must believe. I do not know whether I could guarantee their safety in Hassanganj. I have no fears for myself, but we could be cut off, isolated. And in Emily's condition …'

'But how can you be sure? All these rumours, and they are nothing more than rumours after all.'

'No, you are wrong. It is much more than rumours now. Ungud brought me news that I cannot ignore. Whatever it is that is a-brewing will boil over before the monsoons, that is within the next two months. It is still possible that it will be no more than a storm in a teacup; that is the view of most of the authorities who, unfortunately, have our governance in their hands. But I cannot agree with them. I do not want the Floods or yourself here for a day longer than is absolutely necessary.'

'I see.'

'No, I don't suppose you do really. Why should you? Most people, including Charles, would consider it crazy to go by the gossip of the roads, the judgement of an old pensioner like Ungud and my own formless intuition. Yet, I trust my own conclusion. I want you to trust it too, and to believe that there is real urgency now; that you must leave here very soon.'

He spoke with great earnestness, his amber eyes full of purpose.

There could be no doubt that he wanted us away in a hurry. No doubt, also, that whatever information he had received from the pensioner Ungud added to that desire. Yet I could not at the same time avoid the suspicion that the wish to be rid of the woman who had discovered him in flagrant moral cupidity, despite the insouciance with which he had earlier treated the matter, contributed to his urgency.

As it happened, there was no need for me to use my persuasive powers on my cousins. The following night at dinner, Charles announced, quite as though he had come upon the idea himself, that Emily and he felt it would be wiser to go to the hills in view of the unpleasant heat to which Lucknow was subject during the summer months.

'Very wise. Very wise,' said Mr Erskine gravely, while I concentrated on my plate. 'When do you think of going?'

'We don't wish to cut short our visit to Hassanganj too much, of course. If you can put up with us, that is: the middle of the month will give us plenty of time to see ourselves comfortably established in Mussoorie before the, er, event.'

'Would it not be wiser to leave yourselves more time? I can make the arrangements in a couple of days.'

'Oh, I don't think so. Emily and I have discussed the matter thoroughly. She feels she would sooner stay here and, in any event, there is no social life in the hills before the end of April, we hear, and we would not like to be long alone in a strange town.'

'As you will,' said our host resignedly. 'I will see to the *dak* arrangements and provide palanquins for the ladies. I take it you will prefer to ride, Charles?'

'Of course!' agreed Charles, though I was certain he was inwardly appalled at the idea of riding two or three hundred miles through a strange country.

'Only two weeks more in dear Hassanganj, Oliver,' sighed Emily. 'I shall hate to leave it.'

'Then you must come back before you sail for home,' replied Oliver gallantly, and there the matter rested.

CHAPTER 11

Day by day the heat mounted—inexorably, swiftly, palpably. Now, from seven in the morning until five in the evening, the house was darkened by split-cane blinds, called *chiks*, hung round the verandahs to keep out the glare, while doors and windows were further shielded by screens woven of the aromatic *kus-kus* root kept damp and sweet-smelling by the spray from the *bhisti*'s goatskin waterbag. Great earthenware pots filled with water were placed in each room to lower the temperature by evaporation, *punkahs* flapped overhead all day and all night, and the ceaseless slap and swaying frayed the nerves only less than the sudden knowledge that the movement had stopped.

We rode now at half-past five in the morning when already the heat would be uncomfortable. It became too hot for needlework, too hot for study, too hot to walk in the garden, and when we wrote letters home the perspiration rolling down our wrists smudged the ink on the paper. Emily became too listless even to be cross. She spent the greater part of her time by the north window of her darkened upstairs room, rereading old novels while her *ayah* fanned her. Charles, making the most of his chances, spent all his time with Oliver, going where Oliver went, doing what Oliver did, very much to his own discomfort. And pointlessly, as I knew. He was raw with sunburn, and soon developed prickly heat in the joints of his arms and legs. Accustomed to the Indian sun all his life, dark complexioned, lean and active, Mr Erskine showed no ill-effects as the temperature mounted, and continued his usual routine with few concessions to the time of year. I sometimes wondered whether he would have shown the same hardihood had Charles not been present; more than once I detected a gleam of sardonic enjoyment in his eyes as he announced some energetic plan for the day and then added politely, 'And of course you would like to come too, Charles.'

The preparations for our departure were put in hand, the bullock-carts for our luggage and the palanquins for ourselves examined, repaired, cleaned and finally pronounced acceptable. Runners were despatched to reserve relief coolies at each of the many stages, and bookings were made in the *dak*-bungalows along the road. At this time of year, with so many families moving north to the hills, it was necessary to arrange everything beforehand. All our many trunks, bandboxes and carpetbags were brought up from the cellars and, while I directed the *ayahs* in the correct folding of gowns, stuffing our bonnets with tissue paper and wrapping our slippers in muslin, I discovered an odd ambivalence within myself regarding our going.

I was in Emily's room, emptying her closet, and the two *ayahs* were busy with the drawers of a tallboy.

'It hardly seems like four months, does it, Em?' I said. 'In some ways it has gone so quickly.'

'Much too quickly. I wish we were right at the beginning again—in December, when there were fires at night and the mustard fields were in bloom. Oh, I wish we had just arrived! I know I shall hate the hills. And I hate leaving here—and Oliver.'

'He has asked you to come back.'

'For a visit! What good is that? No, I have been hoping all this time that perhaps he would ask Charles to stay on here—for good.'

'But why should he?'

'It would be the sensible thing to do, if he meant to make Charles his heir. Charles would have to learn about the running of the estate, after all, and what better master could he have than Oliver? I had hoped so much, even though I knew it was not reasonable, and prayed every night that Oliver would say something about it before we left. Oh, I know it's silly. I know Charles has no real right to Hassanganj ... to expect anything more from Oliver. But ... well, I have been happy here. Happier than I ever was since we left home ... since I got married. I don't know why. Charles said once it was because I was flattered. Because I enjoyed living in a "vulgar luxury"—those were his words—that he could never provide me with! Perhaps he's right. I don't know.'

I was silent at my work and felt unwisely wise. Poor Emily! Of course she was flattered. The way Oliver Erskine treated her—the gifts, the gentle consideration, his almost excessive thoughtfulness—would flatter any woman. No doubt he had used the very same methods to preserve the contentment of those shadowy young ladies who had 'visited' him for protracted periods in his youth, the wiles of a sophisticated and unscrupulous man. And Emily had fallen victim to them, as surely as had the shabby little adventuresses he had once employed them on. I looked intently at my cousin, leaning back in a big chair, wearing only a loose wrapper, with her hair down her back, and realized, as I should have realized long before, that her expression, so malleably sweet, so yearningly soft, was the expression of a woman in love. Of a woman in love with Oliver Erskine.

Well, now here's a pretty kettle of fish, I thought to myself ruefully, for I was not seriously worried. I felt I knew Emily. She had always been susceptible to the other sex, had always enjoyed using her feminine arts upon them. She had dreamed herself in and out of love with every neighbourhood boy from the time she was fourteen. Certainly she was now a married woman who should know better, but her marriage was unhappy, she was still very young—and the object of her affections was Oliver Erskine. I knew his opinion of Emily, and I knew that any misery her ill-directed affection caused her would be her own doing. But we would be leaving Hassanganj in three days. Once away from our host's immediate ambience, Emily's fancied passion would soon wane and, as soon as the baby came, Oliver, his gifts and his attentiveness would be thrust into the same limbo of her mind which held her memories of the boys of Mount Bellew. But I was glad our departure was to be so soon, all the same.

The next afternoon Emily and I had *tiffin* alone. The men had ridden over to the McCrackens' plantation so that Charles could make our farewells, and we did not expect them back until dinner, indigo being a subject that absorbed Oliver as much as it did the McCrackens.

'I'm rather glad Toddy-Bob is to come with us to the hills,' said Emily. 'I don't like the wretched little fellow—do you remember how rude he was to Charles at the Residency that night?—but at least he is dependable. I should hate to make that long journey with only black people around us. Toddy at least speaks English!'

'Of a sort,' I admitted. Though I had grown quite fond of Toddy myself, I could not admire his original syntax. Recently he had not ridden out with his master when Oliver's duties took him away from the house, and I had become accustomed to his subdued whistle on the verandah whenever Emily and I were at home. Ishmial with his curved *tulwar*, his bandolier across his velvet chest, and those fiercely curled whiskers, now took the place of the little man behind Oliver. I had a well-founded suspicion that Toddy-Bob had been appointed our watchdog.

After lunch we went to our rooms. I had held out for as long as possible against the Anglo-Indian habit of spending every afternoon in bed and asleep, but the gathering heat had defeated me. Now, when the whole house was filled with a heavy, hot somnolence and nothing stirred in the sun-deadened park, I too went to my bed, unlaced my stays, kicked off my slippers and fell into a deep uneasy sleep.

I have no idea how long I was asleep that afternoon before I became aware of a knocking on my door and a long wailing cry in the background of my consciousness. For a moment I lay still, trying to focus my blurred senses, feeling the stickiness of the coverlet beneath my bare shoulders, of sweat under my chin and pouring down my neck. Then I was fully awake and struggling into my wrapper as the knocking grew louder and more insistent. I stumbled to the door. Emily's *ayah*, eyes rolling in her frightened brown face, met me with her palms joined in a gesture of submission and apology.

'It is coming! Aie! Aie! *Missy-sahib*, the *baba* is coming!'

'What? It can't be!' I grabbed a handful of shoulder and white muslin *sari*, and shook the woman until her teeth rattled. 'The baby is not due until the end of next month. It cannot come now!'

'No! No indeed! But it comes, *Missy-sahib*. It comes now!'

'You stupid thing,' I muttered between clenched teeth, 'Emily *Mem-sahib* ate cucumbers in vinegar for *tiffin*. She has indigestion!'

'Yes! No doubt that is it. But the *baba* also—it comes now! And the *Chota-sahib* is not here, and the *Lat-sahib* is not here, and only the gods know what will happen to Emily *Mem-sahib* for she has the hips of a ten-year-old girl!'

I did not wait for the end of the sentence, but rushed down the long corridor to Emily's room, determined that if force of will could do it, force of invective if need be, I would keep that damned brat from making an appearance. Only two more days, two more little days, and we would be clear of Hassanganj. In another week Emily could have all the babies she wanted, triplets if she liked, in the cool, pine-scented air of the hills. But not here in this place of secrets and conflict, suspicion, threats and ill-matched people. 'Dear God,' I prayed to my neglected deity, 'dear God,' with my hand on the door-knob, 'please, please don't let it be the baby. It mustn't come today!' Both Charles and Oliver were away and I was alone with a responsibility I could not avoid and knew not how to take. It was Charles's duty to be present at the birth of his child, not mine. And only Oliver would know how to get the doctor and the midwife; I didn't. So the baby could not, must not, come today! In the midst of my worry, I found time to wonder how I was so sure that Oliver would manage the situation, when Charles's wife and child were involved. But so much I knew.

The long, high wail had ceased, and I realized that it must have come from the *ayah* at my door and not from Emily, who lay on her big bed looking very white and frightened but none the less composed. I pulled my wrap and my confidence around me, and went to her.

'Now what's all this talk of the baby coming?' I asked with forced jollity. 'You know that's very unlikely. It's not due for another six weeks and they say first babies are always late anyway.'

'I know, that's what I've been telling myself, Laura. But I really think it must be, all the same. I've … I've had a backache all day. I said nothing, since I thought it would pass, and then about an hour ago these pains started and they are worse now.'

'A false alarm! Nothing more. Everyone has them. Don't worry about it; just lie as comfortably as you can until they pass off. They will, Emmie, they will!'

'Do you really think so? I don't want the wretched baby to come early, Laura, but…'

'Now don't say any more. Lie still and try to sleep. When you wake up, you'll find the pains have stopped. I'm sure of it.'

Emily shut her eyes obediently and I sat down near her to wait. In ten minutes her eyes were open again. In half an hour the pains were forcing her to bite her lips, and at the end of an hour she was writhing on the bed and gasping with relief as each spasm passed.

'It's no good, Laura! I'm so sorry, but it's the baby, it must be. It has gone on so long now and it's only getting worse!'

'I can see that, Em. I'll … I'll have to send Toddy out to find someone to help. Mrs Camp has had six children. She'll know just what to do and she seemed a nice practical sort of person. And when Oliver gets back, he'll be able to find a doctor for you.'

'But the nearest doctor is in Lucknow … that's what frightens me, Laura.'

It was what frightened me too, but I could not let her know it.

'Well, very often midwives are much better than doctors, and I'm sure Oliver will manage to get one nearer than Lucknow. Take it gently, darling, I'll be back as soon as I can.'

Drat it, I fumed to myself as I left the room. All I knew of childbirth was that it was a protracted business, particularly with a first child, and that not much could be done until the end. But when the end came, eventually, someone with a modicum of knowledge of the procedure had to be available, and that someone, I determined, was not going to be me. I was as ignorant of the whole business as a nonagenarian monk!

I scrawled a note to Mrs Camp, and asked her to come to us as soon as possible. Toddy-Bob was sitting on the back verandah chewing tobacco and gazing vacantly at nothing. He had an astonishing facility for relaxing in any position, born no doubt of his days as an ostler's boy watching horses in London. He sprang up when I appeared, the blankness of his expression belied by the shrewd appraisal in his eyes. He knew what was going on upstairs and for a second I wondered whether I should mention the matter outright and ask him who in the vicinity was most likely to help. But upbringing was too much for me.

'I have a note here, Toddy,' I said. 'It's urgent and very important. Please deliver it yourself and wait for an answer from Mrs Camp.'

He took the note and examined it politely.

'Sorry, miss,' he said, handing it back. 'Couldn't do it.'

'You couldn't do it!' Wrath almost made me stutter. 'Why not? Haven't I just told you it is very important?'

'Yes, miss, and that's as may be. But I 'as my orders quite clear like.'

'And what might they be?'

'To stay in this 'ere 'ouse and never to leave it while the Guv'nor isn't around like.'

I had been right then; he was our watchdog.

'But, Toddy, this is an emergency! I will take full responsibility and explain to Mr Erskine that it was I who sent you—against your own wishes. Please, Toddy, it is desperately important!'

'No go, miss. First, because Toddy-Bob takes 'is orders from no one but the Guv'nor, nor never 'as. And second because Toddy-Bob 'as never gone against them orders nor doesn't aim to now.'

I was defeated.

'Then, well, I suppose one of the other servants will have to take it. Will you arrange it, please? Tell them how urgent it is. Mrs Camp must have the note as soon as possible!'

'That wouldn't do neither, miss,' he said with decision, but regretfully.

'Now what do you mean?' I held in my annoyance and spoke with honeyed sweetness.

'Mrs Camp aint 'ere, miss. She's gone to the 'ills, a week ago.'

'You're sure?' I could not hide my dismay. 'How do you know; you could be mistaken?'

'Not I, miss. She's gone all right and all the nippers too. Seen 'em!'

I sat down on an old cane chair to think. What else was there I could do? Mr Camp's assistant was not married and neither were either of the McCrackens or Mr Baird. The only other women I knew were in Lucknow. Had Toddy-Bob, his equine features gravely triumphant, not been watching me, I might have wept.

'It's a *dai* you'll be wanting, miss,' he volunteered after a pause.

'A *dai*?'

'Yes, miss; like a midwife—a nurse, you know.'

Nothing can ever be hidden in an Indian household. Here now was Toddy-Bob in full possession of the facts.

'Yes,' I agreed, further subterfuge being pointless, 'we do need a midwife!' I said it as though midwives were as rare as pearls in clamshells.

'I can get you one of *them* all right, miss.'

'Can you! Oh, Toddy, how?'

'Why, every village has two or three, miss. Bit rough like they may be, but they manage to bring the nippers into the world just the same as any.'

'You mean a … a native woman?'

'That's right. Like I said—a *dai*.'

'Oh, no! I'm afraid not. Mr Flood would never hear of that!'

'Well, that's the best I can do, miss, and one of 'em did all right by the Guv'nor.'

Naturally, I thought to myself, with Yasmina in mind. A native woman would not want anything but a native midwife. Having accepted the fact of Yasmina's parentage myself, I was hardly surprised that Toddy-Bob should blatantly mention the matter.

''Is ma was 'ere you see, miss, alone with the old people, and a *dai* come and pulled 'im into the world with nary a bother!'

'Mr Erskine himself?'

'Certainly, miss! Who else?' He regarded me warily.

'Oh! I ... well, I'll have to wait until the gentlemen come in anyway. Thank you for trying to help.'

Slowly I went indoors and Toddy-Bob looked after me with one eyebrow cocked, his lips already pursed in his nearly silent whistle.

The long afternoon dragged slowly into evening. Emily's room was close and hot despite the efforts of the two *ayahs* and myself. While they took it in turns to fan her, I tried to cool her face and forehead with cloths wrung out in cologne and iced water. The two fat Indian women watched her intently, almost obscenely, and now and then exchanged comments in their own tongue. They knew how Emily was progressing, they knew what to expect, but when I questioned them they broke into such torrents of excited explanation that I could not understand a word. Neither my *munshis* nor Mr Benarsi Das had included the vocabulary of midwifery in their Urdu lessons.

As night approached, Emily began to moan and cry out at frequent intervals, and each time she did so I clenched my teeth and swore under my breath at my own ignorant helplessness. And each time she moaned, the *ayahs* shook their heads and looked knowingly at each other.

It was almost dark when the men returned.

The *chiks* had been rolled up to let in the cooler night air and the lamps had been lit when, hearing the approach of horses, I left Emily and ran down the wide staircase to break the news. I might have saved myself the trouble. As they entered the house, the news I had to give them was announced by Emily herself in the form of a piercing scream, clearly audible on the floor below. Both men stood stock still, frozen into immobility by the unexpectedness of that sound in the big quiet house.

'It's Emily,' Charles whispered.

I nodded.

'The baby? It's coming?'

I nodded again.

'Oh, my God!' He flung down his hat and riding crop and took the stairs three at a time.

Oliver also removed his hat and placed it carefully on the carved chest beneath the elephant skull.

'Well,' said he deliberately, 'that's all we need!'

'She can't help it, Oliver,' I said defensively. 'It's six weeks early, and I'm as sorry about it as you are, believe me.'

'That's a comfort! Have you got everything you need? I take it you can deal with this situation yourself, now that it is upon us?'

'No!'

'No what? What do you mean?'

'We must have a doctor! I know absolutely nothing about it. How could I? I'm not even married, and no one talks to unmarried women about such things. Oh, Oliver, I know I'm a fool not to know, but it's the truth. Please help us to find someone. I wrote to Mrs Camp but Toddy says she has gone to the hills, and I don't know of anyone else. We must find a doctor!'

'Good God, woman, pull yourself together! It would take two days to get a doctor out here, and then there's no saying one would come. You'll have to manage on your own. The *ayahs* will help you. They always know everything. It's their business to.'

'But I don't understand them well enough, don't you see?'

'Then they'll manage without you. Just leave them alone to get on with it.'

I shook my head helplessly, and sat down suddenly and inelegantly on the bottom stair. 'It's not as simple as that,' I said. 'They have managed to indicate that Emily is having a difficult time. She ... she is too small!' I hoped he would understand without further explanation. He did.

His expression softened a little. He looked down at me in silence for a moment, biting his underlip in thought.

'A doctor is out of the question. The first thing to do is to find out how things are going. Come up with me and fetch out one of the *ayahs*.' He started up the stairs as he spoke, and I got up and followed him.

Emily's *ayah*, who came to the door at my summons, broke into a long and involved explanation when she saw Oliver. He listened attentively, asked a few questions, then dismissed the woman with a nod.

'Yes, it's as you say. She is having difficulty and things can only get worse. The *ayah* says ...' He broke off in mid sentence at the sound of a sobbing cry on the other side of the door. When he spoke again, his voice was gentler.

'There is one possibility; if you will accept it.'

'Anything! Anything is better than this!'

'The *ayah* says Emily and the child will die if she doesn't have help. I'm sorry to be so blunt. There's no other way. We have a woman here whom the *ayah* says is sometimes called in for this kind of thing ...'

'You mean a *dai*?'

'She's not really a *dai*. Where did you learn the word?'

'Toddy-Bob.'

'I see.' He grinned faintly. 'No, Moti is not a *dai*, but she has very thin long hands and some experience of dealing with such ... such situations, I believe. The *ayah* tells me she can help Emily and I see no alternative.'

'Then get her, for pity's sake, get her quickly!'

'Wait!' He looked at me intently in the light of the lamp at Emily's door. 'You should know one thing first. You have already met Moti.'

I tried to read in his face an explanation for his delay, and slowly I understood. Moti. I had already met her. Then she could only be the woman in the old tower.

Somewhere in the recesses of my muddled mind I felt I should be shocked. No gentleman would ever have considered introducing his native mistress into the presence of ladies, whatever the reason. But, though I saw the necessity for outrage, I felt none.

'You mean ...?'

'Yes.' His tone was deliberate and unapologetic. 'Moti, Yasmina's mother.'

'She doesn't like me,' I said confusedly, remembering the venomous outburst that had met me in the tower.

'It won't matter. She has no reason for disliking Emily. And in any case she would do what I asked of her.'

'Then, please, get her quickly!'

'Very well.' And with a final searching look into my face, he went.

I walked into Emily's room. Charles stood at a window looking out into the darkness, clasping and unclasping his hands behind his back. His wife lay still and quiet for the moment, all colour gone from her face, her golden hair, black now with perspiration, stuck to her forehead and cheeks. I touched him on the arm and motioned him out of the room, following him. 'Oliver has gone to get someone who ... who can help Emily,' I said, closing the door behind me.

'A doctor?'

'No, a woman. A ... a sort of midwife. It's the best he can do.'

He nodded, but did not seem to be listening; I knew he was waiting for the next moan or cry. When none came, he turned to me, and I saw his eyes were full of tears.

'Laura, don't let her die! For God's sake, don't let her die!'

'Oh, Charles, there's no likelihood of her dying,' I lied. 'She is only having a baby, and we'll soon have skilled help. Come now!'

'You don't understand, Laura. You can't! Emily never wanted this baby. Any baby. I forced ... it on her. If she dies, I'll have murdered her!'

He spoke with such intensity that for a moment I could say nothing. I remembered instead, that night in Calcutta and the sound of Emily's sobs in the darkness; and later her unhidden terror at the knowledge that she was pregnant. Both were memories I should not have been in a position to recall, and the knowledge that I was party, however unwillingly, to his shame and her degradation brought hot colour to my cheeks. I disguised my own feeling of inadequacy with anger.

'Don't be so melodramatic!' I said sharply after a moment. 'This is no time to speak of such things!'

'There is never a time to speak of such things,' he admitted with bitterness. 'But one cannot escape living with them.'

'Now look, Charles, you are anxious and over-emotional on account of it, but listen to me. Many women feel as Emily does about a first baby, particularly when they are as young as she is. They see motherhood as a threat to their independence, a curtailment of their enjoyment. Oh, I know you and Emily have not been getting along too well, but that's to be expected, too. It ... it's the sort of growing pains of marriage; but when the baby comes, things will all be different ... for you both.'

'No, they won't. They can't be, Laura. I ... I have been such a clumsy, selfish fool! She was only a child, but I couldn't have patience. I wouldn't wait. I know she will never really forgive me. She has said more than once that she hates me, and she means it. I know she means it.'

'But she will grow up. In time she'll see things as you saw them.'

'No. And it will do no good if she does, because I have grown up too. That's the hell of it!' He walked a few reflective paces down the corridor and then came back to me, head bowed, hands in his pockets. When he spoke, he kept his eyes on the floor.

'I swear that when I married her, I loved Emily, Laura—not you!' I drew in my breath ready to protest, but he went on: 'I could never have married her without loving her. Or at least thinking I did. She was so pretty, so gay and ... bright! I couldn't keep my eyes off her face—and she's so graceful and light in all her movements, so deft with her pretty hands. I loved her voice and her laughter; all her ways. I'd never seen a girl like her. I was her slave, Laura. I gave her everything I could; everything she wanted. But I wanted ... I wanted something in return as well. She never gave it to me. Not willingly. I tried to be patient, but once we were married she continued to treat me as her ... her cavalier. Not even her favourite one. Just the most constant! And then I ... well, then I lost patience. I took what I wanted. And that was really the end—for us both. When I realized that, I turned to you. You know I did, don't you, Laura? You always had time to listen to me, the kindness to ... to sympathize, to understand, so that gradually I came to believe I never had loved Emily. God knows, perhaps I never did. But when I married her, I thought I did!'

'Please, Charles,' I said gently, 'you don't need to tell me all this, indeed you don't. You are overwrought. In the morning you will be ashamed of ever having mentioned these things. Please don't go on. In fairness to Emily, if not to myself.'

'Yes, I must do the right thing, must I not? But tell me, where can "fairness" be found in an unhappy, unfulfilled marriage like ours? Oh, I know; between us, Emily and I are producing a new human being, but believe me we have no chance of any real marriage for all that. And it's my fault. That is what I have to live with. Can you understand, Laura?'

I understood too well. Once, and not so long ago, I would have known a degree of guilty joy at his admitting that he loved me. But now—well, I suppose I too had 'grown up'. I felt compassion for him, but also found in my mind a marked distaste that he should have spoken as he had at such a time.

'Perhaps I can understand, Charles,' I admitted, 'but none of this is my business, least of all now. You shouldn't be telling me your inner recriminations and hidden guilts. We all have them, after all, and you made your own choice. It's only right—only manly, Charles—that you should stand by it now. And in silence. Emily has had her share of suffering too.'

308

'God, do you think I don't know that? That's why, Laura, you must not let her die. If only she will live, I swear, I swear on everything that's most holy to me, that I will make it up to her. Don't you see … if she dies … I could not live with myself?'

'She will not die,' I answered brusquely. 'And we all, sometime or other, have to learn that we are less than we think ourselves.'

He looked at me for a moment almost with wonder, almost as if he had never seen me before.

'How hard you can be,' he said slowly. 'How hard you have become!'

He moved away from me up the dark corridor lit by little pools of yellow light where the lamps hung. I think he intended to come back to me, looking for more sympathy or understanding, support perhaps most of all. But I was unwilling to give it. I watched him for a moment, his comely head bowed, his hands clenched by his side, then turned and went in to Emily again.

Sitting in the hot, dim room by Emily's bed, I wondered what my Aunt Hewitt would have said to the way in which her first grandchild was entering the world, unwanted by its mother and with only the help of a native woman to usher it into life. But Mount Bellew was too far away, too unreal; and, hard as I tried to conjure up a memory of my aunt's face and tone of voice, to remember her views on propriety and expediency, I could confront myself with nothing more than a vague recollection of warmth and kindness. Perhaps, after all, she would have understood; would have done the same as I was doing on behalf of her daughter. I had to hope so. Here, in this foreign room that smelt of limewash and the coconut oil the *ayahs* used on their hair and the betel-nut they were fond of chewing, it was easy to believe that I had no alternative.

Somewhere, far away, a pariah dog yelped shrilly, and within the room a captive cicada iterated its maddening click from a cranny in the woodwork.

CHAPTER 12

Oliver was so long returning with Moti that I began to wonder whether he had been unable to persuade her to come. When I realized we might still be left without help, I prayed for her presence, forgetting, not caring for her position in his household; all I prayed was that the woman forget her dislike of me sufficiently to be of assistance to my cousin. Why had she disliked me in the first place, I who had never set eyes on her before? And what was it that Oliver had said when I had told him of her dislike? Something like 'She has no reason to dislike Emily,' which implied that she did have a reason to dislike me, despite the fact that our first encounter, on that afternoon when Yasmina had led me to the old tower, had also been our last.

Of course, I suppose I understood him immediately, but women being as they are, I had decided to withhold recognition of my own understanding until I was able to analyse it, and, as it were, throw up a guard. Oliver had implied, though now I was inclined to think it too delicate a term, that his mistress was jealous of me. There could be no other interpretation, knowing what I knew. So then, having dragged the matter into the light and dissected it as I sponged poor Emily's head, I became angry. I raged at Oliver Erskine, at his mistress, at his unwarrantable conceit; but chiefly at his unpardonable breach of all decency in bracketing the two of us (however nebulously) together.

But below the sound and fury and all the stinging eloquence of my dumb anger, I was conscious of a strange small singing in my heart whose meaning I could not decipher and whose origin I would not trace. Perhaps, left to myself then, I might have reached the source of that secret, uninvited joy but, even as I first felt it, the door opened and Moti entered quickly in a swirl of satin and a scent of musk, so inappropriate in that dark and pain-filled room.

The *ayahs* greeted her with twitters of relief. She threw me one brief look, discarded her veil of gauze, and set to work.

It was a strange night we spent, a night that seemed at times to have no ending. I soon realized that there was nothing I could do of practical assistance but, being reluctant to leave Emily alone among strangers, I withdrew only as far as a chair in the corner of the room where she could see me plainly, and I could watch the three dark women at their work: the *ayahs* attentive and obedient to every gesture of Moti's, and Moti authoritative and decided, working and waiting with a calm assurance which did much to make the hours endurable for me at least. But sometimes I cringed with my eyes closed and my hands clapped over my ears, and prayed and half cried for an end that would not come.

And then at last, and quite abruptly, it was over. Emily lay at last quiet on the wreckage of her bed in a stupor of exhaustion, and at her feet Moti crouched, drenched in perspiration, with a small pink fragment of humanity in her lap and a look of purest triumph on her face.

An hour later, unable to believe that I had ever been tired, ever been frightened and sickened by the sights and sounds of childbirth, I carried my little cousin downstairs to make the acquaintance of her father.

The brothers were in the library, Charles hunched on a chair and Oliver spread out comfortably on the long sofa that had held Ungud. The sun had been up some time, but lamps still burned, lending the room an air of desolation, augmented by the remains of a meal and empty glasses and decanters on a table, and many cigar butts scattered on the hearth. Charles, I saw at a glance, was very drunk indeed and fast asleep.

Oliver got to his feet leisurely as I entered and politely wished me 'Good morning.' For answer I held the baby out to him. He advanced cautiously and poked her with his forefinger. 'Hmph! Devil of a lot of trouble you've caused, sir,' was his greeting to his niece.

'Miss,' I corrected.

'Oh, girl, is it? No way of telling when you see 'em like this. Is Emily all right?'

'I think she will be. She's very tired now. Exhausted.'

'And—this—is quite strong?'

'A very bonny child indeed,' I assured him—that being a useful phrase I had heard on similar occasions.

'Nothing wrong with it, then?'

'Well, of course, she is rather small—please don't call her "it"—but small babies are often more healthy than large ones, so we must hope for the best.'

'Good! Well, young woman, your father's no credit to you at the moment. Doubt whether he'd even know what you were. I think we had better let him sleep it off before making the introduction, Laura.' And he looked aside at Charles's heavily recumbent form.

I had not seen Charles drunk before. He was an unlovely sight, lying in a shaft of all-revealing morning sunlight, with his shirt unbuttoned, his boots off, his mouth hanging open and his moustache stained with claret and tobacco. My disgust must have shown on my face, and Oliver, calmly getting into his alpaca jacket, laughed.

'Don't look so damning,' he said. 'He's only drunk. He has every reason for becoming so, and I encouraged him.'

'I'm sure you did!' I retorted, and was immediately sorry for the censorious note in my voice.

He buttoned his jacket and passed a hand over his hair.

'Come now, Laura, let's swear a truce. You have discovered all my iniquities and I have admitted all your excellences. Is that not enough to form the basis of a more—cordial—relationship?'

'Oh, I'm too worn out to quarrel with you this morning.' And, with the realization that the first exhilaration of holding the baby in my arms had worn off, I was glad to seat myself in Old Adam's great leather-covered chair. 'You are the most exasperating man. I never know where I am with you.'

'Hmph! Because your ideas, regarding me anyway, are preconceived ones,' he announced blandly. 'And you are a trifle too fond of making judgements.' He looked again at Charles, who was snoring horribly. 'He's your hero, I'm your villain. And regardless of any indications to the contrary, so we must remain. You want us both to stay neatly labelled, as you have labelled us, and either of us deviating an iota throws you into a panic or a temper. Poor Charles has slipped badly in your eyes this morning by looking so like a ... a besotted tramp. Not your idea at all of what an English gentleman should look like, is he? So I suppose it will, take you days to work him back into his favoured niche in your affections. You'll have to think up a fine set of apologies, explanations and excuses, instead of just admitting that your Beau

Ideal is capable of becoming blind, stinking drunk. Like any other man.'

He was smiling as he spoke, but this was no jesting matter.

'You're talking nonsense!' I got up to go.

'No, I'm not. I just want a little fair play. But now, last night I did you something of a favour, didn't I?'

'A favour?'

'In bringing you ... Moti?'

'I would hardly call it a favour. Least of all to me. If it was a favour, and I see it as no more than your Christian duty, it was to Emily. However, I had meant to thank you.'

'Spare me your thanks—for that! What you should be thanking me for is realizing that you would have the good sense ... the ... the intelligence to accept her services. That is what I meant by my favour to you; that I trusted you to behave like a human being rather than like an English, er ... maiden lady.'

'And you accuse me of preconceived ideas!'

'Oh, come now! Let's not spar. However you may consider it, I paid you a compliment, don't you see that? So, as a result, don't you think I could go up a step in your estimation, just as poor old Charles, for getting drunk, has gone down one?'

'But you behaved no better than I expected,' I assured him. He regarded me suspiciously for a moment, but before he could speak, I went on: 'You behaved just as I knew you would. I was sure you would do all you could for Emily, and me, in spite of your growls.'

'Did you indeed?'

'Yes, and though you may be right in thinking me too critical and too fond of my own opinions, I am capable of changing them, and I hope I am honest enough to do so whenever I see that I am wrong.'

'Well, I'm damned! The woman is admitting that she can be wrong!'

'Don't be caustic. I'm doing my best, and it was *you* who just said we should be friends.'

'I certainly did not! God forbid!'

'Well there you are, you see. We don't even speak the same language.' I shrugged and turned to the door. 'I must go and find something for this child to sleep in.'

'Oh, but we do!' he said with decision, his eyes on my face. 'We speak just the same language—but, however, for the moment, you choose not to understand me. Very well, then. But would you be good enough to find Toddy and tell him to come and help me to put our hero here to bed?'

'Certainly, and I suppose I should congratulate you on remaining sober yourself?'

'No need at all. I was under no strain. After all, it was not my baby!'

When I got back to Emily's room, she was sleeping soundly. The *ayahs* had washed and changed her and put fresh linen on the bed, but she looked as frail as a crushed rosebud, with deep shadows under her eyes, and cheeks and lips still drained of colour. The *ayahs*, tired but willing, moved about putting the room to rights, but of Moti there was no sign. At their suggestion I constructed a makeshift cradle from the bottom drawer of a tallboy, fitted with a pillow and the tiny sheets and shawls Emily and I had sewn. I placed the baby in it with some ceremony, but she, instead of settling to sleep, elected to open her unfocused eyes and bawl. I wanted to wake Emily to perform her maternal function but, when I asked her *ayah*, the woman smiled pityingly at my ignorance, then dipped the corner of a clean handkerchief into a mixture of tepid water and sugar she had been preparing, and popped it into the infant's mouth. Within seconds, she was sucking contentedly, and within minutes she was asleep.

BOOK III

MOFUSSIL

'Consider how much more pain
is brought on us by the anger
and vexation caused by ill acts
than by the acts themselves …'
Marcus Aurelius

CHAPTER 1

The small girl survived her unorthodox arrival and flourished under the ministrations of the two old *ayahs* and a third employed solely for her benefit.

Her mother responded less quickly to the attention with which she was surrounded, and for a week or so I knew great anxiety on Emily's behalf. She seemed unable to rally her energies, but lay quietly all day, her eyes closed, uninterested in anything, even the infant in its absurd drawer-bed beside her.

Charles remained invisible throughout the day of his daughter's birth, the 14th of April. Emily never asked for him, and I was grateful that I did not have to lie to explain his absence. When that night he entered her bedroom as I was spoon-feeding her with chicken broth, he looked both shamefaced and ill. His eyes met mine briefly as he approached and I saw in them not only awareness of the condition in which I had found him at dawn, but a memory of what had passed between us on the previous night. He stood at the end of the bed looking down at his wife and child.

'Emily? Emmie? How are you?'

'All right,' she replied in a whisper.

'The baby? I have not seen it yet.'

'Over here, it's a girl.' Emily opened her mouth for another spoonful of soup and refused to look as her husband came around the bed and bent over the drawer.

'She's nice!' said the infant's father. Her mother did not disagree.

'Very nice! Very small, though, don't you think?'

'They are always small.'

'Oh, yes, I suppose so.'

There was a pause as the new father cast around for something to say, while Emily continued to sip stolidly at the soup.

'Emmie, is there anything you want? Anything I can get you?'

'No.'

'Cannot I do anything for you? Would you like me to … to read to you?' Obviously a sudden inspiration.

She shook her head.

'Nothing at all I can do? Anything? I'd like…'

'No, nothing!' And she turned her head away as though the interview was at an end.

'I'll … I'll come in again later, then.'

Charles tiptoed out of the room and Emily continued silently with her meal. My heart ached for her, and for him, but there was nothing I could do to right matters between them.

Dinner that night was a depressing affair of long silences punctuated by heavy sighs from Charles and brief bursts of pointless conversation between Oliver and myself. Once, after a particularly deep sigh, Oliver caught my eye and made a *moue* of mock despair. I frowned heavily to reduce him to order, whereupon he fetched a huge sigh from his boots, compelling me to smile hastily into my napkin. Charles excused himself directly he had eaten and went to his own room; Oliver settled down to his port and I went out and walked up and down the dark verandah to try to cool myself in the open air. I enjoyed the freedom of strolling in the warm darkness unencumbered by shawls and wraps. It reminded me of the sociable, comfortable Italian nights of my childhood, when the villagers promenaded the little square below our villa, laughing and gossiping by yellow lamplight, and the scent of camellias and orange blossom mingled with the salt sea air. Here it was great bushes of pale hibiscus that glimmered through the dark and the scent came from fronds of pink and white quisqualis cascading over the verandah rail. There were crickets in the grass, the sudden moo-like moaning of a conch shell and the inevitable pi-dog barking in the servants' quarters. So different, but because of the warmth and the southern sense of freedom, so much the same.

'So, Laura, it appears that his wife has not yet forgiven poor old Charles. I hope you have?'

'Oh, she knows nothing of what happened last night.' I turned to face Oliver as he joined me.

'No? Then it must have been alcoholic remorse.'

'Remorse of some sort, certainly. Must you be flippant?'

'But why the sighing? What else has happened—or should I not know?'

'You already know. As you have said yourself, they do not love each other.'

'Ah, I see. Poor little creature.'

'Whom do you mean—the baby?'

'Emily. Isn't she happy, then, at least about the infant?'

'I don't know. She has scarcely looked at her. And refused to look at Charles either.'

'Poor little woman; that's too bad. Can I see her?'

'Why not?'

'Come with me then—now!' And he walked with his quick light stride into the house, followed by me.

Emily did not open her eyes when we entered her room, but I knew she was not asleep. The *ayah*, who had been fanning her, gave me the fan and I sat down on the bed.

'Emmie, you've a visitor,' I began softly. 'Oliver has come to see how you are and inspect the baby. Isn't that kind of him?'

'Oliver?' She opened her eyes and smiled at him where he stood, looking quite at home, at the end of the bed. 'Oliver's always kind,' she whispered and put out her hand. He took it and sat down without ceremony on the opposite side of the bed to me.

'Are you feeling better now?'

She nodded, still smiling.

'Good. And the baby? I haven't really seen her yet. Can I have a look?'

A shadow crossed Emily's face, and she turned her head away from the drawer. 'If you want,' she said.

Oliver bent over the drawer and pulled open the shawl with one finger.

'Good heavens, it's tiny! Here, young woman, let's have a closer look at you.'

Before I could stop him, he had scooped the baby out of the drawer and was holding her up to examine her. Her milky eyes fluttered open for a moment, then closed again tranquilly as Oliver cradled her in his arms and in a most professional manner. I almost expected him to say 'Diddums!', and watched with astonishment, the fan idle on my lap, as he continued his scrutiny.

319

'She's going to have very fair hair,' he said after an appreciable pause. 'Look, Emily, there's a little yellow curl at the back of her neck.' Without turning her head, Emily slid her eyes around and threw a resentful look at her daughter. 'And her eyes—well, difficult to say as she won't open 'em, but her eyelashes are as dark as yours already, so I'll wager her eyes are going to be blue like yours too. What would you like them to be—blue or brown?'

'Don't care!' returned Emily coldly.

'They'll be blue—not a doubt of it—and her nose is certainly yours. Not much of it yet, but what there is is yours. And, look, her chin too, and the way her eyebrows arch. Quite extraordinary! You must have noticed the resemblance yourself, Emily? There's no mistaking it.'

'No ... she just looks like a baby to me. Any baby!'

'But you're wrong. Isn't she, Laura? This infant is exactly what you must have been at the same age. Quite enchanting.'

I gritted my teeth and threw him a warning look. He was overplaying his hand. But Emily did not realize it. For the first time her expression betrayed a flicker of interest.

'You're joking,' she said doubtfully. 'She's not really like me ... is she?'

'The image! I don't see how you can have missed it. Here, have a closer look yourself.' And he held the baby towards her mother. Emily hesitated, then pulled herself up against the pillows, and took the white bundle from him. Oliver watched her gravely as she settled the child in the crook of her arm and looked down on it.

I watched Oliver. I had begun to think I knew him well, but I had never seen his face so serious, so earnest, so understanding. Just in time I remembered what an excellent actor he was, or I might myself have melted. He bent over and placed his finger under the baby's chin.

'Look, Emily, she is just like you—though I don't expect she'll grow up half as beautiful. But now, well, she's lovely, isn't she?'

'Yes! ... Yes! She is nice, isn't she? A nice little thing, really.' And she pushed away his large hand the better to see the tiny face.

'Very nice. It's just as well Charles can't be shamed by her looking so like her mother, because there's not a trace of her father in her that I can see.'

'No?' Emily's interest grew to avidity.

'Not a trace. Not a feature that is Flood. She is all Hewitt, my girl. Pure Hewitt!'

320

'Yes, I believe you're right. And, oh, Oliver, do look at her little hands; see the minute fingernails, all so perfect!'

Oliver drew back, smiling, and watched as Emily rather hesitantly kissed one small hand, then examined it again for further evidence of perfection. He drew in a deep breath and gave me a glance that was scarcely less than triumphant.

'Oliver, what about ... do you think her toes can be as perfect?'

'Have a look.'

'Oh, but she's all wrapped up ...'

'Unwrap her, then. She's your baby, isn't she?'

'Yes! Yes, she's *my* baby!' And Emily swiftly unwrapped the shawl to reach the problematical toes.

I don't believe she noticed when we left her. She was too busy gloating, doting and crooning over her newfound treasure.

I shut the door behind me and walked downstairs with Oliver in companionable, and, for once, easy silence.

'You know,' I said judiciously as we gained the drawing-room, 'that was a very nice thing you did.'

'I did? What did I do, apart from congratulate a mother on her child, which, I believe, is fairly customary?'

'And also apart from lying like a trooper and stretching your luck to the winds! I was afraid you were not going to get away with it, particularly when you pointed out how little the infant resembles its papa.'

'Well, that's true enough, in all conscience.'

'And the marked, astonishing, resemblance to its mama?'

'Well, that only needed pointing out. The rest was just ... well, maternal instinct, I suppose.'

I laughed and then we stood smiling at each other amiably in the light of the chandelier.

'You're a fraud, Oliver Erskine,' I said; 'an absolute fraud. All the trouble you take to get yourself disliked and condemned, and beneath your cynicism and hardness you're very nearly as sentimental and ... and squashy ... as a new mother yourself.'

'Oh, come now. That's a bit hard ...'

'And you handled that infant as to the manner born; yet I can remember being told, and on good authority, that you "couldn't abide nippers".'

'No more can I! Most unreliable objects—at both ends. I was mighty glad to hand over that parcel of incipient squalls I can assure you.'

'I wonder whether I'll ever understand you.'

'And yet, I'm such a simple man, Laura.'

'You are not,' I said vehemently.

'But I am. That poor girl upstairs, all she really wants, you know, is something of her own, something to love. Isn't it better for her to grow into a foolish mama rather than a bitter wife? And the brat's going to need a loving mother, after all; there's nothing extraordinary in divining that much.'

'I wonder. And I wonder if Emily will ever realize how much you have done for her tonight?'

'Certainly not. She's much too silly. Anyway, it would all have come in time. I just hastened the process a little perhaps.'

'You did much more than that. She was determined not to love the baby because ... because it is Charles's.'

'I had gathered as much. Which was why I played on the Hewitt features. Poor devil. He'll probably be made to feel out of things for the rest of his life. But he could have managed his own affairs with a little more ... er, finesse, don't you think?'

Knowing what I now knew of those affairs, I had to agree. 'Oh, absolutely!' I said, never realizing how far I had travelled from my original estimate of Charles. Or, indeed, of his brother.

'Possibly. As to that, little imagination was needed by me. You cannot know it, I suppose, but I was abandoned by my mother. My father died when I was four.'

'Oh, Oliver.'

'Now don't waste your pity. I lacked nothing. From my grandparents I received more love, more cherishing, than any mother could have given me. I was spoilt ... indulged, I suppose ... in a way no boy should be. But still, I always knew I was not as other boys.'

That I could understand. Reared here in Hassanganj, heir to the estate, surrounded by servants and retainers, and used, from birth, to the deference and respect that that position gave him, he must have had a hard time of it among boys brought up in more prosaic circumstances. As if in answer to my thoughts, he went on: 'Of course, I saw few children when I was a child; but at thirteen I was sent to school in France, and the young gentlemen of the academy favoured with my presence had the deuce of a good time reducing me to size. Can't blame that on my mother, of course, but perhaps, had I had a mother at all, I would not have felt quite as... as out of things, as peculiar. My boyish sufferings might have been less acute,' he ended, with a laugh.

'What a lonely little boy you must have been.'

'Probably. I was not aware of loneliness at the time; but, sometimes, of an enormous discontent, which was probably due to loneliness. And while I was certainly over-indulged, I was also made to learn my responsibilities at an early age, something else that set me apart from my contemporaries. I must have been an abominable little brute: self-important, too contained, precocious! An amalgam of all the least endearing qualities of youth.'

'Yes, I expect you were,' I agreed. 'You've improved with age.'

'Thank you.' He laughed.

I had never before thought of Oliver as a child; it is not easy to envision a strong and assertive character in the days when it was still malleable, open to influence, immature. Now I saw him, very distinctly, trying to content himself with the companionship of the old, earnestly endeavouring the role assigned him, yet remaining, despite his efforts, a lonely and rather pathetic small boy. That my conclusion was accurate, and that the memory of that lost childhood had remained with him, was proved by his evening's work with Emily and her baby.

For a space we enjoyed a ruminative and intimate silence; then he said, 'You must get Emily back on her feet as soon as possible. I want you all out of here in a hurry.'

'More news?' I was too used to him to resent his phrasing.

'Nothing explicit. I don't want to run the risk of you being cut off here in Hassanganj. And you will all be better out of the heat.'

'It will be some weeks before we can move. Emily had a very hard time, and she has not been strong for weeks. The heat, I suppose. I'm sorry we are such an anxiety. Another few days and we would have been gone.'

'And the baby would have arrived on the road! No, better this, even though it means a delay.'

'I'll do my best. You have endured more through the presence of your guests than you had bargained for, unfortunately.'

'Not at all. In fact, it's a curious thing, but there have been moments when I have really felt the benefit of a woman's presence in the house.

No, don't laugh, I'm serious. Things have been—well—better ordered; more comfortable, since Emily—or rather you, for I know it is you who have done the actual supervision since Kate left—had a hand in the housekeeping. Sometimes I've even had a fancy to see a woman of my own sitting at the head of my table, entertaining my guests, concerning herself with my well-being. I must be getting old. It's a fancy I have never entertained before.'

'But not unnatural, surely?'

I had seated myself and Oliver now stood before the empty hearth, leaning one arm along the high, marble mantelshelf.

'Do you think it could work?' he asked after a short pause.

'What?'

'Well—marriage. I suppose it would have to be marriage. For me, I mean?'

'I doubt it,' I replied seriously, for he seemed serious.

'Why not?'

'Well, you're too old! Too set in your ways, at least. And you've had everything your own way too long. I don't think you could adapt yourself to another personality. And of course you would have to.'

'Hm, perhaps you are right.'

He put his hands in his pockets and stood frowning at the floor.

'The thing would be, of course, if not much adaptation were needed. If I were to find my … my "complement"—I believe that is the term, is it not?—perhaps I would have a better chance?'

I made no comment.

'You cannot agree?'

'I cannot see you finding a "complement".'

His frown grew more pronounced, but my suspicions awoke when I saw his lips twitch very slightly.

'Well, but now, tell me honestly; just supposing I were lucky enough to find my true complement … my prospective helpmeet, do you think that my … er … well, the matter that you so summarily discovered in the old tower one afternoon, do you think such a departure from the conventional norms could be forgiven me?'

So this was what the easy intimacy of a few minutes ago could lead to. I stood up and readied myself to leave the room.

'I have no idea,' I said frigidly, 'and it is not something I care to discuss!'

'But, Laura, please don't go … one moment! I'm only asking your advice, quite genuinely, I do assure you.'

I hesitated. Being asked for one's advice is always flattering.

'And admit it, now, you are the one person who knows sufficient of my—er—situation to advise me without prejudice, are you not? Do you think … could a well brought-up young woman overlook such a matter, do you suppose?'

'I am sure I do not know. It would depend on the young woman.'

'No? Well, but could you, for instance, any young lady of your background and upbringing … even your temperament and education … could you, let us say, forgive such a thing? Supposing you loved a man?'

'Yes,' I answered unwisely but without hesitation. 'I suppose I could—if I loved the man very much, of course.'

'Of course! Thank you. That is all I wanted to know.'

'But,' I added sternly, unable to resist the luxury of admonition, 'if you intend to look for a wife, I would advise you to amend your ways. First!' And I walked to the door.

'That piece of advice, at least, is unnecessary,' he said. 'But thank you all the same.'

And opening the door he wished me a polite goodnight.

A couple of days after her birth, Emily and I decided the baby was ready for her first airing, and at sunset I carried her on to the verandah.

With their feet on the extending arms of their chairs, brandy-*panis* in their hands, Oliver and Charles took their masculine ease before dinner. Charles, who still had only the slightest acquaintance with his daughter, looked both pleased and alarmed when I placed the child in his arms, and Oliver watched sardonically as his brother attempted the role of nursemaid, rocking the baby rather feverishly in his arms.

'Has it got a name yet?' Oliver asked after twitting Charles for his lack of fatherly expertise.

'Please don't refer to her as "it",' I objected.

'Well then, has *she* got a name yet?' he amended with good humour.

'Oh, I think I'll leave that to Emily,' Charles answered. 'She'll think of something suitable.'

'More likely a whole string of names. Her mother, your mother, her grandmother and your god-mother, aunts without number and all her closest friends, they'll all have to be included or risk giving offence. You'll have to be firm, Charles. It could end up "Euphemia" ...'

'We don't know any Euphemias,' Charles pointed out.

'... or "Eustacia"! Much better take it upon yourself to dub it Mary or Ann and leave it at that.'

'Well, I don't know that I can ...' Charles began to object, as I took the baby and allowed him to return to his brandy.

'She already has a name—a very beautiful one,' I broke in as I prepared to return indoors. 'Emily has decided on "Pearl".'

'Oh! Well, it's nice enough, I suppose, though I don't believe it is a family name, is it?' Charles said.

'Well, Pearl she is to be,' I assured him, and then retreated hurriedly as, the connection made, Oliver took the cigar from his mouth and burst into laughter, to the bewilderment of his brother.

For it was I who had told Emily that 'Moti' is translated by the English 'Pearl', and nothing would satisfy her but that her daughter should bear the name of the woman who had brought the child safely into the world.

CHAPTER 2

The mountains now were seldom visible.

All through the day, the sky was more bronze than blue: a gong of bronze trembling soundlessly under the onslaught of heat reflected from the parched plains of India. Distances disappeared in a stifling haze and in the evenings the horizon disintegrated into a long bruise, purple and livid, where the sun, which none had seen but all had felt, slipped into a night scarcely more bearable than the day. Only occasionally, when the moon rose, a suggestion of serrated silver to the north reminded me that the mountains were still there.

I doubted now whether I should ever see them. The trouble forecast by a few, ignored except intermittently by the many, was no longer a matter for conjecture.

Remote as we were, inaccessible as I had thought we were, now Hassanganj was on the way to somewhere, Lucknow, and two or three times a week we shared our meals with travellers posting hurriedly to and from the capital of Oudh, giving news or seeking instructions: soldiers, civil administrators and merchants anxious for their future, all with stories to tell, opinions to give, alarms to share. I became conversant with the names of half a dozen small European communities within a few hours' ride of Hassanganj, and realized for the first time how artificial our isolation had been, how much more due to Oliver Erskine's character than the character of the terrain. For our host, the boundaries of Hassanganj were the limits of the acceptable world.

All who came to the house knew his name and situation; Hassanganj and its master were difficult to overlook. But often, as we ate our heavy meals in an atmosphere which advocated living on air, I became aware of the hostility and suspicion with which Mr Erskine was regarded by his neighbours, a hostility engendered more, I thought, by ignorance than animosity. Not that Mr Erskine exerted himself to dispel that ignorance.

Usually he sat at the head of his table, listening courteously enough to what was said, but in a silence that enraged the bold and intimidated the frail. But when he was aroused, and I will say that what roused him was usually stupidity, he did not hesitate to disagree or condemn with just that same sardonic bluntness he used with his intimates. His manner was a nice combination of arrogance and reserve, and I guessed he used it deliberately as a shield to foil the advances of his fellows.

'A man with a lot of friends,' he once said to Charles, who had ventured to criticize his lack of cordiality, 'is like a dog with a lot of fleas—always restless and generally uncomfortable. Give me one or two fine ticks I can really work on.'

I smiled when I heard this and, little as I condoned his disdain for his fellows, I sympathized with his desire to channel his interests deeply rather than severally, for this was my own bent. Moreover, few of the men, and they were all men who called in at Hassanganj, had intellect, education or imagination enough to commend themselves even to me, much less to a man as critical as Mr Erskine. He seldom bothered to conceal his derision of the type of Englishman who tried to produce around himself in India the same atmosphere that he had enjoyed, or more probably wished he had enjoyed, at 'Home', and Charles and I suffered many uncomfortable moments trying to lead the conversation away from such matters as the impossibility of finding a good sausage, or sufficient gentlemen to make up a cricket eleven, or servants conversant with how afternoon tea was served in Chichester.

These reflections on past comforts were probably largely defensive; it took a hardened newcomer to wander through the vast Hassanganj rooms and submit to the ministrations of the Hassanganj servants without some betrayal of astonishment, while the luxury of the furnishings, and the splendid accoutrements of the dinner table often reduced the stranger to silence. It amused me to realize that no section of the Europeans who visited us in those days could altogether forgive Mr Erskine his wealth, his ability or his self-sufficiency. By tone and inflection, rather than any actual comment, it became clear that the military chose to see him as a sybarite, the planters as an amateur, and the officials as a meddler; I suppose because he combined something of all their trades with such unwarrantable success.

I believe he knew, and quite enjoyed, the opinion in which he was held. What he could not realize was that his most unforgivable characteristic was his self-sufficiency, for this was so much an integral part of him, and owed so little to deliberate cultivation, that he was unaware of it.

However, not all the gentlemen who passed through Hassanganj were deserving of Mr Erskine's censure, and one morning, at the beginning of May, I found my shipboard friend Mr Roberts taking *chota hazri* on the verandah with my host. He had travelled through the night, and had decided to take advantage of the proximity of Hassanganj to rest in comfort during the day.

'I had not hoped for the pleasure of finding you still here,' he said, as we sat down.

'We did not expect to be here ourselves, but the baby arrived rather less than opportunely, so here we are.'

'So Mr Erskine has just told me. Mother and child are well, I trust?'

'Pretty well,' I said, while Oliver added, 'Confound 'em!'

'Yes, I can imagine, Mr Erskine, that you are anxious for the welfare of your young relatives; this heat, y'know, apart from anything else.' And though it was not yet six o'clock, Mr Roberts mopped his face and pointed out that the Brain-Fever bird was already calling, a sure indication that the day was to be a torrid one.

'All the same,' he went on, 'they are certainly more comfortable here than they would be elsewhere, and probably a good deal safer too.'

'You bring more alarms and rumours of war, then, Mr Roberts?' I sighed and settled back for yet another recounting of the incidents and symptoms I had heard so much of recently. What would it be this time?

'There are plenty of them about, Miss Laura,' Mr Roberts answered, while Oliver watched him lazily through half-closed eyes. 'I think I may safely say that this has been the most disquieting journey upriver I have ever made. Most disquieting. This business in Barrackpore, you're heard of it of course, Mr Erskine? I remember how good your system of information is.'

'Perhaps. There have been a number of incidents. Which one do you mean?'

'At Barrackpore. A sepoy of the 34th Infantry, inflamed they say by *arak* or *bhang*, ran amok, tried to incite his fellows to mutiny and cut down a couple of his officers. Could have been serious; very serious. Fortunately, the man in command there—you will have heard of General Sir John Hearsey, of course—was sufficient to the occasion. With his two sons, undeterred by the fact that the sepoy was still armed, he rode out to where four hundred men of the 34th had stood by and watched the attack on their officers without protest. Seeing him approach, the sepoy, one Mangal Pandi, lost his nerve and turned his musket upon himself. He did not die then, but was executed some days later.'

'Hm,' commented Mr Erskine, 'that was a mistake.'

'What else could the General have done?' retorted Mr Roberts with indignation. 'The man had to be made an example of.'

'That is very military thinking from you, Mr Roberts. Do you not see that this man—what did you say his name was?'

'Pandi, Mangal Pandi.'

'Mangal Pandi is now not only an example but a legend. Worst of all, a martyr. Making martyrs is a mistake, as the Jews once discovered to their cost.'

'There was no alternative, surely? Particularly at a time like this.'

'Most particularly at a time like this, it should have been avoided. Ignominious dismissal would have served General Hearsey as well, or penal servitude, or even an execution, delayed until the matter was forgotten.'

'Well, perhaps you are right. It is disturbing. Very disturbing.'

We sat in silence for a time. The Brain-Fever bird's call reached a frenetic crescendo, and then gave way to the three-note despair of a dove.

'You have had no trouble here, of course?' Mr Roberts commenced again.

'Not yet, but I'm sorry to say there is no "of course" about it. Hassanganj is unlikely to escape the flame once the tinder is lighted. If it is allowed to be lighted.'

'But surely, oh, come now, Mr Erskine, matters are very different here in the *mofussil* to what they are in Calcutta, or any cantonment? Why, you haven't even a police outpost on your land.'

'No. If trouble comes for me, it won't be from the military element. I have tried to be just and a fair landlord; my people are probably as contented as any in Oudh. No, if we encounter trouble, it will come from another direction—my neighbours on three sides.'

'Ah, *talukhdars* all. I had forgotten. But your relations with them have always been good, have they not?'

'Generally, but what will that matter if it comes to every man for himself? One of them, I think, I can be fairly sure of … Wajid Khan,

Laura, if it's any comfort to know it. But the other two are acquisitive gentlemen both. Certainly neither would hesitate to put a bullet in my brain if it would mean an extra parcel of land for themselves. And, frankly, I wouldn't blame them. Resettlement is an injustice, and they feel it more than any.'

'Naturally.'

'Even if the trouble is confined to the Army, believe me, our friends the *talukhdars* of Oudh are going to make capital of it. They don't care a damn about caste; all this rot about crossing the sea, defiled cartridges and so on means very little to them. Their grievance is a great deal more practical. They have been dispossessed of their rightful inheritance. Give them half a chance to win that inheritance back, by whatever means, and they'll take it. As I would.'

'Yes, yes, I take your point.'

'In Oudh, at least, any form of insurrection could be rightly termed a war for independence, Mr Roberts. Would you not agree?'

'I would agree that that is how the *talukhdars* will look on it.'

'They will be waging it too, Mr Roberts; make no mistake about that.'

'Well, I am grieved to hear of this. I confess I had given the matter no very serious thought and, bearing in mind the unique stability of Hassanganj in the past, the equity with which you have dealt with your people, and your *rissal*, of course, I had thought that you must be undisturbed. Now I can see why you should be anxious.'

'My *rissal*, forsooth! Four dozen brigands with matchlocks. They could be bought by the next *talukhdar* for an extra rupee a month. They are mercenaries; Rohillas most of 'em. And mercenaries are for sale to the highest bidder. They bear me little personal loyalty; and they'd bear their next employer just as little. No, Mr Roberts, I am a realist. I cannot depend on the devotion of any but a handful of personal servants, and those I would not strain to the point of denying their own people.'

'You have of course a perfectly legitimate title to your land?' Mr Roberts spoke as though he doubted it.

'Perfectly. A deed of gift signed by the Nawab Asaf-ad-Doulah in 1795. But what of that? The *talukhdars* around me consider themselves the rightful owners of their properties, but that meddling fool of a Settlement Officer Thomason decided he knew better and that the land belonged to the *talukhdars*' tenants. Which it doesn't, mind you. Neither by Mogul law, nor by Oudh law nor by decent common sense. Having been dispossessed by the superior and most worthy legislation of the British, do you think when their hour strikes, they are going to hold back from taking what belongs to a Britisher?'

'No, I see your point. This issue has been somewhat obscured in my mind by the military aspects of the situation. But of course what you say is very true. Thomason's measures were most ill-advised, even though he acted on behalf of the *ryot*, whom you must admit, has known little consideration from the *talukhdars*.'

'Everything, Mr Roberts, has been done too hastily; and in ignorance and arrogance. Now it is too late to mend matters. What disgusts me most is the indignation with which the news of the trouble here will be received by our lawmakers in London. How furiously they will disclaim their mistakes and blame all on the base ingratitude of the heathen Indian who has the temerity to love his lands with just the same grasping fervour with which every noble MP loves his manor set in ancient English fields.'

'Yes, yes indeed,' Mr Roberts sighed, though he managed to look, in spite of the heat, very cool and contained in his pale grey breeches and alpaca coat.

Heat haze already clouded the clear morning sky and, in the pause that followed, my eyes lingered on the long vista of lawns and gardens, giving way in the distance to wooded parkland and a glimpse of the top of Moti's tower thrusting through the foliage of mangoes and sal woodland that formed the confines of the park.

I had become so accustomed to it all: the vast spaces, the huge pink house, the army of servants, the quiet routine of the day. I knew the names of the gardeners now and of all the house servants. I knew how many children they had, and where they lived, whether in the servants' quarters or in the village beyond the park. I knew, too, a little of how they lived, and how small the contentments were they cherished: a bare mud-walled room, a string bed, one meal a day and, after work, a pull at the communal *hookah* while their children scrambled in the dust around them, and their friends told long countrymen's stories of crop failure, water shortage and sudden flowering after God-given storm. I had learned a little about their gods, and I had an inkling of their fears: the fear of disease and unexplained death, enemies in this world and the next, uncountable, unnamable ghosts and bogies and hydra-headed devils, and the *bunnia* who owned them body and soul. And of their rare delights I knew something too: chanting processions to the temple or the mosque, marriages with cymbals and hand drums, bride and groom made modestly blind by strings of marigolds hanging before their faces, and a great *bhoj* to follow with mountains of sweetmeats and spiced pastries. From being strange, all these things had entered the fabric of my reality, woven day by day, in custom and monotony, into the warp and woof of my own mind.

Peaceful, placid, simple! Could it be possible that I had been so wrong, that my people had been so wrong? Could these thin brown men, shanks gleaming in the sun as they tended flowers, really turn on us, betray us, kill us? That morning the thought was inconceivable.

And then Mr Roberts turned to me and said he had recently come upon the Wilkins family again. They were in a small station a little to the east of us; the Major, like Wallace Avery, had been seconded to civilian duties.

'It's one of these new stations they've created. Merely a police post really, but Major Wilkins has a subaltern and a few sepoys under him, and a civilian assistant of some sort; so he is a happy man.'

'How many Europeans are there?' asked Oliver.

'Six or seven, no more.'

'Hmph!' Oliver's grunt expressed disapproval. 'And there's a woman there?'

'Two,' I informed him. 'Elvira would never leave her Ma and Pa. Isn't that right, Mr Roberts?'

'Oh, yes, Miss Elvira's there, and the poor young civilian looks rather hunted.'

'Pity,' said Oliver.

'I did try to hint, you know, that the ladies might be better placed in Lucknow, but Major Wilkins wouldn't hear of it. His men could be relied on, and so forth and so on. You know the usual attitude?'

'I know.'

'For myself, well, the unrest is almost tangible, particularly here in Oudh, but our people either will not or cannot realize it. Up and down the river I have found the same extraordinary complacency in the face of flagrant insubordination. Among the military, that is. The planters know what is happening. And the civil administration—sometimes.'

'Henry Lawrence realizes, thanks be to God,' commented Oliver in a tone that indicated his respect for the newly appointed Chief Commissioner of Oudh. For Henry Lawrence had won the admiration of all who knew of the strength, efficiency and probity he had brought to his administrative duties in the Punjab. It was these qualities that had brought him now to Lucknow, to placate the *talukhdars*, reassure the sepoys and ameliorate the effects of the measures instigated by the Chief Settlement Officer, Mr Thomason.

'Yes, indeed! I hear he is fortifying the Residency and laying in provisions in case matters deteriorate. It is something.'

'Very little more than nothing,' retorted Oliver. 'A waste of time. The Residency is incapable of fortification. Think, man! How can you adequately protect a cluster of buildings like that, perched on the highest point in the area, one flank right on the river, the others deep in the city, none of it more than partially walled. It is a preposterous position to strengthen.'

'It is all he can do.'

'True. His battle was lost last year with annexation. Now all he can really do is keep matters from coming to a head; and if there is any man who can do that, it is Lawrence. But his jurisdiction is only Oudh. And there's a hell of a lot of India outside Oudh, Mr Roberts, a hell of a lot.'

Mr Roberts looked at me uncomfortably, not knowing how well used I was to Mr Erskine's language.

Having completed his business in the upper sections of the Doab, Mr Roberts was on his way downriver to Calcutta again. As an indigo trader, the waterways were the main transport for himself, no less than his commodity, and his life seemed to hinge on what he referred to fondly (and inaccurately, as there were several) as 'The River'. The conversation soon reverted to indigo exclusively.

He left again that evening.

'I wish my forebodings on the ship had not been fulfilled, Miss Laura,' he said as he shook my hand. 'God only knows what is in store for us, but we must hope to meet again before long in happier circumstances. I shall look forward to renewing our acquaintanceship when things are better; at least you could not be in safer hands.' And as he turned away to mount his horse, he threw me a half-whispered aside over his shoulder. 'A great man in his own acres, Miss Laura! But where's the hawk?'

I laughed, and watched him ride away down the avenue.

'You have a very good understanding with Mr Roberts,' observed Oliver drily, as we went indoors. 'What did he say to you as he left?'

'A joke,' I answered. 'Just an *intimate* joke.'

'Indeed?' said Mr Erskine.

CHAPTER 3

I remember the day Emily got dressed and came down for breakfast for the first time—Sunday the 10th of May.

None of us had expected to see her and it was with relief that I greeted her appearance, for otherwise I would have had to endure once again the chastening experience of being the sole audience (alone I could hardly be termed a congregation) of Charles's weekly prayer meeting. Oliver had been polite enough to stay and hear the lessons and collects read by his brother for the first two or three Sundays after Christmas of our stay, but had then decided that Sunday morning was the only time in the week when he could give the elephants from the indigo factory the sort of attention they needed; *mahouts* these days were not what they had been, and the elephants' welfare could not be left to chance. So that had left me, during the time that Emily was indisposed, with the sole responsibility for the heartfelt 'Ah-mens' that Charles expected.

That evening, when the sun had set, Charles took Emily out in her little white governess cart for an airing. As we watched them go slowly down the drive, Emily's white dress glimmering ghostlike in the dusk, Oliver said: 'Well, thank God for that. It won't be long now before I can get you all out of the place.'

'Oh, but she's not fit to travel yet,' I exclaimed. 'She's up and about, but she has no strength, Oliver. And we can't take the risk of her ... of her not ...'

'Not being able to feed the child,' he offered helpfully.

'Precisely. I'm afraid you'll have to put up with us for some time yet.'

'How much time, Laura? Before she can be put into a palanquin and sent to the hills? It will mean very little exertion for her—I'll see to that.'

'A fortnight, three weeks perhaps. I'm doing my best, Oliver. I'm trying to build her up, making her eat and so on. But we can't take risks.'

'Ha!' exclaimed my host rudely. 'Risks, the woman says!'

'Oh, do be sensible,' I said irritably. 'For the last three months you men have done nothing but rumble and grumble to anyone who would listen to you about the trouble that is to come, but be honest now, and admit that in all this time there has not been even one really significant incident here, let alone an alarming one. I declare, I am tired of the whole business, all this hurried coming and going, the alarms and rumours, the atmosphere of tension and ... and fear, and nothing ever happening!'

'Would you want something to happen?'

'No, of course not, and I don't believe it will either. I'm not going to force Emily beyond her strength for the sake of your ... your forebodings. You must just put up with us until I feel she is fit to travel.'

'Laura?'

'Well?'

'Is it only because of Emily's health that you are so reluctant to leave Hassanganj?'

'Certainly! What other reason could I have?'

'I can think of a couple. Leaving Hassanganj is the first of a series of steps that in the end will mean your severance from Charles. I have not forgotten that you intend to leave Mount Bellew and take up an—ah—"position", I believe you termed it, when you get back to England.'

'Oh, for heaven's sake! Use your common sense,' I flung at him without bothering to contradict his assertion.

'No? Not that? Well then, could it be, I wonder, that you have become fond of ... the place?'

'Well, yes, I have. In a way. I like it here. And I'll never live in this way again, I suppose. I'll miss it. But not enough to want to stay on here once we can get away without endangering Emily,' I added firmly.

'Ah, well. It was just a thought. Pity. I'll miss you too, you know,' he said after a time. 'And I don't mean all of you: just you yourself.'

'I can't think why,' I said morosely. 'I've done nothing but bicker with you since we arrived.'

'That's what I'll miss, I expect. I've enjoyed having a sparring partner.'

'Then you'd better find another,' I said ungraciously.

The governess cart was in view again, and I went out to meet it, leaving Mr Erskine puffing his cheroot on the verandah.

Then, a couple of mornings later, Charles dropped his hat into a shallow pool covered with scum and waterlilies when he was out after green pigeon. By now he seldom went out shooting—the heat made the sport less than inviting—but Emily had expressed a desire for jugged pigeon, and he had gone out to shoot her some birds. If he had used his common sense, he would have returned immediately after losing his hat, but doggedly he had ridden on through the open fields from grove to grove in pursuit of his quarry, and by the time he had got back to the house, not only were his face and neck beetroot red, but he was ill with headache and nausea.

'Sun stroke—but mild,' commented his brother without sympathy, and Charles was put to bed with a pad containing crushed ice on his head, and a lump of rocksalt to suck. I had fetched the salt myself from the sack in the cellar where it was kept, not knowing the use to which it was to be put; when I did, I protested that it would make poor Charles even more thirsty than he was.

'Probably,' concurred Oliver, 'but it will cure him of the sun. I don't know how or why, but I know it does. My grandmother used this remedy on me more than once, and I've seen the villagers use it too. Stop clucking and stick it in his mouth!'

Knowing better than to quarrel with the nostrums of Oliver's grandmother, I did as I was told.

'He'll be up in a couple of days, which is more than he deserves for his lack of sense,' said the elder brother, while the younger groaned piteously through the lump of pinkish salt, unable to open his eyes because of the swollen state of the lids.

'Poor Charles!' I whispered.

'Silly fool!' said Oliver, and we withdrew to let him sleep.

That same evening, Toddy-Bob brought us the news of Meerut. He had been sent into Lucknow for some much-needed articles for the baby and Emily, although I knew that Oliver had been reluctant to let him go. Covered with dust and sweat, he burst into the drawing-room where Oliver and I were sitting together in uneasy domesticity after dinner, and before even pulling his tall hat from his head, blurted out: 'It's happened, guv'nor! They're up! They turned on their h'officers and slaughtered the lot of 'em—women and nippers too! Word come of it on Wednesday, and I rode back like 'ell's blazes as soon as I'd foraged things out!'

338

'No doubt, Toddy?'

Oliver had got to his feet, and the two of us had our attention riveted on the small dirty man, his eyes popping in excitement and his hands clawing convulsively at his ridiculous headgear.

'No doubt, guv!'

'Sure it's not just a bazaar rumour?' Oliver repeated as Toddy-Bob strove to collect sufficient saliva in his mouth to enunciate his words.

'No, no rumour, guv'nor, s'elp me! It's Gawd's own truth! Massacred the lot of 'em, the dirty 'eathen bastards, shot their h'officers on the parade ground, fired the 'ouses in cantonments, and set free the prisoners.'

'When?'

'Last Sunday. On a *Sunday*, guv'nor!' He was as shocked as if he were a devout Christian and believed the world contained only others like himself.

'What else?' Oliver's lack of excitement made me want to shake him. Surely this was not the time to be so clinical, so detached.

'There's been trouble in the lines in Lucknow, already, and they say as 'ow the women, ladies that is, 'as all to go and get theirselves shut up in the Baillie Guard. S'truth, guv'nor.' Toddy wiped his forehead with his sleeve. 'The *chowks* are like all 'ell broke loose with people sayin' this and that and the other, but there's big trouble already, and what they say in the bazaars is only the beginning! They say—in the bazaars—that the 'eathen soldiers from Meerut 'ave gone on to Delhi, guv'nor!'

Toddy's boot-button eyes almost left their sockets as he imparted this intelligence.

'That's unlikely, anyway. They'd have been stopped before they got to Delhi. Meerut has more white troops than any other cantonment in the province.'

'Yeah.' Toddy was entirely unconvinced. 'But that's what they say!'

'Well, if that's all, Tod, you'd better go and get something to eat.'

'*All!*' muttered Toddy bitterly, as he moved to the door.

'Ah! And Tod …'

'Guv'nor?'

'I think you had better have a dram or two tonight. For your health's sake.'

'Gawd bless you, guv'nor!' said Toddy fervently, and closed the door. The ecstasy on his face at receiving permission to drink was more than even the gravity of his news could counter, and I was smiling as Oliver came back to his chair.

'I trust we will not have to call on him for help tonight,' he said, 'for he'll take my dram or two to mean a bottle or two.' Then, more soberly, 'Well it's come then, Laura. Here is the alarming incident you were talking about, and if even half of what Tod has heard is true, it is very alarming indeed.'

'Meerut is an important place then?'

'The main depot of several of the Queen's regiments, and also of some native regiments. If officers have actually been killed, and I think that much is true, then it is mutiny of the Army. All the Army, I expect. At least in this province. And from there, it must spread.'

He sounded tired and depressed, and for the first time I actually believed that he was in danger of losing his home, his estates, all that made his life worth living.

'You'll have to stay now willy nilly,' he said. 'If you could get away tomorrow, there might be a chance for you to reach Mussoorie before the thing spreads. But with Emily, and now Charles, laid up, damn him, I suppose that's out of the question?'

'I'm afraid so. Oh, Oliver ... I know we must be a wretched burden on you at such a time. I wish it had happened otherwise.'

'Can't be helped. We must just make the best of it.'

Though Toddy-Bob had been emphatic that his intelligence was correct, it was still possible for me to withhold belief that British women and children had been slaughtered along with their menfolk. It was not that I was sufficiently sentimental to think that sex or age could materially alter the gravity of murder; it was just that nothing in my admittedly limited dealings with the natives had borne even a shadow of suspicion or animosity, and I hesitated to think them capable of deeds which I would have been reluctant to ascribe to my own race. So I was not frightened for myself, or indeed for the Floods. More cogent was the fact that Oliver Erskine, a white man, was in possession of a large tract of India which would most understandably be coveted by Indians, should the mutiny of the Army spread to the civilian population.

'What will you do now, Oliver?' I asked. 'Or, rather, what would you do if we weren't here?'

'Nothing to do. Except wait. Make plans, I suppose, in case the worst comes to the worst and we have to run for it. But that won't be for some time yet. Perhaps never. Henry Lawrence is a good man, you know. And he's still in control of Oudh.'

'Will he be able to handle the *talukhdars*?'

'God knows. I don't. I couldn't handle them myself, that much I know. But that's because I sympathize with them. Very soon perhaps I'll be in a position to sympathize with them even more deeply. Funny, isn't it? And they'll never realize it because of the accident of my white skin! Have you ever thought, Laura, that almost all the things that divide people from each other are accidental? Colour, race, religion. Which of us can influence how or what we are born? Yet we judge each other by these accidents. If it were not so, if my affections, my understanding, my deepest loyalties, were taken into account, I would be as much an Indian as the Maulvi of Fyzabad himself. But because I have a white skin, they'll cut my throat with pleasure. And I'm too much of an Indian to blame them for wanting to!'

'You do really associate yourself with them, don't you? I mean, haven't you any loyalty to England?'

'Some. But I could forget it much more easily than I could forget my affection for Hassanganj. My land, my people, my life are all here. England isn't important to me. Nor France. But this ... this is! This is where I belong, you see, Laura. And no one, neither the white man nor the brown, for very different reasons, can believe that I am honest in saying so.'

I found it difficult to believe him myself. No one could grudge his affection for Hassanganj, nor his pride in it; no doubt the satisfactions he discovered in his isolated life among the Oudh peasantry were, bearing in mind his temperament, more rewarding than anything he could have had in England. But yet? When the moment of severance came, should he ever have to make a final decision one way or the other, would he really find it easy to deny his birth? I did not think he would find it easy; but neither did I think he would find it impossible, as for instance, Charles or any of the other men I had met in India would find it impossible.

'What are you brooding about now?' he asked, noticing my silence.

I laughed. 'As a matter of fact I was thinking about you,' I answered him. 'I was wondering what you would really do if it came to the pinch and you had to choose between Hassanganj and your life, perhaps. Or your future anyway.'

'It is a choice I will never have to make, never fear. Hassanganj is mine, and here I stay.'

'Even if the *talukhdars* think otherwise; if they run you off the place?'

'I would very sensibly remove myself for the moment. But I would be back in due course. I have a better title to my land than most of my neighbours have to theirs. They might want it; they'll probably try to take it, but don't you see, Laura, whatever is going to happen, whatever form this trouble takes, it can only be temporary? The British have gone too far to withdraw. They are more now, have been more for a couple of generations, than just a parcel of traders defending their right to barter; they have put too much into this country. They have too much to lose to allow themselves to be pushed out. We are the real rulers of the entire peninsula. Alien, bungling, often unsympathetic, we may be, but the thing is a *fait accompli*. In time, the situation will right itself and the British will regain control of Oudh and all India; meanwhile, we all have to suffer the consequences of the apathy, ignorance and stupidity of our people at home. That's about what it amounts to; let us hope that the lesson we have to learn will not be too hard bought.'

'I would hate to think of Hassanganj abandoned by the Erskines,' I said, trying to imagine the contingency.

'There is only one Erskine,' he reminded me. 'There's the rub! But now, we are wasting time in thinking of imponderables. I don't want to alarm you, but as you know what you do, I would be glad if you would help me by making some small preparation yourself—as a possible safeguard. No more.'

'Of course. What can I do?'

'Some time, sooner rather than later, get together a bundle of clothes and so on, toilet things—I leave it to you—the sort of things you might need if we had to leave hurriedly and you hadn't time to pack. And do the same for Emily, but don't let her know it. And don't let the *ayahs* know either; they're curious old harpies. I take it you have a wardrobe or a drawer you can lock?'

I nodded.

'Good! That's all. Take as little as you can, and don't worry, it is most unlikely that you will need any of it, after all. What about money? Have you any cash?'

'Enough.'

'Good. Sew it into whatever … er … garment you wear next to your skin.'

I got up, thinking I would prefer to be employed in these matters than worrying about what might come, and went to the door. But Oliver stopped me.

'One moment. Have you ever used a gun? A pistol?'

'No, of course not.'

'Well, it doesn't matter. If you have to, you'll find you can shoot a man with the most practised. Come to the library a moment, will you?'

He made his way down the dimly lit, horn-hung corridor. I followed him apprehensively. He lit the lamp on his desk, unlocked a drawer and took out a pistol, which he opened and examined carefully. He clicked it shut and held the weapon out to me.

I took it with reluctance. It was a clumsy thing and heavy in my hands.

'Don't be scared. It's not loaded,' he said, smiling. 'Hold it like this, see …' He demonstrated, and then gave me a course of instruction on how the thing worked, and how to work it. Again and again I practised cocking it, firing it, loading it and unloading it, cocking it again, firing, unloading and so on. At the end of three-quarters of an hour, I was handling the weapon with confidence, if not affection.

'Good!' said my instructor. 'I believe you have the makings of an accomplished assassin. Now, I am going to load it, so don't fiddle with the damn thing more than you can help. Hide it, but in an accessible place, and don't forget you have it. If we have the opportunity, I'll take you out to practise firing it.'

He loaded the weapon and handed it over, butt first.

'Don't point it at *anyone*,' he said, quite unnecessarily, 'unless you intend to kill them, and if you intend to, make a good job of it! By the way,' he added as an afterthought, 'you won't need it if I am in the immediate vicinity. I shall be only too happy to put a bullet in your head to save you from … ah … the ultimate outrage.'

'Good heavens! Is that what all this is for?' I asked, genuinely astonished.

'Certainly? What else?'

'I thought it was to protect my life,' I answered him, whereupon he threw back his head and roared with laughter.

'An indomitable realist,' he chuckled, fixing me with an appreciative eye. 'Don't let my old-fashioned notions deter you, m'dear. If your life is of more value to you than your virtue, by all means relinquish the latter for the sake of the former, and accept my congratulations on your common sense!'

He laughed again, as I cast round furiously for something withering to say; but before I could speak, he went on: 'As a matter of fact, you are nearer the mark than you realize. I have armed you because I took it for granted that you would share the misconception of most young Englishwomen in India. But if we do run into trouble, it's much more likely that they will want your life rather than your person. Whatever your own opinion of your attractions, most Indians, bar the very lowest, would consider any, ah—commerce—with a white woman a defilement. Though of course, in time of war ...'

'Thank you. I will know now what to expect!'

He came round the great leather-topped desk to where I stood with the pistol in my hands. At the other end of the book-lined room, I could make out Old Adam's chair in the shadowed window alcove, and the lamplight just sufficed to glow dimly on the copper and silver-chased bowl of the hubble-bubble beside it.

'Laura, I don't want to frighten you, but it's best to be warned, isn't it? At least, I believe you would wish to know the worst.'

'Naturally. Though I wish things were rather more definite. It's the uncertainty, not knowing what will happen, or when, that I find wearing.'

'And I, believe me! I'm sorry that ... that your stay in Hassanganj has not been pleasanter. You've had more than your share of alarms to contend with.'

'Oh, there is no need for you to say so. Indeed, we have been most comfortable and ... and happy,' I said, but not with entire truth.

'I have been trying to see all this as it must appear to you, a young girl from a sheltered home, straight out from England, but I'm afraid the exercise of imagination is beyond me. Except, of course, that you must have cause to be more alarmed and agitated than you have allowed yourself to appear—by many things.'

'You are wrong,' I corrected him. 'I am not a young girl, and I am only indirectly straight out from England. Nor was my childhood particularly sheltered. You are trying to make me see with Emily's eyes. We are totally different people, with very different backgrounds. There is no need for you to worry about me, I assure you. I learnt early to take life as it comes.'

'Yes? Well, perhaps that is why I find you so ...' Then he stopped, laughed, and shook his head. 'Never mind! Not now. Perhaps it's too late. Or perhaps it's too early.'

'What is?' I asked, puzzled, but he just shook his head again, smiling.

'Go on. Off to bed with you now. Pack up your duds. It will give you something to think of. And don't ... don't be frightened, Laura. The worst might never happen.'

CHAPTER 4

My memories of the following weeks are blurred and confused. So much happened in other parts of India, even involving people we knew, but nothing touched us directly. Life in Hassanganj continued as it had always done, and perhaps the very fact that we had lived in such isolation for the past five months, cocooned in self-sufficiency, made it harder for us to believe that the tempo of our placid days could change and be engulfed by violence.

I had made up two neat packs of clothes and other necessaries for Emily and myself, and locked them away together with the pistol, trying to realize that these precautions were indeed necessary, not merely the sort of action taken by a character in a schoolboy's story. But as I worked in my big white bedroom under the swaying *punkah*, I found I lacked the imagination, or perhaps the experience, to envisage what circumstances would ever make them necessary. I was trying to anticipate seriously what seemed to me manifestly absurd, and this feeling that we were play-acting, that nothing was quite real, continued with me to the end. God knows why, for the following days brought us enough authenticated news to disquiet us to the point of alarm. I suppose Hassanganj's characteristic, if somewhat bizarre, atmosphere of stability had something to do with it.

At the end of the week, we heard that the bazaar rumours reported by Toddy-Bob were only too true, and that the mutinous sepoys from Meerut, having murdered their officers, set fire to the cantonment and freed eighty-five of their fellows from the cantonment jail, marched that same night to Delhi and placed themselves under the banner of the last of the Mogul kings. Then the telegraph wires had been cut and no further news had come, but few could doubt that, incited by the Meerut rebels, Delhi, the last stronghold of the ancient glory, would also rise in arms.

Hardly a day passed now without someone—a lone officer, perhaps, or a whole family—stopping at Hassanganj for a hasty meal and to disburden themselves of their news; but, even if this had not been the case, information would have reached us, more mysteriously perhaps, but none the less speedily. For one thing, Ungud was now fully recovered, and I often caught a glimpse of his meagre form edging away from the direction of Oliver's library. But more potent than any single source was the age-old system of communication that operates throughout India: the wells where the women gossip; the village tanks and groves where people gather in the dusk; the *serais* or halting places where travellers tell their tales all along the dusty ways that snake across the country; the roads themselves, always, however far from habitation, busy and alive; and the natural communicativeness of a people reared on curiosity and seeing no virtue in reserve.

No European could fail to be aghast at the news that the insurgent sepoys had been allowed to march from Meerut to Delhi without stay or hindrance. That they should attempt to do so was understandable; that they should manage to do so unbelievable.

'But what, after all, could be more natural than that they should want to place themselves under the man they believe to be their legitimate ruler?' pointed out Oliver. 'In their eyes, what they are doing is not rebellion; nor insurrection nor mutiny. It is an attempt to throw off foreign domination, and remember that is what the Indians have been doing with various degrees of success for the last three thousand years. It was bound to come, I suppose. If not now, then in ten, twenty or fifty years' time. But having come, their first instinct would be to place themselves under their king, doddery old puppet that he be.'

'You speak almost as if you condone them, sir,' observed our guest of the moment in an affronted tone. He was a major in the 71st Native Infantry, a round-faced man with large but dispirited whiskers and a pompous manner. Charles was with us also that evening, taking the air on the verandah. He was over the sunstroke, as Oliver had promised, but was plagued by boils and prickly heat.

'At least I cannot condemn them for wanting what, in their place, I would also want. Their methods I do not condone,' said Oliver.

'I'm glad to hear it,' said the visitor. 'The stories circulating in Lucknow regarding the Meerut massacre are too horrible to repeat!'

347

'Nevertheless, we have heard them all, several times over, and with many variations,' observed Oliver laconically.

'Then I cannot understand how you can have even a vestige of sympathy with the devils.'

'But I didn't say sympathy. I said understanding,' pointed out Oliver carefully.

'The same thing, in my view!'

'No doubt, but not necessarily in mine. Or not in all cases. Where I can place neither sympathy nor understanding is with the commanders in Meerut. They were on the spot and yet made so little attempt, not to halt matters—perhaps that was out of their power—but to raise the alarm in Delhi. One man on a good horse would have been enough to warn the city. But no one had the wit to realize it.'

His tone was scathing, and Major Ingham, rightly reading into it a condemnation of the military mind, huffed and fidgeted, but ventured no reply. For, indeed, the story which had come to our ears of that Sunday night in Meerut was no credit to the workings of the martial intelligence, but an indictment of the lack of initiative consequent on too acquiescent an acceptance of discipline.

The match set to the torch of Meerut was once again the abhorred Enfield cartridge. Advised of the sepoys' objections to this cartridge, Lord Canning, the Governor General, had ordered that, since the cap could readily be removed with the left hand, the teeth should not be used for uncapping—a wise, if partial measure, which, had it been followed, might have averted much that came later. The military, however, from the Commander-in-Chief, General Anson, through senior officers down to ignorant, newly-arrived subalterns, objected to this compromise as a point of pride, and ignored the directive. In Meerut the commander of the 3rd Light Cavalry, by reputation a vain and puffed-up man, now decided to use the favoured and elite 'skirmishers' of his own regiment to prove to their companions that an order from a British officer was inviolable. The skirmishers were paraded and ordered to pull the cartridge caps with their teeth as laid down in regulations. Eighty-five of the ninety men refused. They were court-martialled, condemned, then stripped of their regimentals and fettered at an ignominious public parade watched by all troops, brown and white, in the station.

After a couple of days of savage brooding on this wrong, on a hot Sunday as dusk drew in, the enraged sepoys rose, released their imprisoned comrades (and the other inmates of the gaol) and turned on their officers. The 60th Queen's Rifles, a white regiment, ready for Church Parade, were ordered out to quell them, but were first required to change their white drill for the Riflemen's dark green considered more suitable for battle, so that by the time they had been issued with ammunition the station was aflame. Swiftly joined by the native police and the *badmashes* of the bazaars, the sepoys cut down any officer they encountered, fired the lines and the bungalows of cantonments, and murdered women and children without compunction. The general in command of the station, Hewitt, a man so fat he took parades sitting in a carriage, and his Brigadier, Archdale Wilson, shocked to paralysis by their *Baba-log* having the temerity to revolt, only added to the chaos with inept and contrary orders and by bickering between themselves. When a junior officer volunteered to lead a contingent of the 60th in pursuit of the mutineers to destroy them before they reached Delhi, his suggestion was refused since it was felt that it would divide the force necessary to ensure the safety of the remaining officers.

So much was fact, as were the terrible accounts of pregnant women disembowelled by mutineers' swords, of others mutilated but yet living who were thrown on the pyres of their own bungalows, of children decapitated before their mothers' eyes, mothers set alight while their children watched shrieking. And, as Oliver Erskine remarked acidly, in the horror engendered by these atrocities it was easy to forget the self-love and the complacent arrogance of the officers whose prideful stupidity had caused the holocaust.

As the month of May wore on, the atmosphere of tension and apprehension tautened almost to snapping point, aided by the unremitting, inescapable heat. I wondered sometimes how much of the alarm displayed by our callers, how many of the rumours they recounted, and what measure of the credence they gave them was due to the sun and what to the facts. It seemed to me that many people had abandoned their homes and possessions, not to mention their positions, for trivial or inadequate reasons, impelled by panic rather than necessity. Some of them, particularly the women making their way to Lucknow, appeared almost to enjoy the novelty of their situation, regaling us with long accounts of how they had secured their possessions—the silver had always been buried, or let down a well, or hidden in the thatch—paid off their dependants and disposed of their pets. Some, indeed, carried their pets with them, dogs, cats and birds in cages, and all were accompanied by so many servants that I wondered what possible functions could have been performed by those who had been paid off. The birds reminded me of Connie's Polly, and I wondered often how that family was faring, and how little Johnny was doing in the heat.

Kate Barry was a more faithful correspondent than Wallace, and we had received several letters from her, the last to tell us that Sir Henry Lawrence had ordered all the women and children from Mariaon, together with the sick of the 32nd Foot, into the Residency.

'It has been a trying time,' she wrote, 'but so far everything has remained peaceable, though you would be saddened to see all the bungalows lying empty now, as even their masters are seldom able to go home. I resisted Sir Henry's orders till I thought he would clap me in irons and have me forcibly removed to the R. So here we are now, my dears, a lot of cats fighting for space on one small roof. The noise (for the defences are as yet incomplete, and an army of coolies is at work on them), the heat and the crowding are horrible, but George says it cannot be for more than a few days, so I do my best to bear it. But protect me from my own sex *en masse*, particularly when my boys are either absent or too busy to throw me a word!'

Emily was up and about now, but pale and languid, which I put down to the heat rather than to her confinement. We tried to shield her from a full knowledge of what was taking place, but sometimes she joined the party on the verandah in the early mornings or at dusk, and then she would cry weakly at the thought of abandoned pets in empty bungalows, and pray that all our friends in Lucknow were safe and well. So far she was unaware that Hassanganj too was threatened, and we took care that she should remain in her ignorance, not a difficult matter since she was always willing to have her attention diverted to Pearl, and indeed thought and spoke of little other than her child.

By the end of the month we had abandoned the pretence that nothing untoward was afoot, for by now the servants, on whose behalf we had dissimulated, were probably in possession of more of the facts than we ourselves. Oliver kept a loaded shotgun beside his bed, and Charles a similar weapon under his, while I took my pistol out of its drawer at night and laid it beside my pillow. I was afraid of it and sure I could never use it but, for all that, it gave me some sense of security.

Toddy-Bob swaggered around with a brace of pistols in his belt, and Ishmial wore his enormous *tulwar* in his.

Oliver continued to ride around the estate day by day, supervising, directing, scolding. Twice a week he held his court in the *kutcheri*, and a group of villagers with grievances would gather under the mangoes to sleep in the heat until their cases came up for hearing. Each morning, the usual line would form outside the back verandah, to lay a complaint against a neighbour, ask for an extra hour's water from the canal, or beg the *sirkar* to be lenient regarding their rent. And each day he heard them all with an equal, comprehending patience; even when we heard the accents of his wrath echoing in the house, we knew it was carefully timed and perfectly controlled. But now, Ishmial sat immediately behind him with his rifle and his *tulwar*, and Toddy-Bob would saunter, whistling, up and down the line, his sharp eyes alive to every unfamiliar face or unexplained bulge in clothing.

June came in, and on the first day of that month we were descended upon by the Wilkinses: the Major had decided that his womenfolk would be better off in the Baillie Guard after all, so gallantly he was attending them thither, assuring us that, of course, he would call in on us again on his return journey. He made this point so strongly that it was difficult to believe he was wholly innocent of having deserted his post, until it transpired that his post had deserted him, the handful of Indian police and soldiers he commanded having informed him politely, but with decision, that they were off to join the king in Delhi, and he would be wise to go to Lucknow.

'The damndest thing it was,' he said, astonishment at the recollection still in his eyes. 'They just marched in, said it wouldn't be any good sounding reveille in the morning as they wouldn't be there and neither would the coolies, and marched out and off! All quite quiet and regular-like and not a shot fired or a harsh word spoken. Extraordinary!'

It was impossible not to smile at the poor man's discomfiture.

'And what has become of the other Europeans in your station?' inquired Oliver.

Mrs Wilkins took it upon herself to reply.

'Oh, well, the Morrisseys (they're just police, y'know) have gone to Sitapore to her brother, and young Mr Snaith decided to stay on where he was. Of course he knows the Major will be returning, and he said it was too hot to travel anyway. And Mr Morrissey says he'll return too, once the rains have broke. But really, Mr Erskine, the cantonments were as quiet as a graveyard with nobody in 'em, and as I says to the Major, what is the use of going back to where there's no soldiers for you to command?'

'Hmph! Very reasonable,' commented Oliver.

'No question of it, my love,' said Mrs Wilkins's spouse. 'I must go back. To my station. To my command. That's why I must go to Lucknow, to report the situation, and make them see that I must have a fresh contingent of men. Reliable, responsible men, not like the others. Damn them!'

Oliver regarded Major Wilkins coolly over the orange he was peeling.

'Perhaps Lucknow won't be able to supply you with reliable men,' he suggested. 'What then?'

'Oh, nonsense! Nonsense! Of course they will. I'll make it my business to see that they do. Can't have the whole *mofussil* running amok because a few dozen sepoys take it into their heads to march off to Delhi. Delhi indeed! And what do they imagine will happen when they reach there? Will their king up and lead them? That silly old man … nearly blind and all as he is? Lead them against their own salt, for that is what it amounts to after all. *He's* never fed 'em, never paid 'em, never taken any interest in 'em. Not as we have. I've spent my whole life among the sepoys, Mr Erskine, and I'll wager I know more about 'em, white as I am, than their old king does.'

'Indeed?' said Mr Erskine, with a scepticism that was hard to ignore.

In the evening, Pearl's *ayah* brought her out onto the verandah to be admired by the visitors.

'Oh, Ma! What a mite it is,' exclaimed Elvira, prodding the white bundle in the *ayah's* arms with one thin unenthusiastic finger; but her mother insisted on taking the child into her own arms, and examined her closely.

'Oh, little pet,' she crooned. 'Oh, how lucky you are, Mrs Flood. I declare, I can't wait until Ellie gives me a grandchild. I just love these little ones. So helpless, y'know, and so pretty. Why this child has a real look of its Papa, hasn't it, Ellie? Look closely now.'

'She has not!' expostulated Pearl's mother. 'She's a true Hewitt. Why, she's more like Laura there than Charles.'

'Oh, no! How can you say that? She's her Daddy's girl all over, aren't you, little darling?' And Mrs Wilkins hugged the child to her massive bosom till she squealed in alarm.

In spite of the single young gentleman whom Mr Roberts had said she was pursuing (would that be Mr Snaith?), Elvira Wilkins was as lethargic as ever. Nothing seemed to move her, neither the present excitements, her unexpected journey, nor seeing us again. One felt that, for Elvira, life held no more surprises, and that she would respond to the Last Trump as if it were the bell at the tradesmen's entrance. I wondered, as we walked over the lawns, whether her inertia was due to having lost her first lover at an early age or whether it was due to too many summers spent in the Indian heat. But there was one emotion to which she was not immune. Fear.

I had led her out into the grounds to show her the house from a distance; the more distant the perspective from which one viewed it, the more likely it was to appear imposing. Close to, it was a shock rather than a surprise.

'It is big, isn't it?' commented Elvira. 'And all them funny knobs and turrets. Like a fairy story almost. You know, a picture in a book?'

'Yes, it is rather,' I agreed. 'But I've got used to it now. I even rather like it.'

'It must be nice to live here,' she went on. 'You know, sort of safe. These flowerbeds ... so nicely planted and that. We've never lived long in one place, but I do like gardens ... only just as I got things planted out, we'd have to move, so I've hardly ever seen my seeds flower.'

'Are you glad you're going back to Lucknow?'

'Yes. Oh yes, Miss Laura! Meelapore, the station Pa was commanding, y'know, has not been pleasant these last weeks. They never seemed to notice things like me, my parents I mean, and I didn't like to say anything. Perhaps it was only the heat after all. But things changed all of a sudden. I don't know why, but I was frightened. The people changed too—our sepoys, you know. They used to look at us ... well, different. And at night, I used to lie in my bed under the *punkah* listening to the drums in the bazaar. I never minded them before, but in the last few days I haven't been able to sleep because of them; they seemed sort of threatening. And they went on for hours and hours. And the conch shells too, and the dogs—they all seemed different somehow. So I'll be glad to get to Lucknow. You wouldn't feel it here, I suppose,

353

not with your relations and Mr Erskine with you. But one can be very lonely in India, you know.'

The Wilkinses stayed the night. At dinner Oliver Erskine watched Mrs Wilkins with an unbelieving fascination as she ate and talked and gestured with her fat white hands. I doubt whether he had ever met anyone quite so free with her comments, and by the end of the meal I was relieved to see that the fascination had given place to appreciation.

'Who would have thought, Miss Laura,' she whispered to me at bedtime, 'that your relations would be such marvellous fine people? All this wealth, and the solid silver forks at dinner. And what a fine man he is, your Mr Erskine. I remember thinking so that night at the Residency, though of course I didn't know him then. And remember me saying that if ever I could help you ...? Me!' And covering her mouth with a pudgy hand, she giggled her way upstairs. Then she paused and looked down at me. 'But mind, I still have it, just like I said I would!' And she patted her skirt in the direction of her knee, and gave me an arch glance before disappearing.

Chota hazri the next morning, which was taken in some state on account of the travellers, was almost a festive occasion. Mrs Wilkins talked as usual, Elvira ate more than all the rest of us put together, and Major Wilkins nodded solemn agreement to all his wife's remarks on the spaciousness, beauty and luxury of Hassanganj and its house. Then their carriage was brought round, Emily and I were kissed fondly by both the ladies, and I knew a moment of genuine regret when, having assured us that they would write the moment they got to Lucknow, they drove down the avenue. A bullock-cart, laden with luggage and accompanied by several servants, had departed some hours previously.

The house was very quiet when they had gone. The *chiks* were lowered, the *punkahs* swung and, in the semi-gloom of the big rooms, we drifted about aimlessly, trying to occupy our minds with something other than apprehension and conjecture.

All morning a dove called in the heat, the three monotonous long-drawn notes irritating me even more than the slap, creak and swing of the *punkah* or the singing of the mosquitoes. The baby was querulous and poor Charles, tortured by prickly heat, scratched and swore with futile malevolence. No one else called in that day and I realized how much we had come to look forward to our visitors. With nothing to distract us, the waiting in ignorance for an unknown evil became doubly hard to bear. It was a relief to know, once dinner was over, that in two or three hours I could go to my bed, hot, sticky and unrestful as it was, and abandon the effort to appear normal.

It must have been about nine o'clock that I went upstairs to superintend the baby's *ayah* performing the final washing and changing of the day. The room was tidy, the baby sleeping soundly but the *ayah* was absent, as was Emily's, who at this hour should have been waiting outside the bedroom door to undress Emily when she went up.

'I suppose they are in the kitchen getting the remains of the dinner and talking their heads off,' I grumbled to myself.

I got everything ready, made Pearl comfortable for the night and tucked her back into bed. Still irritated at the lack of dependability so obvious in the servants of India, I went downstairs and reported the *ayah*'s failure in her duty.

'Wretched woman,' sighed Emily. 'She's very scatterbrained, but I don't suppose we shall need her for long, so there is no point in making a fuss now.'

'But your bed hadn't been turned down, or your night things put out, or your washing water brought up, so your woman must be with her, wherever that is. They've no sense of time, that's the trouble!'

I am not normally a lazy woman, or an irritable one, but in such heat we all tended to make mountains out of molehills, and this small break in routine seemed unforgivable.

'Both of them off together?' Oliver looked up with belated interest.

'Both of them,' I answered crossly, and returned to my book.

Reading was not a pleasure: the lamp attracted all manner of insects so that one was continually slapping or brushing them away or picking them out of one's hair or clothing, but it was better to attempt to read than to sit idle and allow the mind to wander.

So busily was I engaged in my battle with the winged and feelered adversary, that I did not notice Oliver get up and go into the house. We were sitting, as was usual at night, on the verandah outside the drawing-room.

What finally caught my attention was the sound of light feet running over the gravel of the path towards the house. I looked up in alarm (almost anything in those days could alarm me) and met Charles's eyes;

Emily was engrossed in *The Lady's Magazine*. A moment later, Moti stood before us, breathing quickly, one hand clutching her veil to her face. Though, of course, he knew of all that she had done for Emily, Charles had never seen her, Moti being a Mohammedan and therefore, theoretically at least, in *purdah*.

'It's all right,' I reassured him, though not before his look of concern had turned to an expression of pleasure. 'It's Moti.'

Moti's dark eyes swept the three of us over the tinselled edging of her veil.

'*Lat-sahib?*' she queried. '*Lat-sahib?*' She was looking for Oliver and I knew directly that her errand must be an urgent one to bring her thus boldly and openly to his house. Before I could attempt to say that I would fetch him, Oliver himself was with us.

'They've all gone ...' he began, then seeing Moti, crossed the intervening space and spoke rapidly to her in her own tongue, while Emily, still in her chair with the magazine in her hands, looked on in uncomprehending surprise.

Moti's answer was hurried and emotional, and accompanied by many gesticulations. At one point, she grabbed Oliver's hand, letting fall her veil in so doing, and made as if she would drag him away with her. He disengaged her gently, shaking his head and laughing slightly, then pointed to us and asked her a further question.

The whole exchange took, I suppose, no more than a couple of minutes, but in that time, I realized from their expressions, from their gestures and the tone of their voices, that what we had feared was somehow upon us; in spite of the heat, my hands became ice-cold and my knees grew shaky.

Oliver must have reassured her. She stood silently for a moment, then went down on her knees on the ground while we all watched her, touched his feet with her forehead, then, getting up, threw the rest of us a perfunctory salaam and walked sedately away. But before the darkness quite enclosed her, she paused and turned a look of such open devotion and yearning to Oliver that, seeing it, I was as ashamed as if I had been discovered opening another's letter. Oliver himself could not have caught it, for already he was speaking.

'No servants in the house except Ishmial and the *abdar*. The *abdar* was sitting in his pantry dozing, waiting for the scullion to come and do the dishes, and Ishmial and Toddy-Bob have just come in from the stables to report that the quarters are deserted. Even Soorie has gone, poor old devil.'

Soorie was the watchman, an old man now, born in the quarters; for forty years he had told Hassanganj the time, striking the hours, the half-hours and the quarters on the great gong in the porch, which was also used to herald the approach of visitors. How was it that none of us had missed its sound? Because we were too accustomed to it?

'But why has he gone, why aren't they all here?' Emily asked with dawning fear. 'And Moti, what did she want, Oliver? She seemed so upset.'

Oliver paused a moment, estimating how much he should reveal. But it was too late now to consider Emily's health and weak nerves.

'She came to warn me, Emily,' he said, 'to tell me that a band of strangers have been seen in Peeplehara. She believes they intend to attack us. Tonight. We must go—now, Emily!'

Emily, understanding at last, had begun to wail like a child, 'Oh, my baby, my baby! Oh, Charles, take us away; why did you ever bring us here? What can we do? Oh, my baby!'

I should have gone to her, but my legs refused to carry me. I was thinking of the unattended gong in the pillared porch, the lantern still beside it on the ground and, beyond the little ring of yellow light, the garden and park dark and deserted, and because of that abandoned gong suddenly menacing.

'Emily, be quiet!' Oliver's voice broke into my reveries. He moved swiftly to Emily's side, took the silly magazine from her lap and drew her to her feet. I thought he was going to shake her. She had her mouth open ready to scream, but he took her hand, put his arm around her shoulder and led her gently to the door.

'Now listen to me, Emily. We have no time for hysterics.' He was stern but kindly. 'Your baby's life will depend on how you conduct yourself in the next half hour. Not on what we do, but on what *you* do, because you can either help us or hamper us. Do you understand me?'

Emily nodded, her knuckles against her lips. 'You must keep calm, Emily, and do exactly what you are told! All right?'

She nodded again, though her eyes were still unfocused with fright.

'Good! Now Laura will take you upstairs, and you must bundle up the baby and whatever clothes and things she needs. Then go and sit quietly with Laura. Don't come downstairs again until I call. Oh, and change your dress. Put on something dark and serviceable—and sensible shoes. Laura!' He beckoned me, and I went to them and took Emily's arm. His mention of hysterics had pulled me together, whatever it had done for Emily.

'And for God's sake, drop those damn fool birdcages,' he added as we turned away.

'What?' I was puzzled.

'Your hoops, woman. The things you wear under those acres of skirt. There's no room for anything fancy where we are going!' I nodded, and we went indoors.

I led Emily up the wide staircase, the utter silence of the huge house making me want to turn tail and run back to the men. Usually, quiet though the house was, there were always small, half-heard noises in the background: the clink of silver as the *abdar* laid the table, the clash of pan lids from the pantry where the food was dished up for serving, the comfortable mutter of the *ayahs* gossiping together between their duties, the swish of the house servants' starched *atchkans*, as they moved from room to room tending lamps or opening windows, the creak of the *punkahs*. I had looked up as we crossed the drawing-room. The *punkah* was motionless so the coolie too had gone, and if we had been sitting in the drawing-room, we would perhaps have had this earlier warning.

The stillness of that *punkah*, even more than the silent gong, brought home the fact that disaster was upon us. Since the start of the hot weather, it had been impossible to ignore the patient figure crouched outside my bedroom, the cord of the *punkah* passing through his splayed toes, a brass pot of tepid water beside him. We did not often see the *punkah*-coolies; they sat hidden from view on the verandah downstairs, or on the balconies upstairs, but I was not yet sufficiently inured to the ways of India to ignore a fellow human being, however humble, who worked so unremittingly for my comfort. They had all gone.

Lamps had been lit along the corridors and in our bedrooms, but they hardly served to dissipate the thick warm darkness that filled the house, exacerbating our nebulous fears. In Emily's room, I extracted her bundle from the recessess of the wardrobe where I had hidden it a fortnight before; then, while she picked up the baby, I got together some of its things and pinned them up in Emily's paisley shawl. Pearl continued to sleep soundly in her mother's arms as we moved to my room.

I changed my dress for a dark poplin house frock, took out my bundle and a cloak, laid the pistol where Emily would not see it and sat down to await our summons.

Perhaps, I thought, this is the last time I will ever be in this high, white, comfortable room, and I looked round it as though I had never seen it before. On the ceiling, a lizard, one of the many I had watched as I lay in bed in the humid warmth, crouched for an instant in waiting, then leapt across the surface of the plaster at a tiny spider angling its way across the sea of white. The spider disappeared; the lizard clicked its throat in satisfaction, and scurried back to its corner to await its next morsel.

'Ugh! Horrid things. How cruel nature is,' shuddered Emily, who had followed my gaze. As she spoke, I remembered our 'birdcages'.

With the hoops removed, our skirts hung too low, impeding our feet, so I fetched a pair of scissors and cut off about four inches from the edge of both our skirts.

'We can't go out like this, Laura,' Emily protested. 'You must put a little hem in. I assure you I have never been in public wanting a stitch or a button in my life before, and I'm not going to start now!' But I paid no attention. For, on opening a drawer to replace the scissors, I had seen there a small rosewood box containing my few trinkets and Wajid Khan's bracelet. I had overlooked it on the night when I had packed my bundle, though I had not forgotten a sewing case, writing materials and my copy of Marcus Aurelius. The contents were of only sentimental value, among them a small brooch of rubies and pearls that had belonged to my mother, but I justified my sentimentality by the thought that no one else would value the things more highly than I did, and slipped the box into the top of my bundle. Then, at last, there was nothing to do but wait.

CHAPTER 5

Sitting in silence on my high brass bedstead, Emily and I waited with the sleeping baby between us, while my small travelling clock ticked away the moments of that 4th of June 1857. I wished I could pray, or at least speak comfortingly to Emily. But, though I had forced myself to gather together our belongings and organize them for swift transport, I was capable of no further effort and could only wait in an apprehensive and strangely sorrowful silence. It was natural to be frightened at such a moment; but I could not account for the weight of true regret that lay on my heart, almost as though I were about to lose my home.

It must have been half an hour that we sat there before the men came upstairs. I heard Charles's footsteps go directly to his own apartment and then Oliver entered my room.

Emily and I got to our feet hastily, but he ignored us and, taking Pearl from the bed, shook her awake, not roughly, but Emily remonstrated with him all the same. Oliver disregarded her, thumped the infant's back, tossed her up in the air two or three times and, when she was crying indignantly, laid her in the crook of his left arm and stuck his brown thumb into her mouth to act as a comforter. Bewildered, Emily and I looked on in silence.

'A drastic measure, but necessary under the circumstances,' Oliver vouchsafed at last, while the baby sucked enthusiastically. 'There is a pellet of opium under my thumbnail, and this young woman will sleep the clock round if we can get it into her.'

'Opium! ... oh, mercy!' breathed Emily.

'It's an old trick known to every *ayah* who has ever had to deal with a querulous child. You'd be surprised at the number of fine English gentlemen who have been reared on the infernal poppy.'

'But she'll die,' whispered Emily, too agonized to snatch the child from him.

'No, but she will sleep like the dead, which is what we want her to do. In twelve hours or so, she'll be as right as rain.'

We watched in fascination while Pearl sucked contentedly, the tears of her awakening still undried on her sweetly rounded cheeks. After some minutes, Oliver withdrew his thumb, examined it with interest and pronounced the experiment successful. All the opium had disappeared down the baby's throat.

'Oh, my poor darling, what have we done to you?' crooned Emily as she took the child. I gathered up our various packages and made to follow Oliver.

Charles and he had worked hard in the downstairs rooms during our absence. At a glance, I saw that they had tried to simulate a frantic departure: furniture had been knocked over as though in haste, drawers and cupboards lay half open, gaping their contents on to the floor. In one corner of the dining-room, a chenille tablecover held a quantity of silver, but one corner hung open, revealing its contents. A loaf of bread stood on the table, with beside it a joint of cooked meat and the knives used for their cutting; off the passage leading from the dining-room the larders and pantries stood open, temptingly, their contents disarranged.

Soon sounds from above stairs told that Charles was producing the same effect of delusory haste in the bedrooms.

'Oh, Oliver … why ever didn't we hide the silver as other people did, and the jade and beautiful porcelain? And, oh, Oliver, all the books! What if they are taken?' For I had realized belatedly that Oliver would probably never see his possessions again, those possessions to which he paid such scant attention, but which nevertheless had been part of his life from the day he was born.

'Why? Because, perhaps, I own too much. Besides, there is no safe hiding place for them in Hassanganj once I have gone. Anyway, I count my life dearer than my plate. Leave 'em enough to loot and they'll lose interest in the chase. Which reminds me …'

He fumbled at his watch chain and took from it a large key, the key to the cellar. The entrance to the cellar was in the pantry nearest the dining-room and often I had seen the *abdar* come to Oliver for permission to bring up the claret or a bottle of port. Now he opened the cellar door wide, descended into the dark depths and proceeded to break bottles. Not many—just enough so that our pursuers should think he had been interrupted in his work of destruction. He clattered back to the dim light of the dining-room, carrying three bottles. One he broke deliberately on the threshold, leaving the remnants to indicate its place of origin; another, a flat green bottle of old brandy, he placed in his pocket, and the third he opened at the sideboard. Then he searched round for glasses, found four and filled them.

'We're going to need a heartener,' he said as Charles came in looking immeasurably pleased with himself for the havoc he had created upstairs.

'Here you are, Emily, drink up!'

'But ...'

'No buts! The infant won't need any sustenance for some time, and if it does the brandy will do it good. Laura, you too!'

I took the glass he handed me and sipped it gratefully. Unreality having descended on us with such catastrophic suddenness, the drinking of neat brandy at such an hour and in such surroundings of deliberate desolation seemed hardly out of the way.

'Now, here's the plan. We haven't a hope in hell of getting away from Hassanganj tonight.'

'Oh, Oliver!' Emily almost screamed, straining the now deeply sleeping baby to her.

'Not *tonight* I said, Emily. But we will get away tomorrow night. And in the meantime we must go into hiding. There are plenty of places upstairs in the attics, but we can't risk remaining in the house, since they will probably fire it. So I'm taking you to the safest place I can think of—but everything depends on your keeping absolutely still and quiet until nightfall tomorrow. Understand, Emily?'

She nodded, but I wondered what sort of hiding place could be safe if fire was to be used against us in this dried-out tinderbox of a land.

'Good. Now Toddy-Bob has already left with the carriage. He is our, er, decoy, so to speak, and a great deal depends on whether he manages to get away and abandon the carriage where I have told him to. Meanwhile, Ishmial is procuring a bullock-cart, which I am afraid is what you ladies are going to have to travel in. Our best chance, don't you see, is to remain here for the moment, while giving the impression that we have left.'

'But where?' began Charles, impatiently.

'Come, there's nothing more to delay us. We will go out by the garden and skirt the house so that we don't pass through the quarters.

I believe everyone has left; they'd be too scared to hang around. But still, there's no sense in running unnecessary risks.'

The moon had already descended and the night was very dark. Outside the house everything seemed quiet and as usual. The air was heavy with the scent of quisqualis and Christmas-pudding tree. Yakub Ali, the *abdar*, helped to carry the bundles, and the glimmer of his white *atchkan* was the only thing visible in the wide spaces of the garden. When I got my bearings, I realized that we were making towards the old tower ... Moti's tower. I had to suppose that Oliver knew his business, but I wondered uneasily whether, if I were a mutineer and knew the facts, it would not be the first place I would make for in search of Mr Erskine.

And then, almost the instant the thought passed through my mind, lights appeared in the distance, coming through the salwoodland that formed the northern boundary of the park. Lanterns bobbed, and torches, held aloft by horsemen, flared suddenly in currents of air then died down again.

'God damn them! Here already!' Oliver swore through his teeth as, with one accord, we stopped.

'We'll never get to Moti now,' I said quietly to him.

'Not a chance, God rot 'em! Now, pick up your heels and follow me.' And he made a tangent to the left. Here the ground was rough, matted with unscythed grass and treacherous with unseen obstacles; but fear carried us over it safely, and within a few seconds we were in the grove of trees in which were situated the ice-pits, those queer beehivelike structures of thatch which had once so captivated my mind with their ingenuity.

Needing no instructions now, we crouched behind the thatch deepest in the shadow, hearing above our own gasps for breath the sound of shouts, hoarse laughter and hoofbeats growing momentarily nearer.

'They'll make straight for the house,' Oliver whispered, trying to reassure us, 'and we are off their route. Just keep quiet until they have passed.'

His voice was calm and, to my astonishment, now that I was nearer true peril than ever before in my life, I felt comparatively collected myself. Every sense was alerted and quivering with a rare sensitivity; never had my hearing been so acute, nor my eyes so fully adapted to darkness, and my mind raced, relating every smallest fact recorded by eyes, ears and nose to a reality already half apprehended. Even my body felt light and capable of extraordinary exertion. This, then, was the experience of danger. I knew now where lay the attraction in climbing mountains or shooting big game. Danger induced a sense of super-normality in the midst of fear that made men, for an instant, the kin of gods ... or perhaps, more accurately, most truly human.

So we waited, holding our breaths, as the troop approached us, and I was glad for no rational reason that I was next to Oliver Erskine, and that his body shielded me from seeing round the edge of the domed thatch.

The noise was not loud; rather, it was controlled and ominous, though men called to each other and shouted. Somehow, it indicated a confidence that was unnerving to us, hiding like foxes in a covert. After what seemed an age, they had passed. We gave them more time, then Oliver peered round the ice-house.

'All clear—but keep your voices down. There might be stragglers.'

'What can we do now? For God's sake, Oliver, we have got to get Emily and the baby out of here,' whispered Charles. 'Where were you taking us in the first place? Can't we make a run for it, before they discover we have left?'

'Not a chance! There's a cellar under the flag floor of Moti's house, she suggested it herself. It would have been safe enough, but too far. Too risky with the beggars all around us.'

'Then what the devil ...'

Oliver had turned his attention to Yakub Ali, who was whispering to him.

'He's right, by God!' he said, turning back to us. 'This is as good a place as any.' He patted the thick thatch of the ice-house. 'This stuff is in two layers, and Yakub says a man can lie comfortably between the two. We'll soon find out.'

He began to pull out large sections of thatch from the edge of the roof, but Yakub, who had been examining the structure, beckoned Oliver to him. He had found a place where the thatch had already fallen out or disintegrated. Peering over Oliver's shoulder into the slit this made, I felt rather than saw a space of about twenty inches between the two stout layers of thatch and dried palm leaves.

'In with you, Laura, and be ready to take the bundles.'

I did not like being the first to enter. There would be insects and mice; perhaps even scorpions, or snakes, and what if … but the thought of the thatch on fire was too awful to formulate.

'Get in,' whispered Oliver again impatiently. 'Even if it doesn't hold, you haven't far to fall.'

I believe he was joking, but at the time his remark added one more fear to my litany of horrors.

All that met me, as I crawled and clawed my way in, was a smothering cloud of dust. I could not stop myself from coughing and, though I did so as quietly as possible, was met by a harsh 'Be quiet, will you!' from below me as the bundles were pushed into the aperture. My eyes smarted, my nose was full of powdery grass and I nearly choked, so that I am not sure how long it took for us all to dispose ourselves around the central cone of the roof and arrange our luggage. But soon everyone was coughing and spluttering, even, as I was pleased to realize, the impatient Mr Erskine. Yakub Ali remained outside, and in response to Oliver's whispered instructions we could hear him stuffing back the thatch that had been displaced by our entrance and sweeping up the odd wisps that must have littered the ground.

'*Khub thik hai ab*!' he whispered, and Oliver thanked him. We could not hear his footsteps as he departed.

'What will happen to him now?' I enquired anxiously. 'Wouldn't he be safer with us?'

'He will be all right. He can make his way out without difficulty. No one will know he was with us.'

'He won't tell them, will he?' I was ashamed to have to suspect, even so negatively, the stolid, prosaic Yakub, always so dignified and imperturbable; but I had thought of the abandoned gong in the porch, and the deserted bedrooms, and the motionless *punkah*. They had all known what was coming, but no one had warned us. No one but Moti. Which could only mean that there was danger to them in their association with us.

'We must hope not,' returned Yakub's master.

'And, Oliver …?'

'Well?'

'Have you thought that they might … they might set these roofs on fire. If they burn the house?'

'Yes.'

'Oh!'

'Sparks won't do it. Too far, and the trees will protect us. They might fire them deliberately, but that's a risk we have to take. They won't suspect us of hiding in these things; there are no doors. The thatch is lifted off when the ice is removed. And they know how—er, delicate, English ladies are.'

'Oh!'

I lapsed into silence and tried to pray; but within moments, the quiet was broken by yells that even in the distance were unmistakably enraged. Our escape had been discovered.

In the dust-filled darkness of our hiding place, we strained our ears to try to make out what was taking place, but it was difficult even to estimate distance correctly. Horses galloped past two or three times in the direction from which the mutineers had come and then doubled back on their tracks towards the house and out through the main entrance to the park. Oliver, listening intently, chuckled.

'They have found the carriage tracks. Must have been a devil of a job in this darkness, even though I told Tod to fill it with fodder and make sure to cut corners across the flowerbeds. Perhaps some of the servants saw it go.'

'They will know we were not in it then.'

'No, it was the closed travelling carriage, blinds modestly down. There were trunks and band-boxes strapped to the back; Toddy took care of that. It will puzzle them, for a time at least.'

'So you had it all planned.'

'I thought so, but I misjudged the time of their coming—for which my apologies,' he whispered back.

'Very clever,' I answered acidly.

The noise continued for hours—all through the long hot night. I wondered why no attempt was made to search the grounds for us, until I remembered the looting and the open wine cellar. Suddenly, a thought struck me.

'If they are Mohammedans they won't drink, will they?'

'Not as Mohammedans. But as looters, I fancy they will allow themselves some indulgence.'

When the early dawn began to force slivers of dusty light through the thatch above us, the sounds outside became more dispersed and, at the same time, easier to recognize. I had dozed a little, but was fully awake to the departure of the elephants, trumpeting angrily at being driven by strange *mahouts*. A little later, the draft bullocks were driven out and then, as the light grew stronger, the horses passed in the distance, whinnying and dancing in distress. I thought of my roan, Pyari, and of Oliver's great bay beast, handled by strangers and perhaps with cruelty, and for the first time felt more angry than frightened. Then, later again, horsemen galloped past us, very close, along the path to the garden pavilion.

'Oh, Oliver! Moti? Will she be all right there?' I asked. 'They seem to be making towards the tower.'

'She's safe enough. She said she would leave for Cawnpore, and by now she should be well on her way. Even if she were here, she'd be all right so long as she kept her temper, but she's liable to throw something at them.'

I remembered her reception of me, and smiled. 'Yakub will have told her why we did not reach the tower. She'll have left by now,' Oliver said again, as though reassuring himself.

Some time after this—the sun was already gaining strength and I was sweating as I lay half asleep with my face buried in my arms—I thought I heard a faint scream, but no one else stirred and I said nothing. By then, the shouts and noise from the house had almost ceased, and I forgot the half-heard scream as we became aware of the smell of burning.

'Oh, Oliver! Oh, the house!' Emily wailed. 'Oliver, they have set fire to the dear old house.'

'Blast them for destructive swine!' cursed Charles, but Oliver said nothing. Beside me, I felt his body stiffen, but he said nothing.

Of that day of heat and fear, of thirst and cramped discomfort, my recollections are acute. Even now, I sometimes wake at night gasping for breath because my nostrils are full of dust, straw and the scent of fire.

The sun rose, swiftly and inexorably, beating down upon us, despite the shade of the little copse in which we lay. The thatch gave us protection from the glare but none from the heat, which was intensified by the airlessness. We could move if we wished to; lie on our backs, stomachs or sides, but every movement created such a choking fog of straw dust that we found cramp almost easier to endure. The thatch was full of rustlings and small movements, and as the light grew, insects of all kinds emerged to run across our faces and hands and tangle themselves in our hair.

The baby slept, a deep uneasy sleep. We had laid her, practically naked, on her shawl, and Emily and I took turns to keep the insects away, the light filtering through the worn thatch serving us to this extent. Sometimes she rolled about disconsolately, uttering little cries, but all in her drugged sleep.

Poor Charles suffered the most, I think. Already raw with prickly heat and suffering from a series of unpleasant boils, he was unable to find comfort but lay sweating profusely and enduring agonies of irritation to save us from the suffocating effects of any movement he might make.

All of us fought thirst. I began to long for water very early in the day, at about that hour when we should have been enjoying fragrant tea on the verandah. I determined to say nothing, knowing that all suffered alike, but when I dozed my troubled dreaming was all of water: of streams cascading down green hillsides, fountains spilling back into rounded basins, leather buckets pouring their limpid contents into the irrigation canals in the garden—even of raindrops beating against window panes. So preoccupied was I with thirst that I felt no hunger at all. Just below us lay a great quantity of ice, stored up from the brief winter frosts, but even if one of the men had risked leaving our hiding-place in daylight, or if we had been able to burrow through the lower layer of thatch on which we lay, a pickaxe would have been needed to free the ice from its bed, and we had none. The thought of it there, just below, tortured me all day.

And all day the great pink house suffered in its death throes, fighting the flames that sought to devour it. So solidly built, roofed with tiles instead of thatch, it put up a long struggle, but the flames won at last, and as the day wore on, our dim refuge was several times illuminated as a great tongue of victorious fire forced itself into the overhanging smoke, to be followed by a roar of falling beams and disintegrating masonry, as part of the roof, or an angle of wall, collapsed into the inferno beneath. I thought of Danielle, of her jade, porcelain and crystal, so lovingly collected over so many years, and of Old Adam's library. I thought of the effort, of the caring, of the time that had been put into creating the oasis of civilization that had been Hassanganj, all gone in one spiteful day, and I came near to real hate.

When the day was at its hottest, I was woken by Oliver shaking my shoulder and holding a flask to my lips.

'Drink up,' he said as I opened my eyes. I shook my head. It was the flask he normally filled with brandy when he went duck shooting in the early mornings. The very thought of that scorching liquor on my dry tongue made me want to vomit.

'Come on now ... it's water. Only water.' Unbelievingly, I took a sip. It was warm and tasted slightly of brandy, but nevertheless it was water.

'Go on. Drink away. We've all had some.' So I raised myself on one elbow and drank. It cleared my head; and my first reaction was annoyance. Why had he kept it from us for so long? Hadn't he guessed how thirsty we would be?

I saw him grin in the half-light.

'We have only two flasks; no sense in telling you until we really needed them. You don't know what thirst is yet, but this will have to do you until five o'clock this evening, so stop grumbling. What did you expect me to have—a *mushak* full?'

Afterwards I fell into a deep sleep, from which I did not wake until late afternoon. The house was still smouldering. We ate hunks of buttered bread and slices of meat that Charles took out of his shooting bag. It was an effort to force the stuff down my throat, but Oliver had warned us that there would be no water until we had eaten and, like children, we obeyed him. The second flask was passed round. Immediately I felt better and my spirits rose. It was cooler now, and in less than two hours would be dark. Pearl was beginning to whimper and her sleep seemed lighter. Emily, I knew, was longing for her to wake, not only to reassure herself of the child's health, but to ease her aching, over-full breasts.

When it had been dark for a full hour, Oliver decided to move. We covered the baby with her shawl, and our own faces with our clothing as he set to work reopening the aperture by which we had entered. He slid his body through it to the ground. I was just about to follow him, when he ordered me to stay where I was. He would take a look around and we were not to stir until he got back.

'You might never come back!' I pointed out irritably.

'True,' he agreed. 'But don't waste time wishing me dead. I'm as fond of my own skin ... as I am of yours!' He was gone before the words had sunk in or I had thought of a retort.

CHAPTER 6

I resigned myself to another period of waiting, but more cheerfully, and it did not seem long before Oliver's voice was telling me to get out, and his hands were pulling at the thatch to assist my descent into the open air. Stiff and cramped beyond bearing, I would have fallen as my feet touched the ground had he not held me upright. His face, close to mine for a moment, was strained and grim, and I realized in the midst of my own discomfort how much he must be suffering at the loss of his home.

After a moment I was able to stamp the circulation back into my legs, and gasped in great lungfuls of smoky air as he helped the others out in their turn. Not until we all stood together in the darkness behind the ice-house, giggling shakily in mingled relief and nervousness, did I notice his clothes. In place of his drab trousers and alpaca jacket, he wore now the baggy pyjamas, long loose shirt and starched turban of a Pathan, with a red velvet waistcoat covering his chest, and crossing it a pair of bandoliers such as Ishmial wore. Probably the things were Ishmial's, I thought, but then remembered the talk in Lucknow so long ago when someone had hinted with disapproval that he assumed 'native dress'. To judge by the ease with which he carried his strange apparel, perhaps they had been right.

'Why, Oliver, how funny you look,' exclaimed Emily. 'Do we all have to dress up like you?' The thought appealed to her.

'Not just now, but later perhaps. First, we have to get out of the compound and find Ishmial and the bullock-cart which I hope he has managed to get for us. There's no one around, neither our own folk nor the others, but go quietly and keep in the shadow.'

Charles took Pearl from Emily and the rest of us picked up our various bundles and followed Oliver, who carried a mysterious burden that had not been with us in the thatch under one arm, and a rifle on the other.

Our direction took us away from the house, but I turned back several times to watch the rosy glow of the smoke still rising from the ruins. Of the house itself, I could see nothing. It must have collapsed thoroughly into itself. Presently, we arrived at the high boundary wall that enclosed the whole park, and followed it for perhaps ten stumbling minutes. Then Oliver, placing his bundle and rifle on the ground, scaled the wall with disconcerting ease and, sitting crouched on the top in the shadow of a tree, gave a low whistle. Instantly, he was answered. In a few moments, amid the lamentations of Emily and only too aware of torn clothing, scraped knees and broken fingernails, we were all over the wall and on the edge of a rutted country track where waited Ishmial (a close approximation of his master now), Toddy-Bob and a bullock-cart.

My relief was great on seeing those two familiar figures, but, wasting no words on greeting, Oliver strode to the cart and came back with a large earthenware jar full of water and a copper container of food. It was native food—*chapattis*, vegetable curry and lentils—and we ate it with relish; having at last had our fill of water, we were able to turn our full attention to our plight.

'Well, that's that,' Oliver grunted, standing up and rubbing his hands inelegantly on the seat of his baggy trousers, while Charles wiped the curry from his moustache with a grubby handkerchief. 'Now get into these all of you, and you too, Toddy-Bob, and no argument!' His voice was harsh and his manner brusque, but under the circumstances, who could blame him?

Oliver pulled apart the bundle he had carried and threw us each a voluminous tentlike garment of heavy cotton called a *burqha* ... such garments as Muslim women wear when outside their homes to protect themselves from the gaze of males.

'Not me, Guv'nor!' Toddy-Bob objected immediately.

'Yes, *you*. God knows how you have managed so long in those clothes as it is.'

'I only been out by night, as you well know—and then I 'ad me 'at off,' Toddy said in an injured tone, removing his high coachman's hat as he spoke and holding it behind his back. 'S'truth, Guv'nor! You can't expect me to wear no Muslim nightgown! Really you can't! Tells you what ... I'll pull me shirt out over me breeches, and snitch a *puggaree* next time I 'as the opportunity. But you can't get me into no *burqha*;

and, Guv'nor, I'm that brown now, I'd be taken for a *bunnia* by me own mother—you know that!'

They measured each other for a moment in silence, and Oliver gave in gracefully. 'Very well, but you'll sit in the well of the cart with the ladies.'

'And I'm really to get into this?' Charles, in his turn, held up the offending garment as though it smelt.

'You are. How else do you propose to hide those luxuriant yellow whiskers? To say nothing of your lovely blue eyes!' Misfortune had not mellowed Mr Erskine's tongue, I noticed, as Charles donned his *burqha* with disgust.

'We will travel only at night; it is customary at this time of year and we will arouse no suspicion. But don't speak to each other when we are passing anyone, keep your shoes covered by your skirts, and Emily, keep the baby under your *burqha*—that shawl is much too clean.'

We set off. Oliver and Ishmial walked beside the cart and the rest of us crouched on the dirty boards of the floor. We were in no way remarkable from a score of other parties we passed: three veiled women and a youth, accompanied by their two stalwart menfolk. Only Toddy's bare head struck a false note, and, by morning, that too had been covered with a dirty white turban. How or when he acquired it, I can't be sure, but once we had stopped outside a village to water the bullocks and had discerned a party of travellers asleep in their cotton sheets not far from us. Perhaps they had the answer.

It was a strange, almost mysterious experience, jogging along the immemorial ways of India while the great indigo arc of the night wheeled its burden of stars slowly above us, and the plain stretched away in its infinity of secret, unexplained life. A dozen times we passed through sleeping villages that might have been the same village, watched by the same ring-tailed, stark-ribbed dogs; shaded by the same groves; watered by the same shallow tanks; inhabited by the same population of skinny old men asleep on string beds beside the road. Villages that looked the same and smelt the same and gave the same inadequate protection to the same undemanding people. And, between the villages, stubbly fields, scrubby pasture and miles of wasteland broken by dry watercourses, with here and there, perhaps, the remains of a mud fort rearing a blacker bulk against the black of the sky. There was such a sameness in the dusty road, the nameless hamlets, the featureless dark landscape, that it became difficult to believe we were moving at all. When the sun gathered strength, we halted in a grove set some way back from the road.

No stretch of country in India, however inhospitable in appearance, is quite devoid of humanity, so it was pointless to look for a place where our presence would not be discovered. The most we could hope for was to blend with our surroundings, and this our bullock-cart, our apparel, and the presence of Ishmial enabled us to do. While we exercised our cramped limbs by strolling through the grove, Ishmial went in search of food and Toddy-Bob built a fire in a stone *chula* at the base of one of the trees—evidence that the grove was a recognized stopping place for travellers. We breakfasted on hot milk and dry *chapattis* and lay down beside the cart to sleep, while the men took turns in watching the approaches to the camp. Sleep came easily, in spite of lying on the bare ground, and it was midday before the heat, the flies and the wails of the baby combined to awaken me. Ishmial and Toddy-Bob were busily employed at the stone hearth cooking, Emily and Charles sat some distance away with Pearl, but of Oliver there was no sign. Toddy said he was on guard, and jerked his chin in the direction of the road.

I found him sitting cross-legged on the ground with his rifle across his knees, gazing abstractedly through the deep shadow of the trees towards the rutted white track, bordered by dusty lantana bushes and clumps of point-leaved cactus, that stretched its monotonous way through the parched land ... back ... back to Hassanganj. He made no move as I approached and sat down beside him.

In the branches above us a troop of monkeys stilled into silence for their noon siesta, but a small grey squirrel, angered by our presence, skittered shrilly up and down the bole of a mango, scolding us, and a flight of green parrots broke the heat haze with a sudden scream of movement.

Morosely, Oliver threw a pebble at the indignant squirrel.

'Well,' he asked, 'and are you rested?'

'Enough, but still uneasy.'

He made no reply, but watched for the squirrel to emerge from its hole so that he could take another shot at it.

'Are we going to manage it, Oliver?' I insisted. 'Do you think we will ever reach Lucknow?'

'We will.' And it was no mere reassurance. It was a statement of fact. I knew him well enough now to realize that he would disdain lying in order to comfort me, so hoped that we would never be in a position where his answer would be less optimistic.

'In another two nights, three at the most, we will be in the outskirts of the city. By that time we should know something of the state of its inhabitants and can make our plans accordingly.'

'Do you think ... do you think they will be antagonistic?' I winced inwardly at that weak word, but was afraid to use a more accurate one.

'Probably. But, having got that far, we should be able to get through the city without undue trouble. So long as the Residency is still open, of course. That's all that bothers me. Tomorrow we should get some idea of how things are going there. How is Emily bearing it?'

'Well. Much better than I had expected. She's hardly even grumbling, and you know how she loves her comfort ... Oliver?'

'What?'

'I want to say how sorry I am. About all this. And the house ... and everything! It's a terrible loss, and I feel that if we hadn't been with you, you ... well, you might have found some way of saving it. You could have done something perhaps.'

'Perhaps,' he agreed. 'But I don't think so, and anyway, you were not responsible. Why do you feel you were?'

'I know we have been in your way. You've said so often enough.'

'I was anxious for your safety. I hoped that whatever was going to happen would happen after you were gone. That's all.'

'I ... I hate to think of it all in ruins, all that you Erskines have built up in Hassanganj. I suppose women are more sentimental about their surroundings and possessions and so on, but when I remember your books, and Old Adam's chair, and your grandmother's beautiful things, I could cry. It's such wanton waste. I think I mind almost as much as if it had been my home and not yours. All it took to make it.'

'It can be rebuilt ... and I'll rebuild it.'

'Yes, but you'll never be able to restore what you've lost.'

'Perhaps I don't want to. Isn't it always a mistake to try to go back, to replace what has once been got rid of?'

'A mistake? Oh, Oliver, you're joking! I don't choose to believe that you are really uncaring of so much association and tradition.'

'No,' he said slowly, as though he had just realized it, 'I am not uncaring; but I haven't the time to care now. When I have, I think I will be grateful for the opportunity of a fresh start. I don't think I'd be much good at patching up another man's dreams. I'll build my own ... and not only with bricks and mortar. Great God, when I think of what I could do with this land, these people, given a little stability, a little time. I don't want help; I can do without encouragement; I have money. But I need the opportunity! Perhaps, Laura, a phoenix will rise out of the ashes of the old house; perhaps this present turmoil is really the birthpangs of something better, something that we can't envisage yet. I'd like to think so anyway.'

I did not really understand him. I was thinking in concrete terms, of the house, of the garden and orchards, but I was glad he had sufficient resilience to take the loss of these things in an optimistic spirit. His next words enlightened me.

'Do you know what the chief exports of Oudh are at the moment, Laura?'

'Exports? No, however should I?'

'Hmph! I thought not. I'll tell you. Soldiers and gold embroidered slippers! Everything else that is produced in the State is consumed, or wasted, in the State. And every four or five years, ninety-eight men, women and children out of every hundred go starvation hungry for eight months on end, often more.'

'And so ...?'

'Well, don't you see?'

'No.'

'It's the question of an economy! Until now, what with the old Nawab's rapaciousness, and the *talukhdars*' eternal quarrels, and all the mismanagement and general stupidity, it's been as much as any man in Oudh could do to provide for himself and his family. But with a stable government, with taxation efficiently administered, with peace ... and most of all with imagination, this province could be again the garden it once was, oh, a long time ago, but it was! There's not much wrong with this soil, you know. It isn't overworked to the extent that the rest of the Gangetic Plain is, and with good planning, good husbanding, an understanding of the rudiments of agriculture—why, it could flower. Almost every acre in Oudh could be put to good use, could grow sugar, indigo, gram, millet, vegetables and mustard, but how much of it is? You've seen yourself. Mile after mile of parched grass supporting a few skinny cows. Not because the land is inadequate, but because men are. Now, with the British in control, the railway will come to us, Laura. And that will mean transport of our goods, our produce, to other parts of India, and to the ports ... to Calcutta. The railway will bring us a market, and force us to rise to the occasion. It will mean development, and development will mean a full belly for more people all the time. The Hassanganj I will build will have to be a very different Hassanganj. That's why I don't want to replace. I want to create.'

The squirrel shot out of its hole and whisked up the bole of the tree, tempting Oliver, but he had forgotten it.

'I admire your strength of mind,' I told him. 'For being able to think of such things now!'

'Do you? But in truth it is cowardice. An escape.'

'I understand,' I said, sure that I did, and comforted to know that he was more capable of sentiment than he would have me believe. He turned his golden eyes on me, and for a moment regarded me in silence; then he shook his head slightly and smiled.

'No,' he said gently. 'Remorse is not yet within your experience.'

I did not answer, not wishing to trespass on his privacy. After a time, he said in his usual rather brusque tone of voice, 'And anyway, it appears that the British are not at the moment in control, that no railway engine belching fire is likely to appear and whisk us to our destination, and that we had better apply ourselves to the problems of the moment. Tell me, seeing that you are so sentimental, did you bring Wajid Khan's *rakhri* with you?'

'Why yes, oddly enough. I only remembered it at the last moment. Do you think it really meant anything to him? I thought it was just a gesture.'

'So it was. Old Wajid certainly never imagined any circumstances in which you could make use of it. But if you do, I am fairly sure that he will feel it incumbent upon him to make another gesture. Particularly if it is taken to him by someone who knows the significance of the thing. Indians are curious people. It's difficult to tell just what they are going to take seriously and what they will dismiss if it suits their convenience. Especially an Indian like Wajid with a smattering of European education. I don't believe he ever intended you to take his protestations of filial loyalty to heart, but he might well take them seriously himself. Honour and all that. And then again, he might not. Still, I'm glad you have it with you.'

'I didn't bring it with any idea of making use of it. It never occurred to me, but of course it might be of real value to us, mightn't it?'

'Don't count too much on your "brother's" assistance, Laura. The times are not propitious to sentiment and I can't see Wajid risking his life for his own mother, let alone an honorary sister. The difficulty is going to be in getting you people through the city to the Residency, and it's possible we may need some assistance there. If he's in Lucknow, that is; he might be in Jamadnagar; if he has any wit, and the situation in Lucknow is worsening, he certainly will be. But it's a thought. We are not in a position to despise any method of furthering our own purposes.'

'How odd it is, all of this. How unreal! To be sitting under a mango tree seriously considering making use of an archaic Indian custom to save the lives of a group of harmless Europeans. Everything, since Hassanganj anyway, has been so peaceful. It seems to me that the peasants don't even know there is trouble afoot. Look at that party making their way along the track … an old man, a boy, and a woman with a child on her hip. Do they understand what is happening around them, Oliver? Do they wish us dead? Do they hate us?'

'No, and if I were to go out there and tell them who we were and ask them for food, they would probably take us to their village and shelter us for as long as we need. We have little to fear until we reach the city: the odd marauding band of mutineers or a party of *dacoits* made bold by the general unrest, perhaps, but those are easily detected. It's on account of people like that that you are wearing a *burqha* and I'm in this absurd get-up, not because of the villages we have to pass through or the *ryots* we meet on the road. I'm ready to swear they'd not harm us.'

'How can you be sure?'

'I know them. I know their history. All their energy, for thousands of years, has been directed towards keeping themselves alive in situations like the present one. All they really want is just enough land to feed themselves, and the peace to nurse that land to fruitfulness. God knows, they haven't had either commodity in sufficient quantity, ever, to risk it in purposeless violence. No, it's not them; it's the organized elements, like the Army, like *dacoits* and the criminals in the cities, whose only aptitude is the fostering of trouble—those are who we must be wary of.'

The party of villagers disappeared round a bend, and the world stilled into the oppressive silence of great heat. Nothing stirred. Even the squirrel had pulled its bushy tail sedately into its hole in a knot of the tree.

'I've an apology to make too, Laura. You're in this mess now because of my lack of judgement.'

'But how could you possibly have known when Hassanganj would be attacked? We all knew the situation, we all hoped that nothing would actually happen. And you did more for us than we could have done for ourselves.'

'I wasn't thinking of that. Old Wilkins, the evening before they left it was, suggested to Charles and myself that it might be a good thing if you all accompanied them to the city. In a sort of convoy. He knew I wouldn't come, of course, but there was no reason why Charles, Emily and you shouldn't go with him.'

'I see. But you refused?'

'No, I didn't. It was Charles who wouldn't hear of it. Oh, Emily's health, his own health, God knows what else. He was acting for the best, I suppose. I have said often enough that it is impossible to make any sort of a stand at the Residency. I believe that still, but neither of us were to know we would have no alternative. All the same, when Wilkins proposed the matter, I could see some sense in it. I allowed myself to be overruled by Charles. And, whatever happens once you reach Lucknow, if you had been with the Wilkins, you would have been spared at least the discomforts and dangers of our present method of travel. For this I apologize. I should not have allowed Charles to have his way. I could have insisted on your leaving.'

'Oh, don't blame yourself. After all, none of us took Major Wilkins or his alarms very seriously, did we?'

'I took his alarms seriously enough. It was his confidence in the garrison at Lucknow that I could not agree with. It seemed to me, or perhaps I only wanted to think, that there was more chance of safety in Hassanganj than in Lucknow. I was wrong.'

CHAPTER 7

We set out again just as the short Indian dusk fell, in that hour when columns of dust creep slowly across the darkening sky and indicate to the knowing the path taken by the herds as they pad homeward to the villages. The scent of that dust hung in the air and mingled with the acrid smoke of cowdung fires; the last of the sunlight slanted long rays low over fields and stubble pastures, glinted briefly on the shining leaves of the mangoes, and then was swallowed in the encroaching east. Freed from toil and sun, the villagers relaxed with their hookahs on housetops and in mud-walled courtyards; women with brass pots on their heads, babies straddling a hip, gossiped on the way home from the well, and the boys bringing in the herds yelled to each other and at their charges and played as they went a crude sort of cricket with a stick for a bat and a small wedge of wood for a ball. So pastoral and peaceful a scene seemed unlikely to be productive of violence, and I had no difficulty in accepting Oliver's opinion that the ordinary countryfolk would do us no harm.

The night passed slowly, peacefully, but in increasing discomfort. Now that we were somewhat used to our situation, and the fine edge of fear had been a little blunted by usage, we became aware of a multitude of petty trials hardly noticed the previous night. It was impossible to find a comfortable position on the hard boards of the bullock-cart. The *burqhas* were heavy and hot and, while they excluded air, they failed to keep out the dust caused by our own passage, which rose in a smothering cloud around us. The unoiled axles of the cart squeaked incessantly and every board creaked in nerve-wracking unison. I developed a headache and my throat and nose were sore with swallowed dust.

At about midnight we made a halt so that Emily could feed the baby. The rest of us were glad of the opportunity to stretch our legs. We were surrounded by a wide vista of fields, grey and featureless in the starlight, broken here and there by clumps of dark trees. I was relieved to see no sign of life, no lights nor smoke nor passing human, and heard only a nearby jackal's manic howl, answered immediately by the cries of his fellows a little way off. There was no moon, though the sky was pale with a myriad stars.

'Thirsty?'

Oliver held out his flask as I climbed out of the cart, unfolding my aching limbs with care. I threw back the face-flap of my *burqha* and accepted a drink.

'We'll stay here till the child falls asleep,' he said as he pocketed the flask. 'That's a grove of peepul trees across that field. It will be cooler there than waiting here. Coming?'

I hesitated. The grove was some distance from the road.

'Oh, come on! Nothing to be nervous of. The others will be here with Emily and don't you trust me? To protect you, that is?'

I smiled in the safety of my replaced face-flap and followed Oliver as he jumped across a drainage ditch and struck out towards the trees, taking a narrow path snaking through the stubble.

'Yes, peepuls. They call them "travellers' friends" in these parts. I'll show you why.'

It was a large grove, the trees so tall I presumed they were very ancient. At the foot of one of the largest was a domed and white-washed shrine such as one becomes accustomed to finding in out-of-the-way spots in India. A garland of yellow marigolds, wilted now, had been thrown over the dome, and two or three earthenware saucers stood before it.

'The spirit has been pleased with the offerings,' Oliver said, pointing to the empty dishes. 'That is something you must remember about these places. The food offered to the spirits by the pious attracts snakes. So always be careful.'

'Not really very friendly to travellers, after all,' I commented.

'Merely an unavoidable hazard. Look at these.'

He reached up and picked a frond of leaves from a low branch. They were shaped rather like ivy but with an elongated point.

'See the pointy tips? That's what makes the difference to a man sitting under a peepul. These trees water themselves, all year round. The leaves retain moisture as it is drawn up from the soil, and at the merest whisper of a breeze the points shed droplets of water to keep the earth above the roots damp. It's always cooler, and fresher, under a peepul than any other tree. The name is justified I think … despite spirits and snakes.'

We sat down on the ground at some distance from the shrine. I was anxious to test his pronouncement, so threw my *burqha* back over my shoulders, leaving my face and arms open to the air. Above us the leaves stirred and shivered as restlessly as aspens; looking up through the boughs to the starlit sky, seen as patches of light through the foliage, I was conscious of a mist-like moisture striking my skin, and within moments was cooler.

Oliver stretched himself on the ground with his arms folded behind his head.

'There's usually a holy man of some sort attached to a place like this; he extracts a toll from wayfarers for the use of the grove. Keeps himself alive on their offerings.'

I looked around apprehensively, fear at once returning.

'Nothing to worry about. If there were one here, he'd have been out to visit us by now, and anyway he'd be unlikely to wish us ill … so long as we paid him!'

I relaxed again and surrendered myself to conscious enjoyment of the coolness. Whatever his shortcomings, Oliver Erskine was a reassuring person to be with.

We sat in silence for some time. I thought Oliver had dropped off to sleep. My headache had abated and I dreaded returning to the cart. In the whispering quiet of the trees, the silence that lay between my companion and myself was deeply peaceful, deeply pleasant.

Then Oliver rose suddenly on one elbow and listened intently to the small noises of the night.

'Do you hear that?' he asked quietly, but not whispering. 'That soft regular creak?'

The grove was quiet but not silent. The leaves susurrated softly, bough creaked sometimes against bough. There were small rustlings in the sparse undergrowth, and occasionally a bird would shuffle on its perch or a fruit bat squeak as shrilly as a mouse. The jackals, too, seemed in uncommonly good voice that night. I would not have remarked the noise myself, but heard it as soon as my attention was drawn to it. It was a sound a shop-sign or a hanging lantern might make on a still night.

'Can't place it. What can it be?' He got to his feet. 'Come on. Let's go and find out what it is.' He reached for my hand and pulled me up.

There was no suggestion of alarm in his tone, but fear was ever present and my heart thumped as I followed him, though I would not let him know it. He walked freely and without stealth, and I took care to follow him closely, eyes on the ground, for there was no path and it was dark beneath the trees.

We had almost reached the far side of the grove when, all at once, he stopped dead, swung round and, gripping me by the shoulders, propelled me in the direction from which we had come.

'Don't look!' he implored, but the agonized exclamation came too late.

In the second that he had stopped abruptly before me I looked up in surprise and, before even he had turned round, my eyes had taken in the ghastly thing swinging rhythmically from a branch at the edge of the trees, the powdery starlight sufficing by its very inadequacy to emphasize the horrors of death by hanging.

It was a woman who swung there. The remnants of a gown dropped from her in shreds, telling eloquently of the talons of the vultures and the snarling leap of the jackal. Long hair still hung from the oddly angled head.

Only a swift impression, a glimpse—but enough! In an instant I had plumbed a hell of degradation. Supported by Oliver's arm, I stumbled away, knowing in the deepest part of my mind that I would be a different person always, living for ever in a more cruel world, because I had seen what I had.

After a few paces we stopped. I was shivering and it seemed natural to allow myself to remain in the circle of Oliver's arms.

'Forgive me! I should not have brought you out here ... but I didn't know!'

'I know, I know,' I whispered, shivering, into his velvet waistcoat. 'I'll be all right in a moment ... pull myself together! The ... the shock. It is so ... so horrible, so horrible!'

'I'm a fool. I knew something was exciting the jackals and, as we walked here, I noticed a group of vultures sitting at the edge of the trees. Full, I suppose. But I thought they were just waiting for some wretched animal to die before finishing it off. But ... God! I couldn't have guessed!'

'No, we couldn't have guessed.'

I burrowed my face into the velvet, trying to erase the image etched upon my inner eye, as I could so easily blot out the dark world around me. I felt Oliver's arms tighten around me, and he put his face to my hair. 'Woman dear!' He whispered Kate's phrase, not now in polite derision, but I could not stop shivering, and so we stood for a long moment.

'Oliver,' I whispered at last, 'it was a woman, wasn't it? A ... a white woman?' I felt him nod his head.

'Poor, poor woman.' I wished I could cry, but no tears would come to cleanse my eyes. 'We cannot leave her there, can we? We must bury her. We must call the others and bury her decently.'

'No time,' he answered gruffly. 'We've got to get on now as fast as we damned well can. That didn't happen any too long ago ...'

'But we can't leave her like that ... it's, it's obscene! I beg of you, don't leave her. It might have been one of us, it might have been me and ...'

'Don't be a fool. Don't say it!'

He put his hand over my mouth roughly and his voice was trembling. For a second his eyes held mine, then he took away his dirty hand and kissed me gently on the lips. 'It will never be you, Laura,' he said with effortful calm, 'I will never let it be you.' And then he gathered me to him again and we stood together for a moment, bewildered and perhaps, for once, equally defenceless.

'Guv'nor?'

Toddy-Bob's hoarse whisper from the darkness was unmistakable, and we stepped quickly apart.

'Guv'nor?'

'Here, Tod.'

'Thank Gawd! I was wonderin' what 'ad 'appened to you. We ought to be movin'.'

Toddy walked towards us in the shadows and I saw his arrival as the work of Providence.

'Please, Oliver ... let's bury the poor thing now that Tod's here? Please,' I urged earnestly.

'We've nothing to dig with,' he answered, weakening, 'and the ground is as hard as iron.'

'But we can't just leave her hanging there. If we could just get her down and cover her up with some decency, with stones, branches ... anything?'

383

'It won't save her from the …'

'I realize that. But for anyone to see her like that! I cannot go away and leave her, Oliver.'

'Very well then. But we must be quick. Tod, come and help me, and you stay here, Laura.'

'Oh no! Not on my own! I'll come with you … I won't watch.'

'Come then, but for God's sake let's get it over with,' he said angrily, moving away.

'What's up, Guv? What's 'appened?' Toddy-Bob regarded us both with suspicion as we walked towards the edge of the grove.

'A woman has been murdered. Up there at the edge of the trees. Hanged. A white woman.'

'Gawd's truth!'

'We, Miss Laura here, wants us to dispose of the remains. There's not much we can do, but I suppose we ought to do something.'

Toddy-Bob whistled his emotion but was otherwise silent as we retraced our steps.

While the men worked—Toddy had to climb the tree to cut the rope and ease the body to the ground—I stood with my back to the scene a short distance away so that I would not hear too much. A jackal howled once, very close, and the rustlings in the undergrowth were full of menace as I knew we were watched jealously by predatory eyes. When Toddy climbed the tree, two or three vultures perched in the topmost branches flew off with a clap of heavy wings to join their fellows outside the grove and wait patiently until the intruders had removed themselves, and their own digestive processes allowed of further gorging. There would be no quiet grave for the victim, but at least we would have done what we could.

So I tried to comfort myself as my eyes probed the darkness around me, and so it was that I discovered the others … but these were lying on the ground in a shapeless huddle of slack limbs, like two dolls thrown in a corner by a petulant child. They were a mere few yards from where I stood, but it was the buzzing of the flies that attracted my attention. Here at the edge of the trees the darkness was less intense, and a sudden concerted movement of the mass of winged bodies, disturbed by something unknown to me, caught my eye.

I think I had a presentiment immediately of what I would find, but I walked towards the buzzing heap, half caught in the tangled roots of a peepul, because I was unable to keep away. I could have cried out. I could have waited until Oliver and Toddy-Bob had completed their grisly task. But like a woman in a nightmare, I went where my limbs took me, drained of all emotion but an overriding desire to make a certainty of mere suspicion. I have no idea when that suspicion entered my head but, gazing down with a sort of mesmerized horror at the evilly moving mound, I found it confirmed. I would have known who they were—no, who they had been—even without the jacket with the silver numerals. She had been so proud of 'the Major'.

After a long, dreadful moment I turned away blinded by sudden tears, and sick. Was it really only two days before that we had said goodbye on the sunny, early-morning verandah at Hassanganj? Elvira had been so cheerful at the prospect of a return to Lucknow and the Major's last words had been 'I'll be sure to drop in on my way back to my station.' Perhaps, had I been capable of thought, I would have admitted that both the Major and his daughter obviously shared the mortality of us all. But that Mrs Wilkins, vigorous, vulgar, overwhelming Mrs Wilkins, should meet an end at all, let alone such an end, was unthinkable. 'My, what grand relatives you have!' I almost heard her voice. And again, from long ago: 'I'm a saving sort of woman and it will be ready for you when you want it.'

I turned away, shuddering with nausea, and leaned my face against the bole of a tree, where for a time I shivered and heaved with sheer physical loathing of the repulsive remains bared to my eyes when the flies rose. The vultures, the jackals, the flies and the heat had all done their work. Most of the clothing had been torn away and lay in stained rags around the bodies, and some of the limbs were almost bare of flesh. The bellies, of course, had been ripped open, and the soft flesh of thighs and breasts and cheeks. The eyes had gone.

I steadied myself and gathering my skirts close, picked my way carefully away from the bodies, then stumbled into a run as though distancing myself from the dreadful sight might somehow erase it from my mind. I had gone no more than a few yards when I stopped. Among the shreds of clothing lying on the bloodstained litter of leaves and fallen twigs, I had seen something, a gleam different from the dull shine of the leaves or the cotton that had been Mrs Wilkins's dress. At first I could not remember what it was, nor why the fact that I had remarked it should be of importance in that horrible moment.

I still do not know what primitive instinct of self-preservation came into play, but then I forced myself to walk back to where I had come from, and covering my mouth and nose with my hands, bent and searched the tragic debris until I found what I was looking for.

Nausea flooded over me. I was cold yet sweated profusely and my hand as it reached down trembled violently. The black satin garter was stained with dust and another substance I would not name to myself, but was almost intact except for the fastening which had given under the wrench of talon, claw or tooth.

By now I was weeping hysterically; I stumbled away, threw myself down behind some bushes, well out of range of sound and smell, and was most violently sick. Afterwards, I lay with my face in the dust and cried, and so Oliver found me, how long afterwards I cannot say.

'Come,' he said gently, lifting me to my feet. 'Come, Laura, we must go now. We have covered her over with stones and branches, and her parents.'

'You found them?'

'When we were looking for you.'

'It was the Wilkinses,' I told him unbelievingly. 'The Wilkinses.'

'Yes, it was the Wilkinses, but there is nothing more we can do for them now, Laura.'

'The Wilkinses ... the Wilkinses ...' I kept repeating as Oliver brushed the dust from my clothing and with his fingers combed the hair out of my eyes.

'Come ... we cannot waste any more time now and, truly, we have done all we can. It is finished now, and we must look to ourselves. Come, Laura, you must make the effort!'

I let him lead me out of the horrible grove without speaking, though my mind continued to repeat 'The Wilkinses!' He walked with his arm round my waist, his other hand holding my two cold ones very close. He almost carried me, and all I could think was: 'It was the Wilkinses.'

CHAPTER 8

My mind was too shocked to allow of personal fear as Oliver led me back to the track and settled me, still crying, in the cart. He told the others, brusquely, of the reason for our delay. Emily cried too, but not for long, and she soon dozed. Charles, who must have had a more accurate idea of what we had found in the grove, tried to comfort me but I could not rid myself so quickly of my experience. For most of the night I sat with my head bent on my knees weeping sometimes, sometimes silent, fighting a lonely battle with memory, imagination and conscience.

Only much later, when the stars had disappeared and all the world lay black and very still before the dawn, did I find time to wonder whether only the jackals and the vultures had marked our presence in the grove. Then fear awoke and banished every other sentiment. I had gathered from words muttered over the body of poor Elvira, as Oliver and Toddy-Bob worked, that both were puzzled as to why the corpses had not been more thoroughly dealt with by the vultures. 'Couldn't have happened long ago or there would be nothing left to bury,' I remembered Oliver saying.

'But they should 'ave passed by 'ere yesterday evenin', guv,' Toddy had objected.

'Something might have delayed them, an accident to the carriage, or to one of the horses, perhaps.'

'More like they was took yesterday and left waitin' like, till the varmints makes up their minds what to do with 'em!'

'Perhaps. We'll never know now, but I don't like the thought that this lot are still in the vicinity, Tod, I don't like it at all!'

Now, jolting along in the warm darkness, I recalled the anxiety in Oliver's tone, and the recollection heightened my fears. Each time we met a group of villagers making their dogged, dusty way, just as we were doing, I shrank back into my *burqha*, wondering whether this would be the moment of discovery. I no longer had much faith in Oliver's estimate of the peasantry; every silent, sheet-shrouded figure we met was menacing. Since leaving Hassanganj, we had travelled by side roads and narrow tracks in order to avoid a press of traffic, but once a party of armed men galloped past us in a hurry. They hailed us, and I closed my eyes in agony, waiting for the denunciation. However, Ishmial responded to the hail with good nature, and the men continued on their way without pause.

Due to the long delay in the peepul grove, we made bad progress that night and, instead of halting at sunrise, pressed on our way until mid-morning. Then we turned off the track in the middle of an unprepossessing waste of barren land, and continued until we found a tree under which the cart was halted and the bullocks unyoked and tethered to pasture. Taking his rifle, Oliver set off to look for shelter and, after an eternity in the sweltering heat, returned to say that he had discovered an abandoned hut that would afford us more adequate shelter from the sun. We ate the remainder of some food from the night before; then while Toddy stayed with the cart, Ishmial strode off to find a village and fresh provisions and the rest of us wearily made our way towards Oliver's shelter.

The hut, a one-roomed edifice of mud and gaping thatch, had probably once been a shelter for cattle, or perhaps for the herdsmen, though there was nothing left to betoken human occupation. Compared to the scorching fields, however, it was cool and hid us effectively from prying eyes, an attribute we were grateful for when at about midday, a herd of cattle passed in the charge of three or four small boys and the inevitable collection of ring-tailed dogs. Hearing the dogs bark a little way off, I resigned myself to discovery within moments. They would surely scent us and investigate the hut. But the same thought had struck Oliver. He motioned us to stay hidden, then walked out of the hut rubbing his eyes as though he had just woken from sleep, and crouching in the gloom we overheard a long, laughing conversation take place between the boys and himself. He came back still grinning.

'They think they have come across the most stupid Pathan horse thief south of the Khyber,' he chuckled. 'I asked them the way to a fictitious village, saying I had lost myself in the darkness and my horse had bolted. Never having heard of the village, they told me just how to find it; if we were to follow their directions, we'd probably find ourselves in Hyde Park. However, they are not suspicious—but we must be away from here before the herd returns to the village at sunset.'

Charles and Emily were soon asleep with the baby, fed and comfortable, lying on my cloak between them. But I could not sleep now, as I had not been able to sleep in the cart all night. I sat upright in a corner seeing sights, hearing voices, thinking thoughts which I felt would never allow me to sleep quietly again.

'Don't you find it stuffy in here?' Oliver whispered after a time; I had thought he too was asleep but, glancing at him in the opposite corner, had found his eyes watching me. Perhaps he guessed something of what I was undergoing from my face. 'Come outside for a while; we can sit in the shade of the hut and there will be a little more air anyway.'

I followed him out stealthily and we seated ourselves, native fashion, on the baked earth, with our backs against the wall of the hut. An arid vista of poor fields and dry waterways stretched around us, and in the distance the herd moved slowly along cropping the short brown grass as it went.

'Poor devils! They can't make much of a living on this soil.' Oliver picked up a handful of dry earth and let it slide through his fingers. 'Dust! Just dust!'

I had thrown aside the face-flap of the *burqha* and swung the heavy folds back over my shoulders in an effort to cool myself, but I was too nervous to discard the thing completely and Oliver did not suggest that I should. Since leaving Hassanganj, our ablutions had been sketchy, to say the least, and what with dust, tears and sweat, I must have looked a sorry sight indeed. I took out my bedraggled handkerchief, sitting there in the hot shade, and tried to clean myself up.

Oliver watched in interested silence, then took the handkerchief from me, spat on it, and rubbed my cheeks vigorously in spite of my protests.

'Don't fuss,' he countered irritably when he had finished. 'A bit of spit isn't going to kill you at this stage.'

'It might at least have been my own spit!'

'True,' he grinned. 'Forgive my lack of gallantry in not thinking of it myself,' and then, after a careful scrutiny, he added, 'What a nice face you have—when it's clean!'

'Thank you,' I said stiffly.

389

'Not beautiful of course, and certainly not pretty. Not plain either.'

'That leaves very little that it can be,' I pointed out, piqued despite myself, for I have never quite learned not to covet beauty.

'Quite the contrary; it leaves a great deal. It's a face of intelligence, and ... generosity. And, though I can't see it at the moment, you have a most magnanimous brow. All good things. Indicative of character!'

'Thank you,' I repeated acidly. 'I suppose I should be glad the bad qualities are not apparent at least.'

'Not apparent at first sight, but there all the same. You have a sharp tongue, a quick temper, are as stubborn as a mule and much too prone to jump to conclusions. You also appear to have a hankering for martyrdom, which does not at all accord with the rest of your temperament as far as I have been able to judge it. I cannot understand it, but I do deplore it!'

He was thinking of Charles, and suddenly I realized very distinctly how wrong he was and what a foolish conclusion he had jumped to himself. The knowledge that I could mislead him, even unwittingly, filled me with an irrational gaiety and I found myself laughing.

'That's better,' he said innocently, 'I am glad to hear you laugh again, Laura.' Then he leaned over and covered both my dirty hands with one of his. 'I'd do anything in the world to blot out the memory of last night for you. I'd have given my right hand to prevent you from ... seeing what you did.'

I was sober again immediately and drew away my hands in the pretence of shading my eyes from the sun.

'You must try not to brood, Laura. It cannot do anyone any good now ... neither the dead nor the living. What has happened has happened. Now it's over.'

'I know,' I sighed. 'And three fairly harmless lives are over too. I know you are right, but it is still so ... recent. I cannot help thinking of it. The dreadful ugliness of it. And wondering whether they ... whether they ...'

'Whether they suffered? But that's just it ... you must not let yourself wonder. We'll never have the answer to that question and you only wound yourself by asking it. You must try to think of something else. Anything else!'

'Surely one needs to be able to think of something pleasant. And have you considered lately how few pleasant things there are to think of now? The present is better met each slow minute as it comes. The past hardly bears thinking of with pleasure because all that we were … all that we had or hoped for … is gone past retrieving. We will never be again, any of us, what we were just a week ago. And the future? Don't ask me to think of that! I am afraid of uncertainty. I am a prosaic and rather limited person, not much given to over-optimism or flights of fancy regarding my own hopes for the future. The truest satisfactions I have known in life have come from setting myself some goal and then working towards it, knowing I was secure enough of time, and health, and opportunity, to do so. What, besides survival, is there for anyone to work towards now?'

'It won't always be so …'

'Perhaps not.' I shook my head helplessly. 'But none of us can know when or how it will all end. So you see … neither past, present nor future are going to supply the material for healing reveries for me. Have you any other suggestions?'

He was looking straight in front of him, legs stretched out, thumbs hooked into the armholes of his red velvet waistcoat.

'Well, yes, perhaps I have. Would it take your mind off your unpleasant memories to know that I love you? That I am, as the novelists put it, "in love" with you?'

The earth halted in its gentle rotation for a full second. The sun spun in its own orbit with the haloed speed of a peg-top thrown by a skilful boy. In the total stillness, the blood drummed against my eardrums with the shattering force of summer thunder.

Then, being me, I released the cosmos to its immemorial patterns and realized that it was the declaration that surprised me much more than the fact.

'Are you really?' was all I could think of to say.

'I am,' he assured me, in so prosaic a voice that I could have been forgiven for doubting it.

'But why now?' I insisted.

'Do you mean, why do I tell you now?'

'Well—yes.' But it was not what I had meant.

'As I said, I hoped it might divert your mind from the happenings of last night.'

'Yes. Thank you! You are kind … as Emily has always said.'

'And that is all?'

'No!' I took in a deep breath of hot dusty air. 'No, of course not. But I don't know how seriously I am to take you?'

'Most seriously. If you will.'

I sat in silence, not looking at him because I knew he had turned and was watching my face.

'What ... what makes you think you love me ... now? Is it something that has just happened?'

'No. A long time ago.'

'A long time ago! And yet I never guessed ...'

'No? Though I gave you so many hints?'

'Hints?' My surprise was genuine.

'So you did always miss them? Sometimes I wondered whether you were not just being coy. Yet I suppose I know why you missed them.'

'I really don't know what to say!'

'You soon will. I've never known you tongue-tied,' he chuckled. 'And as you are so clinically interested in the why's and the when's, well, having met my brother and his wife, I felt no need to ask them to spend the winter in Hassanganj. Five minutes of their company was enough to tell me that a week or so, at most, would be as much as I could stand of them. Then I met you, if you remember, and by, I believe, our third encounter I decided I had to know you better. If I am correct, it was that eventful afternoon in Cussens's bungalow that finally decided me. Since then ... well ... it has been one long slow slide into subjection. And a damned sight more pleasant than I ever imagined such a progress could be, too, despite sundry alarms which sometimes boded badly for my intentions!'

'That afternoon ... at Major Cussens's bungalow? Oh come, Oliver! Now I know you are joking. When I made such a fool of myself?'

'No, Laura, I am not joking. Indeed I love you. In fact, if you will forgive the superlative, I love you ... well ... desperately.'

I had kept my eyes away from him but now I turned and looked into his face. The expression I discovered in his strangely coloured eyes filled me with such confusion that I was forced to look away again.

'Please don't,' I whispered. 'You're embarrassing me.'

'Good! You cannot be quite indifferent, after all.'

No easy reply came to me, and coyness, whatever he thought, was never part of my character. For the expression on his face had toppled my precarious assurance and with it all the judgements I had made of this man who said he loved me. In his amber eyes I had seen an unequivocal honesty of emotion which nothing in my upbringing, my experience or my imagination had prepared me to encounter. I was afraid … and as much of my own feeling as of his. With him, I knew now, no reserve would be possible, no withholding, no comfortable subterfuges, no concealments for the sake of self-preservation. And what he was prepared to give, he would demand in return. I would be engulfed, annihilated, by the strength of his feeling, by the force of his idea of me.

But I was not sure that his idea of me coincided with my knowledge of myself. He would expect a quality from me which I was not certain I possessed.

'I told you once that I had watched you more than you imagined. Do you remember? I could not tell you then of the interest … or the delight, with which I watched you, a delight that grew deeper with every day you passed in Hassanganj. I wanted, you see, to discover whether there was any chance you could be happy, feel at home, in the sort of life Hassanganj had to offer. Not many women could, I suppose … at least not many of the sort of women that I have met in India. After a while, and perhaps I only wished it so, but I began to believe that you liked the life, the old house, even the solitude. You were never at a loss for something to do. You never complained of the lack of company, or of the discomforts due to the isolation. And so I began to hope that perhaps, given time, I could prevail on you to share Hassanganj with me. And then … well, this damned trouble started. But I was not wrong, woman dear, was I? You could be happy in Hassanganj?'

'Yes … yes. I enjoyed the life. I could be happy there.'

All at once I found my two hands enclosed in his.

'With me?'

I looked down at the lean brown fingers clasping mine, and for a moment gave myself up to a vision of what life with Oliver Erskine might be—a vision of happy dependence. It would be pleasant, I allowed myself for a moment to think, to resign myself to a stronger will, to acquiesce to a profounder intelligence, to be directed by a wider experience. There would be great, and real, satisfaction to be found as wife to the *sirkar* of Hassanganj, and there was no doubt in my mind that, in time, that would again be Oliver's position in life. There would be wealth, and the security that wealth can give and, on a less materialistic plane, opportunity to influence for the better the lives of the people among whom we lived. More particularly, I acknowledged that I enjoyed his company and conversation and respected his attainments. Oliver Erskine was a man on whom I could rely, to whom I could always turn, and who would not fail me. My own conduct in the last weeks had shown me how much I trusted him, for in all the alarms of the days past it had been he who had directed me, and to him that I had gone for help—not Charles. Lastly, I felt, despite Moti, that once he had given himself, he would be faithful in a way unguessed at by more moderate men.

As though he had divined something of my thinking, he spoke: 'About Moti ... well, that's finished. Quite finished. You know the worst of me, Laura, all of it, I believe. Will you not give me a chance to show you the best?'

I dared not meet his eyes again, but I smiled. I already knew so much that was good in him. It would not take much learning to be happy with him. And yet ...!

My mind returned to the enraptured period when I first knew Charles, the breathless ecstasy of those first few days when I had discovered my love for him and could live in the hope of it being returned. Those faraway few days before Emily returned from Bournemouth and all my hopes fell to ashes as her small bronze boot in the grass set the hammock swaying.

That was what love was. That was what love should be. Not this deliberate assaying of worth, this detached examination of qualities. Love should need no accountant.

'Don't think so much,' he said at last, as still I did not speak, and there was great tenderness in his tone. 'Don't try to analyse and dissect. Don't be so obstinately set on seeing your way, on being right. Oh, my little mule, stop kicking! Forget your head and just this once trust your heart!'

He was pleading with me. I looked up at him, but now his eyes were guarded.

'I'm afraid it is my heart I am guided by,' I answered apologetically. 'I think you want something that I cannot give you. I can't pretend to feel what I don't, Oliver.'

'Would I want you to pretend?'

'No.' So much was patent.

'You have no need of pretence with me, Laura. Never will have.' He sighed and took his hands away from mine.

'So it's still Charles, eh? I'd have sworn you were over that. Could it be that you are only pretending to yourself that you love him, for old time's sake?'

'But I don't! No, it's not Charles and I am certainly not pretending anything at all to myself in his regard.'

I might not love Oliver, but I could not have Oliver thinking I still loved Charles.

'Oh, I'm not denying,' I went on, as he folded his arms and stared across the colourless fields, 'I'm not denying that I thought for a long time that I did love Charles. To begin with, perhaps, I really did. He was so handsome and elegant, and I had known so few young men. But that's all finished now. I think it has been finished for even longer than I realized, perhaps because I didn't want it to be. I know I can't make any sense to you. Men are so different about these things: all black and white and clear cut and quite unable to appreciate the gradations and changes in a woman's feelings. But it is finished. I've grown up, I suppose. It's strange, you know. I thought this journey to India in his company, seeing him with Emily, would be the cruellest thing I'd ever have to endure. At the beginning it was. Then, well, I found I wasn't thinking of him so much, or if I were it was with criticism, and now, though I can remember quite well how I once felt about him, I no longer feel it. Feel anything for him. You must believe that, please?'

'Good! Familiarity generally does breed contempt, you'll find.'

'That's putting it a little too strongly. But at least, in this case, familiarity seems to have put an end to romantic dreams. That much I will acknowledge.'

'Good again. Romance is for dimwits and cowards!'

'What a dull, prosaic world we would have if everyone thought so.'

'Nonsense. Reality is far more interesting than romance.'

'Interesting? Possibly for the strong-minded. But never as pleasant.'

'Hmph!'

We were silent for a time. Heat haze shimmered over the ground and only the tops of the few scrubby thorn-trees were visible, like corks bobbing in a sea of soda water.

What a peculiar place to receive a declaration of love, I thought, and from Oliver Erskine of all people. Everything lacked reality: our situation in this baked terrain, our fugitive condition, our unfamiliar clothing. I was very tired, very hot, and conscious of my own lack of cleanliness; no doubt these physical discomforts played a part in keeping realization from me, even the true realization of what Mr Erskine had just told me.

Had things been different, had he declared his love in the drawing-room at Hassanganj, or in the garden at Mount Bellew, had my world been safely balanced on security, familiarity and hope and not overthrown by fear and flight and the horrible evidence of sudden death, I suppose I would have been young enough and female enough to have enjoyed thinking over my conquest. I would surely have felt flattered, no doubt complacent too, however little I loved him. I would have realized that it was no mean thing to bring a man of so positive a temperament to my feet, and perhaps the very flattery of it would have led me to think I could love him in return or, at all events, desire not to lose my power over him.

But my little times were too badly out of joint to permit the tender triumphs of courtship. His declaration, almost casual as it was, had certainly surprised me, and for a moment stirred me to the recognition that it was genuine, and even briefly touched my heart. Yet for many reasons I was incapable of any response, and the chief of these was that all my faculties were bent on the justification of what I had done the night before. For, although the emotion engendered by the dreadful deaths my friends had met with was genuine, I had been kept awake through the long night and the hot morning, not by the vision of their decomposing bodies lying unattended in the peepul grove, but by the fear that I had done them yet another wrong in robbing them. In robbing the dead. Twice during the night I had brought myself to the point of throwing away the wretched black garter that I had thrust into the bosom of my dress; and twice I had desisted. It was of this I thought as we sat in the hot shadow, so close together—and not of Oliver.

'Oliver?'

'Yes?'

'Please help me.' Tears of exhaustion and self-pity rose to my eyes as I spoke.

'What is it, Laura? You know I will.'

'I ... I did an awful thing last night. At least I think it was an awful thing now, but then I only remembered that she said I could always call on her for help, that it would always be ready for me. I didn't think of it as thieving, but perhaps they have relatives and then I will certainly have to send it back. Everything is so dreadfully uncertain and there's no way of knowing what we might need money for, cash for, before we reach Calcutta, and none of us have very much with us. But if they have relatives, I will send it them back. I promise I will!'

'Who? What? Send what back?'

'Mrs Wilkins's garter.'

'What are you talking about?'

He put his hand under my chin and forced me to face him. Seeing the tears, he wiped them away with a fold of my *burqha*. 'What is all this, Laura? Now start from the beginning and tell me.'

'It was on the ship, that's where it began. I had looked after them, Mrs Wilkins and Elvira, when they were ill, and I suppose they were grateful, although I didn't do any more than they would have done for me or anyone else, I'm sure. But afterwards, when they were well again, Mrs Wilkins showed the garter to me. I think it was the last day on board. She always wore it, and she said India was a hard place for a young girl and that if I ever needed help—money, you know—I was just to write and let her know. She had sold two already, but she was a thrifty soul and there would always be enough for me.' I gulped and sniffed.

'You mean there was money in the garter?' He began to look less puzzled.

'No.' I shook my head. 'Jewels! Pearls and rubies and a very large emerald. I didn't think of it at first. Not when I found them. But then I remembered, and I went back. The … the flies … they were so repulsive! But I got it, and then I went away and was sick. It was horrible, Oliver, horrible! A terrible thing for anyone to do, and I know I was wrong. Robbing the dead is a crime. Oh, Oliver, what am I to do?' I wailed.

'Where is this thing?' he asked.

I took it out and gave it to him. He examined it minutely, much as I had done in such different circumstances on the ship ten months before. He pulled a few stitches at one end, making an aperture, then shook the garter vigorously. Four milky pearls and a ruby fell into the palm of his hand. He whistled in admiration.

'Magnificent!' he exclaimed. 'If they are all as good as these, you are almost a wealthy woman.'

'But they are not mine. I don't want them. Don't you see, I stole them! I went back and found them near Mrs Wilkins's dead body!' I enunciated each word very deliberately so that he would understand. He regarded me blankly for a moment, then the corners of his mouth twitched and, burying his face in his hands, he gave himself over to laughter.

I sat watching his shoulders shake and wondered whether my misdeed had been too much even for him. Did men sometimes have hysterics as women did?

When he looked up, there were tears in his eyes, and for a while he could not speak. Every time he tried to, he would catch my anxious eye and something would set him off again. At last he leant back against the wall and mopped his perspiring face with the tail of his turban.

'Oh, my jewel,' he gasped, started to laugh again, but controlled himself. 'My queen amongst women. My angel of expediency. My saint of common sense. There are no words good enough for you!'

'Stop it, Oliver. You're teasing me, and a moment ago you promised to help. I am really worried about what I did.' But something in his face, a suggestion of disbelief, perhaps, prompted me to smile as I spoke.

'You have absolutely nothing to worry about,' he assured me solemnly. 'No woman capable of retaining her practical good sense in spite of what she experienced on such an occasion as last night need ever worry. About anything. Anywhere!'

'But that's just it, don't you see? I'm ashamed of having done it, but I'm even more ashamed of being the sort of person who could think of doing it. Emily ... well, you know it would never have entered Emily's head. She would never have thought of the jewels, or that they might be useful to her, with those two poor things lying there in that awful condition. Perhaps I wouldn't have either, ordinarily,' I allowed myself, 'but now with everything so upset, we might very well need more money than we have with us. It seemed such a pity to leave them there.'

'No, don't. Please Laura, don't explain. It would start me off again, and I can't bear any more. Oh, my God!'

'But are you sure? You don't think I was very wrong to do it? Honestly?'

'Tell me, what would have happened to that ... that thing, if you hadn't taken it?'

'The jackals ...'

'Yes, but then someone, sooner or later, would have found it and discovered what it contained. There is no one in the world so curious or so rapacious as an Indian peasant. Have you thought what would have happened if the men who killed the Wilkinses had discovered it, as well they might have done?'

'No.'

'They would have bought guns, ammunition, supplies with them to use against other people like the Wilkinses. Against us, perhaps. They would have made good use of them, believe me.'

'Yes—but after all, those were ... enemies.'

'Would Mrs Wilkins sooner her enemies had her jewels than her friends?'

'I suppose not.'

'You said yourself she had offered you her help. Now, in a wrong way but at the right time, she has given it to you. And tell me, how did she come by the things in the first place? Did she buy them?'

'No! Oh, she told me all about it. The Major, only he wasn't a major then of course, got them after a battle ages ago, in one of the states, from the coat of a dead princeling, Mrs Wilkins thought ...' My voice trailed away in confusion.

'Oh, no! Oh my God! I'm off again!'

This time I was able to join in the unseemly laughter with only a trace of remorse left in my mind.

* * *

That evening, as we made our way back to the cart to resume our journey, I made an opportunity to have a few words alone with Oliver.

'I am sorry,' I told him, 'that I am not able to feel for you as you would wish me to. I am very ... grateful for your regard.'

'Are you?' He was striding along with his rifle over his shoulder, and I had to hurry to keep up with him and out of earshot of the others. 'But I don't want your gratitude, Laura. There's no place for gratitude between two people as matched and equal as us. I'm willing to wait for what I want from you. I always get what I want—in the end!'

And with a grin he lengthened his stride and left me to pick my way onward alone.

CHAPTER 9

We travelled steadily all that night and until the early afternoon of the following day. Ishmial had managed to procure a strip of canvas from somewhere with which he roofed the wall of the cart so that its occupants were protected both from the sun and curious eyes. We had decided again to press on by daylight, for now Lucknow was only a score or so miles away, but the pace of a bullock-cart is scarcely hectic, however harshly the driver may yell at his long-suffering beasts or however cruelly he may twist their bony tails.

As we drew near the city, even the side roads that we were using became busy with traffic, with other carts and shabby horse-drawn *gharis* and *ekkas*, with mounted men and throngs of villagers, with sometimes bands of sepoys marching in ragged formation or half a dozen *sowars* on fine mounts who galloped in the middle of the road regardless of pedestrians. And the closer we got to Lucknow, the more obvious became the atmosphere of tension, of crisis around us. Several times we stopped boldly at roadside *serais* where Ishmial bought food, watered the bullocks and made use of the opportunity to ask questions and listen to gossip, that gossip of the Indian roads that travels faster than a message by telegraph, and carries more of actual truth than any newspaper. The information was not reassuring; it became apparent that all the north-eastern section of the Indian peninsula was now in turmoil—all Oudh, Bihar, and Bengal, to say nothing of Delhi itself. The sepoys we saw swaggering along so arrogantly were all mutineers, most of them making their way to Lucknow from small stations up-country. As I watched each party pass, peeping through the slit between the canvas and the top rail of the cart, I wondered whether these were the men who had attacked the Wilkinses. Oliver thought it possible that the dreadful deed had been done by the Major's own men, who had known his intentions and seen him set off with his family and his cartload of baggage, a powerful incentive to murder in the present times.

So far, we had managed to skirt the towns and larger villages, but now we could no longer avoid passing through them on our course, and each of the little towns, with its tall balconied houses cut through by narrow alleys crowded with people, indicated clearly the mood of the country.

The *bunnias* were doing a roaring trade, the streets outside their little shops solid with sepoys buying food, as watersellers and coffee vendors, with their conical copper jugs and their tinkling bells, moved busily among the crowds. On the balconies, women of doubtful virtue, for they were unveiled, watched the comings and goings and engaged in high-pitched conversation with the soldiery beneath them. Even the usual smell of an Indian bazaar—of rotting vegetables, filthy drains, hot oil from the sweet shops, dust, urine, cheap sweet perfume, and incense coils and sweat—seemed to be heightened in the heat and excitement, and the stains of red betel nut juice, spattered on every building, were ominously like blood to my nervous eyes.

The sun reaching its unbearable zenith forced us to halt, and some distance off the road we took shelter in a clearing of what seemed to be a large stretch of forest. For the remainder of the day, the only people we saw were a couple of woodsmen with their axes, and a woman going home from market carrying her purchases on her head, singing to frighten away animals and evil spirits. It was quiet and we slept away the hours of heat in the shade of the trees. After we had eaten in the evening, Oliver asked me to give him my *rakhri*. He had discussed the matter with Ishmial, and they had decided that, not knowing what state the city was in, it would be well to have an adequate escort to protect us through the maze of narrow streets. Oliver had bought a sheet of paper and a bamboo pen, and now sat down and wrote a letter to Wajid Khan in elegant Urdu, explaining our position and asking for some men of his household to see us safely into the Residency.

'I have been politely but pointedly expectant of his help,' he said, 'assuring him that I know he could not in honour disregard such a token as I send him. It might do the trick; anyway, he can only refuse. I have taken care to be rather vague as to our whereabouts, just in case … And if he does refuse, well, we will still be the better off for Ishmial's news of the city.'

Then he arranged a meeting-place with Ishmial, folded the floss-silk bracelet in his letter, and Ishmial tucked it into the folds of his cummerbund, salaamed and set off.

I experienced a moment of desolation as his tall form disappeared among the trees; now we were truly diminished, five Europeans and a baby alone in a hostile land. Fatigue and uncertainty bred in me a sense of hopelessness, and I told myself that we would never see Ishmial again. After all, why should he return to us? We were merely a responsibility, a liability, perhaps even a danger to him. What did he owe us that he should risk his safety for us? Toddy-Bob, too, seemed downcast at the going of his friend and sat whistling and whittling in a most dejected manner until we retired.

We were to meet Ishmial at dawn at a *serai* only a couple of miles further along the road, so that we could enter the city with the countryfolk taking their produce into the bazaars, whose numbers would give us a certain protection. At sunset we doused the small fire we had made to cook on and lay down to sleep, Emily and I stretched uncomfortably in the cart with the baby, the men on the ground beside it. The three of them were to take turns, as usual, to remain awake and on guard. Eventually we slept.

I seemed to dream all night. Not dreams of terror, but curious disjointed memories of scenes and people intermingled absurdly in improbable situations: my Aunt Hewitt sitting in the Hassanganj fernery knitting a tie on thin steel needles that became, somehow, Ishmial's bandoliers; Emily declaring that Toddy-Bob always ate all the cucumber in vinegar at *tiffin*; a pile of Indian sweetmeats, covered with flies, as I had often seen them in the bazaars, all moving together, and Oliver Erskine assuring me that he never wore slippers made by Moti. Whatever the dream, I was hurrying; but my legs were leaden and, despite the effort I made, I knew I was missing something very important.

After an eternity of frustration I awoke, sweating, and lay looking up at the circle of stars above the clearing. It was very still, much quieter here in the forest than it had been in the peepul grove two nights before. But something had disturbed me; something was amiss.

Then I heard a very small sound, a clink of steel against the stone, such as a nail in a boot-heel might make; no more. My mind leapt to alertness. My face was uncovered, but the *burqha* covered the rest of my person. For some time, I heard nothing more, and concluded the sound had been made by whichever man stood guard. But I took the precaution of easing one hand out of my *burqha* and covering the butt of my pistol, which lay hidden in the folds of my clothing. I dozed again. Perhaps I actually slept. Then my eyes were wide open and I saw a form, black against the brighter black of the night, bending over the side of the cart with one hand outstretched, and in that hand a knife. In the same instant I saw the starlight glint on a broad silver bracelet which Emily wore on her right wrist. Unconscious of any formal reaction or process of thought, I tightened my fingers round the trigger of the pistol and fired directly into the dark bulk of the body, angling the weapon upwards from where I lay.

The noise of the single shot echoed round the clearing with terrifying intensity, frightening me much more than the knowledge that I had caused it. I saw the figure impelled backwards by the force of the bullet and for an instant glimpsed a dark, surprised face tilted to the stars before it fell out of sight, making no sound. Then the baby wailed, Emily shrieked, and Oliver, Charles and Toddy-Bob were all around us. I crouched in a corner of the cart, trembling, while my mind cleared and the men milled round the cart investigating the body and demanding explanations of Emily, who was only capable of crying distractedly and pointing to me.

Oliver came around the cart and placed both his hands on my shoulders. 'Good girl,' he muttered. 'Good girl. Now you have your cry and you'll feel better. You saved us, Laura. Bless you!'

Being told to cry, like a child advised to weep away its disappointment at a missed party, dispelled any desire I might have had to do so. Besides, my memories of what I had seen in the peepul grove were still too vivid and, though Oliver obviously thought I would be overcome by remorse and guilt at having killed a man, I was conscious of no such laudable sentiments. What bothered me was that I might have made a frightful mistake: it might have been Charles at whom I fired so instinctively, looking in at his wife and child asleep in the cart. But then I remembered the knife glinting in the starlight and my mind eased; it was the sight of the knife that had made me press the trigger, not an unthinking reaction to fear. I had done it in conscious self-defence, and at such a time and in such a place, who would blame me?

'Well, you're a cool customer. No denying that, Miss Hewitt. And now, since you are not going to have hysterics, would you mind telling

403

us what happened—quickly!' Oliver grinned as he spoke, and I pulled myself up and told him the little I had to tell.

'Perhaps I was wrong to shoot. I should have given myself time to think. I could have screamed, at least.'

'You could have indeed and by the time you'd stopped screaming you'd have been dead yourself. Just remember that.' And he turned away.

'You stay here, Charles. Toddy, take that side and search the thicket. There may be others. I'll go this way, and Charles … shoot at anything that moves; we'll call out when we are returning to warn you that it's us.'

They disappeared immediately into the undergrowth. Charles sat on the tail of the cart, with his pistol cocked in his hands, trying to soothe his wife, and at the same time blaming himself for having slept on guard, for this was how the intruder had managed to approach the cart so closely.

'I'll never forgive myself !' he said with painful guilt. 'I must have dozed. Everything was so quiet; it seemed so unlikely that we would be disturbed, and I suppose I just, well, let myself sleep. Oh God, when I think what could have happened! You could all have been killed while I slept!'

'Oh, don't exaggerate!' I snapped back. 'One of us might have met our end, but no more. He couldn't have seen Oliver in the lee of the cart, or Toddy-Bob under the trees, and if he saw you at all, he probably took you for another woman who would run rather than resist.'

'It was my fault,' he insisted, 'all my fault …'

'Well, yes, so it was,' I had to agree, 'but there's no point in going on about it now, Charles. Oh, Emily, do stop snuffling like that.'

'But,' protested Emily, 'it … it's still down there; I can see his feet. Oh, Charles …!'

And the snuffles became a full-blooded wail again. I put my arm round Emily, drawing her head down on to my shoulder so that she would not see the corpse; I had no wish to see it myself, and could understand her feeling of repugnance. Charles got up and walked nervously to and fro, peering into the thick darkness of the jungle. It vexed me to see him, usually so controlled, undone by his own involuntary lapse. I had been shocked at seeing him drunk on the day of Pearl's birth, but seeing him like this filled me with embarrassment as well as pity. I prayed (but whether for my sake or Charles's I could not say) that Oliver would be forbearing with him and hold his tongue; knowing Oliver's temperament pretty well, I did not think he would.

Only much later did I begin to take in the fact that I had actually killed a fellow human being.

That was after Toddy-Bob had returned, leading a well-saddled horse, followed in a few moments by Oliver and the intelligence that there was no sign of any other men.

'Probably a lone deserter from a cavalry regiment, broken away from his comrades and more anxious to return to his village than reinstate the King of Delhi. Poor devil!' He turned the body over with his toe. 'Well, he'll never have to bother about his crops again. That was a good shot, Laura. Blew his chest in.'

'Oh, don't, Oliver! How can you be so unfeeling?' I was standing on the far side of the cart, having no wish to examine my handiwork. 'I've been thinking; if he was alone, he might only have been a thief, mightn't he? He had seen Emily's bracelet, and perhaps if we had given it to him, he'd have gone away.' But my theory didn't sound plausible even to me.

'So, and what was the knife for then, picking his teeth? Here, have a look at it, Laura, that should still your uneasy conscience.'

But I shuddered and turned away as he held the weapon out for my inspection. It was long and thin, a dagger I suppose one would call it, and a glance was sufficient to determine its deadliness.

To my relief Oliver ignored Charles, who was hovering about still with pistol in hand, like a schoolboy waiting outside the headmaster's study, and turned to Toddy as he stuck the knife in his belt.

'Undress him, Tod. The jacket won't be much good, but his breeches and *puggaree* are more appropriate to our supposed state in life than the things you are wearing; and you can clean up the jacket and sling it over your shoulder. Then throw him into the *nullah* over there. Nobody will be expecting him, so nobody will miss him, but we don't want to leave any traces. Harness up the bullocks, Charles. We'll get going immediately.'

So it was that the party which left the clearing was very unlike the one that had taken shelter in it a few hours before. There were still three women and a baby in the covered cart, but beside them now rode a Pathan with his hand on his hip, his rifle in the saddle holster for all to

405

see, while the cart itself was driven by a small man in the uniform of a *sowar* of the 7th Native Cavalry.

The rendezvous was reached ahead of time.

Light just tipped the topmost branches of the dusty wayside trees, but the *serai* was sleepily astir. Smoke rose lazily from a dozen cooking fires, pariah dogs crept out from under carts to search for food among the huddled bodies and the hooves of bullocks and horses, and mynas began to scold in the trees. One or two men carrying brass pots made their way down to the inevitable tank to make their ritual ablutions; the *bunnia* threw back the shutters of his shaky wooden booth, yawning hugely, and began to range his flat baskets of rice, lentils, gram and bright red chillies on old sacks laid on the ground before the booth. The clearing was redolent of woodsmoke, cow-dung and the sour scent of the scum-covered tank.

Ishmial was there before us, and with him four stalwart figures in bedraggled livery, carrying flintlocks and clubs. We found them discreetly situated at the edge of the camping ground; they had been cooking, so we ate what they had prepared, Emily, Charles and I (as befitted Mohammedan females) remaining in the cover of the cart, while Toddy and Oliver squatted with the men around the fire and Oliver interrogated Ishmial regarding the state of the city.

Lucknow, so Ishmial said, was in chaos, its inhabitants in a state of hysteria and liable to erupt at any moment into open and uncontrollable violence. The already vast population was augmented daily by the arrival of mutineers from outlying posts, armed, aggressive and anxious to prove their metal in combat. All the British, the troops from Mariaon, civilians from the city, together with their womenfolk, had been ordered into the Baillie Guard, while Mariaon Cantonments, that pleasant suburb of shady avenues and peaceful gardens, was deserted, its bungalows looted and burned.

In great haste, earthworks and fortifications were being thrown up around the perimeter of the Residency ('Still! Good God, that should have been finished weeks ago,' Oliver exclaimed in English when he heard this), but the work was unfinished and when the rains broke, as they soon would, further work would be impossible.

'It is said in the city,' said Ishmial with awe, 'that Lawrence *Sahib* has issued orders that no private property and no holy places must be destroyed, and so, as almost all property is private and every man's home is holy, to him, many buildings still stand which should have been thrown down. Is this not the foolishness of the *feringhi*?'

'It is,' agreed Oliver grimly. 'But is the Residency still open to access? Do people come in and go out freely?'

Apparently they did. The English troops came and went and supplies streamed in from the bazaars, such loads of *dhal*, rice, *atta*, and sugar as made the *bunnias*' eyes gleam daily more brightly. 'For they believe, *Sahib*, that soon they will have it all back again to sell a second time—when the *Sahib-log* have been destroyed.'

The police had mutinied too, and the city lay open to anarchy. The more prudent of the wealthy natives had withdrawn to their country estates, leaving their town houses to be looted and burned by a mob who acted without discrimination or favour in its lust for destruction. Wajid Khan also would have left Lucknow, but there was smallpox in his house near Fyzabad, and his estate near Hassanganj was too far away in these times when the roads were as dangerous as they had been in the days of the Thugs.

'But these things are done at night, *Sahib*. Today we will traverse the city and find everything as it has been, except perhaps that it is quieter. The people sit in the houses and wait, watching for some sign, and only when darkness falls, the *badmashes* come out with their *lathis* and their knives.'

We were silent when Ishmial ended, each of us occupied with his own vision of our immediate future, for I had tried to translate Ishmial's words to Emily and Charles as he spoke them.

Then Oliver got up and came to the cart. 'Well, that's it then. The Residency it will have to be, little as I care for the sound of it.'

'Was there ever an alternative?' asked Charles.

'I had half an idea of trying to cut down to the Ganges, to Cawnpore. You might have been able to get some form of transport there to take you to Calcutta. But matters are too far gone for that, I'm afraid. It looks as though we must be grateful that the Residency is still open. Wajid Khan has sent a couple of palanquins, they are quicker than the cart and more comfortable. Also quite private. He is a most thoughtful gentleman is your brother, Laura.'

We descended from the cart, unloaded our few possessions and transferred them to the palanquins, shabby affairs hung with dirty cotton curtains. The bearers sat smoking impassively and merely watched us as we worked. It struck me that they were somehow hostile to us, but then I realized they did not know the *burqhas* covered white women, and they would never have thought of helping their own womenfolk.

It was decided that Emily and Charles should share one palanquin while I took Pearl with me in the second. Emily was reluctant to part with her child, but when it was pointed out that she would be cooler and more comfortable with me than crowded in with her parents, she agreed. Ishmial and Toddy-Bob would lope beside us along with the bodyguard, and Oliver, I presumed, would bring up the rear on the *sowar*'s horse.

I was glad to climb into the odd conveyance and know myself safe from the curious eyes of other travellers, some of whom, chewing neem twigs to clean their teeth, had lounged up to our part of the *serai* and were watching our movements with that open interest which so disconcerts the conventions of the West. We were comfortably disposed and about to set off when Oliver parted the curtains of my palanquin and sat down on the flock mattress which formed its base. He had not shaved since leaving Hassanganj, and he smelt. But so did we all, I suppose.

'Comfortable? No bugs?' He glanced around the inside of the palanquin's dusty hangings and ran a thumbnail along the seam of the mattress. 'None in sight, but that doesn't mean there aren't any. However, your journey won't be long, and there are worse things after all.'

Mosquitoes whined in the curtained dimness of the palanquin, and flies had swarmed in as Oliver lifted the dirty cotton to sit down; but I had not thought of bugs—or the more likely fleas. I shuddered away from the greasy bolster and examined my surroundings with new distaste. Oliver laughed at my reaction, then covered my hand with his own.

'Goodbye, Laura,' he said softly, his eyes fixed on mine. 'I wish many things that have happened had not happened; even more, I wish many things that did not happen had happened. Still, regrets of that nature are pointless now. I can do nothing more for you for the moment, but some day—it will be a different story. In the meantime, will you think of me sometimes? Kindly, if possible?'

'What do you mean? Surely you are coming with us? You are not leaving us now, Oliver. You can't!'

'But, m'dear, can you imagine me holed up with a lot of my compatriots in the Residency for more than a day without defecting to the mutineers?'

Of course, he was joking. He had no option but to come with us, for he certainly could not return to Hassanganj.

'Oh, do be serious!' I snapped, drawing away my hand from his clasp. 'What the devil else can you do? And do you think we are going to like it any better than you? What are you talking about, Oliver?'

'I'm just saying goodbye and good luck, as a well-conducted host should do when he speeds a parting guest.'

'You do mean it!' I said unbelievingly, watching his dirty face and conscious of the whimsical tenderness in his eyes. 'You really do. But, Oliver, you can't leave us now. You mustn't!'

'But I must, Laura. I'll explain it all sometime. I still have other affairs to attend to before matters get worse. Important affairs, I'm afraid, that cannot be delayed.'

'But ...' And I paused to marshal my forces of persuasion.

'Well?'

'I believe we are still in danger. Grave danger. I understood most of what Ishmial was telling you about the condition of the city. We will be in danger every step of the way with the people in the mood they're in. You surely see that? How can you leave us now?'

'The Residency is still open. You heard that too, I presume? Within an hour and a half you will be there, safe and sound among your friends. It is no distance from here, Laura, which is why we chose this place to meet. You have Wajid Khan's men, and Charles, and I am leaving Toddy and Ishmial with you too. They have their instructions, and you know they can be relied on.'

'And what do we know about Wajid Khan's men? They might be cut-throats or *dacoits*; they certainly look it. What could Toddy and Ishmial do against so many, if there is any trouble? And as to Charles, why he's as much a stranger here as I am, and anyway he is not ... not as reliable as he should be.'

At these words Oliver laughed. 'Laura, I believe you are the most unscrupulous woman I know!'

'Perhaps,' I acknowledged. 'But you know that what I say is true; and, anyway, what affairs can you have now, with Hassanganj gone and your responsibilities with it, that are more pressing than doing your duty by your brother's wife and child, to say nothing of me?'

'None that you would acknowledge, perhaps,' he said with something near bitterness in his voice. 'But I have them all the same.'

'But quite apart from us, apart from getting us to the Residency, has it not occurred to you that you might be needed here—if matters get out of hand and there really is a battle or something? Don't you believe your presence would be necessary at such a time? There are those who will put a more ... more sinister interpretation on your abandonment of us, and of your people, at such a moment.'

I felt myself growing angry. Why was he always so trying? Why did he have to play into the hands of his detractors in this way? This was cowardice; that was what most of the men I knew would say, to refuse to assist one's fellow countrymen in such a crisis.

Perhaps he saw the genuine alarm on my face, for he took my hand again and patted it to reassure me.

'Believe me, Laura, if I thought I could be of real assistance to you now, or even, believe it or not, to the others, I would come with you. But I know I have done as much as I need do now for your safety. No harm can come to you, and I truly do have something urgent to attend to. Very urgent.'

Something in the way he spoke prevented me from asking what that urgent business was, and to be truthful I was far more concerned about my own immediate future than his.

'Then ... then when will we see you again?' I asked after a moment.

'Does it matter?' There was more to the question than the words, so that I looked down at my hands in his and answered disingenuously, 'We would not want to leave India without seeing you again.'

'I doubt whether you will be leaving for some time.'

'Then you do intend to return to Lucknow?' And I looked up to find him watching me intently. 'Oh, Oliver, do say you will come back—just as soon as you can. It will be so ... so dangerous for you alone in the *mofussil* now.'

'Your concern is very touching,' he said gravely, but with a twitch at the corner of his lips. 'Unfortunately it is more than ever true at the moment that what man proposes, God disposes. I cannot say what my movements will be. As to being alone in the *mofussil*, well, that's what

I have always been, and I prefer it that way. Within limits, of course, and even those limits are very newly acquired ones!'

I knew precisely what he meant by the last remark, but any pleasure I might have derived from this oblique acknowledgement of his need for me was swamped in anger.

His attitude was intolerable. The eccentricity, the intractability, the almost perverted desire for privacy which I had so often heard stigmatized in my erstwhile host, these unamiable qualities must have their root, not in marked individuality, as I had begun to think, but in unvarnished selfishness. There was no excuse possible for him. I drew myself up and as far from him as the confinement of the palanquin allowed.

'I see!' I said very coldly. 'Very well. Far be it from me to deter you. But before you go, allow me to say, Oliver Erskine, that I think your attitude is altogether reprehensible, and your action quite unforgivable. I believe you are the most self-absorbed, and … and downright cowardly man I have ever had the ill-fortune to meet. And that I should be forced to this opinion of you, after all these months, and all that you have done for us, and …'

I don't think I expected him to be downcast and he certainly gave no indication of taking my strictures seriously. Instead, he laughed so heartily that I became uneasy about the others waiting outside hearing it and trying to ascribe a cause to the laughter.

'That's the spirit!' he said. 'That's your fighting form back to normal. Now I know you will get through whatever trials may befall you with flying colours. That blaze in your eyes would scorch the beard off a mutineer at a hundred paces. As to the rest, woman dear …' He paused to recapture my hands which I had drawn away from him. 'I will come back—for your sake—and as soon as I can. You have shamed me into it. Anyway, I don't believe I could stay away from where you are now. I will come back to you—for you!'

Then he bent suddenly towards me and, before I could make a move to escape, had pressed his hard stubbly lips against mine. He released my hands and placed his arms around me, drawing me close against his chest.

'Back to you—for you, Laura! I promise,' he whispered as he drew away at last. For a moment he laid his cheek against mine, then stood up, dropped the curtain of the palanquin and was gone.

411

I heard him mount the dead *sowar*'s horse, call a farewell in Urdu and gallop away down the road we had come, the long road to Hassanganj.

The darkness of the stuffy palanquin was suddenly welcome. I needed its privacy in which to weep.

CHAPTER 10

'*Uttho*! *Uttho*!' the bearers cried, and in a moment I was heaved up in my curtained darkness that smelt of coconut oil, betel nut and greasy cotton and we were on our way.

The palanquin swayed rhythmically as the bearers jog-trotted through the crowded, now fully-awake *serai*, crying themselves a clear passage through the vehicles, livestock and people with a sharp, nasal note of warning, then settled into a more regular rhythm as we gained the broad, rutted road, their bare feet making no sound in the yellow dust. I could not guess the direction we were taking but, through the curtains, could hear muffled voices, sometimes the cries of vendors selling water, fruit or parched gram; I could hear the squeaking axles of bullock-carts and the rattle as a high-wheeled *ekka*, its tiny platform under a roof of thatch crowded with an entire family, drove past stirring up a cloud of dust. I heard horses canter past, and once we passed a line of camels wearing their special brass bells, while often the deep slow note of an elephant bell served to remind me of peaceful mornings on the verandah at Hassanganj. There seemed to be a throng of people around us, all making their way into the awakening town, and I hoped heartily, now that Oliver was gone, that Wajid Khan's retainers would prove reliable.

The motion of the palanquin soon put Pearl to sleep and, as the moments passed, my first anxiety for our safety grew less, and my mind dwelt more on the behaviour of Oliver Erskine. There was no point in weeping, so I wiped my eyes, sniffed and set myself to discover the reason for his behaviour. Always unpredictable, this latest step was inexplicable. To have accompanied us so far, through so many difficulties surmounted with such resourcefulness; to have used ingenuity and energy in assuring our escape to begin with and then the safe continuance of our journey; and now to leave us when our bourne was in sight, was beyond my comprehension.

Perhaps he was right; perhaps we were now as safe as he could make us. Wajid's response to the bracelet could only mean that he intended to keep faith with us and I had no real fears of the set of bravos he had sent us, whatever their appearance. But our safety could not explain Oliver's refusal to come to the Residency, and neither could the cynical nonsense he had spoken about not fighting his compatriots' battles. He had turned back in the direction of Hassanganj, but what could he do once he got there, with no house to live in and possibly with a hostile, or at least an intimidated populace to deal with? He must have had a better motive than wanting to view the burnt-out shell of his home by daylight, but I could not find one. Even Moti would by now be in Cawnpore, so her welfare could not have drawn him back.

I puzzled the matter over in my mind for a couple of miles, I suppose, and then, when the bearers slowed down because of some obstruction before them, I ventured to peep through the slit of the curtains and saw Toddy-Bob, a bedraggled figure in a cavalry uniform several sizes too large for him, walking by the side of my equipage with a dejected look on his face. I hissed and, when he looked up, beckoned him closer so that we could speak English without being overheard.

'Toddy, why didn't you return to Hassanganj with Mr Erskine?' I asked innocently, although I knew he had remained on Mr Erskine's order.

''E wouldn't let me, miss.'

'Oh. And Ishmial?'

'Nor 'im neither.'

'You mean he's gone back to Hassanganj quite alone?'

'Yes'm.'

So that much was determined anyway.

'Toddy, why did he leave us?'

' 'E didn't want to, I reckon, miss. 'Ad to. On account of the nipper.'

'The nipper? Pearl?' I looked down to make sure she was safely asleep at the foot of the palanquin.

'No'm.' This was one of the days on which Toddy-Bob needed to be drawn.

'Who then?'

'His own nipper, miss. Yasmina.'

Of course. A sense of disquietude, of shame almost, overcame me at hearing Yasmina so described. Certainly she was Oliver Erskine's child, but I had never heard it put into words, never framed the thought consciously even in my own mind.

'But surely … I mean, why cannot she be looked after by … by her mother? I thought they were to go to Cawnpore?'

'Yes'm. That's right. But her mother's dead. Killed.'

'Oh, Toddy, no!'

'Yes'm! They got her right enough, the bastards. Soon as they found the 'ouse empty and you gentry gone. Must've known, y'see, that it was she what …'

Yes, it was she who had warned us, and I understood it all. I remembered the blistering day in the thatch of the ice-house, and how I had thought I had heard a cry from the direction of the tower, but had said nothing. Oliver had said something though; what was it? Yes, he had said the following day, 'Remorse is not yet within your experience.' And later, by the hut, he had said, 'About Moti, it's finished. Quite finished.' What a conceited, self-regarding fool I had been not to have wondered at the flat note of bitterness in his voice as he spoke both sentences. He must have found her when he left us in the thatch and came back in the Pathan clothing, carrying the bundle of *burqhas*. He had been irritable and impatient. Once or twice that night I had addressed him without getting any response, but had put his abstraction down to fatigue.

To fatigue! Poor Oliver, and poor Moti, to whom we all owed so much, to whom Pearl owed her life twice over.

'You see, miss.' Toddy-Bob was suddenly eloquent. 'Moti was a lady—for a native, that is. She wasn't no common bazaar woman as he took up with. She 'ad a proper family, and a big 'ouse and all, down Cawnpore way, and they, 'er family I mean, well, they didn't like it by 'alf when she took up with the guv'nor. Muslims they were, so it weren't caste and that, but they 'as their ideas of right and wrong same as any, and to get 'er away at all, 'e 'ad to do the right thing, settle her proper and agree that if 'e got tired, or married or such, well, 'e'd give 'er a right pension and see 'er 'appy. All drew up it was by a *maulvi*. 'E 'ad 'er for seven year; there were another nipper, older than Yasmina, a boy, but 'e died when 'e was no more than a mite. Married they was, as near as you can get in this 'eathen country, and more so than many I could mention. That's why, you see, 'e, the Guv'nor I mean, 'as to get Yasmina back to 'er granddaddy for 'er mother's sake. 'Tis only right that he should. She can't be brought up in the quarters like a servant, however you sees it, and what else can be done with 'er?'

'How did Yasmina escape?' I enquired with a catch in my whispered voice. The small girl with the great velvet eyes, had she seen her mother killed?

'Hanifa, the servant woman, 'ad taken 'er down to the cellar, where you and the other gentry should 'ave gone.'

'But why, why did they kill Moti? Wasn't she as much an Indian as they? I could understand if it had been one of us.'

'Yes'm. But she warned the Guv'nor. And then there was the way she 'ad been livin' with a white man. They don't like it; anyway not now they don't.' He shuffled through the dust, looking at his feet in embarrassment. 'Mind, 'e'd 'orse-whip me if 'e knew I'd told you all this. It's 'is business, and I've no right ... but there's things as you should know ... now.'

'Yes, of course I see that, and I certainly won't mention it. Tod ... what can he do with the child now? Where can he take her that she will be safe?'

'Oh, as to being safe, 'e could fix 'er up with someone in 'Assanganj, I suppose; Yakub Ali's family, or one of them. But it's on account of 'er ma, you see; 'e reckons 'e must take the nipper back to 'er ma's family, and well, explain like, personal, how it come about that she were killed. 'E'll take 'er down to Cawnpore.'

'But he can't. I heard him say this morning that he had some idea of taking all of us there, to go downriver to Calcutta, but we hadn't a chance of getting through.'

'Yes'm. That's so—for you. But 'im and Yasmina'll get through just fine. No bother about that; not if 'e sets 'is mind to it.'

'I see. I wish, though, I wish very much that you had been with him. I don't like to think of him, of them, alone at a time like this.'

'Yes'm. Me too!' said Toddy with heartfelt fervour, and I closed the slit in the curtains and leaned back on the greasy bolster to consider this latest information.

Moti! How well I remembered that first occasion I had seen her. Moti, vehement, enraged, with small fists balled aggressively, snatching Yasmina away from me and thrusting her into the arms of the serving woman, Hanifa. She had hated me then, so, somehow, she must have divined, or at least feared, the nature of Oliver Erskine's feelings for me, discovered them more quickly and accurately than I, the object of them, had been able to do. So many things, circumstances, odd words, actions, were falling into place now that I had the key to his behaviour. Of course Moti hated me; I was a threat to her happiness, her love, her way of life. I did not trouble to wonder how she had guessed his interest in me, for I know that a man can keep little of his true self from a woman who loves him.

There was one thing further I had to learn from Toddy-Bob. I parted the curtains again, and found that we were now in the city itself, jogging along a narrow, malodorous lane, cleft between blank walls and strangely empty of human beings.

'Tod,' I whispered when he had drawn near. 'What will Mr Erskine do when he has taken Yasmina back to her grandparents?'

'Dunno, miss.'

'But didn't he say?'

'No, miss. 'E didn't know, I expect. Things is powerful upset at the moment, miss.'

'Yes ... yes, I know they are, but, Tod, what is there he can do? Is he likely to stay in Cawnpore or go back to Hassanganj, or what? I can't see what point there would be in his going back there, but perhaps ... I suppose he might?'

' 'E might. No tellin', miss. Though as you say, 'e won't have much to do there. I dunno. 'E might come 'ere I expect.'

'To Lucknow?'

'Well, it would be sensible, miss, though, mind, I'm not saying as 'ow 'e would. 'E don't seem to pull well in span, so to speak.'

'He gave no indication, then, of when you could expect to see him again?'

'Not when, miss, 'e couldn't, now could 'e, with none of us knowing where we'll be in a week's time? Things might've blowed over, and if they 'ave, well 'e'll turn up, I expect. But 'e did say as 'ow we was to keep our eyes peeled for trouble, and that when 'e saw us again, 'e 'oped to 'ave a good report of us. 'E meant me o' course; 'e knows 'e can trust Ishmial, seeing as 'ow bein' a Muslim 'e don't drink.'

'Oh, then it could be weeks, I suppose, before we see him?'

'Yes'm. It could. But if you was to ask me, well I'd think 'ed make it his business to see you right; you and Mr Flood and 'is lady, that is. See you safe on the way to Calcutta,' he ended, and there was no mistaking the note of hope in his voice at the prospect of this end to our vexatious intrusion into the masculine fastness that had been Hassanganj.

'Yes, I see.'

The hour and a half in which we had expected to be in the Residency drew out to nearly two hours, and still we jogged along in the darkness of the palanquins, as the heat mounted and the odours of the bazaars we traversed grew insupportable in their intensity, then faded to an unpleasant afterthought in the nostrils. Sometimes there were crowds of people jostling the bearers, sometimes even pressing inwards the curtains of the palanquin; at other times we seemed to be moving in isolation, when the only sounds were the shuffle of the bearers' feet on the beaten dust of the roadway. It was stuffy in the palanquin; Pearl slept restlessly, tossing her arms about in the heat, and after a time, lulled by the movement and the heat and the darkness, I too must have dozed.

I awoke with a start. The palanquin was stationary, and around us voices were loud in altercation: strange voices of the guards, the bearers and the onlookers, the familiar tones of Toddy-Bob and Ishmial's deeper, gruffer accent. I had no idea where we were, and was afraid to part the curtains and look out. I strained my ears, trying to make out what was being said; two or three times I heard the name 'Wajid Khan', but the rest was lost to me, so many people spoke together and spoke so quickly. At last the curtains were parted. I shrank back into the darkness of the corner in which I sat, but it was only Toddy-Bob.

'A spot of trouble, miss,' he said uneasily. 'There's some sort of trouble going on up the road. A shop's been set on fire, and a lot of *badmashes* with clubs is gettin' set to make things 'ot for the poor devils in the bazaar. Looks ugly, right enough, and the bearers is refusin' to go on. Can't say as 'ow I blame 'em.'

'Then what's to happen, Tod? Where can we go? Must we turn back?'

'Nothin' else to do, miss. The bearers are talkin' about going back to Wajid Khan's place. Seems like it's the best thing to do. Can't think of no alternative!'

'Oh, surely we can take another route? We can't be far from the Residency now, we've been travelling such a long time. Surely we can take some road that skirts the area where the trouble is, and still reach the Residency?'

'I'll see, miss.'

There was another pause for the sort of heated, acrimonious exchange which in India only means that several people are exchanging views. Then Toddy thrust his head into the curtain again.

'No go, miss. The bearers say as 'ow this 'ere is a sort of dead end. We got to get through that square to reach the Residency, or go back almost as far as Wajid Khan's house anyway. They reckon it would be a good thing to 'ear what he 'as to say, first; then if 'e thinks it's safe, we can go round, the long way by the river.'

'You'd better consult Mr Flood,' I said, remarking the look of pain on his face as Toddy ducked his head out of the curtains. He did not mind consulting me, but was reluctant to give Charles the impression that he was now in Oliver's position of authority. Toddy was back in a few moments, which had seemed long because I could hear from their voices that the bearers and guards were becoming restive at the delay; up ahead of us there was shouting and screaming as the fire took hold.

' 'E don't know what's for the best, miss. Didn't think 'e would!' Toddy paused.

'But you think we ought to go back, don't you, Tod?'

'I think it's the only thing to do right now, miss. If this trouble up 'ere spreads, the 'ole city might be riotin' in an hour. I seen it 'appen before. They get worked up about next to nothin' and next thing you know, they're all chargin' down the *chowks* ready to murder their own mothers. Best to lay low like, till we see what's goin' to 'appen.'

'Very well,' I sighed. 'You'd better tell them to turn back. We will have to throw ourselves on Mr Khan's mercy, I suppose, and leave later on when things have returned to normal.'

We moved at a much smarter pace returning than coming, and alighted in the courtyard of a large house, glad to stretch our limbs and feel sunlight on our faces. The bearers grunted and groaned and rubbed their shoulder muscles, but stood around until Charles had remembered what was necessary and handed a fistful of silver to their leader. Meanwhile, Emily and I looked around us curiously, and Ishmial went in search of someone to send for Wajid Khan. After a time he came back and said we were to wait in the inner courtyard, so we picked up our bundles and followed him through a high archway into what was obviously the hub of the household.

This courtyard was only slightly smaller than the first and was lined by the ground floor verandahs of the great house. On the opposite side to where we stood another archway led into a third court, where probably the servants' quarters were to be found and the stables and coach-houses; for, as we stood in the deep shadow of the verandah trying to accustom our eyes to the darkness, our two palanquins were carried through and into the far courtyard, followed at a more dignified rate by the guards.

We stood for some time watching the life of the household progress around us, with as little attention given to our presence as if we had been invisible. On one of the verandahs, preparations were being made for a meal. A cook squatted against a pillar and made the paste for his curry, working the spices on a piece of red stone shaped like the headstone of a grave with another rounded stone which he held in both hands and ground in disciplined, rhythmical strokes over the heap of curry-leaves, peppercorns, coriander seeds, fenugreek and turmeric. I could smell the garlic and ginger from where I stood, and realized suddenly that I was very hungry. Near the cook a couple of women scoured copper pots with wood-ash and wads of grass, and another winnowed the black spots and twigs from orange lentils with a cane winnowing basket. Another cook watched a pan simmering on an iron brazier, sometimes fanning the red-hot charcoal with a fan of plaited straw. Near us a woman sat with a child in her arms, watching another little girl toddling about in the shade before her; I wondered whether these were the sisters of the boy I had rescued. Several beds stood about haphazardly on the verandahs, the crude native beds of string called *charpoys*; one of them held a recumbent form, and on another, whose grimy mosquito netting had been turned back on the bamboo poles that held it, a man, wearing only his nether garments, sat and yawned and scratched his sagging belly and the mat of grey hairs on his brown chest.

Servants, coolies, tradesmen came and went, bringing in charcoal, vegetables and round baskets of fruit. Some carried their wares through to the servants' quarters, some stayed to offer and haggle and eventually leave their merchandise on the verandah. As I watched, I became aware of other figures sleeping in the deep shade against the wall, or gossiping together with long intervals for thought, or moving pointlessly from one group to another. Once the half-naked man on the bed clapped his hands and, as if from nowhere, a servant appeared with a large inlaid box which he laid at his master's feet, while with the contents, leaves and betel nut and sharp white lime, he prepared the wad of *pan* which had been called for. The man on the bed took the plump green tricorne, shoved it in his mouth, and chewed thoughtfully, while the servant replaced the parrot-beak shears with which he had sliced the betel nut, picked up the box and disappeared. After a while his master spat a long stream of red juice at the base of a pillar, and subsided, content, on his bed. I was glad, for I had noticed that he, alone among the folk in the courtyard, had been watching us, and there was something in the unswerving gaze of his yellowed eyes, some hint of expression in his fat, loose-lipped face, that made me uneasy.

'It is very unlike the way an English house is run,' Emily whispered softly. 'So many people doing nothing in particular, and cooking and sleeping in the open air. And sleeping at such an hour! There seems no system or order, and yet Oliver said Wajid Khan is of very good family.'

'So I believe,' I agreed. 'Their way of doing things is just different to ours. And I have no doubt that they have worked out some system that suits them in this climate. But,' and I looked around me, to find the fat man on one elbow gazing at us again, 'I expect these are only hangers-on, poor relations and so on. The more important members of the family will live upstairs, and the ladies, of course, will take their air on the roof.'

'Poor things! Shut up by themselves all day long; no wonder the house is so badly run.'

We had been waiting a good half-hour when at last a servant appeared and ushered us to Wajid Khan. He was a young man, from his appearance and clothing an upper-servant of some sort, and he had a bold eye and impudent manner that I at once disliked. As we were going, the fat man on the bed called out a question to which the young servant made a careless, laughing rejoinder, but I knew that what I had found disturbing in the fat man's gaze was that something in our appearance had aroused his curiosity. Yet we had kept our hands covered, and Pearl, who was so very white, was safe beneath her mother's *burqha*.

Wajid Khan met us at the top of a bare stone staircase, an uneasy, forced smile baring the wide gap between his two front teeth. He motioned the servant away impatiently and led us into a room that at some time had been half-heartedly furnished in the European manner. A fine ormolu table stood under an enormous chandelier which was innocent of candles and whose lustres were chipped or missing; four or five chairs stood around, and in one corner a very large majolica plant-pot stood on a three-legged bamboo stand. The pot contained three peacock feathers. There was no *punkah*, and the layer of dust on the table was a sure indication of how little the room was used. The lot of us had crowded into the room and, while Emily, Charles and I sat down with our host, Toddy and Ishmial stood with arms folded in a corner.

'What can I say?' Wajid commenced when we were seated. 'Oh my! What can I say? My house is honoured. Of course it must be honoured but, Miss Hewitt, I am telling you that it is bad that you do not go straight to the Residency.'

Charles had thrown off his *burqha* when the door was shut, and Wajid's eyes kept sliding towards him apologetically while he addressed me.

'We could not help it,' I said. 'We tried to make the bearers take us on, but they said it was safer for everyone to come back here. They must have told you there is some sort of trouble, and we couldn't get past it without danger.'

'Of course. There is trouble every day now. Every day someone's house or shop is burned, every day the *badmashes* come out and break the heads of the populaces with their big sticks. There is much trouble, much trouble.'

'We are very sorry to have caused you so much inconvenience,' Charles said politely. 'I trust we will not be on your hands for too much longer. It was just bad luck, I'm afraid. I believe we were nearly there.'

'That is so. So they say. Yes, that is so. But now, the question is, sir, what thing are we to do? Tell me that, sir!'

'Why, we must make another attempt,' Charles answered. 'Is there not another road, by the river, that we could take?'

'Certainly! Oh, certainly, there are many roads. But the point is, you are not yet on them, you are in my house, and how to get you from my house to the road, that is the question!'

Wajid Khan was sweating; beads of perspiration had formed on his forehead and cheeks and slid, as I watched, into his fine black whiskers. It was very hot certainly, but I believe his discomfort was occasioned more by fear than the temperature; having guessed that, I realized we must have even more to fear than he. But why? He had shown his good intentions by sending us the palanquins and the guards. It was no fault of ours that we were in his house, and what was there to stop him sending us on our way again? I banished the thoughts of sleep and food which had begun to trouble my mind, and shook myself alert.

'Oh, sir!' His liquid brown eyes besought Charles, and then turned to Emily and myself. 'Oh, misses! This is a fine kettle of fishes, I am telling you. I am already besetted by so many disgraceful questions, and now one more. What can a man do?' Then he held up a plump, pink-palmed hand for silence, shrugged his fat shoulders under the muslin shirt, sighed and tried to explain.

'It is my family, you see. Believe me, if it was only I, oh, how happy I would be to do all in my power to assist you. How kind you were to my little son, Miss Hewitt; can I ever forget that, can I? No, of course I cannot forget; therefore I say, whatever will happen, I, Wajid Khan, will see that his friends are safe and in good hands. It is not my intention to abandon you to … to those wretches in the bazaars. No, nothing like that, never fear. But then, I am asking myself always, what can I do? This is my house, but it is not only I who live in it. There are many … very many people living in this house, my brothers and my uncles and my nephews, and their wives and children, and sometimes their wives' families also. So many, I cannot count it. And I am afraid, sir, that not all my relations are cultural men like me. There are people in this house who take opposite opinions to me on many things, and in times like this, such people can be very dangerous. And, of course, I have to think of my own children. That is only right. You must agree that is the first thing a man must do.'

He stopped and mopped his face and neck. His shirt was sticking to his flesh in islands of damp. Charles muttered and looked uncomfortable, and I saw Toddy-Bob's black eyes fastened unwinkingly on our fat host. I was beginning to see where Wajid's difficulties lay, and my heart sank. Then his eye fell on Ishmial.

'Ah, yes! This is the man who brought me the *rakhri*. I recognize him.'

He spoke rapidly to Ishmial in their own tongue, and Ishmial made a monosyllabic reply.

'Yes, you see, I have asked him and he said that I have done everything in my power. How quickly I chose my best men to send to guard you.

Never would they have let you down. And I had to do it all in secretness. And then they too had to go to you in secretness, for if my uncle, one uncle—oh, such an unloving man!—had come to hear of what I was doing, then surely he would have put an end to it. This uncle of mine, and other men in the family, they do not want to help the *feringhi*—oh, excuse me, misses, the Europeans. They are all too anxious to come to fisticuffs, I am telling you. They think this is the end of the British power in India, and they want to get the British out of Oudh. This also I am telling you so that you can see how difficult it is for me to have you in my house; and yet, now that you are here, how am I to get you out of it?'

There was silence in the extraordinary room for a moment, as Wajid's protruberant apologetic eyes roved from face to face. Then Charles cleared his throat and spoke on rather a high note.

'I think there is only one thing to do. We must leave you at once. Of course, we can appreciate your difficulties, and we do not ask any further help of you. No doubt we can make our way to the Residency alone. Our servants are well acquainted with Lucknow and can guide us and, for the rest, well, we must take a chance on our clothing being a sufficient disguise.'

Wajid rolled his eyes and flapped his hands. 'Oh, sir, sir! Do not think of such rashness, I beg of you!'

'Then what the devil do you want us to do?' Charles asked impatiently, getting to his feet.

'Only wait a little time, and I will tell you. But to go out of this house now, and be seen going out, that will be worse for all than if you stay—and that will also be difficult.'

He sighed again, and I was sorry for his genuine distress of mind.

'You see, sir,' he admitted at last, 'it is known to my relatives that you are in the house. In such a house as this who can keep secrets? Already they have been to me to say that you must be sent away, and—oh, what an ashamed man I am to have to say what might happen? I have been hearing such terrible things in these days, and you yourselves, do you not know how badly matters stand between your people and mine?'

Charles sat down again, winded, and Emily, whose expression had changed from bewilderment to understanding to fear, began to wail, much to the perturbation of the soft-hearted Wajid, who looked as though he would like to join her.

'Then what do you suggest we do?' I asked at length.

It must have been nearly midday, and it was difficult to think coherently in the heat, but I had forced my mind to work out the implications of Wajid's explanation of the situation. One thing was evident: he felt he had already redeemed his honour by sending us the palanquins and the guards in response to the *rakhri*. He had gone to some lengths to point that out, as much for the benefit of his co-religionist, Ishmial, as for ours. Apart from this, what was explicit was that he could not count on his household forbearing to harm us if we left his house, and what was implicit was that he could not be certain of them if we remained in the house. It was, as he said, a 'pretty kettle of fishes'.

'What do you suggest, Mr Khan?' I asked again, for he had not answered the first time, but was sitting silently glum, one fat leg crossed over the other, jiggling on a nerve, and cracking his knuckles methodically as he stared at his patent leather slipper.

'You must stay here, miss. It is not good, but for the present it is the only thing.'

'But you just said …'

'Yes, my relations would sooner that you went. But in my house they will not dare to touch you. I am master here, I am telling you. I am thinking that if you will stay here quietly, then in a day or two I will find some way of getting you to the Residency, some private and acceptable way to all.'

A day or two. That could mean anything, any length of time at all, and who knew what might happen even within the next few hours?

'Yes! Yes, that is it. Now I have it.' He slapped his knee with gratification. 'There is a little piece of the house near the ladies' quarters.'

'The *zenana*?' queried Charles.

'That is correct! Near the *zenana*, where ordinary peoples may not enter. There are two-three rooms and a courtyard. Oh my, how private, and there you will be safe as houses. At the moment, it is not usable, and you will be so comfortable, you will see. My wife, oh, how delighted she will be to have you under her roof!' His changes in mood were electric, and now that he had found a solution, he beamed happily, rubbed his hands together and laughed. 'This is it, most certainly. You will be very fine and comfortable and, meanwhile, I will see how things go and make arrangements.'

'What sort of arrangements?' Charles asked suspiciously.

'Oh, that I cannot say. Perhaps I will get word to your friends in the Residency or perhaps the animosities of my relations will be forgotten. This often happens, does it not?' he asked optimistically. 'But, whatever it is,' and he lifted his hands, palms outwards, to underline his words, 'this I can promise: that in one, or at most three days, you will be happily safe with your families in the bosom of the Residency. Do you not agree?' he ended on a note of anxiety.

We had no option, so we agreed and he hurried away to attend to the matter. When he had left, Ishmial went and stood with his back to the door. We waited again, a long time, in that stifling room.

'Of all the impossible luck!' Charles growled. 'We were damn nearly there, and then this! I don't like it, I don't like it by half.'

'What else can we do? Apparently we can't just walk out. I think he is really trying to help us, and I suppose if his family are ... er ... disaffected, we must be a considerable embarrassment to him, Charles,' I said.

'Oh, no doubt of that. But how do we know we can trust him? Nobody who knows us is aware that we are here, either. He or one of his precious relations could do away with us all and no one any the wiser.'

'Oh, Charles, don't!' said Emily faintly.

'No, Charles, don't!' I agreed. 'There is no point in taking that position. I believe he will do the best he can by us, and we have no alternative but to trust him.'

We were silent for a moment, and then I said, 'Toddy, what do you think, you and Ishmial?' For it seemed to me that Ishmial alone of us all could estimate our unwilling host accurately.

'Wouldn't like to say, miss,' replied Toddy dubiously. 'They're a changeable lot at the best of times.' He turned and spoke to Ishmial, who replied at some length. Toddy grunted. ''E says, miss, as 'ow no 'arm will come to you, not while the *Burra-begum* knows 'ow things is. She's the one 'ose little boy you saved in the bazaar that time. 'E says it's probably on 'er say-so that 'is nibs sent the palanquins and that. Last night when Ishmial brought the *rakhri* 'ere, there was no end of a takin', and 'is nibs went off to the *zenana* for a big talk with 'is ladies, and then when 'e come out 'e did like 'e said 'e did, fixed everything up in a 'urry and private-like.'

'Well, we must thank God that he is such a devoted husband, then,' said Charles sourly.

'Oh dear, I do wish Oliver was here!' Emily sighed, tears in her eyes. 'He's such a dependable man, and would have known just what to do. I don't believe any of this would have happened if … if he had been with us. He would have made those wretched bearers take us another way. He's so resourceful. I wouldn't be nearly so frightened if he were here. Oh, Charles!' And Emily bowed her head and wept. I was so anxious, and so hungry, that I felt very much like joining her. It occurred to me to wonder what explanation, if any, Oliver had given his brother for his sudden return to Hassanganj, but I was too dispirited to enquire. No doubt, manlike, Charles would have been satisfied with some story about Oliver salvaging the remnants of his possessions from the ruin of the house.

One further blow was to strike us before we were taken to the rooms Mr Khan had apportioned us. We were parted from Toddy and Ishmial.

'It is because of *zenana*,' Mr Khan explained with the apologetic shrug of his fat shoulders. 'I myself am enlightened man and think little of such matters, but my ladies, and some of the other men, if they were to see your servants coming and going here, in this part of the house, there would be questions, and then trouble.'

'But then, what will happen to them?' Charles asked. 'We want them near us, of course.'

'Oh, of course, of course, they will be near you; in the servants' quarters. I will treat them just the same as I treat my own. They too are guests. No one will be troubling them, that I am telling you.'

'It'll be all right, sir,' Toddy said gruffly. 'We'll make out, and we'll be 'ere when you wants us.'

'Of course!' Wajid echoed heartily, 'very much all right!' But I think we all reached our lowest ebb as Toddy and Ishmial turned and walked down the stone staircase away from us. I was worried about Toddy in particular; he certainly was as brown as a *bunnia* as he had once pointed out, but I had no confidence that his disguise would bear up to a close scrutiny, and I hoped he would allow Ishmial to do the talking. I knew that he had lived among natives for many years, but still, I was very uneasy.

CHAPTER 11

We descended another staircase, traversed several cavernous corridors and at last Mr Khan opened a door and ushered us into our apartment, a suite of three lofty rooms, opening one off the other in a line, with, at the end of them, the usual *gussulkhana* or bathroom.

We were at ground level again, and each of the rooms opened on to a small courtyard completely enclosed by the blank, windowless walls of the house, in the centre of which stood a hideous marble fountain and a couple of lemon trees. There were no doors between the rooms, merely high Moorish archways cut in the walls; chandeliers of great splendour depended from the ceilings of the three large rooms (also candleless, I noticed gloomily) but, apart from these, several fine Persian carpets and a few bolsters, the rooms were empty. Later, three string beds were brought to us and, as a concession to Western habits, three circular cane stools. The rooms were cool, however: huge frilled *punkahs* flapped dangerously near the chandeliers, operated by coolies sitting on the inner corridor, for I saw the ropes disappear through holes in the walls in that direction. Of course, if this section were truly part of the *zenana*, no *punkah* coolie could sit on the ladies' verandahs, and later, when we had time to examine our surroundings, we noticed that the courtyard could not be overlooked by any curious eyes. We were certainly private, and by the time Wajid Khan, having besought us to make ourselves comfortable and promised us food, had departed, I realized that we were perhaps too private.

We discarded our dirty *burqhas*, washed and, when the food arrived carried on a huge brass tray by a thin female servant we attacked it with enthusiasm. Then, since it was the very hottest time of the day, we were thankful to lie down on the carpets and sleep until the cool of the evening restored us.

Wajid Khan came at nightfall to assure himself that we were comfortable. He was followed by the same servant girl, bearing a platter of elaborate sweetmeats donated by his wife; but nothing was said of our departure and, after a few moments of polite platitudes and shaky syntax, he left us.

The first two or three days passed quietly and not unpleasantly, despite our anxiety. Charles was inclined to grumble at being confined to the tiny courtyard for his exercise, and Emily discovered bugs in her bed, but I think we were all too worn out, physically and emotionally, to have any urgent appreciation of our position. Each evening Khan came in most punctiliously; and, each evening, he said that he was 'Still thinking, but tomorrow, undoubtedly tomorrow, something will be occurring to me.' Apart from him, we saw no one but the servant girl, and morning and evening a sweeper woman who slipped into the courtyard through a small door in the wall to perform her unenviable duties and refill the great earthen jar of water. Twice a day food was brought us, delicious food: curries of various sorts, vegetable dishes and unleavened breads of many different types, and in the evening fruit and nuts as well. Our clothes were taken away and washed, and it was purest luxury to know ourselves clean again. I could have been quite content in Mr Khan's household but for the feeling, at first unadmitted to, that we were prisoners.

We used to go to bed early. When darkness fell, the servant girl would bring us a couple of lanterns but, since the wicks were never trimmed, they smoked; so it was pleasanter to put them out and retire. In any event, as we discovered on the first morning, sleep in an Indian household is impossible after sunrise. The early hours are the favoured time to strive for musical accomplishment, and we were always woken at dawn by hideous wailings on stringed instruments, often accompanied by dirgelike nasal singing that went on and on interminably. For though the world could not see us, we could hear it, and at night I would lie on my string cot and listen to all the varied noises of the huge household and, beyond it, the constant, hive-like murmur of the city—and try to diminish my sense of isolation by distinguishing and naming to myself the various cacophonies of bazaar and kitchen and stable and street. At night, the doors into the courtyard were left open for the sake of coolness and I could watch the stars change position as I waited for sleep to come, but I never caught the glimmer of a lantern other than our own, or glimpsed the gusty flicker of a torch, so immured were we in the depths of the sprawling house. At first, our absolute isolation had spelt safety but, as the days passed, it became increasingly menacing. It was as though we were at the bottom of a deep black well, could hear but not be heard, could look upwards and only the stars could return our gaze.

On the seventh evening Wajid Khan sent word that he could not visit us as usual since his wife was ill.

The message was brought by the servant girl, who had been put at our disposal because of her slight knowledge of English. She was a pathetic little creature whom I guessed to be a half-caste on account of her yellowish complexion and dark grey eyes. We were informed that she had spent the first few years of her life in a mission in Agra (hence the English) but, beyond that, she would tell us nothing of herself or how she had come to find employment in a Muslim household.

'It is the smallpox,' she added, when she had conveyed the message about Wajid Khan's wife verbatim, her eyes wide with apprehension. 'It will sweep through the house now like an evil wind. Many will die!'

'Smallpox? Are you sure?' Charles's voice was sharp with alarm.

'Already one has died. One of the servants. It is smallpox!'

The girl glanced quickly from face to face, then backed out of the room salaaming, leaving us alone to face this new peril in our own way.

'We must get out,' Charles said quietly when the door had closed behind her. 'It is suicide to stay here. If one of us were to fall ill, what chance would we have of recovery without a doctor or civilized attendance, or even medicines?'

'Quite. But how?' I asked. The door the girl had used was our only communication with the rest of the house, and we had learnt that a large man with a curved sword in his belt always locked it behind her. There was the other little door in the courtyard, but it too was locked, as I had discovered.

We discussed our predicament from every angle, wracking our brains for some solution to the problem; not for the first time I cursed the fate that had separated us from Toddy and Ishmial. If we could only get word to them, then perhaps they could obtain help for us from the Residency. Sometimes it seemed that they must surely go to the Residency on their own initiative to report our whereabouts, but in cooler moments I knew this to be unlikely. After all, no harm had come to us, and we had no real justification for thinking that any would. Not until now.

When Wajid Khan failed to appear on the third evening running, we sent him a message by the girl, saying we would like to speak to him. He made no response, so Charles wrote a note on the flyleaf of his Bible. The girl—her name was Ajeeba—assured us that she had delivered it, but we received no answer. Several more days passed, days of such acute frustration and anxiety that I do not care to remember them. Closely confined, ignorant of all that was taking place around us, ridden by unformed fears, the three of us gave way to nerves and bickered and squabbled among ourselves like children. Everything was an annoyance. Of course the heat was now almost unbearable. The rains were due to break any moment; the sky was leaden and heavy with unshed water, but still the searing wind of the Indian plains, the *loo*, kept us indoors even during the early mornings, so hot it was, so laden with cinder-like particles of dust that stung the flesh and burnt the eyes.

But whatever the inclemency of the climate and the uncertainty of our position, we did not make sufficient effort to behave with dignity or calm, and at length the only way we could keep the peace was by keeping to ourselves. I would retire to one room with Marcus Aurelius, Charles to another with his Bible, and Emily would sit on her little stool with Pearl, crooning and crying until her loneliness drove her to one of us for comfort. Poor Emily; she had so few resources, and always sooner or later she would hark back to Hassanganj, and how happy she had been there, and how she was sure that Oliver would have found some way out for us.

'If he had done his duty by us, we wouldn't be here now!' I snapped back more than once, and Emily would sigh and say, 'I can't think why you dislike him so much. He was always so kind, and I remember thinking, when we saw his portrait in Calcutta, I thought I should be frightened of him. Oh, I do wish he were with us.' And she would wander away to annoy Charles.

At the close of a day so stifling that I had lacked even the energy to open my book, but had lain on my bed half dead with heat and *ennui*, Ajeeba told us that the *Begum* was dead.

She was weeping quietly as she spoke, standing in the warm light of the lantern with the big brass tray containing the remains of our meal in her arms. A very hot curry had rendered me a little less inert and, impelled more by curiosity than sympathy, I decided to try to draw her out. We did not know which wife it was that had died, and I had an uneasy remembrance of Ishmial telling us that we would be safe so long as the *Burra-begum* spoke for us. I did not want to ask a direct question, so resorted to circumlocution.

'I am sorry to see you weep. The lady must have been a kind mistress to you.' The girl nodded, sniffing. 'Have you worked for her long?'

She nodded again. 'And my mother also.'

'Your master must be very sad. But she was not his chief wife, was she?'

'Of course she was!' The girl was indignant that I should be so ignorant, or perhaps because of professional pride. I suppose there was more honour in serving the chief wife in such a household than any of the others.

'She was the mother of the heir, as well. She ... She ...' The girl gulped. 'She had promised me a dowry. Because my mother died in her service and I have no father. She had promised it to me!'

'And now what will happen? Will you lose your position?'

'There are other *begums*.'

'Will they give you your dowry?'

The girl shook her head violently, and I knew what had elicited the tears.

'I am sorry to hear that,' I said politely.

She looked me directly in the eye, and said with malice, 'You will be in trouble now too. It was the *Burra-begum*, my mistress, who pleaded for you, because of what you had done for her son. And she sent me to wait on you; that is why I am here now. But the next wife is jealous for her own son. She has no cause for gratitude to you.'

'How do you mean pleaded for us?' I asked coldly. 'One would think we were in some sort of danger, but Wajid Khan would never hurt us. We are *rakhri band*.'

'Huh!' grunted Ajeeba. 'That was before! Now he is frightened. He thinks that when the Maulvi, and the others, know that he has sheltered *feringhis* in his house they will be very angry. He is frightened for his property. The Maulvi has greedy eyes for land. He is doing all other things like the other great men of Oudh. He is raising levies on Jamnabad, many men are to fight for him, many are already here, in the back courtyard; they sit and smoke and tend their weapons and say what dreadful deeds they will do when the fighting starts, and it will start very soon now. It will be worse than Meerut, worse than Delhi, it will be much worse, for there will be many more men, more sepoys, and the *talukhdars* and *zemindars* will lead them, so that it will be like the old times. Such killing!' And the wretched creature licked her lips and forgot her tears.

'The Maulvi?' That must be the man whom Oliver had mentioned as being the neighbour of Wajid Khan near Fyzabad; the man from whom Wajid had probably learnt more than he cared to tell of the *chapattis*, the Maulvi of Fyzabad.

'Yes,' the girl went on, after a moment. 'All things my master does like the other great men of Oudh, and more, much more, for he is one of the greatest. But when they find that he has sheltered the infidel, then who knows what will happen? He has much to lose, and what man wishes to risk his possessions for strangers?'

'We do no one any harm,' I pointed out reasonably. 'And it was Wajid Khan himself who wished us to stay here until he had arranged a way of taking us to the Residency. We have nothing to fear.'

'So?' But the girl was not convinced. 'There have been other *feringhis*, in the bazaars there is much talk of them, who also have taken refuge in the houses of our people, and then one day, who knows why, word gets around, trouble is caused, then they are led out and … zut!' She drew her finger across her throat. 'They are dead!'

Fortunately Charles had taken Emily into the courtyard for a breath of fresh air. There was a ring of conviction in the girl's words, so that I could not delude myself that she was merely repeating bazaar gossip.

'Well,' I said gravely, trying to give the impression that I was suddenly cast down, 'that will be a pity because we were going to reward you handsomely for your services to us—when we got to the Residency. Now perhaps you will have to do without your reward as well as your dowry.'

I turned away, but from the corner of my eye saw her stiffen, and a look of cunning come into the meagre yellow face. I continued out of the room, satisfied that if there were any hope in that direction, the next move must come from her. I said nothing of this conversation to the others, beyond telling them that the *Begum* was dead.

Sleep eluded me that night. I lay in the oppressive darkness of the empty room and listened to the distant stir of countless human beings pursuing their secret lives by flickering lamplight in the malodorous lanes and crowded bazaars beyond the wall. Sometimes the thin notes of a bamboo flute would rise above the murmur of movement; sometimes a woman would shriek, or a child cry, or a dog yelp as it was kicked out of the way, and the throb of drums rose and fell in incessant accompaniment. The dull unceasing mutter should have been soporific but my mind was too active to allow me to sleep.

Endlessly I turned over all the implications of our presence in the house of Wajid Khan, in an effort to anticipate what was to come. Would he ever let us go? Could he afford to? I tried to put myself in his position, to understand him without emotion and without judgement, and remembered every word he had spoken in an effort to determine his motives. He was not a cruel man, of that I was sure. He had a gentle nature, was indolent and anxious always for the easy way out. But he was not very intelligent either, and his silliness, coupled with his love of ease and his fear, would make him an easy target for a stronger character. I recalled uneasily the disquieting interest of the fat man, scratching his belly on the courtyard verandah, and the smart, over-confident young servant with his impudent curiosity. How many more were there like them in the household, men, and women perhaps, much more capable than Wajid of strong feeling, of single-minded passion, of long-suppressed hatred, relatives jealous of his position, retainers harbouring a grievance, ready to threaten him if he did not dispose of the *feringhi*? So long as the *Burra-begum* had been alive, we were safe, even if imprisoned. But with her death, our lives were jeopardized. Little by little, our presence, already an affront to his relations, as he had himself admitted, would become an affront to him too, as they worked on him for our undoing. He would hesitate, demur, argue, complain querulously at not being master of his own house; he would storm and swear, probably even shed tears of self-pity because his family could not appreciate the dilemma in which he found himself. But slowly he would be worn down. One night, some hot night such as this, he would throw his hands to heaven, shout so that all could hear that he never wished us to be mentioned in his presence again, and someone would interpret this as Wajid in his shrinking soul wished it to be interpreted. I had learned myself that for most of us it is not the deed but the witnessing of it that really strikes home. He would know nothing of what followed, of course. Had he not commanded that we were never to be mentioned again? But on some breathless night, or on an afternoon when all the household slept the sleep of great heat, a handful of men would come in, lead us out of the house, and then ... well then, as Ajeeba had expressed it, 'Zut!' All would be over.

At dawn I rose, red-eyed but alert, convinced that our only help lay in arousing the avarice of shifty little Ajeeba. It was not a hope of robust proportions.

Some cat-and-mouse instinct made me take care to be unavailable when Ajeeba was in our rooms, but that night she hung about busying herself with trifles until she could speak to me alone. She came to the point with admirable bluntness, and I was hard put to it to disguise my relief that she had brought up the subject.

'I cannot take you to the *bilaiti* Residency,' she muttered, half an eye cocked at the door, behind which the eunuch stood. 'But I could help you if you give me money. Here. Now.'

I was so nervous I was almost taken in. Later, I was to thank God for the sudden flash of wit that made me reply, 'How would that be possible? We have no money here. We would first have to get it from our friends in the Residency.'

'You have none?' She didn't believe me.

'None,' I answered shortly. 'Did you not see how we came, in borrowed clothes and borrowed palanquins?'

'Your friends would surely give you money? You do not lie?'

'Why should I? And how do I know that you would be able to help us, supposing we need help?'

She thought that over.

'I think you will need it,' she said coldly. 'Just now, Wajid Khan is heavy with grief: he thinks of nothing but the *Burra-begum*. But in one or two days, he will remember you again, and then who knows what he will do?'

I shrugged indifferently. 'I cannot help that. *Jo hoga, so hoga*'— What must happen, will happen.

Happily she was not easily deterred.

'You could get word to your friends, no?'

'How? I do not see my servants, and whom else could I trust?'

'Me?' It was half entreaty, half suggestion.

'No.' I shook my head firmly. 'You would take the money and go away to your village, leaving us here to Wajid Khan's mercy. Oh, no!'

She protested her innocence, but she was a poor actress, and I had uncovered the weak plottings of her avaricious little mind. She looked at me with marked respect, coupled with uncertainty, as she vowed her innocence of any evil intention.

I held up my hand for silence, and took a thoughtful turn around the room.

'There may be a way,' I said judiciously. 'Perhaps there is a way after all, if you are willing to help us.'

She waited breathlessly for me to explain myself, but I turned away from her again, and once more paced the length of the room.

'Do you know where our servants are: the big Pathan and the small man with the horse's face?'

She nodded, contemptuously I thought. 'They were here, in the house. I saw them sometimes, but a few days ago they went away.'

'Away?' I echoed, hopes dashed.

'Yes, not far away though. They live in the bazaar. This I have heard said.'

'You could find them?'

'Of course! They are strangers; everyone will know where they live.'

'You could take them a note? A chit?'

She nodded.

'Very well, we will see. If you bring me back a note from them in the morning, I will know you are to be trusted, and then I will send them to the Residency for the money. They will get the money; there is no doubt of that. But you will have to come with us for at least part of the way before you are paid. You understand?'

Again she nodded, this time with resignation.

'If I do this, I will have to go with you. I could not come back here. They would kill me!' This was a point I had overlooked but it appeared to be an added safeguard. 'But first: how much money? Remember that I risk my life and lose the only house I have known. This is much to do for infidels, and I must have much reward.'

'Three hundred rupees. One hundred for each of us. That is a great amount.'

I did not know what would constitute a fortune to such a girl, but was going on the worth of three or four pearls from Mrs Wilkins's garter, for the amount of cash we had with us was trivial. Apparently, and much to my relief, my premise was more than adequate, for the girl licked her lips and agreed to the amount so quickly that she probably felt I would think better of my generosity.

'Good. Then wait a moment and I will write.'

I tore out the back page of Marcus Aurelius and, with a stub of drawing pencil that had been in the pocket of my dress when I left Hassanganj I printed a short message to Toddy-Bob, instructing him to send me something to indicate that he had himself received the note. It would be too easy for it to find its way into other hands, and I had to be very cautious.

'You read English, I suppose, as you have been in a mission school?' I said holding the paper out for Ajeeba's inspection in a gesture of trust that was far from sincere. She took it and examined it minutely, but then, to my satisfaction, shook her head and returned it saying, 'Once I read, but now no more. It is many years since I was in mission, but I remember the prayer of *Esoo Masie*.' And she began to intone with downcast eyes and swaying body: 'Our Father, which art in heaven ...'

There was no way of sealing the note, so I folded it and gave it to her. If it found its way into the hands of the fat uncle on the verandah, or the sly young servant, it would be the end of us. On the other hand, if it got to Toddy, well, he would at least know that all was not well with us. I knew a crushing moment when I wondered whether Toddy himself could read, but remembered having once seen him spell out the sporting column of an old newspaper on the verandah at Hassanganj. In any event, I was sufficiently sure of his resourcefulness to know that if he had difficulty in deciphering my note, he would find somebody trustworthy to read it for him, even if it meant going to the Residency.

His answer was in my hands at six o'clock next morning.

'Dear Miss, We come out here because things looked hot in the house. Waiting your orders, yrs, respctfl. T.Bob.'

Immediately, knowing this time that I was truly laying my head in the lion's mouth, I wrote another note, telling Toddy to delude the girl into thinking that he was off to the Residency to obtain money, and asking him to fix as safe a rendezvous as possible for the following night.

Anyone but Toddy-Bob would have needed to be told more of the facts, but I relied on him to act without question, and I smiled to myself as I imagined how he would expatiate to Ajeeba on our influential and wealthy friends, and also the horrors that would overtake her if she betrayed us. No doubt but that 'Sir 'Enry 'imself' would play some part in his fantasy.

When Ajeeba had gone, I felt safe in confiding my hopes to Charles and Emily. The day, hot and wearisome as any other we had passed in that house, was borne more easily as we thought of the night, and we spent much time deciding which of our possessions we could best do without; for, though we had brought little with us, our bundles were still too heavy to be carried with comfort, and we would have to make our way to the Residency on foot. In the end all we left behind were our night-caps, some lawn petticoats and two heavy cloaks. I discarded also my little trinket box, but took the trinkets tied up in a handkerchief, and at the last moment, very unwisely, discarded Marcus Aurelius. I could not know then how often I would stand in need of his philosophy.

We were ready with our bundles and our *burqhas* at ten that night. Ajeeba had told us when she brought the evening meal that she would come for us at 'about midnight', so we had a long wait, made no more comfortable by the knowledge that it was still not too late for her to change her mind. She arrived, at last, at about half an hour after midnight. The last thing I had done was extract three pearls from the garter, wrap them in a page of Marcus Aurelius and put the little packet in my pocket where it would be easily accessible. Then I refastened the garter round my leg, where I had worn it since the day when Oliver had persuaded me that I had committed no great crime in taking it.

The pearls, lying in my hand for a moment, brought back that dry and windless morning, and I heard again Oliver's voice, 'Think of this then; I love you.' Tears, which I chose to consider nostalgic, stung the back of my eyes, and hastily I wrapped up the pearls and put them out of sight.

Our escape from the house of Wajid Khan, when it came, was simplicity itself, despite the perfervid imaginings with which we had filled the hours of waiting. There was no hurried, dangerous flitting through the corridors of the great house; no guards to be bribed; no sudden alarms to bring our hearts into our mouths. It was almost an anticlimax to the days of anxiety, the planning and the tension.

Ajeeba simply led us to the small door in the courtyard wall, used by the sweeper woman, and opened it. Beyond lay a dark and smelly passageway under the bulk of the house, and beyond that again a narrow lane skirting the house and opening into a bazaar. Our only anxious moment came through Pearl, who whimpered as we crossed the courtyard, but the folds of her mother's *burqha*, beneath which she was hidden, served to muffle the sound effectively.

Ajeeba, never looking behind her, led us swiftly through a tangled maze of stalls and shops and little alleys, and so quick was our passage that I retain only a blurred impression of shrill voices chattering at the lamp-lit stalls, hurrying feet, pressing bodies and light and darkness succeeding each other through the eye-slits of my *burqha* with great rapidity.

'Psst.'

In the angle of a wall behind a large mosque, Toddy-Bob and Ishmial lurked in waiting. They pressed our shoulders joyfully, thanked God in divers tongues, and laughed, but softly, while Ajeeba watched the pantomime with a suspicious expression on her yellow face. When our mutual satisfaction had been expressed, Toddy-Bob drew me apart.

'We 'as our doubts of that wench, miss, Ishmial and me. She done like she said she would, but who knows if that's the end of it? We 'as a plan of sorts. Ishmial will take you to a friend of 'is in the bazaar; it's no good trying to get into the Residency at night, see, with everything locked up and sentries all around. Proper suicide it would be. They're gettin' that nervous, they'd blast off at their own daughters if they appeared done up in them *burqhas*. So you lay low where Ishmial takes you, and I'll join you in the morning.'

'Oh, Tod, you're wonderful! I don't know what we'd have done without you,' I exclaimed, for what could be simpler than for Ajeeba to accept her reward and then put the populace on our trail. It was a contingency I had not thought of myself, but Toddy had been ready for it.

'Yes, well!' He cleared his throat in modest agreement.

'But you must pay her, Toddy. She has risked her position, if not her life, for us, after all.'

'Certainly, miss,' And then as an afterthought: 'What with?'

'Oh, yes! I have it here; she needs a dowry, you see, and I think she can sell these for a handsome sum. Mr Erskine told me they were very fine.' I passed over the packet surreptitiously, for I had not wanted Ajeeba to see the transfer. 'Three pearls. I ... I happened to have them by me.'

'Yes'm.' Toddy's face was a mask, but I could guess what was going through his mind.

We parted: Toddy-Bob and Ajeeba going one way—her farewell, once the packet was in her hand, was quite cordial—while Ishmial led us through further small bazaars and along more smelly alleys till we came to the shop of a *halwai* or sweetmeat vendor, and through it to a room behind. The room was small and amazingly dirty for a storeroom of edibles. A lantern was brought us and we tried to make ourselves comfortable, but there was nothing to sit on but the floor, and I reconciled myself to another sleepless night. It was a small price to pay for safety.

When the sun rose, light filtered in through a slatted window set high in the wall. The room was crowded with sacks of flour and sugar, earthern jars of clarified butter smelling rancid in the heat, baskets of parched gram and lentils, great brown wheels of solid molasses, bottles and tins of spices, sesame seed, poppy seed and dill seed, all the ingredients needed in the manufacture of the rich sweets and spiced pastries that were our host's stock in trade.

There was little air in the storeroom and, as the heat rose, so the smell of the rancid butter increased. When the *halwai* began his cooking soon after dawn, the smell of hot oil from his cauldrons added to our discomforts. We had to perch Emily on a sack of flour, for she had seen cockroaches moving on the floor; but she was scarcely comforted by her position, as a rat gnawed at the sack she sat on.

We turned our backs while she fed Pearl, but when the *halwai* came in with a bowl of fish cooked in sour curds to form our breakfast, though we thanked him politely, we let it lie on the floor. The stench in the room had taken away appetite.

The sun was well up when Toddy joined us with a self-satisfied smirk on his face. He vouchsafed no explanation of how he had 'dealt with' Ajeeba, and a sixth sense warned me that it would be impolitic to enquire. He ate some of the fish with enjoyment, then sat back and told us of all that had taken place while we were separated.

'Didn't they suspect that you were not one of them, Tod?' Emily asked.

'No'm. Not at first anyway. We kept to ourselves; you can do it in them big houses with so many comin' and goin' all the time, and there was more people comin' in every day, so the crowds 'elped us. Ishmial did the talkin' mostly, and I made an effort to look stupid so they wouldn't want to draw me out. The men who came in were soldiers, you see, miss, at least what they fancies is soldiers—must 'ave been a 'undred of 'em more or less—so when things become really crowded, and some of 'em wants to know too perticular where we come from and that, well, we thought it best to move on. We didn't go far, miss, and every day Ishmial would go in and 'ave a *bāt* with some lads as 'e took up with in the stables. We kep' in touch with what was going on, you can be sure, and when Ishmial 'ears that the *Burra-begum* 'as gone aloft, well, you can imagine 'ow we feels!'

'It didn't occur to you to go to the Residency, and report our position?' Charles spoke with some irritation.

'No, sir.' Toddy surveyed Charles with an unrepentant eye. 'We was told to stay by you, and we stayed. Anyway, what would have been the use of goin' to the Residency? Wajid Khan would 'ave said 'e knew nothing of you, and things is that delicate at present, none could 'ave forced their way into his 'ouse. Not even Sir 'Enry. Least of all Sir 'Enry. 'E still thinks 'e can calm things down if 'e only acts like a gentleman and keeps his powder dry, like!'

'But the Residency is still open? It's three weeks since we've had any word from outside, Toddy, and we know nothing of what has been going on.'

'To be sure, sir, it's still open. And they're still trying to get a wall around it, so they say. Still! S'truth, what the Guv'nor will say when 'e 'ears that! Not that we seen many Englishmen. Not seen none, come to think of it. But then, you never did see 'em in these parts. Always kep' to their own cantonments and the big streets.'

'What else, Tod?' I prompted, as he fell quiet. 'What else has happened?'

'Nothing much, not 'ere, that is. Course there's talk, lots of it. The *talukhdars* and *zemindars* are fetchin' in their soldiers, just like Wajid Khan is, and they sit around sharpenin' their *tulwars* or causin' trouble with the women. Proper 'orrid it is, the goings-on we come to 'ear about. They say as 'ow Delhi is all cleaned up, no whites left alive there, and now there's a batterin' goin' on in Cawnpore. Well, that's not far off and, as I sees it, if they've started on the shootin' there, they'll start 'ere pretty soon too. Stands to reason, like.'

441

The mention of Cawnpore reminded me of Oliver Erskine, but I could not ask Toddy whether he thought his master was safely away from the place before the 'battering' started, since I could not tell Charles and Emily what errand had taken him there. They thought he was still in Hassanganj.

So we talked away the uncomfortable hours. At midday, we were brought more food, and since by this time we had accustomed ourselves to the stench and were extremely hungry, we ate what we were given. Then we dozed for a while, but at two o'clock sharp were wakened by Ishmial, who had decided the safest time for us to make our way across the city was when most of the people were stretched on their string cots or the filthy roadways, sleeping away the greatest heat of the day.

We were now at a greater distance from our objective than we had been in Wajid Khan's house, for Ajeeba had led us back through the city and away from the river on which the Residency stands.

Perhaps because of fatigue, the fear of discovery hardly troubled my mind, but as we walked endlessly under the deadening heat through the somnolent streets of the city, I began to fall into a sort of lethargic hopelessness. My bundle, small as it was, was heavy; my *burqha* impeded every step as my feet dragged through thick dust and noisome mounds of garbage left to putrefy where they were thrown. Few people were abroad; even the bullock-cart drivers slept on the shafts of their vehicles as their beasts plodded unerringly to familiar destinations.

Charles carried Pearl under his *burqha*, and Toddy had taken Emily's bundle, but it would not have been right for Ishmial to be seen carrying anything while he had womenfolk to do it for him. True to his role, he strode ahead of us, his musket on his shoulder, with Toddy close behind him, while we three supposed females kept at a decorous distance to the rear. The very monotony of our progress through unfamiliar but strangely similar streets added to our fatigue. I began to feel that everything had been going on too long. I was sick of fear, of suspicion, of hostility, and was tired to death of the whole unbelievable situation in which we found ourselves. My resources had petered out, and I felt that I had never had the sort of character to deal with the crises through which we had passed. Too much had been expected of me, of us all. Now our luck was running out; we would never reach the Residency. At this last moment, something must happen to kill our final hope. The gates would be locked, or we would be discovered. Too much had happened over which we had no control, and which we had never provoked. So many were dead: Moti, the Wilkinses, the *sowar*, the *Begum*, whose delicate hand, henna-tipped, I had glimpsed fingering a jeweller's little boxes. For all I knew, even Oliver Erskine was dead. Almost I longed for discovery and a sudden end to tension.

A roar broke out behind us, and I knew my longing was to be fulfilled. Men shouting, hooves clipping rapidly on stone, many hooves, and a rumble of carts and a jingle of harnesses.

'Why do they need so many to take us?' my numbed mind asked. 'We have no strength left. We're too tired to run away.'

I would not look behind, but clutched my bundle and doggedly put one blistered foot before the other. Let them cut me down from behind, I thought; I have faced enough.

'Sir! Sir! Please, sir, wait. The Residency, we are near it, aren't we?' I heard Toddy cry anxiously.

'Good God! You an Englishman?'

'Yes, sir! As English as the Queen—Gawd bless 'er Majesty—and so are my friends here, savin' the black one and 'e's as good as one.'

'You had trouble?' The young officer's bright blue eyes swept over us enquiringly, as we halted and turned to face him.

'You might call it that,' agreed Toddy with dignity. The officer reined in his horse and stared down at us with amusement and interest, which grew into a great guffaw of laughter as Charles, his patience tried beyond bearing, threw off his *burqha* and stood revealed in his breeches, shirt and sweeping golden moustaches.

'Sir, we would be grateful if you could direct us to the Residency by the shortest route,' he said curtly, cutting short the newcomer's mirth. 'We have come a long way and the ladies you see have endured a great deal, to say nothing of my infant daughter!' He held the child up for the officer to see.

'Sorry, I'm sure, sir. Had no idea,' the young man said, taken aback. 'Straight on and then to the right. Make towards the river, and you can't miss it. You'll be all right now, sir, half a platoon of Britishers are coming up behind you. It's the detail sent out to fetch in the crown jewels of Oudh. You're just in time, sir. We're to be invested tomorrow, they say.'

It was Sunday, the 28th of June 1857.

BOOK IV

BAILLIE GUARD

'Nothing happens to any man
which he is not formed by
nature to bear.'
Marcus Aurelius

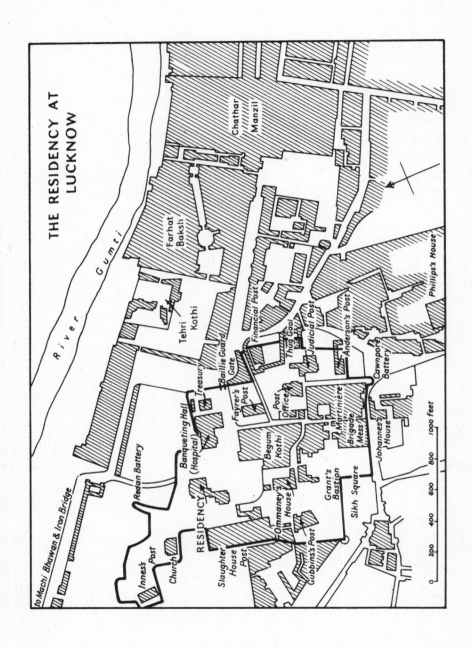

THE RESIDENCY AT LUCKNOW

CHAPTER 1

We followed the road that leads from the city through parks and gardened palaces, past the soaring minarets of the Imambaras, bending then towards the river and the Residency. At the top of an incline, we found the brass-studded gates of the Baillie Guard wide open to receive us.

Wide open and welcoming, though for three long weeks we had imagined them barred. For a moment I paused to take in that open gate. I knew I would never see a finer sight than the unpretentious arch of snuff-coloured stucco, flanked by two smaller arches neatly pillared in the classical style, through which now the remnant of the State of Oudh was conveyed as I watched, on bullock-carts, in carriages, on ammunition floats and gun limbers, on the backs of elephants and in the swaying panniers of camels, while armed men, on horseback and on foot, lined the roadway, and wheels, hooves and feet churned up a choking cloud of thick white dust.

The hot, lowering morning had developed into an afternoon dark as night and ominous with the far-off rumble of thunder. The whole world, arid and exhausted, waited in sullen longing for rain—the first downpour of the monsoons. As I dragged my blistered feet up the slope and through the gate, I noticed a familiar group of the birds called Seven Sisters at the gatehouse door, ragged grey feathers fluffed out, eyes cocked apprehensively skyward, waiting only for the first big drops to dart shrieking for shelter.

Emily, with Pearl in her arms, had been lifted up by a kind soldier to sit on the tailboard of a cart on which, among boxes, crates and bundles, was a throne or state chair of some sort wrapped in a piece of dirty sacking. Free of his *burqha*, Charles strode beside her, and I followed, with Toddy-Bob and Ishmial bringing up the rear of our little procession. Apathy fell away as we neared our journey's end, and I knew the others shared my excitement at the sight of that open gate; yet as we passed through, all we could do was smile our relief to each other with tear-filled eyes. Only Ishmial remembered his God. As we found ourselves at last truly within the Residency walls he dropped to his knees and pressed his forehead to the dust.

During the long starlit nights in the bullock-cart, and sometimes even during the first days in the house of Wajid Khan, I had allowed my thoughts to linger on this moment, imagining the greeting of old acquaintances, the surprise, the delight, the unbelief with which we would be received, savouring prematurely those sensations of ecstatic relief and triumphant accomplishment which I felt we must all know at such a time. In my fancy the Residency had looked as it had done when I first saw it on a mild November afternoon of late sun and pale sky: elegant buildings gay with striped awnings and painted shutters, lawns neatly mown, hedges clipped and gardeners moving about the flowerbeds spraying the blooms with water from their goatskin *mushaks*—an enclave of order and tranquillity. It had been pleasant to anticipate moving among those lime-washed houses, walking along precise gravel paths under the shade of mighty gold mohurs laden with flaring orange sprays, or tall flame-of-the-forest trees, offering their scarlet cups to the pure sky, for in dreams all flowers bloom together—and pleasanter still to know that once there, we would find friends, support and commiseration, as well as clean beds and familiar food.

But now, had I not recognized the Resident's house itself, or rather its short hexagonal tower on the summit of which the flag hung motionless under the livid sky, I believe I should have thought myself in Bedlam.

Gone were the trees that I remembered so fondly; gone the neat hedges, the shrubs and flowerbeds; gone the white palings and tile-capped walls that divided one house from the other; gone even the lawns and the gravel walks. In their place stood great piles of ammunition, pyramids of ball and shot, mounds of stores and equipment, tents and huts, shelters of thatch, sacking and bells of arms, carts and carriages, limbers and *doolies*, wheelbarrows—and guns. The grass had been trampled into the hard earth by soldiers and coolies, by horses, mules, bullocks, camels and elephants. Everywhere there was movement, everywhere noise and dust.

Here a group of civilians drilled under the supervision of a perspiring, red-coated sergeant; there a party of soldiers stacked up kegs and cases of stores and quickly thatched the completed piles; white men in shirtsleeves and brown men in loincloths worked side by side fortifying buildings with sandbags and banks of earth, while strings of skinny-legged coolies bobbed past carrying baskets of earth on their head with which to strengthen the glacis; and through the hurrying labouring throng gun bullocks pulled guns to new emplacements, and mules, their harnesses jingling, drew loads of ammunition to places of safety. Under the purplish light of the banking clouds, the scene was weird and threatening. I could make nothing of it; I could not see the purpose that underlay the confusion. Yet it was clear that, although so many worked with desperate concentration, although the air rang with shouts and orders and neighing of horses, camel bells and the trumpeting of elephants, there was over all that chaotic scene a sense of suspended animation, as though everyone and everything, men, beasts, the buildings themselves, were waiting.

The soldiers who had accompanied us in were soon swallowed up in the throng, and for a time we wandered hesitantly around, jostled, shoved but otherwise ignored, looking for a familiar face, or someone of recognizable authority to whom we could turn for advice. Two or three times Charles stopped men hurrying by and asked for Major Barry, but each time an unknowing shake of the head was the only reply. I scanned every group we came to, looked eagerly into each abstracted face, hoping beyond hope to find the one countenance that I knew must come to our aid. Toddy-Bob and Ishmial too, I noticed, were searching for that one particular face and, despite myself, hope grew in me that perhaps Oliver was already here, among all these strangers, all these busy, preoccupied men, and that soon we would come upon him. It was a foolish hope. If he had returned to Lucknow, he would surely have come to the house of Wajid Khan before the Residency? So much that was improbable, impossible, had happened over the last weeks, that it was difficult for me now to order my mind to only reasonable expectation, and I followed Charles and Emily with an almost eager hope.

Then Charles spoke to a grimy, shirtsleeved soldier, pausing for a moment on his spade, who, having heard our predicament, took us over to a middle-aged officer.

'So, just got in, have you?' said the officer, looking with an unsurprised eye at Emily and me in our *burqhas*. 'Had some trouble, I see. And with a baby too! Well, you are lucky to be here; another day or so and you'd have found yourselves shut out. We expect the attack any time now; the devils have closed in all around us. Can't think myself what they are waiting for; not that we haven't had a few skirmishes already of course, but nothing to what they are preparing to mount.'

'Do you mean there is going to be a … a battle, sir?' Emily anticipated my question, alarm in her tired blue eyes.

'No, madam,' answered the officer, a kindly man with a round red face and sandy whiskers. 'No battle. A leaguer. We are about to be besieged.'

'Oh!' The martial terms meant little to Emily and not much more to me. However, with the evidence before me, I was prepared to believe that a siege was liable to be as alarming as a battle, especially when I recalled the account I had read of the siege of Sevastopol, of the suffering and privation, sickness and starvation endured by the troops in the Crimea. But I was too tired to feel added alarm, too sure it was better to meet whatever might come in the company of our fellow countrymen than be forced to endure alone, so I followed the officer in stoical silence as he wound his way through the crowds.

'Don't know where we can quarter you,' he said. 'Place is bursting at the seams as it is. Parties have been coming in every day from stations in the *mofussil*, some of 'em in a really bad way. But the first thing to do is to see that you are down on the quartermaster's list so that you can draw rations. We might be holed up here for some time, you see, so we have to be careful of what food we have. Have you any firearms?'

Charles replied that he and Toddy-Bob had pistols, but made no mention of mine, so neither did I.

'Well, that's better than nothing,' the officer commented. 'You and your man will be issued with muskets in the morning. And, er, the black gentleman is trustworthy, I presume?' He nodded towards Ishmial.

'Eminently,' returned Charles shortly. 'It is largely due to him that we are alive.'

'Quite so. Well, we shall issue him with a musket too then. Believe me, we are going to need every man that can hold a gun, black, white or brindle.'

He was not much interested in where we had come from, or how we had arrived, once he had assured himself that Charles was not a military man, nor yet in the service of the Government.

'Hm, just visitors, are you? Well, your stay in India is going to turn out livelier than you expected!'

Later, when we had heard the stories of some of our fellow escapers, we understood this lack of interest. Our adventures were in no way noteworthy, for few had entered the Residency during the past month whose stories were any less remarkable than ours; many had met with greater terrors, and some with tragedy.

We had stood to one side to allow a gun to rattle past, when I caught sight of a familiar black bonnet bobbing towards me.

'Kate! Oh look, there's Kate! Kate! Kate!' I cried and, as soon as the passage of the gun allowed me to, darted across the path to Kate, who had stopped and was peering through the dimness in an effort to make out who had called her.

'Oh, Kate! Thank heavens we have found someone we know!' And I hugged her so hard that she squealed, looking up at me with her bonnet awry and tears in her bright periwinkle eyes.

'Laura! Oh, my dear, you here too! And I was so sure that nothing could ever happen to you in Hassanganj.' And then as the others joined us, 'Emmie dear, Charles—and, oh, Toddy! And Ishmial!' She kissed Emily and Charles, and nodded, smiling through tears, at the other two, patting each of them on an arm so that they would not feel left out of her welcome.

'It's good to see you, indeed, but so sad as well. So Hassanganj has gone too?' She blew her nose in a large man-sized pocket handkerchief as she took us in: Charles in dirty shirt and breeches, Emily and I with our *burqhas* thrown back over our shoulders to reveal grimy dresses, Toddy-Bob with the *sowar's* breeches wrinkling round his ankles, and the *sowar's* bullet- and blood-scarred jacket over his shoulder. Only Ishmial in his stiffly starched turban, his red velvet waistcoat and crossed bandoliers, with his *tulwar* stuck in his cummerbund, must have looked to her much as he had always done.

'Yes. Hassanganj has gone, but we are safe at last, Kate. Quite safe.'

'Thank God in his goodness for that! But where,' and she looked around, 'where is Oliver? Why isn't he with you? Surely he came?'

'He isn't here then?' I asked in a small voice, though Kate's surprise at seeing us had been sufficient indication that he was not. 'We ... I ... thought he might have arrived by now. He brought us as far as the outskirts of the city, and then went back to ... to attend to something in Hassanganj. We have been in Wajid Khan's house for three weeks, and I felt sure he must have come straight here, thinking we would be here before him.'

'Wajid Khan's house for three weeks? How extraordinary! But no, I've seen no sign of Oliver and I'm sure I should have done if he had arrived. But don't worry about him, m'dears. He'll turn up like a bad penny, never fear. Though he had better hurry or he'll find himself on the wrong side of the fence for sure!'

The sandy officer, who had become restive at the delay, caught her attention.

'These are friends of mine, Will,' she said. 'I know you are busy and I suppose you are trying to house the poor creatures, so shall I take them over and find them quarters?'

'Bless you, Kate—if you would? You'll see them stowed away more comfortably than I could anyway. She has pull!' he informed us with a wink. 'See that they are put down for rations, and scrounge as much else as you can too, with my blessing; blankets and mattresses are going to be in short supply once the hospital fills up, so get all you need now.' With which cheering advice he left us, saluting smartly though he wore no jacket or cap.

As he walked away a party of ladies emerged from a long, low, barrack-like building and stood on the wide verandah just near us, laughing and talking. They were very correctly dressed in light gowns of muslin and poplin, amply frilled over wide hoops. They wore bonnets and in their white-gloved hands carried prayer books and hymnals. I realized it must be Sunday; the days of the week had had no significance for us for nearly a month, and what struck me was the ordinariness, and expectedness of the ladies' attire. I could not take my eyes from the sight of so many neat gowns, polished slippers and pretty bonnets; they were all so clean, spruce and well cared for. Among the ladies were a few with whom we were acquainted, but we did not draw attention to ourselves. We were about to move away, when a number of officers in full uniform came on to the verandah, hovering around a thin, stooped man with sunken eyes, prominent cheekbones and a wisp of grey beard.

'Sir Henry,' Kate whispered to Charles, as the gentleman came down the verandah steps and passed by us. 'Sir Henry Lawrence. Poor man, he's not at all well.' She tapped her chest significantly. 'When you are settled in, I must introduce you to him. I don't believe he had arrived before you left Lucknow, had he?'

'No,' answered Charles, 'but we know something of him; Oliver has a great regard for his judgement and knowledge of the country.'

'And he, believe it or not, has a great regard for Oliver.'

I wondered how Kate had discovered this, and whether it was generally known that Oliver Erskine had been in communication with Sir Henry Lawrence since the latter's arrival in Lucknow. Probably; so few things are ever secret in India.

My eyes followed the frail figure curiously as it passed out of sight. He had looked sad, almost bitter; and, though he had attended politely to the men with him, he had not smiled. Gossip said that his wife's death three years earlier had left him a broken man; that his disagreements on policy with his disputatious brother John, now provincial commissioner of the Punjab, had embittered him; that the lung disease from which he suffered would have killed him but for the steely will that had made him accept the administration of Oudh, where he hoped to prove his own way right in opposition to his brother's harsher theories of government. Gossip called him a sage—or a dreamer; a scholar and a soldier; a saint, sometimes a fanatic. To me he had looked a sick, tired and comfortless man. But it was to him we owed whatever measure of safety we enjoyed in the Residency.

As the last of the congregation came out from the room in the Thug Gaol that did duty as a church, the heavens at last opened. A tremendous clap of thunder followed streak lightning that split the purple clouds, and a second later a few enormous drops of rain cratered the powdery dust at our feet and we ran for shelter. Tired and depressed as I was, I had to laugh at the elegant ladies putting up diminutive parasols to shield themselves from the breaking of the monsoon. Later, much later, I was often to remember that futile gesture as a true symbol of our human situation during the terrible months that followed.

CHAPTER 2

Much later that evening, when the first frenzied cloudburst had abated to a steady downpour that drummed on the roofs and turned the thick dust into a morass of yellow mud and washed the last of the light from the angry sky, we found ourselves housed in two small cells of that same building, the Thug Gaol, outside which I had caught my first glimpse of Sir Henry Lawrence. By then, with our bundles stowed on the two string beds which were all the furniture the cells boasted, we had learned to consider ourselves lucky to have even so inadequate a refuge.

What a comedy that hunt for accommodation proved, and how pointed was the lesson it taught me: namely, that for all our superior talk of Christian culture, political democracy and Western civilization, the British system of caste is as tenacious an evil and as impervious to the onslaughts of disaster and crisis as is that of the Hindus whose prejudices we so complacently condemn!

The trouble was that we could not be tidily pigeon-holed into any of the accepted strata or sub-strata of local society. We were manifestly not military; neither were we administrative, covenanted or non-covenanted civilians; we had no claim on the professional men of Lucknow, nor on the tradesmen. We were merely the guests of a remote and unpopular *zemindar* and planter, and this fact precluded us from all but the least salubrious accommodation.

Perhaps I am being too sweeping; certainly every building in the enclosure was packed to capacity, but nevertheless I had the feeling that we were turned away from most of them more because of our social ambivalence than their lack of space. The best houses, those in which resided the permanent civilian administrative staff of the Residency, the houses of Mr Gubbins, Mr Ommaney and Dr Fayrer, had taken in the wives and families from cantonments when Sir Henry Lawrence had ordered them into the Residency five weeks earlier. The wives and families of the officers, that is; the families of the men of the 32nd Foot had been housed in the *tykhanas* and subterranean rooms of the Residency itself. We were latecomers and could not be housed with our social peers; neither could we hope to move in with the rankers' families since we were civilians, even could our social superiority have been overlooked. Of the other buildings not devoted exclusively to officers or men, one housed the schoolboys and masters of the Martinière School, one was full of unaccompanied women and children from the *mofussil*, others had been taken over for the families of covenanted officials, clerks and writers, and one, which was practically empty, was considered too dangerous a place for women, for its defences were still non-existent and it was near the enemy lines. It began to look as though we must share the restless fate of the Wandering Jew.

As a last resort, Kate decided to throw us on the mercy of Mrs Gubbins herself. Mr Gubbins, though contentious, overbearing and unpopular, was of a generous disposition, but when we arrived at his house wet and muddy, it was to be informed by the Gubbins's starched and starchy maid that her mistress was 'not at home'.

'Stupid females!' stormed Kate, as we walked into the rain again. 'They pay morning calls, leave cards on each other and gossip away their days as though they'd never left their dreary villas in Surbiton or Bournemouth—or seen their bungalows in cantonments go up in flames either. Most of them arrived here with so much baggage and furniture, birds and pets—Mrs Germon even brought her piano— you'd think they were settling down for a protracted holiday, instead of making ready for a siege!'

In the end, it was the sandy officer who had first befriended us who took us to the Gaol and installed us in the two small whitewashed rooms, while Kate regaled him with a spirited and not entirely accurate account of the reception we had received at the various houses, and Toddy-Bob and Ishmial, still homeless, stood on the verandah with the rain gusting over them, looking bewildered and depressed.

'Sorry about it, Mrs B,' apologized Captain Emerson. 'But we can't force 'em to take your friends in, you know; they are still private houses! I thought they'd be more hospitable, though, which was why I let you take them over. However, this place is at least weatherproof and in the second line of defence, so they'll probably be safer here than in the Doctor's place, or Mr Gubbins's come to that.'

'Oh quite, quite, Will! No one's blaming you, dear boy! But now we must have some more furniture, and you must find a billet for Ishmial. Toddy will have to sleep in the kitchen with you, Charles, for the moment.' We had already termed the larger and lighter of the two cells the kitchen, since there was a primitive fireplace in one corner.

'I'll go and see about the blankets and so on now, and your man there will be billeted quite snugly down in the native lines.'

Captain Emerson took Toddy-Bob and Ishmial with him when he went, and after a time they returned laden with four bedding rolls, such as are issued to the troops, together with a tin mug and plate for each of us. Another expedition saw them return with a rickety table, two kitchen chairs, a stool and two thin mattresses. Somewhere along the route Toddy-Bob had also managed to 'collect' a wooden packing case, fitted, illegally we felt sure, with a pillow of real down; Pearl was thus provided with a cot.

When everything was in place and we had eaten the sketchy meal which was all we had the energy to prepare, Emily and I lay down gratefully on our string beds while the men spread their mattresses on the floor of the other room, all of us beyond caring that previous occupants of our quarters had been mass-murderers awaiting the scaffold! The Thugs for whom the Gaol had been built were members of an Indian religious society who earned merit for themselves by strangling unsuspecting travellers with a knotted handkerchief. Their secrets had been discovered and their activities suppressed within recent years by Colonel John Sleeman, a former Resident at the court of Oudh. I thought of Colonel Sleeman with the deepest gratitude that night. And of Oliver Erskine with anxiety …

There were two or three shops in the enclosure, still fairly well stocked, and on the following morning, the rain having cleared away, we purchased some further small comforts for our rooms: cooking pots, a lantern, an enamel bowl for washing, cutlery, and various other useful articles, as well as food to supplement our rations.

It was as well we did, for on that day Sir Henry Lawrence summoned into the enclosure the remainder of the troops from Mariaon Cantonments, and with their coming our situation would become more crowded and correspondingly less productive of comforts.

Now that I was adequately rested and fed, I began to react in a less supine manner to the circumstances in which I found myself, and with

Kate's help came to a better understanding of all that had happened while we had been in the house of Wajid Khan. No reliable information had penetrated to us there, not even rumour—bar the manifestly biased stories recounted by the girl Ajeeba—and even when we had left Hassanganj the situation had been so confused and reports so contradictory that we had no true idea of what we could expect in Lucknow or what would happen in the foreseeable future.

The petty incidents and minor outbreaks of April and May, those unfocused, ineffective symptoms of a radical grievance, had been but the tinder set to kindle the flame which had leapt to monstrous life at Meerut and spread so swiftly and disastrously to Delhi. Now all Hindustan, all that part of Northern India watered by the great rivers and known as the Gangetic Plain, from Bengal to the Punjab, was in revolt. Meerut, it seemed, had been the signal for the mutiny of the army of Bengal, as Oliver had feared, the blazon that encouraged every aggrieved sepoy to desert his post, break his 'salt' and rally to the banner of the Emperor. In his rose-red fort at Delhi, the last of the Moguls, senile and almost blind, spent his time writing poetry, while the men who had been summoned by the magic of his name and ancient state, the men whom he had never led and now could not control, plundered, burned and killed. One by one the British strongholds fell.

Meerut. Delhi. Allahabad and Agra. Then Ferozepore and Aligarh and a hundred smaller posts. At last Cawnpore, only forty miles away, had fallen too.

It had been on the Queen's birthday, the 24th of May, that Sir Henry Lawrence, merely as a precaution, had ordered all the women and children from Mariaon Cantonments, together with the sick of the 32nd Foot, the only Queen's regiment in the district, into the Residency. The order had caused some alarm, but soon, Kate said, everyone had settled down to the novel, picnic-like existence, refusing to take the threat of danger seriously until more than a week after their entry into the enclosure, when the 71st Native Infantry mutinied, fired bungalows in cantonments, murdered several officers, and then were joined by the greater part of three further native regiments. After that, alarm heightened: the murdered officers had been known personally to many in the enclosure. Other intelligence as bad came in day by day from outlying posts and small stations, brought in by fugitives who had escaped with only their lives; women who had seen husbands murdered by the men they had commanded for years; husbands whose wives and children had been slaughtered or burned to death in blazing thatch-roofed bungalows.

No one now could dismiss the reality of the danger, but not until the day of our own arrival, that day on which the news had come of the fall of Cawnpore, had even Sir Henry been certain that the Residency would be invested by the mutineers. For a fortnight past, knowing the entire country was in revolt, he had pressed all measures to fortify his little stronghold, in spite of the fact that the only troops he had to defend more than six hundred women and children were one British regiment much depleted by illness, about seven hundred native troops, some of whom at least were thought to be disloyal, and a hundred and fifty civilian volunteers. At first he had hoped that relief, or at least reinforcement, would arrive from Cawnpore, but early in June it was known that Sir Hugh Wheeler, the commander of that garrison, was himself besieged in an inadequate entrenchment by the forces of the Rajah of Bithur, better known to the Europeans of the district, with whom he had been on most amiable terms, as the 'Nana Sahib'. This intelligence had made apparent the fact that, due to the inadequacy of communications, the incendiary state of the country and the difficulty of transporting troops in a land without railways or metalled roads and whose waterways were now controlled by the enemy, the only remaining hope was to strengthen the Residency, concentrate all Europeans within it, and prepare to withstand a siege.

'So now there can be no doubt that we shall be besieged?' I asked Kate, as we walked back to the Gaol from the shops.

'Well, there is no reason now why we should not be; with Cawnpore gone, we are entirely cut off, you see. Besides, the servants have begun to leave. A lot of them went yesterday, and this morning my own *ayah* and bearer, who have been with me for years, have not shown up. That, my dear, is much more significant than all the tidily worked out theories of the pundits round Sir Henry.'

'Gone, have they? Then how are you going to manage, Kate?' asked Charles.

'Oh, I'll be all right. George and I have quite a snug little room in the King's Hospital with the other officers of mutinous regiments. The lads there have so many servants some of them at least are bound to stay on, and I'm sure they will put me in the way of whatever help I need. Of course I'm not much of a cook, so George's girth will probably diminish. But it looks as though we are not going to have very much to cook anyway!' she ended cheerfully. 'Oh, Charles, I nearly forgot to tell you. George asked me to say if you, Toddy and Ishmial will go up to the Resident's House at about ten, he will see about arms and ammunition and so on, and have you detailed to your posts.'

'Good! I presume we will be officially called volunteers from now on?'

'You will, and a marvellous bunch of brigands you are too: French, Italian, German, Swiss, Irish, of course, Goanese, Eurasians and I don't know what else besides. Oh, and Laura, a friend of yours is among them—Mr Roberts.'

'Mr Roberts! Good gracious. Poor man, I thought he must be safely in Calcutta by now.' We had not had time the night before to think of anything but our own predicament, but now the mention of Mr Roberts made me curious as to others of our acquaintance who might be in the Residency. Yes, Major Dearden, Captain Fanning and Major Cussens were all somewhere about, said Kate in reply to my query—and also poor Wallace Avery.

'Wallace here too? And Connie and Johnny?' Charles sounded pleased to know his cousin-in-law was at hand, but Kate stopped in her tracks, her hand over her mouth.

'I had forgotten! Of course you can't know about … about what happened. Just as we could not know what happened at Hassanganj. Connie is dead. And Johnny.'

'Oh, no, Kate, not Connie! Poor Connie! What happened?' I asked, shocked.

'Nobody's very sure—and it's impossible to get Wallace to say. It seems he must have been away for a few hours, and when he got back the bungalow had been burned, and Connie and Johnny were dead.'

'Good God! Were they burned in the house?' Charles asked.

Kate shook her head. 'I believe not. He found them in the garden— bayoneted I think, but as I say, one can't make him talk. He has been here for about a fortnight, and we've all tried to comfort him, tried to get him to unburden himself. He just shakes his head, and the moment he's alone gets out the bottle. He's so thin now, Laura, you won't recognize him. We can find no way of helping him.'

'Oh, poor fellow! Poor Wallace, there seems no end to his unlucky streak,' said Charles, while I remembered watching the shabby buggy drive out of the gate, followed by the bullock-cart of baggage with Polly in his cage on the top. 'Good girl, Connie, good girl,' the parrot had squawked as the last flutter of Connie's handkerchief had disappeared. Irrelevantly, I wondered to myself what had happened to the bird.

'You must find him out, Charles,' Kate said, 'and talk to him. Perhaps having someone of his own will make him more communicative—and he was always fond of Emily and Laura. He needs to talk, poor fellow, not shut away all the horror and grief in his own mind to dwell on, as he is doing.'

'But of course, as soon as I have seen George.'

'Yes, and George can tell you where to find him. I'm sure I don't know where he is, or where any of the men are now in this confusion. But George will direct you.' She shook her head sadly, and we walked back to the Gaol in silence to break the news to Emily, who had remained behind to feed Pearl.

It was a long, trying day. The sky darkened, the heat gathered under low clouds, but no more rain fell. Emily and I put away our few possessions, swept out the rooms with a twig broom, tried to cook an edible meal on a fire set between three bricks on the floor, and waited for the men to come in and eat it. Then there was nothing more for us to do but sit on the hard chairs in the sticky heat and pursue our own thoughts. During the morning the last of the troops from cantonments, British and native, marched in cheerfully to add to the congestion, and our neighbour on the Gaol verandah, a very fat woman with an immense bosom and an immoderate number of chins, told us joyfully that her husband was among them, so now all would be well. Something in her manner put me in mind of Mrs Wilkins, and Mrs Bonner, like Mrs Wilkins, had one thin and puny daughter, named Minerva.

Although we tried to keep busy, it was impossible not to think of Connie Avery; but we did not talk of her.

And always, lurking behind every other thought in my mind, was the thought of Oliver Erskine. What had happened to him? Where could he be? What was there to keep him away from Lucknow now? Had something happened to Yasmina? Had she fallen ill perhaps; or, worse still, fallen into the hands of the mutineers? But they would not surely harm a child of their own blood? Not like little Johnny Avery. It was said that no one was kinder to children than the Indian, no one more foolish, fond and indulgent. They had not indulged Johnny.

But not even the thought of Johnny's death could for long deflect my mind from Oliver. He had meant to come straight back to Lucknow. Of that I was sure. So something untoward must have happened to keep him from his purpose. Had someone penetrated his disguise, perhaps? Or some of his own tenants or retainers at Hassanganj betrayed him to the rebels? Or could it be that he had changed his mind after all, and decided to remain in Hassanganj? No, that was impossible. How could he stay there with his house burned, his servants fled, and even Moti, who could have harboured him, dead? In my mind, I went back over all the stages of the road we had travelled together: the dusty mud villages that had seemed so full of hidden eyes; the crowded *serais* and lonely camping places; the long stretches of rutted track running between sun-baked fields. Anywhere along that road he could have met with discovery and death. And yet ... and yet there was something inconceivable in the thought of Oliver lying dead in some dry ditch. I could imagine the scene well enough but credit it not at all. Something of his own belief in his capacity for survival, something of his confidence in himself, had infected me, so that I could not see him overcome by circumstances which, after all, he had deliberately chosen to meet. And, as my anxiety waned, its place was taken by familiar irritation with the man and anger at his thoughtlessness and lack of concern for the rest of us. Surely he must know that we were worried about him? But that was the last thing that would make him change whatever plan he was pursuing.

CHAPTER 3

When night fell, Charles brought Wallace to us.

Charles had spent most of the day drilling with Toddy-Bob and the other volunteers under the eye of a sergeant of the 32nd, in the space in front of the Residency where once, so long ago, they had seen each other for the first time.

'Hullo, hullo, hullo! How good it is to see you two dear ladies again!' Wallace attempted to greet us with his old convivial heartiness and kissed us both with clumsy fervour; but, as I drew away from him and looked into his face, tears ran freely down his pale, sagging cheeks, and, abandoning his attempt at cheerfulness, he sat down suddenly on the stool, put his head in his hands and cried like a baby. Charles, embarrassed as men generally are by expressed grief, turned away and, with his shoulder against the door post, surveyed the night outside, while Emily and I looked at each other in wordless alarm. I had never seen a man in tears either, and could think of no way in which to meet the situation. It was Emily who, with a true instinct of sympathy, knelt down beside him and put an arm around his shuddering shoulders.

'Poor Wally,' she murmured. 'Poor Wally. Don't mind crying in front of us. We are your family and must share your grief, you know. We are here to help you in any way we can. Oh, Wally!' And she leaned her head against the table, and wept along with him. I doubt whether she was weeping for Connie and little Johnny; more likely she wept not for them but for the manner of their death? Perhaps her tears were really for herself and Charles and Pearl who, quite unwittingly, were now involved, without understanding or blame, in a force that brought death and mutilation, sorrow and shame, destruction and despair to ordinary people—people with no pretentions to power, people without intentions of evil, people just like herself. I think she wept for the incomprehensibility of life. But whatever the reason for her tears, the very fact that she shed them helped Wallace to master his own emotion. He sat up and mopped his face with a well-worn handkerchief, then looked from my strained face to Charles's back with a little shrug of self-depreciation.

'Sorry for this exhibition,' he apologized. 'The shock, you know. Had no idea you were here; never thought Erskine would be affected by all this in Hassanganj as we have been … here. I knew ours wasn't the only station that had been disturbed, but Hassanganj—well, one wouldn't think a place like that could come to any harm. Still! Who would have thought that we … that Connie …' He stopped, and the ready tears sprang to his protruberant eyes again; but he sniffed and squared his shoulders. Then he fumbled in the pocket of his jacket and produced a bottle of brandy which he set on the table before him.

'A little something … to … to celebrate your safety, y'know. We are lucky enough to have a good supply of spirits down in the mess, and I felt we should, all of us, share a drop tonight. Come, Charles! I shall not give way again. Let us have some glasses, cups, anything we can drink out of. Laura, I expect you are the housekeeper here, as you used to be in Mariaon—where are the glasses?'

I looked at Charles for confirmation. He nodded to me silently, then came to the table and sat down on an upended packing case which made our fourth seat. I got down our tin cups, and Wallace, with a hand that trembled visibly, poured the brandy. Emily brought a dipper of water from the earthen jar in the corner of the room to add to the liquor, but Wallace waved it away from his own cup, and quaffed the contents with one gulp.

The wavering yellow light of the lantern fell on a face that, but for its pale eyes, was almost unrecognizable. Wallace had been a rotund man, with a ruddy complexion and a cheerful expression. Now his face had slipped away into folds of slack, putty-coloured flesh, his eyes were red-lidded and underscored with shadow; even his sandy moustache was no longer carefully waxed and curled, but drooped raggedly over slack, moist lips. His eyes were dazed and thoughtless, and put me vividly in mind of how Connie used to look by five in the afternoon.

'Wallace.' Charles broke the silence in which we had all been sipping the brandy. 'Wallace, will it help you to tell us what happened? Sometimes to talk of a thing eases the pain a little. You know how fond we were of Connie and Johnny; you know we do not want to talk of her simply from curiosity. Can you tell us what happened?'

Charles's voice, well-modulated and pleasant, was full of kindness. But Wallace, after looking up from his mug for an instant, shook his head, and poured himself another liberal measure from the bottle.

'I ... I don't know. I don't know what happened, and that's the truth. If I did know, dreadful as it probably was, I think I could bear it better. But I wasn't there, you see. I ... I don't know whether they burned the bungalow and then, then, killed Connie, or whether they got her first, or anything. If I could only be sure that Johnny—if I could only know that they had no time to realize what was coming to them, but ...'

He shook his head again, passing a sweaty hand over his eyes.

'You see, we were both called away, I and the police fellow, Jenkins, who lived in the next bungalow. There had been trouble in a village down the road the night before, and the *thanadar* sent for us to make a report. Some pandies had passed through, demanded food and, when they didn't get it, had set fire to the native police station and one or two other buildings. We were away a couple of hours. On the way back, we smelt the smoke before we were in sight of the bungalows, and somehow we knew something was wrong. We rushed back ... but it was all over. It must have been the same lot that had attacked the village we had visited. Must have been hanging around all night, and when they saw us ride off, decided to ... well, the bungalows were blazing merrily. There were only the two families in the station. Mrs Jenkins and her two children had been killed on the verandah of the house—our house, that is. They had come across to keep Connie company while I was away. Knew Connie was nervous and didn't like our black brethren at the best of times. The fire had reached them, but we knew it must be them because ... because ... we found Connie near the servants' quarters, and Johnny a short distance away—in a bed of cannas. Orange cannas. His *ayah*—you remember Parbatti?—was still alive, but she died before she could tell us anything. And that was all. There were no troops in the station, just a few police. They helped us to bury ... them, and then I decided to come back here. Jenkins was going to stay on, but I advised him to go to the police barracks in Hodipore. Perhaps he did, I don't know. But there was nothing for me to do there. Records had all gone with my office; everything. Anyway, it was apparent that everything was falling apart, and I thought, I thought I would be more use here, than stuck away on my own in the *mofussil*.'

'Oh, Wallace, how you must hate them!' Emily clenched her hands round her mug so tightly that the knuckles showed white. 'To kill children! What fiends!'

Wallace looked at her in mild surprise and shook his head.

'No, Emily. I don't hate them. I hate myself. It was my fault that Connie and Johnny were killed. All my fault!' And, though he spoke without bitterness, it was with the deepest conviction.

'Good God, Wallace, you mustn't allow yourself to think like that,' broke in Charles hurriedly, while Emily looked at Wallace in alarm. 'You could not have prevented it even if you had been there. They would have killed you too without a thought. Don't blame yourself, old man.'

Wallace shook his head again in a tired manner, looking directly at me.

'I was to blame, nevertheless. Laura knows the truth of the matter.' And, as I made to interrupt him, he held up his hand to silence me. 'No, my dear, it's of no use trying to hide things any more. I am not interested in what people say of me now.' He turned to Charles. 'Laura knows that the real reason we had to leave Lucknow was not because I had been transferred to do a difficult job, but because my colonel wanted me out of the way on account of my gambling and my debts! If I had not been such a confounded fool about cards and horses, and everything else one can gamble on, Connie would be on a boat now and halfway to England.'

'I thought you were in difficulties that last few weeks before you left Lucknow. Wallace, why on earth didn't you apply to me? I could have seen you over a rough patch.'

'It was more than a patch, my dear chap; and I had lost more than Connie's passage money and the wherewithal to set her up in a cottage in England. I shall be in debt for the rest of my life. Which is one more reason why I would so much sooner be dead.'

'You are not just to yourself, Wallace,' I said. 'Why do you not also tell them that it was because of Connie that you gambled in the first place? Because you wanted to do so much more for her than your income allowed you to?'

'Because I'm not sure any more that that is the truth, Laura. Oh, I thought so at the time. But I fooled myself over so many other things, perhaps I fooled myself over that too. Anyway, it was directly due to my debts that Colonel Hande rusticated me, so it was due to that that Connie and Johnny were killed. Shan't fool myself on that point anyway! If I had had the sense to keep my money in my pocket, instead of piling it up on the baize night after night, we would not have had to leave Lucknow. At the worse, Connie and Johnny would have been brought in here with all the others, and, and … well, I didn't have the sense!' he ended bleakly.

There was nothing we could say to dissuade him in his reasoning, and it was a relief when, after another stiff drink, he got up to go.

'I'll be needing that,' he said, as he got unsteadily to his feet, recorking the bottle and slipping it back into his pocket. 'We're to go out in the morning, I suppose you have heard? Sir Henry means to intercept a party of mutineers approaching from Cawnpore. Suppose he knows what he's doing; but I wish we could be a little more certain of the black gentlemen who remain with us. Don't like the temper of the Sikhs myself. Don't like it a bit. Still, perhaps it will be the answer to my problem.' And he smiled wryly as he wished us goodnight.

Emily hardly waited for him to descend the steps before turning to Charles with the question that was in all our minds.

'Is it true, Charles? Is Sir Henry going out in the morning, and will you be going too?'

'Good grief, no, girl! I won't be going. I may be a volunteer, but I'm scarcely a soldier yet, you know. Thank heavens for it too, because my feet wouldn't carry me as far as the gate!'

'Oh, I'm so glad!' Emily flopped down on a chair in relief. 'It would be dreadful if you had to go out and we were left here on our own. I couldn't bear it!'

'Well, it won't happen just yet. Not that this is going to be a serious affair. One account has it that there are several thousand mutineers on their way here to reinforce their brothers, and another that there are just a few hundred. I should imagine the latter estimate is the correct one, and I can't think Sir Henry would risk the men he has to defend this place if he wasn't sure that his losses would be negligible. I imagine he just wants to make an example—show them there is still fight in us. Nothing more.'

The entrenchment was astir very early the following morning. By six o'clock we had eaten our meagre breakfast, Charles and Toddy-Bob had gone to their respective posts, and Emily, Kate and I went hurriedly to a vantage point on the upper verandah of the Banqueting Hall, from where we could watch the departure of the troops. Even so early, the strength of the sun as we walked out of the Gaol gave warning of an unusually hot day.

Emily and I had never before witnessed such a sight, and it was with interest rather than alarm that we watched the mustering of the men. We still knew too little of war to be immune to the romantic enthusiasm engendered by bright uniforms, fine horses, great guns, and the stirring sound of bugles, of harnesses clinking accompaniment to the rolling drums, of incomprehensible shouted orders; so when Sir Henry Lawrence appeared on the steps of the Residency, we joined in the cheer with which his men greeted him.

'Well, we're off!' George Barry paused to call to his wife as he led his horse into position. 'A prayer for us all, my dears. It's going to be a hard hot day, even if we never fire a gun, and I've just heard that the 32nd are going out without their breakfast.'

'Poor lads, but why?' Kate called back.

'God knows,' her husband answered as he swung into his saddle. 'Some damn-fool mix up about the commissariat, I suppose, but there's no time to right the matter now if we want to get this business over before mid-day. *Au revoir*!' And with a salute he was gone.

The 32nd, every button of their scarlet jackets fastened, every pipe-clayed crossbelt snowy, were already marching down the slope and through the Baillie Guard. The guns followed, each drawn by its team of four horses, the lead horse ridden by one artilleryman, his comrades following their charge in close order; then ammunition wagons drawn by mules or bullocks; then the Sikh cavalry—tall men, full-bearded and blue-coated, on tall horses—followed by a group of mounted volunteers and the officers of mutinous regiments like George Barry, faithful men, dispirited because they had no troops to command. After these, through the gate lumbered an elephant drawing a huge howitzer, the only one we had, so Kate said. Then the staff and, among them somewhere, Sir Henry. More cavalry followed, and, at last, ominously, a few horsedrawn ambulances curtained in blood red.

The clear morning sun glinted cheerfully on scarlet jackets and white turbans, on the satiny flanks of well-kept horses, on the great, dull bulk of the elephant, and the great, dull barrel of the gun it hauled;

on the blue coats of the Sikh *sowars*, and bright pennants fluttering in the morning air. Even when the tramp, rattle and creak of their passage had died to a far-off hum, the sun struck answering sparks from lance-tips and bayonets and the brass spikes on helmets, as the long, awkward line of men and beasts wound its way across the pleasant parks and wooded land towards the distant village of Chinhat.

The enclosure was curiously desolate when they had gone. Groups of soldiers stood about idly and in silence, wishing perhaps that they had had a part in the foray. The coolies employed on the earthworks took advantage of the general lull to drop their shovels and baskets and squat down for a hurried pull on the small thin cheroots, called *biris*, extracted from the folds of their turbans or loincloths. Women, many with babies in their arms, stood in knots talking in low voices, unwilling to return to their quarters with only the prospect of an empty, anxious day before them.

And the sun gained strength by the moment.

Kate, glad of company, returned to the Gaol with us. We could guess her anxiety, but she gave no sign of it, busying herself cheerfully in helping us to tidy our rooms and showing us how to roll up our bedding and stow it away in approved military style. Ishmial, who would normally have insisted on performing these services, had been given a musket and put in charge of a labour gang, and Charles and Toddy-Bob were by now busy drilling once again.

When we had finished our housekeeping, Kate took us to visit acquaintances in other buildings, and after an hour spent listening to the ladies of cantonments complaining of their servantless, comfortless state—and all of them far more luxuriously housed than we—Emily, who still tired easily, went back to Pearl, who had been left in the charge of our fat neighbour, Mrs Bonner, and Kate and I sat ourselves down in the shade of the earthworks to watch the progress of the fortifications. It was very hot and humid, but more bearable outside than in the close darkness of our rooms, and the unfamiliarity of what was taking place around us diverted my mind at least from physical discomfort. The previous day I had bought myself a large-brimmed straw hat that saved my eyes from the worst of the glare, and with my collar turned back and my sleeves rolled up to the elbow, I felt myself as well equipped to meet the climate as even Mr Erskine could have hoped. I owned no hoop now, nor even half the number of petticoats generally considered decent, and was far more comfortable for the lack of them.

From where we sat, we had a good view down into the entrenchment on the one side and, on the other, over the low wall at the summit of the glacis, could look into that part of the city which approached the enclosure.

The coolies now were back at work, and the labour of strengthening the fortifications, and indeed of erecting the fortifications themselves, was continuing with all possible speed, in spite of the heat and the inadequacy of the materials. Near where we sat, a labour gang was crowning the glacis with sandbags and erecting entanglements of wire and branches. On the further side of the wall, pits had been dug and planted with pointed stakes, while four-pointed spikes, known as crows' feet, were forced into the earth between and about the pits—measures that, in the event of a successful assault, would delay the enemy sufficiently to enable our men to withdraw to the second line of defence within the walls. I was not versed in the art of war but, even so, these precautions seemed to be not only archaic but inadequate. This impression grew as I continued to look around me. In no place was the wall even as high as the buildings it enclosed. One stretch of the perimeter was still unwalled, and a screen of bamboo, sacking and thatch had been hastily thrown up to supply the deficiency. In places, buildings themselves formed the fortifications, their apertures barricaded with boards and sandbags, even furniture, and guns mounted on the roofs. In another spot, a low board fence was laboriously banked up with earth from the coolies' shallow baskets. But perhaps these primitive defences would not have seemed so alarmingly insufficient had not the city itself edged so closely to their line, had not so many substantial houses abutted almost on to our fortifications.

I was only a little reassured by the seeming placidity with which the life of the city continued beyond the barricade. Along the streets and alleys leading away from the Residency the people of Lucknow pursued their various ways, stopping sometimes to view the progress of our labours, but generally too busy with their own concerns even to pause. Certainly, none gave any sign of hostility; but it was known that guns were already in place in the upper storeys of many of the buildings around us and from time to time figures appeared in the windows, watching us.

We could even make out the colour of their clothing.

CHAPTER 4

'Now, you must tell me everything,' Kate said when we had sat in silence for some time. 'What happened at Hassanganj? Why did you go to Wajid Khan's house instead of coming straight here? And how is it that Oliver Erskine isn't with you, child?'

I drew a long breath and began, knowing that Kate would want the truth.

'I hardly know where to start, so much has happened and all of it so little what we could ever have believed would happen!' She was silent and attentive as I told her of our last days at Hassanganj and the journey to Lucknow, only shaking her head when I got to finding the bodies of the Wilkins family and clucking in disbelief when I confessed to having shot a fellow human being.

'Incredible!' she breathed, as I paused to take stock of what remained to be told. 'Incredible, except that I have heard so many other accounts like yours in the last couple of weeks, and some of them have ended in greater tragedy. But when I think of what you all must have suffered! You must often have given up all hope of reaching safety. And Emily, poor little Emily, how wonderful that she has borne up so well. I would not have thought it of her. Truly, motherhood is a remarkable thing. But Oliver—what made him desert you at the last? He cannot have returned to Hassanganj. There would be no point to it, for the moment anyway.'

'No, there was a point to it. I am not sure that it is something I should mention, even to you, but I know you will not be satisfied with less than the truth. I count on your discretion, Kate. As you know, he came with us as far as the outskirts of the city. Everything seemed calm enough that morning, and he had arranged with Wajid Khan to send an escort for us, thinking of course that we would be brought straight here to the Residency. He ordered Toddy and Ishmial to come with us, and I suppose he had no more idea that Wajid Khan would play the traitor and, well, hold us prisoner, than we had. Naturally, we had expected him to come on with us, so.what was our surprise when he cheerfully bade us goodbye, and galloped back the way we had come. I was thunderstruck. Then furious. And then curious. A few discreet questions of Toddy-Bob finally elicited the real reason for his departure. He had gone back in order to take his little daughter, Yasmina, to her grandparents in Cawnpore. Yasmina's mother, you see,—her name was Moti—had been killed by the mutineers on the night of our escape. It was she who gave us the first warning.'

'Oh ho! I begin to see. And all of this came, I suppose, as a dreadful revelation to you?'

'Yasmina's parentage, no. I had been aware of it for some time. Moti helped Emily at the birth of the baby. But of course I did not know that she had been killed, and the awful part is that I believe I must have heard it—when it happened. I heard a scream, but no one else did, and so I ... I did nothing about it.'

'Sure, and what could you have done? You'd only have been killed too—all of you. And were you, then, very shocked when you learned about Mr Erskine's domestic arrangement?'

'Yes. Of course I was. At first, anyway!' But I smiled at Kate as I spoke. She was not the woman to be upset by such a discovery, and under the scrutiny of her blue eyes I found it difficult to remember any time when I had been. Perhaps it was becoming clear to me that my initial outrage had been due to wounded pride rather than injured virtue. She returned my smile with understanding and settled herself more comfortably against the earth wall.

'Just like the fool!' she snorted after a thoughtful pause. 'Not the business of the woman—that could happen to any man living alone as he has done for this age past—but to make himself responsible for the child. Quixotic nonsense! He could have arranged to have it cared for by—well, by one of the servants or something. But, that's much what I would have expected of him. None of the Erskines had a sense of proportion about their responsibilities.' She sniffed in a manner that indicated approval, despite her words.

'And so he took the child to Cawnpore, you say? I'd feel easier about him if he hadn't gone there, supposing he got that far. I suppose he did?'

'I should think so. He was wearing Pathan dress, as I told you, and Toddy said he'd have no difficulty. He knows the country and the people so thoroughly that I have no fears for him in that respect.'

'Aye, but the country and the people as they are today? That's the trouble!'

'But you have never seen him in his native things, Kate. He just melts into a crowd as though he belongs to it. And he has great forethought; he organized everything, planned our escape and so on, long before there was any need for it. Of course, matters began to go wrong from the very beginning, but he was always up to the occasion, even though the mutineers really surprised us. I think that annoyed him more even than the burning of his house. He does so like to believe himself omnipotent in Hassanganj and he was furious at having—well, not been caught napping, exactly—but being given so little time! Perhaps he had relied too much on the servants. I don't know. Anyway, they had all disappeared that night, except for the old *abdar* and Ishmial, of course, all the house servants and the *punkah* coolies, everyone. Just deserted him after all these years.'

'He must have expected that. He would know the poor wretches had no option once the pandies were in the vicinity.'

'Pandies?' I broke in, puzzled by the term.

'The rebels. Our lads have nicknamed them "pandies" after the mutineer who attacked General Hearsey in Barrackpore.'

'I remember now. He was executed, wasn't he, as an example?'

Kate pulled a wry face. 'Yes, but anyway, Oliver would know that his servants had their own homes and families to think of, you know, like the rest of us, and with all the rumours and strange stories that have been flying around for this age past, why, he would be the first to realize that they would go when the time came.'

'Perhaps you're right. He certainly wasn't unduly surprised when I told him the *ayahs* were not in the bedrooms that night. Annoyed, more.'

'Hm! And when he left you to return to Hassanganj, did he say he would come back here?'

'Yes.' And I thought of what he had said: 'I promise—I'll come back to you—for you.' But to Kate I said only, 'Yes, he said he would come here. Quite plainly. In fact I … we were almost sure that he would be waiting here for us when we entered. All the time in Wajid Khan's house we expected him—or half-expected him, anyway. I suppose we should have realized that he would have suspected something at once if he had come here and not found us, but still, one couldn't help hoping … And we had so little idea of what was going on, even in the house, let alone in the city or out here in the Residency.'

'Yes,' Kate sighed. 'If there were only some way of knowing what was really happening anywhere! Cawnpore isn't far off, but we know nothing but that there have been negotiations going on with the Nana Sahib, and now Wheeler has capitulated to him. It's curious to think of the Nana Sahib as an enemy, y'know. Everyone who was ever stationed in Cawnpore speaks well of him. He was quite the gentleman; very polite and amiable and fond of joining in the local jollifications. It's very strange. But at least we can hope that he proves a magnanimous victor in the light of what we know of him.'

'You knew him personally?'

'Well, we met him. In the old days. A small man with pudgy hands, I remember. Very correct in his dress. Not much like an Eastern prince, I can assure you.'

'Rather like Wajid Khan, in fact?'

'Precisely. Westernized, that's what he was. Though, mind you, they said even then that he was secretly very bitter because Lord Dalhousie denied him the throne and the pension of the Peshwa of Poonah on the grounds that he was only an adopted son. Adoption has always been a recognized method of succession in India, so of course it must have seemed to him that Calcutta was merely using it as an excuse to annex his lands. I own it would have looked that way to me, particularly if I had never been anything but a model retainer to the government and not even extravagant or profligate as the Oudh people were. Sure, and we do make such blunders out here. And yet, Cawnpore was such a pleasant place in the cold weather. As Lucknow used to be.'

'Do you think … could it be possible that Oliver is somehow cut off in Cawnpore? So that he can't get away again? Would that be why he isn't here, Kate?'

'I don't know, woman dear. But it might be indeed. Perhaps he joined General Wheeler …'

'Oliver throw in his lot with the military? Never!'

'But he might have had to, y'know. However little he liked it,' said Kate drily. 'We can't be sure that he had any alternative.'

'In that case, then, he is now a prisoner of the Nana's?'

'Most probably.'

'Well, it would explain why he isn't here, I suppose. And if I could be sure that was the explanation, I wouldn't worry about him.'

'Why ever not, and the poor fellow cooped up in some smelly native gaol?'

'Because if he's not dead, you can take it from me that he's not uncomfortable either. I never knew a man more able to take care of himself.'

'Well, sure, and what a lot of thought you have given to his character,' Kate said slyly. 'I must hope that your idea is correct, m'dear. I would far sooner imagine Oliver comfortable than dead, and I know you'll agree with me.'

'Well, yes. But Kate, we can't be sure, can we? That he isn't dead, I mean?'

'I think it unlikely. You have just said yourself that you never knew any man more capable of looking after himself. I agree with you entirely, and I'm willing to wager that in a couple of weeks' time when this is all over, he will stroll in quite unconcerned about the lot of us, and never guessing for a moment what an amount of anxiety he has caused.'

'Oh well, I wouldn't say I'm anxious really. But of course, one must be concerned, and he was a very attentive host to all of us, was he not?'

'He was that!'

'So naturally I would like to know he is safe, as would we all.'

'Oh, naturally!' Kate agreed.

There was a deliberately vague expression in the eyes that met mine, and I looked away hastily, confused by Kate's percipience, and in doing so caught sight of a familiar figure, half-obscured by a large black umbrella, picking its way through the debris below us.

'Kate, look! There's Mr Roberts ... Mr Roberts,' I called, 'Mr Roberts—up here!'

Mr Roberts cast a startled glance upward, then waved his open umbrella and scrambled up the rubble of the glacis to us.

'Miss Laura! But how nice—and yet, no, how sad!' He laid aside his umbrella and took my hand in both his own. 'I know you won't misunderstand me, and truly I am delighted to see you again, but in these circumstances,' he nodded at the guns, 'it is a pleasure that I would have deferred. And is it not an irony, Miss Laura, that it should be the fulfilment of my forebodings, those "croakings" which our mutual friends in Calcutta so much derided, that should serve to bring our paths together again? I caught a glimpse of Mr Flood last night, and guessed that Hassanganj must have met the fate of so many other places.'

We exchanged truncated versions of our adventures. Mr Roberts had been pursuing his business in Lucknow when word had come that Agra and Allahabad had fallen. Since his trade depended on the river, and the river was now, if not in enemy hands, at least untenable for trade, he had seen no option but to enter the Residency with other tradesmen and businessmen of Lucknow. 'But I am a man of peace, Miss Laura, and I must confess that I am ill at ease in all these martial preparations and rumours of war. To say nothing of the discomforts, which, if my findings are correct, are going to increase before they decrease or disappear. Do you know,' he nodded his head with great solemnity to mark his point, 'the situation is absurd, quite absurd! We are almost entirely unprepared for the situation the military gentlemen consider will develop. Look around you, Miss Laura—Mrs Barry! Can even you believe that these … these *piffling* precautions are going to keep at bay a large, well-armed and, it appears, most earnest enemy? For more than a few hours at most?'

As much the same conclusion had already entered my mind, I could not disagree with him, but Kate objected mildly.

'Sir Henry has been doing his best to fortify this position and provision it adequately for weeks past, Mr Roberts. It is not *his* fault that matters have come to a head so quickly. I am told he has expected something like this ever since he arrived in Lucknow, but he was reluctant to let the natives know of his suspicions until there could be no further doubt. He took a risk, but surely a necessary and well-considered one? Our preparations may look sketchy, but they are as much as anyone could do in the time. And perhaps you forget, we are not dependent solely on the fortifications, such as they are. We have plenty of artillery and a fine force of fighting men—and the mutineers are leaderless. George says that that will prove the most important factor in our defence, and that, without their white officers, the pandies will accomplish little.'

'As little as they have already accomplished in Meerut and Delhi— and now Cawnpore? That little will be enough to see us all with our throats cut, Mrs Barry, if you will pardon my saying so!'

'In Meerut and Delhi we were surprised, and in Cawnpore obviously overwhelmed by superior numbers ... But here we know pretty well what to expect, and there is no man in this place, bar, perhaps, Mr Gubbins, who does not accept Sir Henry's judgement of the situation. Not a man who does not believe that we can hold out against the pandies until help arrives, as it must do very soon.'

'I can only hope so, Mrs Barry! For I have been making a few enquiries about our numbers and so forth, and I have no hesitation in saying that I am most alarmed.

'Colonel Inglis, of the 32nd, you know, was kind enough to ask me to dine with him last night. A very helpful man; very informative. Now, including the civilian volunteers and the Eurasian drummers, there are just over seventeen hundred men in this entrenchment capable of firing a gun. That is, of Christians, the men of the 32nd Foot, the fifty men of the 84th whom the unfortunate General Wheeler sent to our assistance from Cawnpore, the officers of various mutinied regiments and, as I say, of volunteers like Mr Flood and myself there are about one thousand. The other seven hundred are sepoys, and the Sikhs among them are widely believed to be—well, let me say ambivalent in their loyalties. Then there is the labour force, all these hordes of coolies, gardeners, *syces* and servants whom you see below us. I would estimate there are between seven and nine hundred of them, all with mouths to feed though they bear no arms. Lastly and most important there are just about six hundred women and children.'

'And so ... ?' said Kate.

'These ... these ludicrous walls, Mrs Barry, surround about thirty-three acres of ground and extend to rather more than 2,000 yards in length. On one side we are wide open to the river and for the rest—well, you can see for yourself how closely the buildings outside threaten us. I dare say they are no more than a couple of dozen yards away in many places and closer in some. Nor is the fact that 2,000 yards of perimeter are to be defended by fewer than seventeen hundred men the worst of our misfortunes. The fact is, Mrs Barry, that we are going to be starved to death if not killed outright. I cannot by any means ascertain that we have provisions sufficient for more than ten days to a fortnight!'

'I cannot contradict you, Mr Roberts,' said Kate, since it was obvious that he was now awaiting comment. 'I only wish I could. I am sure your facts are incontrovertible. However, while I am an old campaigner and fairly used to contemplating disaster of one form or another, it is not quite kind of you to draw Miss Hewitt's attention so explicitly to our situation. There are many imponderables which cannot show in your accounting, to begin with, and which therefore render your sum incorrect, I firmly believe! True, we are too few. But we are well equipped. True, our walls are flimsy, but my spirit, at all events, is stout. And I know I am not alone in having full confidence in Sir Henry. Above all, there is still time. After today's engagement it may well be that we can forget the whole threat of a siege or leaguer, or whatever you choose to call it ...'

'To my mind, it can be called nothing more heroic than a blockade. And that will be bad enough when we are all starving!'

'Really, Mr Roberts!' said Kate impatiently. 'You are lacking in all tact! And in common sense. Gloom always invites disaster!'

'Perhaps. I prefer to face facts, and as to tact, my dear good lady, this is no time for tact, I do assure you. Miss Laura and I are old friends—indeed, I think I may say familiar companions—and I believe I know her character well enough to think she would prefer to have the facts than facile reassurances. Miss Laura is very far from being a frivolous girl; she is a most sensible young woman.'

He meant to pay me a compliment, but, as always, this too-often reiterated summation of my prosaic personality had the effect of chilling my heart. Why did no one ever see that I was other things as well as sensible? Not that I was unduly alarmed by Mr Roberts's statistics; figures never made much impact on me, and I was inclined to think that the studies of my dear Mr Roberts—so correct, so dependable, so anxious to learn as well as to teach—were motivated as much by unfamiliar alarm as by expected curiosity.

There was no need to take his prognostications too seriously, I felt, and, after some further debate, the heat, the dust and the noise drove all three of us indoors.

CHAPTER 5

I persuaded Kate to share our midday rations with us for George's safety must continually have been in the forefront of her mind, so we returned to the Gaol together, joking rather unkindly about Mr Roberts's old-maidish alarms. Pearl had been fractious and Emily was consequently ill-tempered. Charles, having soaked his feet in cold water and salt, was just easing them back into his boots, when we entered the kitchen. I set to work immediately to produce something to eat, for Charles had been assigned to the battery in Dr Fayrer's post, and was to report back as soon as possible. Toddy-Bob, whose rations I had cooked along with ours, did not appear, so we sat down without him.

I thought it was the time-gun that in military stations is fired at midday and automatically my hand went to the fob-pocket at my waist to check my watch. But before I could take it out, the thunder of the gun was followed by a sharp, hysterical crackle of musket fire. For a moment, we sat immobile, our eyes questioning each other's. Then Charles jumped to his feet.

'It's come!' he shouted in a high, unfamiliar voice, and, as we stumbled to our feet, he grabbed his rifle, slung his ammunition pouch over his shoulder, and rushed outside, with me close behind him.

The heavy somnolence of the afternoon was shattered by more than the firing. As I and many another ran out into the savage sunlight, pandemonium broke loose: every coolie, tally-clerk and servant in the enclosure gave vent simultaneously to yells and wails of distracted panic, dropped whatever they were doing and made for shelter. The tide of non-combatants running for cover was met at every door and gateway by soldiers and sepoys, still shrugging into jackets and buckling on belts, intent on reaching their posts. There were shouts of 'Stand to your arms,' 'Attack! An attack!' Women screamed and children cried ... and the chatter of the guns gained strength.

'Come back, Laura! Come back! At least put on a hat,' called Kate with inspired irrelevance. She stood on the verandah, with Emily's scared face peering over her shoulder. Charles, shoving his way through the running, yelling crowd, had soon disappeared, and, suddenly realizing my own stupidity in following him, I returned sheepishly to the verandah.

'What is it?' Emily asked in bewilderment. 'Are we being attacked, Laura?' As though I were in a position to know more than her.

'Yes, yes, it's an attack,' said Kate soothingly, 'but it's only a warning. Nothing more, so don't be alarmed. We've had several of these skirmishes, but no one has ever been hurt, in spite of the noise. I do wish the coolies wouldn't howl so. Most unnerving! George says the pandies probably just want us to know they really have the ammunition for the guns. Come in now, girls, and finish your meal. We don't have to starve yet.'

Her calm, even amused tone of voice reassured us, and we sat down to our abandoned plates. But the food stuck in my throat and my stomach and chest felt constricted. In spite of the heat my hands were cold.

We were under fire—yet only a short time ago I had thought that only soldiers could know that experience.

Emily had no more success in swallowing than I.

'Oh, where can Charles have gone to?' she said after a time, pushing away her untouched plate with a gesture of distaste. 'Surely he should be back by now? You'd think he'd have more consideration for me. For all of us.'

'But he is considering us, m'dear,' said Kate mildly. 'He's at his post—where he should be, and where he must remain until the alarm is over and he is no longer needed.'

'But Kate, we are being *attacked*!' objected my cousin. 'Surely they can't expect him to stay away when we are in danger. His place is with me. I need him. I ... I'm frightened.' And she began to cry with her blue eyes wide open, the tears cascading down her pale face unheeded, as she looked for assurance from Kate to me.

I went over to her and hugged her shoulders.

'There there, Emmie,' I comforted. 'We're not really in any danger, and you wouldn't want Charles to do less than any of the other gentlemen after all, would you?'

'Yes, I would!' she gasped between sobs. 'I want him with me. I have a right to want him here, and his place is here. I know you don't understand, Laura, but I'm his wife, and so I'm his first responsibility, don't you see? Not some wretched gun!'

'But, Emmie, every other man in the place is at his post, and most of them have wives too. And just think of George ...'

'No! Why should I? George is different. He's a soldier and it's his job to fight, but Charles isn't; he's just a ... a visitor, and they have no right to keep him away from me.'

'Oh, Emmie! We can none of us think like that any longer, don't you see? We are all in this ... this trouble together; we all have to play a part ...'

'Stop fussing over her, Laura!'

Kate stood up and wagged a finger at Emily across the width of the table. Her blue eyes were cold and hard.

'Now listen to me, my girl,' she said, addressing Emily. 'This is no charade we're acting, and if you think it's bad now, just wait until they really start to batter us from across the wall! I don't like it any more than you do. I don't like the guns, the noise, the way we have to live, but believe me, neither do the men. And the fact that we women are here makes it all ten times worse for them. The only thing we can do, the only thing we are asked to do, is stay quiet and keep out of their way. Fussing and crying and behaving like a spoiled child, as you are doing, is the best way of getting your Charles hurt, perhaps even killed. Yes, I mean killed! If he has you on his mind, don't you see, if he has to worry about you because you're too silly to put a good face on it and hide your fear, he'll get careless about his own safety. Believe me, we're all going to need our wits about us to come through this at all. Anxiety, lack of concentration, make a man take foolish risks, and foolish risks mean early death!'

She paused for breath.

'Do you understand me, Emily? Do you see why you must take a hold of yourself and not behave like this in front of Charles?'

'I suppose so. But I still think it's not right that he should be away from me.'

'That's as may be; but, for his sake, keep your thoughts to yourself. Pull yourself together and let's have no more tears. Now come on! Be a good creature and mop up. Tears always upset me.'

Emily did as she was told, but reluctantly. I could not escape the realization that she had wanted Charles to come back to the safety of the Gaol for her own sake, not for his.

All afternoon the firing continued: ragged musket and rifle fire interspersed now and then with the heavy roar of ball and shot. After a time, when no reports of disaster reached us, we settled down to it pretty well, only jumping when the large roundshot whirred laboriously through the hot air to fall through a roof or bring down the corner of a building.

When Charles eventually limped back, his shirt dripping with sweat, he plunged his head into the basin of cold water, and then, as he rubbed his hair, informed us ruefully that he had been given the undramatic duty of seeing that the labour gang kept at their work of digging burial pits for animals. This was a formidable task, for there were scores of horses, camels, gunbullocks and elephants within the enclosure, and Sir Henry had directed that if our situation worsened, all surplus creatures were to be destroyed.

'Quite apart from the work, there's not enough room,' Charles said, munching hungrily, for we had kept the meal he had not had time to eat. 'And it's damned difficult to keep those poor devils at it with the firing going on, to say nothing of the heat down there by the river. The ground's like iron, in spite of last night's rain.'

'But then, what can be done with the animals, I mean?' I asked.

'Heaven knows! Even the river is too far, if we are closely invested, that is. For the moment, I must just keep the damn fellows digging for all they're worth. By God, it's hot down there! No shade and the ground reflects the heat; and the glare from the water is almost the worst.'

'Has anyone been hurt by the firing, Charles?' Emily asked hesitantly.

'Not yet,' her husband answered, stuffing a handful of biscuits into his pocket. 'Or rather, not badly. But as I was coming back I heard that they have begun to loophole the houses near the perimeter, so I expect the pandies are stepping things up. I must go. Don't know when I'll be back, so eat when you want to.'

'Oh, Charles, don't be long … please!' Emily looked as though she would cry again given half a chance, but one look at Kate, frowning from a corner, made her think better of it.

Sometime too, during that first long hour of fire, though we were not aware of it, Sir Henry Lawrence galloped into the enclosure with the bitter intelligence that the battle of Chinhat had been lost.

Instead of the few hundred mutinous sepoys from Cawnpore he had expected to encounter, he was met by a force of six thousand men, well-mounted, well-armed and excellently disciplined, and the battle had fast degenerated into a rout. News of our defeat soon reached the city; the populace, wild with excitement, hurried to throw in its lot with the sepoys, and even as Charles stood in our kitchen talking to us, our men fought their way through the now openly hostile streets, back to the Residency.

We women had received strict orders to remain under cover and, in truth, we had no desire to venture out, so were spared the pain of witnessing the return of the brave little army we had watched setting out in the bright morning light.

All that evening and through the night they limped in, exhausted, bewildered, dejected, carrying the dead and the dying and the many who had fallen victims to the sun. No one knew that night how many men had been lost, but the Howitzer had been taken, and four of the other guns.

The entrenchment rang with stories of how the defeat had happened, as the men who had been left behind hurried to their wives and friends with the stories, often conflicting, of the men who had gone out. Rumours, suppositions, garbled versions of the truth, we heard them all with equal alarm and pity. Some said that the mutinous sepoys, armed with six fine guns, had fought with courage and cunning worthy of their erstwhile officers; that the native artillery, and a large number of the Sikh cavalry, seeing the steady white turbanned tide of the mutineers cresting the brow of an incline, had overturned the guns and galloped their steeds over to the enemy without firing a shot; that our men were exhausted by a hard day's work and a hard night's drinking before they set out, hungry and thirsty; that the muskets of the 32nd, so long unused, were clogged and could not be fired. On two points only were all the accounts agreed: we were outnumbered six to one, and the day's most potent enemy had been the sun.

Kate remained with us through the night. It was impossible to sleep, and we sat on the hard wooden chairs in the shifting light of our lantern dozing, waiting, straining our ears to try and make out what was happening outside. The small room was stifling and stale in the heat; the oily smell of the lantern was almost unendurable, but none of us had the courage to put it out. After a time, Charles stretched out on one of the beds in the other room, where Pearl in her box slept quietly.

The firing that had been sporadic during the afternoon increased in intensity as the night wore on and our attackers were joined by the mutineers whom we had so signally failed to deter at Chinhat. All the buildings around the perimeter were now loopholed for rifles, and heavy guns mounted on roofs and upper storeys were brought into play. Many of our own men snatched only a couple of hours' rest on reaching the enclosure, before relieving others at the defences.

It must have been about three o'clock in the morning when Wallace Avery and Captain Fanning knocked on the door in search of Kate, to tell her that George was dead. They had come upon his body as they stopped for a short rest at the Machi Bhawan, a fort some five miles away along the side of the river, and that was all they knew.

It was almost as though Kate had expected their news. She nodded two or three times as they spoke—her bright, lined face suddenly very old—and, when they had finished, sat for a moment in silence looking at her hands holding her blue rosary beads. Then she put the rosary in her pocket and stood up.

'Thank you, Wally,' she said. 'You were very thoughtful to come to me directly. I could have been waiting such a long time. I ... I think I would like to go back to my own quarters now.' She picked up her bonnet, Emily and I kissed her wordlessly, then Captain Fanning and Charles took her over to the King's Hospital. A burst of noise entered the room as the door was unbarred briefly to allow them to leave, and then Emily and I were left facing Wallace alone.

He had a handkerchief twisted round his forehead, and a mass of congealed blood stained his cheek. He shrugged as the door closed, then sat down wearily on the stool.

'God, what a blasted awful day!' he said thickly, drawing a dirty hand across his eyes. 'What a bloody mess! You'd think my luck would have changed, wouldn't you? All those poor devils dropping around me like duck on a *jheel*, and all I manage to pick up is a scratch on the forehead and a pair of blistered feet. Oh, my God, what a pitiful, bloody awful mess ... and I'm still alive at the end of it!'

'You're being saved for the gallows,' I said witheringly, and set about making some tea. At that hour of the morning, I had scant patience with Wallace Avery, particularly in view of the news he had just broken.

'You didn't see George until ...' asked Emily hesitantly.

'No. Not a sight all day. Then Fanning came upon his body on the back of a cart. Both legs had gone. I expect he died at once. God, I hope so! There were dozens of others in the Machi Bhawan, dead and wounded, but mostly dead. We wanted to bring him back, but there was nothing to carry him on, and anyway we couldn't have managed it. Done up, you know. Poor old George. Decent chap. Dearden, he's gone too. You remember him? A bullet got him straight in the gullet, not two yards away from me. He was alive, so we put him on a limber, and later on, when I had time, I went to look at him. Dead. The sun, I suppose, as much as the bullet. Look, I even lost my helmet when I was hit, but the sun wasn't enough to do for me—not lucky Wallace! Saved for the gallows is right. No thanks, no tea for me, I'm in search of something stronger.' We made no move to stop him; and he lurched to his feet and staggered into the noisy dark.

George Barry, comfortable, quiet George Barry, lay somewhere on a bloody limber with both legs shot off, dead. We made tea and drank it gratefully, making no attempt at realization.

Kate was denied even the scant comfort of a funeral.

The next day, the remnants of the force from the Machi Bhawan were brought into the Residency and the fort was blown up. Sir Henry Lawrence had intended to keep it garrisoned to act as a threat to the country people, in the same way that he had hoped the Residency would deter the city, but the losses at Chinhat forced him to abandon this scheme. Every man alive was needed now at the Residency, and sooner than have the great supply of ammunition stored at the Machi Bhawan fall into the mutineers' hands, the place was destroyed.

Charles, I remember, had just come in and was lighting his pipe when a thunderous report and a shock like an earthquake caused him to drop the match and burn a hole in his breeches. The lantern jerked off the hook that held it over the table and was extinguished. In the darkness Emily screamed; I leapt up, knocking over my chair, and Pearl, woken from sleep, began to wail in protest at the prevailing confusion. Toddy-Bob had been sitting in the shelter of a pillar on the verandah, whittling and whistling, when the twenty thousand pounds of powder and a vast amount of musket shot went up with one tremendous roar. His knife slipped, cutting his forefinger, but he was so astounded by the display of pyrotechnics suddenly enlivening the dark sky that he forgot to staunch the blood, which then dripped down his clothing for some moments unsuspected, and next morning produced many exclamations of commiseration from the ladies of the Gaol, with most of whom Toddy was already on easy terms.

Shortly afterwards, the great wooden doors of the Baillie Guard were drawn to and barricaded with earth, sandbags and baulks of timber. Guns were mounted to command the approaches to the gate. No one now could enter or leave the enclosure, and we were truly in a state of siege.

There had been no word of Oliver Erskine.

CHAPTER 6

Our world now shrank to the confines of the enclosure and became, as the days passed in heat, noise, smells and suffering, as close an approximation to hell as any of us were capable of imagining. The daily battle for survival, the almost hourly search for ways and means to continue a rudimentary and unrewarding form of existence, served in those first days to deflect our minds from the grosser evils around us. Not that we were insulated from the realities of cruel death and crippling injury; not that we were unaware of what our men faced; not that we lacked imagination or feeling, or even information. But for most of us women, cooped up in tiny rooms like those in the Thug Gaol, or in underground cellars in other houses, the conditions in which we found ourselves were so far outside our experience that it took all the physical and mental energy we could muster to adjust ourselves to them.

Very few of us had ever turned our hands to domestic matters— even a private's wife in India has servants—and now we found ourselves without servants, without light and with the minimum of fuel or food to cook on it. The rations alone posed me a daily problem in ingenuity in making them edible. We received beef, rice, lentils, the coarse, stone-ground flour called *atta* and salt. No butter, no milk, no vegetables, and our private stock of tea, sugar and jam would last no great length of time. Moreover, the meat was always so tough it could only be stewed, and was often so largely bone that only a broth was possible. By the time we had worked ourselves into some sort of routine, by the time we had realized that no efforts of ours could produce a palatable meal, decrease the heat of our quarters or increase our physical comfort, we had also somehow learned to accept the more fearful implications of our state. God tempers the wind to the shorn lamb—and many a delicate lady forced for the first time to cook on three bricks on the floor, cut up her meat with nail scissors, and deal unaided with mice, rats, cockroaches, ants and scorpions, had reason to be grateful for even such unpleasant aids to forgetfulness.

There had been a short pause in the bombardment after the great explosion that sent the Machi Bhawan sky high—the pandies clearly were trying to decide what would happen next—but then they redoubled their fire and all through that night and the following day and night the guns never ceased.

The Thug Gaol was in the second line of defence—in other words, there were buildings and entrenchments between us and the enemy. But, though we were relatively protected from rifle fire, round shot, shell and ball threatened us as much as anyone else. On that first night, exhausted by the day's alarms, we managed to sleep in snatches, but woke often to the unremitting din of the guns, of exploding shells, of falling masonry, and once, most horribly, to the screams of a wounded horse.

My string cot stood just across the little room from Emily's, and we had placed Pearl in her packing case against the inner wall to protect her as much as possible. Happily innocent of our predicament, the child slept soundly through the noise.

'Laura?' It was the faintest whisper. Emily was learning consideration, but the noise the horse made in its agony, until someone expended a merciful bullet on it, had driven away any possibility of sleep.

'Yes?'

'Laura, aren't you frightened?'

'No. I'm terrified!'

'How long will it go on?'

'I don't know. Days perhaps.'

'I ... I hate the noise, all the crashes and bangs and the horrid whiny bullets. I can't think properly with it.'

'I know.'

'Do you suppose ... do you think we'll ever really get out of this, Laura?'

'I expect so. Sir Henry would have thought of something else if he had felt we wouldn't be relieved—very soon too.' What was the point of telling her that Sir Henry had had no alternative but to stay?

'But could he have known it would be as bad as this?'

'I imagine so, and we must face it, Emmie; it might even get worse before it's finished.'

'I ... I still can't believe it's happening to *us*!' she whispered unhappily. 'To *me*. If Charles had been a soldier or something—but we are only visitors! We should be in Mount Bellew, not here. It's summer there, Laura. The garden must be full of roses and delphiniums and lupins. And the apples will be ripening in the orchard. I can't seem to realize that this is real. Why should it be us? How can it be us?'

'Yes, I know,' I said again, sighing. But my thoughts did not take me to Mount Bellew. I wondered how Hassanganj looked now, the house a burnt-out ruin, the gardens already running riot with weeds grown doubly fecund in the monsoon rain, the grass in the park waist high. I saw as clearly as though they were before my eyes the mountains rearing out of the dark belt of the *terai*, flushing pink at dawn, silver in the moonlight, and the long fields of canary mustard under the soft spring sky. I thought of Old Adam, all his labour, imagination and love reduced to mere memory in a few mortal minds. I thought, too, of Oliver. Where was he? Why had he not joined us? I believe I prayed for him.

'Laura?'

'Yes?'

'I might die!'

'Nonsense!'

'Or you might.'

'Certainly not!'

'But I might, I really *might*, and if I do and you don't ... I want you to know some things that I am thinking now ... I want you to know I won't mind about Charles ... if you want to marry him, I mean.'

'What?' I sat up abruptly in the darkness. 'Oh, Emmie, for heaven's sake be sensible! You are not going to die and I am certainly not going to marry Charles. Turn over and go to sleep.' It was ridiculous to think of marriage, any marriage, on such a night, and I must have giggled.

'No, don't laugh. It's very difficult for me to say this, but I've had ... so much on my conscience ... and I've known, oh, for a long time, that he cared for you. I'm not being noble or anything. I don't love him. You know that, so I'm not even jealous, not really, and if I ... go, I'd sooner you had Pearl than anyone else. You'd be good to her for her own sake, as well as for Charles's. I've made such a mess of everything. But I want you to know.'

'Now, Emmie, you are being absurd. In a week or so we'll be out of this and you'll be sorry you ever spoke so. We are both tired and frightened, but there's no point in allowing yourself to get morbid and say such silly things. Anyway, I could never marry Charles. I don't love him.'

'You don't? Honestly?'

'No, Emmie, I don't!'

'Oh dear! What a silly waste of time it all was then.'

'What do you mean?'

'I was so sure you loved him, when we first knew him. And I thought he was beginning to look at you as though he might love you. That's why I set my cap at him. I couldn't have borne you to get married before me!'

A sudden silence filled my mind, blotting out the noisy night.

'And was that the only reason you married him?' I asked very quietly.

'I don't know. Perhaps. I thought I was in love with him, for a time. But it didn't last very long ... and I've been very unhappy. Really unhappy.'

'Yes. It was a very silly waste of time,' was all I could say in my bitterness.

'Of course, now that I have Pearl I can bear it better,' she continued, unmindful of my tone. 'She's going to be such a comfort to me, and I'm going to see that she has everything, just everything that a girl can have. Always! If only, when this is all finished, I mean, if only Oliver would ask Charles to remain on in Hassanganj, for always. He is always so good to me, and I know I could be happy again there. And that's another thing. If I should die, will you be sure and tell Oliver how grateful I was to him? For his kindness to me, his thoughtfulness. I've wished, so often you can't imagine, that Charles was a bit more like Oliver, but of course I know that's impossible. But you will remember to tell Oliver how ... how much he meant to me, won't you?'

'I'll do no such thing, for the simple reason that I'll have forgotten this absurd conversation long before we see him, and anyway, you'll have every opportunity to tell him all you want to yourself. Thank heavens that poor horse has stopped. It's nearly dawn. I'll get up and make some tea. It'll cheer us both up.'

'But you said we must save what we have.'

'It's nearly breakfast-time, so I might as well get the fire going before the sun rises. Charles will be in soon, and I can keep the same tea warm.'

While I wrestled with kindling and charcoal and put a pot of water on to boil, I meditated on our conversation and the ironies of fate. A month before, such frankness would have been as impossible to Emily as to me. And even a month ago, could I have told her with such conviction that I did not love her husband? I smiled wryly to myself as I realized how radically we had altered, Emily, I—even Charles. Not so long ago I would have been filled with confusion, guilt, and—who knows?—perhaps even a wild hope by Emily's words. Now they had no importance. True, I had known a certain bitterness when she confessed that she had set herself to attract Charles just so that I would not 'get' him. But it had soon passed. Perhaps I had always known it, after all. Some time, perhaps, I would know a justifiable anger at the moment of thoughtless spite on Emily's part which had led to so much unhappiness for all three of us. For I had been truly unhappy for a time, as I believed she was now and as I knew Charles was too. It was a matter, however, that would have to be faced and dealt with in the future, if we were to have a future. For the moment, remembering to be properly frugal with the tea leaves was of more importance.

While I waited for the water to boil, I opened the door and looked out into the gathering light of the new day. It was like no other dawn I had ever seen, for the entrenchment had not slept and there was no sense of a gradual awakening after rest. Everywhere men were on the move, working as they had worked all through the hours of darkness, hauling guns to new positions, shoring up the defences damaged in the barrage, building screens of bamboo and sacking to cut off the view of lanes and open spaces from the enemy marksmen in houses outside the walls. Other fires than ours had already been lit and I could scent wood-smoke over the smells of dust, cordite and open drains, and the light, when it came, was of the same dead yellow as the dust that filled it.

'Oh, Oliver, where the devil are you?' I thought inelegantly to myself for the fiftieth time that night. 'Where the devil are you?'

I kept the tea warm, but Charles did not come in until some hours later. He had spent the night on duty in Dr Fayrer's garden, up near the Baillie Guard. The house was full of women and children, in spite of its exposed position, and a battery had been thrown up in the garden while the roof was used by riflemen. Charles was filthy, his face black with smoke and sweat, his eyes bloodshot, and his clothes smelt of gunpowder.

'Bad news!' he said as he entered and stood his rifle in a corner. 'Sir Henry's been wounded.'

Behind him Ishmial, who had constituted himself Charles's orderly and seldom left his side, leaned dispiritedly on his musket.

'Sir Henry! Oh, Charles, surely not?'

Emily stopped washing Pearl in the enamel basin and looked up aghast.

'A shell got him, while he was resting in his upstairs room in the Resident's House. He was going to move out of it this morning, they say, because it was too exposed to fire, but the shell came in through the window and burst in the room.'

'But he'll be all right; he'll live, won't he, Charles?' asked Emily.

Charles shook his head. 'The doctors can't do anything for him. No hope. They have moved him across to Fayrer's, but the pandies seem to have guessed what has happened and have turned all their fire on the very verandah he is lying on. Somebody here is informing them, blast 'em! Look, I must get back as soon as possible. Just wanted to see you were all right. Give me a bite of something to take away, if you have it.'

'But, Charles, you've been up all night!' expostulated Emily.

'So has everyone else,' returned her husband shortly. Emily compressed her lips and turned her attention to Pearl, while I reheated the tired tea and watched the two men gulp it, still standing.

That evening, when Charles at last returned to snatch some sleep, he was drained of all colour, and when we enquired about Sir Henry, he only shook his head and muttered, 'Dreadful! Dreadful!' He lay down fully clothed on Emily's bed and turned his face to the wall, but I do not think he slept.

For two days Sir Henry lived on in an agony hardly ameliorated by the doctors' chloroform, and his awful screams, clearly heard by all the men of Fayrer's post, unnerved them far more than did the guns of the mutineers. It was Toddy who brought us the intelligence of his death, early on the morning of the 4th of July, the fourth day of the siege.

'Proper blessin' 'e's gone,' he announced solemnly. 'Yelled like a stuck pig for two days. 'Orrid to 'ear 'im, it was—proper 'orrid.' He meant no disrespect.

In moments of crisis, when many people are confronted with a single emotional reality, atmosphere becomes almost tangible. So it was with us that day, as we were overtaken by a collective anxiety that one could almost grasp. We had lost our leader. No doubt many of the garrison knew Sir Henry well enough to feel a personal grief, a private sense of loss, but for most of us his thin stooped figure had come to mean an embodiment of decision and of wisdom. Who could take his place? The fear we had begun to accustom ourselves to surged up into something like panic. All day the guns spat viciously, the bullets whined and buildings crumbled under the fire; but, for all the noise of war, the enclosure was quiet with a heavy, inward quiet as men reckoned their chances, eyes meeting eyes in silent question, and women sat in the smothering darkness of their quarters, trying to come to terms with terror.

'A disaster, Miss Laura! I have no hesitation in expressing myself so strongly. A disaster! The worst that could befall us!'

Mr Roberts had called in on us soon after hearing the news. He carried a rifle, as did every other man but, unlike the other men, he managed to look neat and almost as clean as usual. Kate, too, for the first time in three days, was sharing the gloom and heat of our kitchen, and the four of us sat round the table talking.

'What is to happen to us now I cannot think,' went on Mr Roberts. 'We may have days to wait before the relief arrives, and who is there among us who can take Sir Henry's place?'

'I believe Sir Henry himself had appointed Major Banks his successor, circumventing old Buggins, which I am sure old Buggins will not like,' said Kate.

'Ah! A successor is one thing, but Banks is not of the same calibre.'

'No, but a good soldier and a good administrator. And then there is Jack Inglis. He'll do too, Mr Roberts, he'll do. They won't replace Sir Henry, certainly, but one man's death should not strip us of all hope, surely?'

'What is the old saw about the hour producing the man?' I asked.

'We must hope so, Miss Laura. We must hope so. But when you reckon the odds against us ... well, this is truly a blow!' He mopped his forehead and then took off his spectacles and polished them. I had never seen him without them before and he looked bare and somehow lost as he screwed up his eyes to see what he was doing.

'Why ... why ...' He shook his head in unbelief and gestured with his spectacles. 'Do you know that it is reckoned that the insurgents have something like forty thousand men to draw on? Forty thousand men well armed and well trained!'

'Forty thousand!' gasped Emily. 'But that's a terrible number. We can't have anything like that on our side, can we?'

'No, Mrs Flood, nothing like that. We have perhaps fourteen *hundred* dependable men within this stockade; that is without the Sikhs, of course, of whose loyalty much doubt is felt and not only by myself.' Having made his point, Mr Roberts replaced his spectacles on his nose with an air of accomplishment.

'Heavens! Then ...'

'Yes, my dear! We are in a very bad situation. Very bad. And now Sir Henry's death has compounded it indeed.' He had no idea of the effect his words were having on Emily, whose eyes had filled with frightened tears as she listened to him.

'And now this news from Cawnpore ...' our visitor continued.

'Cawnpore? What news is there from Cawnpore?' Kate asked suspiciously.

'You mean you have not heard?'

'Only what everyone else has heard—that Wheeler has been forced to treat with the Nana Sahib.'

'Ah, but there is more, I'm afraid. Mind you, it's not official yet, but it is being said that Mr Gubbins has received information that there has been some further trouble in Cawnpore. Treachery on the part of the Nana, most probably, and that there are no survivors of the garrison. But, as I say, I have not heard this from any official source, and one must bear in mind the potency of rumour in a situation like the present one.'

'No survivors? It can't be, Mr Roberts. Surely it cannot be?'

'So it is said, Miss Laura. Had you any friends in Cawnpore?'

'No, that is, there is a possibility that Mr Erskine was there.'

'Mr Erskine? But why should he be in Cawnpore, of all places? I can understand that if life in Hassanganj proved untenable he might want to reach Lucknow, but Cawnpore, after all, is quite out of his way.'

'I hope you are right, but Toddy-Bob thinks he had some business to attend to there, and ... and I know he had friends there about whom he was anxious.'

'Well, that is unfortunate. If, of course, there is anything to this rumour, and there very well may not be. We must remember that.'

Kate caught my eye across the table and smiled to reassure me, then turned her attention to Mr Roberts.

'This is not the time, Mr Roberts, as I thought you would have had the good sense to realize, to repeat rumours! And that is ...' But she was interrupted by Emily, who, though she had followed the conversation, was obviously not thinking of Cawnpore.

'But Kate, is it true—are there really so many pandies against us? Because if there are, then we have no hope, have we? How can we possibly keep them off? Oh, Laura, we are all going to be killed, aren't we?' Emily began to weep.

'Now do you see what you have done, Mr Roberts? You've scared the poor little creature out of her wits. You really have no business to go around spreading alarm in this fashion. Surely we all have enough to contend with?' Kate spoke wrathfully, while I comforted Emily. Mr Roberts, honestly surprised at being taken so seriously, stood up in some confusion.

'My dear Mrs Flood, forgive me. I had no idea that you could still be in ignorance of the true position. I was just making plain the facts as I see them, and I certainly had no wish to add to your ...'

'Yes, yes, Mr Roberts, but I think we have had enough hard facts for one morning. I am sure you are needed somewhere else.' And without further ceremony, Kate opened the door and ushered him out, still apologizing.

'Hush now, Emily! He's a fussy little man and can't see the wood for the trees. Don't cry, child. There is absolutely no way of knowing how many men are on the other side of the wall; no responsible man would even hazard a guess, so pay no attention to Mr Roberts.'

Kate sat down again. 'Sure, and don't I know 'em. They're all alike, these know-all, fussbody civilians, and never a one of 'em has laid eyes on any angry man. Figures! Statistics! Information! They never reckon on such a thing as fighting spirit! And what's more, there is one fact that our Mr Roberts is doing his best not to face, and that is that he is plain scared himself!' She sniffed her disapproval. 'So cheer up now, Emmie. He doesn't know what he's talking about, believe me. We'll manage without Sir Henry if we have to, and without Mr Roberts's forty thousand men too. Irresponsible creature that he is!' She sniffed again.

'I hope there is really no truth in the other matter he mentioned,' I said.

'Oh, couldn't be, woman dear. Just Mr Roberts again; though, mind you, old Buggins is almost as much of an alarmist himself. The

Nana Sahib would never descend to treachery. Remember he was a friend of ours. To fight us is one thing. But treachery? Never!'

'What were you saying about Oliver? Is he really in Cawnpore?' Emily asked through her handkerchief as she wiped her nose.

'Toddy-Bob said he might have gone there, but just for a few days. On some business he had to attend to in regard to Hassanganj, I suppose,' I replied, deliberately vague.

'Then he'd have been with General Wheeler, Laura?'

'Not he! You should know him better than that, Em. Can you see him joining the military? In anything?'

'Well, I do hope not, because if there has been trouble in Cawnpore, then he might be involved in it.'

'Never! He is undoubtedly safe in Hassanganj and happily reconciled to remaining there until all this is finished. He must know that he could not get through the city to reach us, and so remaining in Hassanganj would be the commonsense thing to do. He'll turn up in due course, when all the unpleasantness is over.'

'Oh, I do hope so! And I wish he was here now, even though I know I sound selfish. I really do; I'd feel so much safer if he were here.'

My tone to Emily had been robust and reassuring, but my mind was far from quiet on Oliver's account. What if, despite his avowed opinions and probable desires, he had somehow become involved in the trouble at Cawnpore? And what if there truly had been treachery on the part of the Nana Sahib? What if …?

But such conjecture was fruitless, and I resolved not to harbour any hypothetical anxiety to add its weight to my actual burdens.

That evening, Sir Henry Lawrence was buried in the churchyard on the river side of the enclosure, sewn up in a grey blanket and in a common grave with eleven other men who had died during the day. Not even for him was there room for a separate grave, or time or labour to dig one. The barrage continued without interruption during the brief service. No bugle sounded as they laid Sir Henry to rest so hurriedly, no solemn roll of drums, no Last Post, no fusillade of honour. Only the rifles and round shot and shell blast of the men whom he once had commanded— on both sides of the barricade.

CHAPTER 7

George Barry, thinking they would prefer it, had arranged for all three Hassanganj volunteers, Charles, Toddy-Bob and Ishmial, to serve together at Fayrer's battery, but the day after the death of Sir Henry Lawrence Toddy-Bob dropped in to tell us that he had 'fixed himself up' at Gubbins's battery instead and, since he would have to sleep there, we would be seeing rather less of him. I was careful not to enquire how Toddy had managed to bring about this transfer; his transactions, of whatever nature, were generally better left severely to him; but I did ask why he had wanted it.

'I thought you had no use for Mr Gubbins, Tod?' I said. 'Why the sudden desire to fight at his battery?'

'Well, and that's true enough, Miss Laura; 'e's not a character as I can admire personal like, not knowing the amount of rumours and such like as is going about regardin' him, 'specially now. You've 'eard that 'e's kickin' up a ruckus about Sir 'Enry appointing Major Banks to take over from 'im?' I nodded. 'And, Miss Laura, did you know that it was 'e who nagged Sir 'Enry into going out to Chinhat? Told 'im it were 'is duty to make an example of the pandies as were comin' from Cawnpore, 'e did. Sir 'Enry, they say, didn't like the idea at all, not knowin' just 'ow many of them there would be, like, but 'e went out because old Gubbins pushed 'im to it. And look what 'appened then!'

'That's the merest gossip, Tod,' I said sternly. 'We have no business to believe such things. It won't do any good to rake it up now that it's finished.'

'Oh, but it ain't just gossip, Miss Laura! I knows a chap as was at the Residency steps when Sir 'Enry galloped in after the battle, and 'is first words were—and this is true, so 'elp me, Miss Laura—'is first words were: "Well, Gubbins has had his way and I 'opes 'e 'as 'ad enough of it!" Them's 'is words exact!'

'Then why ever are you so anxious to protect his house?'

'Simple, Miss Laura. Because of what's in it!'

'Oh, Toddy!' I said more in sorrow than in anger, while Emily giggled.

'Well now, Miss Laura, you knows 'as 'ow I wouldn't do anythin' dishonest, like. But it's come to my notice that a man can come by a fair amount of stuff at that battery, and all quite legitimate. Buggins hands out cigars and sugar and even beer, so they tell me, and I got to thinkin' there was no use passin' by such an opportunity. Never knows when we might need a little somethin' extra, for the nipper perhaps or if one of us got took sick, so it's best that I should be there. That's all.'

'Well, it's a good safe place, I gather, and Mr Gubbins was in a position to provision it adequately, so I hope you will be happy there. But don't forget us, Tod. We'll miss not having you here.'

'Gawd love you, no, miss. I shan't forget you. Not till the Guv'nor gets in leastways, and after that, well, I'll be free to mind me own business. Not that it's any 'ardship keepin' an eye on you, mind, but a body gets to feel a bit tied all the same.'

'You feel tied to—me?'

'Yes, miss, only natural as I would.'

'But how ... why ...?'

'Because the Guv'nor says 'as 'ow you was to be the special care of me and Ishmial. 'Spect he figured as 'ow Mr Charles would do right by Miss Emily, but you had no one, like,' he finished lamely.

'Well, that was very good of Mr Erskine, Toddy, and I appreciate his thoughtfulness, but please believe yourself as free as air. I am only too happy to exonerate you from all responsibility for my welfare.'

'That's as may be, miss, but the Guv'nor 'asn't said so, and I'd a deal sooner wait for the word from 'im.'

'Well ...'

'Oh, no trouble, miss! Leastways, I'd sooner put up with you than the trouble the Guv'nor would make for me if 'e were to find as 'ow I'd neglected me duty. So if you don't mind ...?'

'Well, so long as you want it your way. At least we understand each other, and I'll try not to be too much of a burden.'

'Thank you, miss.' And Toddy touched his cap and swayed off with his rolling gait, clutching his bedding roll to his bosom.

'Well, that's one mouth less to feed,' I said as he disappeared. 'I hope Mr Gubbins's largesse will come up to his expectations.'

'And how truly considerate of Oliver Erskine to give you *two* nursemaids!' remarked Emily acidly. 'Perhaps if he had known just how little comfort my husband would be to me, he might have let me have a share in one of them at least.'

'Oh, Emily, it's no good adopting that attitude, surely? Charles can't be here more than he is, and that's all there is to it. You must face up to it. We are as protected as anyone can be in this building and he knows it; you can't expect him to keep running in to see how you are doing every hour or so.'

'I have seen him for precisely forty-five minutes in the last twenty-four hours, Laura. I think he owes me more time than that.'

'And, Emily,' broke in Kate quietly, 'I think you owe him more understanding ... and indeed more sympathy. Use your imagination, girl! Have you any idea of what it is like trying to snatch some sleep, fully clothed, with a gun firing no more than a few feet from you every few minutes?'

'Then why doesn't he come and sleep here like a decent Christian?'

'Oh, you make me lose all patience, Emily! Do you think he wouldn't if he could?'

'Yes! Yes, I do think just that! I think he would much prefer to remain with the other men, in the ... the excitement and ... and companionship, than come here and have to remember his responsibilities as a husband and a father. He is just selfish!'

'Kind Lord Jesus, forgive her!' prayed Kate in exasperation. 'Emily, you are coming up for a good painful jolt, and I'll be glad to see you get it. And that's the truth.'

'Oh, of course, it's always I who am in the wrong! I must always pay for other people's mistakes, mustn't I? I've heard it all so often, from Charles and Laura and you, Kate, in your own way. I'm giddy and thoughtless and spoilt, and life has always treated me too kindly. Well, it's not treating me kindly now, is it? And it hasn't treated me kindly ever since we stepped on to that wretched boat to come out here. Nothing has gone right for me since—nothing! Charles doesn't care for me, doesn't even consider me as he should, and I'd like to have seen you, Kate Barry, having a baby in Hassanganj without even a proper midwife; and then that dreadful journey when we expected to be killed every minute, and now this! I didn't ask for any of it. I wasn't brought up to deal with these things, so it's not my fault if I can't. And … and it is, it *is* up to Charles to see that I don't suffer too much, whatever you say, Kate. I …' But here she burst into tears of tired indignation, and ran into the other room where the beds were, to weep in private.

'Lord, now what have I done?' said Kate contritely.

'Nothing more than I have wanted to do for some time,' I replied. 'It won't do much good though. But perhaps a good cry will clear the air for a while. We mustn't be too hard on her, Kate. She has had a harder time than you realize, and she is very young.'

'Weren't we all—once?'

'But we didn't have to put up with this!'

'You're right. I must learn to hold my tongue. All the same, m'dear, it was rather charming of Oliver to appoint Toddy as your bodyguard, now wasn't it?'

'Yes, it was. I only wish Toddy didn't let it weigh him down so.' And we both laughed.

She went back to her own quarters soon afterwards, and stayed away all next day to allow the upset to be forgotten. Emily was silent and sullen, and when Charles came in that evening pleaded the customary female headache and retired to her bed sooner than have to entertain him.

'Something the matter?' he whispered as she went. Everything said in the one room could be heard in the other.

I shrugged and shook my head with a finger against my lips.

'Oh!' he said, understanding, and then in his normal voice, 'Well, I can't be bothered with what's going on here, but we have one more serious worry, which will give you something else to think of, Emily.' Hearing her name, Emily came to the communicating archway and listened.

'Mining! The devil only knows why they want to go to the trouble of mining when one good assault would have them inside in no time, but if you girls hear anything unusual underfoot, you're to report it immediately, understand?'

'Mining? But what is it? I don't understand,' Emily objected irritably.

'Mining is mining—digging tunnels, burrowing if you like, under the ground till you think you are in the right spot to effect a breach. Then a barrel of powder, a fuse, a match and—whoosh!—up goes the tunnel, defences and all and, with any luck, you have your breach in the defences. That's all it is. Simple. And it could be deadly. So keep your ears open; not that I expect you're in a position to hear much in this place. But you never know.'

'What can be done about it?' I wondered. It seemed an intricate method of attaining a simple end, for I still did not realize what effect a breach would have, though I had a vivid mental picture of the defences themselves.

'We'll have to countermine. Drive our own tunnels towards the pandies', and blow theirs in before they can damage ours.'

'But how will we know where they are?' I objected.

'We'll hear 'em, that's how. As I said, you must listen for them, picks tap-tapping away at the earth, that sort of thing.'

'Much chance we have of hearing anything in this racket,' I pointed out, and set to work to prepare a meal.

The siege had been in progress for two or three days before I realized that the noise of gunfire would never stop. For some reason, mostly ignorance of how such matters are normally conducted, I had expected peace at night, at least after the initial effort, and perhaps a lull at midday, as though the combatants would keep normal working hours. But the firing never ceased and seldom even diminished by night or day. The pandies knew our weakness and their own strength, and it stood to their benefit to allow us no respite. If what Mr Roberts had said was true, if there were really between 40,000 and 60,000 men ranged against us, they could afford to man their guns every hour of the twenty-four. For us it was a different matter. And now this new threat of mining considerably increased the already acute sense of insecurity.

I think it was that same night that Pearl first refused the breast. She was now nearly three months old and, in spite of the alarms of her short existence, had given us very little trouble. She had a placid temperament, always until now had taken her food with enthusiasm, and had quickly accustomed herself to sleeping in any conditions. Now, she went off her food, and the sound of her almost perpetual, hungry little wail tired us more cruelly than the guns. Remembering how the *ayah* had given her sugar and water the day she was born, I tried to tempt her with a similar mixture, but she would have none of it. For two anxious days she tossed and fretted on her hot down pillow, a pitiful sight, with her small limbs covered with red heat rash and mosquito bites, and boils breaking out in the sweaty little joints of her legs and arms.

She became the focus of attention not only for Emily and myself, but for Kate and the menfolk as well. I never knew whether I wanted to laugh or cry as I watched Ishmial in his crossed bandoliers, his musket propped against the box, bending over and trying to soothe her. She seemed to get thinner and more white under the angry rash by the hour.

Dr Darby came in for a moment on the second day. The child wasn't ill: it was the heat, the conditions—he could do nothing. And he went away. Mrs Bonner, who had come in to hear his diagnosis, wagged her head in solemn agreement as he went.

'Ah, that'll be it, I expect. The heat decline. Poor mite, but there's nothing to be done.' She sighed and went back to her own room.

That evening, Toddy-Bob dodged on to the verandah, pulling behind him a goat on a piece of string. Our hearts leapt at the sight, but our consciences were still active, and we were too familiar with the way in which Toddy-Bob 'came by' things to be delighted.

'For the nipper,' he announced proudly, hauling the protesting animal into shelter. 'Very strengthening, goat's milk is.'

We regarded the prize in silence for a moment. It was a fine nanny with bulging udders.

'How—where did you get it, Tod?' asked Charles dutifully, but without really seeking enlightenment.

'Well now, sir, it were like this.' Toddy pushed back the sun helmet which he wore in place of the turban—his tall coachman's hat must by now have been forming an unusual part of the landscape of India. 'There was a lady lived up back of the Begum Kothi with seven of these 'ere useful creatures, and she turns a tidy penny sellin' the milk. Turned, that is!'

'Turned?'

'Yes, sir. She's dead. The cholera!'

'And so?'

'So, 'appenin' to 'ear of 'er goin' like, I nips up there at the double and buys it.'

'You *bought* it?' Surprise, not disbelief, made me emphasize the verb, but Toddy was offended.

'Yes, miss,' he confirmed with dignity. 'I bought it, with money. Me own money, too. A present for the nipper!'

'Oh, Toddy, forgive me! I certainly didn't mean to hurt your feelings. I think it is the most noble thing you could ever do. I was just so startled by seeing ... it ... and ...'

'That's all right, miss,' he conceded loftily. 'If you can find a jug, I'll see what I can do about milkin' 'er.'

'Oh, yes. Of course. You ... you can milk then?' I had been entertaining visions of having to attempt it myself.

'Well, no, miss. Not strictly speakin'. But I'm game to try.'

So he squatted down behind a pillar of the verandah and, watched interestedly by the rest of us from the doorway, in a surprisingly short time had mastered the knack and handed over a bowl of warm, frothy milk.

Pearl accepted it. We had to feed her with a spoon, but slow as the process was, it was exhilarating to see her bend her small head forward in her mother's arms for the next mouthful.

'Oh, Toddy, you are a dear,' smiled Emily, tears of relief in her eyes, while Charles clapped him on the back and declared him a 'capital fellow'. Toddy smiled deprecatingly and, accompanied by Ishmial, who was as delighted as the rest of us, took his gift round to the courtyard in the centre of the building where he hoped it would be relatively safe. There was no shelter for it, but when the rain came, our neighbours said, they would not object to it being tethered on the inner verandah.

Pearl, content at last, settled into a quiet, soft-breathing sleep, and her elders, for the first time in two days, took some interest in their own food.

Late that night, when the men had returned to their posts and Kate to her quarters, and just as Emily and I were preparing ourselves for sleep, there was a knock on our ramshackle door.

'Oh, drat! What now?' I grumbled, as I carried the lantern across the kitchen and opened the door.

A woman stood on the verandah, the largest woman it had ever been my experience to gaze on. Not that she was fat. Just big. She filled the frame of the six-foot door from top to bottom and from side to side so adequately that it could have been a coffin especially built to hold her.

I blinked, too surprised to speak.

'Are you the leddy with the goat?' she asked without preamble as I looked at her. My heart sank at the words. Dead of the cholera indeed!

Here, truly larger than life, was the rightful owner of our most valued quadruped.

I nodded, still speechless, but now with alarm.

'I saw it without in the bittie court,' the woman went on, 'and a fine milkin' animal it is. I'm a proud woman, and not one to beg, but, mam, 'tis my laddie, my wee Jamie! He's awful sickly, and though I have more milk than a dozen nannies, it'll no bide in his belly. Too rich it is for him, poor mite. But I was thinkin', when I saw the goat, if I could mebbe have a wee drop of its milk and add water to it, the bairn might settle.'

'Oh! Is that all? You only want some of the milk—not, not the ...?'

'Yes, mam,' said the woman, looking me straight in the eye. 'That's all. A wee drop o' the milk for my Jamie.'

'Why, yes! Of course. We have plenty.'

Relief made me generous. We had each had milk in our tea that evening, but there was ample remaining. I ushered her into the kitchen.

'Who is it?' Emily wanted to know from the bedroom, and when I explained, echoed my offer, so I made our visitor sit down and poured out a cupful of the milk.

'Now, you drink this yourself first,' I said. 'I'm sure you've seen no more milk than we have, and will enjoy it. And when you've finished, I'll refill the cup for your little boy.'

The woman lowered herself on to a chair, her bulk seeming to fill the small room. I hung the lantern on its hook and, as she sipped with small, obviously 'company' sips, I examined her.

In spite of her height, she held herself as straight as a ramrod, not stooping, as do so many tall women to disguise their inches. She was neatly dressed in a grey gown covered by a spotless apron. Her large flat face was homely and the expression in her pale eyes stern; her nose was long and thin, her mouth wide; her head was crowned with heavy braids of magnificent auburn hair. Face and figure together gave an impression of quiet but massive strength.

'Thank you kindly, mam,' she said when she finished the milk and put the cup down in the mathematical centre of the table. In spite of her size, or perhaps because of it, she was extremely precise in all her movements, and sat with her large feet close together and in perfect alignment with each other.

'You're welcome,' I replied. 'Now, let me rinse your cup and then I'll refill it for Jamie.'

'Thank you kindly,' she said again. 'My name's MacGregor, mam, Jessie MacGregor. My man was Corporal James MacGregor of the 32nd—killed at Chinhat. It's like as if the bairn kens he has no daddy now. It breaks my heart to see him just lying below in his bit bed, never greetin', or eatin', or movin'.'

'You've had the doctor to him, Mrs MacGregor?'

'Oh aye—he came! But he could do nowt. He said the bairn had the fever, but there was nae physic to give him. So I havena' been after him again. He has enough to do above in the hospital wi' the laddies, the good Lord kens.'

She got up.

'Come back in the morning for some more milk,' I said. 'And I do hope it will do your Jamie good. My cousin's little girl took it gladly, so perhaps Jamie will too.'

'That's my hope,' she answered briefly, then added, 'You're right kind and Christian, mam, and may the Lord have his hand on you.'

When she had gone, I realized that I had not even commiserated with her on the death of her husband. I recalled that morning scene as we had watched the 32nd, bawdily cheerful even if unfed, march off to Chinhat. So one of them had been Corporal James MacGregor. But after all, what was there that I, a stranger, could say to his wife? I put out the lantern and went to bed.

CHAPTER 8

No rain had fallen since the great storm on the evening of our arrival in the Residency, and its absence was regarded with mixed feelings by the garrison. The military element was glad of the respite and made use of it to continue the work of strengthening the fortifications, even under constant fire. Many of the buildings were by now so badly shaken by the barrage that the first heavy rain would bring them down; so every day's delay in the arrival of the monsoon was valuable in providing time to strengthen and repair those that could be repaired, or for providing alternative arrangements for the people still living in the houses that were beyond hope. But for the rest of us, everyone, and particularly the women, longed and even prayed for the rains to break. Cooped up in stifling rooms with doors and windows shuttered against the gunfire, we were driven half mad by prickly heat, boils, insects and by boredom.

But day after insufferable day the sun glowered in the haze of a colourless sky, oppressive and exhausting, and we moved in a daylong twilight, drenched in perspiration, scratching ourselves raw, unable to find a remedy even for the flies that tormented us. They were everywhere: small nimble black ones, and slow iridescent bluebottles, all plump and active as a result of good living on the carcasses of the dead and the wounds of the living. They swarmed over our food in droves, drowned themselves in our precious milk, crawled busily over bare arms and faces, stuck to our eyelids, even entered our mouths as we spoke or ate. Their constant hum and buzz mingled with the high whine of the mosquitoes that attacked us the moment we were still, and the noise and the nuisance frayed our patience to snapping point a dozen times an hour. Cockroaches lurked in the corners of the rooms; the string beds harboured bedbugs; sometimes scorpions scuttled in, tails up, out of the heat; and fleas hopped visibly on the earth floor.

We had no remedies for these pests and, though we suffered from them acutely, they were more easily disregarded than the smell, which rose steadily in the continued dry heat to really stupefying proportions.

I use the singular advisedly, for although many odours formed the components, their combination produced one loathsome, inescapable and indescribable effluvium of filth and decay, which penetrated the remotest corners, clung to clothing, skin and hair, and settled over the entrenchment like an evil miasma.

The chief trouble was that we had no adequate means of disposing of the dead—either human or animal. Before his death, Sir Henry Lawrence had given orders regarding the slaughter and burial of all superfluous animals, but the Battle of Chinhat had intervened and we were besieged before the directives could be carried out. On the day following Chinhat, most of the native labour had decamped, leaving the burial pits for the animals undug, and it had been considered ghoulish to prepare too many graves for the garrison in advance. So now, having finished their duties at gun battery or shot-step, the men went directly to work on the pits; many collapsed, several died at this work, from exhaustion, heatstroke and enemy fire. Still the animals sometimes lay for days where they had died before time could be found to haul them away and bury them. Then it became the practice for such carcasses to be thrown over the wall down near the Slaughter House, along with the entrails and viscera of the gun-bullocks that were systematically slaughtered to form our meat ration; yet this, while it spared the garrison the sight of horses, bullocks, even camels falling to gelatinous shreds in the heat, did nothing to sweeten the air.

Human remains met a fate that was hardly better, merely a little more dignified. The graveyard was in a peculiarly vulnerable position and each night one mass grave only, necessarily shallow for lack of time, was scratched out of the baked earth. There, each evening, that day's toll was buried and covered hastily with a layer of dry, friable soil and a sprinkling of lime or charcoal. The stench of decay was so appalling that frequently the men on grave duty or the mourners at funerals were carried back fainting to their quarters.

Nor was this all. The sanitary arrangements, always primitive in India, suffered as much as the grave-digging for lack of labour; few sweepers remained to dispose of what was gently referred to as 'night soil', and what arrangements there were were inadequate for the swollen population now occupying the entrenchment. Drains were blocked by fallen masonry and everywhere water and excrement gathered in nauseous open puddles, breeding flies.

Smoke hung low in the hot air, smoke from the guns and from the multitude of wood and charcoal fires on which we cooked, and mingled its fumes with the acrid smell of cordite, the sour scent of sweaty bodies, and the limey odour of shattered masonry. And everywhere the yellow dust seeped in as ubiquitously, as pervasively, as the smell.

When Emily fell ill, it was natural to attribute her fever and lack of appetite to the terrible odour, and at first I did not allow myself to worry. We were comparatively safe in the Gaol; we had milk for Emily and Pearl, and, as well, I had hoarded a few other small comforts brought to us from time to time by Toddy-Bob, Mr Roberts and Wallace Avery—sugar, a few candles, a tin of biscuits, a tinned tongue and a bottle of cologne—this last from Toddy-Bob! Emily could not eat anything I prepared from our daily rations, but warm milk sweetened with sugar was nourishing and more than many other invalids had.

'It's the tertiary ague,' Mrs Bonner had announced when she looked in on Emily. 'No doubt of it. I've been a martyr to it, off and on, for twenty years. Very trying, my dear Mrs Flood, very debilitating, but not fatal, I do assure you. Just look at me!' And all her many chins wobbled in a chuckle. 'Just keep her quiet, Miss Hewitt, and, of course, if I can be of any use, you must just let me know.'

'Well—it could be,' Kate said dubiously when I told her of Mrs Bonner's diagnosis, 'but I think the fever is too high. We must pray it is not a contagion. Try to keep her cool. Let me stay here tonight, my dear. I can be of some use in fanning her, at least.'

I gratefully accepted her offer and we took it in turns to wield the palm-leaf fan for hours on end, but on the third day Emily's fever rose alarmingly, red spots appeared on her face and we knew she had smallpox.

Ajeeba had told us—how long ago it now seemed—that once smallpox entered a house, it would go through it 'like an evil wind'. We had thought that in escaping from Wajid Khan's house we had escaped also the contamination of the disease, and perhaps we had; but only to find it awaiting us in the Residency.

As soon as the spots appeared, I sent Charles for a doctor—any doctor—but it was hours before one could spare a moment to come.

When he did arrive, Dr Darby took Emily's pulse, examined the spots and shrugged hopelessly.

'I can do nothing,' he sighed. 'If she has a good constitution and good care, she'll pull through. Others have. I have some headache powders I'll send you, but that's all. When she becomes delirious, she'll be reaching the crisis. Let me know and I'll look in again. I wish to God I could be of more help, but …' He shrugged again and went away wearing the angrily hopeless expression that all our doctors wore.

For three days and nights Charles, Kate and I watched beside the sick girl. There was little we could do apart from fanning her and keeping away the flies. The fever made her increasingly restless, dried her mouth and cracked her lips, but we had no salve with which to ease them. From somewhere (and we did not ask) Toddy-Bob produced a beautiful cut-glass jug full of barley water, which we made her sip, and we tried greasing her lips with morsels of butter that we also owed to Toddy.

Between his duties at Fayrer's battery and his watch beside his wife, Charles slept even less than the invalid. One night, while I stood and watched him drink a cup of tea I had taken him, I realized he had grown old before my eyes. Never robustly built, he was now so thin that his fingernails looked too big for his fingers. His moustache was untrimmed, his eyes sunken, and furrows had appeared on the brow I remembered smooth and bland with confident well-being. Worst of all was the expression of despairing guilt in the eyes that met mine briefly in the wavering light of the candle.

'Pray, Laura,' he whispered as he gave me the cup. 'Pray that she lives. I must have time, just time, to earn her forgiveness. If she dies, it will be the end of my life too.'

'I do pray—constantly,' I told him.

'God!' he muttered, holding his head in his thin hands so that I had difficulty hearing him. 'I would so gladly suffer and die in her stead. So gladly. I have even told her so, but she always turns away from me. If only she will live, I will teach her to come to me with love. Oh, Laura, she must not die!'

Remorse is a poor substitute for love, I thought to myself, and it's a poor woman who cannot tell the difference. But, naturally, I held my tongue.

'I am rested and will stay with her now, Charles,' I said. 'It is time you took some sleep. You do her no good by neglecting your own health.' But he would not leave her bedside, so I joined him in his watch and together we sat the noisy night through to the dawn.

We had been besieged for a fortnight—an eternity. It had been six weeks since we had left Hassanganj.

Only six weeks ago our lives had been secure, comfortable, holding out the hope and indeed the expectation of all the small, important factors from which we humans build our happiness, with however much trial and travail.

Only six weeks ago all that we had gone through, all that we had suffered, all that we were now anticipating was not only outside our experience but beyond our imagination. Six weeks had been sufficient to cleave a chasm that could never be spanned between the girl I had been and the woman I now was.

I thought with a bitter humour of the self-contained, smug, all-knowing creature who had so often congratulated herself on her handling of the silly storms at Mariaon and Hassanganj, who had felt so worldly wise at being able to deal even with the vagaries of Mr Erskine's domestic affairs without self-betrayal. All those teacup tempests, the Avery finances, Emily's unwanted pregnancy, the discovery of Moti's status, Pearl's birth. How they had exercised me, and yet how unimportant they had been, how small, in relation to the last great fact of death which I was now confronting. Emily might not die of the smallpox, but what was there to assure me that I would not? I knew how contagious the disease was, and how devastating, and, as I cooled her brow with cologne, I could not help wondering how soon I might be lying in Emily's place. If I were to succumb and face death even more nearly, how would my life appear to my dying mind? Would I be satisfied with what I had fashioned of my days?

Charles, bent over the single candle, was reading from Emily's little black-morocco Bible, and I was alone with my thoughts.

To know that there are no more chances, I said to myself; no possibility of explanation or apology; no time to make amends. Knowing that, what would be in the forefront of my consciousness? As though in answer to my question, the little room was shattered with sound as a shell exploded against a wall opposite our windows and forced the flare of its flame through the cracks in the ill-made shutters, briefly lighting the room. Charles looked up with a frown, and then went back to the Bible.

Mistakes, I said to myself, my mind lightened as suddenly and as brightly as the room had been. Mistakes! How often I had been mistaken. How grossly, wilfully, I had chosen to misunderstand not only the people around me, but myself. How easily I had always missed the substance for the shadow, and how beguiled I had been by empty appearances. Yet I had liked to think of myself as judicious, cool, balanced, not easily swayed. I had even persuaded myself that I detected the recognition of these qualities in others' eyes. Yet all I had really been was a shallow, self-contained, selfish girl, almost as ignorant as Emily—but Emily at least had never had pretensions to superior wisdom and worth as I had had.

Self-knowledge is bought with pain, and I winced as I recognized the presumption and pride in my own character and remembered my many lost opportunities to give understanding to others. If I had not indulged my infatuation for Charles, I would have known, much sooner, how Emily had suffered in her marriage; and if Emily had not felt that Charles's love was mine, she might have found it possible to give him the affection she had deflected to Oliver Erskine. Had I been able to accept the reality of Charles, instead of clothing him in the romantic dreams of a girl, perhaps my response to Oliver's declaration of love could have been more affirmative. So many mistakes, misunderstandings, misconceptions! It would be regret for these that filled my mind in my last moments, and as I mulled them over, strong and living, the last one returned to fill my heart with unbearable poignancy. Oh, Oliver, where are you? Where are you? I cried silently in the unsilent dark.

As soon as the smallpox had appeared, Mrs Bonner had taken Pearl into her room to save her from infection, but explained that, under the circumstances, that was as much as she could do. With her own 'dear ones' to think of, she could not be expected to run the danger of contagion by helping to nurse Emily. Since no one had asked her to help, no one quarrelled with her refusal to do so. But Emily missed Pearl, and a dozen times a day I tried to explain why the child could not be with her mother. Often in her restless sleep Emily would mutter audibly to herself and, sitting beside her, I would catch the word 'Pearl' reiterated with anxious love. On one such occasion, after a flow of incomprehensible words, she smiled sweetly in her sleep and said with great tenderness 'My love ... Oliver.' Charles was in the room with me; as he caught the words, he looked at me, then knelt down and buried his face against his wife's sick body, and I saw his shoulders shake with sobs.

On the third night of the smallpox, Emily seemed easier, and I lay down to rest, hopeful that she would indeed 'pull through' as the doctor had said. Perhaps she would have recovered—many others did, despite the lack of medicine and proper care—but early on the following morning the dreadful symptoms of cholera appeared, and at three o'clock the same afternoon she died. She would have been nineteen years old in a few weeks' time.

We were all with her when she went, except the baby. Charles held her hand, Kate and I knelt by her bed. Toddy-Bob was in the kitchen whittling into the fireplace and Ishmial sat cross-legged just inside the kitchen door, with his musket across his knees and an expression of deep dejection on his face.

Emily had been unconscious for some time and only Kate, I believe, realized how near the end was. None of us knew the moment her soul slipped from her body. Then a waxy blueness spreading around her lips told us she was no more. Charles leaned his head on her hand and wept despairingly, and Kate, with tears streaming down her face, joined her hands, bent her head and began the *De Profundis*:

'Out of the depths I have cried unto Thee, O Lord,
Lord, hear my prayer and let my cry come unto Thee ...'

Her voice faltered, then rose again, intoning David's great song of lamentation, while outside the guns roared, and inside the whine of mosquitoes rose to a crescendo. That day the barrage was particularly heavy, for a couple of days earlier the mutineers had swarmed into the tall house of an Armenian merchant named Johannes that stood only a few feet outside our walls. They had posted snipers in the tower and installed several heavy guns, which were now showering us with an extraordinary assortment of missiles, from nails and bolts to ramrods and tins packed with splintered glass. But we heard nothing of the noise that afternoon. Only the mosquitoes and Kate's voice praying.

We did not have much time to prepare Emily's body for the evening burial.

Charles clung to Emily, and Kate needed all her powers of persuasion to make him leave the room. At length he calmed down sufficiently for

Toddy-Bob and Ishmial to lead him away somewhere to recover, and Kate and I set to work. I had no tears, though I would gladly have wept, but the strain of the last hours had given me a headache so bad that I could hardly see as I moved about the room doing Kate's bidding. We washed the wasted body and dressed Emily in her only spare gown, a flowered poplin with lace collars and cuffs. Then I combed her hair, rebraided it and wound it around her head. The smallpox marks were already fading in the pallor of death, but her face bore no memorial of the young girl who had left Mount Bellew. It was a mask, no more; vacant, bluish-white, the purple lips drawn back from the teeth and the protruding cheekbones deepening the violet under the sunken eyes. She looked old, and I was frightened. Kate remembered to remove her rings and handed them to me for safekeeping. Slipping them into my pocket, so that later I could give them to Charles, I remembered poor Emily's wedding day and the pride with which she had danced around the drawing-room showing us her newly bedecked hand.

We had no winding-sheet or shroud, so, crossing her thin hands on her breast, we laid her on a clean grey blanket from my bed and sewed her up in it.

At sunset Ishmial, the strongest of our men, carried her down to the cemetery in his arms like a child, followed by Charles, Toddy and Mr Roberts. Wallace Avery did not yet know of his cousin's death. Women were forbidden the graveyard, so Kate and I could only stand on the verandah with our neighbours and watch the strange little procession move away into the growing dimness. When it had disappeared from view, the other ladies on the verandah murmured their sympathy and went back to their rooms. Kate kissed me and made her way back to the King's Hospital to rest.

Pearl was still with Mrs Bonner, so for the first time since our arrival in the Residency I was absolutely alone in the two small rooms.

No doubt it would have been more correct of me to pray, or perhaps to read the Bible, but I could not endure the idea of sitting still, so, sooner than move aimlessly about the rooms, I decided to give them a thorough cleaning. Ignoring orders to the contrary, I threw open the windows and doors leading on to the two verandahs, seized the twig broom, which was all I had to work with, and swept every inch of the floors, having first pushed our few pieces of furniture outside the doors. Then I swilled water over the hard earth floor, and, while it dried, stripped Emily's bed; heedless of our shortage of such necessities, I piled the soiled mattress and her blanket and Kashmir shawl (which we had used to protect her limbs from mosquitoes and flies), together with the few garments she had used while ill, all together in a heap in the inner courtyard and set fire to them. The goat, tethered near by, looked on with its full yellow eyes, chewing placidly the while, and desultorily flicked an ear.

The flames took hold, leaping upwards briefly in the steamy malodorous twilight, and I sat on the verandah steps watching them, holding my aching head in my hands, suddenly drained of all will, all energy.

What had happened to them? Where had they really gone? The Wilkinses and Elvira, Moti, Connie and Johnny, Emily? Even the *sowar* in the forest clearing? They had all, in one way or another, affected my life so deeply. Where were they now?

In Heaven, the parsons would say; in eternity. In oblivion, my sceptic father would have answered me. I had no doubt that I would, personally, infinitely prefer oblivion to the conventional idea of Heaven, yet I could not rid myself of a stubborn desire to believe in some form of continuance for the human spirit after death. Mere conceit, I heard my father say, a symptom of the self-love in which we foolish mortals pass our days. But it could be some ancestral common sense. I found it then, I find it now, difficult to believe that personality is more ephemeral even than the memories it holds—or leaves behind.

How potent such memories may be, I discovered for myself that evening. Because I was so tired and bewildered, because I had so long suppressed my emotions, they now took revenge on me, and I found myself imagining the dead alive, all with such vividness and clarity that I heard their voices ringing in the deserted courtyard, remembered the style and colour of their clothing and seemed to glimpse their characteristic gait and gestures in the gathering obscurity of the evening. Mrs Wilkins in her purple dolman trimmed with bugle beads of jet, Emily's green sprig muslin dress, poor Elvira in her girlish and unsuitable white, and Connie in the bedraggled yellow gown at the ball. I could smell them too. Connie always smelled more strongly of peppermint even than of gin, and Mrs Wilkins moved in an aura of patchouli, while everything that Emily owned was scented with violet cologne.

It was, however, the clearly heard and immediately recognized tones of their voices—each individual voice, carrying to me across time and the grave—that affected me most poignantly, and I turned my head in consternation from point to point, searching for the beings who uttered the words I had forgotten but now heard spoken.

'I think we shall do very well in India!' Oh, Emily, in the pride of life! She had such a light voice, like a child's. And then the deeper tones of Mrs Wilkins, rather vulgar. 'I'm a saving sort of a woman, and it will be there when you want it.' 'Come Polly, good Polly, say it after me, "Good girl, Connie, good girl!" ' ... . And Elvira's customary squeak, 'Oh lawks!' Then I seemed to see a swirl of gauze above the shine of satin pyjamas in the smoke of the fire, and heard—I swear I heard it— the glassy tinkle of Moti's innumerable bangles.

I shook my head, half laughing and half weeping at the lively memories of the dead that played about me so insistently, and took myself in hand. This would not do. I was edging myself into hysteria, and there was Pearl to think of. Soon she must be washed and fed and put to sleep. So consciously I shut my mind, forbidding all associations entrance, and tried for a few moments to live solely in my senses.

It was still hot and the reflected warmth of the courtyard walls beat down upon me. I made myself experience inch by inch the feel of warm air on my bare arms, neck and face. I licked my lips and tasted the salt sweat. My feet, encased in heavy shoes, were swollen and painful, and my dress, whose bodice stuck to my damp body like a plaster, dragged the slatternly folds of its dirty skirt in the dust. Smoke from the pyre of bedding filled my eyes, throat and nose, but the scent, I suddenly realized, was pleasanter by far than the air we normally breathed, and I gulped it in thankfully. The noise of the guns, unremitting as ever, I hardly heard, but when a flight of fruit bats passed across the murky sky, the slow clap of their leathern wings drew my eyes upwards.

Looking around me, I discovered that there were others beside myself in the courtyard I had thought deserted. A couple of women bent over a tiny fire built on the wide verandah, and in a corner three children played with a box on wheels, loading it with stones, then sending it crashing against the building to upset and lie, wheels spinning, on the summit of its load. Not far from them, a man with a bandage round his head and another on his leg lay propped against the plinth of the verandah, rifle by his side. He was asleep.

In the centre of the courtyard stood a tree. The upper branches had been shot away and, since none lay below it, I could guess that they had been gathered for fuel almost as they fell. The leaves had withered and most had fallen, killed by the drought perhaps, or more probably by the fumes of cordite and gunpowder, and the tree stood bare and broken, raising truncated limbs to the bloodshot sky. I could not make out from what remained what type of tree it was. Yet squirrels still inhabited it, the small grey squirrels that are an integral part of any Indian garden. Fascinated by this mercurial, chattering life sustained by the dying tree, I watched them flick their bushy tails over the three black fingermarks that Rama's blessing had left on their neat little bodies, beady eyes bright, small claws twinkling up and down and along the branches, noisy and aggressive, screaming imprecations at imagined insults, then stopping suddenly to wash a face or scratch behind an ear with total concentration. They were alive. Each small body was filled with all the life it could hold or, for the moment, needed. Perhaps they were hungry, for who could spare them a crumb? But they knew no fear, no foreboding, no loss, no recognition of mortality. They did not even know they were alive—as I now knew I was alive.

And I *was* alive. Still alive.

My head ached, my eyes burned, my throat was scorched and my feet hurt. I was tired to a point beyond exhaustion. My clothes were adequate only to cover my nakedness. My body smelled and my hands were filthy. My hair, long unwashed and soggy with sweat, had not been combed in a day and a night. I hated the feeling of my own unkemptness and cringed at the picture I must present. I feared the present, saw no hope in the future, could not endure the thought of the past—but for all that I was alive.

Soon it was too dark for me to see the squirrels in the ruined tree. The children were called indoors to eat and the wounded man hoisted himself to his feet with the aid of his rifle and limped away. One of the women on the verandah doused the little fire with a cup of water, while the other carried a pan of food into their room. A comparative silence fell with the darkness. Only the guns remained and I no longer heard them; for, sitting alone in the dark heat of that unhappy night, I formed a fierce determination to stay alive. It was more than a determination. It was a presentiment, a foreknowledge that I *would* survive. I could not have analysed how I arrived at this resolve, this certainty, but I remember hugging it to myself, exultant in the midst of grief and shock and loneliness. 'I will live!' I kept saying to myself, half as statement, half as resolution. 'I will live! I will live!' I would meet whatever came— sickness, injury, anguish. I would meet it and endure it and vanquish it. And I would live actively, meeting my days with open eyes and a pliable mind, in the knowledge that I was living the only life I would have to live. I would adopt no acceptable role of patient endurance; I would wear no admired mask of resigned suffering. Acceptance, I suddenly realized, was the virtue of the inert. But I was alive ... and I would fight my life in order to live it.

Over the past weeks I had become an unwilling intimate of death. I had seen it come to the young and the old in horrible forms, had witnessed the dissolution of healthy bodies, and every nauseating breath I took reminded me of what lay in wait for my own tired bones and aching limbs should I succumb. But I would not succumb. I could not succumb.

For another voice I now remembered with the clarity of life spoke to me, with other words—words which forbade me the ease of death. As I remembered, I spoke them over softly to myself, knowing them to be a true memory and no fancied whisper from beyond the grave.

'I will come to you—for you!'

His tone, as always, had been cool and unemotional. He had stated a matter of fact, and that fact I now believed in as surely as I had learned to believe in my own survival. He would come and I must be ready and waiting for him. That was why I must live, why I *would* live.

At last I stood up wearily to go indoors. The fire had fallen to a heap of white ashes and glowing sparks, all that was left of the earthly remnants of my cousin Emily.

Before I turned away from the fire and the night, I shut my eyes and prayed aloud, 'Oh, God, please let him come as he said he would. Oh, God! Please let him come soon. Soon!'

CHAPTER 9

The rains broke in earnest at last, and within hours the entrenchment had become a morass of mud and evil-smelling slush. While the rain fell, we could rejoice honestly in the sound of the solid drumming on the flat roof of the Gaol; even the sight of small runnels of water seeping over the lintel of our doorway and entering the kitchen was almost welcome. The smell, that had so distressed us, abated, and for a short time we were refreshed and invigorated by the downpour. But then, when it stopped, the sun came out in strength, the ground steamed and bodies streamed with perspiration in the sweltering heat.

This pattern was to repeat itself day after day for two and a half months. Nothing and no one was ever truly dry, whether because of the rain or the sweat that followed it. Charles had but two shirts to his back, and, though I did my best to keep one clean and dry, such was the dampness of the atmosphere that he often changed from a shirt that was dirty and wet to one that, though clean, was almost as wet as that he had discarded. Fever flourished then; rheumatism became rampant, and often men manning the guns shivered so with the ague they could not touch the port-fire to the breach. Anything left on the floor or hanging against a wall became green with mildew in a few hours. Our dark rooms were horrid with the pursy bodies of large black spiders; at night monsoon toads sat in the puddles and croaked in shattering unison; fat, armoured beetles hurled themselves into whatever little pools of lamplight still remained, and minute mango flies, silent and almost invisible, added their quota of stings to flesh already raw with mosquito bites.

The day following Emily's death found Kate moving her possessions into our rooms. Two rooms, however small, were considered too much for one baby and a woman (for Charles was now expected to sleep at Fayrer's post), and had she not done so I would have been afflicted with a stranger's constant presence. The arrangement suited us both: we were company for each other, understood each other's tempers pretty well, and I was glad to have Kate's assistance in dealing with the baby. We both dissolved in laughter the first time we tried to wash Pearl's small slippery body in the inadequate tin bowl. One childless widow and one spinster between them made a poor showing at motherhood. And the baby and I were a comfort to Kate, too, whose loss was so recent and who, I knew, grieved deeply, though in silence.

Of Charles we saw less than ever. Once a day he came to the Gaol for something to eat and hung dutifully over his daughter for a moment or so. But he had little to say to anyone, seemed relieved when he left us, and I knew was volunteering for every possible extra duty that would keep him at his post. In my heart I was grateful to be allowed to forget him for long passages of time. Toddy-Bob found time each day to milk the goat, whom we had named Cassandra, and often Mr Roberts dropped in to see how we were getting on. Occasionally Wallace Avery came too, but he was becoming increasingly incoherent and, selfishly, we were always glad to see him depart.

Our few visitors were almost the only break in the routine of our day. Mrs Bonner, indeed, would have been very willing to spend the best part of her waking hours informing us of her past grandeurs as the 'First Lady' of her husband's station, but we soon learned that it was very easy to dampen her social enthusiasm by complaining of some slight indisposition, preferably of the baby's, since Pearl could not be asked suspicious questions. The word 'contagion' bore an even more terrifying connotation in Mrs Bonner's mind than did 'pandy'. For the rest, with too little work to do and too many hours to do it in, the irritation born of boredom was difficult to control, and it was always with relief that, as soon as the sun set, we ate our meal and made our sketchy preparations for bed.

There was no more oil for the lantern and our few candles were too precious to be wasted; they must be kept for a crisis, or perhaps a celebration, for day by day we hoped to hear of the approach of the relief. Then one day we realized gratefully that Mr Roberts's estimate of our food stores must have been wrong. We had been besieged for a full three weeks and there was no indication that we were running out of supplies.

On the morning of the 20th of July we awoke to absolute quiet and the strange knowledge that for several hours we had slept undisturbed by gunfire. Charles took advantage of the fact to come in for breakfast; he said the pandies had not fired a gun since midnight. It was not known what had deflected their attention from us, and a few hopeful souls considered that they might have got wind of a force coming to our aid and withdrawn to meet it. I put some of the previous night's *chapattis* on the table for Charles and a jug of warmed-up tea, but before we could start eating, the familiar shout of 'Stand to your arms!' caused him to raise his eyebrows resignedly, shrug, shoulder his rifle and go out without haste or alarm.

Everything remained quiet, however, while Kate and I swallowed our unappetising meal and for some time afterwards. Then Toddy-Bob arrived to milk the goat. From the studied innocence of his expression, I knew he was somehow breaching discipline—no doubt there were strict orders for every man to remain at his post during this abnormal quiet—but the milk was vital to Pearl, so I made no comment but poured him out the last of the tea and gave him a few *chapattis* to pass on to Charles. It would take Toddy out of his way, but I was anxious that Charles should eat. Toddy had just trotted off with his odd bowlegged run, when the entire room rocked, and a roar, submerged but deafening, filled the air.

A moment of complete silence followed as the garrison reacted to the shattering blast. Then there were frenzied shouts of: 'A mine! A mine!' 'By God, we've been breached!' 'Stand to your arms! To arms!' Women along the Gaol verandah shrieked and cried out for their husbands, and men, heedless of everything but the desperate urgency of the moment, ran headlong for their posts. I rushed out on to the verandah.

A great cloud of dust-filled smoke was billowing up over the river side of the entrenchment. Just as I gained the verandah steps, searching for someone who would pause long enough to answer my anguished questions, the great guns of the Redan Battery which overlooked the river belched into action. A few seconds more and I was coughing and spluttering as the dense yellow smoke engulfed me, and above the guns came the terrifying, open-throated roar as the invisible pandies surged into the charge, yelling their war-cry of *'Din! Din! Din!'* in answer to the bugle's shrill exhortation to battle.

I retreated to the kitchen, none the wiser as to what had actually happened, and found Kate, chalk-white and trembling as she knelt, saying her rosary, the blue beads held to her lips with shaking fingers.

'This is the end, woman dear,' she whispered with closed eyes, pausing in her 'Hail Marys' as I entered. 'This must be the end. I had prayed that it wouldn't be this way for you ... oh, I had prayed!'

By now I was sufficiently versed in the 'arts' of war to know that if our defences had been breached by the mine and the assault that must follow succeeded we would not see the sunset.

For a moment I could not but share in Kate's uncharacteristic certainty of our doom, for in the name of holy common sense how could our men, decimated as they were by casualties and sickness and weakened by fatigue and hunger, hope to stand out against even a moderate-numbered but determined force? The long silence, that grateful quiet to which we had wakened, had been no more than a final respite before the end. In my mind I saw the fatal gap in our ridiculous stockade, saw the pandies bring up their guns, their elephants and their cavalry, then the assault force swarm through the breach and overcome the defenders. And then—what then? Then it would be our turn. My stomach lurched in fear, my hands grew cold and my mouth was so dry I could not speak. There would be a carnage then, a dreadful letting of blood, a massacre! I would be part of it, and Kate and oh, God, no— Pearl.

I went to the baby's box and picked her up. The explosion had wakened her but she was not crying. As I raised her in my arms, she chortled and made a grab for my hair. I buried my face in her soft neck and, doing so, remembered the odd certainty of survival that had overwhelmed me on the night that Emily was buried. I felt it still. I knew it was irrational, childish, probably silly too, but I was absolutely certain that whatever I need fear it was not death. Not now, at any rate.

Curiously comforted by this inner assurance, I went to Kate with the baby in my arms.

'It's all right, Kate,' I said, as her sad blue eyes regarded me over the blue beads. 'Truly. I don't know how I know it, but we will be all right. Believe me. You mustn't give way now, my dear. They'll never get at us, Kate; our men won't let them. So come now, we'll go into the bedroom, shut the door and windows and wait until it's over.'

'You don't understand, Laura dear. You don't understand,' she said tearfully as she got to her feet. 'If we are breached ...'

'But I do understand, and a mine exploding does not necessarily mean a breach. At least, we can hope that it does not, can't we?'

'But there is no way our poor men could fight them off, don't you see? There are too few of us … and I … I don't want you to be … !'

'I am not going to be ravished, raped or slaughtered—or if I am, I refuse to think about it beforehand! Now come, Kate darling, pull yourself together. It is just not like you to give way so. Let's go and sit on the beds and make ourselves comfortable.'

'I know. I'm so sorry. I'm just a stupid old woman, but I'm so frightened for you and … and the baby, poor mite!'

I do not know what crazy reasoning prompted me to take Kate into the inner room. Only a cotton curtain, hung from a bamboo pole, separated it from the kitchen. Kate, however, seemed to derive some obscure comfort from the move, and settled down on her string cot while I put Pearl back into her box.

I made sure the single barred window was fastened, then returned to the kitchen and secured the two rickety doors that led on to the front and courtyard verandahs; but before doing so, took a quick peep outside. There was nothing to be seen. A thick fog of smoke and dust obscured everything and our long verandah was totally deserted.

The rest of the day is in one sense a blur and in another sense the most vivid memory I have to carry me through old age.

It was too dark in the little room for me to do anything but sit with folded hands on my bed, listening to Kate's endlessly repeated prayer and the soft click of the blue beads passing through her thin mottled hands. Pearl, most amiable of infants, slept quietly until, at midday, I roused myself to give her milk. We had no heart for food ourselves. Mrs MacGregor had not called in for her milk that morning, and I wondered how the day was going with her and with sick little Jamie in the fetid darkness of the cellars beneath the Resident's House—the *tykhana*.

Outside, the noise of battle increased and it was soon apparent that our assailants had encircled the entire entrenchment. The din became deafening, even in the small, shuttered room, as explosions shook the plaster from the ceiling, rattled the wooden doors in their frames and, on one occasion, forced the window inward against the bar that fastened it so fiercely that it never again closed completely. A concentrated and vicious cannonade, such as we had not before experienced, screamed and shattered into the shaky buildings surrounded by their ephemeral protection of mud, bamboo and sacking. Ball, shell, grape, canister, rifle and musket, the enemy used them all. Our building was hit several times. Just after I had fed Pearl, an eighteen-pounder dropped through the roof of the verandah and landed with a great thud on the stone not far from our rooms, then rolled harmlessly into the mud, where later we discovered it. Not long afterwards a shell burst in the inner courtyard, and only a few moments later another exploded in front of the Gaol, showering our doors and shuttered window with shrapnel. For six long hours we crouched in the dark trying to make out from the sound only which way the battle went; twice during those hours, the thunder of the guns was rivalled by the shrill note of bugles, of drum beats mounting to a crescendo, the frenetic skirl of fifes and the pandies' menacing roar of 'Din! Din! Din!' Each time Kate murmured grimly, 'That's another force they're bringing up!' Then the firing would grow stronger until the martial music was drowned by the yells of the attackers, the shouted commands of our own men and the screams of the wounded.

'Hail Mary ... Our Father ... Glory be. ... Amen!'

Kate prayed, sometimes with closed eyes, sometimes aloud, but unflaggingly.

I listened to her. I believe I tried to unite myself to the intention of her prayer, but prayer in such moments avails me little and I did not follow her example. The breathless heat in the small room sometimes weighed me down into a doze from which I would waken gasping, half smothered by my own sweat. I fetched a pitcher of water and a rag with which I tried to cool Pearl's body and refresh my own face. For the most part, however, I had only my thoughts, my memories and half-forgotten hopes to help me through the long succession of apprehensive hours.

Where was Oliver Erskine? Where could he be? A prisoner of the Nana in some noisome prison in Cawnpore, or safe with Moti's family, sleeping away the afternoon of this fevered day under a tree in some pleasant courtyard? Could he have tried to return to Hassanganj, be living in some shed or storeroom in the park, trying to gather his people around him and rebuild already what had so recently been destroyed? Or could he, after all, have escaped downriver from Cawnpore to Calcutta, there to constitute himself a thorn in the flesh of every complacent civil servant unlucky enough to run across him? I had no way of knowing, or even guessing, and shortly memory and imagination took the place of conjecture in my mind.

Now that I knew the reason why he had left us at the outskirts of Lucknow, it had become difficult to think of this 'desertion' with anger. It was a foolish, quixotic thing he had decided to do, yet I was glad he had done it. To be more accurate, I was glad that he had thought it necessary to do it. That single act indicated a sensitivity to the needs of others which, though I had discerned it in his character before, I had not fully appreciated.

Emily had appreciated it, though. How many times, I wondered, had I heard her say, 'Oliver's so thoughtful ... so considerate.' Now, as in my mind I played out the memories of our pleasant days in Hassanganj, I recalled a score of incidents that instanced that consideration of others, and of myself. Why was it that I had blinded myself to his merits with such enthusiasm? Could it have been fear? Had he always held an attraction for me that I was reluctant to admit because of the unlikelihood that I would have any attraction for him? Had I insisted on dwelling on his shortcomings only to save myself from being overlooked or superseded in the regard of a man I could love?

He had told me he loved me, and had added that I had missed the many hints he had given me of his feeling. At the time, and for many days thereafter, there had been small leisure or opportunity for me to examine this surprising assertion, but what had remained in my mind through the weeks of separation were his last words to me as the palanquin was lifted and I was borne away to the house of Wajid Khan: 'Never fear, Laura, I will come to you—for you!' They had reverberated around me, the echoes of those words, in the steamy courtyard on the night of Emily's death, and at last I realized that it was they alone that had filled me with the strange certainty of my own survival. Had I not found, after all, the best possible reason for clinging to life? I was in love.

Love was something, so people said, that must grow slowly and sweetly, nurtured by knowledge, appreciation and shared experience. When I considered the matter, it was plain that I had gained a pretty thorough knowledge of Oliver Erskine, that my appreciation of him had advanced greatly since the early days of our acquaintance, and that we had certainly shared some of the most curious experiences ever to fall to the lot of law-abiding English folk.

True, a barrier of misunderstanding and misinterpretation still stood between us; that must come down before we could grow towards each other. But honesty forced me to admit that all the misinterpretation and most of the misunderstanding had been on my part, not his, and even as I did so, the last wavelets of both ebbed swiftly into the tide of the forgotten past, leaving my mind clear and acceptant as new-washed sand.

Certainly Oliver lacked all those qualities that made Charles the man he was. Oliver could never be considered genial, kindly or open. He was inclined to be dictatorial, was quick-tempered and careless of moral convention. Yet there were other excellences than those exhibited by Charles. Oliver was himself and, I admitted without a qualm, more than Charles would ever be. Oliver had imagination and insight; he was slow to judge and, for all his anti-social protestations, tolerant of others; he was quick to act and decisive in action; there was a strength in him that I both admired and feared; yet he was capable of true gentleness. He was the last man in my acquaintance to whom the tender epithet 'lovable' could be applied; yet now, quite suddenly, I knew myself to be in love with him.

A sudden rush of feeling, compounded of regret for my past shortsightedness and of an aching desire for his presence so that I could amend matters, brought tears to my eyes. I let them fall unheeded. In that dark room, on a face dripping with perspiration, no one could have remarked them.

The acknowledgement of my love, total now, flooded over me like a golden, light-filled warmth, filling me with joy. 'I love him! I love him!' I kept repeating to myself, as the cruel cacophony of the battle continued outside. 'I love him ... and he loves me. I know it. He loves me!'

Made restless by my inward and inexpressible delight, I went into the kitchen and paced its length from front door to back door with quick blind steps. I heard nothing of what occurred beyond the fastness of these rickety planks, saw nothing of the smoke-grimed murky room they guarded. All I could see now was Oliver—my love—and all of life in a new light.

I did not allow myself to dwell on the old tower and Moti, but fled delightedly back to memories of things we had shared and enjoyed together. The morning rides through the dewy fields; my struggles with Urdu, and Oliver pretending to read at his desk as I worked, but always aware when I was in difficulties; afternoons when we wrestled together with catalogues, inventories and plans in the library; and evenings when we sat alone with our books before the fire, the only sound a falling log or the rustle of a turned page. Why, I could reconstruct an entire day of happiness from these piecemeal memories. I made up my mind to live that happy day over on each of the days I must exist through before I next saw him; and such was the euphoria of my mood, that scanty memory seemed almost enough to keep me in the state of bliss I then experienced.

Briefly I was recalled to the present by another blast close to our window. Pearl, whom I had placed on my bed, stirred and whimpered. I went in to her and soothed her with a little water; then returned eagerly to the ecstasy I now found present in my most prosaic memories. My mind's eye followed Oliver with love, as he strode swiftly about the house and grounds of Hassanganj or sat on his great bay gelding, one hand on his hip, straightbacked and commanding. I watched his lean brown hands on the reins, heard his voice, smiled at his laugh, looked again curiously into the strange tawny eyes under their heavy brows, those eyes that had last looked into mine from a face grimed and stubbled with beard but full of searching tenderness, full of understanding love.

That, I decided, was when I had learned to love him, though I would not then admit it. On that morning when he had ridden away from me to risk his safety and perhaps his life for his child.

At about three o'clock the firing slackened and by four o'clock the entrenchment was for the second time that day filled with an unnatural quiet.

Kate had dozed, exhausted by her praying, and I, lost in my new-found joy, remained unaware of the silence until she sat up and called out, unbelievingly, 'Laura, it must be over! Listen! Listen to the quiet! We must have beaten them off, Laura. We're safe. Our lads have beaten them off!'

Recalled unwillingly to the moment, I unbarred the kitchen door and the two of us stepped hesitantly on to the verandah, blinking in the harsh sunlight.

Along the verandah, other doors opened and other women, many with babies in their arms or holding children by the hand, crowded out. They were as ignorant and as anxious as ourselves, and the sudden silence kept them speechless as their eyes, like ours, searched for information. That silence, after so much noise so long continued, was as painful to our ears as the strong sun was to our dark-accustomed eyes. It was almost frightening.

Over the entrenchment a dense pall of smoke wreathed and wraithed between and around the shattered buildings, and the stench of cordite was such as to overpower the more usual smell of putrefaction.

As we became accustomed to the light and the smoke, figures became apparent in the haze, men, exhausted and silent, sitting in the shade of a wall, or stretched on the muddy earth, still holding fast to smoking muskets or rifles. Some walked slowly to their billets, black-faced and red-eyed; some limped; some stumbled and remained where they fell; some helped a comrade, some carried stretchers to the hospital; some just sat where they had stood, heads bowed between their knees, shoulders heaving with exertion. All were quiet. Cheers should have rent the smoky air, wild hurrahs of triumph. But fatigue had felled them when the enemy had failed; and now that the impetus to movement was over they collapsed where their knees buckled under them in motionless silence.

I ventured down the verandah steps and moved hesitantly through the smoke a little way, picking a path between the debris and mud. Soon I recognized a familiar figure stumbling towards me, and ran forward to intercept him, since he seemed not to have noticed me.

'Wally!' I cried, shaking him by the arm to get his attention, so sunk was he in his own thoughts and fatigue. 'Wally, do tell me? Is it all right? What's happened? Is it really all over? Oh, Wally, we know nothing but surely we have not ... capitulated?'

He stopped, shook the sweat out of his eyes and looked at me.

'Eh? Laura? Capitulated? Good God, no! We licked 'em!'

'We've won?'

'Won? How can we? No, but we've beaten 'em off for the moment. Until the next time.'

'They've drawn back then?'

'Yes. Right back. There'll be some quiet tonight, with any luck. We're all right, Laura. All right.'

He shook away my hand with some impatience and moved away in hurried anticipation of his quarters and his brandy.

I turned back to the Gaol with tears of relief sliding down my sweaty face and, as I did so, caught sight of Charles coming towards me, with Ishmial behind him carrying their two guns. Even at a distance, I could see that Charles was hurt, and I hurried to him.

'Don't touch me, Laura,' he implored as I reached out. 'I'm not much hurt really, but don't touch me.' I had put out my arm to help him.

'But what has happened? Where were you hit?'

'My shoulders and upper back,' he grated through clenched teeth. 'Nothing much; a shell exploded some way behind me, and I have been peppered with spent shrapnel and muck. Just let me sit down for a while, and then you and Kate can have a look at it.'

'Oh, Charles! I'll run for a doctor, or Ishmial will, I'm sure!'

'No need. Anyway, you won't get one to come. Just let me have a rest and then you can get the damned stuff out yourselves.'

We sat him down gingerly on the box in the kitchen, and I made some fresh tea, extravagant in my use of leaves. When Charles had drunk his wordlessly and greedily, Kate cut away his shirt and examined his back.

'Well, I've seen a lot worse than that in my time, m'lad. You were lucky not to have been nearer the big bang, were you not?'

'I know. It killed two men; blew them to bits, I hear. But this is bad enough for the moment. If I hadn't been standing in a bit of a trench, I wouldn't be able to sit down this side of Christmas.' And he tried to laugh as he laid himself face down on Kate's bed.

'Good. That's the spirit. Now I want hot water, scissors and a darning needle. And open that window, Laura. I need all the light I can get. Light two candles and get Ishmial to hold them for me, and you, Laura, you had better get to work on something to eat. Even that ghastly stew of yours seems almost appetizing at the moment, and I'm sure the lads can do with something hot too. Now, out of my way, girl. Ishmial—here!'

Ishmial hastily finished his mug of tea, wiped his moustache with the back of his hand and took the lighted candles from me. I was relieved to be exempted from watching or helping with the operation and turned my attention to the bullock meat and lentils. For over an hour I was left alone to stir the unsavoury amalgam in the pot and think my oddly happy thoughts, which had immediately reverted to Oliver the moment I was alone. At the end of that period, Charles emerged, white but more comfortable, with his torso bandaged in strips of my only linen petticoat, and Kate behind him looking complacent and pleased with her handiwork.

Somehow Toddy-Bob, down at Gubbins's battery, had learned of Charles's injury, and just then appeared with a bottle of brandy hidden under his jacket and a screw of paper containing six sugar lumps concealed in his sun helmet. These offerings were accepted without demur or enquiry and, as I poured out a generous measure of the liquor for Charles, I blessed Toddy's forethought in getting himself transferred to Mr Gubbins's post. Toddy looked wistfully at the bottle as I placed it on the shelf, and Kate, following the direction of his eyes, smiled.

'Oh, come now, Laura!' she protested. 'This has been a trying day for us all, and I think a dram would do me almost as much good as Charles. Surely you wouldn't dream of sending Tod away without a heartener on such an occasion?'

So I took down the bottle again, and we each had a drink, while Charles, feeling better for the food and brandy, and with a hint of colour returned to his dirty cheeks, gave us an account of the day's battle.

The mine directed at the Redan Battery, our largest, strongest and most important strongpoint, had been ill-laid and, instead of breaching our defences at the vital point, had exploded harmlessly, if alarmingly, much short of its objective. No doubt the pandies had been disappointed by the failure of the mine, but ready mustered for attack as they were, had hurled themselves into battle, flinging wave after wave of men against our walls while their guns opened a murderous cannonade into the entrenchment from their vantage points surrounding us.

'I never thought I'd live to see the end of them,' said Charles. 'My rifle barrel got so hot, my palms are blistered ... see! There was no end to the devils: they just came on and on and on. We'd beat them off at one point, only to see them bring up reinforcements at another; then the ones we'd beaten off would regroup, be joined by more, and attack again before we had time to wipe the sweat from our eyes. I swear I didn't know there were so many blasted sepoys in all India! They fought splendidly too, and I'm damned if I can guess why they let us beat them off and win the day into the bargain. Around three o'clock, the firing began to taper off and soon afterwards the ceasefire was called. God knows why. There were still thousands of them milling around below us, though their ardour had certainly been dampened.'

'They called for a truce, the bastards!' Toddy said with satisfaction. 'To remove their dead, like. There's 'undreds of the beggars lyin' in the muck outside, dead as mutton or gettin' on that way. 'Orses too, and gun-bullocks and that. Thank Gawd they 'as the decency to want to bury and burn 'em all proper like. Think what the smell would be like if they didn't!'

'Oh, Tod!' Kate remonstrated, but it was impossible not to smile at Toddy's mixture of unction and common sense; the stench would indeed have been intolerable had the dead been allowed to rot at our walls.

'Yes, 'undreds of 'em ... and I'm not exaggeratin' either, mind! You cast your blinkers over the parapet and you'll see 'em bein' taken away by the cartload. And shall I tell you how many we lost?'

I frowned discouragingly; I did not want to hear the numbers or names of our dead. It was sufficient to know that we few friends were still safe and together. But Toddy disregarded my glare.

'We lost four whites killed and a dozen wounded, and maybe a dozen of our own 'eathens gone to their 'eathen 'Eaven. Four, mind you, just four!'

'But how can you possibly know?' queried Kate with scepticism. 'Everything is still so confused, surely.'

'Sure enough! But I been down in the 'ospital 'elpin' to lay 'em out, like, mam. Makes it me business to know them as 'as gone on account of the auctions, like. No sense in losin' time at the sale of a man who didn't have nothin' I might want. But when I gives a 'and to sewin' them up, I gets a pretty fair idea of a party's effects, if you follow me. Now tomorrow or the day after there'll be pretty pickings, I reckon, on account of two of the gonners bein' gentlemen, like.'

He accompanied his words with a satisfied smirk so droll that, in spite of the morbid matter of his discourse, we all laughed. The possessions of the dead were generally auctioned soon after burial, and, though at first the custom had been considered deplorable, now we were all used to bidding for the clothing, stores and little luxuries of our comrades and friends, there being no other way of supplying our own lack. As time went on and casualties grew heavier, it was quite common for a jacket or a pair of boots to change hands several times without ever being worn by their successive purchasers.

But, though our losses were so few on that day of the first assault, one of them at least was of the utmost importance to us. Cassandra, the goat.

When Toddy went into the courtyard to milk her, he found she had been blown to bits by the shell that had bombarded our doors with shrapnel. As he commented mournfully when he returned with the news, there was not even enough of her left to make a meal. Terrified by the initial explosion of the mine, then anxious to soothe Kate, and later lost in my new and private world of love, I had not given the animal a thought all day. If I had remembered it, I would certainly have brought her into the kitchen, for one odour more or less would have been more than worth the animal's safety.

'Oh, miss, miss!' Toddy turned to me with something like agony on his strange features. 'Oh, miss! And what's goin' to 'appen to the nipper now?'

He had realized sooner than we that the shell had killed Pearl as surely as it had killed the goat. Without the goat's milk, she would die. There was nothing else on which we could feed a three-month-old infant.

The room was suddenly hushed. The mosquitoes whined and the fat blue flies buzzed contentedly as they explored our empty plates.

Charles laid his head on his arms folded on the table, and I sat down slowly, thinking of the dreadful days that must follow as the baby starved. I wished I was sufficiently Christian to ask God to give me strength to bear another's suffering, but I was not. I did not pray; instead I railed against the Fate or Deity that could allow the agony of the innocent. 'Let us all die!' I raged silently to whatever power it is that has the arranging of such matters. 'Let us all die! We know why we die and what has caused our death; perhaps we have even deserved to suffer. But this child has harmed no one. Let her not die so cruelly, so horribly. Oh, let her not die. Take me!' I hardly knew what I said, nor to whom I was saying it. My ideas of religion were rudimentary, but not so elemental that they could countenance a vengeful and vindictive God, so I suppose it was the Devil with whom I attempted to bargain.

I shut my eyes and for a moment was overwhelmed. No sight I had seen until then, not Elvira Wilkins's body swinging half-devoured in a starlit grove, not Emily's swift unlovely dissolution, not the casualties carried past our door on bloody stretchers, had affected me as now I was affected by the figments of my own imagination: the tortures endured by a small child dying slowly of hunger, while her elders watched in helplessness. I felt physically ill with apprehension.

'I won't let it happen!' I swore, clenching my fists till my fingernails bit into my palms. 'I won't let it happen!' I must have spoken aloud without knowing it.

'Sure and what can you do, woman dear?' Kate asked hopelessly. 'What can any of us do?'

She stood looking down at Pearl as she spoke. We had given the child the last of the morning's milk, though it was 'on the turn', but it had not been enough to satisfy her and she beat the air with small balled fists and cried for more.

'Surely ... surely there must be other goats? In fact I know there are. We must find out who they belong to and ask for some of the milk. We can pay for it. They must let us have it if we pay for it?'

Toddy shook his head.

'No go, miss. There's too many other children needin' it. I heard only yesterday that Mrs Inglis had turned away one of the gunner's wives because 'er goats are givin' only enough for 'er own nippers. Stands to reason! She feels about 'ers as we do about ours!' Even in that moment of despair, I warmed to Tod's possessive plural.

'Cows then?' I insisted. 'There must be some cows somewhere.'

'All dead or dry by now, miss.'

Nonplussed, I fell silent.

'If ... oh, if only we knew someone who could act as wet-nurse,' Kate said, but without hope. 'Perhaps ... I suppose we could enquire. I suppose we might just find someone who would be willing to ...'

'Of course! That's the answer! Why didn't I think of it before?' I jumped up.

'Oh, don't hope too soon, Laura dear,' begged Kate. 'We have no certainty of help in that direction. We might not find anyone.'

'But we *have*, Kate, we *have*. Mrs MacGregor! She ... she told me that she ...' And I stammered to a halt. Mrs MacGregor had said that she had more milk than a dozen old nannies, but just in time I realized that I could not report her verbatim in the present company.

'Mrs MacGregor will help us. I feel sure of it. I'll go over to the Resident's House now and see her. It is still quite quiet and the sooner we can arrange it the better, even if it means that Pearl has to stay in the *tykhana* for a time. I know Mrs MacGregor is a good, safe, reliable woman. I just know it.'

I owned no bonnet, but I tied on the large sun hat I had bought after our arrival and tidied myself as much as was possible for my first 'social' call.

'Heavens, girl, you can't go alone. I'll come with you,' said Kate, but I pointed out that someone should stay with the querulous baby.

'I'll take you over, miss,' volunteered Toddy. 'Mr Flood 'ad better stay quiet for as long as 'e's allowed.'

But Charles had got up and was waiting for me at the door.

'Thanks, Tod,' he said, 'but she's my daughter and it's only right that I should make this small effort on her behalf.'

'But your back; it must be very painful,' I demurred.

'It will do. Come along, Laura, don't fuss!' he replied, and the two of us set off.

CHAPTER 10

The insurgents, still busy with their dead and wounded, spared us their fire, and the evening was almost disquietingly still.

For over three weeks I had not been more than half a dozen steps from the Gaol verandah, and what I observed around me as we walked to the Resident's House that evening brought home to me more clearly than any words or detailed explanations the desperation of our position.

Every building was holed with shot and scarred by bullets and shrapnel. Walls had collapsed under the barrage and the rain; roofs had fallen in; porticoes stood precariously supported by half their complement of pillars; shutters hung crazily from smashed windows; balconies sloped at odd angles, and doors on upper storeys gaped open, leading into air.

We picked our way through mounds of rubble and shattered furniture, doors and window frames that had been carefully collected for fuel, edging around stinking puddles of greenish mud, and so chaotic was the destruction, so complete the transformation of the neat and orderly cluster of buildings I remembered, that had Charles not been with me, I would have been hard put to it to find the Resident's House. As we moved through the debris, men, spent with the long day's fighting, were already at work again, carting or carrying away the rubbish, the crumbling pillars, mounds of bricks and lumps of masonry, to be built into the breastworks damaged in the fighting. 'We are even using files and books to stop up the gaps now,' remarked Charles wryly as he helped a soldier to lift part of a mahogany sideboard on to a barrow.

In every nook and angle, weary men bivouacked under the tattered remains of tents or shreds of striped window-awnings; tiny fires, jealously watched, glowed in the dusk under the cooking pots, and the men's laundry—ragged shirts and toeless socks—fluttered from strings stretched between the ruins. The shirts swaying in the windless air put me in mind, incongruously enough, of the flag, and I looked up to see it hanging inertly on the top of the tower of the Resident's House. It had become something of a joke and latterly a challenge to keep it and its pole atop the tower. At the beginning of the siege it had been forgotten, and in the confusion of those first days, no one had bothered to lower it at sundown. So it had flown bravely through the first days and nights until, inevitably, the flag pole was shot away, when immediately it became a symbol. Now it was a matter of the utmost concern that, as soon as it came down, which happened frequently, it should be mended and replaced, and everyone, from the smallest Martinière schoolboy to the most cynical old brandy-soaked Bengal hand who had never so much as looked in its direction in the days of prosperity, was anxious to volunteer for the hazardous duty of setting it back in place.

It was difficult to keep memory at bay as Charles and I walked under the shaky portico and up the few steps leading to the entrance. There had been so many lights that November night: such a galaxy of chandeliers, such a flowering of candles in silver candelabra, well-waxed furniture, gleaming mirrors and the sheen of satin and silk. I remembered laughter, the clink of glasses and the hum of conversation—and music; the men smart in their bright uniforms, the women floating like iridescent bubbles in their extravagant skirts. I thought of it as another life lived by another woman; yet it had been less than nine months ago.

Now, a single dirty lantern smoked on the floor of the entrance hall. There was no furniture; it had been built into the defences or used to block up the windows of the first floor. The upper storeys were empty—the building being the favourite target of the pandies—and the inmates had been evacuated to other buildings or to the ground floor and cellars or *tykhanas*.

Stepping carefully over the recumbent forms of men who slept fully dressed on the floor, we made our way into the building and down a flight of stone stairs leading to the subterranean rooms where the wives of the men of the 32nd were quartered.

A series of large apartments opened before us, connected by great arches and ventilated only by inadequate slits set horizontally in the walls at roof level. No windows, no doors and little light combined to produce a sense of confinement. The place was like a dungeon—a densely populated dungeon.

Families crowded every inch of floor space, each huddled round some article of furniture or homely treasure—a brass bedstead perhaps, or a studded chest, or simply an old armchair losing its stuffing—that had come somehow to represent home and hearth. On mattresses laid on the bare stone the sick lay, many of them with their faces turned to the wall and away from the restless children, who ran and played noisily between and about their elders. Women nursed infants while gossiping with their neighbours; others washed the family clothing in whatever receptacle would hold water; some tended the sick, or sewed by the tiny light of a tallow dip. Some just sat apathetically on their mattresses with their hands in their laps. One old toothless woman combed her long white hair.

Moisture ran down the walls and oozed up between the flags as we trod on them, and the whole place reeked of damp and stank of ill, unwashed and crowded humanity. Compared to this, the air outside was almost sweet.

But tonight the *tykhanas* too shared in the relief and exaltation engendered by the repulse of the assault and, with their muskets beside them, men sat among their families recounting the glories of the day. Smiles shone on proud faces and lit up tired eyes, and as we entered, someone said sardonically, ''Ere's another of the 'eroes, give 'im a cheer, girls!' A few voices cheered, more laughed and a woman said, ''E's more of a 'ero than my Jim! 'E's wearin' a bandage. My Jim slep' behind a gun all day!'

'We really did for 'em today, didn't we, sir?' said another. 'Do you reckon we'll be out soon now?'

'I'm afraid not,' answered Charles, embarrassed by the attention. 'We'll have to hang on a while yet. But can you tell us where we can find Mrs MacGregor—Mrs Jessie MacGregor?'

'Mrs MacGregor?' The woman shook her head doubtfully.

'Course you can, Annie!' broke in another. 'It's Red Jess the gentleman means! We calls her that, y'see, sir, on account of 'er 'air.'

'Red Jess! Oh, 'er! You'll find 'er at the far end of the next room. Up there see, under the skylight.'

We thanked them and made our way carefully between cooking pots, bundles and babies to Jessie's portion of the room. At first it was difficult to locate her, there was so little light and so many people. But at length we discovered her sitting bolt upright on her mattress, with her legs stretched out before her, and her skirts neatly tucked in around her ankles. She held her baby, wrapped in a shawl, in her arms.

She did not seem to notice our approach, but a woman nearby, seeing us pause beside her, came to me and touched me on the arm.

'Ma'am, is it Jess you're wantin'?'

'Yes,' I answered, while Jessie continued to stare at the opposite wall with unblinking eyes.

'Oh, ma'am, make 'er give 'im up! Last night it 'appened, and she's sat there like a statue all this while and let none of us lay a finger on 'im.'

'But what ... I don't understand,' I whispered back in puzzlement.

'It's her babe, ma'am, Jamie. 'E died yesterday ... but she won't let 'im go. Just sits there 'olding 'im, and whiles she sings hymnsto 'im as she used to when 'e was crying, and whiles she rocks 'im and cries 'erself. 'Taint right that 'e shouldn't be buried proper, ma'am, like all the others!'

My heart sank, both at the information the woman gave me, and at her expectation that I should get Jessie to relinquish the little bundle. I wanted to turn away and leave the big woman to her grief. Before long she would recover from the first shock of sorrow and give up her child to her friends. I was an interloper, after all; I had no right to interfere, and I wanted more from a woman who already had given too much. But there was Pearl. I seemed to see her in her box, tossing her small body about angrily, demanding sustenance with outraged wails. I had to make the attempt. So, motioning back the woman and Charles, I went to the mattress and sat down beside Jessie.

'Jessie?' I began hesitantly. 'Mrs MacGregor?'

To my surprise she answered immediately.

'My bairn's dead, missie! My Jamie's left his mam.'

'Yes. Yes, I know, Jessie. I'm so sorry—so very sorry for you.' And I paused, not knowing how to continue.

'He was just sleepin', miss, and the hand of God touched him. I didna even hear his whimper. He had the fever, the doctor said, but he took the wee sup milk whiles, and I was hopeful that he'd mebbe tak' strength. He was such a good wee bairn, missie, and so bonnie. And now he's dead!' She turned her large, flat face towards me for the first time, and the expression in her eyes was puzzlement more than grief.

'Is it my wickedness that makes him tak' them from me, miss? Three bairns I've borne to a good man, and all been tak'n.'

'Oh no, Jessie, it's not your wickedness—not anyone's wickedness …' But she didn't seem to hear. Her eyes were abstracted and she spoke softly, almost wonderingly, to herself.

'Whiles I'm a wee mite thrawn; and my temper's nae o' the best. But I've aye done my duty … and I have a lovin' heart. The gude Lord knows I loved them a'. My man drank, but I suffered him. And when the other bairns went, I sorrowed but didna fret. Jamie was all I had left. Why did my Jamie have to be tak'n too?'

'I don't know, Jessie. I don't know why any of these horrible things are happening. Our own baby, our little Pearl …' But I could not continue. I bent my head, and tears of bewilderment, exhaustion and grief flowed from my closed eyes. I was certain that my last resource had failed. I had heard of many a woman losing her milk for lesser reason than Jessie had.

'Ah, and is your bairn dead too then, missie?' She bent towards me and her voice had a hint of warmth in it.

'No, not yet!' I managed to say between sobs. 'But she will die—you see, the … the goat was killed. Today in the assault. We have nothing to feed her with, now that her mother has gone.'

'Ah! Poor mite. Mebbe my Jamie's better off after a'. Who knows what disasters are yet to come to us a'.'

'Yes. Perhaps he is the luckier! I came here, Jessie, to see if you could … could feed her. We thought a wet-nurse, if we could find one—but we didn't know about Jamie or I shouldn't have bothered you just now.'

'No, no! We must a' think of our own first, missie. That's only right. Ah! … poor mite, poor mite.' And she sighed deeply, looking down at the bundle she held, so that I could not tell whether she referred to Pearl or to Jamie.

I wanted to go away and come to terms with this fresh disaster alone. But, though I had failed to receive help, there was no reason why I should not try to give it. I wiped my eyes on the edge of my skirt and sniffed.

'Now, Jessie, we must see that Jamie is given a good burial.' And I used the arch, hypocritical tone usually used of the dead by people unconcerned.

Jessie's arms tightened convulsively round the macabre bundle, as she regarded me with stony eyes.

'What is it you're meanin'?' she asked suspiciously.

'We must have Jamie buried, Jessie. Won't you give him to me? We'll find a little box for him and put his pillow in it, and Mr Flood and Toddy-Bob will take him to the graveyard. It's not right for you to keep him now ... now that his soul has gone to God.'

I nearly choked on the words, but could think of no other way to reach her. Perhaps she was a religious woman.

'No ... No ... He's my bairn, missie. I canna let him go.' She spoke slowly, as if she were explaining something difficult to a child. I shook my head firmly, though I had little hope of succeeding where her intimates had failed.

'Yes, he's your bairn, Jessie, no one denies that, my dear! But he's gone to his Father now, and you must let them be together in peace.' I was not at all sure whether I referred to Corporal James MacGregor or his Maker, but Jessie understood me to mean her husband.

'Yes. Yes, that's true,' she agreed hesitantly. 'He has ... he has gone to his Da. They are all there together in the heavenly land, all together now—savin' their poor old Mam!' And all of a sudden she thrust the little body at me and collapsed weeping on the mattress.

We did as I had promised her. Toddy-Bob found a packing case, and I laid the little body in it, wrapped in its shawl with its head on the pillow. Then Toddy carried the box down to the graveyard, accompanied by Charles.

I held Pearl in my arms as I watched them take the same route they had taken with Emily's body. I burrowed my face in the wispy down of Pearl's hair, and wondered bitterly how long it would be before her father carried her away too. She was fretful with hunger and I could do nothing but walk her up and down the verandah in the unfamiliar peace of the night, and croon to her. After a time, she dozed, and I put her in her bed, but as I did so, she awoke again and immediately began to cry. Bending over her, in tears of despair myself, I tried ineffectually to soothe her. I wanted to die and so escape the days to come.

And then, as I knelt weeping beside the box, a determined voice behind me said, 'Missie, that bairn'll no sleep till she's supped. Let me tak her. Red Jess has all the wee girl needs to soothe her!'

And Jessie, her hair well brushed, her clothing neat, took two long strides into the room, unbuttoning her bodice as she came.

CHAPTER 11

Red Jess moved in with us on the following day, laid her mattress between our beds, stowed a small tin trunk away in a corner and thereafter was in undisputed control of the household. She never again mentioned her Jamie, and I never heard her speak of her husband and other children; but she devoted herself to Pearl with such ferocious intensity that the rest of us were soon asking her permission to fondle the child. She fed the baby, washed and dressed her, crooned her to sleep and, when the firing was heavy, sang her mournful Covenanters' hymns, which strangely, in view of their dire content, seemed to soothe the child. Had I not been so grateful to see Pearl fed and well, I believe I would have become jealous. As it was, Kate and I would sit transfixed, watching the enormous woman nursing the little girl, or jump to do her bidding as she ordered us to take this away or fetch the other to her, while the men tiptoed around the room as if it held an invalid, and smiled and bobbed ingratiatingly whenever Jessie bent her pale eyes upon them.

A couple of days after her arrival in our quarters, she summoned me from the bedroom in which I had been trying to patch a pair of Charles's breeches with a scrap of green baize.

'The wee man wants you, missie,' she announced, 'and he looks unco' downcast.'

Toddy-Bob stood in the doorway wringing wet, rain streaming down his face and dripping from his clothing to form a pool on the earthen floor. But the men were in this condition at least once a day, so it was not his dampness that alarmed me. I thought at first that he had been drinking, his face was so pale and his eyes so bloodshot, but a closer look convinced me he was sober, though perhaps sickening for one of the agues or fevers which had become so frequent among the garrison. So I put the pot on to boil, for our tea still held out, and I could think of no other panacea for any indisposition.

'Take off your boots and sit down, Tod; your feet will dry by the fire,' I said as I took down our mugs and laid them on the table. Silently, he did as he was told, then sat with his hands on his knees, licking his wet lips and swallowing so that his Adam's apple wobbled up and down his scrawny neck.

'What is it, Tod? Are you not well?' I asked, laying my hand on his wet shoulder.

He shook his head and blinked.

'Not ill, miss,' he managed to say huskily. 'Bad news, miss!'

At once my mind went to Charles. He had been on guard all night, and in spite of the heavy rain, the pandies had been active.

'Tell me,' I whispered. 'It's ... Mr Charles?'

A sharp look came into his cold black eyes, and his glance held a hint of contempt or resentment; I could not be sure.

Again he shook his head. 'No, miss—not 'im.' He swallowed again and, with his head lowered, said almost under his breath, 'The Guv'nor, miss. He must be dead!'

'No! Oh, no!'

For a moment I was too shocked to question his assertion, but stood still and watched with curious concentration the tears trickle down his cheeks and join the drops of rain on his wet face. He clenched and unclenched his hands convulsively on the patched serge of the dead *sowar's* breeches.

''E must be, miss! 'E ... 'e went in to General Wheeler's entrenchment in Cawnpore!'

'He joined General Wheeler? But that's impossible. Why should he? And ... and ... anyway, how can you know, Toddy?'

I forced my mind to work, forced it to consider, to question so that I should not have to face the mental image that Toddy's words immediately produced. I could see him so distinctly, grimy and unshaven, sitting on the edge of the palanquin that morning of our arrival in Lucknow, and heard the subtlest cadence in his voice as he said, 'But I will come back. I'll come to you—for you!'

'Toddy, how can you know that he went to Wheeler?' I demanded sharply, dropping to my knees beside him and shaking him to draw his attention. He was crying openly now, and gulped, watching my face, as I went on.

'You know he'd never do a thing like that. Even if he was in

Cawnpore, there was no necessity for him to join Wheeler. He was probably there no more than a day, only long enough to leave Yasmina in her mother's home. He ... he probably didn't even know that Wheeler was being attacked, and if he did, why, you know, Toddy, how he felt about the military and ... and ...'

'Miss! Miss! I just seen Ungud.' Toddy halted my words with an upraised hand. 'Ungud came in last night with a message. Dunno yet what it was, but I'll find out. I saw him just as he was goin' out again. Wanted him to come to you but he 'ad to get out while it was rainin'— not so much firin', you see. He told me, he *told* me, miss, that 'e knew the Guv'nor had gone into the General's entrenchment, an' if 'e done that, 'e's dead, miss. There's none of 'em could have lived after what the Nana did to 'em. None of 'em, miss.'

'The Nana. But, Toddy, we have only heard that he was treating with General Wheeler. Do you mean ... ?'

''E done for 'em, miss, the lyin', thievin' bastard. 'E done for 'em all. They never 'ad no chance. Ungud says 'e 'eard from Moti's family like, that the Guv'nor went into the old General's entrenchment—an 'ospital it was—and no good to no one needin' protection from a sparrow. They put up a fight, though, and then, after a bit of a *burra-bat*, the Nana agrees to let 'em go peaceful like, lays on elephants and *palkis* and boats for 'em to go downriver to Allahabad. So then, well 'e lets 'em out, like 'e says, lets 'em all climb into the boats—thatched boats they was, and in no way enough to carry 'em all, but all they 'ad. Lets the boats push off, but 'alf of 'em was grounded on the sandbanks, and then, when they was struggling to get into midstream, 'e 'as 'is blasted pandies open fire! The thatch caught immediate like. Oh, Gawd, miss! It must of been 'ell on earth with all them nippers and women ... and the wounded. The men they slaughtered, and as many of the ladies and nippers as they could before the Nana sends to tell 'em to bring them ashore—but not the men. Ungud says 'e 'eard that one boat got away, but 'alf the men on it was dead or wounded and the pandies got it lower down. There ain't no chance for 'im, miss. The Guv'nor must be dead.'

He bent his head and sobbed, holding his sleeve across his eyes and sniffling convulsively just like the Cockney urchin he had started life as.

'No! No! Oh, my God, Toddy, it can't be true!'

'Yes, miss, it's true enough! And it weren't only the pandies on the shore; there was cavalry 'idden in the bushes on the river bank, and when the firin' starts, the troopers charges down into the river on their 'orses and cuts down everythin' before 'em with *tulwars*.'

'Did Ungud see it then?'

No, not 'im. But 'e 'eard it all, from the pandy sepoys in Cawnpore. It 'appened near a month ago now, and it stands to reason, miss, if the Guv'nor 'adn't been killed, 'e'd 'ave been 'ere by now. If 'e 'adn't gone in with Wheeler, that is, because 'e was only a day's ride from us, and if 'e 'adn't gone in—well, 'e would have come straight 'ere, wouldn't 'e? 'E'd 'ave been 'ere long afore us, miss. Oh, miss, 'e's dead!'

'How did Ungud know all this?' The voice was Kate's. She and Jessie had come in and listened silently as Toddy broke his news to me. 'And who is Ungud anyway?'

'He's a pensioner from Hassanganj. He was one of the men who came in response to Sir Henry's call at the end of May. Oliver used to employ him as a … a messenger.'

'That's right, miss,' confirmed Toddy huskily. ''Twere Sir 'Enry as sent him out, before Chinhat, to keep a eye on the Nana, like. But the pandies pinched 'im and kept 'im in Cawnpore, near two weeks before they let 'im go. Suspicious they was, but they couldn't fix anythin' on 'im. 'E 'ears all the gossip, the *bāt*. You don't know what a bazaar is like, miss, nor native lines, you don't. They sits around the fires in the evenings, the sepoys do, and they talks and tells tales, and they boast, and correct each other's tales, 'cause they know 'em all so well. One of 'em, that Ungud 'eard yarnin' with 'is pals, said as 'ow 'e'd seen a big Pathan with light eyes carryin' a wounded woman to one of the boats and 'angin' about in the water afterwards. 'E guesses the Pathan is a white man, you see, and watches 'im, like, for a while, and 'e tells 'is pals what 'e seen …'

'But, Tod, that's not enough to go on!' I burst out desperately. 'It need not have been Mr Erskine at all. It could have been some other man; after all, perhaps … I'm sure they must have been as short of clothing there as we are here, and would put on anything that covered them, and Mr Erskine would not have …'

Toddy shook his head and looked at me pityingly. 'No, miss. Don't think that, miss. It were 'im all right. You see, when the first man tells what 'e seen, another chimes in and says as 'ow 'e'd seen the big Pathan too, and it weren't no Pathan but the Sirkar of 'Assanganj. So then they asks 'im 'ow 'e knows and 'e says 'e and 'is family were from 'Assanganj, one of the villages like, and that 'e knew the looks of *Lat-sahib* Erskine, turban or not, as well as 'e knew the looks of 'is own pa. It were the Guv'nor, all right, miss.' He spoke with tired patience, and I realized he wanted to spare me the pain that must follow on unfounded hope.

I sat back on my heels and looked into his sorrowful face; perhaps my eyes spoke more eloquently than my lips could at that moment.

'Poor miss,' he whispered, and Kate crossed herself and said, 'May the Lord have mercy on his soul.'

'And Amen to a' that!' responded Jessie solemnly, having little idea of whom we were talking.

When Charles came in that night, I knew as he entered the room that he had seen Toddy-Bob.

'You know?' I asked, to break the silence.

He nodded.

'Do you think it can be true, Charles? Would Oliver have gone to Wheeler?'

'What else could have happened to him, Laura? He couldn't stay in Hassanganj, and there was nowhere else for him to go if he didn't come here.'

They all said that, so it must be true, but I still didn't believe it. It was not that I didn't want to believe it: I was incapable of having any views on the matter either way. If they all said it was so, then it must be so, but what they said meant nothing to me.

I must have behaved with a laudable and detached calm as we ate our meal, and sat for a little while trying to talk. No one could have guessed from my appearance or manner that I had a right to feel more than a decent amount of regret. Neither Charles nor Kate could guess at all that I knew of Oliver Erskine, let alone all I had learned to feel for him. And although then I felt nothing, part of my mind was already shrinking from the knowledge that I would have to bear my grief, when it came, without sharing or sympathy, and carry the burden of my loss in secret.

My life over the past months had been a series of avoidable, and now tragic, mistakes and it was the acute awareness of this that kept me from the realization of Oliver's death. First, I had to come to terms with my own conscience, forgive my own stupidity; then, purified by compunction, I would learn to face his death with fortitude. But not yet. Not yet. For the present, I would live in a half world of overactivity numbing my mind with the effort of appearing normal—normally polite, normally interested, normally frightened, although I was none of these things.

The whitewashed rooms were never cleaner or neater than during the days that followed. Sometimes I washed the mud floors three times a day; I polished our cooking pots with wads of grass and wet ashes as the village women did; I mended every rag in our possession with beautiful, precise stitches, then washed them with suds made from boiled gram, our soap being hoarded for Pearl. When all other methods of occupying myself failed, I turned to wick-making—pulling threads from petticoats and plaiting them together until the strand assumed a sufficient thickness to glow without burning up when placed in an earthenware saucer of thick, smelly tallow. I think I would have sold my soul for a library, or even a single book. In the past, I had always managed to assuage my ills by reading, and very often had inadvertently come across some particular work that strengthened me to meet misfortune or explained to me the intricacies of whatever predicament I was facing, teaching me philosophy and bringing me courage. Now, I had only Emily's small morocco-covered Bible, and the print was so close that even had I had the desire to read it, the darkness of our rooms would have made it impossible.

The long, hot nights were the worst to bear. The tallow for our saucer dips was hard come by, and since we had only two candle-ends remaining, we had formed the habit of retiring soon after our evening meal. The three of us would lie for hours awake, each feigning sleep to reassure the others, each unhappily occupied with sad memories and thoughts too heavy for expression. Sometimes it seemed to me that the accumulated regrets and fearfulness of we three bereft and lonely women weighed down upon us as near tangibly as the heavy, insect-loud darkness that pressed against our open eyes.

I would listen to the staccato crack of the Enfields, playing mental games to keep from thinking, counting the number of cracks between booms of the big guns, or between the explosions of one shell as they lit up the room briefly sometimes, and the next. I would listen to the toads croaking in the puddles and would try to fit the words of a poem to the broken rhythm—croak, craw craw craw, croak craw, croak—but the beat was never consistent. I would recite the poems to myself then, pages of Scott, Cowper and Wordsworth, and I found that I had picked up quite a lot of Mr Tennyson too, without knowing it. Every journal and newspaper in England had printed his poem on the Charge of the Light Brigade, and, though I had never learned it, preferring the lyric or sonnet form to the ballad, I had retained, as had the rest of England, those two lines that go:

> *Their's not to reason why,*
> *Their's but to do and die.*

I quoted them to myself with unrepentant bitterness, seeing in them now an allusion to our own situation, though not to my state of mind. The unthinking acquiescence that had made six hundred good men charge to certain death in the name of military discipline had never struck me as heroic. I saw no reason to admire them, or the system that had formed their mentality, though I never had the hardihood to say as much at home at the time! But still, it seemed now that ours *was* but to do and die, however little we liked it.

For one thing I was grateful: no one spoke much of Oliver. Living in the constant presence of death as we did, hearing day after day that some one or other of our comrades whom we had come to know, perhaps like, had died suddenly, horribly, a sense of self-preservation kept us from the sort of lugubrious reminiscence which can bring comfort to the bereaved in normal circumstances. Never did one hear, 'poor so-and-so, do you remember how he used to do such-and-such?' and similar remarks. We accepted the fact of death, then turned our minds consciously to living. It was the only way. We never mentioned Emily, either, or George, or Jessie's husband and children. Our griefs we kept private for the common good. We had no need to bring ourselves to a realization of the transience and mutability of existence; rather we needed to escape that realization. So we accepted the passing of our friends and loved ones, and then sorrowed for them in silence.

Toddy-Bob had taken Ishmial away and told him his news in private, and we did not see either of them again for two days. I wondered uneasily whether they were absenting themselves from their posts as they were from our kitchen, but Charles reported having seen Ishmial at the most dangerous sector of the walls, where the enemy outposts were a mere dozen yards from our own, dancing like a dervish, brandishing his smoking musket and screaming abuse at his opposite number on the other side, who was responding in kind!

On the evening of the third day, Ishmial staggered on to the verandah carrying the limp form of Toddy-Bob on his back. He dropped the little man like a sack of flour on the kitchen floor, and stalked out again wordlessly.

Toddy-Bob was very drunk.

Red Jess, who by this time was in full charge of our establishment, cocked an experienced eye over the steel knitting needles on which she was manufacturing socks for Charles, and remarked resignedly, 'I doubt he'll no be sober till the morn.' And laying aside her knitting she tidied him away in a corner of the kitchen, on a blanket fetched from her own bed, thoughtfully placing a bowl beside his head.

'He'll be the better of his grievin' when he's slept away the rum,' she assured me, and returned to her socks.

Later, as I was clearing up the kitchen before following the others to bed, Toddy awoke, and regarded me warily through one side-set eye.

'Miss, I bin drinkin'!' he informed me unnecessarily and with a hint of truculence.

'Yes, Tod, but ... well, you have an excuse this time.' What did it matter after all? Perhaps if I could have found release in liquor, I would have been drunk too.

'Oh, miss!' He sat up quickly, then clapped his hands to his head and winced. 'Oh, miss!' he repeated, when he had recovered from the initial shock of assuming an upright position. 'What'll we do now? Me and Ishmial? What'll we do! Me 'special? What can I do?'

I did not know what they could do, so said nothing.

'I've no 'ome, miss; leastways no 'ome but 'Assanganj. No family neither, miss. I got nowhere as I can go to now—when this is finished, I mean. Maybe it won't finish ... for me. Maybe I'll catch my wallop before that there relief ever comes. I swear to God, miss, beggin' your pardon for cursin', but I 'opes I does! I really 'opes I does!' He wiped his nose on a sleeve, and screwed up the one beady eye that I could see.

'With the Guv'nor gone, there's no place for me to go, no place at all. You see, miss, 'e were like me mother and me father all put together. 'E picked me out of the gutter when I was 'ardly more'n a nipper, and I been with 'im ever since. Always with 'im. It were in London. Me Dad run off; don't ever remember 'im. And me Ma drank like a belly-cut wasp at a jam jar. There was seven of us, different pa's I think we 'ad—we all looked mighty different anyway—and we never 'ad no money. When we was big enough we 'ung around the public 'ouses and the 'ostlers' yards, beggin or runnin' messages or 'oldin' 'orses and that, anything that would make a penny or two. Me Ma, though, she could pick the pocket of a h'archangel and him never know it. When she was sober, of course. I spent all my time 'angin around 'orses. 'Orses was the only good thing in me life and the only thing I cared about. I wanted to be a ostler or maybe a coachman, but there was no use in 'opin' 'cause no one would give me a place. No one to speak for my character; they all knew me Ma in them parts.

'So anyway, one day the Guv'nor come along and give me 'is 'orse to 'old. I'd seldom seen the like of such a beast, and such leathers! Soft as a lady's shoe the saddle was. So we 'as a friendly chat like about the animal, and 'e congratulates me on the amount I knew about 'orseflesh, and then 'e goes inside.

'While 'e's eating along comes me Ma, with the littlest nipper on 'er hip. That's 'ow she worked, see? She'd whine a bit and pinch the kid till it yelled and then say she had nothin' to give it to eat—which were true enough often—and the party would likely take out a penny and give it to her. As 'e turned to mount, she'd have spied the right pocket, see, Ma would fall against 'im or mebbe drop the nipper and do her stuff.

'This day she tries the same game with the Guv'nor, while I 'olds the 'orse's 'ead. Right worried I was, too, and angry when I see 'er come, 'e'd been that decent with me, interested and polite-like, like 'e always is when he understands, you know?'

I nodded silently, thinking of Emily whom he had also understood.

'Well, Ma fumbles the job, the Guv'nor catches 'er with 'er 'and in 'is pocket, grabs 'er and then grabs me too, 'cause I'd yelled out to warn 'im. Ma wriggles out of 'er shawl, drops the kid at the Guv'nor's boots and scarpers.'

A slight smile flitted across Toddy's face at the memory.

''E looks after 'er, quite cool, you know, and asks: "She is a thief," says 'e. "Why did you warn her?" Now that stung me. I'd been tryin' to do right by 'im, 'adn't I? "It was you I was warnin'," I says, "and I wish I 'adn't. She's my Ma. She don't mean no harm, but we got no pa and with all the young 'uns at 'ome" … and so on … chatting 'im up, like. I thought 'e'd report me mother to the Runners, anyone else would of, or the magistrates, maybe, and then what would happen to us, eh? Instead 'e puts 'is chin in 'is hand and takes a long look at me. Then suddenly, 'e bends down and smells me breath.

'"Drink," says he, disgusted, and I felt proper ashamed. "How old are you, boy?"

'"Don't know," says I. "Twelve year, maybe, maybe more."

'"Why do you waste your pennies on liquor? You're hungry too, or look it." So I tells 'im I drinks because I like it and me Ma does too, and I never remember bein' anything but 'ungry. By this time I'm blubberin' a bit, and me little brother is roarin' and the 'orse is gettin restive with all the noise.

'Maybe I should 'ave scarpered then like me Ma done. But there was something about the way 'e was lookin' me over, considering, that made me stay.

'Well, to cut a long story short, instead of calling the Runners 'e takes us, me and the little chap, Ned, to a chop 'ouse and buys us a dinner like we'd never 'ad. Then he makes me take 'im to my mother. 'E yells at her a bit, says she should be in gaol but then the nippers would all starve, then gives 'er a fiver and says he'll give me a chance to earn a 'onest penny workin' with his 'orses. Me Ma don't mind. All she thinks about is the 'undred shillings worth of gin in her mit. So 'e takes me away, first to the 'otel he lives in, then to France, and then 'e brings me out 'ere. Sixteen year ago it is now. I never looked back, miss. Not once. 'E pays me reg'lar. Feeds me reg'lar. Trusts me. And Ishmial teaches me all as I 'adn't already learned about 'orses. 'Is father— Ismial's father—was a Pindari 'orse thief, and a very knowin' man. And I plays it square with the Guv'nor all these years. Never snitched a farthin' from 'im, and when I 'as to drink, I does it reg'lar like—with 'is permission. That were the only condition 'e ever made. No drinkin' exceptin' with 'is say-so. It were worth it, miss. Never regretted it a day. Not till now. And now, well, miss, I 'as it in me to wish 'e'd never set sight on me, nor never tried to make nothin' of me. 'Cause without 'im, miss, I'm done for. I got nothin' left!'

For a while we were silent: Toddy propped on an elbow looking into the darkness, and I sitting on the stool beside him looking at Toddy. Outside the guns spat sporadically through the steady thunder of the rain, and the toads croaked. Both of us were trying to adjust to the emptiness of life, and I envied Tod his right to express his grief.

'Miss Laura,' he said after a time, very quietly. 'You know how I feel?'

'Yes, Toddy, I know,' I answered, and he lay back on his blanket and wept.

CHAPTER 12

Ungud had carried no written message into the Residency on that first visit of his on the 22nd of July, and at first Mr Gubbins, who was head of the Intelligence Department, had been reluctant to believe his words. He and his staff had examined Ungud thoroughly, then ordered him out again to bring written confirmation of his news, which if it were true was heartening indeed, for Ungud said that he had seen the British once more in control of Cawnpore. Probably the authorities had tried to keep this intelligence to themselves until it was confirmed, but in twenty-four hours we all knew that General Havelock, with a small force, had defeated the Nana Sahib, burned down his palace at Bithur, retaken Cawnpore and was now preparing to march to Lucknow. The garrison, as a whole, received the news cautiously; none of us was eager to give way to hope. But on the 25th, Ungud materialized again, this time with a letter from Lt. Col. Fraser Tytler, giving substantially the same information and, moreover, promising to relieve us within the week.

Then we allowed ourselves to rejoice, if only for others, for Ungud had brought other news as well. We knew already of the Nana Sahib's treachery to General Wheeler's Cawnpore force, and among us were the wives and children, the fathers and mothers of the men who had been mown down by the Nana's guns just as they thought they had attained safety. There were many besides myself who feared sleep because of the vision it brought of a river flowing blood and ablaze with fire. Now, we learnt that the women and children who had jumped clear of those sinister boats and been dragged out of the water by the Nana's inexplicable moment of mercy, had met an even more ghastly fate. For eighteen days they had been kept in a comfortable house near the Nana's palace, the *Bibighar*, wellfed and treated kindly. Then, one morning early, five men with freshly edged swords, had entered the guarded house. When they emerged at midday all the women and girls, the children and babies at the breast, lay slaughtered like cattle in rooms ankle-deep in blood.

'It is too dreadful to contemplate! Too dreadful! And, Miss Laura, when I realize that the same thing may very well happen here …!'

Mr Roberts, our harbinger of doom, mopped his brow with a clean but crumpled handkerchief. He derived some sort of strength, I believe, from trying to keep his clothes as neat and spotless as they had always been, in spite of the difficulties presented by lack of soap, hot water and a smoothing iron. He was regularly to be seen darning his socks, a sight which called forth no little ridicule from his peers.

He had brought us the news of the massacre of the women and children, and in doing so had gained a measure of relief for himself at the expense of Kate and Jessie, who had both had many friends among the victims.

'The bodies—what was left of them, that is—frightfully mutilated they were, and hacked to pieces—were thrown down a well in the compound of the house. Such barbarism is scarcely to be credited. And from the Nana! Why, I remember the man myself well. I often had occasion to go to Cawnpore, and really he seemed a most unexceptionable, gentlemanly native. And the children! It is said that two of them … !'

'No!' Kate almost spat the word at him. 'No, Mr Roberts! I will not listen to any more. What you have told us is enough! I … I knew so many of the women—and their babies. I had known them all my married life. Poor Polly Danvers—she must have been over sixty; she must have been there, and I remember her as a young woman lately married, who was very kind to me when I first came out. And young Martin Dodd's wife, Agnes. They have been married only six months. He's here, poor boy. They were expecting their first child. Agnes was only eighteen. And Barry O'Connell … he left a wife and five children in Cawnpore, and he's lying in the hospital with a stomach wound. Oh, God, I suppose I should go to them. But I can't, Laura, I can't! Perhaps later, when we have got … accustomed to the thought. But I can't yet!'

'No, no, and where would be the sense o' that?'

Jessie's voice was muffled. She had put her large hands over her face, but the tears ran down her cheeks in spite of them and dropped on her broad grey bosom. She rocked to and fro on the little stool, and each movement of her body produced a protesting squeak from the cane.

'And where would be the good of going to anyone but the Lord in such a time? What comfort would ye have to give?

'There's many a one among the dead that I ha'e lived wi', marched wi', grieved wi', nursed and joyed wi', these many hard years past. Bairns that I helped their mothers to born; laddies I made the breeches for, and wee girls that ha'e helped me bath my Jamie when he was hardly bigger than my hand. They were kin of mine, though not by blood, but in sufferin'. We bore each other's woes, we women in the regiments. And we had the greater woe than weal. The men could drink and curse and whore to buy a wee while's peace, to forget the heat and dust and dirt, the loneliness and the fear, in rum or a boughten woman's dirty arms. But we had no such comfort. We bore our bairns painfully in strange places, to lose them o' the heat or cholera or flux before they'd brought more than worry to their mothers' hearts. We suffered our men in their drink, nursed 'em when they were ill, followed 'em when they marched, and few among us hoped for any comfort greater than a belly big with child. Aye, we'd see the young ones come, so fu' of hope, and age an English lifetime in a year. And then to die—in such a way, in such a place, by such a hand! The ways of the Lord are passing strange, passing strange!' Her voice died away, and even Mr Roberts was silenced. For a while only the mosquitoes said their say. Then Kate spoke again.

'Will we never understand them?' she said slowly. 'Why should the Nana have gone back on his moment's mercy so cruelly? What can have made him do it? How could they hinder or hurt him? Why did he change his mind twice? You would have thought that he could not bear to harm the objects of his own clemency. Anyone else, but not them surely?'

'Oh, Mrs Barry, if we had the answer to that,' said Mr Roberts, 'but, well, we do not know enough of what was happening, or of what the Nana thought would happen. Perhaps he was frightened of what would befall him if they were found in his keeping, though that messenger man ... what's his name?'

'Ungud?'

'Ungud, yes, he said no hair of their heads had been harmed until that morning. The Nana must have known, you see, that General

Havelock was very near. Perhaps he panicked. Perhaps he was really more evil than he appeared. How will we know until they catch him?'

'And yet, you know, I may be a blathering old fool, but I'd stake my left hand that man wasn't evil. Weak perhaps, but he hadn't an evil face. Something, or someone, influenced him. God forgive me for my softness at such a moment, but I cannot believe it was his doing!'

'Certainly, it is hard to credit, very hard to credit. But then, my dear Mrs Barry, so are most of the things that have happened to us all in the last couple of months. The messenger said that the town of Cawnpore is a desert of ruined buildings. Much had been fired or destroyed before our forces arrived, and then when our men found the house and the well, they went mad and completed the work of destruction. Such a pleasant town it was in the cold weather. Though always dusty, of course. Very dusty ...'

The daily ration of rum or beer allowed to each man was hardly enough to inebriate a kitten. After the news of the *Bibighar* massacre had filtered through the garrison, however, we were overtaken by a wave of drunkenness. A few drank for the sake of relief; after all, whatever had happened at Cawnpore, General Havelock was on his way to help us. But many more drank to kill their grief and shock. It was a mystery where the liquor came from but, whatever its source, it was consumed in a quantity sufficient to immobilize some of the batteries for hours on end. But for the lucky fact that the enemy were unusually quiet for the succeeding few days, we would have been in very real danger of being overthrown ourselves.

Once again, the optimistic among us suggested that the pandies had gone to meet Havelock's advancing force, but on the following Sunday another mass attack was launched against us.

Ungud paid us a visit shortly before it commenced.

He had become something of a hero to the garrison, and when he walked on to our verandah, the other women crowded round to see him and ask him questions. Some who had been bereaved by one or other of the Cawnpore massacres begged tearfully for more details, trying to force him to give them a crumb of hope. But to all the questions, all the suggestions that perhaps he was wrong, perhaps some few had escaped, at least from the boats, he would only shake his head and repeat, '*Sub murgya hai*' (They are all dead). When he was going, he touched my feet with his forehead and said: '*Mem*! The *Lat-Sahib* was a man ... but they cut him down like dog.' I was glad Toddy-Bob was not there to hear.

Then the attack broke out. It was the worst we had so far endured, but of short duration. We hoped the pandies knew their days of power over us were nearly over, and exulted when the firing died away to a ragged stutter of musketry and finally silence.

The assault was not even a topic of conversation for long, for that night someone entered the Resident's House and stole a selection of the King of Oudh's jewels—those jewels with which we had entered the enclosure a month before. The plan had been to bury them, along with a quantity of other treasure, in front of the building. No one then could have dug them up without being observed. But in those first chaotic days, no labour could be spared to dig the pits, and the treasure had merely been locked away in one of the rooms.

Charles laughed as he told us what had happened.

'Well, it shows at least that someone has faith in our relief really materializing,' he said. 'I own that I wouldn't have the spirit to think of future wealth in these circumstances!'

I did not find the matter very entertaining myself. I had noticed that Toddy-Bob was wearing that day a new and splendid pair of cord breeches; they must have cost a small fortune at the auction of some officer's effects, and Toddy-Bob was not, as far as I knew, a wealthy man. Or had not been. But I held my peace.

As women will do under any circumstances, the three of us, Kate, Red Jess and myself, had fallen into a routine of housework: Jess was responsible for Pearl, Kate made the beds and kept the rooms tidy, and I washed the floors and wrestled with the cooking. None of us had enough to do, and time hung heavily on our hands. We had no books except Emily's Bible and Kate's prayerbook. Jessie, who could not read, was probably the luckiest of us; she could not guess what she was missing. She had, however, an extraordinary memory, and in the evenings, when Pearl was tucked into her box for the night, she would recite psalms, or the poems of Robert Burns or the Ettrick Shepherd, or sing us hymns promising glory to the virtuous and sulphurous hells to the sinful. She never missed a word and could recite and sing for an hour at a stretch without repeating herself. Otherwise, she was not communicative. She looked askance at Kate's rosary beads and practice of crossing herself when she heard of a death. At first, she would just purse her lips and pretend not to notice, but eventually, curiosity got the better of her.

'Yon wee beads?' she asked truculently one evening. 'What do ye *do* wi' them?'

Kate's bright eyes twinkled. She explained the sequence of prayers: how the Hail Marys said on the ten small beads served as a measure of time during which one was expected to think of some moment in the life of Jesus Christ—his Birth, Death, Resurrection and so on—the large beads between them, on which the Lord's Prayer was recited, serving as a reminder to change the scene so to speak.

'Weel,' Jessie said doubtfully when Kate concluded, 'there's nae much wrong with what I can see o' that. I willna say the Papish prayer to the Virgin, mind, but when ye tak the big beadie in your finger, sing out and Jess'll give glory wi' ye!'

My culinary efforts did not occupy me for very long each day; the hardest part was trying to get the tough gun-bullock meat into an edible condition. I used to whack it between two flat stones on the floor, and then shred it with Emily's nail scissors. Even so it was tough and tasteless. Apart from my stew made of the beef (without vegetables) and rice and lentils there was little variation possible. To eke out the tea, we drank toastwater—slightly charred *chapattis* covered with boiling water and then allowed to steep. We got used to it.

I longed for occupation and could find none. All of us became irritable and snappy, and quarrels and stiffnesses were common among the ladies of the Gaol. We kept ourselves to ourselves as much as possible, much to Mrs Bonner's annoyance, for she had constituted herself the mentor and social arbiter of the Gaol. Morning calls were no longer possible except within the Gaol itself, but Mrs Bonner would put on her bonnet and sail down the inner verandah each morning at ten to do her duty by her neighbours; or rather, those of them whom she considered within her social *milieu*. She could not forget that she had once been the First Lady of a station—a very small station, Kate informed me sourly—and so she condescended to give unwanted advice and encouragement, even to those unfortunates on whom she absolutely could not call—the women of the lower orders. She formed the habit when the weather and the firing permitted, of singing hymns on the inner verandah each evening with those of the ladies who had not had the courage to withstand the suggestion, and it was to escape the unction in her self-satisfied voice as she warbled at the Lord that I, one night, closed the door behind me and seated myself on the steps of the outer verandah.

It had rained heavily all afternoon and toads were hopping into position near the puddles to begin their chorus. Mrs Bonner would have competition. Of course there was gunfire: the crack of a musket now and then, sometimes a sharp burst as two or three marksmen fired simultaneously. Once a shell burst above the Redan Battery, but two men passing at the time never looked up or broke their stride. We knew enough to recognize that the pandies tonight were not in a serious mood. The sky had cleared; a few pale stars grew bold and shone as I watched, and the western horizon was washed with green light that lent a brief unearthly glow to the tumbled buildings.

I closed my eyes and leaned my head against a shot-scarred pillar, wondering without much interest when our relief would really arrive. We had had a false alarm on the previous day: firing had been heard in the direction of Cawnpore and a strong force of pandies had crossed the Iron Bridge and rushed off in the direction of the firing. Like lightning, word had spread that Havelock had arrived. Men cheered, women rushed out into the open, congratulating each other on their deliverance; some even climbed on to the roofs to watch for our troops, and those of the wounded who could walk left the hospital, grabbing their weapons as they did so, in order to harass the natives still surrounding us as Havelock fought his way in.

But someone had made a silly mistake. There was no relief in sight, and dejection supplanted the enthusiastic cheers as we crept back to our rooms and the men turned once more to their guns. Excitement had not been unreasonable, however, for it was over a week since we had received word that the relieving force could be expected in 'five or six days', and it could not possibly be delayed more than a few days longer.

A few days more and it would all be over. I would be free to go home, free to walk on fresh green grass and breathe pure air; free to wear new clothes and eat good food; free, at last, to make plans.

But what plans were worth the making now? What was there left for me to do, but go back to Mount Bellew for a time, and then start work in some strange household, giving lessons to spoiled children? Yet, for the days between the first assault and Ungud's first visit, I had felt that all the best of life was mine for the grasping. Now Oliver was dead, and with him my moment of hope and happiness. Long ago on the ship Mr Roberts had commended my resignation as philosophy. But he had been wrong. I had never allowed myself to expect much from life because I was frightened of what would happen to me if my expectations were unfulfilled. But no amount of careful self-deception can protect one from experience. I had found myself and the promise of joy in the strangest quarter and had known that promise voided in the cruellest pain. Sometime, somewhere, a long way from here, the pain would ease, but never again would I experience the ecstasy of those few days when I had realized, and been prepared to admit, my love for Oliver Erskine. I was no longer a girl; I was dowerless, sharp-tongued and plain. And even had I not been all those things, there was only one Oliver Erskine. I would never know his like again. The thought of Charles never crossed my mind.

As I sat there, Mr Harris, the young chaplain, staggered out of the dusk towards me with a handkerchief pressed to his mouth, and subsided on the steps of the verandah, shivering with suppressed nausea. Mr Polehampton, the assistant chaplain, had been dead a fortnight, so now Mr Harris was forced to carry out all the duties of his office alone. It was not the first time I had seen him in this condition; the stench in the graveyard was now so unbearable that every evening poor Mr Harris was rendered violently ill by the time he had finished reading the burial service over those who had died during the day, and people said that often he would get back to his quarters and vomit for a couple of hours at a stretch. I ran into our kitchen and brought him out a mug of water.

He sipped it slowly with his eyes closed, mopping the cold perspiration from his brow, and shuddering as though in ague.

'Thank you,' he whispered, putting down the mug. 'Thank you, Miss Hewitt. I can never get used to it down there. It is truly terrible!'

I nodded sympathetically, and when he made to get up, restrained him with my hand.

'Sit still a while,' I begged. 'A little rest will do you good. Your wife must get so worried seeing you like this. Recover a little first.'

He allowed me to persuade him. 'Yes. I must say it is pleasant to sit still. I never realize, though, how tired I am until I do sit down, so I try to keep on my feet as a. rule. There is so much to do. I must not stay long; the men in the hospital are expecting me, though with the light gone there is not much I can do for them. Not many of them want to pray!'

'Well then, to wait won't hurt them, will it?' I assured him. He was a fussy, anxious man, but he was doing his best to carry the double load, and I respected him for it.

'There is more to do than ever now, in the hospital I mean, since the doctors decided that it was no longer proper for the ladies to be there. Letter-writing and so on, which the ladies used to do, falls to my lot now, and with everything else as well ...'

'Letter-writing? But what on earth for, when they can't be delivered?'

'Ah, well, the wounded, the dying rather, are sure that we will soon be relieved, and they want their people at home to have a last word from them. It's natural. Poor fellows, they always want to sound brave and cheerful, so that their families won't know how bad things have been with us.'

Three widows, one of them Mrs Polehampton, had volunteered to help in the hospital, and had been given a room in the building to save them the risk of crossing the open ground between their quarters and the hospital. Now, so Mr Harris said, the conditions were such that no ladies could be expected to endure them; and, though Mrs Polehampton and her friends had protested, for the last ten days they had been lodged in the Begum Kothi and forbidden to go to the hospital.

'None of them is strong, you see,' he said, 'and two of them are elderly. But they were a help—a great help!' He sighed resignedly.

As he spoke, an idea came to me—an idea which had been presenting itself half consciously to my mind since I had heard of Oliver's death. I needed occupation and I had to learn to think of something other than my own heart's emptiness. Surprising myself almost as much as I surprised Mr Harris, I seized time by the forelock and blurted out, 'Will they let me do it, Mr Harris, what the other ladies did? I'm young and healthy and have no responsibilities—no ties either,' I added quickly as he began to expostulate.

'Oh, my dear young lady!' Mr Harris was thoroughly shocked. 'Certainly not! The authorities would never hear of it, and rightly too. After all, the other ladies were much older than you, and experienced. Married, and ... and so on. Why, it would be most improper for a young girl ...'

'But, Mr Harris, I am *not* a young girl! I am twenty-four years old. Certainly I am not married, but I can't help that. And I have done quite a lot of nursing. I looked after my father for two years before he died, and here, when my cousin got cholera, I nursed her too. Oh, Mr Harris, it would be the saving of me if I could do something useful. You have no idea of the boredom and inertia we suffer cooped up with absolutely nothing to do.'

'I understand, Miss Hewitt, and I must commend your wish to help others, but really, you have no idea … This is no well-ordered, adequately provisioned hospital that we have here. We lack everything, medicines, bedding—even clothes for the wounded. No, no, Miss Hewitt! You must put it out of your head.'

I could have shaken the silly man. He thought I would have the vapours at the sight of a naked male. Perhaps I would indeed—the first time. But I would recover myself and get used to it.

'Now listen, Mr Harris, please,' I begged, 'I'm a practical sort of person, and reasonably steady. Honestly I am. I know what you are thinking—that I will be shocked. But I won't! I've seen many worse things than naked bodies, or even wounded ones …'

'Indeed she has, Mr Harris,' Kate said calmly, as she seated herself beside us. 'She has even killed a man. I'd take her if I were you. She don't weaken easily and I'll be glad to come along with her.'

'Mrs Barry, Mrs Barry, I would have expected you to support me, and here you are in collusion with the young lady! But surely you see the impropriety of even suggesting it?'

'Well now, Mr Harris, and I'm not sure that I do. But I can see a lot of impropriety in allowing men to die without even the small amount of comfort we two could bring 'em. No, Mr Harris. Divil take it, but I can see no impropriety at all in Laura's suggestion.'

'Well … I …' By this time Mr Harris had forgotten his nausea under the concerted attack of two determined females.

'And anyway, Mr Harris, what about the Birch girls? I know they are still doing their mite in the hospital. No one can keep them away, isn't that so?'

'Yes … but well, they are a special case, after all; their own brother, and the fact that they have lost so much—their father and so on, and as you say—well, they can't be kept away. In any event, they do not come regularly.' As though this was a mitigating circumstance.

'But they do go to the hospital?'

'Yes,' he sighed. 'They do.'

'Hm! Well then, there is a precedent to be followed. We will follow it!'

'It is a waste of your time, Mrs Barry. The authorities will never hear of a single young lady helping in the place. You have no idea what it is like, or you would not even think of it. I can understand Miss Hewitt's being carried away, but you, well, you know something of what is involved.'

'Only too well, Mr Harris, only too well. But now, tell me, if by any chance we did get permission to help the sick, you would not really object to our presence, would you?'

'If you mean, would I help you to get permission—I would not!'

'But you won't stand in our way if we do?'

'The matter will not arise!' said Mr Harris in a pontifical tone, and got to his feet. 'A kind thought; indeed a noble thought, Miss Hewitt. But unfortunately, quite impracticable.' And having raised his sweat-stained hat, he hurried away.

'Hm! We'll see about that!' said Kate as we watched him go. 'Now why ever didn't I think of it earlier? Woman dear, you're a genius!'

It took her several days to accomplish her purpose. She lobbied them all: Brigadier Inglis (now Officer Commanding the garrison), Father Adeodatus, the doctors, even Mr Gubbins. She wrote letters and waylaid the great as they hurried past our verandah, and at length she got her way. I never knew how she finally prevailed, but I imagine the doctors, harassed beyond conventions by the number and state of the wounded, were the first to succumb to her blandishments. However it was done, eventually the authorities relented so far as to allow the two of us to visit the hospital for one hour *per diem* in order to write letters and read prayers to the wounded. Nothing else was to be allowed us, and no more time. We were to go immediately after the midday meal, when the firing usually slackened a little while the pandies attended to their cooking, and should we be killed in the discharge of these trivial duties, no one would be held accountable but ourselves.

'We can start tomorrow,' Kate said joyfully when she had imparted these directions. 'And now we must get Toddy to "come by" paper, pen and ink.'

CHAPTER 13

When I had gone to the Resident's House with Charles to find Jessie MacGregor on the day of the first assault, the sight of the tall building had recalled to my mind a happier occasion and I had been able to compare its condition with the way I remembered it nine months before. No such sentimental ruminations were possible as Kate and I approached the Banqueting Hall, which now housed the hospital, on that August afternoon; we were in too great a hurry to reach its shelter to waste time in reflecting on its past.

In the elegant colonnaded building, I had once waited for Captain Fanning to bring me iced champagne, and, while waiting, had heard a stranger's voice enunciating unwelcome sentiments about the women who thronged its rooms. 'Women mean emotion,' that voice had said, and the equation I now knew was valid. Without women, Cawnpore would have been merely one more inglorious episode in a long history of martial ineptitude and civil ignorance. But because women had died there, every white woman in India, including ourselves, was potential victim, martyr and burden all in one. Had there been no women in Lucknow, the city would have been evacuated; no entrenchment would have been necessary, no leaguer possible. Men who were dead would be living, men dying would be well, men maimed would be whole.

I did not formulate these thoughts as Kate and I sped sweating through the heat, starting involuntarily at every shot which rang out as we went. The men were inured now to fire and never ducked, and even we, when we were in our rooms, noticed none but the closest explosions. But neither of us had ever been under fire in the open before. That night, however, safe again in my bed, I reflected on what I had seen and remembered Oliver's words; and then, though I could grant the justice of his sentiment, I could have no inkling of the depth of indignation which would be fired in every English-speaking country and in Europe by the murder of a few score white women and children in a dusty Indian town. I could not know of the great endeavour being made on our behalf, or the frantic haste with which that endeavour was being turned to action. Who could have guessed then at the torrent of rage, revenge and bitterness that had its fount in the well at Cawnpore? But I had learned during that single hour in the hospital the extent of the sacrifice and suffering which our presence demanded from our men.

The long ground floor room which constituted the whole of the hospital since, for safety's sake, the upper storey had been evacuated, was so dark that we had to pause at the door to allow our eyes to accustom themselves to the gloom. We knew that, in order to induce the pandies to spare the hospital, prisoners, including a couple of the Princes of Oudh, had been lodged in rooms in the north wing of the building; but, though the enemy was aware of the fact, the building was under constant attack. Every window and door was barricaded, a fact which banished light and raised the temperature, but had not prevented one man from being shot dead through the head, and several others from being wounded as they lay on their beds.

The room was crowded to suffocation with iron bedsteads, string cots, mattresses laid on the bare floor, and rush mats lacking even a mattress—all so close together there was barely room to pass between.

The air was appalling. The heat of the shuttered room served to accentuate the myriad horrid odours resulting from tropical diseases and the sweetness of gangrened limbs. The *punkahs* moved but could not freshen the evil effluvia, and the men lay sweating, gasping for breath, unwashed and unshaven, many still wearing the clothes in which they had been wounded. There were no sheets, no pillows, and the blankets on which they lay were stiff with filth. Bluebottles buzzed over pools of vomit and excrement on the floor; over plates of uneaten food, medicine glasses, mugs of tepid water and the tins in which leeches disgorged the blood of the wounded.

Perhaps, had we been able to discern all this as we entered, we would have turned back then and there. Our eyes, however, were slow to mark details, though our ears were immediately assailed by moans and sighs, the delirious ravings and unconscious mutterings which were to become the invariable accompaniment of our efforts.

Dr Darby looked up from a man he was attending as we entered.

'Ha, Mrs Barry, you're here,' he said gruffly. 'I don't know that you should be, but I suppose I can't keep you away now. Like those Birch girls. This is no place for women, but I can't say I'm sorry to see you all the same. Mind, no meddling with the nursing. Write their letters, fan 'em, keep the flies off, give 'em water, and tidy up the mess, if you can face it. But nothing more. And don't pester the poor devils with prayers. Save those for yourself. Who is this with you?'

'Miss Hewitt,' answered Kate serenely.

'Well, mind you do as I say, young woman!' he admonished me. 'And keep away from this section. Not fit for you. Over there are some of the convalescents. See what you can do for them. Now be off, keep quiet and stay out of my way. And if you intend to faint, do it outside and don't come back again. Haven't time to bother with sensitive females.'

He turned back to his patient, and we picked a path towards the men he had indicated. Dr Darby's pregnant wife had been in Wheeler's entrenchment in Cawnpore, and it was not difficult to forgive him his brusqueness.

Most of the men were too ill and miserable to do more than regard us dully as we passed them, but one or two smiled and one waved a bandaged hand at us cheerfully. 'What, no broth nor jelly?' he enquired sarcastically as we passed.

We did not accomplish very much that afternoon. Only two men wanted letters written, and I believe they were accommodating us. The one I wrote went something like this:

Dear Nell,
The pandies got me in the left foot, but it is mended. If you ever get this, I wish you to know as how I often think of you and Ma and Pa. We have fought them off till now, and otherwise I am well and happy as I hope this finds you.

I looked up, expecting more, but the lad (he was no more) asked me to sign his name. 'Can't say much to 'em, can we, miss? Wouldn't want them to worry. Anyway, where could we start?'

For the rest of the time, I moved among the beds with dippers of water, which I fetched from a bucket just inside the door. I felt self-conscious and responded shyly to the calls of 'Water, ma'am!' or 'Please, miss, water 'ere,' taking care to keep my eyes averted from the bare limbs and scantily bandaged wounds of even these so-called convalescents. More than once, only a quick drink from the communal dipper kept me from an ignominious retreat outside. An elderly man, who saw me pause before taking water to a man who had asked for it, gave me a smile and a wink. 'You feels it more'n we do, miss,' he whispered. 'We got used to the smell, and it's better'n bein' dead after all! Don't take on, miss. There's worse things than this.' I wondered if there were.

Kate did better than I. She knew many of the men, and could talk to them about their families as she fanned them. Her manner was forthright and easy, but pity and embarrassment constrained me to silence.

There were several doctors in the entrenchment, but too few medical orderlies. The few men who were on their feet did what they could for the others, and the smaller boys of the Martinière School pulled the *punkahs*, fetched food and water, swatted flies and fanned. Other help there was none—either for doctor or patient.

After a bare hour, we walked out into the sunlight in silence, too preoccupied with our impressions to bother about the bullets.

The next day we returned. And the next.

Gradually, the regulation hour became two, and we did more than keep the flies off and pass the dipper round. Soon we were washing the patients and feeding them. Then, emboldened by the Birch girls' example, we watched the doctors dress wounds so that we could do the same. Before long, we were dressing wounds ourselves.

My embarrassment soon disappeared; we were in no position to value false modesty, and, though the doctors still protected us from the worst of the sights, nothing could guard us, or the other patients, from the sounds a man made as he underwent amputation. What was even more horrifying than the victim's agony was the knowledge that it was useless. No man ever recovered from losing a limb.

Often, in the evenings, I stumbled back to our rooms nauseated and trembling, and swore that I would never set foot in the place again. Night after night, I left my food untouched and went to bed to sweat in anguish at remembered scenes. Then my mind would grow cruelly calm, and the worst scene, the one I feared most and fought most strenuously to forget, would crowd into my thoughts: Oliver cut down by a trooper's *tulwar*, drowning in that river of blood. By morning, I was always ready to escape from it back to the hospital. I could forget him there—sometimes.

So the month of August wore on. It rained, and when the rain stopped we sweltered in the steamy heat. Our rations were cut; the tea was finished. The men were without tobacco or sugar. No one had seen white bread for nearly three months, and the *atta* (coarse wholemeal flour, ground in hand mills) with which we made our *chapattis*, induced an irritation of the bowels and consequent diarrhoea.

Twice in a fortnight the wall was breached, and twice we beat off the insurgents, but the danger that had at first seemed a joke, mining, had become a major preoccupation.

Evening after evening, the lookouts watched for the sudden flare of a rocket that would tell us General Havelock was really coming. But night after night, they watched in vain.

It would be fatuous to pretend that we became accustomed to the conditions of our life: rather we became, to some extent, inured to them. We could not disregard the heat, the boils, the noise, the lack of food, the evil smell and the fatigue. But we learned to minimize them in order to cope with the more acute distresses. Men got drunk, despite the fact that there was no longer a ration of liquor; they fought their friends, stole each other's paltry possessions, went whoring when the opportunity offered, and cursed their fate with colourful energy. And they fought. Women wept and worked, nagged and bickered, gossiped and lied, and sighed for better days. And they suffered. The cohesion of interest and endeavour produced by the first fear fragmented as we became accustomed to living in it; we became again, but less pleasantly, our true, individual human selves.

To all this, the petty selfishness no less than the hidden heroism, I became a party now that I was free to move around the entrenchment. The men became accustomed to seeing the Birch ladies, Kate and myself running between our quarters and the hospital, and almost always we found ourselves accompanied for protection. What good our protectors could have done against a pandy's stray bullet was beyond my comprehension, and certainly no one but the enemy would have harmed us. I had soon realized that it was easier to face the enemy's fire for two brief periods a day than to endure the anxious monotony which was the lot of the other women, but the men insisted on treating us as privileged beings. Presents came our way, pathetic little wisps of paper containing a crumbled biscuit, or a little sugar; once, three buttons on a card! I think the fact that we were willing to talk to the men in the hospital did more for them than any of our other amateur ministrations. We heard many an unhappy story of unfaithful wives, dead children or anxiety for parents left alone in some small out-station overrun by the mutineers. We could do nothing, but we were willing to listen; and the look of relief that came into a man's eyes when he had given verbal form to his sorrows and worries was worth all the time we spent in this way.

We made friends, too, and chief among these was Llewellyn Cadwallader, one of the Martinière schoolboys who helped at the hospital.

Llewellyn was perhaps twelve years old, though the tired eyes in his wan, coffee-coloured face belied his youth. The son of a Welsh road inspector, his mother had been a Eurasian girl who died giving birth to Llewellyn's young brother, Sonny. The two little boys had been placed in the Martinière at an early age, and the school was almost all the home they had ever known. When the trouble broke out, they had been brought into the Residency with their comrades, but of their father, who had been pursuing his work somewhere in the district, nothing had been heard.

'It is not, miss, that he is dead,' Llewellyn assured me stoutly, 'only far away.' I hoped very much that he was right. He was a quiet child, with an elderly manner and a resigned outlook on life. One day, shortly after starting work in the hospital, I had rewarded him for some service with a little sugar given me by one of the wounded.

'It is a very good thing, sugar,' he announced solemnly when I told him what the paper contained. 'Very strengthening! I will give it to Sonny. He is very small, you see, miss.'

He placed it for safe keeping in his pocket, and after that, as soon as I appeared in the hospital, he was by my side and never left me till I went. Though he spoke seldom, I soon realized that he heard everything (including a great deal that he shouldn't have) and was a walking encyclopedia not only on the conduct of the siege, but also of the besieged. Being bilingual, and in addition free to move where he wished, his information, if not always accurate, was extremely varied.

It was he who told me of the prevalence of 'light infantry', as the more delicate females termed head lice.

'They've all got it now,' he said with satisfaction. 'Not only us boys and the soldiers, but the officers and even the ladies. They've been going to bed with their heads tied up in scarves, but it didn't work.'

'Surely not, Llew!' I stopped. Why should we ladies not have them? We had known for weeks that the men were plagued with the wretched things, and everyone realized they were catching. Immediately, my scalp began to crawl.

When I got back to the Gaol that night, I got out Emily's little nail scissors, which I used to shred the meat, and went straight into the bedroom. There was little light and no mirror, and my hair was thick and heavy, but I hacked away and soon my hair, my best feature, was lying in red-brown coils on the earth floor. Having satisfied myself that the worst of the job was done, I went into the kitchen to ask Kate to trim the ragged ends.

'Lord have mercy on us!' cried Kate.

'Och now, Miss Laura!' said Jess.

And Toddy-Bob, who had been sitting on the floor in a doze, leapt to his feet, and then broke into a guffaw of rude laughter at the sight of my shorn head.

I explained the purpose of my desperate deed amongst mingled laughter and recriminations.

'Frightened of a louse!' exclaimed Toddy in disbelief, while Jess announced that I looked 'for a' the world lak' a bonnie wee boy, but I doubt ye'll find a husband lookin' that way.'

They would not allow me to view myself in the square of spotted mirror which we kept above the table, until Kate and Jess between them, aided by advice and comment from Toddy, had brought some neatness to the edges of my locks. What I then saw was sufficiently depressing to make me wonder what I had looked like to begin with.

Just at that moment Mrs Bonner chose to look in on us.

'But, my dear, of course you'll have to wear a cap now,' she said, having taken me in with pursed lips.

'I haven't one,' I answered shortly.

'No cap? But surely, at least a bed-cap? You must have a bed-cap?'

I shook my head, impatience mounting. I had brought one with me from Hassanganj, true enough, but now perhaps one of Wajid Khan's servants was wearing it.

'How ... singular,' breathed Mrs Bonner. 'I can't think how you manage. I confess that I could not bear my cruel lot so well if I didn't see the necessity of retaining as much as possible of my former ways. I try to keep to a timetable you know, very much like the one I pursued in Kaliaganj. One must discipline oneself, even in moments of *extremis*.'

'Must one?' I asked sourly. 'I haven't enough time to think of a timetable.'

'No? Well, I'm sure the hospital must take up a great deal of your attention, of course, and I'm sure it is very noble of you to work there as you do.' She stopped, reflectively, and then went on. 'My Minnie had some fanciful notion of joining you, but, of course, I put a stop to that immediately. She has such a generous nature, gets quite carried away by her own good-heartedness. But, as I said to her, "Well, Minnie, my dear, that sort of thing just doesn't become women like us. We must be content to give dear Papa all the comfort and support he needs when he comes home. That is a truly ladylike vocation, and it is always well to know the bounds beyond which the genteel cannot go." She's so young and enthusiastic.'

'Quite!' said Kate decisively. 'And when her poor papa is carried into the hospital some fine day, missing an arm or a leg, it will be a comfort to him to know how properly she is being reared.'

'Quite,' agreed Mrs Bonner complacently. And then in another tone of voice. 'Quite!' She left soon after.

When the others had gone to bed, I sat for a time in the kitchen, fingering my short hair sadly. I had propped the door open for the sake of air, and could hear the rain splashing on the verandah and the bass chorus of the toads.

After a time I picked up the tallow dip and went to the mirror. I scarcely recognized myself, and looked with curiosity at the stranger's face—thin and pale, with deep shadows under the eyes, and cheekbones oddly protruberant—in the guttering light of the little wick. I had never been blessed with beauty, but now I was worse than plain. I was ugly. My mouth was wide; I had liked to think it indicated humour, but now there was a new set to the lips, firmer, but also bitter. In two and a half months I had aged out of my own recognition. The short hair looked horrible. I looked at my reflection for a long time, trying to remember myself as I had been, but the tired eyes, sad mouth and cropped hair made my task impossible. Two tears of nostalgia for my lost youth slid down my thin cheeks.

'Don't cry! Oh, Laura, don't cry!'

Unknown to me, Charles had entered the room, and my eyes met his as he looked over my shoulder, his face very near mine.

'Please don't cry, my dear—not you,' he whispered, and then he smiled. 'Oh, your hair. I see what is the matter now. But ... it looks quite charming, honestly!'

'Liar.'

'No, honestly! But you've got so thin. I hadn't noticed before.'

'So have we all ... and hard and old.'

'Hard? You? What nonsense! You've always had more heart than was good for you. Or me, come to that!'

He put his hands on my shoulders, and we regarded each other in the mirror. He was thin, too, and his moustache was badly trimmed. I tried to smile but, for a moment, emotion, and even more pure fatigue, overcame me, and more tears came, so that I turned and buried my face in the open collar of his shirt. I wanted to tell him, to tell someone. I wanted to say, 'Oh, comfort me now for my love's lack, as once I wished to comfort you for yours. Console me for my mistake, as once I would have consoled you for yours.' If I could, I would have wrung sympathy from him, and understanding and strength. But I knew it was no good. In that moment, when we had looked at each other in the mirror, I had not really seen him. I had looked behind him for that pair of eyes that once in Hassanganj I had found beyond his in the mirror, and known as I met them that they had seen more than I had seen myself.

'Laura? What is it? These tears are not for your hair? Oh, my dear, you must not cry. What can I do?'

'Nothing.' I drew away, and took out my handkerchief. 'I'm sorry, Charles. It's just that I am so tired, and nothing seems to get any better, ever. I ... I'm just tired. That's all.'

He took my chin in his hand and tilted my face upwards into the light of the dip.

'Yes, you're tired. But that's not all, is it? What is it, Laura? Let me help you. You know how I ... But something's changed you, hasn't it? You're not the same, not the same at all; though you try to be. Is it fear?'

'We've all changed. We must all change to survive. Don't be silly, Charles. Everything changes all the time—people, events, everything. It's only right that they should.'

'Is it? But I haven't. Not that much anyway. You know that, Laura, don't you?'

I nodded. It was the only thing to do. I had thought of him so little over the past weeks that perhaps what he said of himself was true. But I didn't know.

'It can't go on much longer. The relief is bound to arrive soon, and then ... well ... then we'll be all right again, Laura, and there'll be so much more to look forward to than before. We'll know so much better how lucky we are, because of all that we have lost and learned here. I expect, in that sense, you are right, and even *I* have changed. Don't let go yet, my dear. Hold on a bit longer, only a little longer. Things will soon be better.'

I nodded again, the picture of female docility, knowing that for me nothing could ever be really better. I was relieved when he turned and went out of the door, shutting it after him. And then, as soon as he was gone, I wished that I had had the courage to tell him what had changed me. Once again I was too late.

CHAPTER 14

Incessant hunger and inescapable fatigue: those are among the evils that I recall most clearly about the siege. We never had enough to eat, and we never had a night's unbroken rest. Even if the enemy were relatively quiet, there would be something else to disturb us: Charles clattering in after a long spell in the mines, longing for food; a bereaved woman bewailing her loss further down the verandah; a drunken soldier creating a *fracas* on his way to his billet. Only the sound of the rain drubbing heavily on the flat roof was comfortable and familiar. Often we would go the night through without ever really sleeping, one ear open for the too-often heard cry of 'Stand to your arms!' the other alerted for the sound of picks and shovels in the earth beneath us. There was no telling where the next mine would be sprung, or at what hour. So far, we had been lucky and the enemy's tunnels had been misdirected. But the next time? Captain Fulton of the Engineers had discovered, in the ranks of the 32nd, a number of Cornish ex-miners. With their help our countermining had become more efficient, but we all were aware of the exhaustless supply of men the pandies could draw on; while as our numbers dwindled daily so did our duties increase.

No doubt Mrs Bonner retired with all decorum, but Kate, Jessie and I never troubled to undress at night. We took off our shoes, unlaced our stays, opened buttons at throat and wrists and lay down fully clothed. Our defences having twice been breached, fear and insecurity were intensified, particularly among the women, who spent much time and thought deciding what they should do should the enemy finally force their way in. Wherever three or four women gathered in the perennial dusk of shuttered rooms, the conversation was bound to turn to this sombre subject.

Listening to their chatter, half-besotted as I was with lack of sleep, I came to the conclusion that every woman in the entrenchment knew someone who had known someone else who had been violated, ravished and slain with unspeakable refinements of torture. The curious thing was that no one who, like ourselves, had managed to reach the Residency, had even been threatened with what was generally termed 'the worst imaginable'.

True, some had lost their menfolk from illness or accident on the way; some had seen husbands and fathers murdered by their own sepoys. Women too, like Mrs Wilkins and Elvira, had met violent deaths, but I could find no basis at all for the ladies' declared belief that the rebel sepoy's sole aim in life was the rape of a white woman. However, every female in the place declared that she would sooner die than submit to 'it', and to this end some had armed themselves with poison, others carried loaded pistols, and the more hysterical declared that they had arranged with a husband or friend to put an end to them with a bullet, as a last act, before shooting themselves. Only a very few, like Mrs Polehampton, had the strength of mind to leave their fate in the hands of their Maker.

I listened to these discussions in silence, remembering the night when Oliver had taught me to handle a pistol. How he had laughed on discovering that I intended to use the weapon to defend my life rather than my virtue! 'It's your life they'll want—not your person,' he had said. 'And whatever your own opinion of your attractions, they would consider any—er—commerce with a white woman a defilement. So you're safe enough there!'

I put forward this view on one occasion, but was met with such a mixture of blank disbelief and outright hostility that I decided to keep my own counsel in future.

'Erskine, did you say? Not Oliver Erskine? The man they call the Brahmin?'

Mrs Bonner had been telling us how Major Bonner had arranged with no less than three of his dearest friends to take over his duty of shooting his wife and daughter should he have met his end before the pandies entered the entrenchment.

'The same,' I answered coldly. It was almost the first time I had heard his name spoken since the news of the massacre at the river, and Mrs Bonner's use of the present tense wrung my heart.

'Oh, well! I can understand how he came by such peculiar notions. After all, it is well known that he is little better than a native himself, in his habits at least.'

'Indeed?' I said icily. I knew Mrs Bonner would never, in any circumstances, have been sufficiently intimate with Oliver to use his Christian name so carelessly, and obviously she did not know that he had been our host. She spent so much time dwelling on her own past grandeurs, that we had never had the opportunity to recount our histories.

'So you know him?' I asked.

'Oh, not well! A most peculiar man he is. Not at all *comme il faut*, and my husband never cared to develop the acquaintance, though of course, in his position, Edgar never needed to be short of friends, and I have no doubt but that Erskine would have welcomed the association. But no, I cannot say I know him well; Edgar would not permit it!'

'Oh, and in what do you reckon Mr Erskine to be deficient?'

'Oh, not only we, my dear Miss Hewitt,' she corrected. 'Anyone who has ever had anything to do with him recognizes that he is—well—an extremist, unbalanced. What normal man would want to live as he does, all alone out there in the *mofussil*, from one year's end to the other, with only the natives around him? A wealthy man like that, why, he could have the best that India has to give. He need never spend more than a month or two of the cold weather on his estate; I can't see what he finds to do there anyway. But as it is, he neglects all his social duties to the rest of the community, and it is well known that he holds the most *peculiar* views. Edgar says he speaks the language just like a native and—' she whispered behind her hand—'of course there has been talk of a "Petticoat Dictionary". He reads Persian for pleasure! I suppose it's the loneliness. It's enough to turn anyone's head, particularly in the hot weather. Edgar has always said that, although he is almost a neighbour— well, not quite in the English sense, you understand, a good day's ride from Kaliaganj his place is—but well, even though Mr Erskine is comparatively near, we could not entertain him. On account of Minnie, you know. Single men of that age so often form unfortunate attachments to young girls, and we do want the best for Minnie. After all, Miss Hewitt,' and she leaned forward confidentially, 'one must keep one's standards, even out here, most particularly out here, and that is just what Mr. Erskine has failed to do.'

I had a distinct impression of the standards Mrs Bonner considered worth maintaining, and was sure that Oliver had not upheld them. I said nothing, and there was a pause.

'But, Miss Hewitt,' and there was a note of suspicion in her voice, 'how do you know so well what Mr Erskine's opinions are—on the matter we were discussing? Do you know him?'

'Oh, I used to!' I said noncommitally, glad that Kate was not present to expatiate.

'And he talked to you, a single lady, about such a matter! Well, as you must admit, he really is not quite the thing, now, is he? Edgar will be horrified when I tell him. He is always so particular about such matters himself, and how right he was to protect dear Minnie from such a man. No wonder you say, "used to", Miss Hewitt. No wonder!'

I made an excuse and hurriedly left the room.

Fortunately for me, I did not have as much time to think of what would happen if the enemy entered the entrenchment as the others had. There were now so many sick and wounded that a couple of rooms in the Martinière post had been turned into an auxiliary hospital, and I could have found useful work for myself every hour of the twenty-four. Only the seriously ill could be visited by the doctors; but almost every one of us was less than well. The symptoms of scurvy now became apparent among us, added to those of tertiary ague, rheumatism and diarrhoea. Teeth became loose in spongy gums, the smallest scratches festered and wounds refused to heal, while a knock on the hand or foot rendered the whole limb bruised and blue. We lacked almost everything now: vegetables, fruit, white bread, butter, sugar, tea and coffee, and it was rumoured that we were coming to the end of the rum and beer. Tobacco was at a premium. While the tea lasted, the men smoked tealeaves, but when this last resource was denied them, tempers were liable to flare savagely, they became morose and depressed and a wave of looting and petty thieving broke out.

In addition to the walls, there were nine batteries of heavy guns to be manned night and day, and the numbers of the artillery had dwindled so alarmingly that now civilians, schoolboys, even—to their chagrin—cavalrymen, were indoctrinated into the mysteries of loading, firing and cleaning the heavy cannon in order to keep them in action. The professional gunners, however, had not yet learned to trust their assistants and spent their time rushing from one battery to the other to assure themselves that all was well.

Our daily more ruinous walls were constantly tumbling down under the enemy fire and the rain, and it was of the utmost urgency to build them up again without delay. There were graves to be dug, ruins to be cleared of rubble and sketchily repaired for use, and guns to be hauled by hand from one position to another. And in all weathers and at all hours men worked on the countermines, or simply sat at the end of a tunnel listening for the sinister sound of a pick deep in the earth.

The rain, which we had so longed for, did little to mitigate the smell of the entrenchment; instead, it provided one more hazard. The stretch of shell-holed land between our walls and the enemy was now verdant with waist-high grass, a splendid cover for pandies approaching the entrenchment.

'S'truth,' swore Toddy, describing the qualities necessary to keep oneself alive. 'By the time we're relieved, we'll all 'ave ears like lynxes from listenin' for the mines, and eyes like cats from watchin' for the pandies. T'aint natural!'

Mr Roberts's shirt was frayed at the collar and lacked buttons, but it was still clean. Like the rest of us, he had lost weight, and his hands, once as smooth and well cared for as a woman's, were covered with boils and scabs; but he still carried his musket as though it were a furled umbrella.

'Have you no news for us of a cheering nature, Mr Roberts?' I asked.

'Ah, the relief! Rumours, Miss Laura. Nothing but rumours. The strain of not knowing is almost greater than hearing the worst. But I cannot understand what is keeping Havelock so long. The military gentlemen, of course, have a great many theories as to why he is delayed, but, after all, he is only forty miles away, and reached Cawnpore, as we know, a full month ago. What can there be to deter him from marching on to us?'

'A roused countryside, and a great city crawling with pandies through which he must cut his way in order to reach us. Among other things,' said Kate.

'Agreed. But it is said that he has a fine force with him. I cannot but feel that he has not been given the facts—about our food supplies, for instance.'

'Come now, Mr Roberts. According to your predictions, we should have died of hunger by the end of July. And here we are still going strong at the end of August. The Brigadier must know what he is about.'

'But it's not only the food. I am increasingly alarmed by the state of mind that seems to be apparent among the Sikhs. I have always had my doubts of them, you know, Mrs Barry; I always felt it would have been wiser to disarm them, or if that were impossible, order them out of the place before the Baillie Guard was closed. Who could blame them now for losing confidence in our ability to withstand the enemy? Not I for one!'

'Nor I, Mr Roberts. And it is just that fact, that, though knowing our wretched position, they have remained with us for so long, that makes me think they will remain until the end.'

'And then, of course, the Cawnpore affair: That alone was enough to make any native in the place wonder whether he wasn't on the wrong side.'

'Not at all! I spoke to many who were horrified at the whole thing.'

'Certainly they would *say* so, but such a signal defeat of the British cannot but have made some impression on their minds, given rise to some doubt.'

'And now, the Nana has himself been most signally defeated. Don't forget that, Mr Roberts. The sepoys will know of that as well as the other. Really, there are times when I lose all patience with you. You mustn't be such an old woman, Mr Roberts; you must learn to encourage optimism, not the reverse.'

Poor Mr Roberts was quite put out by her manner and words; Kate never learned to temper her tongue to the shorn male's vanity, but what she said was true. We needed to husband our hope, not squander our emotional energy on vague presentiments, half-formed fears and groundless suspicions. Life was so little pleasant now that dejection had to be fought off as consciously and aggressively as the pandies. Sometimes, lying sleepless on my string cot in the unquiet dark, I had caught myself wishing that the end would come, almost longing for the cessation of effort, of grief, of recurrent fear, that was all that death could mean for so many of us now. Only the thought of Pearl, only the guilt her mother's memory still roused in me, only the knowledge that some few men in the hospital were the better for my presence, kept me from surrendering to the lethargy of abandoned hope.

Mr Roberts shrugged. 'I did not mean to alarm you,' he said stuffily. 'I will keep my views to myself in the future.'

'Yes, please do,' grinned Kate, unrepentant, and we all fell silent for a while.

Kate's words were brave ones; but how many of us at that time, including her, had any real expectation that help would arrive before we had been breached and the enclave entered, or at best starved out? From the beginning of the siege, it had been common knowledge that one determined push on the pandies' part would be sufficient to overwhelm us, and the question continually in the minds of the garrison was when the final assault would come. So far, we had beaten off three major assaults, twice the walls had been breached, and no one knew why the enemy had allowed themselves to be repelled without accomplishing their object. Perhaps it was the lack of leadership that George Barry had declared would be more useful to us than a regiment.

And then, at midnight on the 28th of August, Ungud returned again from Cawnpore with another message, this time from General Havelock himself.

The authorities, judging the matter to be of a cheering nature, posted up a copy of the message for all to read.

My dear Colonel,
I have your letter of the 16th instant. I can only say do not negotiate, but rather perish sword in hand. Sir Colin Campbell, who came out at a day's notice to command, upon news arriving of General Anson's death, promises me fresh troops and you will be my first care. The reinforcements may reach me in from 20–25 days, and I will prepare everything for a march on Lucknow.

Yours v. sincerely,
H. Havelock.   Br. Gen.

Kate and I read it on our way home from the hospital. Dusk was falling, and sheeting rain added to the darkness. A soldier lit a lucifer and held it up, protected by one hand, to help us read the communication. He was shivering with ague, and his clothing was soaked.

'Another month, it looks like, ma'am,' he said to Kate, as she turned away from the paper, and thanked him. 'Another month—of this!' An all-encompassing shrug indicated the desolation of our surroundings— the rain, the sound of the guns, the mud that squelched in our shoes as

577

we moved—and I saw in it also the man's hunger, his fever, sleepless nights, restless days, and all his fears and hurting memories.

'Yes, another month. It will be hard, but at least General Havelock has been honest with us. It will be no more than a month, I am sure. He is a man of his word, they say.' Kate was trying to cheer the man, a thin fellow with pinched features, dull grey eyes and ginger whiskers. His expression, half furtive, half watchful, combined with his physique and features, told of a childhood in some city slum, always unsatisfied, always deprived—of food, education and hope.

'Aye. But a month, ma'am. 'Tis a long time to go on like this. Is that truly what the General says in his letter? I haven't the reading; 'twas one of my mates as told me. Would you, maybe, say out the writing for me to hear for myself?'

Kate did as he requested and spoke a few words of encouragement to him before we walked on.

'How the military mind does love a flourish,' I said acidly, and declaimed into the teeth of the rain with appropriate gestures, "Do not negotiate—but rather perish sword in hand"! What happens, dear Kate, to us wretched swordless females?'

The rain was warm, and one's bare skin met it without flinching as it does at chilly English rain. It produced also, a false sense of security against the guns, wrapping us in a cocoon of grey water that obscured our vision and muffled our ears, so that we hardly hurried as we passed from the shelter of one building towards that of the next.

'Oh, didn't you know? We are to be herded together into one house and blown up—all together in a jolly bang!'

She spoke lightly, but I knew she was not joking. With the memory of Sir Henry Lawrence's final directions, and the example of Cawnpore ever present in their minds, the authorities had worked out some such plan. The touch of the rain turned colder as I remembered that there were now only seven hundred and fifty men to defend us, and a month of fighting still to come. But I ignored the tremor of fear, refusing to take Kate seriously.

'But surely not,' I exclaimed in a tone of well-bred horror. 'Not everyone! Perhaps there are others like me who would sooner form part of a *talukhdar*'s harem?'

'Ah, then let me advise you to apply at once for permission to the recognized authorities, civil and military, and in due course, perhaps even in good time, you will receive the appropriate permit ... in triplicate, of course.'

'Thank you. That I shall do.' And we made the last dash to the Gaol verandah in a gale of unworthy laughter.

Later that evening, Ungud came again to see me.

The enemy had of late directed much of their attention to the battery in Mr Gubbins's garden, so Toddy-Bob was not with us, but Kate was there to interpret when I got lost in the flood of Ungud's words.

The little man squatted on the floor with his back to the wall, wizened and nearly naked, his staff laid carefully beside him.

He had had great difficulty in getting away from Cawnpore with General Havelock's message, and for ten minutes or so we had to hear an account of his ingenuity and hardihood in managing at length to do so. The rebel sepoys were massed on the north bank of the Ganges at Cawnpore, but our relieving forces, after a succession of minor battles, skirmishes, and what seemed to me pointless comings and goings, were now assembling in the town to await their reinforcements and then push through to our relief. The Nana Sahib, having been defeated at Bithur, was licking his wounds in Fatehpur, and British forces were expected to re-enter Delhi within the month. All this was of consuming interest to Ungud and, as he expatiated on each detail with the enthusiasm of a military strategist, his long sinewy hands cast strange shadows in the light of the dip, as he used them to bring home a point or describe a manoeuvre.

Then his monologue took suddenly a more interesting turn. The enemy, said Ungud, were on the point of making a great assault upon the Residency. There would be no less than eleven thousand sepoys concerned, and they would have the help—'*they* say,' said he—of natives within the entrenchment. We had returned to the question of the loyalty of the Sikhs. Perhaps Mr Roberts would, after all, have the satisfaction of being in the right, though if he were, he would have scant time to enjoy his triumph.

We thanked Ungud for bringing us his news, and said we were sorry we could offer him no tea, not having any ourselves. He made the usual deprecatory gesture, palms upwards and a shrug of the shoulders. Then he looked at the floor between his feet for a moment, apparently in deep concentration. Kate, Jess and I regarded him in silence, sure that more was to come.

'This is not all,' he said at last, looking directly at me. 'I have other news, but whether good or bad, I cannot say. It is not the concern of Inglis *Sahib*, or Gubbins *Sahib*, but of us of Hassanganj.'

I watched him attentively.

'It is said ... No!' He stopped, thought a moment and started again. 'This I know, it is true, there is an officer, Lieutenant Delafosse, who is now with the General *Sahib* in Cawnpore.'

I could not immediately see any relevance to Hassanganj in this piece of information, but my heart beat faster as I awaited further enlightenment.

'This officer,' he went on slowly, his eyes never leaving my face, 'this officer was at Cawnpore. On the day of the boats.'

So then I understood. One man had survived the Nana's treachery. But why had Ungud mentioned 'us of Hassanganj'? I had never heard of Lieutenant Delafosse.

'Go on, Ungud,' Kate said quietly. 'What is it you have to tell us?'

I could not have spoken with such composure. I did not want to hear how Oliver had met his death, even supposing this man Delafosse really knew.

'With this officer, there were many other men on the boat. Many were wounded, some dead. But the boat, for two days, sailed down the river, and then, though I cannot tell how, when most of them had been killed by the Nana's men who harried them from the banks, this officer, and some others, all ... escaped! He is alone now. And has yet only reached the *bilaiti paltan* in Mangalwar. But, Miss-*sahib*, if he has done so, cannot the others who were with him—four, five, more perhaps—cannot those others reach safety too?'

Still I waited for some word that Oliver had been among the men who had drifted down the river in the single fugitive boat. But when Kate put the question to him directly, Ungud shook his head. He had not himself spoken to Lieutenant Delafosse, but had heard of his presence and this much of his story in the lines. All were speaking of it. It was, and Ungud again turned his eyes on me, it was surely possible that even more of the Nana's intended victims had escaped, for on that one boat there had been 'many men', and Delafosse and his companions, who had somehow managed to drift further down the river on a raft, were not necessarily the only ones left alive.

'Is it not possible—' here he wagged his head and hands in concert to emphasize his hope—'is it not possible that the *Lat-sahib* lives? Surely this can be thought of now?'

During the first part of his recital, though I tried not to allow it, I had known a flicker of hope. By the end I had realized that I was listening to just another *kahani*, those longwinded tales, lacking point or purpose, that are so dear to the Indian heart, and mean so little to the brisker Western mind. Perhaps one man had survived the carnage at Cawnpore. Perhaps even more than one had escaped. But what chance was there that Oliver should be among them? Ungud had clutched at a straw. And then, mercilessly smothering that flicker of hope with douches of cold reason, say he had escaped by some incredible piece of luck, what was the likelihood of his ever reaching safety? At large in a hostile country, most probably injured or sick, his existence was threatened a hundred times an hour. No! To hope against hope when the odds were so unequal was sheerest folly.

Ungud was disturbed by our reception of his story.

'It is good to hope!' he insisted, with puzzlement on his seamed brown face.

Kate shook her head. 'One man only, that you know, out of all the many men who were there, has lived. Let us leave it at that.'

'*Han! Han!*' he agreed, quite unconvinced. 'But what of the others who were with him? Lieutenant Delafosse himself thinks that some of them must live.'

'Perhaps! Perhaps! But there is treachery, Ungud, hunger, accident, animals, exhaustion. All these could have put an end to them since Lieutenant Delafosse last saw them. And, anyway, we do not know that the *Lat-sahib* was one of them. What is the good of thinking he might have been? What is the good of hoping with so little foundation? Better let us forget.'

'Such are the words of foolish women,' Ungud muttered bitterly as he got to his feet. 'But I am a man and a soldier. The *Lat-sahib* was a man, and, though he was no soldier, I say this: if a man could survive by fighting, by cunning, by strength of arm or sureness of aim, then the *Lat-sahib, my sahib*, has survived. This I believe, and thus I shall hope.'

He salaamed and left us, dignity and disappointment equally present in the set of his thin naked shoulders.

BOOK V

RELIEF

'That which does not make a
man worse than he was, also
does not make his life worse, nor
does it harm him whether from
without or from within.'
Marcus Aurelius

CHAPTER 1

August became September and we entered the third month of the siege, though few besides those zealous ladies addicted to the keeping of diaries realized the fact. For most of us, the conduct of our lives had become no more than the continuation of an unbreakable habit. We had to live, so we ate what came our way, snatched sleep as we could and worked on, but without interest and often without active hope. We endured. Even the alarms inherent in our situation which had so terrified us in the first days had been repeated so often and in so monotonous a pattern of unlucky death or miraculous escape that we almost welcomed any event or disaster serious enough to be remembered with clarity. I know that not many of us were buoyed up by the promise of General Havelock's relieving force, at least after the initial surprise, for nothing changed for the better. The rain continued, the heat never abated, our enemy's guns thundered on. Each day brought its deaths, its quota of wounded to the hospital, its sicknesses to the women and children in damp cellars and dark rooms. Only the insects thrived and proliferated, and the sole cheerful sound in the entrenchment was the chorus of the toads.

The only discernible result of General Havelock's communication was that our rations were cut by half. For myself, I was so sick of the endless repetition of *chapattis*, lentils and gun-bullock meat, I found little deprivation in the smaller amounts issued to us. But the men, always overworked, always tired, were also constantly famished, and one day as Jessie was piling up leathery *chapattis* on a tin plate for our supper, a private of the 32nd, seeing them from the verandah, rushed into the kitchen, slapped a silver rupee on the table, grabbed two of the *chapattis* and made off with them.

'I ran after him wi' the siller,' Jessie said, recounting the incident. 'I said he was welcome and more to a' we had and no payment necessary, but he had stuffed his maw so fu' he couldna speak and he just shook his head at me and slunk away like a thievin' pi-dog in the bazaar, and wi' the same desperate look in his eyes. Och, Miss Laura, what are we comin' tae when a Christian man behaves like a starved beastie?'

'It is my considered opinion,' averred Mr Roberts, who was with us at the time, 'that this measure of halving the allowance of food is unnecessary. Quite unnecessary.'

'What?' Kate and I exclaimed simultaneously, and Kate continued, 'But Mr Roberts, for weeks past you have assured us that, if the pandies did not get us, starvation would. Now, when it seems that the authorities have some reason to concur with your opinion, you about-face and declare them wrong!'

'Quite so, Mrs Barry, quite so. But I was speaking yesterday to Mr Simon Martin—the Deputy Commissioner, I am sure you know him—and he told me that Sir Henry Lawrence had ordered him to make provision for three thousand persons for six entire months. That was, of course, before the siege commenced.'

'And Mr Martin did this?'

'Certainly. Of course there was a great deal of confusion at the time, the military gentlemen insisting on purchasing and laying in their own provisions, despite the steps taken by the civil authorities, so no precise estimate of what is available is possible. But it is a great deal more than sufficient to see us to the 10th of September. A great deal more indeed.'

'Well, I know for a fact,' Kate went on after we had digested Mr Roberts's information, 'that there are still sufficient of those wretched Commissariat bullocks to last us all for weeks. Not that I wouldn't sooner starve, mind, but I know they are there!'

'Precisely, I too have heard, and indeed seen with my own eyes, that there is ample meat. If one may dignify it with that appellation!'

'Well, I suppose someone knows what they are doing,' Kate said grumpily.

'You don't look any too well tonight, Mr Roberts,' I broke in. 'Are you coming down with a cold? Almost everyone has one at the moment.'

He had been sniffing constantly since his arrival, well-ordered, gentlemanly sniffs to be sure, but sniffs all the same, and there was a pinched look to his red-tipped nose. His grey alpaca jacket was still neat and as clean as his own inexpert hands could make it, but it hung on him and the hands folded on his knee were thin and trembled visibly.

'No, no, Miss Laura, no cold at all. I am quite well, remarkably so indeed when I think of what others are suffering. I could do with a pinch of snuff, of course; nothing would steady my nerves more quickly … but!'

'I am sorry we cannot offer you that; but a drop of toast-water before you go perhaps?'

'No, thank you, my dear. I must get back to my post.'

He made his adieux and turned to the door; then hesitated before turning back to us, saying, 'By the bye, I have not seen Toddy-Bob for some days past. I trust nothing has happened to him?'

'Oh, Toddy's indestructible, thank heavens,' I assured him. 'I expect he's been too busy, for even we have not seen as much of him as usual.'

'Then would you be good enough to ask him to come to me, when he has a moment free? He does the odd small commission for me, as I am sure you know. A most helpful chap really, and there is a matter I believe he could attend to more satisfactorily than I could myself.'

'Of course. We'll send him around to you directly he appears.'

'Thank you. Thank you very much.' He lifted his correct grey hat, stained at the band but still in shape, and departed.

'He is looking seedy, don't you think, Kate? I do hope he is not sickening for something.'

'He's been sick for an unco' number of years, if ye were to ask me!' Jessie put in dourly before Kate could reply.

'What do you mean, Jess? He has always looked well to me.'

''Tis the habit, d'ye ken? I'm thinkin' he has it bad. There's a look about them that has been takin' it for some time and then can find nae more.'

'What habit?' I remained unenlightened.

'Opium,' Kate said quietly, while Jessie regarded her knitting in silence.

'Opium? Mr Roberts?'

'I have suspected it for some time,' Kate said.

'But he's so self-contained and … and proper! Are you sure?'

'I'd be very surprised if he were the only gentleman among us suffering more from the deprivation of opium than of food. Very surprised! But not all the money in the world can buy what no longer exists in this place.'

'Aye! There's none to be had by any, and that's the truth. Not even a bittie wee pipeful left among the lot o' us!'

'How do you know, Jess?'

'The wee man was tellin' me. 'Tis he who did the findin' of it for Mr Roberts—when it could be found. No doubt but that is why the poor gentleman has nae seen him!'

'Of course, Toddy-Bob! I should have known. He has even left a couple of packets with me for Mr Roberts when he couldn't wait to see him himself. I thought they were tobacco or snuff.'

'Well, 'tis the Lord's hand nae doubt. If yon gentleman can weather these next few weeks, he'll be free o' the hankerin'. An' that will be a blessin'. 'Tis the expense, ye ken, the sair expense!'

As silence fell between us, my mind went back many weeks to my bedroom in Hassanganj and to Oliver standing with the baby in his arms and saying, 'There's many a fine English gentleman who has been reared on the infernal poppy!' But I was still capable of surprise.

Ungud's account of Lieutenant Delafosse's escape from Cawnpore, unspecific as it was, had disturbed me, despite my resolution not to indulge an idle hope. When he left us, he had sought out Toddy-Bob and Ishmial who must have proved a more sympathetic audience than we three women, for on the following evening Toddy walked in on us, looking more cheerful and less debauched than he had for several weeks past, and I realized that he, at least, had clutched at Ungud's straw. There was no avoiding the subject however much I wished to, and when he had beaten the likelihood of Oliver's escape back and forth between us for some time, I could have screamed, 'Stop, oh, stop! I will not be unreasonable; I want no belief in the impossible; I cannot leave myself open to further anguish!' But I restrained myself, for it was so obvious that Toddy-Bob needed to hope as much as I feared to. I listened to his reasons but determined to dismiss them from my mind.

Which, of course, was impossible.

At night now, I lay thinking not of the desperate carnage at the river, nor of the few happy hours I had spent in Oliver Erskine's company, but imagining his reappearance in my life. When I scolded myself for this foolishness an insistent voice at the back of my mind would repeat, 'But it is possible. Only just possible. But surely possible?' As it is seldom that cold reason is the victor in a conflict between head and heart, and with all my heart I wanted Oliver alive, sooner or later I would catch myself protesting, 'Of course it's possible! More—it's even probable. Remember what Oliver was like.'

But always, at this point, that other small voice—of reason—would point out icily, 'But what right have you to hope for the life of one particular man amongst so many?' And only when the shadow-fight of right reason with rebellious hope had exhausted me would I sink into a restless sleep.

Then, once again, our individual struggles were merged and forgotten in a common effort, as through a long day we withstood the attack Ungud had foretold, the fourth major assault the pandies had launched against us.

Once more our men managed to repel the attackers, but when it was all over, for the first time the garrison showed no exhilaration, no triumph. I believe we all felt that day that nothing had been achieved by our efforts but an added margin of fatigue, suffering and near despair, and when Charles visited us at nightfall he told us how through all that long day of shattering noise our men had fought in almost total silence. The silence of exhaustion.

One cheering fact emerged, however. The native troops of the garrison, including the Sikhs on whom so many doubts were focused, had fought with dedicated ferocity. There was nothing else to cheer us, and that one reassuring fact was not sufficient to lift the spirits for long, for all of us suffered to some extent from depression and lowness of heart. The weather changed too, becoming suddenly much cooler, so that the shelterless men at the batteries were now shivering from cold as only a few days before they had shivered from ague. All the tents and rolls of canvas had long since been built into the stockade.

Charles was again wounded in the fourth assault, but again not seriously. A shell splinter cut through the calf of his left leg but, though no bones were broken and he insisted on hobbling about his normal duties, the wound would not heal. In the hospital every man was showing similar symptoms: small wounds, sometimes mere abrasions, remained open, often growing larger and festering despite prompt attention. 'It's the diet,' Dr Partridge said when I questioned him. 'We are suffering from scurvy, as sailors do at sea when they can get no fresh fruit or vegetables. There's nothing any of us can do about it. Blood's bad; lacks something that contributes to the healing process. Lemons help, but what hope have we of lemons here?' He had turned away shaking his head wearily at the thought of the mountain of insuperable problems he was expected to deal with.

That evening when we were assembled for supper, I told my household what the doctor had said.

''Course!' Toddy-Bob jeered. 'Everyone knows that; that's why the blackies go over the wall every night—to get theirselves a handful of *sag*, to add to their lentils. They're in better fettle that we are by a long shot too.'

'They get over the wall?' exclaimed Kate, horrified.

'Sure, ma'am—reg'lar. They always likes this green stuff, *sag*, in their curries and that, you see, and now they just adds it to their *dhal*, their lentils. They say it does 'em good. I'll get you some if you want.'

'Oh, no, Tod. You mustn't,' I protested hurriedly.

''Old 'ard, miss. Toddy-Bob 'ops over that wall for nothin' nor no one, so don't worry your 'ead on that one. Not as there's much 'oppin' to do, mind. There's places in this bloody wall of ours where you can just open a door or slip through a 'ole into the long grass and no one any the wiser. It don't need no 'eroics, or there wouldn't 'ave been so many desertions. Them Christian drummers, you remember 'em, miss? They just pushed open a door and walked out, like. *And* left the door open. The stuff's bin comin' in the same way too, see?'

'Stuff?'

'Yes, miss. Messages. To the blackies from their friends outside. And tobacco. Rum for a while too. And ...' He stopped.

'And opium?' Kate asked shrewdly.

'Well yes, ma'am. That too.' Toddy blinked his button eyes.

'Is that how you have been managing to supply Mr Roberts?' Kate continued sternly.

'He asked me, ma'am! An' I never took a penny for it, seein' the cruel packet he 'ad to pay the *sowar* I got it from in the first place. Never made a penny off of 'im, I didn't. Didn't seem 'ardly right to me. I ain't never touched the stuff myself. Seen what it does to a man. But the old gentleman, well 'e really needed it, like—see? So I just obliges 'im. When I could, that is.'

'And you can oblige him no longer?'

'No, ma'am. First, because the Sikh *sowar* who sold it to me 'as took 'is passage to a better world. Then, because there's no more comin' in. The pandies thought more of us would desert to get it, see—

590

and we might of—but then word gets round they kill deserters anyways, like them chickaboo drummers, so, well, that's it. None of the stuff around any more. Not for commercial purposes anyway.'

This intelligence of Toddy's brought home to me how little we women knew of what was going on around us. My horizon had been somewhat extended since Kate and I had started visiting the hospital, but even so I had not caught a glimpse of the world outside the wall since the end of June, and even the world within the wall came to us largely by hearsay. With a few exceptions even the men who led us were to me, at least, only names. Sir Henry Lawrence I had glimpsed but twice on our arrival; his successor, Major Banks, killed soon after his appointment, I never to my knowledge set eyes upon. Mr Gubbins I recognized, as I did Brigadier 'Bluff Jack' Inglis who was now in command of the entrenchment. But there were a score of other names I heard and used myself day after day whose owners were as remote as the prominent characters mentioned in a newspaper. As in a newspaper, also, it was the heroes and the villains who were most frequently mentioned and whose death or injury caused most comment. So, when one of our great heroes, Captain Fulton, met his end, Mrs Bonner braved a heavy rainstorm late at night to run down the verandah and tell us of the fact, and though I had probably never even seen the gentleman, my heart sank a little on hearing of his death. Captain Fulton, a young, high-spirited Engineer, had controlled and directed the mining operations within the entire entrenchment. Cheerful, energetic and unconventional, it was inevitable that his personality should form the kernel of one of those myths fastened upon as inspiration by people in peril.

'He had dined with Mr Gubbins,' Mrs. Bonner confided tearfully. 'Afterwards he went out into the garden with his field-glass to try and make out what the pandies were doing across the way—and was killed. All in a second, Miss Hewitt. The back of his head was taken off by a nine-pound shot, but Major Bonner says that when they laid him out on a bed no one could have told what killed him. So awful, Miss Hewitt, his face was quite unmarked. But just … just a mask!'

Kate crossed herself. 'Glory be, but that's a sore loss that we'll all be feeling. A sore loss.'

'Second only to that of Sir Henry himself,' Mrs Bonner concurred, for once in harmony with Kate.

My birthday falls on the 16th of September, so I remember well the date when Ungud came to tell us he was going 'out' for the third and last time.

Toddy-Bob had donated a bottle of brandy for our celebration. No one asked where it had come from, and even the thought of the men in the hospital failed to rouse my conscience as I allowed the warmth of the spirit to slide down my throat.

Charles was with us, but Pearl, exhausted by the attention given to her new accomplishment of clapping hands, had been put to bed. Ishmial sat on the verandah, a silent benevolent spectator to our festivity. As a Muslim he could not be tempted to the brandy, but the equally God-fearing Jessie agreed to a tot and became more loquacious and Scottish with every sip. I had hoped that Mr Roberts could be with us but his visits of late had been less frequent and I had had no opportunity to invite him to the 'party'. Wallace Avery we had seen only three or four times since Emily's death, and from all accounts it was probably as well he was not with us.

We were sitting in comfortable silence with the doors open, watching night close over the entrenchment, when Ungud, naked but for his loincloth and carrying a staff in his hand, appeared on the front verandah. He salaamed politely, but refused to sit down. He was still hurt at our reception of his story of the escape of Lieutenant Delafosse.

'I cannot stay,' he said gruffly. 'I go out again—now!' He looked directly at me as he spoke and there was an aggrieved note in his voice. 'I do not go out because I wish to know what has happened to Havelock *Sahib* or the *bilaiti paltan*, though that indeed must be known and that is what *they* think. I go out to find the *Lat-sahib*—or to find news of him. Inglis *Sahib* has paid me much; enough to keep a man such as I am, with all my relatives, for my life. Now he says he will pay me again, five hundred English pounds, if I come back with news of Havelock *Sahib* for him. I do not need the money, *Mem*. I do not want the money, *Mem*. But if this is the only way I can find the *Lat-sahib*, then I will take it. But I go not for the money but for the *Lat-sahib*. I will come back with the information the *Sahib-log* need. But first I will find out the truth about *my Sahib*. And if I find the truth this time, then I will go out no more. Whatever the truth may be.'

He paused and surveyed us all with something between sorrow and disdain. He was a skinny little man, and his brown skin had taken on the grey tinge of age, though he was probably younger than he looked. As he stood in the doorway, with the light of the dip playing on his bent shoulders and thin shanks, we were aware of an immense strength of purpose, a great devotion and an admirable dignity in his air and bearing. I felt humbled by his belief in himself and in his master and ashamed that I was incapable of the like.

'If I do not return,' he continued, speaking slowly so that I should have no difficulty in understanding. 'If I do not return, and the *Lat-sahib* lives, then tell him that Ungud died in his service—and in that of the *Raj*. That is all, *Mem. Salaam*!' He lifted his staff in salute and padded away into the hostile night.

'Poor devil!' said Charles pityingly.

''E'll be all right, sir,' put in Toddy sharply. 'And if anyone can find out anything about the Guv'nor, it's Ungud. Good luck to 'im, that's all I can say!'

'And Amen to a' that,' agreed Jessie tranquilly.

For some reason Ungud's visitation, like the abrupt apparition of an angry hurried ghost, cast a gloom over our party, and before long we corked up the precious bottle of brandy and bade our guests goodnight. The brandy put me to sleep quickly, but several times I woke to find Kate also awake. At last she voiced the thought that was disturbing our rest.

'I'm wondering and wondering if he'll manage to get through the city.'

'Perhaps he's out already,' I whispered.

'Not out of the city, so vast and sprawling as it is.'

'He's done it before, Kate.'

'Surely, but God help the poor creature just the same. I believe he meant it when he said the money meant nothing to him.'

'He'd have little to spend it on, anyway. But there's no doubt he is truly anxious to find ... to find news of Oliver. He and his family for generations were born at Hassanganj. Oliver means something to him.'

'Aye, he was always a man that inspired devotion was Oliver. When it wasn't loathing, that is. Just like his grandfather before him. There were no half-measures about the Erskine men.' She sighed and again tried to sleep.

I had no doubt that Ungud would perform his errand for the *Sahib-log* with success. He would contrive to make his way through Lucknow to where General Havelock was waiting to push through to our rescue, ascertain the reasons for the General's delay, and return with his intelligence to Brigadier Inglis.

But how could he possibly hope to discover Oliver's fate?

I knew something now of the vast populations that throng any Indian city, populations that eddy and surge like the waves of the sea but with less explanation. They come and go, these anonymous multitudes, from the seething bazaars and tenements to homes in scattered hamlets, always restless, always on the move, their peregrinations appearing to Western minds as mysterious as they are frequent, drifting for no discernible reason from city to village or from one tumbled dwelling to another precisely like it. Now, to confound confusion, armies marched and countermarched over the tired plains of ancient India, erasing each other's paths as they went, fighting, marauding, plundering, laying waste the anguished husbandry of the patient men who tilled the battlefields and ploughed the new-made graves. Where, in such a maelstrom of movement, among so many conflicting streams and passing currents, could Ungud hope to discover the trail that Oliver might have left behind him? The notion was absurd.

I watched anxiously for Ungud's return, nevertheless.

Six days passed without bringing news of him, but then, on the 23rd of September, Charles told us that Ungud had returned the previous night with news that General Havelock would 'without doubt' be in Lucknow within a fortnight. I, personally, received the news with small enthusiasm. There had been so many other times when the relief was heralded as being 'no more than a week', or 'within five or six days', or 'certainly no more than a fortnight' away, that now my scepticism was not to be overcome even by the delight of the men in the hospital.

'Only think on it, miss!' one of the wounded said to me that afternoon. 'A couple o' weeks and this'll be be'ind us. Clean air, miss, and real bread wi' butter inches thick on it, meat as don't crawl off'n your plate by its tod, and all the rum a man can drink!'

His method of expression was perhaps primitive, but the sentiment behind it was universal. Everybody in the entrenchment had drawn up a favourite menu with which he hoped to celebrate deliverance, and even the longed-for letters from 'Home' took second place to food in one's mythology of liberation.

I tried to share in my patient's enthusiasm, but a dead weight of fatigue and apathy allowed me only to mouth the acceptable words. I felt nothing.

I was glad to leave the hospital and wait for Ungud's visit, hoping he would have some news for me as well as Brigadier Inglis, but darkness fell without his coming. We ate and eventually the others went to bed. Still I waited. Mosquitoes whined in the small room and, despite the drop in temperature, it was stuffy, so I dragged my stool on to the verandah. Musket and rifle spat irregularly in the darkness but I hardly heard them, intent as I was on picking up the shuffle of one pair of bare feet moving towards me. Men talked in low voices where they sat on the verandahs snatching an hour with their wives, cleaning their weapons as they talked. Occasionally someone passed, softly whistling a snatch of a song, and in the distance I caught the strains of female voices raised in treble hymns. Children wailed the thin, tired wail that all children had acquired during those months, and up the verandah I heard the drone of Mrs Bonner's voice as she read some 'improving' literature to Minerva at bedtime. A gun was manhandled to a new position amid grunts of strain and tired swearing. Far away a sentry barked a sharp 'Who goes there?' at the officer on duty making his rounds. These things I heard, but what I listened for was Ungud, and Ungud did not come.

I told myself that he was too exhausted, or conversely that he had been sent out again immediately with another message. But when I eventually snuffed out the wick in the saucer dip, I could acknowledge to myself that he had not come because he had no news to give. He was ashamed to admit the failure I knew I must accept.

CHAPTER 2

I was too tense and tired to sleep that night, or perhaps, more truly, too disappointed. After hours of restless darkness, day broke and I forced myself to continue the routine of my life. I dressed, washed and ate, did my few chores and then accompanied Kate to the hospital, but I hardly knew what I was doing. I moved among the beds like an automaton, too tired to speak, sometimes not even hearing when I was addressed, and eventually my exhaustion became apparent to others than Kate. At midday Dr Partridge mixed me a sleeping draught and ordered me back to the Gaol with instructions to take it immediately I got indoors. I complied gladly, and as the draught took effect, sank gratefully into unconsciousness.

I slept, with two brief intervals of wakefulness, for nearly twenty-four hours, and at that Kate had to waken me.

'Come now, Laura,' she said as I groped my way through mists of sleep. 'Come now, it's time you were stirring. I've a bite of food here, two English biscuits and a pot of tea that Dr Partridge sent down for you, good man that he is. Poor love! You're plain tired out and small's the wonder, but sit up now and sup your tea while it's hot, for there've been great doings while you've slept and I'm dying to tell you of them.'

'Oh, Ungud's been!' I said at once.

'No, not that, at least not yet, woman dear, but he'll come. No, but the relief's here. The relief is really here!'

'The relief?' It was odd how difficult it was to understand Kate, let alone believe her. The landscape of my dreams still filled my mind with another felt but unremembered reality, and it was long since I had allowed myself to think of our deliverance as probable, still less as imminent.

'Sure and you're still fuddled,' Kate laughed. 'Drink your tea and then you'll feel more able to take things in.' So I gulped the weak potion, while Kate watched me. When I put down the mug, she refilled it.

'Well now, that's better. The doctor's say you needn't go in today. There's no need, so lie back and rest again.'

'No, no!' I protested. 'I must go. Tell me all that has happened while I dress. We'll never be relieved but the once, Kate, and can you really expect me to miss it while I rest?' As I spoke, my own words brought the fact home to me and I jumped out of bed in a hurry to see what was happening.

'Oh, Laura, they're here! Thank God, thank God, they're here! And I don't mind admitting it now, but there've been times and a plenty when I felt in my old bones that we'd all of us die here! There's the faith of a God-fearing Christian woman for you! But when we heard the guns yesterday afternoon, and then again this morning, we couldn't believe our ears. Who in their senses would have thought that gunfire would one day be the sweetest sound our ears could hear? None of us would let ourselves believe it, mind, and Jessie even swore she couldn't hear 'em, so that she wouldn't be disappointed when they stopped.'

Kate sniffed and wiped her eyes free of tears.

'But such a night it's been, wondering whether the guns would start again this morning, and then when they did, they seemed to be farther away again and I nearly died, I'm telling you truly. I nearly died. But now … I should have let you sleep on, but oh, my dear, we've shared so much, it was the wish to share this too that made me wake you, for now there can be no doubt. They're here. Close to us. Close!'

'They must be in the city then?'

'Fighting through the city, and may God guard the poor lads in those narrow streets. 'Twas madness to come that way, but come they have.'

I believed Kate now, but full realization evaded me until I walked into the steamy midday heat and experienced for myself the electric sense of anticipation that animated the whole entrenchment.

The men were at their accustomed posts, crouched behind abutments and under the lee of the walls, scarecrow figures in ragged oddments of clothing, rake-thin, often hatless, but armed still, and there was something in the set of heads and shoulders that spoke of the crazy jubilation each must have felt. The enemy still fired in on us, but desultorily, as though they were looking over their shoulders. No one regarded the fire. As Kate and I walked down to the hospital, I realized that everyone with legs to stand on had come out into the open air. Men who normally would have been snatching rest between their duties stood about chewing on empty pipestems, jesting among themselves, and groups of women and children, pale from three months spent indoors, stood on verandahs blinking into the sunshine, hands cupped to ears for the sound of Havelock's guns. The guns were there too, and, not far away, the steady chatter of musketry and rifle fire, often overlaid by the deep belch of a big gun, though whether these were the pandies' or the relievers' none could say.

As Kate and I entered the hospital, a shout went up from a lookout. The natives were leaving the city. 'Lines of 'em,' the sentry yelled, 'with bundles on their 'eads and nippers on their backs—over the Iron Bridge now, they're pourin' over it!'

I shuddered as I thought of what must be taking place in the city. Who could blame anyone for leaving it? Those streets so narrow, always crowded, obstructed by booths, bedsteads and bullock-carts; livestock everywhere, the great bulls nuzzling imperturbably in the gutters. That was how I remembered it in peace. Now the ordinary people, the small tradesmen and artisans, the beggars, the cripples, the women with their multitudinous children were fleeing, leaving the streets as our troops forced their way through them and as, from every shuttered window, rooftop and high balcony, death rained down indiscriminately on soldier and civilian.

The smelly semi-darkness of the hospital was more than ever a penance that afternoon. I longed to throw responsibility to the winds and rush up on to the walls to see for myself what was happening. Yet, armed with a dipper of water and my fan, I set about my accustomed duties, while Kate, Miss Birch and her sister-in-law helped the doctors to organize provisions and space for an added quota of wounded men. Our relief would be dearly bought.

Before long, the newcomers' guns could be heard even in the hospital. Those of our patients who could walk dragged themselves to the verandah and shouted each new item of information to their mates as they heard it, while their bed-bound comrades lay fretting on their cots and mats, swearing with irritation, and watching the door with anxious eyes. It was useless to try to soothe the excitement, so all I could do was relay the scraps of information as I heard them and scold the little Martinière schoolboys, jigging with anticipation and frustration, into their dull task of pulling the *punkah* ropes.

When the shadows outside were lengthening, I sat down for a moment on a vacated cot to mop my face and take a drink of water. The man lying quietly in the next cot was unknown to me. He must have come in the previous day when I was sleeping off Dr Partridge's draught, and I, too accustomed now to death, knew by looking at him that he was dying. His eyes were open and his hands lay still by his sides. When my gaze moved down his blanketed body I saw the abrupt termination of the contours of his limbs and realized, with familiar sick pity, that he had lost both legs.

He must have seen the direction in which my eyes moved, and when I glanced back quickly at his dirty, unshaven face, he smiled faintly.

'They're too late for one of us anyway, miss,' he whispered. 'Just my blasted luck!'

'You must not think that,' I countered with instant hypocrisy, and reaching out covered one hand with my own. 'You must have the will to live. That's what helps, more than any doctor or physic and now … now with help so near there'll be more surgeons, supplies. They'll be able to do so much more for you than we could do for the others.'

He shook his head slightly but continued to smile politely.

'Sure, miss. I 'opes so. For the next lot. But me, well, miss, 'ow's a man to make a livin' with no legs? Pandies got one. Dr Darby took the other. Not much of a life left for a man, miss, not without no legs.'

I was silent. Beneath the dirt and stubble on his face, I could discern the dazed tranquillity of shock. His resources were at an end. He sighed and closed his eyes. I wondered whether I should ask him whether he wanted a letter written to his family but, before I could speak, a sudden deafening cheer startled me to my feet. I retained my hold on the man's limp hand, however, more, I believe, to placate my fear of my own death than to bring comfort to his dying, and so we remained in a tenuous and ephemeral human communion in the gloom of the long room as cheer followed cheer, each louder and more triumphant than the last. Every man, woman and child in the garrison must have added to the uproar, except the dying man and myself, for even the wounded in their beds raised their voices. I heard the cheers; perhaps I even rejoiced in them. I do not know. All I remember is the feel of that cold, coarse-skinned hand in mine and the sensation of anguished inadequacy

that filled me as Llewellyn Cadwallader rushed up to me with brilliant
eyes and gasped, 'I saw 'em, miss! We all saw 'em: coming up from the
city and fightin' all the way. They are really here, miss! Really here!'

'Did you hear that?' I whispered as Llew made off again. 'The relief
is here at last.' I hoped to cheer him, I suppose.

The man nodded with closed eyes, and I sat down again, clasping
his hand now with both my own. After a few moments his lips moved
in a whisper so low that I had to bend to catch his words. 'Poor
bastards,' he said without rancour; and then again more softly still,
'Poor bloody bastards.'

He smiled very slightly, then his eyes flicked open and I caught an
expression of immeasurable surprise. He drew in a deep breath of air;
then his head moved gently to one side, the mouth still open, and he
was dead.

What followed is history. The books today call it the First Relief of
Lucknow. For us that day it was simply 'the Relief'.

As Llewellyn sped from one end of the room to the other, telling of
what he had seen, the noise outside increased to a pitch that was near
frenzy and the clamour around me swelled as the sick cheered and
whooped and banged tin cups against tin plates, and clapped and called
to each other, and sent their leechtins, caps and long-cold pipes spinning
to the ceiling in a delirium of joy. No one tried to quieten them; the two
doctors stood with great grins on their tired faces and the Birch girls
and Kate hugged each other and cried and hugged each other again.

Only the dead man and I were silent. I never learned his name, but
as I gazed down at the dead face amid the triumphant hullabaloo of the
living, I tried to reconcile what had happened to him with what was
happening around me. The thought of his passive resignation filled me
with bitterness, not admiration. I had probably seen him often during
the last three months, one of the many men who had grumbled and
joked and whored (when they could), got drunk and fought and endured
around me, all unwillingly condemned, like me, to a tawdry little hell
of other men's devising. Why was he dead now? One more day, a
handful of hours, and he might have lived to see his family and home
again. I tried to remind myself that he had died doing his 'duty'; that
he had died selflessly, nobly, for others. That he was a soldier meeting
no more than a soldier's fate. But the sentiments rang hollow. He was

a dead man who should have been alive. There was no explaining it; no justifying it. Baffled mentally and emotionally chilled, I pulled the grey blanket over his insignificant features and prayed, perhaps without sufficient piety: 'Well, God—if there is a God—make it up to this poor soul, if he has a soul!' It was not much of a prayer but the most I could manage. Perhaps the tears which came spontaneously to my eyes as I turned away made up for the unconvinced tenor of my words. It was a moment in which I despised my own fated humanity and could only hate the injustice of the whole human condition.

But, weak as all our emotions must be in the changefulness of time, I did not long remember that wasted life, and now cannot even reproach myself for my swift forgetting.

The cheering continued, wild and uncontrolled. Never since have I heard anything like it, for it drowned even the reverberations of the guns. The boys of the Martinière, bless them, had all made off while I was occupied with the dying man; the Birches, too, and Kate were nowhere to be seen. One of the sick, seeing me hesitate as I wondered whether I too should run outside as the others had, egged me on.

'Away with you now, missie,' he said. He was elderly, with a wisp of grey beard and a bandaged head. 'Run off and see them come in. Go on, there's not a man here who will miss ye for the next while and it's not a sight as you should miss. Fancy what you will be able to tell your children and your children's children. Away with you. I seen what you just done, missie, and that lad has no need of any of us any more.'

I untied my apron and walked with as contained a step as I could to the door. The hospital stood just to the right and a short way up from the Baillie Guard. From the crowds gathered in the irregular rectangle made by the hospital, Dr Fayrer's house across the road, and the Resident's House, as well as from the sight of several extra guns brought to bear on the gateway, it was not hard to deduce that this was to be our relievers' point of entry. The shot-steps of the walls adjacent to the Baillie Guard were thronged with men looking out towards the Hazrat Ganj, and amongst them I glimpsed Wallace Avery with Mr Roberts beside him. I intended to approach them to ask what they saw but came instead upon Charles, just descending from the roof of the hospital where one of the guns was stationed, and grabbing him by the sleeve demanded to be told what was happening outside the range of my eyes.

'Laura! Go indoors immediately,' he began in furious alarm, and as a matter of fact so many bullets whizzed over us that I had every intention of obeying him, but not until I had learned what he had to tell me. The pandies, I suppose, had redoubled their firing to dampen our spirits, but were failing entirely to do so.

'In a moment,' I replied, resisting his pressure on my arm, as he tried to direct me back towards the hospital verandah. 'In a moment, but first tell me what is happening outside. I've been shut up in the hospital all afternoon—I must know! What did you see, Charles?'

He dragged me into the comparative shelter of an angle of ruined wall, muttering at my foolishness.

'Nothing you would want to see. It's hell out there for those poor devils. What on earth made them choose that route, right through the most crowded part of the city, God only knows. You remember the Hazrat Ganj and the streets leading off it? Should all have been destroyed before the siege began. The minute our chaps entered, they were caught in a murderous crossfire from the windows of the upper storeys and the roofs. No defence possible. No room to manoeuvre, to return fire. It's a death trap, nothing else. God knows I'm no soldier, but I could have done better by my men than that. They're lying out there in the mud in scores, and more falling every minute. We are supposed to be giving them what cover we can with our guns, but it's hand-to-hand fighting out there, Laura, and you can't do much with artillery in a *mêlée*.'

'But they will get through to us? Oh, Charles, surely they must get through to us now? They are not going to be beaten back?'

'Of course not, silly! They're here. A few hundred yards away, no more. They'll be making the final dash across the broken land outside the gate very soon. It's a matter of minutes now and I've got to get back. Stay here, Laura, or better still let me get you back to the hospital?' I determined to stay where I was, and Charles was too hurried to dissuade me.

The ladies on Dr Fayrer's verandah, directly across the road, waved to me to join them, but there was such a press of bodies around me that I could not push my way through to them, and since no one paid any attention to the pandies' bullets, I caught something of the general courage and remained in my shelter of broken wall.

The crowd surged impatiently around me, and obstructing all approaches to the Baillie Guard, so that I could not see how our rescuers would be able to force their way into the enclosure at all, once the gate was open, for as yet it was still barricaded. Men worked feverishly at clearing away the rubble and timber that had been shored against the heavy wooden doors when they had been closed after the battle of Chinhat. Using spades, picks and bayonets, they dug and heaved at the baulks of old wood.

There was no lack of ribald advice from the onlookers. One man yelled to a comrade: 'Eh, Bert! Get on with it will yer? Even if they doesn't want to come in, I'd like to get out!'

I was still smiling at this exchange when the laughter became a tremendous unbelieving roar, as a horse complete with its rider was dragged by the reins over the wall just near the arch of the gate. I caught only a glimpse, for immediately beast and rider were obscured by dozens of men anxious to congratulate the very first member of the relief to enter the Residency. I did not give much thought to his identity then, beyond joining in the lusty cheer of welcome. Later I learned that the horseman had been General Outram, who, having in fact led the relieving force though he had surrendered the honours to General Havelock, insisted on being the first man to enter our walls.

The gang at work on the gate redoubled their efforts, and man after man among the onlookers laid down his rifle and got to work to clear a passage, for other horsemen now followed the lead of General Outram, their animals scrambling splay-legged and snorting over the battered masonry. Within minutes these were followed by a horde of Highlanders, who leaped over the wall, firing their muskets in the air and uttering bloodcurdling whoops as they came.

Then pandemonium broke loose truly, the newcomers adding their measure of cheers and yells to those of the relieved. Women and children rushed out of the buildings to greet their deliverers, crying, laughing, even kissing the men, who grabbed up children and placed them on their shoulders and thus continued on their tumultuous way into the enclosure. I wept myself, such was the general emotion, knowing that never again would I live through a moment of such high drama. After eighty-eight days of death and despair, we were at last relieved.

Then the eerie note of the pipes added to the confusion around me, and I could see the piper standing on a chair in Dr Fayrer's decimated garden with a crowd of women and children around him, for everyone had forgotten the battle still being fought around us. Hungry for news of relatives or friends at Cawnpore, our people fastened on every man who entered, plying them with eager questions: What happened? Are there any survivors? Time and again I heard variations on those words, and time after time watched a head shake sadly in reply.

I too had a question to ask, but standing there alone with my back to the warm masonry of the shattered wall, watching with tears the event that we had dreamed of for so long, I felt oddly withdrawn and isolated, as if I alone of all those present had no true part in what was happening. I would have left if I could, gone back to the stuffy darkness of our rooms to try to quieten my mind and heart. But, though now the crowd was beginning to disperse, leading away the relievers to feed and house them, I stayed where I was and watched their comrades come in, watched the work continue at the gate ... just watched.

At length—perhaps it was for this I had remained so long?—the last of the barricade at the gate was cleared and the singed and shot-holed remnant of the great wooden doors swung apart. I caught a glimpse of what had been road sloping away from the entrance, trenched and shattered by shell, littered with the detritus of war, along which straggled a waver of weary men dragging their feet in the bloody dust and stumbling over the corpses of their companions.

Dusk was upon us, the quick uneasy dusk of India. The joyous tumult of the welcome had dropped to a busy, satisfied hum. A few stars winked in a gauzy pale-green sky over Dr Fayrer's house. Small fires came to light and the scent of wood-smoke was borne on the warm breeze of evening. Faces became indistinguishable, tallow dips gave a faint radiance to windows, and still I lingered, shivering despite the warmth and suddenly overcome with a dreadful melancholy.

India gives a moment, between the setting of the sun and darkness, when man is forced to recognize his own mortality. Creation then stills to a breathless hush before the dark finality of night; all eyes look inward, the most fervent heart grows chill and old memories of sad happenings beat at the mind like bats. Reality recedes and sorrow for things unguessed at stings to tears. It is a moment that nurses negation, that fosters awareness of omnipresent tragedy, unmasking each man's knowledge of inevitable failure. It is seldom that one escapes the insidious languors of this moment. Alone, a man will bow his head and surrender; in company, a sudden hush falls on friendly talk as each feels the flick of the wing of mutability. Then, after no discernible length of time, as though a blindfold were pulled from the eyes or a heavy hand lifted from the brow, the world struggles back to the familiar and, quietly still, one turns with relief to the necessity for effort. Long breaths are drawn unconsciously, well-remembered faces are seen as if for the first time, as the hush is dispelled by a barking dog, or the protracted exhortation of the *muezzin*.

It is a strange moment, instantly recognized by any who have known it, perhaps incommunicable to those who have not, and it caught me there in the angle of crumbling wall as night drew in on that 25th of September. Overwrought by all that I had witnessed that day, my mind a turmoil of conflicting impressions and emotions where death was accompanied by triumph and triumph's only end was found in death, I succumbed willessly to the smothering pressure of depression, feeling to the very bones of my soul that all man's struggle was in vain.

I saw, yet did not see, the gang at the gate pick up their tools and move leaden-limbed and slow from the scene of their labours. I recognized in their bowed heads an echo of my own feelings, which were reflected again in the scattered groups of men caught in silent immobility, who like me lingered on for no good reason and watched that strangely gaping gate.

Then, when the weight of melancholy was all but unbearable, the spell was snapped.

A party of officers appeared under the arch of the gate, supporting, almost carrying, a slight figure in white breeches and a long blue, or grey, coat. I knew by the deference with which he was treated that this man was someone of importance, but it was not he for whom I watched and I would have given him no further thought but, gratefully released from the *accidie* of gloaming, would have made my way homewards, had not a man beside me sucked in his breath with surprise and exclaimed, 'It's Havelock! By all that's holy, Havelock himself!'

I looked again, more attentively. The man paused on the heap of rubble just within the gate. He took a long look at the position he had striven for so long to reach, while his staff stood round him in an anxious group, watching him. General Havelock bent his head as though in prayer, then nodded to the men who held his arms and advanced, stumbling, up the slope.

Thus Henry Havelock entered the Baillie Guard, quietly and without the fanfare that had met his men. Without even a welcome.

I was almost alone now. A few women still lingered, halting the soldiers as they came in to beg for news of their loved ones. At last I too turned away. I had forgotten everything and everyone to whom I owed a duty: Pearl, Kate, Jessie, the men in the hospital. I had forgotten myself, my hunger, fear and long weariness, but not why I remained when others went. Every man that passed, every tired form had borne my earnest scrutiny. It mattered not that they were all in uniform and he would not be; that they were short, perhaps, and he tall; that this man used his rifle as a crutch and that man was carried by upon a litter—I devoured them each with anxious eyes, seeking, searching, longing. But Oliver was not among them. I knew I had no reason so to hope, but as I turned away the tension of my vigil snapped and fatigue struck me like a blow.

I thought for a moment of Ungud, wondered why he had not come to me, wondered where he was, wondered whether he would ever come to me now to admit his failure.

CHAPTER 3

As I walked down the verandah of the Gaol towards our rooms, I found myself feeling much as the Prodigal Son must have felt as he returned to his father's house. Our kitchen door was open and light fell on the flagged floor of the verandah, while inside I heard voices and laughter and the sound of feasting. Music was provided by a harmonica player a few doors down with a rendition of *The Londonderry Air*.

Two young men sat at our table, smiling self-consciously, as Jessie ladled stew on to tin plates and Kate did the honours with the drinking-water jug.

'Ah, here you are then! Where ever have you been?' she said as I walked in. 'Jess and I were getting worried about you, especially since we have guests, house guests, too. I have asked these young men to stay the night with us, uncomfortable and all as it is; at least our floor is dry, and it's threatening rain tonight they say. Just till they get settled in their own billets, but sure who's going to worry about any but the wounded on such a night as this? Now this is Billy Miles, Laura dear,' and Kate introduced the taller of the two young men. 'Used to know his parents well, and indeed I knew Billy too when he was just a nod from nowhere, and now here we are met again by chance, after years and years! And this is Corporal Albert Dines, also of the 64th Foot. The two of them got in together and have been together this weary while, it seems, so will not be parted now. Jessie has cooked us a stew, and we were just about to get started.'

I sat down and watched our guests, pretending not to be hungry. Jessie's stews were no more appetizing than mine were, but every gristly morsel disappeared, though I noticed that Kate had taken only *chapattis* and lentil broth.

Since it was a celebration, the lantern had been lit instead of our usual tallow dip, and I watched the shadows play on the youthful faces and wondered what it was they had seen to produce so old a look of experience in youthful eyes.

After the stew we had tea which came from Lieutenant Miles's pack and chocolate which came from Corporal Dines's, and when these good things had disappeared, Corporal Dines foraged in his pack again and came back to the table with a bottle of whisky. The mugs came out again, the whisky went down and we all felt better.

Lieutenant Miles described the march up from Cawnpore, the skirmishes and delays, and the battle at Bithur at which the Nana Sahib had been decisively defeated. He told us that many more troops were on the way out from England to quell the Mutiny.

'I received a letter from home last week. They say the excitement is more even than that caused by the Crimea. All England is outraged, all Europe, even America …'

It was a comfort to him to know that the loneliness of our struggle was only physical, and that far away, over thousands of miles of strange countries and cruel seas, our people felt for us, thought of us, organized assistance for us. He would have continued with what was in his letter, but Toddy-Bob entered the kitchen—Jessie said he must have smelt the whisky—and soon had the temerity to ask the question that had been on the tip of all our tongues.

'You were there, then? In Cawnpore?' he said when I had explained the presence of our guests. 'Did you see it—the house, I mean?'

Corporal Dines looked at his young officer and shuffled his boots unhappily.

'Yes. We were there,' Billy Miles replied for both.

'What really 'appened?' Toddy pressed them to answer. 'We've 'eard nothin' but rumours, you understand, and a body's got to know the truth sometime.'

The boys glanced at each other uneasily; then the corporal sank his face into his mug of whisky, shaking his head as he did so.

'I … I was in the house, but some time after it … it had been cleaned up,' said Lieutenant Miles. 'Even then, it was … it was not … pleasant. Corporal Dines was with the first detachment to enter, the day after we took Cawnpore. It … he … it affected him very deeply and he would prefer not to talk about it. Anyway, it is not something that is easy to discuss before ladies. Especially with ladies …'

Toddy turned disappointed eyes on us, and I could see him making an inward resolve to buttonhole Corporal Dines at some future date.

'Boy,' Kate said sadly, 'and wasn't it the ladies who did the dying there?'

'Yes, ma'am ... but, but there's no need to ... to talk of it. And they're dead now, poor ladies!'

'Yes, they're dead. Mrs MacGregor and I both had many friends among those women, whom we had known all our lives. It would ease us to know even the worst. There are few things harder to bear than not knowing.' She looked directly at me as she spoke, and I felt the tiredness return to my bones and remembered all the sleepless nights and tearless days of the past weeks and thought of the many yet to come. She was right. Not knowing is the hardest thing to bear.

'It ... when it came to them at last, it must have been quick!' Young Miles swallowed and stared down at his plate.

'At last?'

'Well, ma'am, there were over two hundred women and children in the *Bibighar*, and they say there were only five of the devils sent in to ... to ... kill them.'

'Swords?' went on Kate inexorably.

'Yes, ma'am, *tulwars*. Very sharp. But ... but we found the hafts of some that had been broken in the work—there in the bloody rooms.'

'Oh, God! May they rest in peace!' Kate sighed, and her hand went into her pocket for her rosary.

The corporal raised his head and rubbed his nose on the back of a calloused hand; then, getting to his feet, he poured more whisky for each of us. Jess, our stern Covenanter, did not demur but was the first to take a sip from her replenished mug.

'The bairns,' she whispered almost to herself. 'Och! The bairns and the sights they must have seen!'

Corporal Dines sat down again and swallowed his whisky at a gulp. He looked round at the table, into questioning eyes. His face was working and there were tears in his eyes.

'Yes'm,' he nodded to Jessie. 'Yes'm—and we ... we seen them sights too! Afterwards and all, but we seen 'em and may Christ Himself curse me if I ever sleeps a night through and not dream of what I seen!'

We were silent. Lieutenant Miles covered his eyes with his hands as though to protect them from the lantern's glare.

'Bert ... don't! There's no use ...' he muttered to his friend, but Dines straightened himself on his stool and continued.

'First thing I seen, ma'am,' he said hoarsely. 'First thing I seen were a nipper—no more'n a year old, maybe—hangin' on a meat hook between two women lashed to pillars on either side of a h'archway. Throats cut ... and ... and blood everywhere. All over there was blood, inches of it on the floor and the walls, and spatterin' right up to the ceilin'. Oh, God!'

'Hey, Bert, steady old fellow! That's enough now. Don't speak of it any more!' Billy tried to pat his companion on the shoulder, but the other shrugged away, shaking his head, while tears cascaded down his grimy cheeks into his bedraggled boy's moustache.

'No, sir! Now I 'as to tell it. Now I've started, and I 'asn't spoke of it to no one in all this time, and they want to know. I ... I got to tell it. Like it was when I first seen it, sir. Since then there 'as been others as 'as seen it and spoke of it—and to me— but *I* got to tell 'ow *I* first seen it myself. Like it is in my 'ead now, sir. Just like it is in my 'ead and afore my wakin' eyes—all the time!'

'Let him talk, Billy,' Kate said gently. 'It will do him good perhaps, and as we have said already, it is better for us to know than to conjecture. Go on, Corporal, tell us what you see in your head, in your own way and in your own time.'

'Well ...' Dines sighed and sniffed and rubbed his nose again. 'Well, we was told off to Mr MacCrae's detachment that mornin' and we marches up to this 'ouse, my mate and me that is, and we stands waitin' in the garden, wonderin' what was up and why we was there. And first—well first, I didn't *see* anything, see? There was this smell. This stink—all over the 'ouse it 'ung and we wonders what it is. Then Mr MacCrae goes in and after a couple of minutes 'e comes out and ... well, 'e starts to throw up all over the verandah. Couldn't stop. One of the men 'elps 'im and 'olds 'is rifle, and the rest of us that was there just waits and ... wonders, like. You know? We was all quiet, no mutterin' or grumblin' like there always is. Very quiet, and seems like the 'ole bleedin' awful town went quiet waitin' for us to go in and ...

'Never 'eard nothin' like that 'ush, ma'am. No birds. No crows nor mynas nor sparrows. Didn't even 'ear a cart go by on the road, or a dog yelp. Then ... well then, an old sergeant, a real tough old bird if ever there was one, 'e pushes in to see ... curious like; but anyway it were 'is job, and when 'e comes out, 'e's whiter'n snow and can't speak. Just stares at us all ... all of us waitin' there in the quiet ... and after a while signals with 'is 'and to us to go in ... but stays outside 'iself. And there's Mr MacCrae still pukin' into a rosebush and groanin' like. God! 'Ow I wish as 'ow I'd never set foot into that bleedin' door. I 'ung back till almost the last, but then ... then ... I goes in, and I see that there babe ... with the 'ook through its little throat, and I seen my mates standin' around them rooms in the stink, all quiet ... still quiet ... like they'd never find words to tell it. Like I couldn't neither—until now.'

He reached for the whisky bottle and all our eyes watched his shaking hand spill what remained of the liquor into his mug.

'There was two rooms, see? Biggish, but not too big, and whitewashed and a courtyard beyond in a 'igh wall—just like lots of 'ouses you see around. It were early—no more'n eight o'clock, I reckon, but ... they'd been there all night in the 'eat and so ... the smell ... the smell was there. And the flies; they was there too, and the only noise we 'eard was them and their blasted buzzin'. Well, at first, I just stands there with my mate, lookin' in like, and not seein' anythin' clearly. Not wantin' too neither after that nipper on the 'ook. But then I starts lookin' around and noticin' things. There wasn't that many bodies in the rooms ... leastways, not enough to leave all the blood, and I wonders what 'appened to the others. Then we walks in and the floor is as ... slippery and sticky, like ... like mud, but it were blood, and after a minute or two my mate says to me "Oh, God! Will you look at them!" And I looks where he points and I sees a row of little shoes, babies' shoes and nippers', all with the feet still in 'em.'

'Lord ha' mercy!' sighed Jess with closed eyes.

'Cut off at the ankles, all them tiny feet. And some of the shoes ... well you could see as 'ow they'd been pretty colours—blood and all you could still see that. Some'ow ... some'ow that was the worst thing I seen, them little coloured shoes with the feet in 'em. But ... but then there was other things too. Legs and hands lyin' around, see, and we begun to see other things that was left—clothin' and ribbony bonnets lying in the blood on the floor, and books and Bibles and parasols with frills—all them things that females likes to 'ave with them wherever they be ... and milk jugs and a scent bottle with a silver top and ... all them sort of things. Toys too. For the nippers. But everything broken and slashed and blood on it. There was 'andmarks on the walls, 'andmarks in blood, and the walls and pillars and doors was all chipped and scarred with the sword slashes. All scarred with bloody lines. Some of 'em ... some of 'em was right low down too, like as if the women 'ad been crouched down, tryin' to escape, or maybe the children ...

'Well, we just stands there lookin' for a while, everyone quiet, like I says, and cryin' too ... then ... then someone shouts from outside—not sayin' nothin' mind, just a yell ... like ... like 'e's been shot or somethin'. So we goes out, very careful. We don't want to slip in that ... you see, and fall into ... and we comes to this well in the garden with a tree near it, and they tells us that ... that it's full of bodies, full of 'acked-up bodies. All them bodies we didn't know what 'ad become of 'em, and they was packed there in that well—just thrown in any'ow with arms and legs and 'eads cut off ... all together. I didn't see that. I couldn't. My mate, 'e takes a look and comes back vomitin' just like Mr MacCrae, and I wants none of it. I wants none of it. I seen enough. And then, as I stands there under the tree, not lookin' at that there well, I sees some funny grey stuff hangin' from the bark of the tree, and ... and it smells right bad too, and one of the others sees me lookin' and he sez, "Brains. Children's brains." They must 'ave swung 'em up by their 'eels and bashed their 'eads against that tree to kill 'em.'

Corporal Dines stopped and covered his eyes with his hands.

'Jesus!' swore Toddy softly.

'That's all I seen, ma'am. I couldn't tell of what I'd seen ... couldn't speak of it, and my mate, 'im as was there that mornin', well 'e was wounded on the way 'ere and I 'aven't seen 'im 'ardly since, or I could 'ave maybe spoken to 'im. But it's a terrible sight I do carry in me 'ead now, ladies. Terrible!'

He put his head down on his arms folded on the table and the rest of us sat for a moment silently watching him.

'Aye,' Jessie said at last, 'there's nair a word a body can say. Nair a word. But, I knew them, laddie. Friends of mine were there, and their bairns. Och! May the Lord hae them in his hands the night.'

'Jesus!' Toddy breathed a second time.

'Watch your tongue, wee man!' admonished Jessie through her grief.

'Many of their husbands, fathers, brothers, are here—with the 32nd,' I said. 'They ... we have all been hoping against hope that what we heard was not true, that there must have been some survivors. But now I think, perhaps, it is better that there were none. To live with the memory of that ...'

'No. No survivors,' Billy Miles said in a tired tone of voice. 'Nothing.'

Corporal Dines got unsteadily to his feet. 'Ma'am, beggin' your pardon, but could I lay down and sleep somewhere? I'm ... I'm that spent, I can't 'ardly see.'

We pushed the table and stools on the verandah, dragged the thin straw-filled mattresses from our beds, and made the two men as comfortable as goodwill alone could make them on the kitchen floor. In seconds, it seemed, young Dines was asleep.

'Thank you, Mrs Barry, Miss Hewitt.' Billy Miles, unlike his friend, hesitated to remove his boots in the presence of ladies, and waited for us to leave the room.

'Sure, and what can you possibly be thanking *us* for, Billy Miles? God knows it is little enough we have to give, in view of what you have done for us.'

'Thank you for letting him talk. He ... he's a good man and a good friend. His home is in the village a stone's throw from my grandparents' house, where I was brought up when Mother and Father were out here. We used to lark around together when we were boys and I was home from Haileybury. When I got my commission, he joined the same regiment, and we've been together more or less ever since. Three days ago he saved my life in a skirmish on the way here. I think he'll be all right now he's talked, but at one time, after Cawnpore, I thought ... I thought he might kill himself. You see ... his sister ... was one of the women in the house. She was married to a private in the 32nd, and ... and there was a child too. That's why I brought him here with me. I would not want anything to happen to him.'

'Divil take my prattling old tongue!' said Kate. 'And me telling him I had friends among those women. As though that gave me some sort of special reason to grieve!'

'Poor boy. Oh, poor boy!' was all I could say.

'He'll be all right now, I'm sure of it. He needs a rest, a long rest.'

'And so do you, Billy Miles. Bed down now, and may the two of you sleep in peace. Come, Laura—Jessie—let us go and leave these boys to sleep.'

CHAPTER 4

It was over.

That was what our minds were full of as we prepared for bed. The siege was ended. In a few days we would be free, and even Corporal Dines's account of the dreadful *Bibighar* was soon overlaid by the realization that at last our ordeal was concluded.

Kate, Jess and I sat long on the two string beds talking softly of the events of the day and of what must soon follow. No more waiting in unbearable anxiety that we somehow had managed to bear. No more hunger. No more constant tiredness. No more dirt, decay and smells. No more sudden horrible death. Only our griefs would go with us when we left and would grow, as time passed and memory dimmed, half-pleasuable and then be wholly forgotten as griefs are meant to be forgotten. In the next room the snores of our guests echoed thunderously as the poor fellows slept for the first time in days, and through the small square window of the bedroom came the stir and bustle of the entrenchment which, all through that long night, knew neither rest nor quiet.

The Baillie Guard stood open and through it struggled an intermittent stream of exhausted men, some singly, some in bands, and the wounded in litters and horse-drawn ambulances, the rearguard of the relief. Brigadier Inglis had sent detachments out from the Residency to reinforce the relief and guide in the stragglers, and there was so much activity that little sleep was had by any but the newcomers. Thank God it was not raining, for there was scant cover for the poor souls.

At about midnight, unable to sleep, I stole outside over the recumbent bodies of our guests, to see for myself what was happening. As I gained the verandah steps I found Jessie beside me.

The first thing that struck us was the number of lights that shone in the darkness; bivouac fires, torches of rags soaked in oil and a reckless number of lanterns. Everywhere windows showed light and doors stood open, affording us glimpses of our neighbours ministering to their deliverers. There were unaccustomed sounds too, horses neighing and stamping, and the jingle of bridle-irons, a camel's sneezing snort and men talking in normal voices, even shouting to each other, unmindful of the volley of musket shots or the shell such unwariness might provoke. And then I realized the strangest thing of all. They had no need to fear a sniper's bullet. For the first time in eighty-eight nights the pandies were not firing into the enclosure.

'Och, Miss Laura, it can only mean that they've gone,' said Jessie joyfully. 'All of them, like the ones that went over the Iron Bridge this afternoon. They ken they're beat!'

She grabbed my hands in her two large ones, and we stood in the noisome light of a torch and laughed, really laughed, loudly and freely, as we had never seen each other laugh before.

''Tis true,' Jessie said at last. 'Now I believe 'tis true. The good Lord ha'e delivered us a'!'

'With the help of Messrs Havelock, Outram and a few others,' I pointed out, but Jessie was too happy to correct my irreverence.

'But will you look at them,' she said as we began to pick our way through the crowd. 'So many of them ... so many—and a' the grand clothin' on them!'

Men were everywhere. They lay with their heads on their packs, rifles beside them, on verandahs, in ruined buildings, on the bare ground, in and under carts, limbers and gun-carriages. They were begrimed with mud, dust and sometimes blood, the sleeping faces lined with fatigue, but the flickering light of fire and torch showed us also that they were well-clothed, well-shod and, strangest of all, robust despite fatigue. Caps, shakos and helmets lay beside them, and often I caught the remembered whiff of tobacco from a glowing pipe.

'Will ye take a look at yon boots?' Jessie breathed in my ear, pointing to a pair of heavy army footwear standing neatly aligned beside their sleeping owner. 'Not a patch on them; hardly a scratch! Och, to think what 'twill be like to wear good shoon again!'

'Yes, but if that lad's not careful, he'll be barefoot by morning,' I pointed out. 'It's as well Toddy's not seen them.'

'Sure they'd be too big for yon wee man,' said Jessie, judiciously sizing up the boots; the man stirred and mumbled as we looked at him, so we moved away.

Small groups sat around fires, sharing tobacco, scraps of chocolate or rum with the men of our garrison, and often we paused if we saw a face we knew among them. The talk was all of the battle to reach us and of the fighting, fierce and bloody, that we learned was still continuing in the narrow lanes and unlit alleys of Lucknow.

There had been a great number of casualties as the troops forced their way to us that morning, so many that it was said General Outram had advised General Havelock to remain outside the entrenchment through the night in order to allow his scattered force to rally before making the final push. Havelock, however, had decided that even one night's delay might see our garrison slaughtered and had ordered the advance to continue.

'I've been on orderly duty, see? Runnin' messages and that for the staff all day,' said a grizzled man with a bandaged hand. 'I were standin' not six feet from the General when we 'alts and 'e takes out his field glasses and runs it over your walls and that there gate. Couldn't see much myself at that distance, 'cept that your walls looked to me like the things nippers build up with their 'ands with sand at the seaside, and not much 'igher neither! 'E looks for a long time, and then 'e shakes 'is 'ead and says: " 'Avin' seen that gate, I will delay no longer!" Like as if them were 'is last words, all solemn. Well, later, when we gets to the Baillie Guard, I see 'is point. 'Ow it 'as stood up so long … well, it's a bloody miracle. All charred it is, and shot-'oled and damn near down. A bloody miracle!'

'We should 'ave waited and paid no mind to the looks of it,' an elderly man said bitterly, spitting a stream of tobacco juice into the dust. ''Tis right cruel, miss. We 'ad to leave our wounded, same as always, but they say—I 'eard it from a bloke what's just got in—the bastards is doin' in the wounded now, seein' as 'ow we managed to get through 'em. Gawd—and them 'elpless!'

'Not for long, matey,' one of our garrison attempted to console him. 'Bluff Jack sent out two detachments from here, and there will be more following in the morning. We're to clear the city of stragglers before midday.'

'Maybe, but that'll be too late for some of my mates. For a lot of 'em.' The old man lay down with his elbow under his head and stared into darkness.

Not long afterwards we came upon Toddy-Bob wandering with careful aimlessness through the huddled forms, and I knew that his errand was, essentially, the same as mine.

'You didn't ought to be out alone on such a h'occasion as this,' he scolded, glaring up into Jessie's white moon of a face. 'You ought to know better than to let 'er out, woman! 'Tis all right for you, maybe, but she's a lady and it ain't fittin' to 'ear the talk that's goin' round tonight. S'truth! It's enough to make me blush like a maiden aunt, and they're gettin' grogged up proper now, so it will be worse. Now you'll be favourin' me if you get back to where you belongs, and I'll make it my duty to see you safe 'ome.'

I would have laughed had I not been afraid of hurting his feelings. There were many other women wandering through the entrenchment in curiosity or perhaps a desire to help; many too who were still seeking news of those they had lost. And by now my vocabulary, known if not used, was as comprehensive as most troopers'. However, I had been aware of the odd amorous glance and wink cast in my direction and the fumbling of a drunken man's hand at my skirt, so I allowed Toddy to grab me by the elbow and lead us back to the Gaol. Somewhere bagpipes were skirling and Jessie hummed to herself as we walked and a pure pale moon shed a light so bright it put out the stars.

It seemed I had just put my head on the pillow when I felt Kate's hand shaking me awake.

We ate our meagre breakfast standing on the verandah so as not to disturb our guests, who were still asleep, and, knowing how urgently we would be needed at the hospital, set off directly we had finished. The clear sky of only a few hours earlier was now heavy with threatened rain, and we made our way to the hospital through a world dark, hot and steamy.

The pandies were quiet in our vicinity but from the city came the sound of heavy firing. The men of our garrison who had been sent out to escort in the wounded and the rearguard of the relief were having a hot time of it. Over the great palace of the Kaiser Bagh and the pretty marble pavilion called the Moti Mahal, the leaden sky was lined with pale smoke from the rebels' heavy guns. We paused a moment on the slope leading down to the Baillie Guard before turning left to the hospital. Through the gateway the road leading to the city carried a slow-moving stream of men, animals, ambulances and wagons for as far as the eye could see.

'Where in the world are we going to put them all?' wondered Kate. We turned towards the hospital and within minutes she had her answer. There was nowhere to put them.

Those of our own wounded who could crawl, shuffle or bear to be dragged from their beds had voluntarily vacated their places to the newcomers. We could now count the number of familiar faces on our fingers, but not all the gratitude and goodwill in the world could extend the capacity of the Banqueting Hall, and within a few hours of the opening of the Baillie Guard every inch of space was crowded—in the main room, in the storerooms at each end, on the verandah. The supply of straw mats and pallets had given out, and men lay in rows on the verandah without even a canvas sheet between their bodies and the stone, while a party of their able-bodied comrades worked hurriedly at hanging tattered awnings from the roof-beams as protection from the impending rain.

Many women of the garrison were already at work helping the doctors, though since they were new to the work, they were sometimes more hindrance than help, and one or two had to be nursed over ladylike attacks of faintness themselves. Not that one could have accused them of over-sensitivity. Accustomed as I was to the smells and sights of that horrible long room, my stomach lurched with nausea as we entered and picked our way over the men to receive instructions from the doctors. On the heavy wooden operating table, impregnated with the blood of all those who had suffered on it over the last three months, an amputation was about to take place. Five men moved forward to hold down the victim, a sixth held aloft a lamp. Dr Darby removed the cigar from his mouth and carefully extinguished it on the ground before putting the butt back into his trouser pocket. He glanced at his assistants, who tightened their grasp on the victim's limbs, and I caught the dull glint of steel in the lamplight as he suddenly bent his head and made the first swift, decisive incision. The rum bottle from which the patient had been drinking dropped with a crash of splintering glass and a scream of mortal agony forced the blood from my face and stopped me short in my tracks with my hands over my ears. At my feet a man clutched at my skirt and buried his face in it, sobbing. For a moment silence filled the twilight and then, no further sound coming from the table, the mutterings, groans and retchings of the other sick resumed. I took a deep breath, cursed with silent volubility, and set about my work.

There were new faces among the medical men, but not yet enough, and where, I wondered, were the supplies that should have come in with the relief?

'This is war, missie,' Dr Partridge grunted when I put the question to him as I bandaged a leg with strips of linen from some woman's tucked and hem-stitched petticoat. 'God alone knows where they've got to—if there were any in the first place. If I could get my hands on some chloroform! A wagon-load of the stuff, that's what we need now. Thank you, that will have to do for this poor fellow. Now, there ... that sepoy two places up. A leg smashed.'

We moved along the row and looked down at the unconscious man. I knelt and tried to peel away the shreds of trouser leg from the wound. 'An ugly one, but I think we can save it. You'll need water there, missie, and here ... take my scissors, but mind you give them back. I think you can deal with that yourself. He's lost a bit of blood, but he's a sturdy fellow and the bone is only broken, not crushed.' His fingers, bloody and expert, explored the limb as he spoke, and the man quivered and moaned without regaining consciousness. 'Now, you clean it up and I'll send along an apothecary with some splints, if we can find any, to set the bone. And here, there's still a sup or two of heartener in the bottom of this bottle. See that he gets it, but after the apothecary is gone. The longer he stays under the better for him!' He wiped his fingers on his leather apron, then produced a flat silver brandy flask from his pocket and handed it to me.

'His caste ...?' I asked anxiously as he left me.

'Mohammedan. Use a spoon to put it between his teeth before he comes around and he'll never know the difference!'

As often before, as I worked on the sepoy's leg, I noticed that the sight of dark red blood on dark skin is somehow less alarming than the sight of dark red blood on fair skin. Indeed, it was difficult to see the blood in the gloom of the room, caked and congealed as it now was on clothing and flesh, so I had to use the utmost care with the scissors. The apothecary arrived with rough splints cut from a board before I had finished swabbing the wound.

'Damn shame, miss, if you'll pardon the expression,' said the apothecary as I made room for him to kneel beside me. 'This fellow is one of our own men, shot by mistake by the relief when they were entering last evening!'

'Oh, no, Mr Saunders!' The apothecary too was one of our men with whom I was well acquainted.

'Yes, fired off a volley at a group of our fellows who had climbed over the wall to greet them. Saw them near the wall, thought they were trying to enter ... and ... bang, bang, bang. None killed, thank the Lord, but a bad business!'

'And you mean he's been here, in this condition, since last evening? Without attention?'

'Miss, we've none of us slept this entire night. All we've been able to attend to were the amputations—or at least the evident ones. For the rest, we could only give them water and food and hope they'd hang on until the supplies arrived. Now it looks as though there are no supplies to arrive. Gone astray somewhere in the city, or most likely been captured or blown up. Over two hundred men arrived during the night and they're still coming in. We've nothing left to use on them. We strip the bandages from the dead now before we send them to the burial ground. Look at that heap over there in the corner. Not even washed and we'll have to use them again. No swabs, ointments, salves, tinctures; not even a headache powder. Leeches and rum, that's all we've got, and soon it will be only leeches.'

'Oh, my God!'

'You're welcome to Him, miss. Me, I can't believe in Him any longer.'

The young man set to work with his splints and cord. Handing over Dr Partridge's brandy for him to administer, I moved to the next man.

So the morning somehow wore away, all of us working with numb hearts to try to bring some comfort to those for whom we had no healing. The heat increased and with it the stench, as for all our efforts men still lay, sometimes for hours, in their own vomit, excrement and blood. It had begun to rain, the usual torrential midday downpour, which reduced the roads of the entrenchment to rivers of slush and raised the humidity to such an extent that inside the crowded hospital it was almost impossible to see for the sweat dripping off one's brow into one's eyes.

I was beginning to feel the strain of the previous day's excitement, the sleepless night and the hard work I had been engaged in for several hours. Outwardly I must have appeared much as I always had done, much as the other women around me did: solicitous, sympathetic and moderately efficient in the unpleasant tasks I performed. But within I was almost as incapable of emotion as the man who died in my arms, and in mid-sentence, as I raised him to remove his shirt.

'He's gone,' I said to Saunders, the apothecary, who was tending the man on the next pallet. 'He's gone—and he was talking!'

Saunders turned on his haunches and finished the work of pulling off the shirt. 'Back wound, miss. Ball or shell fragment too near the heart, I expect. Moving him was enough to kill him. Now don't fret, miss, you couldn't have known and when your number's up, it's up!' He turned away.

There was no sheet or blanket with which to cover the dead face. I crossed the still-warm hands over the bare breast, pulled down the eyelids, and rose to my feet, feeling nothing, not even the rough kindness in Saunders's brusque words. Mindful of our necessities, however, I tossed the dead man's shirt on to a nearby heap of dirty bandages.

It was nearly noon. Above the vehement rain the guns of the Kaiser Bagh could be heard. I wondered whether I was hungry, decided I was not, but that I must have some fresher air very soon or earn Dr Darby's contumely by fainting or vomiting over my next patient. Slowly I worked my way on to the verandah, shaking my head dumbly at beckoning hands of doctors and patients alike.

Outside and away from the open door into the hospital, the air was better. I picked a path to the edge of the verandah, and was grateful for the feel of warm rain on my hot, wet face. The world had disappeared behind sheets of solid grey water, the buildings nearest the hospital, the Resident's House, the Treasury, Dr Fayrer's house, only visible when the downpour veered for a second and afforded a momentary glimpse of their ruined wraith-like forms.

A little revived in body if not spirit, I leaned my cheek against the damp pillar to which I clung in order to feel the rain on my face, and surveyed the scene around me.

The generous architecture of an earlier day had endowed the Banqueting Hall with a wide, arcaded verandah. Once the pillars that supported its considerable length had supported also the flowery masses of jade-leaved quisqualis and the brazen trumpets of bignonias.

The red tiles had been polished to a brightness that reflected Chinese lanterns and fairy lights.

I wiped the rain and sweat from my face with my sleeve and looked around me.

The climbing plants were long gone, and with them some of the pillars. The shot-holed roof sagged threateningly and the worn canvas and old awnings with which it was now repaired did little to keep out the rain. The bright tiles were smashed and men lay, sat and sprawled on the soaked stone, propped against the wall, the pillars or the backs of their companions. Some shivered with ague, teeth chattering; some moaned; one or two muttered in delirium; most endured in a silence that was itself agonizing. Doctors, apothecaries and the few women moved among them, and those of our own wounded who were capable helped their new comrades with a few poor means at their disposal: a mug of water, a hand with the unlacing of a boot on a swollen foot, or a shoulder to lean a bandaged head upon. They were still arriving, the wounded from the city. If a man could walk, he was sent on up the slope into the entrenchment to find what accommodation and assistance he could. If not, his comrades on the verandah drew in their legs, hunched closer and made room for him on the sodden floor.

A cauldron of gun-bullock soup was lugged out and the women on the verandah prepared to serve it. I should be doing the same inside, I knew, so I filled my lungs with a few deep breaths of air, pushed my damp hair back from my forehead and was about to return to the ward, when through the rain I glimpsed what I thought was a familiar figure helping yet another wounded man toward us. Curiosity made me pause for a moment as they approached.

It was Ungud, but with a cotton sheet wound around his skinny form to protect him from the elements. That, then, was why I had not seen him, I thought. He had been sent out again to act as a guide to the relief. When they were near enough, I called to him, indicating a vacant spot on the very edge of the verandah where he could deposit the man he was helping. He nodded and made towards me, without surprise. The verandah rail had been taken for fuel, so all he had to do was disengage the man's arm from around his shoulders and allow him to slide down to a sitting position on the plinth. The man remained upright but slumped against a pillar and, as he did so, I saw blood dripping down his arm and over the slack fingers resting on his knee.

'Thank you, Ungud,' I said wearily, wondering whether the wound was something I could take care of myself or whether I would have to go in search of a doctor. He would have a long wait if the latter.

'Give him water!' ordered Ungud peremptorily, instead of shuffling off after salaaming, as I had expected him to do. 'The blood is nothing, but he is tired, too tired. Feed him quickly and let him sleep!'

Something in the small brown man's tone of voice, in the proprietorial manner in which he stood looking down anxiously at his erstwhile burden, made me take a closer look at the man.

He was dressed in a ragamuffin accumulation of clothing: cord breeches and native string-soled sandals, a soldier's grey-back flannel shirt, and a white helmet with a brass spike at the top. His head was bowed on his chest and the peak of the helmet came low over his forehead so that all I could see was an unkempt brown beard covering the lower part of his face.

'Miss-*sahib*! Food and rest. *Juldi!*' Ungud said again.

I took a grip on myself. This was no time to give way to fancifulness. I had waited and I had hoped; I had longed for the improbable always, and believed in the impossible sometimes. I must not now allow my heart to beat with such ridiculous haste because of the tone of voice of a damp and dirty native pensioner.

Merely to still the clamorous thudding of my heart, I knelt beside the man and gently lifted the helmet from his head. The lock of sun-bleached hair that fell forward over his forehead had choked me with tears even before the stubbly black lashes parted over the hazel eyes.

'Do as he says, Laura,' said Oliver, trying to smile, 'I'm … thirsty.'

He fell against me, fainting.

CHAPTER 5

No qualms of guilt assailed me as I deserted my duties, and I gave no single thought to the other men in the hospital who needed my help.

We laid him on my string cot. Jessie boiled water and tore her last remaining petticoat into bandages, while Ungud and I pulled off the string-soled sandals and cut away the sleeve of the grey shirt to attend to Oliver's wound, a jagged slash on the inner side of his right arm just above the elbow. I had by now garnered enough experience of such matters to realize that the wound was an old one, partially healed, that had broken open anew under some undue exertion. It bled freely, but I knew I could stop the flow.

'Aye, and many's the one I've seen like this one after a hand-to-hand,' commented Jessie, as she brought in water and bandages. 'He had his arm upraised to strike, d'ye ken, but the other man sidestepped smartly to the left and brought his weapon down just that mite the sooner, making for his enemy's arm. "Butcher Cumberland's cut" the lads ca' it, and 'tis many weeks old, too.'

We worked together to staunch the blood and then bound up the wound and laid the arm across Oliver's chest. He never stirred. He bore no signs of other injury severe enough to account for his unconsciousness, so I had to suppose the wound had broken open more than once and that loss of blood, lack of food and exhaustion accounted for his weakness. On the soles of his feet were scars and scabs of severe lacerations, some of which now oozed blood. These too we cleaned and bound.

Having satisfied himself that his *Lat-Sahib* was in competent hands, Ungud went away, returning presently with Toddy-Bob, who burst into the room without preliminaries and then, on seeing his master's apparently lifeless body stretched on the bed, promptly burst into tears. While Jessie hushed him, attempting to explain that all was well with

Oliver, I fetched the remainder of the birthday brandy and slipped a spoonful of the neat spirit between Oliver's teeth. He shuddered a little but his eyes remained closed, so I repeated the dose two or three times, my anxiety mounting as each time he failed to respond. Then at last he heaved a long sigh and his eyes fluttered open. For a second or two he gazed around the room, taking in nothing; then his eyes focused on the white frightened blur of Toddy's face and his lips twitched in a smile.

'Tod.' The whisper was so faint it would have gone unheard but for the light of recognition in his eyes. 'You here?'

'That's right, Guv'nor,' answered Toddy, edging nearer. 'We're fine, me and Ishmial too. I'll fetch him in a moment.'

Oliver then looked enquiringly at Jessie's vast bulk as she peered down at him with worried interest.

'This is our dear friend, Jessie,' I explained, speaking for the first time. 'She lives with us—here in these two room—and looks after us all.'

'Laura!' he exclaimed on hearing me, in a stronger voice. 'Laura!' He paid no attention to my explanation of Jessie's presence. 'Where are you?' I was kneeling by the bed and a little behind his head, so he had to turn to see me.

'Laura, are you ...'

'Yes, I'm here and well. You mustn't worry about anything, just rest and get well and strong. There'll be plenty of time to talk later, but now we are going to bring you some food and then you must try to sleep.'

'Laura ... Laura.' His voice dropped away and his eyes searched my face wonderingly. Then he lifted his left hand and touched my cropped head.

'No hair?' he asked in a puzzled way. I had forgotten my hair, forgotten the curious sight I must present to someone unaccustomed to my present appearance.

'I had to cut it off. Lice.'

'Oh!' He laughed silently. 'Look funny.'

I nodded in agreement. His hand slipped to my shoulder and stayed there. I covered it with my own and laid my cheek against his wrist. He sighed and closed his eyes; then in a moment and in another tone of voice said, 'My arm's done for.'

'Nothing of the sort!' I protested immediately. 'It's a clean cut, it will mend in time.'

'No. No good,' he insisted quietly. 'Sabre cut through the muscles. Useless. Useless now. Weeks ago, but ...' And he slipped back into unconsciousness.

So he remained, on the borders of consciousness, for two days and nights. Sometimes he knew us all and spoke rationally. Then at other times he would address us by strange names, give us orders in Hindustani or English, mutter feverishly, flinch and toss himself about in the bed. Once he shot up, his eyes wide open in terror, and yelled, 'Dive, damn you! Dive! Dive!' Often tears slid out from his black lashes into the unfamiliar whiskers and, like many of the sick in the hospital, even his quieter moments were marked by groaned curses.

Late on the first night Dr Darby came to see him at Kate's request. Knowing of the doctor's own terrible bereavement—he had lost his own wife and baby at Cawnpore—I protested at his being bothered, but Kate replied, 'The work is what the poor man needs just now. It will help him more than sympathy.'

So he came and cleaned the wound and redressed it, examined Oliver thoroughly and confirmed Oliver's own diagnosis of the sabre cut. 'He'll never use that arm again,' he said gruffly. 'Muscles cut through and the bone chipped, which is why it won't heal. Chips are probably still working their way out. Try compresses. Keep him quiet. Not much fever just now, and try to keep it down. You know what will happen if I have to amputate! Otherwise, he's shocked and exhausted. Don't worry about the unconsciousness; Nature's method of keeping him still. He'll mend in time. Or his arm will, anyway.'

For those two days and nights, no thought entered my head that was not in some way connected with Oliver and the miracle of his return. I was with him almost constantly, poulticing the angry wound, cooling his head with water and vinegar to reduce the fever, feeding him when he was sufficiently conscious to swallow with a gruel of arrowroot, which the resourceful Toddy had somehow come by.

It was Toddy, too, who told us of how and where Ungud had found Oliver. When Ungud had gone out for the third time, shortly before the arrival of the relief, he had heard from sources we could only guess at that a *sahib* had been living for some weeks in a village about halfway between Cawnpore and Lucknow, protected and tended by the villagers. The hint had been sufficient to make him find the village, only to be told that yes, a *sahib* had been there, wounded and ill, for many weeks, but that a couple of days previously he had insisted on setting out on foot to try to join General Havelock's column. This was, so said the villagers, madness, for he was still ill and weak. They feared he must have been captured or killed long before he could meet his fellow countrymen. Ungud had tried to trace the fugitive's trail as he returned to Lucknow, but without success. He did not forget the incident or the unknown man's intention, however. When the relief arrived on the 25th of September, he heard that more than one white man had joined the force on the way up from Cawnpore; hope had revived and on the following day, early in the morning, he had set out for the city. He had found Oliver among a party of the ambulant sick and wounded in the last straggle of the rearguard. The rest we knew.

'It's a miracle in itself,' I said, 'that he wasn't in one of the *doolies* of sick that were wiped out by the pandies.'

'Maybe.' Toddy was sceptical. 'But 'e never give up, you see! Ungud never give up. Not like some of us!'

Kate, Jessie and I took it in turn to watch beside Oliver all night, and I would start awake after the short rests Kate forced me to take and rush into the bedroom to assure myself that his presence was more than a dream.

Charles visited us as often as he could during those first two days but never found his brother conscious. Toddy-Bob and Ishmial insisted that only they had the right to wash and change their master and for the rest of the time practically took root on the verandah, where they remained whittling and dozing night and day, all their duties forgotten and somehow evaded.

Others also came to enquire and exclaim: Mr Roberts and Wallace Avery, acquaintances of the old garrison (I was astonished at the number who knew him and who because he was a survivor of Cawnpore suddenly chose to develop their acquaintance) and neighbours from the Gaol. Many strangers bereaved by one or other of the massacres at Cawnpore came to hear with sad pleasure of this one prayer that had been answered.

'Mr Erskine, no less? Oliver Erskine of Hassanganj? How extraordinary!' Mrs Bonner commented, quite forgetting a previous conversation in which his name and character had been mentioned.

I had not seen Mr Roberts in a fortnight, and such was the change in his appearance that for a moment I almost forgot my invalid. He had been getting thinner all through the siege, like the rest of us. Even Mrs Bonner's many chins now hung above her bosom flaccid as the sails of a becalmed ship. But Mr Roberts was more than thin; he had shrunk, shrivelled up, and his usually ruddy complexion was faded and blotched. His hands trembled constantly and he sniffed, twitched and blinked his red-rimmed eyes without ceasing. He remained, however, as polite and concerned as always.

'Oh, thank God, Miss Laura! Indeed it is good to hear one piece of truly splendid news in this sad time, and there is no one of whom I would sooner hear it than Erskine. As remarkable a thing as I have yet heard. To have survived Wheeler's entrenchment and the massacre at the river. But, then, he is a remarkable man, Miss Laura, a remarkable man, as I am sure you have discovered. A little eccentric, perhaps, and somewhat maligned by those unacquainted with him, but a remarkable man.'

'I remember you saying something of the same sort, but perhaps a little less complimentary, on the ship one day. Do you remember?'

'Remember? The ship? What ship was that?'

'Why, Mr Roberts! The *Firefly*—the ship that brought us all out to India.'

'Of course! Forgive me. My memory is not what it was, you know, and I seem to find it harder to concentrate these days. The privations, I suppose. I'm not a young man, after all. And I said ... you say I mentioned Mr Erskine to you? On the ship?'

'Yes. We were very curious about him. None of us knew much about him or how he lived and you gave us a little lecture about the *zemindar*'s life. I confess that at the time I only half believed you, but then, later, you rather hinted to me that Mr Erskine was a ... a rogue, I think was the term.'

'I said Mr Erskine was a rogue? Surely not, Miss Laura?'

'Well, I believe the word was mine, but you did agree to the definition.'

'How strange. Of course there were many people in Calcutta to malign a man whom I had, at that time, never met. But as you know, I have had much reason since to form the most favourable opinion of his capacities and his character. Much reason!'

I had intended only to tease my old friend, to cheer him up and make him laugh at the memory of my ignorance and curiosity, but had only succeeded in upsetting him. He blinked, twitched his head and fingered his lips in anxiety.

'Well, I also have had occasion to change my opinion of him,' I said to soothe him. 'I made many mistakes in reading his character and now I am so thankful that I have the opportunity of admitting those mistakes.'

He appeared not to have heard me, but after a moment he shook his head and said in a bleak way, 'Yes, women do find him attractive, I believe. Attractive. It would be difficult for you to escape that attraction, living in Hassanganj as you did, and almost alone. Do not allow yourself to get too attached, dear Laura, to anything or anyone. Sooner or later one loses all, you know. Everything. Do not invest too much of yourself in another. It must end in pain. Always pain.'

'Oh, come now, Mr Roberts! These are gloomy words. Surely this is a time for rejoicing and not mournful bodings of ill?'

'Of course, you are right. And yet ... and yet I hope you will remember what I said. It is a mistake to lose oneself, in love or business ... or anything else. A grave mistake!'

Before I could reply, he rose, took my hand and pressed it in his own dry and scaly one and walked unsteadily into the night.

'Ah, poor man, poor man!' sighed Kate, who had been sitting with us. 'He's in a bad way. And no way for anyone to help him.'

'Is it the opium, Kate? He has aged ten years.'

'The want of the stuff. Maybe if he can hang on another few weeks, he'll be as good as new again, but ...' She shook her head sadly.

On the third morning after his coming, Oliver opened eyes that were for the first time bright with interest and not fever. His forehead was cool and he asked for food, so we propped him up and gave him a mush of rice and lentils that Kate said would be more strengthening than the arrowroot. He ate hungrily, insisted on feeding himself with his left hand, and while he ate his eyes wandered around the room and from face to face. I suppose he was trying to get his bearings.

'Thank you,' he said as he finished, pushing away the tin plate with an impatient gesture I remembered well. 'I'm glad to see you have some food here. We had understood that you were starving.'

'We've managed,' I assured him, settling him more comfortably while Kate removed the plate and mug, and Jessie, having clucked her approval of his appetite, took the baby out for an airing.

'Out!' he gestured peremptorily to Toddy and Ishmial who were inclined to linger. As they left the room, he said, 'Alive, well, even adequately fed!' He shook his head unbelievingly, then placed my hand against his lips and kissed it. When he looked at me again, there were tears in his eyes but he only said, 'Thank God!' He turned his head away from me so that I would not see the tears and, still holding my hand, murmured, 'So much I have to know. So much I don't know. Tell me.'

'Not now. When you are stronger. There'll be all the time in the world later. Try and sleep now. It will do you good.'

'Don't leave me, will you? Sleep ... is not always very pleasant just now. Let me wake to find you here.' I told him there was nothing I would sooner do than remain with him, and in a few moments he fell asleep again, still holding my hand in his.

There was a recurrence of fever that night but by morning he was again cool and sleeping peacefully. That day he seemed stronger, slept less and in his waking moments talked and asked questions to which he now demanded answers. He ate a respectable meal in the evening and then asked to be propped up in a sitting position for a while.

'For a very short while,' I assented officiously as I made him comfortable. 'You must not try your strength.'

'But that is just what I intend to do,' he retorted. 'Feel much stronger, pain's less and tomorrow begins to look like something more than only a possibility. I believe I'm on the mend.' He stretched his gaunt form under the blanket, flexed the muscles of his sound arm and arched his neck to relieve the tension in his shoulders.

'Laura, come here.' He patted the bed and I went and sat down beside him, realizing that for the first time our eyes were on a level. He looked large and bony and rather threatening, bulked up in the bed against the pillow we had devised of folded cloaks.

A heavy storm of rain resounded on the flat roof of the Gaol and splashed in spray on the stone of the verandah, deadening the occasional far-away gun. The room was dank in the damp heat, quiet and dark. A saucer-dip on a box beside the bed threw shadows on the whitewashed wall but gave little light. Oliver's long hand groped for the dip, then held it up close to my face. His gaze moved over my features, thin now and in their thinness plainer, and over my cropped untidy hair. Carefully he replaced the lamp, then stretched out his hand again and made it follow the route his eyes had taken a moment before, touching gently my brow, eyes and cheeks, my chin and hair, and at last lingering for a moment on my lips.

'I cannot believe it yet,' he said at last.

'That you are here?'

'And you with me.'

'I know. I had given up hope.'

'Of the relief?'

'No—of you!'

A pause. 'Glad?'

'Yes.'

'Happy?'

'Very.'

'Why?'

'You know why.'

'I was right, then?'

'So I discovered.'

'When? How?'

'Little by little. Now and then. Here and there.'

'Elucidate!'

'You are talking too much. We will go into it later, when you are stronger.'

'Now, at once! Or I'll get up and walk out!'

'You couldn't reach the door.'

For answer he swung his legs out of the bed and made as though he would leave it.

'Very well, very well,' I agreed in real anxiety, for the sudden movement had made him sway in an attack of faintness as he rose. I pushed him back against his pillow, but gently, and replaced the blanket.

'Be quiet and stay still and I'll tell you ...'

He smiled and took my hand. 'Go on, now tell me when you realized you loved me, for I always felt you must—eventually.'

'It was during the first big assault against us. In July. I thought I would be killed before the day was out, and though I was frightened I knew suddenly that I was more frightened of not seeing you again than of dying. An awful feeling of loss, of lost opportunities. Nothing rational about it, of course, but they tell me there is little rational about love at the best of times. But ... losing you was worse than death.'

'I know, I know. I had that, too, and for such a long time.' As though the memory of that time recalled too clearly its pain, he dropped my hand and placed his own over his closed eyes. 'Go on,' he prompted in a muffled voice.

'But ... but even before that, on the night that Emily died ...'

'Emily's dead?'

'Yes, she ...'

'Tell me later, go on ...'

'Everyone was frightened and ill and hopeless, and I was too. I didn't know what was going to happen to us, how we would manage, and then I thought of you and I knew I had to stay alive, somehow, to ... to tell you ... well, all sorts of things. That I had been wrong about you and you had been right about me and ...'

'Not what I want to hear!'

'And ...'

'Say it!'

'Why can't you say it first?'

'I've said it. Don't you remember? Outside the hut that hot morning when we were travelling here? Your turn. Say it, Laura!'

'And—that I thought I could love you.'

'Not enough. Admit it.'

My hand was again captured and I found his amber eyes looking straight into mine. I was trembling despite the bantering tone in which this exchange had been conducted. He tightened his grasp on my fingers and almost pleaded: 'Admit it! Once, please?'

'I love you.'

It was not so hard an admission to make after all; so I rushed on. 'I love you. I believe I must always have loved you and I am sure now that I always will.'

He leaned back and put my hand to his lips, eyes closed. Then, holding my hand against his bearded cheek, he said, 'Are you quite sure it is love? Could it not be pity? Finding me at last in this pathetic and pain-racked condition might have proved too much for your female sensibilities and have nothing to do with your heart.'

'Pity? For you? Nonsense!' I protested, in an effort to respond to his tone, though, gazing at his face with its closed eyes, marked with deep lines of suffering, the mouth set in a new habit of silent endurance, a face very different to the one I remembered, I was indeed very near to pity for him. Not only because of his physical pain, either, nor the tormenting memories for which a hand over his eyes was the best amelioration. There was something else now written on those familiar features that wrung my heart, a suggestion of bewildered guardedness, uncertainty, in short a lack of assurance most unlike the entrenched self-confidence that I had once considered so arrogant. He was vulnerable and knew himself to be so, and guessing this I realized that banter was no longer a defence but a hesitant invitation to pursue the conversation in greater depth.

'I would not want to pity you,' I said, seriously. 'And you would not want me to. But cannot you accept my compassion—along with all the rest that I feel for you? It comes of an understanding that would perhaps surprise you. All those months of fencing with you in Hassanganj, while they delayed the acknowledgement of my love to myself, did help me to decipher your character, and some, at least, of your necessities. Were it not so, I could not read your need of me so plainly now. Oliver, I can love you just as well in your weakness and what you feel is your inadequacy, as I will when you are well and strong again. Let me accept you as you are. Oh, my darling, open yourself to me. I so much wish to be honest with you—in all my moods and tribulations.'

I felt tears against the hand he held to his face, but the eyes remained closed, and quiet filled the room.

'It has come true,' he whispered at last, shaking his head in disbelief, and smiling slightly.

'Oh, Laura! It is so hard to believe, after ... that ... that I should live to hear you speak as I so often wanted you to. With love. There were times in the entrenchment when I believe I would have died without protest had I had the memory of a few words of ... of intimacy with you, to make me feel I had gained something in living. My memories, and I lived by them, were sweet—but there had been nothing between us like ... this.'

His eyes flicked open, bright with tears.

'I was right about you. From the beginning. I knew you could love me as I wanted to be loved, in parity and sharing—and passion. Oh, Laura, you have given me such a sense of ... of freedom. I cannot express it. Such a delight.'

He shook his head again and brushed away the tears from his eyes with my hand, on which his grip had tightened as he spoke.

'Laura! No more "fencing" now?'

He held my eyes with his. I shook my head, silently, seeing in them again the naked strength of emotion that had unsettled me so deeply outside the herder's hut on our journey to Lucknow. But now I did not glance away to escape, nor attempt to quiet my own inner tumult.

'There is no need, my heart,' I said softly, as I leaned forward and placed my lips against his, and his hand loosed mine, and his arm encircled me.

CHAPTER 6

The following days passed with the swiftness and sweetness of a summer wind as I realized that Oliver was on the mend and truly with me. He grew stronger and slept less almost by the hour, and with the return of strength there came the return of curiosity, impatience and all his normal humours, good and bad. Soon the confinement and inactivity began to irk him and I had to use all my ingenuity and powers of persuasion to try to keep him quiet. I spent much time telling him of all that had happened to us since he bade us farewell at the *serai* on the outskirts of Lucknow: of the house of Wajid Khan; of our flight and all we had endured since entering the entrenchment. Of his own experiences he said nothing, and I would not question him until he felt himself able to talk of them without too much distress.

'Poor little Emily!' he exclaimed when I described to him the manner of my cousin's death. 'Poor little thing. She wanted so little, yet it was so much more than she ever received. Nineteen years old and dead! Still, she could have met her end in a more ... more dreadful way. That's one thing to be grateful for. And Charles? How did he take it—with relief?'

'He takes great comfort in his religion now and, well, frankly we have all had so much to think of that I have never discussed things with him. We have endured; I suppose he has had to do the same. That's about all I know. He doesn't live here with us. He's at Dr Fayrer's post and only visits us when he can get away in the evenings. Often we don't see him for two or three days at a time, if he gets off too late at night or when things are very bad.'

'Good.'

'Oh, Oliver!'

'Don't pretend annoyance. You know damned well I could never be quite sure of how you felt about him, whether you had really got over him as you once assured me you had. Worse, I was certain of how he felt for you, Emily or not. Just as well I did not know of her death; my time in Cawnpore would have been even less comfortable than it was.'

His own mention of the place disturbed him. His eyes became abstracted and he sighed, his hand stroking his moustache nervously in a gesture that was new but often repeated.

'It must have been terrible; don't think of it, Oliver.'

I moved to the bed, sat down and kissed him on the brow, removing his hand from his moustache and holding it closely. The expression on his face, full of remembered pain and disgust and fear, wrung my heart. I needed to comfort him, to reassure him. In the past I had often felt that I disliked the assurance amounting to arrogance in his face, yet now I would have given much to see it replace the look of inner and inescapable suffering upon his features.

'I cannot help but think of it. It never altogether leaves me, even yet. I was there all through, you see, all through.'

'But why? Why did you stay?'

'For the best of reasons—the only reason. I couldn't get away.'

'Little Yasmina ... she wasn't there too, was she?'

He looked at me with suspicion and annoyance.

'How did you know?'

'Toddy. He told me you were going back to Hassanganj to take her to her grandparents, but I never guessed at the time that you would stay in Cawnpore.'

'Blast him for a blab-mouthed fool!'

'But was she with you?'

'No, thank God, she wasn't. She was safe in her mother's home. Still is, I hope. I got there, oh blazes! I can't remember when exactly. Early in June, anyway. It was, now let me think, yes, the day after old Wheeler ordered all the Europeans, Eurasians and the loyal sepoys into his crazy "Fort", as they chose to call it.'

'Do you want to speak of it now? Perhaps later ...?'

'God, I want a smoke now! A fat black cheroot ...'

'I'm sorry. Perhaps I can ask Toddy to try and come by some. He did once before ...'

'Doesn't matter. Just thought of it on the spur of the moment. Shows I'm better, doesn't it? First time I've yearned for tobacco.'

He paused, his eyes still far away, then went on.

'Do I want to talk of it? No. Nor remember it, nor ever think of it again, nor hear it mentioned. But I cannot escape it. I cannot. In my dreams; waking; when you are talking to me, sitting close beside me; even when I have the comfort of your hand in mine, like this, I see things, remember scenes, hear sounds. I have no control over them. They just swim up out of my memory and I see them as clearly as I see you, hear those ... those dreadful sounds as distinctly and actually as you hear that gun being hauled over the rubble outside and the strain of the bullocks against the yoke and the crack of that whip. No, I don't want to talk of it, yet ... will you let me tell you? Some of it? Not all. Some is ... some must remain in my mind, only in my mind. I do not want you to know all of it. Ever!'

'As you wish. If it will help you, but don't distress yourself.'

He laughed softly, with bitterness. 'I don't need to distress myself, woman dear. It has been done for me. All done for me.'

He hauled himself up against the folded cloaks, wincing slightly as he moved his damaged arm, and sighed deeply.

'Why was I there, you ask? Why indeed? I delivered the child to her grandparents, made what explanations and ... and apologies I could, fixed up the money end of things and so on, and then intended to come on here, to Lucknow. There was no point in my returning to Hassanganj. When I returned for the child, I found the place a desert, everyone had gone back to their villages or joined the pandies; not a servant visible, not a horse or a cow or an elephant. The factory lay empty, the indigo rotting in the vats and stinking to high heaven. Everything around the house had been—devastated; the house itself, of course, just a shell, but they'd stripped the vegetable gardens and the orchards, ruined the machinery of the wells, burned the stabling and quarters, wrecked the contents of the carpenter's shop and the tinsmith's and the blacksmith's. Or stolen the stuff, I suppose. There was nothing left. I spent a rather curious hour wandering among the blackened bones of the Erskine pride. Very odd thing to have to do, you know. Very odd!

'Anyway, Moti's people told me that the road to Lucknow was still open, there were troops coming and going, and apparently Wheeler, mistaken as always, had despatched reinforcements from the 84th to Lawrence here just a couple of days before, and that decided me on Lucknow, even if Hassanganj had been practicable. Not, you understand, that I had gained in heroism or martial aptitude since

637

leaving you, but, well—you were in Lucknow, so that was where I wished to be too.

'I mounted up early that morning and set off. Passing through the outskirts of Cawnpore, firing broke out. Not the first I'd heard, either. The rebel sepoys, aided by the local *badmashes* and town bullyboys were on the rampage, looting and burning everything remotely connected with the whites, rushing in bands through the streets, shouting, screaming and firing their guns into the air or at any hapless bystander in their way. I was going carefully, taking every precaution to keep out of their sight, when a couple of Eurasian women rushed out of a dilapidated bungalow and called to me. They thought I was a Pathan and, therefore, unimplicated, and offered to pay me well if I would accompany them to Wheeler's entrenchment. They were too frightened to move without a male of some sort in attendance, poor creatures. All they wanted was to remain in their home and so had decided to ignore the orders of the previous day, but the rowdies convinced them of their mistake. I spoke to them in English, and they nearly wept with relief, I can tell you! So, I found myself, shortly thereafter, helping to pile them, their baggage and their poor old mother (she was blind and nearly crippled) into a cart and harnessing up their broken-winded nag, and away we went.

'Fortunately we did not have far to go. I thought I'd do my part by them, see them safe and set off at once. We arrived at the entrenchment about nine in the morning, I suppose. God, what a morning, hot as hell's blazes! I rode in with them to help them get settled. Had to carry the old woman in to one of the buildings, then fetch some of their stuff while they disappeared, the two young ones, to look for stabling for the horse.

'And that was my undoing. I believe they must have led my horse away with theirs. Probably didn't believe I wanted to trust myself to the populace and leave the safety of that blasted Fort. Hell! The irony of it … I'd told them I was moving on to Lucknow. Or perhaps the damned animal bolted; it had reason enough. I don't know.'

How often I had lain in bed at night shivering with fear as I envisioned the ridiculous insufficiency of our fortifications— the sacking, bamboo screens and firewood that in many places were all that protected us from the enemy. Now, however, as Oliver described to me what he had found in Cawnpore on that first morning, our stockade seemed in comparison almost invulnerable. The Residency did at least enjoy the slight advantage of being placed on an eminence.

General Wheeler had chosen as his strongpoint a level plain, several acres in extent, close to the sepoy lines and a mile or more from the river. In the centre of this plain stood two long barrack buildings, high-ceilinged and wide-verandahed, that had once formed part of a hospital. The buildings were of masonry but one, the larger, was roofed with thatch. These were the nuclei of the fortification, and around them a wall had been thrown up, a wall of earth four feet high and two feet wide at the top, forming a parallelogram around the barracks and a well, and within this tawdry protection had gathered by that first morning about a thousand men, women and children. Outside the walls the plain stretched flat and open to the enemy on all sides, except for the ruins of some buildings that the General had paid a fortune to have demolished and which now provided the pandies with excellent cover. Outside the enclosure, to the west, were several half-completed brick buildings, which became outposts and had to be maintained at all costs through the entire siege. The single well within the enclosure, the only source of water through three long weeks in the hottest part of the Indian summer, was totally exposed to the enemy.

'Mud walls four feet high and nowhere impregnable to a bullet,' said Oliver with a bitter smile. 'The excuse was that after seven rainless months the ground was too hard to work; true enough no doubt, but there were no proper emplacements for the guns—not so much as a pile of sandbags between the others' artillery and our own. God, when I think of it! Wheeler could have chosen the Magazine to go to earth in. A good site, easily strengthened, well protected. Or any of a dozen other places along the river. But that billiard table of a place, not a tree for shade, entirely indefensible, he chose that! Well, he's dead now, poor devil, and his wife and son; they say his daughter was dragged off by the pandies at the river …

'Of course, I didn't take it all in at the time. Couldn't see a thing for the crowds clamouring for living space. I got the old lady settled in one of the barracks that was already so packed with women, children and servants, all squabbling and crying to each other, I was damned glad to get out of it again. Just in time to hear old Wheeler announce to some of his officers that he had received a message from the Nana Sahib saying he was about to attack. So I thought to myself, "Well, Oliver m'lad, this is where you get going," and I looked around for my horse. It had gone; nowhere to be found. Word got around immediately of the attack, and panic took over.

'Most unpleasant thing, panic, Laura. Women screamed, children cried, husbands yelled orders to their families, and every coolie, *ayah* and servant in the place, and there were scores, added to the uproar. Fright. Plain blue funk. Not at all a nice thing to see happen to anyone. I managed to get hold of a young officer, explained I had lost my nag and asked whether there was anywhere I could buy or borrow one. He just laughed in a singularly ugly manner and informed me with some heat, justifiable under the circumstances, I suppose, that now even cowardly wogs like me would have to stay where I was, since, whatever about the horses, no one could leave the Fort. Had I been lucky enough to find an animal I would have proved him wrong by jumping it over that damn-fool wall. However, we'd hardly finished our little exchange when we heard a bugle call and at almost the same moment the first roundshot whistled over our heads and smashed into the barrack behind us, maiming a native woman. They kept that average up pretty consistently too; one shot, one life—or at least a limb!'

For the first few days provisions had been ample, even luxurious, and everyone had fed on sealed salmon, asparagus, tongue and wine. But soon the rations comprised a handful of parched gram, lentils and rum, sometimes supplemented by soup made from horsemeat, and later from pariah dogs. The Nana Sahib's blockade was total.

The well in the centre of the compound was a deathtrap; early in the siege the machinery had been shot away and man after man, day after day, died drawing the leather bucket up by hand for all its sixty feet. There was no equitable system of apportioning the water. Those among the women who had friends prepared to risk themselves, or who could pay a private soldier for a mug full, were the lucky ones. The rest sucked on leather straps, went thirsty for hours and days in heat of over 130°, and died for the want of it. Heat-stroke killed half a dozen men in one day alone, a day so scorching that muskets exploded in the hands that held them.

The stench in the enclosure was appalling: no sanitary arrangements whatever existed and in the barracks women and children soiled themselves in their clothes sooner than leave their negligible shelter. Cholera, dysentery and gangrene took their toll and added to the odour. Each evening the day's quota of dead was lowered down a dry well just outside the walls, where in the terrible heat the bodies soon putrefied, adding their stench to the rest.

The noise was, if possible, more dreadful than the heat or the smell, the noise made by hundreds of wounded, ill and despairing human beings, meeting their own deaths and combating the frightful witnessing of their friends' deaths in the only way open to them, screams, shrieks and sobs of terrified sorrow. And minute by minute, the guns of the enemy shattered the two poor shelters, flattened the walls and decimated the huddled inmates, never stopping, hardly ever lessening.

Oliver's thin brown hand moved hesitantly over the straggly moustache.

'I have always considered it an unpardonable impudence to believe the Deity small enough to have thought of Hell,' he said after a thoughtful pause. 'Those three weeks convinced me I was right. The Almighty knows well enough He has no need to provide a facility that His creatures can devise so excellently well without his help.'

Kate and Jessie had both come into the bedroom and were listening silently as he spoke, sitting on the unoccupied bed in the gloom.

'But what possessed poor Wheeler?' Kate wondered. 'Surely he must have known what to expect?'

'I don't know. Perhaps he thought, like a lot of others, that his *Babalog* would never turn on him. After all, he had an Indian wife, had spent his entire life with the sepoys; he must have thought he knew them well enough to have confidence in them. But that ridiculous position, Kate, and then to try to hold it against such odds—in June, without water, shade or food! Without guns either. We had eight nine-pounders. The others'— I noticed he never spoke of the 'enemy', always the 'others'— 'had everything you could think of from twenty-four pounders down to six-pounders. And God alone knows how many men. And yet Wheeler ... History will try to make him out a hero, I suppose, canonize his efforts. Yet the whole damned business was an act of criminal folly compounded by indecision, a dire misreading of the signs and times, and unbelievable lack of plain common sense.

'No hope; we had no hope at all of maintaining that position or of being relieved, yet day after day we went on while people dropped like flies around us and the dead became the envied of the living.

'I was one of the lucky ones; I seldom went into the barracks. Once I had managed to establish my credentials with the military, I was congratulated on having a rifle and told off to join Mowbray Thomson at Barrack No. 2, one of the outposts. He's here, they tell me; I'm glad to know he made it too. It was a hot spot in every way, believe me, but, my God, it was better than watching what was happening in those barracks. Occasionally I had to go in with a wounded man or for supplies or something, but I never went willingly. The sights and the sounds; and the smells. Little children, two and three years old, legless, armless, a mass of blood, their screams cutting through all the other dreadful noises, and nothing could be done for them. For anyone. Almost every day someone went insane. There was an unfortunate missionary fellow—started raving one day, pulled off all his clothes and danced around, mother-naked, shouting the foulest obscenities till he had the good luck to die. A baby died drowned in its own *ayah*'s blood and a ... a woman was ...! No. That won't do. No good lacerating you with my memories. You have your own, no doubt.'

His lonely hand came out to meet mine, and he lay back against the cushion with eyes closed.

'Hadn't you better rest now, Oliver?' Kate said. 'You have been talking a lot and it won't do to overdo things so soon. Tell us the rest tomorrow.'

'No,' he shook his head, his eyes still closed. 'Now I've started, I can't stop. I don't want to upset you, but ...'

'You won't upset us,' she replied. 'We have heard so many terrible things recently, and talking does ease the mind, they say. Tell on, then, boy, tell on.'

'After a few days of the non-stop battering they were getting, those two buildings were almost as dangerous in themselves as the pandies' guns, but there was no other shelter—even from the sun. Then, about two weeks after the start, one evening a caracasse of sulphur and tallow struck the thatched barrack, where most of the sick had been gathered together with the soldiers' families. There was a wind blowing ... the hot wind ...'

'I know; we felt it too in the house of Wajid Khan, the *loo*.'

'Perhaps on that same day,' he murmured, 'that same awful day.' A long pause ensued as he remembered it. He shuddered.

'In that heat everything was tinder. In seconds the roof was ablaze, thatch and pulverized brick and beams smashing in on the occupants, most of them too badly wounded to move. Their screams ... in that hellish, stinking twilight! It's those I hear so often, Laura ... those terrible shrieks of burning men and the smell of burning human flesh. Their relatives ... some of them ... watching. Seeing, hearing what was ... happening to them.'

The shudder became a nervous shiver, and I thought the fever might have returned. I hushed him like a baby, cradling his hand in both my own, but he went on.

'The worst ... the worst was always watching ... others. Suffering, dying ... and not being able to do anything—anything—to help!

'That was the end really. The fire should have been enough. After that the only shelter the women and children had was in some shallow trenches and a few tiny "go-downs" where the heat was so monstrous the children could not breathe. Women were confined in those ditches, bore their children in the full glare of the blazing sun, the guns and every passing eye.'

'Dr Darby's wife was one of them,' Kate said quietly.

'Yes. He's here, isn't he? They got her, though. At the river.'

He paused again, his teeth clenched to try to stop the shivering. Kate and I glanced at each other anxiously.

'Some days later, when the heat of the burned-out barrack had died down sufficiently for us to approach it, we found forty charred bodies among the ashes. And the fire had taken the few medical supplies that had been laid in. By then, though, as many were dying of the heat and sheer despair as from the effects of the guns.

'I remember one afternoon, the day after the fire, I think, it was so hot my palms came up in yellow blisters like balloons from handling my rifle; my head was cracking open with pain, the sun had got me, I suppose, and I'd had no water all that day. I dropped down behind the ruined walls—all that remained of No. 2 post by then—to try and recover a little in the shade thrown by the wall. I found another man there before me, and was just about to ask him to move over a bit when he looked up at me, with the sly, determined expression of a child defying its father, put his revolver in his mouth and pulled the trigger ... And I ... I was so tired ... so uncaring really, that I sat there ... with his blood ... and brains bubbling on the hot stone. Steaming. The water from the well, you see, was often pink with blood. Some couldn't take it, whatever their thirst, or if they did they brought it up at once which made matters worse. Dried them out even more. That chap, I knew, had not had a drink in two days. More perhaps.'

For a further week the purgatory had continued, and then on the 25th of June a lone woman, wearing ragged European clothing and with a child at her breast, was seen approaching the walls bearing a white flag of truce. She brought with her a letter conveying the Nana Sahib's offer of terms.

'We had no option of course, though when it was learned that the Nana wanted us out of the entrenchment that same night and would not hear of our evacuating it in the morning, he was sent a message saying we had enough powder to blow ourselves and his entire army to blazes. If that is an option. The next day Azimullah, the Nana's aide, agreed to treat with Wheeler, though the poor old devil was so far gone by then, everything had to be decided by his officers.'

'And you, did you trust in the terms, Oliver? Did you expect treachery or not?'

'No, I did not expect treachery. I could see no point in it. They'd given us the drubbing of a lifetime, after all. Oh, we'd hung on, but they'd got us out of Cawnpore, made the point, to their own satisfaction anyway, of the Rajah of Bithur's ascendancy in his own territory. There was no point in treachery. What could they gain by slaughtering a few hundred starving whites and Eurasians and a handful of loyal sepoys?

'What's more, the terms they agreed to were pretty well generous: carriages and litters for the wounded as far as the river; elephants and whatever else was necessary for the women and the baggage; even sixty rounds of ammunition to be issued to each man before leaving; boats to get us to Allahabad. It was as fair as we had a right to expect from any adversary. No, I did not expect treachery. I was wrong, apparently, though I have still to be persuaded of it. Yes, I have still to be assured that it was on the Nana Sahib's own orders that we were shot down at the river.'

'But, Oliver, who else could have given the order?'

'You know these people, Kate! You know the intrigue and the wrangling and pushing for place that goes on in these petty courts. There's always someone trying to edge out the present incumbent, or trying to placate him or win his favour. It could have been any of a dozen men, probably—close to the Nana and hoping to gain some private end by taking matters into his, or their, own hands. Or perhaps no one gave the order. Perhaps … perhaps it was all a mistake.'

'How could it have been? I don't understand …' I put in.

'I know. Seems inconceivable. I'll try to explain.'

Jessie had left the room to feed Pearl in the kitchen; it was quite dark now, and we called to her to bring in the saucer dip. Oliver was looking drawn and again we suggested he defer telling us the rest of his story to another time; but he shook his head and continued.

'There was a curious want of consistency in the way the others treated us after the guns were handed over and our surrender became a fact. On the one hand courtesy, even consideration; on the other a ... a deliberate flouting of what we had a right to expect from men who had shown such courtesy. The Nana sent his own ceremonial *howdah* to be used by Wheeler's elephant, yet the *mahouts* refused to order the elephants to kneel, so the only way they could be mounted was by hauling oneself up by the tail. I heard that one sepoy spat in an officer's face, yet I saw others weep when told of a former officer's death. One party of women had their possessions torn from them by the sepoys; yet other sepoys, many others, went out of their way to help by carrying children and assisting the wounded. I don't know why I should be surprised by the inconsistency. They were human, and humanity is inconsistent. Why should I be puzzled by the fact that the memories men harbour are as different as their temperaments or their faces? And impel them to different actions?

'We must have looked a weird, a pathetic sight, setting off for the river and ... safety. The elephants with their garishly painted heads, one bearing a silver *howdah*; the wounded in a long string of carts and litters; the rest of us struggling along on foot, all closely guarded by sepoys and watched by a horde of curious citizenry. It was already hot ... and we took our smell of blood, decay and filth with us. Washing, as you can imagine, had not been among our priorities when half a cup of water could cost a man's life. The men were in tatters, the children nearly naked; some of the younger women wore only the bodices of their dresses over their pantaloons, their skirts having been ripped up for bandages. Poor creatures, their shame and embarrassment as they walked along in their own excrement. Almost everyone wore a bandage somewhere; even the most robust and lucky of us.'

'You too?' I asked, though he had not mentioned his arm.

'Yes, me too. I'd bound my feet in the remains of my red velvet waistcoat. I'd lost my shoes one night, when trying to get some sleep; I'd taken them off and placed them on top of a wall nearby. Thought they'd be safe from my comrades, and so they were, but not from a shell that exploded on the other side of the wall and blew them and the wall to smithereens.'

'You must have been injured too?'

'No, only a little dustier and dirtier than usual. The walls retained the heat, so we tried to sleep in the open, away from them. That saved me. I was lucky, but my feet were soon blistered and cut about by walking on the baking rubble, so I tore up the waistcoat. Compared to most of the others, I was in the pink of form. Most of the women and children had been injured too in that damned worthless barrack, though I saw one female trotting along carrying a parasol and a little dog! Most had little left to carry but themselves.' He laughed slightly at the memory.

'Well, the *ghat*—the landing stage, Laura—was about a mile away. When we arrived, we found the boats drawn up as had been negotiated, forty of them, thatched and provisioned for the journey down to Allahabad, each poled by ten boatmen; everything in readiness. Now tell me, why would a man who was preparing to have us all killed go to such lengths to set the scene? He had had to scour the area for the boats and pay the boatmen a fortune for taking us. And the provisions were on board; I saw them. Why should anyone provide food for people whom he knew would never have the chance to eat it? Wouldn't it have been simpler and cheaper if he wanted to do away with us to arrange for our collective demise back in the entrenchment, when we had surrendered our arms? He could have done it then, you know. No question but he could have done it then. Why the elaborate charade?'

'It's what I said to Mr Roberts when I first heard of it,' put in Kate. 'Do you remember, Laura? And why should the Nana then rescue the women only to have them butchered later? 'Tis truly incredible. But we'll never know the truth of it now, I expect. Unless and until they capture him, or one of his lieutenants.'

'Yes. Why did it happen? That question, Kate, will exercise me for the rest of my days.

'Anyway, there we were at the *ghat*, five or six hundred of us all told, I suppose. On the near bank was a wide beach backed by trees where we were all crowded, and on the far side the trees came down to the water, which was very low and full of reeds. The embarkation was a lengthy business, everyone, well or sick, having to wade through the water or be dragged or carried to the boats that stood out in midstream. It all went smoothly; no incidents. Not much help from the boatmen, but perhaps none was to be expected. The sepoys who escorted us dispersed the crowd that had followed the column and stood around watching, chewing *pan* and talking. It was altogether a very Indian occasion, unhurried, muddled, casual.

'I remember looking round and feeling a strange sort of peace descending on me. It was all so familiar; to me, so ... so pleasant. Even the sight of heavy shade, dark, almost cool, under the trees was a delight. There were crows watching us curiously from their perches, a flock of mynas, parrots ... and a woodpecker at work high up in a tree, and a kingfisher skimming over the muddy water downstream. God, I believe I was almost happy for a few minutes, finding all those everyday things which we had forgotten about for so long, still as they had always been despite what we had gone through.

'I suppose it took us about an hour to get everybody aboard, and a damned tight fit it was too. Boats built for four passengers carrying ten and twelve, so overloaded most of them were aground. I was standing in a boat, looking around me, as I say, with some pleasure at being in the open again, when I heard a bugle, just a couple of notes such as a bandsman produces when the band is warming up before a performance on the *maidan*. For a second nothing happened. Then ... then all of a sudden I saw the native boatmen leap out of the boats and make for the shore ... and heard the crack of a rifle.

'All hell broke loose immediately. And what a hell! There ... there were cannon hidden in the reeds of the Lucknow shore and sepoys rushed out from among those shady, bird-filled groves on the Cawnpore side and raked us with musketry. In moments the dry thatch of the boats was aflame; then cavalry charged into the water with drawn *tulwars* and hacked at the people as they leaped screaming from the burning boats, and I remember thinking, almost immediately it happened, "Hell! Why did we fire first? We fired first!" '

'The bugle call, Oliver?' I protested. 'Surely it was a signal? If not why were the cannon in readiness, or the sepoys waiting in the trees?'

'I don't know. I just don't know. Perhaps they expected treachery from us; we had arms and ammunition after all?'

'Treachery! From a couple of hundred debilitated and wounded men such as you describe?'

'I know; not a sensible deduction. But—what if the Nana were not entirely sure of his own men, the ones who accompanied us, I mean? Their officers were among us. Or what, and this is what truly haunts me, Kate, what if the cannon and the sepoys were there to protect us— not murder us? A ... a precaution in case the Cawnpore people took it upon themselves to finish us off? The Nana, from what I heard in the entrenchment, had been most sympathetic to the British, offered much good advice which had been taken. Even that note he sent in on the first day announcing he was about to attack; it was taken as a threat, but it could have been a warning ... from a man forced to it against his own will. The terms he'd made with us, too, were magnanimous.'

'But that bugle call? What was it then?'

'I don't believe it was a call, a true call. If it was, then the final notes were lost in the firing. To me, it was like some stupid sepoy, a recently appointed bugler perhaps, playing with his new toy. Experimenting with it.'

We all fell silent. In the kitchen Jessie crooned to Pearl, and smoke from the fire she had lit to heat the soup drifted into the bedroom.

'God between them and all harm, but Oliver, boy, do you really think all those lives were lost because of ... of a mistake? That our shots invited, or provoked, the ... rest?'

Oliver said nothing for a moment. The flickering light of the dip accentuated every furrow on his face, and in every line was bitterness.

'I cannot be certain, Kate. I do not know enough and I suppose I never will now. But I believe it might have been due to a mistake, yes! We were all on edge. Jumpy. Remember what we had gone through in those three weeks, and many of us, most perhaps, were expecting treachery. Perhaps if we had not been allowed our guns ...'

'Oh, Oliver! That's a terrible, terrible thought ...'

'Yes,' he said, 'I know. I have lived with it through these months.'

Again there was silence until I put in hesitantly, for the other two seemed absorbed in their musings, 'What happened then, Oliver? Was that when you were wounded?'

He nodded.

'I ... I just stood there for a minute or two, aghast, not knowing what to do, not even thinking of what I should do, and something hit me. I don't know what, perhaps the prow of another boat, or an oar. I lost my feet and fell into the water, but Mowbray Thomson and another man grabbed me and I managed to regain my feet. I hung on to their boat, it was drifting now; somehow it had come off the sandbank that had held it, and all I could do was hang on and hope for the best. I couldn't see. My eyes were full of muddy water churned and splashed by the horses and people throwing themselves into the river; and explosions. Then I lost my feet again. The river was very shallow there, a couple of feet in depth, no more, but we must have drifted into a deeper channel, for I found I was floating and I let go one hand from the side of the boat to wipe my eyes. That was when … my arm went. I looked up just in time to see a *tulwar* descending on the arm still hanging on to the boat. It was too late to let go and dive, and the steel caught me. Slashed right down to the bone. The *sowar* could have ended me then, but somebody on the boat got him with a rifle and we all went down—the horse, the *sowar* and me, into the filthy water, bobbing with bodies now and seething with fallen flaming thatch. The noise! I cannot convey it. The sound of terror, absolute terror: screams, shouts, the human shriek of wounded horses, the *sowars* yelling "*Din! Din! Din!*" as they swept down among us, and the shots and explosions ringing out over it all. On and on the shots rang out.

'It's difficult to know what happened next. I must have disentangled myself somehow from the horse and the *sowar*, and surfaced. I remember someone trying to haul me aboard the boat. A boat. I don't know whether it was the same one, though it seems likely, since apparently it was the only one that moved downstream and got away.

'I was … in a bad way. The pain was frightful and I was half drowned to boot. No!' He shook his head at himself. 'That's not right. I felt nothing at the time; the pain only started later. But I was half-drowned and choking, and suddenly I felt myself falling again, back into the river. I don't know why my hand had been released by my would-be rescuer. Probably a bullet got him too.

'I fainted then, I suppose. Nothing is clear after that. I seem to remember that awful screaming and crying on and off for hours, but it might have been only moments. Then for a long time I heard nothing, knew nothing.

'It was afternoon when I came to. The sun was blazing down directly into my eyes, as I lay in the water on my back with my head and shoulders caught against some roots and driftwood that had got stuck on a sandbank. If they hadn't been there, those roots, I'd have drifted on and drowned, I suppose; been killed certainly. As it was, I must have looked pretty dead already, not worth the bother of wading into the river to make sure of anyway. After a while I began to be aware that things had quietened down; the odd shot, some activity on the bank higher upstream, but I had floated or been dragged quite a way, and I could see nothing. I was losing a lot of blood and must have been caught up in the driftwood some time, for the shallow water around me was red. I could not stop the bleeding and, frankly, hadn't the interest left to try, but I did attempt to ease the pain by lowering the wound into the water. I suppose I drifted off again after a while.

'When I came round the second time, the sun was going down. I was on land; I could feel the harsh grass under my neck and cheek, and I remember wondering how in blazes I had got there. I had a cracking headache, even worse than the arm, and could only think of my thirst. Sunstroke, I suppose. I lay there for a while, trying to make things out, waiting for something to happen, and then I found I was not alone. An incredibly ancient Indian squatted on his haunches a little way from me, pulling on his *biri* contentedly, watching me. When he saw my eyes move, he beckoned and a woman appeared, and they both stood looking down at me, wondering, I suppose, what the hell was to be done with me.

'I managed to croak, after about the third try, and the woman went away and returned with a brass pot of water.'

'They had found you? And rescued you? Natives?' I was frankly incredulous.

'They had found me, rescued me and went on rescuing me. Natives!' His tone was scathing.

'I'm sorry, but surely, in the light of all that has happened to both of us, my surprise is natural?'

'Hmph!'

'What happened then?' Kate said impatiently.

'Well, they were on the way back to their own village after attending a wedding in some place on the far side of Cawnpore. They had a bullock-cart. They told me later they thought I was a Pathan. I was wearing the same kit I had when I set out from Hassanganj—never even washed. My beard had grown during the siege, since we had no water to shave in, and I had clung on to my turban like grim death, and damned glad I was to have it too. I used to wrap the tail around my face and tuck the end into the folds at the side to keep the smell out; it probably saved me from sunstroke a dozen times. Apparently the turban was still on my head when they found me, ducking or not. They had sat and watched me for a long time, trying to make out whether I was dead or alive. When evening came, the woman's curiosity had got the better of her and she had waded out and pulled me ashore. And there I was. They had passed too late to hear the shooting on the river that morning; but, seeing a great many sepoys still riding and marching around, and being simple folk, had decided to hide up in a grove until nightfall. Which was why they had been able to keep an eye on me for so long.'

'They never tried to hurt you? To give you up to the pandies?' I was still incredulous, and basely when I remember Ungud, Ishmial, Moti and so many more.

'They never even questioned whether I wanted to go with them, or considered the risk they were running in taking me. Just loaded me on to the cart and away we went. The village was about twenty miles this side of Cawnpore. They were the poorest of the poor: untouchables—the old man was a shoemaker and leather-worker, or had been in his good days. They had a hut some way out of the village and a scratch of land. They hid me and protected me, fed me and nursed me to the best of their ability until I left—about a week ago. Ten days?'

'Did the other villagers know of you being there?'

'They must have. They kept away so carefully.'

'Glory be! But you're being kept for hanging, lad. No doubt of that.'

'That's it, Kate,' I agreed. 'When I think of how much blood you must have lost, and the pain you were in ... How did you pull through?'

'Fever was a help. God tempers the wind to the shorn lamb. I don't know whether it was some disease, sunstroke, or just the wound, but I was delirious a lot of the time to begin with and didn't feel or remember very much. After the first few weeks, I began to worry about the damned arm, though. Could see it was useless, but it wouldn't heal up. Kept breaking open and suppurating, and the fever kept returning too. One day I awoke from a doze to find a pariah puppy licking the pus away while I slept.'

'Oliver! No! Ugh!'

'Now there's a delicately nurtured female for you,' he commented ironically to Kate. 'No sense! That little ring-tailed pup, with its yellow eyes and its eternal cringe, put me on my feet again. I remembered that once when I was a boy my grandmother had told me not to interfere when my pointer bitch licked an injured puppy's bleeding cut. "She's healing it," my Grandmama said. "There's something curative in a dog's saliva." So, well, having no other medication, I decided to give it a try. Made a point of inviting little Fido back every time I saw him. He became quite a friend.'

'And it helped?'

'It certainly improved. Healed quite well. Looks a mess as you can see; I suppose it should have been stitched up when it happened. But it closed after a fashion, stopped suppurating, and only opened up again when some cloddish private knocked it with a musket butt on the way here. He seems to have made a thorough job of it. Still, as you say, Kate, I am obviously being saved for hanging! And now ... now, if you don't mind, I think I would like to sleep. I think now I *can* sleep.'

CHAPTER 7

Having told us his story, Oliver seldom again mentioned his experiences in Cawnpore or in the village to which his rescuers had taken him. Sometimes, perhaps, he would recall some incident too absurd or funny to keep to himself and he would recount it, smiling. More often the recollections that swam to the forefront of his mind during the days of his convalescence were unhappy, and I would find him lying back on his pillows, grinding his teeth and knuckling his eyes as though in pain, or to shut out some insistent vision too horrible to remember without a groan. Sometimes, too, he would call me in his peremptory fashion and, when I went to him, would hold my hand to his lips, eyes closed, or put my fingers over his eyes, as though their presence would in some way exorcise the devils in his mind. Then he would release me very tenderly and say gruffly, 'Be off about your business, woman. Idling while there's work to be done?'

For me, the small dark room where he lay was all there was of reality during those days. When I was not with Oliver, I was thinking of him, cooking some mess for him, trying to find him clothes, or talking of him to our visitors. Not unnaturally, however, our friends had other things on their minds than Oliver's well-being and before long their anxious or despondent talk made me realize that nothing much had altered in our situation, despite the relief, and that in fact in many ways we were worse off.

For the relief had failed. Instead of being rescued from the Residency by the forces of Generals Havelock and Outram, the relievers themselves were now incarcerated with us and as completely cut off from help from the outside world as the original garrison had been before the 25th of September.

I can no longer remember what I had myself expected from the term 'relief'. Probably something impractical, such as marching out of the entrenchment with bands playing and ranks of immaculate soldiery snapping to attention as we women passed down their precise and warlike lines. Among the men, there had always been two distinct schools of thought: there were those who had hoped for a strong force that in a few swift engagements would release us from our imprisonment, retake the city of Lucknow, and from there quell the insurrection in all of Oudh. Others, more realistic, hoped only for aid sufficient to liberate the Residency and get the dependants to safety, while the men of the Old Garrison remained on to battle for the city and await the coming of a superior force from Calcutta. The second alternative was the most popular, and at times it seemed to me that all most men needed to really enjoy a war was the absence of their female responsibilities. But perhaps my judgement, made in pique, was a little cruel. What no one had envisaged was that, having been rescued, our rescuers would then be shut up helplessly with us within the enclosure.

For General Havelock, having learned what had befallen General Wheeler's force in Cawnpore, of the massacre at the river and the later butchering of the women, and understandably anxious that the like fate should not befall us in Lucknow, had marched to our rescue with too small an army. Of the three thousand men who had gathered in Cawnpore to come to our aid, four hundred were sick or wounded and were left behind; an additional five hundred men, together with most of the supplies and several thousand camp followers, had been left at the Alum Bagh, a palace in a large walled park, only four miles distant from us as the crow flies, but from the nature of things now inaccessible. In the close and bloody fighting in the city on the 25th and 26th of September, two hundred men of the relief had been killed and over three hundred wounded. The strength of the relieving column had thus been halved between the time they had mustered in Cawnpore and the day they entered the Baillie Guard.

'For don't you see, Miss Laura,' Mr Roberts explained patiently, 'if over five hundred men were lost coming through the city when unencumbered even by camp-followers, think what the casualties would be if they were to try to fight their way out again, taking with them some six hundred women and children, to say nothing of the sick?'

'But surely, with our own men to help them ... ?'

'There are only nine hundred and eighty of us left, Miss Laura,' Mr Roberts reminded me solemnly, 'of the 1,720 of the first counting.'

'And so we remain and endure? Just as before?'

'Except that I believe it will be rather worse. I do not envisage starvation. I believe that the opinion that there were a great deal more provisions available to us than Brigadier Inglis was ever aware of, has now been verified. We will certainly eat, even with the added numbers now with us, but less than we have been eating so far. And the cold weather is almost upon us and we have no warm clothing. The unfortunate men of the relief, indeed, arrived with two days' rations and what they stood up in, their thin summer uniforms.'

'And how long are we to "endure", Mr Roberts? Has anyone indicated any length of time?'

'No, one cannot be sure, Mr Erskine. But weeks, no more. Merely a few weeks.'

Mr Roberts was looking better than he had done for weeks; not quite his old self, but the trembling in his hands was less, his colour better and his sniff almost gone. I commented on his improvement after he had left us.

'Perhaps, having had to be without the stuff for so long, he has overcome the craving, Kate.'

Oliver looked from one face to the other with interest.

'More likely he has found a new source,' Kate replied.

'But how?'

'Oh, a sepoy, or some canny private soldier, perhaps, guessing he would find privation here, bought up a supply in some Cawnpore bazaar and brought it in with him. Let us hope Mr Roberts does not have to do without again before too long.'

'Opium?' asked Oliver.

We nodded.

'Funny how it gets the most unlikely ones,' he said without surprise.

'I think he is much lonelier than he would like people to know,' I said. 'He is a sensitive man, and craves companionship. He must have had a sad life since his wife died and his daughters married. No real roots or home. I suppose books can't provide everything, even for him.'

Charles had entered our quarters for his evening visit to Pearl just as Mr Roberts left, and stood now leaning against the doorjamb with his daughter cradled in his arm. She was satisfied after her meal and dozed contentedly, holding Charles's forefinger in her little hand. She was now so active and so curious about her small world that we all knew relief when she fell asleep.

'The suppliers of the stuff should be shot,' he muttered angrily. 'No man should be allowed to become dependent on the fumes of a wretched weed. It's degrading!'

'So is liquor, if you allow it to be,' pointed out Oliver.

'True—but this stuff! We've had some trouble because of it only today, down at our post. One of the sepoys, a decent fellow who has done his duty well all through, suddenly put down his musket, hopped over Fayrer's garden wall and walked out into the no-man's land beyond where the earthworks are going up for the extended position. Shot before he'd gone ten paces. His friends told us he had located a supply among the relief, but having no money, could not get hold of any. Just gave up in despair and decided death was preferable.'

'You were right then, Kate,' I said.

'Unfortunately.'

'What is this extended position you mention, Charles?' asked his brother.

'Oh, I keep forgetting what an old hermit you are. A somewhat sybaritic one, mind you, lolling back there on your pillows, being waited upon by this band of devoted women, but, of course, you can know nothing of what is going on outside. I suppose you are familiar with this place, though, as it was before the trouble?'

'Reasonably.'

'Well, the area Lawrence managed to enclose and fortify, the area we have been living and fighting in all this time, is pretty confined, particularly now with so many extra men, to say nothing of the grass-cutters, grooms and servants that came in with them. As soon as Outram got in and weighed up the position, he decided to extend the perimeter. We've been busy clearing out the houses beyond the present walls—spiking guns, blowing up batteries, blowing down mosques— the idea being to enlarge the entrenchment to include the Farhat Baksh Palace and the Chathar Manzil to the south as far as Phillips's house to the east. Give us a lot more room for living and make things a little less convenient for the gentlemen over the wall. There've been sorties every day, pitched battles some of 'em, and of course we've had our reverses, but the palaces are all but enclosed now and Havelock's men are living pretty "cushily", I can tell you, in marble halls tricked out with precious stones. We tried to clear the road to Cawnpore, too, so that Outram could withdraw with some of his men to the Alum Bagh, but now that so much grain and flour has been discovered here, that idea has been given up. Not but what some variety in the meals would have been most acceptable to us all if he had been able to get through to his supplies!'

'What's he like, Outram? You seem to be so much in the know.'

'A great chap and a good soldier, Outram!' Charles answered. 'A thorough-going gentleman to boot. Why, do you know what he did when he arrived at Cawnpore, to take over command from Havelock?'

'Not an idea. Military gossip isn't much in my line at the best of times.'

'Well, but you must know it was Havelock who took Cawnpore?'

'I had heard.'

'He arrived in Allahabad straight from the campaign in Persia and was ordered to take command of the British infantry, artillery and volunteer cavalry and get to Cawnpore with all possible haste. Well, of course, he was too late to help you people there, but he tried, and by heavens he had a hard time of it too.'

'Poor fellow!' sympathized Oliver.

Charles paused and blinked, not quite sure how to take this, then went on: 'Delays, diversions, muddle, illness, battles and sorties all the way, and then, having taken Cawnpore, he discovers that he is to be superseded, at the behest of Calcutta, by Outram. Enough to embitter any man, don't you think? And Outram must have realized it, for when he reached Cawnpore, after Havelock, he waived his right of command and asked Havelock to accept his services in the capacity of Civil Chief Commissioner, and a volunteer, until Lucknow was reached. Handsome, I call it. Only a big man could have done that.'

'Very well bred. Most genteel, in fact. But damned confusing to the poor beggars under 'em!'

'How do you mean?'

'Nobody knew whom they were to obey,' Oliver expatiated. 'Each generous general was giving way to the other with great punctilio, and the result was chaos. Even in the few days I was with them, I saw only too clearly what happens when two tails try to wag one dog. Outram, as you say, Charles, is a gentleman. He confined himself to suggestions. But Havelock also is a gentleman and so treated all Outram's suggestions as orders. Except, of course, that when Outram advised a respite before pushing on into the Residency, Havelock for once insisted on his own opinion and moved in—with woeful results, as was apparent when I came in with Ungud the following day.'

'Havelock's only human, after all.'

'A holy human too, so they tell me. A regular praying mantis.'

'And in your opinion that is to his discredit?'

'No ...' Oliver considered the question. 'But it is not automatically to his credit, shall I say?'

Charles jiggled his daughter in his arms in an access of irritation and burst out, 'By heavens, Oliver, I don't know how you do it! After all you have been through, after all that you have been saved from ... to have no faith!'

'Now why should you say that, Charles?' his brother queried mildly. 'I did not say I had no faith. I merely said that praying does not, in my view, automatically make a good man; still less a good soldier.'

'Now hush, you two!' I broke in. 'You squabble like schoolboys the minute you set eyes on each other. Cannot you see, Charles, that he is only baiting you? Don't play his game.'

Charles was too stung to be quiet.

'I ... I know, Oliver, that what we have suffered here has been nothing in comparison to what you underwent in Cawnpore, but ... but nevertheless, we all, and I personally, have known grief and loss and ... and great anguish. For me to find a man like General Havelock, a true Christian, a gentleman and a great soldier, living his belief with humility and courage in the face of mockery and criticism and ... in spite of everything, is ... is a true inspiration.'

'I'm delighted to hear it. Inspire away, Charles, inspire away. But accord me the courtesy of allowing me to hold my own opinions.'

'You don't ... why can you not ... Oh, be damned to you, Oliver!' And Charles thrust the baby into my arms and strode out of the room, followed by Kate.

'Now there's a right-minded fellow, Laura. Damning his own kin for no good reason, and when he should be giving a good example to the heathen!'

'You shouldn't tease him so, Oliver. You know, he really is very convinced about his religion.'

'Yes?'

'Yes. He always was in a way. Don't you remember the Sunday morning services after breakfast in Hassanganj? The collects, lessons and Lord's prayer?'

'Do I not? I had a dread that one day his natural instincts would get the better of him and he'd launch into the sermon too!'

'Yes, that was why the elephants had to be inspected on Sundays!'

'Not entirely. I could not bear your too evident admiration, your somewhat overzealous participation. I knew it was out of character for you to indulge in piety, so I looked for the cause ... and found it.'

'That must have been in the very early days of our visit to Hassanganj. But now, well, it's different with him, Oliver, and you must realize it. Emily's death was ... he feels responsible for it. I know it's absurd, but I can only guess what he went through when she died. I know what he suffered when he thought she was going to die, when the baby was coming. Guilt and remorse, and the fear that he could never make amends. In a way it is as well we are here and going through all this. In more normal circumstances, I believe he would have fared worse, after Emily's death. As it is, he has taken to the Bible and prayer and ... well, you must admit that that is better than drink!'

Oliver chuckled. Then chuckled louder. Then broke into a great guffaw of remarkably robust laughter for a convalescent.

CHAPTER 8

Dr Darby had decreed ten days' bed-rest for Oliver. Since the fever had broken, he had improved in health and spirits at an extraordinary rate, so I was not surprised when, on the eleventh morning, as soon as he had finished his breakfast, he commanded Toddy to shave him, since he intended to get up and go out. 'Get rid of these blasted whiskers, Tod,' he ordered. 'They make me feel like a flea in a blanket.'

'Don't do nothin' for your appearance neither, Guv,' commented Tod as he went in search of hot water, gram flour and a razor.

Toddy had attended two or three auctions of dead men's effects, and when he had finished shaving Oliver, Ishmial carried in an assortment of trousers and shirts and a corduroy shooting jacket, to see which would best fit his master. Presently, supported by his two retainers, Oliver limped out of the bedroom and into the mild golden sunshine I was enjoying on the verandah.

None knew better than I who had nursed him that he had lost weight, but seeing him clothed and upright, I was shocked at how bone-thin he had become. The shabby cast-off clothing hung on him, the trousers were some three inches too short, exposing bony ankles above the string-soled native sandals in which he had arrived in the entrenchment. The bushy, untrimmed whiskers had been disposed of and I looked into a face as chalky white as Pearl's and even more angular than Kate's had become. The large nose protruded over the wide well-formed mouth, more compressed now than I recalled it, and bearing the unmistakable imprint of tension and pain. The amber eyes still glowed with life and at that moment were merry at the thought of the sight he must present, but they had sunk deeper under the heavy brows and looked dark against the pallor of his face. Their expression, too, had altered in these hard months. There was a tolerance, a kindness even, now apparent behind the customary quizzicalness of the gaze I encountered.

'Will I do?'

'Beautifully—but for the shoes.'

'Oh, Tod has found me a splendid pair of boots, but my feet are not yet healed. These things are more comfortable for the moment.'

'And they will prevent you from running away,' I pointed out.

A couple of days later I returned to my duties in the hospital. Jessie was delighted to stay at home again with Pearl and the household chores, but it was with acute reluctance that I left Oliver, for to me every moment away from him was a moment of life wasted.

So engrossed had I been in his welfare, so oblivious to everything outside the magic of his presence in our two dark little rooms, that I found myself walking through an unfamiliar world. Guns still boomed at irregular intervals, but at a distance, and because of the enlargement of the enclave, the morning was innocent of musket fire. The buildings through which I walked were as ruined as I remembered them; but where, only two weeks before, I had had to clamber over mounds of wreckage, keeping a wary eye out for shaky walls or crumbling brickwork, now the lanes were cleared and the rubble mounded in neat piles where it could most easily be employed in repairing or reinforcing the walls. For months I had seldom caught even a glimpse of a woman as I had hurried to and from the hospital. Now the females of the entrenchment strolled with their children in the October sunshine, gossiping and laughing in the easy assurance of safety, and more remarkable still, beyond the great open gates of the Baillie Guard, men moved in freedom over the war-scarred terrain so recently alive with pandies and their guns.

Conditions and space in the hospital were better at least. Large tents had been erected beside the Banqueting Hall and in addition the upper storey of the building, now considered safe from enemy fire, had been sketchily repaired for use. One could move between the beds without fear of stepping on a wounded limb, but otherwise not much had changed. There were still no medicines, no panaceas, no instruments. No bedsteads, mattresses or pillows. No strong broths, no port-wine jellies, no puréed vegetables appropriate for the sick. And it was getting cold now; the chill of the stone floor on which the men lay bit through the straw pallets and rush mats and was scarcely ameliorated by the single dirty blanket that was each man's portion. There was more help, of course: several doctors and orderlies and a few apothecary-assistants had come in with the relief. I sighed to myself, however, as I looked down the dark familiar room; there were far too many faces I recognized from two weeks before and, of those I missed, how many were recovered and how many in the graveyard?

I was welcomed back with warmth by Dr Partridge and soon worked myself into the familiar routine of the ward, but all the old zest and interest in what I was doing had disappeared. I did what I could with whatever skill and compassion I commanded, but now I longed to leave the place almost as soon as I had arrived and, with so many others helping, felt no compunction in the fact that my hours were shorter. With what delighted relief I took off my apron, pulled on my shawl and hurried back to the Gaol each afternoon, and with what joyous recognition I entered the smoky little kitchen to see my invalid, often with Pearl in his arms, sitting on a stool watching Jessie cook the evening meal while he spun her outrageous yarns of his sinful youth in Paris.

For a reason known only to himself, Oliver had decided to exert his charm on Jessie, and she had succumbed immediately. He never ordered her about as he did the rest of us, called her 'Mrs MacGregor' most respectfully, asked her advice and deferred to her opinion—or at any rate gave her reason to suppose he did. I wondered what was behind it. Oliver seldom did anything without a reason.

As he grew stronger, so he became more restless, and a few days after my return to the hospital he set off one morning to find himself employment. He had not wasted his time since regaining his feet. Each day he had spent hours practising writing with his left hand and, though always accustomed to being shaved and laced into his boots by Toddy-Bob or Ishmial, he now decided that these were tasks he must do for himself, with his left hand only. Then there was pistol practice. He conceded that he would probably never again be the marksman he once was with rifle or shotgun, particularly since there was no ammunition to spare for training, but there was no reason at all why he should not regain his old skill with the pistol. He would sit on his stool, sometimes with the baby cradled against the useless arm, and try with dogged patience to regain speed and ease in loading, cocking and arming the weapon with his single hand. All these tasks, necessary or unnecessary, were frustrating in the extreme to a man as quick and precise in all his actions as Oliver had been. Cawnpore might have taught him endurance, might have brought him to a gentler tolerance of his fellow human beings, but not even Cawnpore could quite curb the impatient irritation that drove him to end every effort with a string of muted curses. And they were muted only on account of Jessie, who was liable to round on him with outrage and scold him like a fishwife for his 'black-talkin', ill-willin' tongue, Mr Erskine, sirr!'

Determined to be useful, he had no difficulty in finding a useful task.

The troops of the relieving force had been armed with the new Lee Enfield rifle, that same weapon whose disputed cartridge had provoked some of the initial incidents of the rebellion. Men accustomed to the new weapon were loath to return to the old Brown Bess, but the garrison was rapidly running short of Lee Enfield ammunition. By chance, a Lieutenant Sewell of the Old Garrison was found to be in possession of a couple of moulds for Lee Enfield bullets, and soon a small manufactory was in production. Oliver discovered that a left hand was as skilful as a right in pouring lead, and having demonstrated this to everyone's satisfaction, found himself with a job to do.

I was almost as relieved as he was delighted; for, much as I loved him, now that he was stronger, his bored and idle presence in the kitchen was becoming a strain on us all, a situation that resulted inevitably in sharp words on my part and enjoyment on his.

'That's my girl!' he said approvingly one day when I had given him the length of my tongue over some unimportant matter. 'Now I know you've come through your ordeal unscathed and with your character unimpaired. All this sweetness and light you've been shedding, this gentle nursing and kind consideration, has bothered me. It's not like you.'

'I wish I could say the same of you!' I retorted sharply. 'Unfortunately your present behaviour is precisely what I recollect of you—and leaves much to be desired!'

'Ah, woman dear!' he sighed in mock repentance. 'Forgive me. What a disappointment I am to you. For weeks you have had a beautiful memory of my lifeless carcass to hang your dreams on and then I turn up, alive and still kicking. So impolitic of me, not to say impolite. All your dreams exploded! If only I could be the man you dreamed of.'

He grabbed my arm as I passed him and drew me down so that I was kneeling beside him.

'You're an idiot,' I informed him comfortably. 'I knew you could never change. I just have to get accustomed to the idea that I can love a man as abominable as I once thought you were, and now discover you to be.'

'I hope it will not be a very painful process of adjustment.'

'So do I—for your sake!'

I laughed and put my arms about his neck.

Having found himself a job to do, Oliver went in search of a billet for himself and his retainers.

'Been with you too long already,' he told Kate, who had protested at his desertion of the Gaol. 'Even I cannot expect you to give up a bed indefinitely, and the lads at the Farhat Baksh have ample room and say they will be delighted to have me as a companion. Now don't fret, Kate. I'll be back and frequently. Military chatter is not much to my liking, as you know. I'm told they keep a scoreboard down there of pandies killed each day; can't say how long I'll be able to keep my tongue among such primitive savages, so I might be thrown out and find myself back among you very soon.'

'But, Oliver, that's just what bothers me. Do keep a civil tongue in your head. 'Twas well enough to speak your mind and offend the populace when you always had Hassanganj to retire to, but now—here, and in these times ...'

'A landless fugitive must learn to mind his manners! I understand, Kate. I'll be good, truly ...'

'No, don't laugh, Oliver. You're in trouble already, you know. Mr Roberts was unwise enough to repeat your doubts about the cause of the massacre at the river to Wallace Avery. Wallace, in his cups no doubt, poor man, passed on your theory to his friends, and by the time it came to my ears in the hospital you were not only expressing a doubt but stating a fact, and everyone declared that nothing more than treason could be expected of "Brahmin" Erskine.'

'Hm, yes, that's not surprising, I suppose. After all, have I not gone "native", as they say?' Oliver laughed, but not pleasantly.

'Kate's right,' put in Charles who was eating with us that night. 'You cannot afford to get on the wrong side of anyone at the moment. "Cawnpore Fever" has most of us in its grip to one extent or another, and pretty rotten things are being done by the men when they go out on sorties. Old men, young women and any and every pandy who comes within bayonet range is despatched with a yell of "Take that for Cawnpore!" You put a foot wrong and it's not without the bounds of possibility that you might end with a bayonet through your back. No one wants to hear excuses or justifications for the Nana and his men.'

'Oh, come now, Charles,' I expostulated.

'No, Laura, I'm not exaggerating. It could happen. Oliver has ... well, devil take it, you must realize it as well as anyone, Oliver, but you have a bad name among the people of this town. Oh, I know it's because they do not know you, could never understand you ... the fact is that you have. Some time ago the entrenchment was alive with rumours that white officers were leading the pandies. White men, anyway. They'd been seen, so it was said, directing an assault ...'

'I remember that,' I put in. 'They were supposed to be Russians, weren't they?'

'I heard they were Frenchmen,' said Kate.

'Whatever they were, one of the men in our battery declared that there were probably any number of planters in Oudh, dependent on the Nawab's largesse and the favour of the *talukhdars*, who might be willing to take a hand against us sooner than lose their property and their rights, and your name, I'm afraid, was one of those mentioned. Made it deuced awkward for me, I can tell you, when I had to come out and say that you were my brother.'

'Oho! Poor old Charles. And what did you do? Tap his claret?'

'Fisticuffs are a poor way of establishing innocence. I told the man he was a crass, ill-thinking fool and walked out of the room.'

'Bravo! And thanks. But I'm surprised I was even allowed the dubious honour of being "white". I believe my erratic opinions and behaviour are generally put down to my having a "touch of the tarbrush" myself.'

'Damn it, Oliver, I'm serious. The men, particularly the ones who came through Cawnpore—though it has affected them all to some extent—are in an ugly, violent mood. You'll find that out for yourself once you move down to the Ferret Box.' (For so the private soldiers had already dubbed the palace of Farhat Baksh.)

'No doubt. But have no fears on my behalf. I swear I shall be as circumspect as Caesar's wife, if for no other reason than to save you further embarrassment.'

The following morning, after breakfast, Jessie and I watched Oliver walk down to the Farhat Baksh Palace, accompanied by Toddy-Bob and Ishmial. His feet had healed sufficiently to allow him to wear the boots Toddy had bought him, but his arm was still in a sling of purple calico figured with orange leaves, the remnant of one of Jessie's gowns. Both Toddy and Ishmial carried various boxes and bundles, for they had not been slow in benefiting from the looting of the several palaces that now stood within our enclosure. Whether directly or indirectly (I never chose to enquire), Toddy had 'come by' all manner of useful articles for Oliver, himself and for us. We had sheets on our beds now, some exquisite French porcelain plates and cups, cooking pans, embroidered shawls and dirty brocaded cushions for our stools. It was with difficulty that we restrained the little man from foraging for more costly articles on our behalf. 'Coo!' he had said in eye-screwed anguish when I remonstrated with him on this point. 'You don't know what you're missin' by 'alf, you don't, Miss Laura. Kashmir shawls soft as silk, and jewels and silver dishes and all manner of fine things—just lyin' around the rooms and gardens, and all for the takin'.'

I had heard accounts from more reliable sources than Toddy of the splendour of the vast apartments through which the soldiers roamed in search of booty, and not a day passed but some private or his wife would offer for sale or barter along our verandah a jade figurine, a fine ring or a jewelled dagger. These things were a temptation, but one which I had to resist. I had no money for baubles, nor wished to load myself with possessions which might again be lost to me before I could reach safety, so Toddy's efforts on our behalf were confined to long-desired necessities.

It was mid-October when Oliver moved to the Farhat Baksh, and the news of the recapture of Delhi by General Nicholson had already worn thin as a topic of conversation. The air was fresh, very nearly pure; a pale sun cast transparent cold-weather shadows, and the wide sky was the same candid blue as little Pearl's eyes. The sunlight glinted momentarily on Oliver's bare head and, despite his tender feet, he walked away from us with the quick decisive stride so characteristic of him.

'Och, and he's a lovely man!' sighed Jessie as they went, with evident satisfaction. 'And so good and generous. Mr Charles, now, is as fine a gentleman as you could wish, but yon—well, yon's a *man*!'

I smiled at her distinction.

'It'll be a real pleasure to work for him,' she went on. 'And to think he could spare thought, and him in his own sufferings, for a poor widow woman like me.'

'Work for him?' I turned a wary eye on my friend.

'Aye. D'ye no ken? As his housekeeper. He asked me. When all this is gone the by, ye ken?'

'His housekeeper? But Jessie, do you know where his house is? Or rather was, for it has burned down?'

'He told me,' she answered tranquilly. ''Tis way out in the country, wi' the mountains to look at an' a'—jest like Scotland, he said it was. He said he's goin' to build a fine new house, but will be needin' a body to care for it, ye ken. When I told him he should tak' a wife to care for his fine house, he laughed and said: "My wife is goin' to have her hands fu' takin' care of me!"'

'Oh, he did, did he?'

'Aye!'

'But, Jessie, you would find the life intolerable. Mr Erskine is by way of being a misanthrope ... I mean, he doesn't care for company, and the place is miles from anywhere. No Europeans, no one to talk to. You'd be so lonely. Besides, surely you want to go home to your own family, your own people?'

'The wee man would doubtless be about the house, would he no'? And I've no kin so close they'd care. I'd as lief tend yon gentleman's house in the wilderness as return to service in some notary's villa in Glasgow. No, no, Miss Laura. 'Twill suit me fine to bide in India.'

She went indoors with Pearl.

'To bide in India.' My heart constricted with a sudden chill at Jessie's words. The three familiar figures had disappeared from view, but I sat down on the steps in the sunshine and gazed unhappily in the direction they had taken.

'To bide in India.' Was that really what he was planning to do? It was madness. The absurdity of the idea was matched only by its futility. To bide in India? In Hassanganj? Now—after all this? He could not, surely he could not still seriously believe he had a life in India?

Hassanganj was gone, and not only the strange old house. I could imagine what had overtaken the mud-built villages with their careful tillage, their groves and arid pastures. War must surely have flamed them too by now, and torn the roads and breached the mud-banked waterways and filled the precious wells with silt. With no defence, no stern *sirkar* to answer to, even had no marauding sepoys swept the area with destruction, what chance was there that the Hassanganj villages had been spared the malice of the *talukhdars*, or the Rohillas, a neighbour's jealousy or an enemy's spite?

There could be nothing left now to which he could return. And if there were, what justification had he for thinking it would still be his? A worn old parchment with the seal of a long-gone nawab? That would not be enough in the new India, for there would be a new India now, so everyone said. The day of the East India Company was gone, scarcely more than a year after that Company had decreed that the day of the nawabs was over. The old methods of administration would, somehow, give way to better, juster, more efficient means of government. Hassanganj, feudal in conception, autocratic in administration, Hassanganj as an entity would be swept away, whatever its state when the rebellion was finally over. And it might be years, I told myself in panic, before peace returned to India.

I was frightened. It had never occurred to me since his arrival in Lucknow that Oliver would expect me to make my home in India. Before the fire and the flight from Hassanganj, I would have known there was no alternative for him, and it would have been acceptable to me. But before the fire I had not realized I loved him, and the dream of the future he had shared with me on the road to Lucknow could not now come true.

Since then more than my feelings for him had changed, and at last, the 'real India' I had wished so much to discover had shown itself to me completely—as my personal gateway to purgatory.

'He cannot in conscience expect me to stay out here now,' I told myself. 'He loves me. I know it. He would never expect me to remain in India.'

As I sat dissecting my reaction to Jessie's simple words, I came to realize that never since the day of the first assault had I envisaged anything but that our unquiet courtship would somehow end in a long and argumentative married life in England. Always England. When, in those first few days of my acknowledged love, I had fed my passion with sweet imaginings of future bliss, the leafy lanes we'd walked had all been English lanes; the morning downs we'd galloped over, all

English downs; the view from the windows of our imagined home, all English views, serene, domestic, familiar. Even then Hassanganj in my mind had been dealt its death blow.

Could he truly be foolish enough to expect a phoenix from such ashes?

The golden radiance of the morning seemed to dim as I cudgelled my brain for answers to questions not yet posed, tried to read my own intentions, determine my own capacities in fairness both to myself and Oliver.

But then it occurred to me that perhaps my anxiety was premature, that perhaps Jessie had merely repeated some idle words of Oliver's, spoken to fill a bored silence or to test Jessie's devotion to Scotland, and that she had wrongly taken seriously. That must be it, I told myself. He was not serious. I hugged this hope to myself with all my energy, for I knew that, in the last analysis, if Oliver did intend to stay in India, then the final choice could only be made by me.

It was not a choice I ever wanted to make.

CHAPTER 9

The garrison had been given the news of the British capture of Delhi on October 10th. Late the previous night, a messenger had stolen into the entrenchment with information for General Outram that the ancient capital of the Moguls was now in British hands, the Emperor and his *begum* had been taken prisoner, and that, despite heavy losses sustained during the battle, a column of the Delhi force was now hurrying to our aid.

'How long will it take them to reach us?' I asked Kate.

'Well, the way the army moves, hardly less than a month.'

Our daily allowances were again cut, and now the six ounces of gun-bullock meat apportioned to each woman included bone. In fact, it was largely bone, so soup and *chapattis* were all we could look forward to twice a day. The cooler weather certainly increased our hunger. Sometimes, if we were very fortunate, we might receive a present of a stringy native fowl or a few vegetables from one or other of our masculine acquaintances who had been out on a foray, but such pleasures were few and far between. There were those among us who tried sparrow curry, and some pronounced it excellent, and Mr Gubbins, his wife and guests, so it was said, still enjoyed milk puddings, sherry and sauterne with their meals, but most of us grew thinner by the day.

The most tantalizing aspect of our situation was that in the Alum Bagh, not four miles distant, lay great stocks of food, clothing and medicines, destined for us but left behind in that palace by General Outram in the belief that it would be merely a few days before our garrison could issue out or the supplies be brought safely in.

Reminiscing with Kate and Jessie, I discovered that it was three full months since we had tasted eggs or milk and even longer since our last slice of white bread.

'Well, it just shows how unnecessary most of the things we were accustomed to really are,' I said, attempting philosophy.

'Och aye!' Jessie agreed over her eternally clicking needles. 'But werena' the unnecessary things of life the good ones!'

''Tis the lads that I pity,' put in Kate. 'God be between them and all harm, and they without tobacco or a sup of the hard stuff when they want it. 'Tis they who've borne the brunt of it all, and I'd dearly like to see them smoking, or even in their cups, come to that. 'Twould be more natural.'

But that was a sober period in the entrenchment—too sober for some—and one day we learned that the bodies of half-a-dozen men who had made a private foray outside the perimeter in search of liquor had been found decapitated.

My return to the hospital after two cloistered weeks of nursing Oliver awakened me to many changes within the enclosure more subtle in effect and more difficult to define than the purely physical betterment effected under the energetic direction of General Outram. The atmosphere within the entrenchment had changed, and for the worse. The place simmered with hidden tensions.

The previous months had scarcely been pleasant, but before the 25th of September, whatever our personal shortcomings and collective miseries might have been, we had fought and endured in a single-minded unity of purpose. We had bickered among ourselves, of course, irritated each other and criticized our leaders, but never with acrimony. The Nawab of Oudh's jewels might have been stolen, but seldom a comrade's tobacco. Liquor had appeared on occasion like water from the Biblical rock, and then been shared among one's peers; and if a woman lost her virtue to a soldier, difficult enough to do in those exhausting days, it was with her own consent.

Now division and dissension had appeared.

The 'Old Garrison', as we had come to be called, tended to hang together and delighted in making light of the privations their more recently arrived comrades grumbled at.

'You should've been 'ere in July; then you'd 'ave known what's what'; or 'What are you squawkin' about? So the meat ain't enough, but it stays on the plate now, not like in August when you 'ad to put a bullet in it afore you could spear it with a fork!' were among the remarks I overheard as I passed among the hospital beds. Not without reason, the new men felt aggrieved that their efforts to reach us were belittled, and there would be sharp reminders of the depredations from cholera they had suffered in Cawnpore, or the losses they had sustained in coming through Lucknow.

Such altercations were trivial, but an echo, perhaps, of the rivalries burgeoning among our superiors.

Our own Brigadier Inglis retained command of the 32nd Foot and the other combatants of the Old Garrison. General Havelock had been given command of the troops occupying the palaces in the extended perimeter, but passed his days in semiretirement in Mr Ommaney's house, reading books from Old Buggins's library. His health was certainly poor but the men felt that the cause of his malaise lay chiefly in the fact of his supersedence by General Outram. And General Outram himself was now in complete control of the entrenchment and all within it.

Both the generals became familiar figures in the hospital, which they visited with conscientious regularity every day. Out-ram, now the senior, but younger by eight years than Havelock, was a thick-set man with a ruddy, blue-veined complexion and penetrating eyes. Open and genial in manner, he was popular among the men, partly no doubt because of the freedom with which he handed out his cigars, though his interest in his troops was obviously humane and genuine. He was well known to the old inhabitants of Lucknow, for he had served a term as Chief Commissioner before going to Persia, from where both he and Havelock had hurried to India on the outbreak of the rebellion. He was possessed of a most delicate sense of fair play which forbade him to eat anything other than what his men ate, or to send a letter to his wife by a *cossid* going to Agra, since his officers were forbidden any private communications. When Outram entered the hospital, the sick became more animated and cheerful; when Havelock came in, they were inclined to shrink beneath their blankets and feign sleep.

Havelock was almost the direct contrary of Outram both in appearance and character. So upright he looked stiff, he was a small man, but slender and well-proportioned, with handsome sunburned features and hair already white. He appeared delicate and tired, and it was said that the diet of the siege, coming after three months of strenuous campaigning, had undermined his health. Kate couldn't abide him, though she bobbed a pretty curtsey like the rest of us when he passed among the hospital beds.

'Too pious—and a pedant to boot,' she told me. 'And you'll not believe it, I know, but I've actually seen him wearing his sword and all his medals at a ball in Calcutta. Of all things! Probably wears 'em in his bath too, I wouldn't wonder!'

Reserved, almost aloof with his equals, General Havelock was distant and cold with his men. They admired him as a soldier but disliked him as a man, and like Kate tended to deride his Bible reading and his proclivity for praying with the sick.

I began to understand what Oliver had meant about 'two tails wagging one dog'. The tails were not even of the same breed. Watching the two gentlemen with interest, before long I came to the conclusion that behind the quiet, almost humble exterior of the Christian soldier, Havelock was self-concerned and prideful, while Outram, for all his suffused face, bellowing laugh and loud manner, was a truly brave and gentle man.

As was natural when so many human beings had so little to talk about, the entrenchment soon throbbed with rumours of acrimony among the three commanders. Outram still wanted to clear a route for the new relief that was coming from Delhi as far as the Alum Bagh, but would not trust either Havelock or Inglis to hold the Residency. Inglis was angry at the way his men of the 32nd were being used to lead the forays and sorties; and Havelock, immersed in his manuals of military history and his Bible, advocated a complete withdrawal of troops from Lucknow as soon as the new relief arrived—which, of course, the other two commanders would not hear of. How much truth there was in any or all of these rumours, we could not know. To their credit, in public the gentlemen concerned behaved with admirable grace towards each other.

Factionalism, having shown itself among the men, the usual grousing of the British private soldier now had an undercurrent of almost bitter resentment. The men of the relief were made to feel their failure as a personal slur, while the Old Garrison would have been saints indeed had they not vented their disappointment in twitting their would-be rescuers for that same failure. There were other evils, too: petty theft and fighting, bred of *ennui*, hunger, anxiety and the disquieting sense that, though our ordeal might be nearly over, its end remained as problematical as ever.

I was sitting one evening on the steps with Oliver, restraining myself from looking towards him too often and too feelingly, for Charles was beside me. Kate and Jessie sat on stools on the gravel path. Oliver was now ensconced in the Ferret Box, but wandered into the Gaol each afternoon as soon as he had finished his stint at the ammunition manufactory. The enclosure was quiet, everyone busy with the evening meal. On a raddled neem tree not far off, mynas scuffled in a scolding multitude for perches and, below the tree, grey-capped crows strode with fidgety pompousness, pecking hopefully in the dirt. A flight of starlings swept silently across the sky like a scatter of seeds arching from the sower's hand, to fall to earth on some aptly furrowed but invisible field. On the roof above us, a covey of brown monkeys sported around a shattered chimney stack, the old ones, grave and cross, squatting obscenely at the base of the stack fleaing themselves, and baring yellow teeth in elderly irritation when the youth of the tribe gambolled too near.

'The sooner we all get out of this the better,' Oliver said after a pause while we watched the monkeys. 'Another wretched girl was assaulted last night, I hear. Great to-do, everyone threatened with the "cat" and worse, but with 1,500 likely culprits, there is not much chance of finding the right one.'

Beside me I felt Charles wince and glance quickly at the females at this mention of the unmentionable in mixed society. Kate and Jessie, soldier's wives both, were undisturbed, and Charles could not know how well I was accustomed to his brother's freedom of speech.

'Och aye! Poor laddies,' said Jessie, busy turning a heel on her needles. ''Tis hard for them when they canna get to the bazaars.'

Charles shuffled his feet, Kate smiled appreciatively at Jessie's uncondemning realism, and I began to see where lay the affinity between Jessie and Oliver Erskine.

The British Army in India marches with three times its own numbers by way of retinue. Hordes and thousands of coolies, water-carriers, grass-cutters, grooms, bullock drivers, elephant keepers, servants, cooks, artisans and tradesmen, and what are euphemistically termed 'camp followers'. For perhaps the first time in the Army's history, the quick dash of Generals Outram and Havelock through Lucknow, leaving their dependants and baggage train behind at the Alum Bagh, had deprived the common soldier of one of his few if illegitimate comforts. This was not the first time that the word 'assault', and uglier, had cropped up during the last few weeks. Kate and I generally waited for each other's company now if we left the hospital late, and I found it ironical that we were probably in more personal danger from the men of our own race and allegiance than we had been when it was necessary to race through a hail of pandy bullets.

'Dirty swine!' Charles grated through his teeth, and against my will I found myself remembering vividly a night in the Chalmerses' house in Calcutta and a cry from Emily that had cut the silence and my heart.

Oliver unfolded his long legs in their short trousers and stretched them down the steps beside me. 'Hmph! Not necessarily,' he objected. 'Mere men, like the rest of us, after all.'

'Aye! And who's ever to ken if a lass is willin' or no',' said Jess, 'wi'out a grab in the dark forbye?'

Oliver chuckled and I had to smile.

'These girls should be disciplined by their parents; kept at home where they belong, instead of being allowed to gallivant all over the entrenchment in the dark with the first private soldier in sight!'

'At home, is it then?' objected Kate. 'Oh, Charles, come now! And do you not know of the conditions in the *tykhanas* of the Resident's House? The crowding and the stench and the noise? Any young girl who stayed in that "home" when she had a chance of getting out of it would be crazy.'

'That's the truth,' nodded Jessie. 'And, Mr Charles, if you're thinkin' maybe they'd have protection in the *tykhanas* from the ill-doin' of the lads, you'd be sair mistook. Och, when I mind the sights, and sounds too, aye, I've seen and heard nights in those rooms. And not only there, mind. Decency comes hard to the likes of a soldier's wife, sir, when ye mind that we're unco' fortunate if we find ourselves in married quarters. Mostly 'tis a bed behind a cotton sheet at the end of a barracks wi' a hundred other souls sleepin' and wakin' around ye. Privacy. Decency. They're not for the likes of us, Mr Charles. The lassies learn that young.'

'Deplorable,' said Charles. 'Absolutely deplorable.'

'Aye, and that it is an' a',' agreed Jess with conviction. When the men had returned to their posts and Jessie had gone in to ready the evening meal—no preparation was necessary since it was the same bullock broth we had eaten at mid-day—Kate and I lingered on in the evening air.

'So she,' Kate flicked her head towards our open kitchen door, 'intends to go to Hassanganj, when all this is finished, to housekeep for Oliver Erskine. You knew, I suppose?'

'She mentioned it. But he must have been joking. The idea is absurd.'

'Why so? A mite premature, perhaps, but all in all a good idea. He certainly needs a housekeeper, and she will need a home. Though what Toddy and Ishmial will think of having their fastness invaded by a woman and permanently is perhaps best left unsaid.'

'Tod gets on with her. There is something similar in their characters for all the dissimilarity in form.'

'A willingness to call a spade a spade?'

'And an ability to turn off the conscience when it interferes with comfort.'

'Quite!' Kate laughed.

'Anyway,' I had to admit, 'if Oliver says it is right, it will be right—for Tod and Ishmial.'

'But not for you?' There was a sly note in Kate's voice. I looked down at the untended hands lying on my stained and threadbare skirt. We knew each other too well now for dissimulation, but I made no reply.

'He's the man for you, woman dear,' she said. 'Surely you see it now?'

'Perhaps. But … there are difficulties.'

'Whenever were there not? But difficulties are made to be overcome.'

I sighed and watched the monkeys cavorting on the rooftop.

'Sure, when he first came "in" it was obvious how both of you felt. I thought it would be plain sailing. He's alive. You're free. And it isn't still Charles who holds your fancy, that I do know.'

'Was it ever?' I wondered.

'Ah, yes—when you first arrived in Lucknow. And even later, in Hassanganj. But then, when Oliver began to put himself out to be pleasant and agreeable, I observed a change. I expect you thought it was all for Emily, as I did at first, but I soon realized that the happier he could keep Emily, the easier she was for you to deal with, and the more readily you could leave her in order to spend time with himself in the library, or riding around the estate, and so on. Very clever, he was; cunning.'

'He was good to poor Emily. She had begun to love him, I believe.'

'Well, sure and that would be no surprise. She needed love, that girl, like a dog needs a pat; may her soul rest in peace. But he—well, Oliver never had eyes for her.'

It was a relief to know my secret was shared, and being in love, there was joy even in speaking of Oliver, so I did not change the subject.

'And you,' Kate went on, 'I thought at first had eyes for no one but Charles. Oliver must have seen it too, and very exasperating he found it, I'm sure. But before long I realized that, whether you knew it or not, there was a sort of ... understanding between the two of you. Can't guess how he contrived it, but there it was; and often when the two of you were talking, the rest of us were shut out completely, and I would get the impression that what you *said* was not what you were talking about at all.'

'You're too shrewd, Kate,' I answered. 'Far shrewder than I was, for I never guessed his regard until we were making our way here through all those horrors. And then he had to tell me!'

'Bless me! And you so intelligent and learned. Ah, well! But don't tell me you turned him down?'

'At the time. I reconsidered.'

'Then what are the difficulties?'

'Perhaps there are none really. Perhaps I am anticipating what will not, or cannot, happen. After all, however much he may want to return to Hassanganj, there is not much chance that he will be able to do so. Not with all the changes that are bound to come when this is over.'

'You mean you want him, but in England?'

I nodded.

'That's a tall order you're placing, Laura, and a hard choice you're giving him. 'Tis his life, Hassanganj.'

'But, Kate, Hassanganj is gone. He must reconcile himself to that, surely? He'll never be allowed to run that place again like a ... a private kingdom, as Emily used to say. He will have to make other plans, find another life, come home to England and settle down like everyone else.'

The bright blue eyes regarded me doubtfully.

''Tis a big stick you are making to beat yourself with. Is it only living in India that is your difficulty? Or do you not truly love him, after all?'

Tears sprang to my eyes and I averted my head as I whispered, 'I do love him, most dreadfully. But I could not live out here now, Kate. I cannot.'

'Well, it's not I that will blame you for feeling so, but I believe in time, quite a short time probably, things will get back to normal. We know so little of what has happened, of course, but ...'

'But I will not get back to "normal",' I interposed. 'I will never forget.'

'Even though, when things have been settled, living in India will be easier for us all, more comfortable, and certainly much safer? The Government ...'

'Perhaps,' I broke in again, unwilling to be persuaded. 'But I want no part of it. I only want to get home and know that the people around me are my own people, speaking my own language, thinking along the lines I have been taught to think. I want to lie down at night knowing there is little chance of the house taking fire and none at all that my neighbours will be shot and killed.'

'And who would blame you for that, indeed? But don't be too hasty. Think well. Give yourself time, don't you see?'

'It's the insecurity, Kate. I'd never for a moment feel truly safe here. I just want to go Home now. Home.'

'Perhaps that will be the best thing. Time works wonders, and he'd wait. He's a contrary divil, mind, as I've often remarked, but not a fickle one, I think. If his mind is set on you, he'll wait.'

I could only shake my head again, for rare tears were troubling me.

'Ah, the pity of the way Fate works things out for us all,' Kate went on with a deep sigh. 'Here am I, loath to leave India, but with nothing to keep me here, and you, with so much reason to stay, wanting to go. All my old bones seize up with rheumatism at the very thought of leaving the sun and the heat and the big dark bungalows in shady gardens, and all the jollities in the cold weather, and the young men who have counted me a friend over the years—my boys. When I think of the bleak skies and the cold grey seas of Home, and of damp people hurrying down slushy streets, and all the poor creatures like me growing old with their hearts in India and their feet on a stranger's hearth ...'

'It need not be like that.'

'For me, it will be. India caught me young. I love it. Here's where my life's been, my memories. Here's where my dead man's bones are— somewhere,' she added, blinking her blue eyes very quickly. 'I belong here, still, despite everything.'

For a moment we were silent with our thoughts.

'That is how I would have to feel if I were to stay,' I acknowledged. 'There was a time when, perhaps, I could have. I was so interested in everything out here; so curious and so anxious to like and understand it. I tried to learn everything I could, everything Oliver wanted to teach me. But India herself has taught me more than I wanted to know. And the wrong things.'

In our kitchen Jessie banged a spoon on a pan to call us to the meal.

'Laura?'

'Yes?'

'Think well. Don't let him go. To be sure, he'll pipe you a merry dance; he's headstrong and so are you, and there'll be many a time when you'll disagree and worse. But difficult as he is, he's the man for you. There won't be two like him!'

'I know,' I agreed sadly. 'I know.'

CHAPTER 10

I would not let my mind dwell on the choice that I might have to make. I had learned that it is wisest to live in the day for the day. Much might yet happen to obviate the necessity for any choosing on my part, and I was young, in love and recently freed from a terrible fear. So I would not think but laughed and sang, and found everyone around me suddenly and unaccountably lovable.

Each day as the quick dusk closed around us, I could look forward to hearing a certain step on the verandah's flags and would hold myself in readiness for a stroll through the inner, safer environs of the entrenchment, or a long softly-spoken talk as we sat on the steps under the chilly new stars with his one arm around my shoulders. My first thought in the morning was to count the hours until I saw him, and often I was too impatient to wait until dusk but would saunter past the hospital to the Baillie Guard and stand looking out between the tall, singed doors as though only the new freedom of this larger vista held my attention. But just to my left, as I watched the morning's work progressing before me, was the battered Treasury building where now Oliver and others, with much ribaldry and laughter, heated lead and filled the moulds for the Lee Enfield bullets, and there was always a chance that I might be glimpsed by him in the course of my early walk. I was, of course, very surprised to find Oliver was already at work, and he would be astonished to find me on my way to the hospital so early. He would walk a few paces of my way with me, enquiring solicitously of the welfare of my 'family' until we were out of earshot, then perhaps reduce me to giggles by addressing me as his *Nur Jehan*, his Light of the World, or his *Dil ki Aziz*, his Heart's Sweetness. If the morning were very blue and gold-limned like an illumination from a Book of Hours, he might recite a few lines from the Urdu poet Ghalib, or a short rhymed poem called a *ghazal*, which, though flattering, was not altogether satisfactory. My Urdu was not up to the high-flown stanzas and, knowing Oliver, I guessed his recitation might just as well have been a lampoon on the unfortunate rotundity of some dead Mohammedan worthy of Lucknow as a paean to my youth or loveliness.

The mornings were now cold enough to require the protection of a coat or cloak, but he owned none and we had nothing suitable to lend him. Eventually Toddy-Bob 'came by' a splendid native bedcover of quilted crimson satin in one of the palaces, and this his master was content to wear, with a hole cut in the middle for his head and hanging over his shoulders, much like the garb of some South American natives.

After a few moments, when my day, my life, my world were all offered up and returned to me exalted in the light of two direct amber eyes, he would bow politely and I would climb the slope, humming with happiness, to my hours among the sick.

Sometimes I was ashamed of this happiness, for it kept me from entering fully into the sufferings of those around me. I did my best, and I hope without impatience, but it is difficult truly to sympathize with another's misery when one's personal reality is all unbounded joy. I knew enough of life not to wish myself less happy, however, and always at the back of my mind was the nagging awareness that I might have to make a choice that would end my joy.

Once again our rations were cut. Now there was no point in trudging up the hill to the Gaol for a midday meal. I contented myself with dry *chapattis* carried in my pocket, and left the hospital a little earlier in consequence. In the hospital, as soon as a man was capable of thought, he thought of food. So did we all. It was a constant topic of conversation with everyone, and when Jessie leaned her head against the wall with closed eyes to 'tak' a spell' from her knitting, or Kate's blue gaze grew faraway and misty with longing, I knew it was not their loved ones they were thinking of but legs of mutton, Devonshire cream, gooseberry tarts and hot scones soaked with butter. Often I woke in the morning on the point of tears because my waking dream had been of a bountiful meal which consciousness had kept me from tasting.

Day by day and for all our efforts, we grew dirtier and more unkempt. Gram flour made a poor substitute for soap for washing ourselves, and our clothing we could only rinse out in clear water. Vermin troubled the sick almost as much as wounds and disease, and I took to wearing a species of turban over my short hair to protect myself further from infestation. The boys of the Martinière were a sorrow to behold: ragged, their rags filthy, barefoot often, with uncut hair and pale bony faces they scampered about the entrenchment like a pack of mangy monkeys, shivering with cold. At my request Toddy made it his business to acquire some more native quilts which he halved and handed out to the boys who helped in the hospital.

When Mr Roberts appeared in our quarters one evening looking almost as slovenly as the boys, I knew we must be nearing the end of our endurance. He had brought me a gift—and, of course, information.

'I am told, and on the best of authority,' he started, with an attempt at his old didactic manner, 'that General Outram is actually advising Brigadier Greathed and his Delhi column to meet and finish off a band of insurgents said to be making their way to Cawnpore before making any attempt to relieve us. Can you believe such stupidity, Miss Laura, such depravity, I might almost say? We are his first and most pressing responsibility and he motions away the only succour we can expect. He is jeopardizing the life of every one of us for some stupid … military tactical fancy. Nothing more!'

'Come now, Mr Roberts, I believe they are doing their best for us,' I replied.

'But does he not see that the longer we remain here, the weaker we all become? By the time any relief does at last appear, we shall not be able to stagger out of the Baillie Guard but will have to be carried out in litters—every last one of us.'

'Perhaps. But I have decided to take the easier course of hoping for the best. It's less wearing on the nerves to cultivate optimism than anticipate disaster, is it not?'

Mr Roberts made no reply. His dove-grey alpaca jacket was ridged with grease round the collar and on the lapels. His shirt (dyed, like all shirts by that time, in curry-powder or ink) was frayed and dirty; even his hands were ingrained with grime. He fidgeted all the time he talked, scratching at a hole in the knee of his trousers, rubbing the tip of his nose, fingering his lips with his dirty fingers, pulling at his beard, shuffling his feet.

We were sitting on the steps of the inner courtyard, catching the last of the sun; on the same steps where once I had sat and watched the sad pyre of Emily's stained possessions take fire in the July heat. The tree in the centre of the courtyard still stood, though most of its branches had been taken for fuel, and the squirrels—they too were thinner now and less sleek—scampered busily up and down the bole and on the broken earth below it. I remembered that July evening, but as though another had lived through it, not I. I recalled the shimmering heat rising into the almost equal heat that did not shimmer; the squirrels, the goat with its enquiring yellow eyes and the children playing with their homemade wagon. I remembered my prayer that I had made in such a strange mixture of despair and confidence: 'God send him back to me—for me!' but now that Oliver had indeed come back to me the need for that prayer and its fervour were hard to imagine.

'You have the advantage of youth, dear Laura,' Mr Roberts said after a long pause. 'That is why philosophy is still possible for you. I wish I could emulate your stout heart and unbowed will. But ...' His hand strayed to his face, picking at the stubble on his ill-shaved cheeks, then wandered down to the small beard, now ragged and perceptibly more white than I remembered it. 'But for me ... I cannot explain it. I can no longer find comfort in my thoughts. In resolutions. In history ... nor even books. I find myself bereft of all the tools with which to build up fortitude.'

His eyes, behind the spectacles, had a lost expression and filled with tears as he ended. He straightened his collar self-consciously.

I put my hand on his knee. 'Dear Mr Roberts, bear up! Don't give way now. We are nearly at the end of it, after all. I don't care what plans or instructions General Outram has, we know now that help, real help, is on its way to us from Delhi. It will be here within days; everyone says so. They cannot be longer than a couple of weeks at most and perhaps not that long. All the world knows our situation now; they will not let us endure this for one moment longer than is necessary. Remember, we are in touch with the outside now. Messages come and go every day. Your alarm is needless, but I do understand it. It's due to the long effort you have made; and discouragement and apathy always accompany not having enough to eat. You know that. Oh, dear Mr Roberts, don't give way now; you mustn't!'

He drew himself upright on the hard step and for a moment I caught a glimpse of my old mentor, contained, pedantic, precise.

'No, no, I am not really giving way. It has become rare for us to exchange such moments of sympathy. There are very few to whom I can express myself as fully and as confidently as I can to you, Miss Laura.

The self-indulgence of expression weakened me, but momentarily, I do assure you, only momentarily.'

'I know. We all need a shoulder to cry on sometimes.'

Again silence fell between us, and my mind immediately deserted the matter at hand, genuine as was my sympathy for Mr Roberts, and flew to Oliver. Soon he would be coming. Usually I waited for him on the front verandah, but today I would let his coming be a surprise.

'We have—I think I may say, Miss Laura, that we have found comfort in each other's company in some strange and diverse situations?'

'Indeed you may, Mr Roberts. Great comfort.'

'My mind is inclined to be a little woolly these days. I hope it is not too apparent, but I do find it difficult to drag my thoughts together. The hunger, I suppose. But one thing never eludes me: my admiration for your character.'

'Come now, you mustn't flatter a poor girl!'

'No, indeed no. No flattery there, merely the plain truth. All through this ... unpleasing military exercise, you have been a tower of strength to those who have known you. I have often wondered how one so young could be so equable, so unsurprised and unfrightened in the face of all our evils. It is not due solely to a good brain, nor the resilience of youth, nor to a disciplined character. It has often puzzled me, that well-spring of strength on which you have drawn since entering the Residency. Now I think I have found the fount of your steadfastness. You are in love, are you not, Laura? With Oliver Erskine?'

As with Kate, so now I saw no need to prevaricate with my old friend. I nodded, smiling—no doubt foolishly.

'I am.'

'And he reciprocates your regard, I trust?'

'I believe so.'

I waited for him to felicitate me, express his delight at my happiness.

But instead he subsided into himself again, and plucked anew at the hole on his knee.

'The last strand has given,' he said, so softly and strangely I hardly heard, and thought I must have misheard him.

'I am pleased,' he then said in a more normal tone. 'I am glad that your happiness is assured. Or rather ... Miss Laura, I am trying to be glad!'

The atmosphere between us changed. I half guessed what was coming and wished it would not.

'I cannot suppose you were ever aware of it, but there was a time, a long time ago now, of course, when I almost allowed myself to hope that I might be lucky enough to influence your affection toward myself.'

'Mr Roberts ...'

'No! I would like to say it all this once, and then go away and never mention it more. Of course, it would not have been an ideal match for you because of the disparity in our ages, and I realized that fully. But I found in your company, in your character, so much ease and contentment that I hoped you felt some of the same in mine. I knew it was unlikely that you could love a man so much your senior in years with any great passion, but a good understanding between the parties, shared interests, like-mindedness, have often proved a sound basis for marriage. And you had given me to understand that your pecuniary situation was not of the soundest. I allowed ... yes, I did allow myself to hope for your hand. At one time. Perhaps I should not be telling you this now, but you will not take offence. I want you to know that I was willing, most willing, to give you more than books and the fruits of my experience in India. In fact, Miss Laura, it is more than *wanting* to give.' He paused, clenching his hands together. 'I did give. I have given you my elderly heart, and in gratitude for so much that you gave me.'

'I don't know what to say,' I said, which was true.

'You need say nothing, my dear. It is enough that you have listened to me with kindness. I know you will not laugh at me or betray my confidence. I am glad you know, and ... and I am also glad it is Mr Erskine who has won you. A formidable rival for me, was he not, Miss Laura,' he asked with a brief attempt at levity, 'but I believe he will make you a good husband. I hope you will be happy. Very happy.'

Emily had been right. All those months ago, thoughtless, frivolous, unhappy Emily had guessed my friend's secret, and I, busy as ever with every concern but my own, had missed the meaning in his interest.

'Goodnight, Laura. Thank you for your patience. Have no fear, we will not need to refer to this again. I ... I am most sincerely glad that you have found happiness; I hope it will endure for all your life.'

We both stood up and he turned to go, while I tried to think of something suitable to say.

'I almost forgot ...' He stopped on the top step and produced a book from his pocket. 'I happened to come across this among my few remaining possessions. You know they commandeered my trunk of books, my three-drawer chest and almost everything else I owned to build into the walls—in July, when the rains came and everything was tumbling down?'

'I remember you telling us. It was a shame!' He had been disconsolate at the loss of his books, old and treasured friends that had accompanied him wherever he went.

'Yes.' He seemed to forget what he wanted to say, then saw the book in his hands and continued.

'I came across it, and recalled your fondness for the Aurelian Emperor and the fact that you had been forced to abandon your own copy. I thought you might like to have it. As a memento of a friend? Please accept it.'

He put into my hands a beautiful morocco-bound copy of Marcus Aurelius.

'I would love to have it,' I assured him soberly. 'I have missed him all these months. I will treasure it for many reasons, but mostly to honour the donor. I will never abandon this copy, I promise you.'

Mr Roberts smiled wanly, gazing at me through his spectacles.

'Dear, kind Laura,' he said, and walked slowly away with bent head, weariness evident in every line of his shabby figure.

I entered our kitchen and sat down. Smoke from the small fire below the soup pot filled the room; otherwise it was empty. For no reason that I could name, I felt upset and alarmed.

I half intended to tell Oliver what had occurred, but remembered my assurance that I would not betray Mr Roberts's confidence; telling Oliver would do so. When he arrived, I merely said that Mr Roberts had visited me and was worried at some further rumours regarding General Outram's intentions. I also showed him the book, delighting in the soft tooling of the binding. On opening it for the first time, I found that Mr Roberts had inscribed it:

For Laura, with Affection and Gratitude.
'The perfection of moral character
consists in this: in passing every
day as the last.' M. Aurelius
Henry M. Roberts   November 1857

'That's so like him,' I smiled, while Oliver read the inscription over my shoulder. 'Exactly in keeping with his character.'

'Is it? He doesn't seem to put it into practice too well.'

'Why do you say that?'

'Opium is not usually the recourse of the philosophical, the self-sufficient.'

'No, I see what you mean. He said just this evening that he seems to have lost the capacity to find comfort in books, studies and observation of life. He was rather sad, Oliver, and he made me sad for some reason too.'

'A full belly is all any of us needs to cure us of melancholia! He'll be right as rain as soon as we get out of here.'

I laid down the book, found my shawl and followed Oliver out of doors for a walk. Kate was back from the hospital and Jessie had brought Pearl in to feed her. The wish for privacy often drove us out of doors, even when the weather was bad, and I sometimes wondered how our courtship would have progressed had Oliver, like Charles when he was engaged to Emily, been allowed to see me only in the presence of a third party. Not that we had the chance to stray very far along the path of impropriety; there were people everywhere, whatever the hour, and Mrs Bonner, who was usually sitting on her stretch of verandah with Minerva when we left, probably took great care in timing the length of our absence, always observed the direction we took and asked with interest where we had been. She had told Kate in accents of sorrow that she believed I had '*une tendresse*' for my cousin-in-law, and Kate had enjoyed telling her there was no relationship and I was perfectly free to indulge my affections for Mr Erskine if I so pleased. 'Oh, but I do hope it is merely a case of propinquity,' Mrs Bonner had sighed. 'Not a suitable match, Mrs Barry. Not suitable at all.' After this, Oliver had made a point of winking at Minerva whenever he caught sight of her and now she started giggling even before he was in winking distance.

The pandies' band-concert was in full spate as we sauntered through the dusk to the Baillie Guard. Each evening rebel bandsmen on the far side of the wall would remind us of the comforts of former days by playing a selection of familiar airs such as *Annie Laurie, The Flowers of the Forest*, and *Auld Lang Syne*. Perhaps they hoped that the musical reminder of pleasant evenings with friends at the cantonment bandstand would serve to depress our spirits, but in fact they were listened to with enjoyment, and even the final impudence of *God Save the Queen* provoked only laughter.

'Tomorrow,' Oliver announced as we walked, 'I am to go down the mines. A listening-post, I believe, is what I am to be entrusted with. It should be interesting.'

'Oh, Oliver, no!' I was aghast. 'You are not well enough yet, and your arm ...'

'I'm as strong as I am ever going to be without a decent meal. It is something I can do, and will relieve the monotony of pouring bullets; believe me, that can become very monotonous. As to my arm—I can hold a pistol in my left hand and at point-blank range—which it would be—even I am not likely to miss if I actually need to pull the trigger; though it seems from what I have heard that one is unlikely to come face to face with one of the others. That ginger-haired fellow, what's-his-name—Kavanagh—he spends half his life underground lying in wait for pandies who never show up or, if they do, either argue with him or run for their own lines. I'll be fine; Toddy has been giving me a short course of instruction as to what to expect.'

'I do wish you wouldn't. There are so many dangers ... a fall of earth could be the end of you. But ... if you've made up your mind, I don't expect you'll listen to me.' He grinned and said nothing.

'I know. I'm fussing. But I know something else too. You are going to be thoroughly uncomfortable and miserable down there. Much more so than you imagine; the mines unnerve the stoutest characters and I'll be surprised if you venture down a second time.'

'Perhaps you're right. We'll see. Meanwhile, let's not talk of mines and martial matters. We've such a lot of things to talk about. All these months past I have been holding long, long conversations with you. Did you guess? In the strangest places and at the oddest times. They were the best I could do, but not very satisfactory. I suspect I too often gave you my opinions simply because I did not know yours, and we've had enough disagreements in the past for me to know there will be more to come.'

'Indeed there will. We shall have a most contentious life, I fancy. I am very used to forming my own mind. I believe you may find it displeasing.'

'Why should I?'

'Well, perhaps you have lived alone too long to learn how to deal with your own will thwarted. As it will be sometimes, naturally. And that will certainly displease you.'

'Never—so long as you do the thwarting. Your slightest wish will ever be my command. You know that.'

'Then don't go down the mines!'

'Ah! Conscience must take precedence even over your wishes. I'm afraid …'

'There you are, you see …'

'And surely you would not have me do less than Toddy-Bob or Charles or all the others to secure your safety?'

I enjoyed the bantering tone of his voice, belied by the tender expression in his eyes, but knew I must be careful not to allow the conversation to edge into the dangerous territory of where these idyllic disputes would take place. To reassure myself, I twined my fingers in the fingers of his left hand safely hidden under the crimson quilt he was wearing. It was difficult not to enlarge upon my dream plans for our life together; but, nervous of what his intentions might be, I preferred not to rock the barque of my frail happiness.

On the verandah of the Fayrers' house the ladies were singing hymns with a group of off-duty gentlemen from their battery. I caught a glimpse of Charles's fair head and waved but he did not see me, so earnestly was he carolling with a hymn book held before his face.

We walked down the slope to the Baillie Guard and across the open space beyond it.

'The final touch!' Oliver chuckled as we went. 'A pandy band playing "The Queen", guns firing, and ladies singing hymns amid it all!' And suddenly I was laughing too.

Each time I viewed our meagre fortifications from outside as the pandies must have seen them, my astonishment at my own safety grew more pronounced. Tumbled, frail, battered before completed, the wall of brickwork, mud, firewood, bamboo and sacking stretched in an often interrupted arc surrounding, but hardly protecting, the ruined buildings I now knew so well.

'Crazy!' Oliver said, as together we paused. 'Crazy. I always said the place could not be defended.'

'But it *was* defended. It is being defended. Oliver, how can you! We are entering the fifth month of the defence and you still say it cannot be done.'

'Why the devil didn't they get on with it?' he demanded of the evening air as we turned back towards the old gate. 'There was nothing to stop them. Nothing.'

'You sound regretful that they never had the fortitude to make the final push that would have meant our end. I believe your loyalties really are as ambivalent as rumour has it!'

'Hmph! Perhaps. Though I incline more to the belief that I am as Ungud is, as Ishmial is, as the pandies should be. I am loyal to my *nimcha*, my "salt". In other words, to the hand that feeds me, though in my case it would be more correct to say to the land that feeds me. Hassanganj.'

A sharp chill made itself felt around my heart, so I began talking nonsense.

'Would you be pleased if the pandies win? I mean over all?'

'Don't be foolish, you know quite well they can't win—over all or any other way. And no, I would not want them to if they could. They would not have the capacity, at this time, to manage their own affairs, their own country, or what we have made of their country over the last hundred years. But I see an old order dying. High time it went too, in some ways. But much that was good, estimable, and to be emulated as I think, will also die. That I must necessarily regret.'

'Oliver, don't you hate them? At all? For what they have done to you, to Hassanganj? To all of us here—and in Cawnpore?'

'No.'

'You surely cannot still find any justification for their behaviour? It has been appalling.'

'I can understand it. In some respects I even sympathize with it. War is appalling, Laura. On both sides. Always. Our own record is not blameless, remember, and in any event hatred destroys the hater more efficiently than the hated. Your friend Marcus Aurelius has something to say on that point—and by the way, I did not know you were an admirer of his; you see how little I know of you?'

'Oh, yes. He's been my greatest comfort for years, but I left my old copy in Wajid Khan's house, which is why Mr Roberts gave me his. But I cannot recall anything about hatred explicitly.'

'No, not explicitly. But he says, somewhere, "The best way of avenging thyself is not to become like the wrongdoer," Do you hate the pandies, Laura?'

'No, I don't think so. But I ... I am repelled by what they have done, and frightened of it. You will say because I do not understand, and perhaps you are right. But they are human, after all, and surely one should expect some sort of human behaviour ... standards ... even though they are not of our race.'

He was silent and I continued, 'I think it is terrible to be confronted with such ... such loathing, such vicious hatred. To have to live among people capable of it ...' Again on dangerous ground, I fell silent.

Oliver sighed and said seriously, 'You are right. The bitterness of this is going to last a long time. A very long time. Yet we have earned it too. We must not forget that, nor allow it to be said of us again.'

The chill around my heart increased, and I turned to him, took his hand and said, 'I love you so much. So much!'

As we approached the Gaol, we saw several people crowding around our door looking into the kitchen: Mrs Bonner and her stout husband and young Minerva, two or three other neighbours, a couple of officers. Immediately anxious, I hurried up the steps. They made way for us without speaking.

'What's happened?' I demanded urgently. 'Is something wrong with Pearl?' But I was at once reassured as Jessie stood with Pearl in her arms, the baby pulling at Jessie's deep red hair with every appearance of good health and spirits.

'Oh, Laura, thank God! Charles has gone out to look for you. We didn't want you to hear from strangers ...'

'What is it, Kate?' said Oliver, as I stood in silence wondering what could be wrong in my world since all the people I loved were present and well.

Intent upon the baby, I only then saw Wallace Avery sitting on one of the cane stools at the back of the room, his head in his hands.

'It's ... oh, Laura dear, it's poor Mr Roberts!' said Kate.

'Killed?' asked Oliver as I waited.

Kate shook her head.

'Hurt then?'

'He has shot himself. He is dead.'

'No! Oh no, Kate! He was here ...'

'I ... I found him.' Wallace looked up. His face was white, his eyes blotched and red with drink and tears. 'My God! Why the hell did *I* have to find him? It was frightful ... frightful.' And he began to sniff and blubber like a frightened child.

Oliver took three strides across the room to where the bottle of brandy that Wallace himself had given us stood on a shelf. He reached for a cup and poured out a tot. 'Here, man, drink this,' he ordered with a touch of the old impatience. Wallace complied noisily, then put the cup down and wiped his mouth with the back of his hand. 'That's better,' he said. 'And, my God, when I remember that I had gone to him to ask for a drink ... and he was there ... finished, all the time I was searching around his bedroom!'

'Wallace, when did it happen?' I whispered.

'I don't know. But not long ago. Couldn't have been.'

'No. He was here only a couple of hours since.'

'Was he? Well, there you are, you see. I ... I had got in from a spell on the guns at the South Face. Not much doing actually, but tedious, d'you know, and I'd been there since midday. Needed a drink to ... to help me ease up, and I found my bottle was empty. Knew old Roberts had a couple of bottles under his bed. Usen't to drink much, not generally, but just lately he had been findin' it more of a comfort like the rest of us. So—well, I trotted down the verandah to his room but he wasn't there. Door was open, of course, so I thought, knowing him, well, he wouldn't mind if I took just a tot or two before asking him. I found a cup, but not the bottles. No furniture, y'know; just a trunk and a string bed left in the place. I felt under the pillows and looked underneath the bed, but there was nothing. Then I remembered. 'He's—he was—a neat sort of chap, very tidy, and he kept a lot of things on the shelves in the bathroom, since there was no table or anything in the bedroom. So ... so I went in and found him. God! Poor old Roberts!'

Tears sprang to his protruberant eyes again and he passed a podgy hand over his face to control himself.

'He ... he ... It must have been hell, trying to screw himself up to the pitch, d'you know. There was a glass, still with a little brandy in it, on the floor beside the bottle. He was very particular, you know, Laura? Very tidy ... and liked everything in its place about him. He must have ... I suppose he hadn't wanted to make a ... a mess everywhere. He'd got into the tin tub and ... and sat down in it—it was empty, of course— in all his clothes and with his boots on. And then ... and then he'd put a pistol in his mouth. There were ... there were brains and bone and hair all over the wall ... and, oh God! Sickening, it was sickening to see poor old Roberts like that. He did ... no one ... any harm.'

I had not wept when Emily had died. The last time I could remember giving way to tears on another's behalf was the night in the peepul

692

grove. Since then, but for my weeping when Oliver had left us to ride back to Hassanganj for Yasmina, tears had proved inadequate to ease my heart. Now, however, I remembered the words Mr Roberts had spoken, half to himself, on the courtyard steps so short a time before. 'The last strand has given,' he had murmured. I had not known what he meant.

Now his meaning had been made clear. Had I not confessed to my feeling for Oliver and his for me, perhaps my poor friend might have been able to continue his lonely struggle until the relief. Bereft of all he had clung to, from his love of scholarship to his opium, at the last he had realized that his affection for me too was a lost cause and had determined quietly to put an end to his misery.

I could have helped him. I knew I could have helped him. I had not really tried to enter his mind—his heart—even when he had been speaking of his troubles, and of his inability to find comfort where once he had found it. I had allowed my thoughts to wander from what he was trying to communicate to me, busying my mind with the anticipated delight of Oliver's coming. Overwhelmed with a regret very close to guilt, and with great grief for the awful isolation in which my disclosure of love had left my friend, I turned and, unmindful of the curious faces of our neighbours at the door, buried my face against Oliver's rough corduroy and wept as though my heart would break.

They buried Mr Roberts the following night, in that same unquiet field where lay Sir Henry Lawrence, Major Banks, Mr Ommaney, Mr Polehampton, Colonel Anderson, Captain Fulton, and all the other men, great or obscure, heroes or frightened fools, who had succumbed to the enemy. Where, too, lay Emily and Jessie's little Jamie.

'They might make difficulties about a burial in consecrated ground,' Charles had hazarded the night before. 'A suicide! ... After all ...'

Kate and I had looked at each other in disbelief, and Oliver, angry as I had ever seen him said, 'By God, if they do, I'll bury him with my own hands—and in consecrated ground. He was a victim of this siege as surely as any man who caught a pandy bullet or was blown to pieces by a pandy shell. He'll be buried in consecrated ground, I can promise you—if that is what Laura thinks he would have wanted?'

I had nodded. Mr Roberts's Christian faith was pleasantly tempered with irony, but he was a man who valued the proprieties. No doubt the authorities reached the same conclusion as Oliver; no difficulties were made by them as to my friend's final resting place, and I felt uncomfortably sure that only Charles had even considered them.

Oliver, Charles, Wallace and some other friends of Mr Roberts's followed the *doolies* carrying the day's dead down to the churchyard, which was still considered too exposed to fire to allow the presence of women. From the Gaol verandah, I watched the *cortège* pass quickly through the dusk, and repeated to myself as a sort of prayer of leavetaking the quotation Mr Roberts had used to inscribe his copy of Marcus Aurelius for my use. 'The perfection of moral character consists in this: in passing every day as the last.' Had he been weaker than I guessed, I wondered? Or in a sense stronger? I would never know now, but I could hope that the stern, uncompromising injunction of Marcus Aurelius had given him some comfort; that, finding he had reached his last day unawares, Mr Roberts had decided to end it in the full if mistaken consciousness of the dignity of what he did. I could allow myself to think of him as fearful of his own future; not unmanned by his own fear.

After the funeral service, our men had returned to the Gaol. Oliver, forgetting or not caring for Charles's presence, had held me and kissed my swollen eyelids and tried to comfort me, and I had gone to him with eager gratitude. We had long since stopped pretending only friendship before Kate and Jess, and I had forgotten that Charles, so little present in the Gaol, might still be ignorant of how matters lay between his brother and myself.

When I pulled away from Oliver, laughing tremulously and trying to pat my hair in place, I looked up and caught sight of Charles in the doorway frowning at us both with an expression close to outrage. As he caught my eye, he turned on his heel and strode away without a word, and had our rickety-hinged door been capable of slamming, he would certainly have slammed it.

'Damn!' said I. 'The cat is really out of the bag now.'

'Would you sooner it were not?' Oliver asked suspiciously.

I shook my head. 'Of course not. But I would have liked to break it to him gently. To have told him ... first.'

Oliver looked at me with a strangely watchful expression in his eyes, but said nothing.

BOOK VI

PASSWORD—'HEROINE'

'Adapt thyself to the things with
which thy lot has been cast; and
the men among whom thou hast
received thy portion; love them,
but do it truly.'
Marcus Aurelius

CHAPTER 1

Since the end of September, native spies and messengers had carried despatches not only to the Alum Bagh but also to Cawnpore. No doubt much of what passed between the commanders of the various posts was secret, but it was common knowledge that General Outram had sent to both Captain Bruce in Cawnpore and Major McIntyre at the Alum Bagh plans of the city of Lucknow and instructions regarding the route to be taken by the relieving column. By the beginning of November we had learned that the Delhi Flying Column was already in Cawnpore, and that in a week or so there would be no less than six thousand men ready to march to our aid. The Alum Bagh was to become the mustering place of all the men, arms and supplies being hurried to us, and someone on General Outram's staff suggested erecting a semaphore for purposes of communication with that palace, which was visible to the naked eye from the roof of the Resident's House. Instructions for making this device were discovered in an old copy of the *Penny Encyclopædia* in Mr Gubbins's library. A few days later the machine was erected on the top of the tower of the Resident's House, near the flagpole that still flew the Union Jack, and we waited hopefully for the bonfire that would signal the readiness of a similar device at the Alum Bagh.

The period that followed was an unsettling one for the garrison. There, on the highest point in the enclosure, the poles, pulleys and weights informed us that we were open to communication with the wider world, yet that world would not answer us. Thousands of men were mustering to our aid less than forty miles distant, but in the bright clear days of early winter, as in the torrid days of summer, our privations continued and increased. The pandies had drawn back their guns and were now playing at what the men termed 'Long Bowls', yet we suffered still the daily quota of death and injury, and the hospital was as full as ever. Indeed, the hospital was a little fuller than it should have been, and in my meddling manner I decided to take it upon myself to expose a malingerer.

Three or four of us had experienced trouble with this man, a hulking brutish corporal of the 78th, who had come in with a bullet in his hand and a gash on his head after a sortie. His hand had healed and he had been sent about his business, only to return the next day draped on a comrade's back, apparently unconscious. The doctors had examined him cursorily, diagnosed a severe concussion and allowed him to be put on a cot which happened to be vacant.

That had been five days before. The corporal had lain immobile under his blanket, but the small grey eyes in his slab of face shifted quickly about the room, following the ladies as they went about their duties. When a doctor approached, the man either feigned stentorian sleep or moaned piteously of his ''ead achin' somethin' cruel'. He was no mean actor and doubtless I too would have been taken in had I not been uncomfortably aware of those small eyes upon me whenever I was in his part of the ward. When I took him water, he clasped his hands round mine holding the cup, pulling them down to his level instead of raising his head as he was quite able to do, so that after two or three such encounters I delegated the duty of slaking his thirst to my friend Llewellyn Cadwallader who, presumably, would be spared such unwelcome attentions. But poor young Llew came in for others equally undesirable.

We who worked in the hospital were fond of the lads who shared our tasks, and it was not uncommon for the ladies to save whatever treats came their way for the boys. In this way Llewellyn had one day been in proud possession of two English biscuits—'Come out of a pretty tin, they did, miss, and with sugar on them,' he told me, exhibiting his treasures. Shortly afterwards I was dismayed to find him crying his heart out, inexpert, snuffly boy's sobs, his face streaked with grimy tears. The two precious biscuits had been taken from him. My temper mounted. Who on earth would do such a thing to a mere child?

'I wouldn't have minded if he'd taken just one, miss,' he sniffed, rubbing his wet nose with the back of his hand. 'I'd have let him have it and not minded really, though they had sugar on them and all, but Sonny should have had his one, miss. He's only little and I wanted him to have one.'

'But who was it? Who took them from you, Llew?' Surely, I thought, no one in the hospital would serve the boy such a trick, and which of the men wandering about the place would even have known he had the things? It must have been one of his schoolmates, I surmised. The usual class bully-boy.

'Can't tell you, miss. He cuffed me, you see, and if I tell, he'll cuff me again proper and worse. He told me so, and he means it.'

Thieving, bullying brute, I seethed to myself, my sense of impotence heightened by the knowledge that I had nothing to offer the lad in compensation. However, there was nothing to be gained in pressing the child for the name of his tormentor, and I watched him wander homeward, trying manfully to still his sobs, a forlorn little figure in the waning autumnal light.

It was time I went home myself. Kate was waiting for me. I went into the ward to fetch my shawl, which I had hung on a nail, and as I pinned it round my shoulders caught Corporal Tuppit's gaze upon me.

'Miss,' he croaked hoarsely. 'My 'ead! Give us one of them cloths with vinegar on. Really, miss, it 'urts somethin' awful. All the time, it does.' With unwilling resignation, I fetched a rag dipped in vinegar and placed it on his low furrowed brow. As I did so he grabbed my hand and squeezed it. 'Give us a smile then, hey?' he leered. 'That's more good to a sick man than a wet cloth.'

Snatching my hand from him, I gave him what I hoped was a freezing look, and turned majestically away, but not before I noticed that his beard was liberally sprinkled with crumbs and powdered sugar.

The following morning, as Kate and I walked down to the hospital together, I turned the matter over in my mind. On one thing I was determined. Corporal Tuppit would be out of that precious bed by nightfall. My mind, however, was singularly devoid of ideas as to how to achieve this object. Certainly I could have reported my suspicions to one of the doctors; no one would have doubted my observations of the man's conduct and Corporal Tuppit would have found himself discharged in double quick time. But I wanted to do more than have him ejected. I wanted to expose him for what he was, a lying, cowardly, thieving fraud, and in this unkind determination, eventually, lay my own undoing.

Towards midday, as I was beginning to think without pleasure of the couple of dry *chapattis* in my pocket, I was helping a sick man to re-lay the blanket on his pallet. I got him settled, but as I tucked the blanket around him, a scorpion, barbed tail curved over its back in alarm, scuttled towards my hand. The man laughed as I quickly rose and stamped my foot on it.

'I remember the time when a lady would've screamed just to see one of them things,' he said admiringly.

'Oh, we're all used to them now,' I assured him. 'Scorpions, spiders, toads, centipedes, rats and mice, ticks and fleas—we've had to deal with them all at one time or another. They don't really do much harm, though the scorpion has a nasty sting, of course.'

'That it has, miss. Had one in my groundsheet once. Stung me bad and I was hoppin' for days. Pain was proper horrid too.'

A sudden illumination filled me.

I searched around for Llewellyn, found him on his way to his meal, and gave him a small lidded tin and certain instructions.

Later in the afternoon Dr Darby came in to do his rounds and I attached myself to him like a docile shadow, the tin, now occupied, safely in my pocket. After what seemed an aeon in my impatience, we approached Corporal Tuppit's bed. Tuppit lay stiff, suffering almost audibly, eyes closed, hands clenched in agony, breathing noisily through his mouth. He was a pathetic sight.

'Well, fellow?' Obviously Dr Darby also had his reservations regarding this patient. Generally his greeting was more cordial. 'How's that head of yours today?'

'Awful, sir.'

'Hm. Curious that. You should certainly be over that cut on your head by now. No fever. Pulse normal ... Hm. I think you'd be better on your feet.'

'Oh, no, sir! Can't do that. My legs, sir, they're numb. Can't feel a thing in 'em. Like dead they are, sir.'

'Oh? Something new?'

'No, sir, been like that all the time.'

'You haven't mentioned it before.'

'I did, sir, to the other doctor.'

'Well, let's have a look then.'

Dr Darby turned back the blanket from the bottom of the bed, exposing a pair of large, calloused and dirty feet, one of which he prodded with a pin taken from his lapel. There was absolutely no reaction from Tuppit. He didn't even blink. But I still had no doubts.

'Hm. You felt nothing?'

'Not a bleedin' thing, sir.'

'Quite sure?'

'Certain sure, sir.'

'Curious. Very curious. Well, stay there until the morning. I'll have another look at you and see what can be done.'

Dr Darby moved along the line and very solicitously I tucked the blanket in round Tuppit's feet, having first inserted the now lidless box between the blanket and the pallet.

I followed Dr Darby. We had moved only a couple of beds down the row, when the dozing afternoon ward was electrified by a succession of blood-curdling yells and the spectacle of Corporal Tuppit, clad only in his shirt, hopping like a madman on his pallet, clutching one dirty foot in his hands and with the most gratifying expression of pure agony on his ugly features.

Dr Darby gave him five minutes to dress and remove himself from the hospital. He was a lenient man, Dr Darby. Any of the other medical men would have put the wretch on a charge, and the time was soon to come when I wished very much that such had been done.

I went back to the Gaol filled with a pleasant sense of accomplishment, and told my story to an appreciative audience. Oliver was eating with us, having appeared just as we sat down, with Toddy-Bob behind him carrying a tin pail of gun-bullock soup containing four potatoes and five turnips—a luxury that had to be shared.

The sun was still above the horizon when Oliver and I set out for our evening stroll. A brief shower in the forenoon had served to lay the dust and wash the foliage of the trees; the air was crisp and almost sweet, and on such an evening of soft light and clear distances it was inevitable that we should make for some high point from which we could look out over our stockade to the palaced parklands surrounding us. We chose the roof of a large two-storeyed house known as the Judicial Post, which was commanded by Captain Germon, a young officer of the Native Infantry. It stood on the south-eastern perimeter of the old entrenchment but, due to the expansion of the enclave, was now a safe point from which to view the surrounding countryside and was a favourite spot on such evenings amongst a populace starved of the sight of woodland, fields and grass. The house had suffered such heavy bombardment for three months that Captain Germon allowed only a few people at a time to risk themselves on its unstable roof. We had to wait a few moments for a party to descend but, as it happened, when Oliver and I then mounted into the open, we found ourselves alone.

The crimson globe of the sun just tipped the dark and gleaming masses of the mango groves to the west, suspended in a shot-silk sky of salmon and silver. Small mackerel clouds of silver-tipped grey, hardly larger than my hand, swam in a diaphanous sea, dissolving, disappearing, reforming mysteriously as they went. Shafts of light, fugitives from the gauzy prison of the cloudlets, cut swathes of gold through foliage and over furrowed fields, and struck brief flame from the gilded domes and minarets before us. Below the gold, the crowded city sprawled in peaceful quiet under a pall of dark cooking-smoke, like a tiger sleeping in the shade. Despite the depredations of war in the foreground, the ruined buildings and the tumbled streets, it was very beautiful.

'Damn it, it's downright beguiling—still.' Oliver smiled, speaking more to himself than to me. 'All these shabby grandeurs and relics of decayed majesty. Wonder what will become of them when this is over? Whether they'll be torn down to make way for more and dirtier bazaars in the name of betterment, or whether they'll just be allowed to fall to pieces with time. Don't suppose anyone will ever live in them again, but I'd be sorry to see them go. Not a one but has its history of treachery and revenge, jealousy and bloody retribution. And sometimes of love. Ghosts too, of course, and rooms that are accursed. Oudh notables seldom died in bed.'

'They still don't,' I pointed out.

'True. And no doubt in time the episode through which we have lived here will prove a veritable quarry of myth and fable regarding the Oudh notables of today. Who knows, perhaps in time even we unnotables will be found to be more than pawns on a political chessboard suddenly overturned in a fit of rage. Good God, I might be remembered as a hero!'

'Then you had better arrange to meet your heroic end before you blemish your record further. If it's left to Mrs Bonner, you will certainly figure as the villain of the piece.'

'Why? It must be three full days since I last tried to seduce her daughter.'

'Perhaps that's the trouble. She told Kate last night that she had a good mind to "enlighten" me on your shortcomings of character and conduct. She didn't want to see me throw myself away on you.'

'And a very estimable sentiment, too. My opinion of the lady soars.'

'Fancy managing to remember all the ill-natured tattling of cantonment tea-drinkings in our present situation.'

'But tattle and tea-drinkings are far more enduring than "our present situation" as you term it. They'll still be continuing long after you and I are mouldering in our well-earned graves. How else can the proprieties be defined—or defended?'

'What a horrid thought; but I suppose you are right. Human beings never really learn anything, do they?'

'Some do. You have.'

'I wonder? I've tried to, but give me a week of comfort and cleanliness and butter on white bread, and I'll probably forget everything I've learned.'

Oliver put his hand under my chin, tilted up my face and kissed me on the lips. Then, murmuring my name, he placed his cheek against my hair, and we stood for a space very close together and allowed our nearness to engulf us in sweetness.

'I'll give you more, my dear,' he said very tenderly, 'never mind what you've learned. Everything I have, or will ever have, is yours now. Isn't it time, Laura, that we had a serious talk ... about the future?'

The moment of decision was upon me. I did not want to meet it. Perhaps, with a little adroit manipulation of mood, I could again have avoided it, but sooner or later it would have to be faced, and suddenly, standing there above the storied pinnacles of the city, with his arms about me I felt strong enough to do so.

'Yes. I ... have been thinking about it a good deal.'

'Good.'

'Oliver, before you say anything more, there is one thing we must clear up.'

'My lurid past?' His lips twitched, but the hazel eyes looked at me with serious attention. 'It shall be as an open book to you, if that is what you want.'

'No! Oh, Oliver, of course not. What's done is done, for both of us.'

'I think it would be better so, but perhaps you feel that there is too much of me you do not know. That my—er—secret life of which Mrs Bonner knows so much will stand between us. Is that it?'

'No. I think there may be something to stand between us, but not ... not other women.'

'What else can there be?'

'Well, Jessie has told me of your offer. She is quite taken up with the idea of running your house in Hassanganj. But—oh, surely, Oliver, surely you don't intend to go back there, or to remain in India at all? Not after what has happened here? What has happened to us all? But ... Jessie thinks you mean it.'

'I do mean it,' he said quietly.

'You really intend to go back?'

'Certainly.'

Perhaps the sun did not dip behind the mangoes at that moment; perhaps the minarets had already lost their light before he spoke. To me, however, that single word brought darkness.

'Hassanganj is destroyed,' I found myself pointing out in quiet panic. 'It's been destroyed.'

'The house has, but that can be rebuilt. The estate is still there and still mine.'

'But how can you know that?' I objected, holding his hand very tightly in both my own. 'The whole country is in confusion and, when they get the situation under control, who knows what the Government may decide ... about your estate, about Oudh, about anything? Everything will have changed. It will have to change.'

'Perhaps. But no one can take Hassanganj from me, Laura.'

'You really think you can take up your life again, just as it was?'

'Perhaps not just as it was. Perhaps I won't want to. But much as it was. In time.'

'And you could forget all you have been through? After your horrible experiences of treachery and barbarity, how can you even contemplate living again amongst such people?'

'They have not all been treacherous—or cruel—and I owe my life to "barbarians" like the leather worker who pulled me from the river. And to Ishmial, and Ungud and ... Moti too, most of all. As do you, Laura. And talking of barbarity, I could tell you tales of the behaviour of our own white-skinned, civilized and Christian fellows that bear dishonourable comparison with any of the evil things done by the others.'

'How can you say such a thing?'

'That is the first totally stupid remark I have ever heard you make, Laura,' he said coldly. 'When did the colour of a man's skin ever control his virtue or lack of it? There have been things done here, in the name of British justice, of course, that are as foul and as vicious in intent as anything those men out there have done to us in the name of their freedom … their right to live in their own way. What they have done has been bad; no doubt of that. But what they did was in the heat of triumph or under the threat of fear—generally irrationally, as I believe. We have done similar things, will continue to do them, without the excuse of fanaticism or hysteria; things like Neill sentencing the Brahmins among the accused of Cawnpore to clean the blood from the floor of the *Bibighar* with their tongues before being hanged. In forcing them to that, he destroyed their souls as well as their caste. They would gladly have relinquished their mere bodies.'

'But that is only what they believed …'

'No man can be more than what he believes, or other than what he believes, in the last analysis. Who are you to be so sure they are wrong and that only our ideas on such matters can be correct?'

'But after what they did to the women and children …'

'I am not excusing them and, God knows, I am not defending them! What you forget is that their own people will be as horrorstruck by that episode as we are. I am only pointing out that not only *they* have been in the wrong, and we have no prerogative of right behaviour. Sometimes I wonder whether we have any hint of it, indeed. Perhaps you remember that among my more unpopular opinions is the theory that we British brought this whole damned rebellion on our own heads by our deliberate arrogance, our inertia and our ignorance of the people we are ruling.'

He was looking at me now as he had looked at me when Charles had found us kissing after Mr Roberts's funeral, with a wary, detached curiosity. His expression cut me more cruelly than his words. I released his hand and walked away from him with bent head. At the corner of the roof I paused and looked with tear-filled eyes over the darkening vista.

'Very well. On this I cannot argue with you. You know much more than I, both of the Indian and of the British in India. But tell me—let's leave the rest aside for the moment—just tell me what you believe you can do in Hassanganj now. What you will be free to do? You know as well as I that everyone is saying the Company must go now, that the country will be taken over by the Crown and everything must change as a consequence. What will you be able to do in Hassanganj? And when?'

'When? I cannot answer that unfortunately. And it is not of any very vital importance. The land will remain, even if abused; the villages may have been burned down, but the villagers will return to them. Perhaps the roads were washed away in the last monsoon, the canals breached for their water. I don't know. But these things can be remedied. These people, my people of Hassanganj, are patient in adversity. If they were not, the villages would long since have returned to the earth of which they are made. Whatever has happened, when I get back I will find them rebuilding their mud houses, scratching out of the hard earth once again the fields that give them sustenance and dignity; returning bit by bit and slow day by slow day to the onerous cycle of their seasonal tasks. To their life. And what will I do, you ask? I will help them to the best of my ability. I will try to repair, to build up, what the folly of my kind and the ignorance of their own have joined in destroying. I will go on living the life and doing the work I was intended for. I have no other option.'

He had not followed me, but when I turned, I found him leaning on the pock-marked balustrade, looking over the city as it faded momentarily into the gathering dusk. From a mosque came the call of the *muezzin*, cracked tenor notes scratching aside the bass growl of the distant bazaars, and the smoke settled closer to the rooftops.

My shoes were now so worn, perhaps he did not hear me as I returned to his side. He did not turn or look at me, and I was not sure he knew I was close to him.

'Oh, woman dear!' And the words were so soft a whisper, I could not have heard them had I not been near. 'You must give me a chance. You must try to understand. There is so much you have no way of knowing—of me and of my life ... and of India. But India is my life, Laura. My only life ...'

CHAPTER 2

After a pause, during which he had seemed to forget my presence, he went on: 'There is so much about me that you still cannot know; give me a hearing.'

'Oh, Oliver, of course! You must see how much I want to understand?'

'Then why should it be so difficult for you to appreciate my point of view?'

For a moment his eyes held mine, then he looked away again.

'Laura … India, as I have said, is my life. To you it is an interlude only, and now an unpleasant interlude; but it is my native land. I am India's as surely as you and your relatives feel they belong to England, and only your ignorance of how things really are with me forces me to say so. You cannot really believe that I, with my white skin, can have as strong an affection for this country as you have for England. Yet it is so, and quite understandable.

'You know my grandfather was granted his land at Hassanganj by the Nawab of Oudh over sixty years ago; my father was born in the old house, as I was myself. Three generations of us now have loved the place and felt it home.

'When my grandfather first went to Hassanganj, it was part wilderness and part desert, damned nearly untouched by human hand unless in destruction. There were no roads, no waterways, no villages; a few tiny, transient hamlets of *gonds* and gypsies only. The land had never been tilled nor the forest cleared.

'Old Adam created Hassanganj. He populated it with the inhabitants of a neighbouring district then suffering a famine; he decided on the best sites for the villages, laid them out and helped build them with his own hands; he pushed back the forest-line, irrigated the scrubland, built roads. He imported the seed for the first crops, experimented with the first orchards, bored the first wells and provided the bullocks to work them. It took him years, and all in the midst of the usual difficulties: the climate, the loneliness, the misinterpretation of his motives by his own people and by the natives. As well, he had the Rohilla raiders to contend with, the jealousy and spite of the *talukhdars*, and the corrupt politics of the Nawab's court. A dozen times in half a century we have had as much reason to abandon the country in disgust, as you feel I now have. But we did not abandon it, and I never will. We have made something where there was almost nothing, Laura, something durable and worthwhile. My grandfather loved India with single-mindedness and passion. My father loved India. I have inherited their love—and with it their responsibilities.'

While he was speaking, his injured arm had fallen out from between the buttons of his corduroy jacket. Impatiently he thrust the limp wrist into his pocket with the aid of his left hand, and glanced at me in embarrassment as he did so.

'Do you not see?' he asked.

'But I have always known how much you cared for Hassanganj, Oliver ...'

'It is more than that. Every man feels affection for his home, yet can leave it when the time comes. Hassanganj is more than my home and the home of my family. It is my life; my work. I can think of no other way of living, no other work to do. That's the difference. And the work has only just begun. Now, after all this ... this wretched business is over, the Company will go. The Crown will take over, and with the Nawab out of the way, I believe things will be easier. I will be able to do much more, and more quickly. With a more stable government, the villages will prosper; within a few years the railway will connect every corner of India, and trade must expand. The indigo has been doing well over the past few years and in a couple more will prove a profitable crop for those of the villagers who have learned from my experiment and are prepared to cultivate it. Then there's sugar. As soon as the railway reaches us, I intend to build a factory where we can process the stuff straight from the Hassanganj fields, and my poor damned peasants will at last see some more tangible reward for their labours than a half-filled belly and an evergrowing debt to the *bunnia*.

'And there'll be other benefits, things I can put my hand to now that were impossible before. Schools in the villages, medical help—by God, perhaps even a hospital if I can prevail on the Government to help me; certainly a dispensary …'

'No wonder they call you a radical,' I commented as he paused, half caught, despite myself, in the sweep of his hopes.

'Is that what they call me?'

I nodded.

'That is a compliment. A real compliment,' he said seriously. 'It is the roots I am interested in. The roots of India. This that is happening here, all around us, is only a beginning, Laura. I do not know what the outcome will be, but I recognize that it is a turning-point. The old ideas by which we have lived here, and which brought us here in the first place, are dead, or at least no longer sufficient to enable us to rule this enormous country—which is what we have now committed ourselves to do. I can only guess at what will take their place, but when everything has cooled down, it will be found that all our notions and expectations will have changed because of an entirely new situation. The British will at last have to forego the extraordinary pretence that they are merely agents of a commercial concern; they will openly become, as they have long been in effect, the only rulers of India. Somehow we—the Government, the Crown, whatever you care to call it—are going to have to create and then deal with a cohesion of interest and direction among all the races, creeds and kingdoms of India, and we are going to discover that we have created out of our tradesmen's lust a creature much larger than ourselves. I doubt whether it will be an angel; I hope it will not prove a dragon! But there, Laura, out there under that smoky sky is one part of that problematical new creature. An infant part, I suppose. Perhaps it will be a couple of lifetimes before it acquires any stature, maybe more. But I want to help it grow, not with money and White Papers in a Parliament thousands of miles away, but with my own effort, my own understanding, my own capacities—such as they are.'

'You're a dreamer of dreams,' I said, mostly to fill the enquiring silence.

'Of only one dream—that I have been bred in.'

Moved by the intensity of his manner, I walked a few paces along the flat roof.

'Laura?'

I paused, without turning.

'What do you say?'

'What am I to say?'

He followed me and stood looking down at my bent head as I pretended to gaze over the almost invisible city.

'I have told you this because I want you with me.'

'I know.'

'In holy wedlock, of course!' he added with a brief resumption of his old sardonic manner.

'I had paid you the compliment of presuming so.'

'My idea in approaching Jessie was that she would make an excellent companion for you. You know and like her well, and I suppose it might be strange for you in Hassanganj at first. She could take all the dreary household tasks out of your hands.'

'And thus leave me free to minister to my master!' I said tartly.

'Oho! So she talked then!' And he grinned, quite unabashed. He was relaxed now, at ease. Apparently he considered his battle won. I turned and looked up at his hawkish face, so thin and strained despite the smile. There was so much I wished to say to him, to explain, even to discover for myself through my own words. All I said, however, was, 'Her exact words were that your wife would have her hands full taking care of you!'

'And so she will,' he smiled, taking both my hands in his one. 'So she will! I'll want you by me every moment of life, waking and sleeping. I want you with me in the office; you were always good with figures and quite a help to me over those inventories, do you remember? I had great trouble persuading Benarsi Das to destroy the perfectly good copies he had made, so that I could give you something to do that would keep you near me. And when I ride to the villages you will come with me, and you will sit in the *kutcheri*, the court, three times a week to see that I temper justice with mercy. We will plan our new house together, and watch it being built together. We'll go shooting and hawking and fishing and will climb in the hills in the summers. I'll teach you Persian on cold winter evenings—oh! and you must continue with your Urdu, of course; it will prove very useful with the women, and the local lingo you'll pick up in no time. By God, how I wish we could start right away! I'm back where my grandfather was, in a way, but with all his experience to help me, and with luck a surer foundation to build on. It will be magnificent, Laura. Exhilarating!'

'Aren't you overlooking one thing?' I said, disengaging my hands and turning from him. I knew he was looking at my averted face steadily but he made no response, and I was furious because my voice quivered as I went on: 'I cannot think of living in Hassanganj.'

Still he remained silent, and I was forced to continue without any encouragement but that of my own unhappy conviction.

'I cannot ... I cannot continue to live in India! I know you do not understand; I cannot expect you to. But it is the truth, none the less. I cannot remain out here. Once before, long before all this took place, I remember feeling the same thing, not so strongly of course. It was when we had encountered the *suttee* procession in the forest. I found myself filled with an overwhelming repugnance for India and everything Indian—because I could not understand it, sympathize with it. Because, I suppose, I knew I could never change it. In time I overcame that. But now, all that has happened to us in the last few months, and to our friends and to you too, Oliver—it has all accumulated and ... and solidified in my mind, so that, while I am trying not to loathe India, I know I will never now love it. Never forgive it sufficiently, I suppose, to live in it without fear.'

'Woman dear, that cannot be the truth.'

'But it is, Oliver, it is! I wish it were not—most truly I wish it were not so, but I cannot bring myself to remain in India.'

'Laura, do you not love me then, after all?'

Tears came to my eyes at the gentleness of his tone.

'Oh, Oliver, I do! You know I do!'

'I thought so—only a few minutes ago. But if you did, you would be able to accept my life here. Is that not so?'

'No! Not under the circumstances. My experience of India has been a great deal more than merely unpleasant, Oliver. It has been terrible.'

'And only that?'

'Of course not. There have been—there were happy times and pleasant ones.'

'As there will be again. I promise you!'

I shook my head. 'Never for me,' I said. 'Never!'

A strained silence ensued, and neither of us moved.

'Then,' he said slowly, 'you are refusing me ... my home and my idea of a good and rewarding life, simply because of what has happened here in Lucknow?'

711

I am sure, now, that that was the truth, so far as there was truth in the matter at all. I took my time in answering, trying to work out in my mind just what had affected my decision. I knew I should have felt complimented by his desire for my companionship as well as my love, and by the confidence he reposed in my understanding of the affairs of Hassanganj; I had always felt that a passion that precluded comradely sharing was not love at all. Yet now some perverse impulse made me see in his vision of our joint life a selfishness in him that overrode my own interests and expectations. Perhaps it was fear at impending loss that drove me to try to mitigate that loss by seizing once again on my old, mistaken interpretation of his character.

I began to speak, coldly and in a precise and distant fashion: 'No. It is not wholly my experiences in this place …'

'Charles?'

'Of course not!' My voice held more of its customary vehemence.

'I wish I could be sure of that … but go on.' And now it was he who was cold and contained.

'I … I can acknowledge the attraction of your plans for Hassanganj, your dream of a useful, busy life—for a man. But quite apart from what I have endured here in India none of your schemes have left room for the fact that I … that I am a woman, and that as a woman I have needs and requirements separate from yours and a desire to fulfil them in my own way.'

'Oh!' For a moment he was puzzled. 'Oh! If you mean *children*, why, you can have as many as you please. Jessie will be there to deal with them!'

In fact I had not given a thought to children, but as the idea presented itself, I seized it.

'Yes—I do mean children,' I agreed warmly, 'among other things. I want to bear my children in safety, knowing they will have the chance of a normal childhood, and not end as Johnny Avery did, or Jessie's Jamie, and so many others. Is that so unreasonable?'

'No, but Hassanganj will be safe for them again, and with Jessie to help you …'

'But Hassanganj will always be India, and what peace of mind would I ever know there now? And you have never taken into account that I may be reluctant to leave my own home and family …'

'But you haven't any.'

'Or that I too have strongly developed loyalties ... and affections.'

'You are rarely sentimental,' he said, almost thoughtfully, as though he were trying to discern another meaning behind my words. His expression had changed from the puzzlement apparent at my first objections to watchfulness.

'I realize you compliment me in wishing me to share your life as fully as you have described,' I continued, trying desperately to explain myself adequately under his wary gaze, 'and once perhaps I would have been able to. But I am no longer the eager, curious young woman I was in Hassanganj. Too much has happened, I have seen and learned too much of matters of which I would sooner have remained ignorant. I have changed, Oliver. And I have learned my limitations. I could not live with my fears. I would always be watchful, suspicious, anxious that once again there would be horsemen in the night and a house on fire. Even with you I could not live in such un-ease.'

'But with peace, Laura, when things are settled ...'

'It is not peace, nor the things that can be settled. The difficulty lies in me, Oliver. I feel you are being over-riding and insensitive in not seeing that. I believe even you will live for a long while looking over your shoulder—in uncertainty. But you will have your work. Your purpose. Whatever you say, I will be much alone, with only my fears— and my memories. I cannot do it.'

'You mean that, Laura?'

I nodded, drained and miserable. His eyes travelled over my face and I became conscious of my horrid fringe of ugly hair, my thin cheeks and sunken eyes and the deplorable condition of my clothing. Conscious, too, that he had not yet understood me. In the silence that enclosed us, I recalled with anguish the many strange endearments he had used to me, telling me in Urdu that I was the light of his world, fairer than the rose and purer than the snow, and also that the ultimate words of love '*jan se aziz*', dearer than life, had been reserved for his lion-coloured acres of Hassanganj.

'What is it you *do* want, Laura?' he asked at last with such unaccustomed pleading that my throat constricted.

'Some ... some security,' I answered quietly. 'A home, perhaps, in some small English town, and a regular, expected sort of life. A quiet life.'

'Surely a husband?'

'Perhaps.'

'A husband like Charles!' His voice cut like a whiplash.

'Oh, you *fool*!' was all I could find to say, and when I looked up with blazing eyes encountered an equal anger in his.

'No, my dear. It's you that are the fool!' he answered and grabbed me to him with his one arm, holding me to him tightly. 'That's who you really want, isn't it—still, and despite everything? Perhaps you've already had a surreptitious sample of delights to come when the conventions allow. From your noble Charles. How many weary hours have been made bearable by the memory of soft sighs, languishing looks and half-expressed aspirations—the tender joys of protracted wooing?'

'How dare you! Let me go!' I was furious, but had to keep my voice low, as Captain Germon and his wife, Maria, were somewhere about in the house below us. And I was hurt, cut to the quick by his words and the tone in which he had spoken them.

'No! Not yet. Hear me out. I've chosen you because I see in you all the qualities I want in the woman who is to be my life's companion. You are realistic, ruthless and honest—generally. You are capable of humour, generosity and sincerity—usually. You have energy and initiative and are as stubborn as a mule. All admirable qualities, and I appreciate them in you as much as I acknowledge them in myself. Your only weakness is that you have been reared to believe a man loves a woman solely because she *is* a woman. I'm no longer capable of that sort of love. I have had it—and often—but it is not enough. But you— you continue to think you must be cosseted as a weaker creature, protected from the buffetings of fate. Though how you can fool yourself that anyone (and least of all Charles) is going to take such a view of your character, after the way you have battled through this siege, is beyond my comprehension.'

'Will you let me go!' I muttered through clenched teeth, near to tears.

'No! Be quiet and listen to me! You say you do not want to be alone with your fears and your memories. What you mean is that you know you will not receive from me the conventional attentions you could expect from a man like Charles. In your heart you want me to dance attendance on you, as Charles would do, and perhaps has done, making you the pivot of my besotted mind. But I am not besotted, I love you with honesty, and I am offering you a great deal more than an ever-ready hand with a chair or a door or a carriage step. Oh, I desire you! Do not doubt that. I want, and intend, to love you, to make love to you, to bed you, whichever the discreet euphemism may be that you best understand and will accept ... not now, woman, at the moment you are about as appetizing as a navvy! But that is what I intend, and by God, Laura, no miss-ish haverings on your part now are going to prevent me. I mean to marry you. The only thing that will stop me is the honest assurance from you that you love Charles—not me. In that case, believe me, I will desist immediately and leave you free to pursue your suburban idyll with him in England. But not until I have that assurance from you will I give up hope of you.'

'How can you speak as you do? Oh, Oliver, you must know I love you and you only.'

'No, damn it! Hoped it, thought it, felt it sometimes—but known it ... never!'

'But I do love you, most truly and with all my heart and have thought that I had conveyed my feeling to you adequately. You are just being cynical. Because you are angry.'

'Cynical? Perhaps. I have had enough experience of your sex to make cynicism pardonable. But the truth is that, even sometimes as I kissed you, I have remembered something. Something that I would sooner forget and cannot.'

'What?'

'The expression in your eyes once, when I caught them meeting Charles's eyes. In a mirror in Hassanganj. Do you remember? You were very embarrassed. And annoyed, naturally.'

'I remember. But that was so long ago. What I felt then for Charles was ... hero-worship, I suppose, or perhaps a sort of aggravated sentimentality. You can call it anything you like. It was not love as I know love is now—with you. You must believe that, Oliver.'

'Yet you have never looked at me in quite that fashion.'

'Oh, nonsense!' I said sharply. 'Now who is expecting the ridiculous inanities of "protracted wooing"?'

'Hmph!' He looked down at me quizzically, then released me, but held one hand. 'Then, Laura, what has all this been about?'

'I don't know. Could it be that we just enjoy quarrelling? Or is it about other things, things quite different to any we have mentioned?'

715

His cheek was laid against my hair, and I could sense his attention to my words.

'Yes?'

'Perhaps ... perhaps it is about the peepul grove that starry night and the poor Wilkinses with their frightful eyeless torn faces and the flies gorging themselves in the opened bellies. Perhaps it is about Elvira, who must have been so frightened before they killed her. Perhaps it is about little Johnny screaming to his death in a bed of orange cannas; or Connie, who must have known what was coming, even though she would not learn the language. Perhaps it is about a scream I heard that day in the ice-house thatch, and a shot I fired into a man's living face. Perhaps it is about the desperate sense of isolation we all knew in Wajid Khan's *zenana*, or about smallpox and cholera. Perhaps it is about ... the awful smell when poor dainty Emily lay dying, or about Mr Roberts shooting himself in despair, or about you lying sunstruck in your own blood on a sandbank.'

I paused and shivered a little in the chill of those memories, and he drew me to him again.

'Or was it perhaps really about me?' I went on. 'All about me? My own fear, my loneliness, my hurt? Perhaps it is really about my hunger, these dirty clothes I have worn so long, the heat and now the cold? Perhaps it is about the fact that I know I cannot live with the chance that any or all of these things might happen again; that I am a coward and tired—old in my soul and bleak in my heart. Perhaps it is because I cannot love your welfare ... more than my own safety.'

He sighed, removed his arm from my shoulders and moved over to the balustrade, where he stood looking down at the almost invisible city.

'Yes. I believe you are right, Laura. You love me—but not enough. If it were not so, you would not allow this ... this episode to stand between us and happiness.'

'You said yourself that I was realistic. I know that love will not always fill my life, or yours. However ecstatic our passion, there must come a time when ... when equilibrium returns, when we will have learned to take each other as a matter of course; and then, well, you would have Hassanganj, your work, your accustomed life. I would have what? A half-suppressed fear, an enormous distrust of the people among whom I lived, and all the disillusionment that this has brought me.'

'But in that time, as you have termed it, of "ecstatic passion", is it not possible that you might have been cured of your fear? That I might have cured you? I would try.'

I shook my head.

'It is too much. Oh, Oliver, my dear, it is too much!'

For a long time we stood together in silence at the balustrade. The night was almost quiet. When at last he spoke, there was finality in his tone and a note of something that might have been resignation.

'I have said—more than once—that we are well-matched and equal, you and I, and it is so. Just now in anger, and in the fear you have yourself admitted, you rejected my wish to share my life with you as fully as I know how and in the only way I know how—in Hassanganj and India. It is not difficult to understand what you feel about India, and I do understand. But I have nothing else to offer you, Laura, particularly since I believe that you can change, and shall continue to hope that you will change.

'Oh, Laura, I too have known days of fear, and many of them, when death would have come as a relief to me. I struggled to stay alive, and to believe in life, because once very briefly I had held you in my arms, and because in the worst of those moments I never ceased to hold you in my mind. So you must allow me to go on hoping—in my own way. I will not bother you further with plans for marriage or a life out here; I will not bother you at all. But I must believe, I will hope that, after a time, when you have been back to England and tried to take up the old life again, you will learn your mistake and let me know. You know that I love you; now believe that I will wait for you in patience and faithfully. But I will not bother you again. It is up to you now to tell me when you are ready to come to me. You must discover your own mind without my interference or aid, so that you will never say that I coerced you into a life not to your liking. Do you understand?'

I nodded, then laid my head back against his shoulder, indulging myself with a moment of sweet physical content. Then I turned and buried my face in his shoulder and felt his arm come around me. Perhaps I expected him to kiss me. It would have been natural.

'I will not ask you again,' he reiterated. 'Now it is up to you, my darling. Oh, my darling!' But though I closed my eyes in anticipation of his lips, I felt myself released, and opened them to find him walking slowly away from me into the cold night.

CHAPTER 3

On the 130th day of the siege we received two welcome pieces of news: the Delhi Column was on its way to the Alum Bagh and Sir Colin Campbell, the Commander in Chief, had arrived in Cawnpore to direct the battle for our relief.

The semaphore stood ready on the tower of the Resident's House, but no signal came from the Alum Bagh. It was surmised that the instructions sent there for the construction of the machine had gone astray, and once again a messenger set out with new plans and orders. The erection of the second semaphore was now a matter of urgency, since there could be no delay in our receiving information as to when Sir Colin actually arrived, or when his force was to march on to the Dilkusha Palace, which would be the last halt before the final thrust through the outskirts of Lucknow to the Residency.

Finally an answering signal was received from the distant palace, and then our anxiety switched to keeping our own machine in workable order, for the pandies took the greatest delight in trying to shoot it down, sometimes managing this feat and often damaging the semaphore.

'Willing to bet the first damned message was safely received,' Oliver said sourly when we heard of the message from the Alum Bagh. 'They were probably just trying to decipher the mixture of schoolboy Greek and worse French in which the plans and instructions were sent, in case they fell into the pandies' hands.'

'What a pity you were not at the other end to lend the assistance of your excellent education,' Charles answered caustically.

'It is, isn't it?' his brother agreed, but before the contention could grow Kate broke in: 'These messengers and spies wear so few clothes, it always astonishes me that they are able to conceal the messages they carry. Can't think where they put 'em; it's amazing any at all get through safely.'

'Oh, not so difficult,' Charles assured her. 'They hollow out the soles of their shoes, or carry them in ready-cracked bamboo staves—so that if caught, y'see, the bamboo will break at an innocent section—and in their hair. Early on, a man got in with a message in his ear and it took the doctors more than an hour to extract it.'

'Or placed in a quill and inserted in the rectum,' Oliver added instructively, but solely to annoy his relative. Before Charles could remonstrate with him on his indelicacy, Jessie nodded over her knitting and said, 'Aye! That would be the best place, no doubt!' and even Charles had the grace to smile.

Our interview on the roof of Captain Germon's post had not resulted in any alteration of Oliver's usual habits. He was with us each evening for a time, but now we remained in the Gaol sooner than go for an intimate walk, for we had learned that privacy held greater dangers for us than any supposed impropriety. That day he had appeared with another gift, a tongue in a hermetically sealed tin.

'Cow's, not horse's,' he had said as he sat himself down on Charles's chair, while Charles went on to the verandah to open the offering with a bayonet.

'Dare we ask where it came from?' said Kate.

'Certainly not. That's Toddy's secret. Only hope it's not flyblown.'

The meat looked and smelled fresh and, when Charles had resignedly seated himself on an upturned box, we each cut ourselves a small slice of the delicacy. Oliver put aside some for Toddy and Ishmial, and after some hesitation we allowed ourselves to be persuaded to finish what remained.

'I was down the mines again today,' Oliver said as we finished. 'You were right, Laura. It is infinitely preferable to be shot at in the open air than to anticipate being shot at down there.' He moved his stool so that he could lean his back against the wall and stretch out his long legs.

'I still think you are foolish to go down, Oliver. You aren't up to the strain, and you couldn't move quickly enough if you had to get out in a hurry. You're too big!'

'I'm not as big as Kavanagh, and he spends so much time down there in the darkness, he'll come up one day to find he's grown claws like a badger. Curious fellow that Kavanagh. You know him, I suppose, Charles?'

'Everyone knows Kavanagh. The biggest braggart and the most confounded bounder in the place!'

'That so?'

'Och, sure now, Charles,' protested Kate. 'The man's had a rough time of it and he's been doing his best for us all, in his way. There's been no one like him at the mining since Captain Fulton was killed, and he's lost a child, you know, and his wife's been wounded too. And did you ever know an Irishman who didn't talk too much?'

'He's very warlike in his attitudes now, but how did he start life?' Oliver asked.

'Oh, just a clerk,' said Charles, 'an uncovenanted civilian. If you ask me, this business has been a godsend to him. Always fawning around the generals and the staff officers and giving advice on the native character and so on. An insufferable bounder. I hear he has a large family and many debts.'

'Well, that would explain his anxiety about money, I suppose. Never talks to me of anything else, and in the intervals spends his time totting up rows of figures on little scraps of paper he keeps in his helmet. I thought he was ill today. Restless as the devil; kept muttering to himself and once I swear he was blubbering about something down in that infernal smelly blackness. Couldn't think what had got into him.'

'Perhaps he has had too much of the mines. Is he becoming a little hysterical from the strain?' I wondered.

'Could be, I suppose. And I wouldn't blame him. I might come up gibbering like a maniac myself one day. Don't like it at all.'

'I was watching the semaphore at work at midday,' Kate said after a while. 'Most ingenious, but a terribly exposed position and the firing was very heavy.'

'The *Baba-log* are using it for target practice,' Charles agreed. 'It's been down a few times now. A fellow from our battery volunteered to put it back together again this morning and was lucky to get down with his skin in one piece. He says the wind up there is enough to cut you in two, never mind the pandies' bullets.'

'There's great interest in the fortunes of the thing down at the Ferret Box too,' Oliver concurred. 'I am told that a couple of excursions up the tower should be good for a Victoria Cross at least. Anxiety to find the courage to volunteer to repair the machine is outweighed only by the anxiety that it might not be shot down again.'

'Still the old cynical Oliver,' Kate observed without rancour.

'Merely because I am entertained by my fellows' careful weighing up of risk versus glory? But I assure you it is true.'

'I've no doubt it is. I heard Captain Masterson discussing what the perks would be if he were to lead a sortie as far as the Tehri Kothi. It took no great eloquence to persuade him only a grave would be his reward, so he stayed within the entrenchment.'

'And why may not a soldier anticipate or plan for decorations?' asked Charles. 'In any other profession, rewards of some sort are part of the inducement to taking it up, and God knows the pecuniary advantages in winning a medal for valour are insignificant enough!' He was heated, and I recognized the look in Oliver's eyes that meant he had achieved what he had set out to do.

'No reason at all. No reason. But I cannot see why I should be considered cynical for merely observing—not decrying, mind you—what is surely a cynical practice.'

'Yes,' Kate said judiciously. 'I suppose it is a little dubious, trying for a decoration in order to get the pension attached to it. But surely understandable; as Charles says, a soldier's pay is scarcely princely and even the small annuity carried by these things can make a difference.'

Later, when the dark had fallen, I went to the verandah steps with Oliver, but he only pressed my hand as he said goodnight. Filled with a sense of incompletion in myself, I watched him walk away. Nothing had really been settled by our long, troubled talk on Germon's roof. We had used many words, but when it came to the point, I felt that we had failed to say anything to each other. As on countless occasions in the last couple of days, I told myself that if he would only give me an opportunity to explain myself more coherently, more plainly, he must understand my point of view and accede to my wishes. It looked, however, as though he had decided not to give me that chance. I knew he loved me. I loved him in return, yet somehow we had not only failed to reach an understanding but had perverted the sense of each other's words and allowed ourselves to be diverted from the main issue by his jealousy of Charles and my justifiable annoyance at that jealousy. We had ourselves erected the barrier that was now between us.

When I got home from the hospital a day or two after the tinned tongue supper I found the whole entrenchment buzzing with talk and the name of Kavanagh on every lip.

'Major Bonner was there, my dear Mrs Barry, actually there with the General and members of the staff when it was all decided, and he never breathed a word to me of what was afoot. He's so responsible, Major Bonner, but I really do think he could have dropped a hint to his own wife.'

Mrs Bonner, sipping toast-water in our kitchen, was not quite sure whether to be pleased or chagrined that her husband had been implicated in the latest drama without her knowledge or approval.

I asked what had happened.

'Well, Mr Kavanagh last night volunteered to make his way to the Alum Bagh through the enemy lines to guide Sir Colin Campbell's column into the city. This afternoon there was a signal flag on the Alum Bagh—and Henry Kavanagh is safe.

'Well, really it gave them all quite a turn!' Mrs Bonner continued. 'You see, apparently General Outram had said that he could only permit the venture if Mr Kavanagh could persuade him, the General I mean, that he could pass as a native. With all that red-gold hair and those blue eyes, I suppose the General thought he was safe enough, and that he would hear no more of the matter from Kavanagh.

'Major Bonner assures me, however, that the General was most intrigued by the idea and by Mr Kavanagh. Quite taken up he was, the General, by the enthusiasm and spirit with which Mr Kavanagh outlined his scheme. And then, of course, Major Bonner says that the General has been worried for some time about getting messages through to the Alum Bagh. He had given instructions that Sir Colin should approach us through the very outskirts of the city, from over the canal, but without a guide; why, you know what those little lanes and narrow roads are like? But Mr Kavanagh knows the place like the back of his hand, so he told the General, and would make an excellent guide.'

Mrs Bonner gently righted the muslin cap on her head and looked a threat at Minerva, who was on the point of bursting excitedly into her narrative.

'Well then, last night after dinner, some of the officers of the staff were enjoying a cheroot when, to their complete amazement, a strange native entered the room—wearing shoes, mind you—and seated himself, actually seated himself, on a chair in the presence of all the gentlemen. Naturally, everyone was both astonished and horrified at this ... this quite extraordinary lack of manners on the part of a native, and two or three of the gentlemen tried to throw him out of the room. Even General Outram did not recognize him at first, for he was wearing a turban, you see, and tight-fitting trousers and a muslin shirt, an orange silk jacket and a cummerbund.' Mrs Bonner, in the best tradition of Anglo-Indian womanhood, who equates a deliberate mispronunciation of Indian words and phrases with social superiority, said 'commerband'. 'He carried a sword and a dagger and had leaned a great embossed buffalo-hide shield against the chair.

'Well, of course, Mrs Barry, when at last someone did see through his disguise, you can imagine the surprise! Major Bonner said he couldn't, actually *could not*, believe his own ears when Mr Kavanagh began speaking English like an Englishman. And—oh yes!—his face, neck and hands had been coloured with lamp black and oil, so that really, the Major says, there was absolutely no telling him apart from a rowdy from the bazaars. Of course, everyone laughed and joked and the General himself wound the turban more correctly, but at last the time came for Mr Kavanagh and his native guide to leave. The most affecting moment it was, Major Bonner says, quite harrowing indeed. It suddenly struck them all that it might well be the last time they set eyes on the brave man. They shook hands and wished him luck and at the last Captain Sitwell prevailed on him to carry a loaded double-barrelled pistol—so that he could despatch himself, don't you know, in case of capture and the sort of lingering death which would most certainly be his in such case.'

'Oh, mama!' Minerva covered her face with her hands and shuddered. Mrs Bonner's many empty chins quivered with complacent pride in the effect she had produced on her daughter.

'Quite, Minerva!' said she. 'Kavanagh was carrying the message and a letter of introduction to Sir Colin in his turban, and Major McIntyre was to raise a flag at midday to indicate that the hero had arrived safely in the Alum Bagh. I declare ... the whole thing has truly been most romantic, wouldn't you agree? The Major says it will constitute an epic for the example of all English young men in the future. And to think that my dear husband has had a part in it all!'

'And he will get a decoration—and the pension that goes with it?' I asked.

'Certainly. And had he failed, I am sure that his grateful country would not have let his family starve.'

'And what of the native spy? What do they say his name is?' said Kate.

'Kanauji Lal, I believe.'

'I trust he has also got through safely?'

'Oh, well, I really don't know, but I expect he must have.' Mrs Bonner had obviously never given the matter a thought, but I could not help wondering just how far Mr Kavanagh would have got without the help of his brown-skinned guide.

'And will his bravery also, I wonder, constitute a shining example for our young men?'

Kate was being deliberately provocative and I loved her for it. While not wishing to denigrate the daring of Mr Kavanagh, it seemed to me that the exploits of men like Kanauji Lal, Ungud, and many others of the *cossids* or native messengers, were even more worthy of praise. Mr Kavanagh, after all, had obviously risked his life deliberately for the gain of himself and his family. The native spies had risked theirs, and repeatedly, in contradiction of all they held most dear on the natural plane, to defend an ancient and honourable but nebulous ideal—the 'keeping of salt'.

I suppose Mrs Bonner made some reply to Kate's acid comment, but I did not hear it, for my mind was once again on my own inner troubles. Here was I, trying to take an impartial view and coming out on the side of the Indian, more sympathetic, more truly appreciative of the Indian's bravery than that of the white man. Would I have been capable of doing the same thing a year before? Before I had begun to know the mind and opinions of Oliver Erskine? Had he affected the direction and tenor of my inmost thoughts so radically? Or was it due more to a justice of mind that my father had always striven to inculcate in me in his eccentric and unorthodox fashion?

But, having thought once of Oliver, I continued to think of him, while our visitor, Kate and Jessie talked on, and young Minerva, sitting on her hands with inelegant eagerness, drank in every word that passed between her elders.

CHAPTER 4

That evening, for the first time since he had left the Gaol for his quarters in the Farhat Baksh Palace, Oliver failed to visit us. Instead, Toddy-Bob loitered in to tell us that his master had drawn a late duty in the new mine being driven under the garden wall of the Chathar Manzil Palace, designed to unmask two batteries of our guns when the time came for us to support the incoming force of Sir Colin Campbell.

My heart sank at this intelligence. I had made up my mind while Mrs Bonner was expatiating on the heroism of Mr Kavanagh to make one final attempt at explaining my mind to Oliver. Rather, that was what I thought I intended to do, but, more accurately, I hoped that a further conversation with him would help me to know my own mind with greater thoroughness and precision. I suppose I was beginning to waver in my conviction that not even for his sake would I consent to live in the *mofussil* of India again, but as usual I was finding it difficult to not only recognize but also admit error. Perhaps what I really wished was to be persuaded to live his life; not given an ultimatum to do so— or else. A justifiable enough sentiment, no doubt, but on the other hand was it not I who had introduced the acrimony into our discussion on Germon's roof, and I, in fact, who had invited the ultimatum?

Toddy had found us, Kate, Charles and myself, sitting at the table writing our first letters home. Jessie, having put Pearl to bed, had settled down by the lantern to her knitting, and when I had finished my own letters, I would write hers at her dictation, for she had never been to school.

I found it uncommonly difficult to compose my thoughts, and not only because they were occupied with Oliver Erskine and my own problems. England, Mount Bellew, my relatives, had all receded so far into the background of my consciousness during these last months that I could not now make them real to my imagination. With so much to tell them, so much to explain, where could I begin, and what would they most want to know? I was relieved when, after looking at a blank sheet of paper for twenty minutes, Charles thrust it away from him and exclaimed, 'Deuce take it, I cannot go on with this! I do not know how to put it, and they will never understand my decision.'

'What decision?' I enquired, in order to postpone the moment of putting pen to paper.

'I have decided not to go home with you and the baby, Laura.'

'But, Charles, whatever else can you do? Of course you are coming home. Everyone is coming home.'

'No, they are not, you know. The women, of course, and the men who are sick or too old or in the Civils, but most of them will be staying on. They are needed here. I … I have been trying to tell you for the last couple of days, but—well, I have volunteered to remain on. With the Army. With the Volunteer Cavalry, in fact, Lousada Barrow's lot. I cannot turn my back on everything that has happened here, and sail home to England as though I have had no part in it and no interest in the outcome. Naturally, if Emily had lived, there would have been no option for me, and no necessity either for me to feel as I do. I have been thinking of it for some time—ever since the relief. I had to face the fact of leaving then, so I began to wonder whether I could.'

'But, Charles, you have obligations to the living too, to Pearl and your mother, even to Emily's father. Have you not considered your position with the firm?'

'I know, I know. I have given it a great deal of thought. As to the baby, she will be well enough with you and Jessie and her grandparents for a year or two. And as to Hewitt, Flood & Hewitt, I believe they will keep my place open for me when they know what I am doing out here. If they don't, well, my own income will suffice for Pearl and myself until I can find something else at home, or perhaps out here, who knows? To tell the truth, Laura, I'd be relieved to know I need not go back to the City. Never was the life for me. I believe I told you so a long time ago.'

'But you are not a soldier, Charles, and to choose to remain out here after all you have been through …'

'I believe I might have made a better soldier than a businessman. It was what I always wished to be when I was young and, don't you see, it is just because of all we have been through here that I feel I must stay?'

'To avenge Emily? That is ridiculous, Charles. A heathen conception.'

'I do not agree with you, and it's not only Emily … all the others too. I suppose you cannot agree with me, but I feel that the least I can do, having lost my own, is to try to make this country safe for the womenfolk that remain. And for those that will come after us, I suppose.'

'It's not your country, Charles. You are only a visitor. It's not your quarrel.'

'But the quarrel has become mine. How could it be otherwise?'

For a moment we were silent, as I thought over this new development and wondered at the extraordinary workings of the male mind. Jessie's needles clicked comfortably on and Kate regarded Charles over the top of the steel-rimmed spectacles she wore for close work.

'And how in the world will you ever find yourself settling down in England again, Charles, after the sort of life you'll be living out here with the Army?' Kate asked eventually.

'I'll face that when it comes. As I say, perhaps I won't have to settle down in England again. Perhaps I'll find something more congenial out here, in the Army—or in Calcutta with my own firm. That is a distinct possibility, after all.'

'I see.'

Another pause; then Charles shifted on his stool and said, with his head bent, not looking at us, 'The truth is, I cannot face going back to Mount Bellew and remembering things as they were when we left it … without Emily. And also, I'll make no secret of it, I have found myself drawn to what is called a life of action. I'd never experienced it before, but I find I enjoy the company of likeminded men, the sensation one knows on completing a hard job well done … the companionship, I suppose. I've never had a real sense of purpose before, and I used to envy Oliver that when I accompanied him around his estate. It's not something one finds behind a desk piling up money for other people's benefit. In any event, however absurd it may seem to you or to the people at home, I have made up my mind. I'm staying here.'

Could he still be thinking of eventually becoming partner and heir to Oliver, as Emily had once wished? It seemed likely and, if so, Charles was taking a step more likely to ensure that outcome than going back to England would have done.

He took up his pen and again drew his paper towards him.

'I will postpone writing to Mount Bellew and Dissham, but I must get a letter off to old Chalmers in Calcutta. They say mail will be despatched as soon as Colin Campbell reaches us, and I want to arrange everything possible for you, Jessie and the baby, Laura. I have already written to my bankers and ordered them to make out a draft payable to you for all expenses. Chalmers will see to it that you find berths on a good ship. I'll leave it to him to decide whether the Cape route or overland will be better. You and Jessie are going to need clothing and so on, so I suggest you spend a few weeks with the Chalmers's, resting and buying what you need. I'm sure they'll be happy to have you for as long as need be. Hospitable people, and after all ...'

'We will be survivors!' I ended with a sigh.

Charles bent to his work, and I again made an effort to compose my mind to correspondence.

It would be spring, more likely early summer, in England when we arrived. I made myself remember the woods around Mount Bellew; new leaves in the chilly air, primroses spilling down the banks, bluebells in the hazel thickets and, later, summer fields starred with daisies and buttercups. Hackneyed things, however lovely—the type of memories that genteel expatriate females write poems about for inclusion in the pious pages of *The Quiver*. The reality of existence in England, even my own existence, would not return to my mind. Yet, that was what I wanted: calm, secure, prosaic England, where I could take myself, my surroundings, my way of life, all for granted. England, where there would be no need to keep my inner forces eternally mustered to battle with the climate, the language, the customs and prejudices and the cruelties of a strange place and a strange race. All I wanted was to sink back into long-accustomed, unthinking, comfortable routine.

But a strange thing happened. When I tried to remember what that accustomed routine had been, I found myself instead back in the routine, very vividly remembered, of the Hassanganj day: the early morning tea on the verandah, the rides, the Urdu lessons, overseeing, with Emily, the running of the house, meals in the stately dining-room, reading at night under the chandelier in the drawing-room with Oliver Erskine opposite me, absorbed in his book.

I pulled myself together. That had gone. The Hassanganj I had known could never now be re-experienced. And the Mount Bellew I had known? Could that be rediscovered? Would I really be able to settle down to being my aunt's dependable right hand again—for with Emily dead, it was unlikely that I would be allowed to leave the house and find a position, as I used to tell myself I some day would. Was dull, pedestrian England, the England of small towns and kindly unimaginative people that I knew, really going to suffice me for the rest of my days? Could I ever submerge the self that had appeared in India, and become again the dutiful, grateful, philosophic poor relation that I once had been?

'I wonder,' I said to no one in particular, 'will they find us very changed? When we get home?'

'Aye! Aye! Unco' changed,' nodded Jessie sagely without glancing up from her knitting. 'Ye were a bonnie bittie lass a twelvemonth since, Miss Laura, and now ye are a woman grown in heart and soul!'

'How do you know that, Jess?' I smiled. 'A good rest and a bath or two, and perhaps no one will know what I've been through.'

'No, no! 'Tis plain to the blindest eye that ye are no thoughtless lass now.'

'But I never was a thoughtless lass,' I protested with some indignation.

'Maybe no', but then ye didna think o' the same things, nor in the same ways.'

That at least was true, and when I found Charles watching me intently, I blushed as I remembered some of the things I used to think about.

Kate leaned her elbows on the table, put her chin on her hands and gazed dreamily at the smoke-grimed wall.

'Indeed, and which of us will ever be the same again? These months will be ... well, like a sort of watershed, will they not? A barrier in our lives, over which we've had to struggle and which will always separate what we were from what we have become. Perhaps every life has to meet some such moment of truth, some point when direction and energy are all diverted into unforeseen channels and we are forced into becoming, if not new people, at least different people.'

'A point of rest? In a lifetime ... in a character?' The idea pleased me. The notion that events might sometimes be focused—like a burning glass—to a point where an inner and vital transmutation was inevitable.

'A wha'?' queried Jess.

'A point of rest. That feature in a painting to which one's eyes are first and most immediately drawn. The focal point of the composition. Everything else radiates out from it or, conversely, appears to lead to it. I wonder ... will this little room, smoky, dark, smelly, full of insects and discomforts, will it eventually prove to have been the "point of rest" of my life? When I am an old lady, on my deathbed perhaps, will it be this small space I remember most vividly, more vividly than Mount Bellew or Genoa, or Hassanganj, or all the other places I will by then have seen?'

'Praise be, an' it's been a safe refuge to us a'!' Jessie said gravely, more at home, in her sane way, with practicalities than philosophizing.

A safe refuge. Yes, that it had been for all of us but one. But had the tiny room defended me from anything but physical injury? I had seen too much of death to value my own life lightly, yet that night I began to wonder whether I had not lost something that was of even more importance than life. Put baldly, the words seem—and are—melodramatic. I had discovered during the past months that, no matter how painful the physical support of life may be, living is always worthwhile. One of the sharpest sorrows I had known was that I had not discerned Mr Roberts's failing confidence in his own capacity for life, had failed to try to imbue him with something of my own hard-won but robust hopefulness. Losing Oliver Erskine would not kill me; would not even make me wish to die. But I was afraid of the long struggle that must ensue to adapt myself once again to living without receiving, or being able to give, love. No, I did not want to die! But only God and I can ever know how little I wanted to live a loveless life.

I found myself longing, suddenly, for Oliver's presence. I looked at my watch. After eight o'clock; surely he must be almost finished with his stint in the mines? He was bound to call in before long. I strained my ears for his step, and joyfully heard a brisk masculine tread mount the steps to the verandah. In my happy expectation, I had almost risen to welcome him, when instead of Oliver, Toddy-Bob, with a large grin on his equine face, his boot-button eyes snapping with excitement, hurried in exclaiming, 'Miss Laura, Mr Charles, sir ... there's a beacon been lit at the Alum Bagh. You can see it from the walls. Sir Colin's arrived and safely! 'Tis a rare fine sight. Do all come out and see it!'

His enthusiasm was not to be gainsaid, although the night was cold. We grabbed shawls and cloaks and followed him into the darkness, through the ruined buildings to a vantage point on the old stockade.

Appearing almost close in the sharp clear air, the beacon blinked in blue flame from the top of the Alum Bagh Palace.

Half-an-hour's ride away, somewhere among the ancient trees that surrounded the palace, Sir Colin perhaps was watching our answering beacon aflame on the top of the tower of the Resident's House, while round him his troops, six thousand of them it was said, pitched their tents, and fed their mounts, cleaned their weapons and discussed the battle yet to come. Half an hour's ride away lay deliverance.

I felt a lump rise in my throat and noticed everyone had fallen silent. Then someone raised a thin cheer from those of us who had ventured into the cold night and bothered to view the beacon. 'Not long now,' an elderly man muttered near me. 'By God, it won't be long now!'

'I tol' you it was a fine sight!' Toddy reminded us triumphantly, almost as though the beacon was all his own invention. Then, after enquiring whether we could find our way back to the Gaol, he took himself off on his own pursuits.

Some of us lingered on the wall, for despite the cold it was a fine night, crackling with starlight. The blue flame among the distant trees held our attention as it rose, then flickered and fell, to rise again with a sudden flare.

It was the first time I had been out in deep night since the beginning of the siege. Intrigued by the novelty, I walked a little way from the others, looking down, not into the city beyond the walls, but at the entrenchment lying quiet within them.

We had long been short of candles and oil for lamps, and the enclosure lay in almost total darkness, with only here and there a glimmer from a saucer dip brightening a window frame. The tumbled remnants of the buildings, bulked against each other in the darkness, gave an impression of solidity and strength denied them in the light of day.

The enemy's fire was so sporadic that it could be disregarded, and the scene below me, dim and disguised, was one of peace. Men went about their business quietly, moving guns and supplies, seeing to their weapons or just gossiping with friends as they chewed on empty pipestems. For a while I stood and watched the quiet movements, then, hugging my shawl around me, turned and clambered along the parapet to a higher point which would afford a better view.

I picked my way for some distance along the shot-step of a fairly long stretch of uninterrupted wall, and then found it would be easier to descend at the point I had reached than to retrace my steps to my companions. I could not hear their voices and, looking back into the darkness, realized that I would not be able to see them even had they not returned to our quarters. Before me a few broken steps led to the ground, and once down I paused to get my bearings. The area was uncommonly deserted and I realized I must have headed towards the river and perhaps was now near one of the far batteries deemed useless and abandoned when General Outram enlarged the perimeter. The ground was hazardous with rubble, brick shards and stones.

Carefully I walked towards the outline of an unlit but substantial-looking building and, as I did so, heard a fall of gravel behind me. No one had been near me on the wall. Certainly no one could have watched me descend the steps to the ground. Alarmed, however, in spite of myself, I stopped and cast a glance over my shoulder; but only darkness and the jagged silhouette of the wall against the sky met my eyes. Again I started off, with senses alert to every sound. I had progressed but a few steps when again I heard the clink of stone against stone behind me. I did not pause, but hurried on, casting about for some sign of a path that would make my walking easier. There could be no doubt that I was being followed. I could hear footsteps, no longer stealthy, and quickened my own. I was in the shadow of a ruined stable. I could see the stalls for the horses, but the gates had been wrenched away for firewood and the beams of the roof had fallen in, bringing their burden of thatch with them. For a moment I wondered whether it would serve if I ran in and crouched in the depths of the debris until my pursuer had passed, but common sense told me he was too close. I broke into a stumbling run and had reached the end of the building when he caught me.

A heavy hand clutched at my shoulder and spun me round. I almost fell, but found myself caught up and looking into the leering, ugly face of Corporal Alfred Tuppit.

Immediately I hit out with both my fists, though it would have been more sensible if I had screamed. The man was strong and had no difficulty in imprisoning both my hands behind my back with one of his. I writhed and wrenched and kicked out at him, but my old worn slippers had no power to hurt.

'Well now, you're a proper smart one, ain't you? Thought you'd played me a fine trick in the 'ospital, didn't you, with your little tin and your insec' and all? But you're goin' to find out your mistake now, missie. Alf Tuppit don't like bein' made a fool of, leastways not by a frozen-faced uppity young woman like you. Goin' to take real pleasure in givin' you what you deserve, young miss, and right now!' His voice was thick with drink and he smelt abominably of liquor and sweat.

'Take your dirty hands off me, Tuppit!' I said breathlessly. 'You can't get away with this. I know your name and everyone knows what a thieving, lying fraud you are. Let me go!' I spoke aloud, which offended the gentleman, who had whispered himself, and he clapped his free hand over my mouth.

'Never you fear. You'll not tell anyone anythin'—not by the time I've finished with you, you won't. Been followin' you I 'ave, ever since you went up on the wall back there. You played right into my 'ands, comin' along all this way by yourself.'

He laughed in my face and the fumes from his breath sickened me. Gagged by his hand, I could use only my eyes and ears to help myself.

Not a light was visible, but I thought I could hear voices far off, men's voices and a child crying. Perhaps we were near the lines occupied by the loyal sepoys. If I could hear them, then they could hear me. Fear lent me strength. I jerked back my head from the imprisoning hand and managed to scream 'Help! Help me!' twice before Tuppit silenced me again. His small eyes were furious and he swore at me, snarling like an ill-tempered bazaar pi-dog. 'By God! You won't want to scream again, not for a whiles you won't!' And he hooked his foot behind my ankles and threw me to the ground.

Even in my alarm, I knew the voices in the distance had stopped. Had they merely moved away, or was someone listening for my scream to be repeated? Frantically I struggled with the man above me, feeling the sharp masonry cut into the flesh of my back and arms. Then, why I do not know, Tuppit's grip on my mouth relaxed for a second and immediately I sank my teeth into his dirty flesh and bit with all my might. He let go, cursing, taking a swipe at my head as he did so, and gave me a savage blow across the ear. I was too busy screaming at the top of my lungs to notice the blow at the time, and finding his grip on me had loosened, I struggled to my knees, still screeching hysterically.

Running footsteps approached, and voices. I screamed louder and Tuppit struck me again as I knelt there, then made off into the darkness. But I could not stop screaming.

'Laura! Laura! My God, what has happened? Laura, it's me, Charles. It's all right now, Laura. All right, I'm here.'

'Charles! Oh, Charles, Charles!' was all I could sob. He raised me gently to my feet and put his arms around my shoulders; my screams gave way to gasping sobs and the sobs to tears.

When at last I calmed sufficiently to know what was happening, I found four or five other men had gathered around, their curious eyes taking in my dishevelled hair and disarranged clothing.

'Come now,' Charles soothed me. 'You'll be better off in the quarters. Can you walk? It's all right, gentlemen, this lady has had a fright of some sort, but I'll get her back to her people now.'

We moved away, the men remaining in a little group to watch us go. We were much further from the Gaol than I had realized, almost at the northernmost edge of the perimeter, and it was not surprising that the area had been almost deserted. We walked slowly, Charles's arm supporting me, and as we went I sobbed out my story.

'I became anxious about you after a time,' he said when I had finished, 'and went back up the wall to fetch you in. I had seen you wander along in this direction and thought you might have lost your way back, since you cannot be familiar with this section. I could not have been too far behind you but I did not see you at all, and if you had not screamed, I would have returned to the Gaol expecting to find you there before me.'

'Oh, thank God you didn't go back, Charles, and thank you, my dear. I was never so frightened before. It ... it was horrible, horrible ... the feeling of helplessness!'

'Don't dwell on it now, it's done with, and I can fix that brute, I think, without your name being brought into the matter. He has a bad name, as you well know.'

'But what can be done to him?'

'Nothing very much, I'm afraid, this time. A few lashes at most, I suppose. I don't want you mentioned and I don't suppose you do either—your name would have to come into it if he were had up on a charge of attempted rape. There's been too much of this sort of thing going on. I believe a certain amount of summary justice without too much enquiry will suit the authorities. They'll be glad to make an example of Tuppit.'

'But what's to stop him mentioning my name,' I asked nervously. 'Telling everyone it was me?'

The thought of the satisfaction the wretched man would have in boasting and no doubt exaggerating the extent, of what he had done to me, filled me with repugnance.

'Don't worry, we'll ensure that he holds his tongue, and is uncommonly willing to do so too. You've nothing more to fear from him, Laura, I promise you.'

I was far from reassured, but it was necessary that Tuppit should be dealt with for the sake of the other women in the entrenchment, if for no other reason.

'I cannot object, I suppose, if my name does come out,' I admitted. 'After all, it was my own fault in a way, first for putting that wretched scorpion in his bed and then for wandering off alone when I knew that … that such things were taking place. But I never dreamed … I couldn't have guessed …'

'Your name will not be mentioned, Laura, I promise you, And the brute will get some, at least, of his just deserts. That too I can promise you.'

As it happened, I never did hear more of the matter and forbore from questioning Charles regarding it. No doubt, as happened at that time, condign punishment was meted out without formality or delay, and perhaps the threat of court martial or even the loss of his single stripe, was sufficient to ensure Tuppit's silence.

We had reached the Gaol, but I was reluctant to go inside and face Kate and Jessie with my tear-smudged face and telltale clothing. We sat down on the lowest step of the flight leading up to the verandah, and I tried to tidy myself. Charles's arm was still about my shoulders and I was glad of it. I leaned against him gratefully and for a moment put my aching head on his shoulder.

'Oh, Charles, I'm so tired of it all!' I whispered. 'I'm sick and tired of the unending ugliness of everything. I'm tired of all the senseless dying and the dreadful wounds I see in the hospital, and of the smells and the noises. I'm tired of being always hungry and always dirty, and

I'm so tired even of being tired. I'm tired of all my wretched memories and the dreams I have at night. I'm tired, tired.'

I began to cry again, but gently, and Charles produced a rag smelling of gun oil for me to blow my nose in.

All through the siege I had fought self-pity, knowing it consumed an energy that could be better employed elsewhere. I think I had been moderately successful in my attempts not to believe that my sufferings were, because they were mine, of a more refined or poignant nature than the sufferings of others. Now, the indignity to which I had been subjected undid a floodgate of regret, remorse and resentment at the whole tenor of my life over the past months. Suddenly everything to which I had been exposed appeared to me not only intolerable but intolerably painful, and for the first time the question, 'Why did it happen to me?' could not be denied. In a flash, all the shocks, ills and sorrows I had been required to meet and contend with swept over me in a mood of overwhelming despair.

'My poor girl,' Charles soothed, stroking my cropped head as I cried. 'My poor brave girl. Don't give way now, it's nearly over. We'll soon be away from here and, once at home, you'll learn to forget it all, to see it in another light.'

'Never,' I sniffed vehemently. 'I'll never put on a nightdress and get between clean sheets, never eat a meal off china plates, never take a hot bath in a comfortable firelit bedroom without remembering what it is like to be without them. The memories of this will have eaten into my bones.'

Charles sighed and I knew he was thinking of Emily and her death. 'In time, other things, other memories, will come to have more importance. You'll marry and have a home and children, do all the pleasant normal things of life.'

'Never!'

'But you will. You're young and life goes on, whatever happens. You are just depressed and shocked by what has happened tonight.'

It was simpler to allow him to hold his own opinion, and for a short time we sat in silence.

'This may be the last chance we have of being alone for a long time, Laura,' he said at length. 'I know, or rather I suppose, that this is not the time to mention such matters, and I do not even know if I have any chance with you now. Am I right in thinking that you and Oliver have

… have reached some sort of agreement? I don't wish to pry. It's none of my business, I know. But, well, he does seem deuced taken up with you these days, and you spend a great deal of time together, it appears. Have you an understanding?'

'No!' I answered bitterly. 'No, Charles, that is the one thing we do not have.'

'But you love him?'

I nodded my head beneath his hand.

He sighed deeply and removed his hand from my head and his arm from about my shoulders; I felt an unreasonable chill of desolation as he did so. There had been a delicious luxury in being supported, even if only physically.

'You know how I feel about you, how I have felt for a long time past. I told you once—at a time when I shouldn't have, I know—and my feelings have not altered. Recently I had begun to form some crazy notion that, if I remained out here until the country was again under control, I'd have done what I could to … to, well, soothe my own conscience in regard to Emily. Not very sensible, I suppose, but I hoped my feeling of guilt would have abated and that when it was all finished I could go home and, with a clear mind, ask you to have me.'

'Charles, I am sorry.'

'I'm too late, hm? Odd! How was it I never considered Oliver a likely rival or supplanter—for I know you did once care for me? Yet it was so obvious.'

'It was not obvious even to me until quite recently.'

He thought in silence for a while.

'But it should have been obvious to me. It would have been, had I been thinking of anything but my own unhappy affairs. After all, he is everything that most women would want. Everything that Emily wanted, in any event. You share many of his characteristics, I believe, and many of his interests too. And I suppose it is not to the man's detriment, even to you, that he is rich, of some importance and the "*Sirkar* of Hassanganj"!' There was an ironical note in his voice.

'On the contrary,' I sighed, 'I wish he were not rich or important and, most of all, I wish he were not the "*Sirkar* of Hassanganj". I cannot live there, and he can live nowhere else. Which is why we have no "understanding".'

'Yet you seemed to enjoy our time there?, You were well suited to the life.'

'But Charles, after ... this?'

'I see. I suppose it is different for a woman.'

Again there was silence. What Charles was thinking I can only guess, but at the mention of Oliver my mind had once more reverted to my problem, my choice. I wondered whether he had called in to the Gaol while I was absent and what he would say—or more probably do—when he heard of my encounter with Tuppit. At once I decided he must never know.

'How do I look now, Charles?' I asked anxiously, fingering the collar of my gown and trying to make my ugly hair as neat as possible.

'Not too bad. A bit puffy around the eyes. That's all.'

'Perhaps they'll think it's relief because of the beacon and everything,' I hoped dubiously. 'You must not mention what has happened tonight. I could not bear anyone to know—not even Kate or Oliver. Least of all Oliver.'

'As you wish.'

I smoothed my skirts, got up and walked to the top of the steps.

'Laura!' Charles laid a detaining hand on my arm. 'One moment before we go in.'

I waited. Along the verandah Mrs Bonner came to her window and banged it shut. Our door, too, was closed against the cold; a sliver of light beneath it and a soft murmur of voices told me Kate and Jessie were still up.

'In view of what you have just said, of Oliver and your not being willing to live in Hassanganj, I must say that ... that my hopes have risen a little again. Perhaps there is still reason for me to hope, and I want you to know that if, when I get home, and you are still free, I intend to ...'

I put my fingers against his lips.

'No, Charles, don't say it. I know what you mean to say, but I cannot allow you to live, however remotely, in false hope. I am too fond of you, Charles. Don't you see, I could not allow you to make a second unhappy marriage? Wasn't one mistake enough?'

'You would be no mistake. You cannot seriously expect me to think that?'

'Loving a woman who cannot return your love would be nothing else. I can never love you—now. Dear Charles, please believe me. I can never love you other than as I do at this moment.'

'I will not believe that,' he said stubbornly. 'I will not believe that. In time …'

'Never, Charles. Never!'

We faced each other in the darkness of the verandah, straining to look into each other's faces. I saw him almost as if for the first time, as in a sense it was. There was nothing left now, I realized sadly, of the confident, happy young man who had left England with his bride eighteen months before. I remembered the fresh-complexioned face with its frank blue eyes and the charming ready smile. A boy's face, cheerful, insouciant.

A man's face gazed back at me now, haggard and thin and not too clean, with unkempt whiskers, and shadows of fatigue and strain under the sunken eyes. A man's face, too, in the quiet determination it expressed.

'Laura,' he said, taking my hand, 'however little you may like it, I will continue to hope. I do not ask for encouragement. I realize that, for the moment, your thoughts and affections are not with me. But you cannot keep me from hoping. You cannot forbid it.'

Perhaps it was the new manliness in his face and manner that touched me; it could have been my memories of him as he had been. More likely it was the fact that I was grateful, not only because he had rescued me from Tuppit, but because his faltering declaration had somehow restored me in my own eyes. I was filled with a gentle, understanding affection for him.

On an impulse I reached up and kissed him quietly on his cheek. He put his arms around me, but not roughly or possessively, and for a moment we stood together in what might have appeared a loving embrace.

In that instant the door of our kitchen opened and even the dim light of the lantern must have sufficed to illumine our two forms entwined so closely together. I swung round, still smiling, expecting to see Kate, and instead found myself confronting Oliver Erskine. He stood stock-still in the yellow light for a moment and I flinched before the mingled pain and anger in his face. Then he smiled, but not pleasantly.

739

'Good evening—and goodnight!' he said to us both with mock cordiality. 'And good luck!' Without another glance, he walked swiftly up the verandah and away from us.

At once I realized the conclusion he had come to.

'No, Oliver, wait!' I cried after his retreating form, all self-respect forgotten. But he did not turn and my knees shook so that I could not run after him.

'Oh, Laura, I'm sorry—he thinks that ... Look, I'll run and fetch him back. You can explain.'

'No!' I leaned against the post of the verandah and hid my eyes behind my hand. 'No, Charles. It's no good ... there's too much to explain now, and I ... I still don't know the answers.'

'Answers?'

'I can't explain,' I said wearily. 'I can't explain.'

CHAPTER 5

Thereafter Oliver Erskine disappeared from my life as effectively as if he had abandoned the Kingdom of Oudh.

I could not sleep that night remembering the expression in his eyes. Stolidly I worked through the following day and hurried home, hoping against hope that I would find him as I often did, sitting on a stool in the kitchen with Pearl in his arms, making Jessie laugh. He did not come, however, not that night nor the next. When the third day passed without a glimpse of him, I was ready to swallow my pride. Every time I recalled the tableau he had surprised on the Gaol verandah on that night, I shivered with chagrin. What cruel fate had prompted him to discover me thus, on the one and only occasion on which I had ever approached Charles with anything like open affection? There could be no doubt of the interpretation he had put on our unfortunate embrace, and I fretted with anxiety to make myself right in his eyes again, wishing I had allowed Charles to run after him and force him to return for an explanation. Yet, what explanation could I make that would not give the impression that I had discovered that I must have him, Hassanganj or no? And was that so? Was it not better to leave him in the belief that I had in truth found a more acceptable alternative?

Confused, wounded by his readiness to believe the worst of me, forgetting, as usual, the excellent grounds I had given him for doing so, dismayed by the panic which filled me as day followed day without his coming, the most cruel fact I had to contend with was, naturally, the misunderstanding. If intimacy between us was to end and our love come to nothing despite its promise, it must not be a mistaken impression that dealt the death blow. He must know, whatever the consequences, that I had not betrayed him. I knew his pride and I knew how much that particular wound would fester. But how could I right matters if, as it seemed, he would not allow me the opportunity?

Then Sir Colin Campbell intervened to make the matter only worse.

On the 12th November, the semaphore was very active and word seeped through to us that Sir Colin had signalled his intention to march from the Alum Bagh to the Dilkusha on the morning of the 14th. The Dilkusha was another of the great, shabby palaces of Oudh, set in a deer park of old and lovely trees, and Sir Colin intended to occupy it before making the final push past the Martinière and across the canal to the Residency. Immediately this message was received, an order went out that neither officers nor men were to leave their posts, day or night, until the relief was finally effected. The enemy, we were told, and in particular the defeated sepoys from Delhi who had poured into Lucknow after Delhi had fallen to General Nicholson, had sworn an oath to take our position with a last great assault and to kill every soul in the place before Sir Colin could reach us.

At night now, the usual cacophony of gunfire and musketry was heavier than it had been for weeks, accompanied by the monotonous drums, the long mooings of conch shells, buglers practising their calls, and often a sudden surge of sound as a whole phalanx of Muslim pandies burst into a screamed warcry of *'Din! Din! Din!'* that would die to an angry mutter, then be taken up again as the loyal sepoys on our side of the wall yelled out in concerted defiance, *'Kump'ny ki Jai! Kump'ny ki Jai!'* (Long live the Company!)

Even Toddy-Bob obeyed the order, though probably not for the right reason, and Kate, Jessie and I saw no more of him than we did of Oliver, Charles, Wallace Avery or any of our other friends. Charles sent messages and dropped in once or twice to see the baby, but they were hurried visits. Pearl was seven months old now, thinner than a child of that age should have been, but of an equable and sunny disposition. She crawled around the floor almost as rapidly as her elders could walk, had learned to pull herself upright with the help of stools and boxes, and anything she could hold in her hands was immediately conveyed to her mouth. On one of his hasty visits to his daughter Charles informed me hesitantly that he had seen Oliver the previous night.

'What had he to say? You must have spoken to him? How is he, Charles?' I asked eagerly.

Charles retrieved the baby from the corner where we kept kindling for the fire, and sat her on his lap. He shook his head.

'He didn't say a word—and wouldn't allow me to say one either. But I think he saved my life.'

'Charles! How? What happened to you?' He did not appear to be harmed in any way.

'I'd been down the new mine leading to the wall of the Chathar Manzil—the breaching mine. It's finished, but a couple of us went down to clear away the debris at the far end, as it was to be readied for firing today. It's always pretty dreadful, you know, squirming your way into the earth in the heat and the damp, and the air is generally foul. I filled a couple of sacks with soil and stones and passed them back to Simmons to haul to the entry, and when I knew he was through began to ease myself out too. There has been a lot of work above ground in that section—trenches and new emplacements and so on—and as I moved back earth kept falling on my head and face, so I was damned glad to find myself within sight of the end. I could hear some heavy guns, but was not worried as I thought they were our own. Well, Simmons passed the sacks up to some others, and crawled out after them. I doused the lantern and started up the ladder too, thanking my Maker that I had survived another trip, and then, just as I got my head into fresh air there was a blinding flash and before I knew what was happening someone had thrown himself at me and the two of us landed at the bottom of the shaft again, covered with earth, the remains of the ladder and the lantern ... and ... other things. The shell had got Simmons just as he'd dusted himself off and was starting back to his billet.'

'Oh, Charles! Poor man!'

Charles was silent for a moment, thinking probably of his own good fortune, and I waited impatiently for him to continue.

'Oliver and a group of others had wandered up to see what was going on, and Oliver, they say, had walked forward to give me a hand getting out, not knowing, of course that it was me. You remember how quick his reactions always were—when we were out shooting and riding ... in Hassanganj? Well, he hasn't slowed up. He must have seen the shell approaching at the same time as my head appeared above ground, and just hurled himself towards me and the impetus threw both of us back down the shaft.'

'But he had saved himself too,' I pointed out, not in disparagement but with great relief.

'Yes,' Charles agreed thoughtfully. 'But I believe his intention had been to save me.'

'Why do you think that,' I wondered, 'if he didn't even speak to you?'

'Because when they eventually dug us out and he realized on whose behalf he had acted so promptly, for a moment I saw an expression on his face … as though, well Laura, as though he was sorry he had done it.'

I said nothing, as in my heart I knew that such might well have been the case.

'It was not hatred, you understand. Nothing so crude.'

Charles was not accustomed to the analysis of motive or emotion, and spent a moment in thought.

'It was more, more … self-hatred, or at least a most acute annoyance with himself. The expression passed in an instant, of course, and then he just nodded in that caustic way of his as I shook his hand and thanked him, then turned on his heel—and walked off.'

Apart from this strange incident I knew nothing of what had happened to Oliver Erskine, and there was nothing we women could do except wait, and hope, and pray, if we were so inclined, that those of our men who had survived so far would be spared the final battle.

The men were 'unco' active' as Jessie put it, making preparations to aid in our own relief when Sir Colin and his force were sighted. Several new batteries for heavy guns were thrown up on the farther side of the Chathar Manzil gardens, and mines were driven beneath the surrounding wall to blow a section of it to pieces when the guns were in readiness.

The atmosphere within the entrenchment in those days reminded me forcibly of my first impression of the place, when, exhausted but almost weeping with relief, we had entered the Baillie Guard and looked around us at the hive-like activity, confused and unexplained, all taking place in an atmosphere of high expectation. The waiting for something to happen was again almost unendurable, the more so for us women, since we had no one now to whom we could apply for information or explanation.

Mrs Bonner was still full of gossip, but gossip that told us nothing we did not already know. We knew the rebels in the city had increased by several thousands; we knew the route Sir Colin would follow in coming to us; we knew the plans our own men would follow to assist him as he fought towards us. What we really wanted to know was just how, even more than just when, we would be leaving.

However, Sir Colin, unlike others before him, was true to his word, and before noon on the 14th we heard guns firing in the direction of the Dilkusha. Soon we could watch their smoke rising in slow peaceful puffs above the trees of the park, and by nightfall beacons on both the Dilkusha and the Martinière indicated that our relievers had accomplished their object for the day and were in possession of both buildings.

As if to warn us not to allow those two far-off flames to raise our hopes too high, the pandies that night bombarded us with a concentrated enthusiasm that put the Old Garrison in mind of the worst nights of July.

Next day brought anti-climax. It had been expected that Sir Colin would push on towards us, but no amount of scanning the treed horizon with anxious fieldglasses could raise the hint of a movement. At noon, troops of the enemy, both horse and foot, were seen to move out towards the Martinière with drums, bugles and fifes, and green flags flying. Then, after an anxious few hours, they were seen returning at a more accelerated pace than they had gone forth, and a few cheers rang out in the garrison at the sight. At dusk a semaphore was discerned on the roof of the Martinière, and after the usual delays, mistakes and rereadings, the message was passed to the garrison: 'Advance tomorrow!'

When darkness fell, Sir Colin began a heavy bombardment of some objective to his left, a ruse to mislead the enemy into thinking he would follow the same route as had the previous relief, for in fact, when morning came, he would approach us by a circuitous march to the right. For a while Kate and I stood on the verandah and watched shells soaring up like tailed comets among the stars, sometimes bursting in flight to light the whole eastern sky with their vicious radiance. It was not so much the pyrotechnics that interested us, as the novel sensation of knowing that those shells and rockets were aimed at someone other than ourselves. When Kate was driven inside by the cold, I remained where I was, glad to be alone in the noisy night with my thoughts.

It was the fourth day of Oliver's absence, the fifth night. The strain of not seeing him was becoming even more unendurable than the waiting for Sir Colin. The latter's arrival now admitted of no conjecture.

It was merely a matter of time, perhaps of only a few hours. But Oliver? Where was he? Could he have left the entrenchment? The idea was absurd, of course, but it haunted me nevertheless.

Early on the following morning, the 140th day of the siege, the garrison began to crowd up on to any roof strong enough to hold a man, to enjoy the excitement of watching Sir Colin's advance.

For a while I too watched from the roof of the hospital, until a neighbour at the rail told me that Sir Colin's troops were storming the Sikander Bagh (Alexander's Garden), a large Mogul park enclosed in brick walls of massive size and height, and that the glints of light we now and then caught between the trees was the sun shining on massed bayonets as the men forced their way in. 'Hand to hand it will be now,' the man beside me murmured. 'Rotten tough going; a bloody carnage it will be, though, once they're in, the pandies will have no escape—not if we have enough men, that is.' I climbed down to the ward, wanting to see no more.

Through the day the battle continued. Building by building, palace by palace, mosque by domed mosque, and garden by garden, the inexorable tide pushed slowly towards us, while the guns grew nearer and the whitey-yellow smoke hung more thickly over the trees. Beyond the Chathar Manzil the new batteries were brought into play, the mines were sprung to breach the wall, and in the afternoon, at Havelock's order, the 'Advance' was sounded and at last our own columns of assault sallied out, cheering, to fight in the open.

That night a further new battery was thrown up at the most forward position we had won, and a howitzer and two heavy guns, with which it was to be armed, were manhandled into position.

Early in the evening of the following day, November 17th, we heard in the distance the sound of cheering. Gradually it grew louder and nearer, as by word of mouth the news travelled with the cheers that General Outram and Sir Colin Campbell had met and the second relief was officially effected.

Later we learned that it was Henry Kavanagh who had led Outram through a tumbled laneway near the Moti Mahal to where Sir Colin waited to shake him by the hand. At the time, however, we merely listened, awestruck, as slowly the cheers grew, travelling through groups of grimy men holding the far-flung palaces, by way of shouts and waved muskets and shots in the air, to signal the men behind them in batteries, earthworks and embattled orchards, until, as the joyful sound approached our populated walls, we knew it could mean nothing other than that the final meeting of the two forces had taken place.

They told us that that same cheer had travelled away from us, through the Shah Najaf and the Sikander Bagh and the Martinière, all the way back to the Dilkusha, so that, had one been able to hear it, the entire route fought over by Sir Colin and his men was loud with the huzzahs of victory.

This second relief, we found, however, was very different to the first.

No swarms of strange soldiery burst noisily into the entrenchment with tears on their faces, swinging children to their shoulders in joy at finding them alive. Most of Sir Colin's troops were needed to hold open the route they had won, and only a comparatively few officers and men wandered through the enclave, viewing with incredulity the paucity of our defences and the shattered structures we had clung to so stubbornly.

They were a different breed of men too, at first view, from the battle-weary veterans of many engagements who had accompanied Outram and Havelock. Blue-coated staff officers, correctly accoutred and adequately weaponed; storied stalwarts of the 93rd Highlanders in tartan and black-feathered bonnets; black-bearded Sikhs in their new drab uniforms called after the colour of earth 'khaki'; the 90th, in the familiar scarlet and white; sepoys of the 53rd Native Infantry in French grey. Strangest of all to our eyes were the sailors of the warship *Shannon* that, bound for China, had been deflected to Calcutta, where the crew had disembarked and marched up-country to our aid, hauling their eight great guns by hand a good part of the way. In their naval blue and still wearing their round straw hats, they were spoken of with wonder by our sepoys as being 'four feet tall, four feet broad and capable of carrying big guns on their heads'.

All these newcomers were so well-dressed, so comfortably booted, that to us it seemed they must be amateurs of war, and we looked on them with a mixture of envy and resentment. Then we began to hear what they had done for us, in their fine uniforms and footgear, and changed our minds. They had fought a deadly succession of battles for our safety, almost within sight of us all the time, each one of which would assume in time the quality of legend. The battle for the Dilkusha, where the pandies fled with the fleeing deer; for the Martinière, whose grey turrets were reflected in its lake flowered strangely with red-coated pandies floating face-down among the water lilies; for the bloody Sikander Bagh, where the toll of enemy dead reached the symbolic number of 1,857; for the Shah Najaf, a strongpoint abandoned in despair by the enemy, fearful the sailors' guns would ignite five thousand pounds of stored powder. Not a foot was traversed without a struggle. The few short miles between the Dilkusha and the Moti Mahal cost Sir Colin the lives of five hundred men.

We ate white bread that night, a small portion each, and butter, and each received an orange and a tot of rum. Letters had arrived too, wagonloads of mail, newspapers and periodicals from home. Kate received several letters and wept as she read them, for her correspondents had not known of George's death. But there was nothing for Charles, Emily or myself; our family could not have known that we had left Hassanganj or even that Hassanganj was no more. As I watched Kate weeping over her letters, I tried again to visualize Mount Bellew and the kind stolid faces of my aunt and uncle, but again the effort failed me. The knot of fear around my heart grew more constricted as I thought of England.

On the following morning we were told that Sir Colin Campbell wanted the women and children to leave the entrenchment that same day. This order did not affect us unduly, for we had few preparations to make and very little to pack; the women in the more favoured houses of the civilian staff, however, set up a cry of outrage that forced Sir Colin to give us twenty-four hours' grace. Then we were told that not only the women and children would be leaving; Sir Colin had ordered the whole garrison to be withdrawn and the Residency completely evacuated.

We had all been aware that the dependants and the sick would leave as soon as the route to Cawnpore was secure, but that the men themselves, all the men, would also have to retire was greeted with downright unbelief.

For one hundred and forty-two days we had fought and endured in the belief that more than our own lives were at stake. I will not plead an altruism amounting to heroism; naturally our own lives and those of our loved ones were our first and most fundamental concern. But yet, when we thought of the matter, we had believed that, given the time and means to retake Lucknow, our long endurance would contribute to the overthrow of anarchy in the entire Kingdom of Oudh, and this belief had helped us to combat more than the pandies' fire. It had given a measure of meaning to our sufferings.

We could forget the hunger, the privation, the discomfort; the sweltering heat of July and the cutting cold of November nights; we could forget the sickness and the suppurating wounds, the smell, the dirt, the lice, rats, flies and mosquitoes. We could not forget the dead, who had died for the same hope for which we had struggled to live. Their lives, we felt suddenly, had been given uselessly.

I suppose we were too tired and strained to be rational, but the knowledge that within a day the old enclosure would lie empty filled some with wrath, most with bitterness and all with a sharp unlikely grief.

In the hospital, to which, having few preparations to make for our departure, Kate and I repaired as usual, the mood of the men was dour. A few loads of supplies and comforts had been brought in for the wounded, and long-cold pipes glowed comfortably as the men muttered and grumbled among themselves. They were all the familiar faces I saw about me, Sir Colin's wounded having been removed to the Dilkusha, but marked with a discontented sullenness that scarcely fitted the occasion. I saw fear written on those plain, unshaven faces, too, for no fighting man could remain ignorant of the long torture of jogging litters or crowded, red-curtained ambulance carts, which would be his lot if wounded.

''E's crazy, miss, and I don't mind what 'e did at Balaclava,' one man said to me, speaking of Sir Colin. 'We got to stay put and beat the niggers back. 'Tain't possible to get us all out and safe away through miles of pandies, nor yet you ladies and the nippers. We'll be slaughtered in our *doolies* same as the poor bloody beggars was when 'Avelock come in!'

'Nonsense!' I countered sharply, because the same thought had occurred to me. 'They are busy clearing a way for us now, digging trenches and erecting cover so that we will be quite safe. And don't you hear the barrage? Those are our guns—a breaching fire on the Kaiser Bagh. The new troops will be with us all the way, they say, and we cannot possibly come to any harm.'

The man subsided, muttering, but I knew I had failed to convince him.

That evening Sir Colin called for a general muster of the combatants of the Old Garrison, every man and boy, white, brown or brindle, who had carried a gun.

It was a long time since a parade had been called in the square before the Resident's House. The last time must have been on the morning of the Battle of Chinhat, when, newly come to martial interests, I had watched with a thrill of excitement as Sir Henry Lawrence led his men, polished, pipe-clayed and swaggering under the eyes of their womenfolk, through the Baillie Guard—and to defeat. Now, four and a half months later, I watched again, but in a very different temper.

Sir Colin and his staff stood on the broken steps of the Resident's House, and had to wait an unconscionable time for our motley collection of men to gather and form up in what they hoped was correct military style.

Sir Colin was a small man, untidy in appearance, with a brown face wrinkled as a walnut under a thatch of curly grey hair. He had many nicknames, from the 'Auld Coudy' of his own Scots of the 93rd Highlanders, to 'Old Khabardar' (go carefully) of the natives, to 'Sir Crawling Camel', as the young officers dubbed him who found his concentration on detail too irksome for time of war. The entrenchment was already enlivened by rumours and stories concerning him. He had fought as a private soldier at the retreat of Corunna, almost a lifetime before. His prowess in the Crimea was known to all, and how at Balaclava, instead of forming his troops into the wonted hollow square, he had thrown them out in a thin extended front that decimated the Russians' charging cavalry, earning for his 93rd the appellation 'The Thin Red Line Tipped with Steel'. It was said of him that, in time of war, he lay down to sleep fully accoutred and wearing his boots, and was so accessible to his men, he was prepared to see them even in his bath.

As we waited, the waning sun pulled long shadows across the space of beaten earth on which the garrison was assembling; a chill wind lifted my short hair as I watched, and I saw Sir Colin shiver slightly and pull his blue patrol jacket closer over his chest. He removed his pith helmet and ran his fingers impatiently through his mass of curly hair, adding to the general dishevelment of his appearance.

Many of the women had gathered to see their menfolk parade, and men of the new relief lounged around curiously, eyeing, in part derision and part admiration, the remnants of our force—something less than five hundred men of all ranks still capable of standing to attention. A further two hundred lay in the hospital.

Justly, the foremost ranks were composed of the men of the 32nd Foot, who had borne the brunt not only of the siege, but of the forays and sorties that had taken place since the first relief. Two hundred and fifty remained of the nine hundred and fifty who had marched into Lucknow the previous December. Behind the 32nd, sternly to attention, stood a couple of hundred sepoys and *sowars*, Sikhs, Punjabis, men of Oudh. Then the volunteer cavalry, long since bereft of their horses: planters, merchants, professional men from the city, and the odd unfortunate traveller, like Charles, cut off in Lucknow by the rebellion. Behind these again were the covenanted clerks and the uncovenanted, and at the very rear fifteen of the older boys of the Martinière School, proudly shouldering the muskets that proved them men. White men, brown men, Eurasians; soldiers, scholars, fortune-hunters and schoolboys. Brave men, all.

A hush fell as Brigadier Inglis, sword raised, advanced to the steps to accompany Sir Colin down the lines of ragged upright figures.

Not a man wore uniform; even the Brigadier, with a couple of pistols in his belt, looked more like a buccaneer than a soldier. A few men wore shakos still; some sported broad-brimmed felt hats; a few had pith sunhelmets or cloth caps, but most were bareheaded. Their breeches were patched and shabby, their shirts dyed in ink or curry powder. Boots were a rarity, shoes were tied together with string; a few were barefoot. Here and there a man proudly stuck out his chest beneath a faded scarlet jacket; the rest, having discarded their makeshift cloaks of native quilts for the parade, shivered in the evening chill.

Sir Colin, very erect, his small white beard out-thrust pugnaciously, marched with military exactitude up and down the tattered ranks. Sometimes he paused before a man for a few words; sometimes he shook his head, in unbelief it seemed to me. On the steps Outram stood with his arms crossed on his burly chest and nodded his head in silent approbation of the scene. Near him, Havelock, supported by an aide, bowed his head in what was probably prayer.

Among the women crowding the area, hardly an eye was dry, for hardly a life had remained untouched by personal tragedy since that last parade on the morning of Chinhat. Of we four females from the

Gaol—for Jessie held Pearl in her arms— two had been widowed on the same day, one had lost her mother, and only I had been bereaved of a comparatively distant relative. Our group was representative of all the other women gathered there.

'George! Oh, George!' I heard Kate whisper to herself, and saw her fumble in the pocket of her skirt for her rosary. Jessie, not much given to tears, sniffed with what was probably sorrow, though it might have been indignation at Kate's tears.

'Well,' observed a burly 'Shannon' standing near us, 'even to a sailor, they don't look much like soldiers, but by all that's holy, they are God's good fighting men!'

'Aye! Oh, aye! And so were them that's gone, lad,' sighed Jessie. 'So were them that's gone!'

My eyes searched the silent ranks for Oliver. Charles I found soon enough among the volunteers, and then Toddy-Bob, whose shortness made a gap in the line like a drawn tooth. Ishmial I could not see; he was probably on the far side of the square, among the other loyal servants who had borne arms with the garrison. But where was Oliver? If I could only mark where he was, I would not let him escape without speaking to him. And then I remembered. Of course, Oliver had not made part of the Old Garrison.

Disappointment brought tears to my eyes. Ever since the parade was called, I had promised myself that at last I would see him, talk to him, explain that night on the Gaol verandah; that much at least I must do. How could I have been so thoughtless, so forgetful? Perhaps because, despite his absence, he had been so present in my mind all through the first months of the siege, I had somehow deceived myself into the belief that he had been physically present.

With so many men now flooding every inch of space before the Resident's House, and with dusk darkening the scene by the moment, I knew there was no use in looking for him among the bystanders, even if he were present, which, in view of his opinions on military matters, seemed unlikely. My interest in the parade immediately abated.

We returned to the Gaol in a melancholy silence, all of us occupied with thoughts of the men we had lost.

There was much to do that night, our last night in the entrenchment. Our first instructions had been that we could take no baggage with us when we left, but along with the twenty-four hours' grace forced from

Sir Colin by the incensed ladies, permission was obtained to carry with us 'a modicum' of personal possessions.

In this respect our little party was more fortunate than the still well-endowed ladies from the private houses for, owning nothing, we had no agonizing decisions to make regarding what should be left and what taken.

All I had was a bundle with a few clothes and the copy of Marcus Aurelius, and in a pocket I had sewn into the inner side of my skirt a packet of Emily's jewels, that Charles insisted I take with me for Pearl's sake. In that pocket, too, was the black satin garter, and my mother's ruby and pearl pin. What extra clothing Kate and Jessie had once possessed had long gone to provide bandages, slings or little dresses for Pearl. Everything else Kate owned had been burned in her bungalow in Mariaon and, as a private's wife, Jessie had never had very much to carry with her on her peregrinations with the regiment.

With our bundles safely tied, we set to work again on our letters, for there was no knowing when we would next have a table to write upon, and we had been promised that mail would be conveyed to Calcutta as soon as we had evacuated the Residency.

After we had cleared away our final evening meal in a mood well compounded of nostalgia and anxiety, Charles came to accompany us down to the graveyard to make our last farewells to the dead. We took Pearl in to Mrs Bonner, so that Jessie could come with us. Minerva accepted Pearl into her arms with a girl's ignorant enthusiasm for babies, as her mother, seated on her bed in a wrapper, was busy giving incoherent directions to her *ayah* on the packing of a vast quantity of clothing and other possessions scattered in disarray around the room. An air of great ill-temper pervaded the apartment, and we hurriedly made our escape before Mrs Bonner took in our presence.

It was a dark night, snapping with cold; later there would be a moon, but now only a few large stars gazed down in icy calm upon our errand, as hugging our shawls and cloaks about us, we entered the sad acre where so many of our friends lay.

At my request, Charles led us first to where Mr Roberts was buried, and we stood for a few moments in silence round the grave, while my mind took me back over the months to a rain-lashed deck and my mackinawed mentor imparting to me his knowledge and love of a country that had killed him. 'Rest well, dear Mr Roberts,' I said inwardly, 'in a book-lined heaven, where all facts and figures are open to inspection and where no question remains unanswered.'

We moved on and knelt for a moment where little Jamie had been buried in a box, his head resting on his pillow. Then we left Jessie to her farewells and Charles led us to the long mound beneath which Emily lay with the others who had died the same day. Kate had no grave to kneel beside; neither George's body, nor Corporal MacGregor's, had been returned for burial. So Kate knelt down beside Charles and myself, and later Jessie too joined us.

No one that night regarded the pandy fire that threatened the graveyard; everywhere dim figures knelt in the darkness or stood, some weeping, some bowed but silent, some holding hands and praying aloud and together.

> *Out of the depths I have cried unto Thee, O Lord, Lord,*
> *hear my prayer …*

As on many other sorrowful occasions, Kate's familiar voice started the great prayer, but this time I could not join in.

I think I was made dumb by the acknowledgement of my own hypocrisy. I could not remember Emily—not as her mother and father or she herself, perhaps, would have wished me to remember her. I could visualize her, with effort, as she had been in death, dressed in her flowered poplin gown with the neat lace collar and cuffs, but her face remained a blur, an impression of the many faces I had since seen in death, never hers. Even her name now was only a word that roused in me a vague sense of guilt and vaguer regret. Yet Emily had been close to me, a part of my life for many years. Once I had known her well; once I had loved her; I had hated her for a time, pitied her often, understood her but seldom. She had been only nineteen when she had died, after great pain and in circumstances that lacked both decency and dignity. I had held her in my arms as a child and brushed her sodden hair when she was dead; I had witnessed her marriage, been present at the birth of her child. None of this now had reality. I could not remember her.

Is this how life must end for us all, I wondered, with distaste more than fear? Nothingness—even in the minds of those who have loved us? Does it really take only a few months to erase the imprint of a personality on the lives and minds of those who loved it, knew it, helped to form it? Emily living, buoyant, gay, beautiful as she had been, that Emily was beyond my recalling. Only a few of her actions had any significance left for me. The fact that she had married a man I once had loved, and then loved in her turn a man who loved me. Poor Emily, she had been as prone to mistakes as I myself, and they were all I remembered her by, those mistakes and delusions.

I sighed to myself as the others prayed. I would have to do better than this, I thought. This state of mind would not be acceptable in Mount Bellew. There would be so much discussion, so many anxious, loving questions. They would want to know whether she had been happy in her marriage, a contented bride and mother. They would want comfort and reassurance, not only about Emily's life, but about her death. Where could I find the words, and where would they find Emily in the carefully chosen half-truths that would be all I could give them?

Kate had finished her psalm and was weeping softly into her hand as she knelt. Jessie too was weeping, quietly and unexpectedly. Suddenly everything became too much for me. I covered my face with my hands and sobs wracked me. I felt myself overcome, not by death but by the cruel transitoriness of life. Emily had been as alive as I was now, yet soon almost the only record of her passing through this world would be the tenderly cherished but figmentary recollections I fabricated to comfort her family for her loss. Little Pearl would have no recollection of her mother, and Charles would soon find it more comfortable to forget any true memories he might have had of his wife. I cried because nineteen years of living could leave behind no more lasting memorial than a few carefully adjusted impressions of a character in a handful of mortal minds.

I tried to control myself, feeling Jessie's arm about me and hearing her soothing murmur, and realized suddenly that it was also for the living that I wept, and in longing, not grief. If my life must end as completely, leaving as little trace as had poor Emily's, then I must live it. Such were my thoughts, as Charles got up and left us, overcome by what he supposed was my grief for Emily. It was a relief to be alone in that sad place with two women who had shared so much with me, and I sought for words to tell them what I felt.

'I ... I have been thinking, trying to think, what I can tell them at home, and oh, Kate ... Jessie, how can I ever do it? I can never convey all that I should about poor Emily, and yet to do less is somehow to ... kill her again. Oh, Kate, whatever can I do? There is so little of her left for them.'

'Och, woman dear!' Kate sniffed through her own tears, taking my hand in hers. 'Why do you rack yourself so? All these explanations you have to make, these responsibilities you feel you must take, they are not yours rightly. Don't you see that, yet? Do you not feel the wrongness in your going home, leaving matters as they would be here?'

'Wrongness? But, Kate, I can't stay out here. I told you so before. I can't stay here!'

I got to my feet clumsily and our three bedraggled figures made a small group beside the long grave in the starlight. The wind ruffled the leaden surface of the river below us, and somewhere on the far side of the entrenchment a shell exploded dully.

'Laura, listen to me,' Kate said, dabbing at her eyes with her cuff. 'They have a saying out here, and it goes something like "to put words between oneself and the truth". My dear, that is what you are doing, what you have been doing for an age past. Sure, what you think you feel for this country at the moment is not important. It will pass. What you know you feel for Oliver is what matters, and all the rest, all this about your going home and not knowing what to say to your relatives and about the baby and all, why that's just putting words between yourself and the truth. Laura, you must not leave Oliver. Face it. You must stay with him.'

'Must I?' Like a dutiful child I was willing to be instructed.

Jessie put her large hand on my shoulder and drew me to her, again like a child in need of comfort.

'Lass, we twa ... we twa hae been weepin' here in the darkness, and on many another night too, for the fine men we had once and hae lost. But you ... do you nae see it? You've been weepin' for a man that lives—and loves you and that you will nae tak'. Sair and lang is the weepin' of a woman for a livin' man, lass, worse by far than our weepin' for the dead!'

'She's right, Laura. You know she's right. Ours must be a long and heavy grieving for the men we loved, but yours ... yours will be regret and remorse and a longing to undo the things you've done and that perhaps can never be undone. You must trust him to know where his life lies, Laura, and trust yourself to him too. Tears and a-plenty will always be given you; no need to buy them so dearly!'

'Kate! Oh, Kate!' I reached my hand behind my back and Kate took it, as I stood with my face buried in Jessie's bosom and cried.

'There now, lassie, there now! Weep well and then hae done with weepin'. Och, but he's a braw man that loves you, and mind, Jess will tak' the wee one home and be back in no time at a' to keep ye company in the fine new house.'

I groped for a handkerchief and, finding none, used the hem of my shawl on eyes and nose, indelicately.

'Now, Jessie, don't bully her. She must make her own decision.' Kate reproved Jessie half-heartedly, and I turned and kissed her leathery, wrinkled cheek.

'I have. I believe I have made my decision—with the help of you both. I suppose it could not be made any other way. I must stay with him, Kate, and trust him as you say. And, Kate, do you think you could go to Mount Bellew with Jessie and the baby and … and tell them everything, and why I am not with you?'

'Sure now, and isn't that just what I have been hoping I'd have to do? I can tell them all the truth I know of Emily, and that will be enough for them, and kind to them and easy on your conscience too, Laura. Your place is here now; you must not lose Oliver.'

'I know, I know!' I said, a sense of relief, of inevitability flooding over me as I spoke. 'I must find him and tell him. There's such a lot to explain to him.'

'You will. Never fear. He'll be bound to come to you in the morning, woman dear. In the morning!'

CHAPTER 6

The morning, however, did not bring him to me.

The families and the schoolboys of the Martinière had been instructed to be ready to leave the entrenchment by ten o'clock on the morning of the 19th November, and by dawn the entire garrison was astir.

During the previous two days, while most of Sir Colin's troops had been busy clearing and then keeping open the route of the exodus to the Dilkusha Palace, our own men had been set to find carriages, carts or palanquins and the animals and bearers necessary for such conveyances as might be discovered. From the outbuildings of the palaces enclosed by the extended perimeter, a medley of equipages were dragged forth for inspection, but most were too badly damaged by gunfire or exposure to be roadworthy, and those that came to light within the old entrenchment were in even worse case. Camels, horses, mules and even donkeys had been rounded up and dragged to the muster, but their numbers were even more inadequate to our necessities than was the number of coolies and bearers who could be impressed into service, and it looked as though a good half of us would have to walk the four and a half miles to the Dilkusha.

Charles had done his best on our behalf, but when by morning he still had only failure to report in his search for anything capable of carrying at least one of us and the baby, we resigned ourselves to a long tramp in shabby shoes, carrying our possessions with us. It was not going to be easy, but at least there would be three of us to take turns with Pearl.

'It is truly dreadful!' said Mrs Bonner, who was sitting in our kitchen with Minerva for the last time, while waiting to set off. 'Such a total lack of organization. My husband has never seen anything like it. We should have been given more time to pack in the first place, and now to find we cannot take away even the few things we have packed because of lack of bearers! Why, I am having to leave behind some of my most treasured possessions: my mahogany sewing-box, the portrait of my father, my second-best set of cutlery and almost all our clothing and, really, it is enough to make one weep!'

She sniffed delicately behind a lace-edged handkerchief. Both Mrs Bonner and Minerva were dressed correctly for travel in gowns of wool, plainly trimmed, with matching cloaks and bonnets. Minerva's sleeves were a little too short, and Mrs Bonner's gown was now a trifle large for her, but both were neat and clean and I eyed them with envious wonder.

'But your servants will help to carry your stuff surely?' said Kate, with scant sympathy for Mrs Bonner's troubles. The Bonners had been assisted all through the siege by a faithful old *ayah* who had been wounded in the leg by the same exploding shell that had killed our goat and a sweeper, the last minion a true luxury we had been very grateful to share.

'The servants? Oh, to be sure. But only the two of them. When I think of the eight we had when we moved in here, and four whole bullock-wagons of our things, almost my entire household goods, Mrs Barry, bar the furniture, of course. And now to be compelled to leave so much of it behind because of the hurried incompetence of ... that carpenter from Glasgow!'

'And have you not considered that to wait for more bearers might well cause you to lose your life as well as your cutlery?'

'Nonsense! With all the troops flocking around? Major Bonner says Sir Colin just wants to get rid of us so that he can engage the pandies in a battle that will bring him even more glory than Balaclava. He was *quite* the wrong man to send to such a ... delicate situation, Major Bonner says. He has no breeding. It's not surprising, I suppose, that he has so little understanding of how a lady regards her sacred household possessions. Not surprising at all. Now, if it had been Sir Henry Lawrence, dear good *gentleman* that he was ...'

'I very much doubt whether anyone could do more for us than Sir Colin is doing,' Kate retorted acidly. 'I believe it is a miracle he got to us at all with all the Delhi sepoys now flooding the countryside and doing their best to stop him. He had only three thousand men left once the Dilkusha was taken, and you know the pandies are thought to have not less than thirty thousand. He led the charge on the Shah Najaf in person, they say, and it is scarcely his fault that there are no carriages nor horses to pull them.'

'Oh, I'm sure he is a very doughty soldier. Very doughty. After all, he came up from the ranks, so why should he fear a charge or two as an officer? But his manners!'

Mrs Bonner settled herself more comfortably and I knew we were to be treated to some further iniquity of Sir Colin's.

'Last night—I think I told you, did I not?—Major Bonner was included in Mr Gubbins's dinner party to honour Sir Colin. Well, as you may imagine, although Mr Gubbins might have some private doubts about Sir Colin as an individual, in his eyes nothing could be too good for Sir Colin as Our Deliverer. Nothing! The table was covered with the best of linen and set with Mrs Gubbins's finest silver and suite of Irish glass. There was fresh meat, vegetables and truffled sausages and all kinds of hermetically sealed delicacies, as well as wine, champagne and old port. Everyone had worked to make the occasion a fitting mark of gratitude and esteem.

'Well, to begin with he was late—Sir Colin, I mean. Then he walked into the dining-room wearing the same blue patrol jacket and brown corduroy trousers he had on when he arrived here. A General Officer Commanding and ... a Knight! And he couldn't be bothered to change for dinner! Can you imagine it?'

'I can. And I sympathize with it. This is scarcely the time for an observance of social graces, such as changing for dinner, Mrs Bonner.'

'Well, that is as may be, though I am sure I would not agree with you. Standards are standards, after all, Mrs Barry, and should be adhered to, if possible, whatever the circumstances. But, as I say, that's not the worst of it. He came to the table, sat down, looked around him at all the food and the servants bringing in the hot dishes, and the wine in the coolers, and ... Mrs Barry, you won't credit it, but he folded his arms and sat through the meal, the entire meal, mind you, without eating a mouthful or saying a word!'

'He did what?' I asked with unconcealed delight.

'Refused to eat a morsel, and at the meal's end demanded of Mr Gubbins why there should be so much in his household that was luxurious when the men in the hospital were denied even necessities. The ingratitude, Mrs Barry! The base ingratitude!'

'Well, bully for Sir Colin!' I crowed, lapsing into the schoolboy vocabulary of my cousins, and to Mrs Bonner's great annoyance. 'That's the best news I've heard since the day Old Buggins's plunge bath took a pandy shell.'

Mrs Bonner's pale eyes regarded me malevolently, and Minerva goggled in alarm at her mother's known opinions being so rudely contradicted.

'Mr Gubbins,' went on Mrs Bonner sourly, and without necessity, 'is the Financial Commissioner of the District and a gentleman. He deserved better at Sir Colin's hands.'

'Indeed he did, and I'm hopeful he'll receive it—in time,' I replied wrathfully. 'Mr Gubbins is a selfish, self-opinionated, complacent and contentious fool, and I don't care a button if he is Financial Commissioner. He is a hypocrite into the bargain, and when I think of our lads in the hospital having to manage with lentils and rice, despite stomach wounds and dysentery and even cholera, why I ...'

'Miss Hewitt!' I was interrupted. 'I cannot think you are yourself when you speak in such a way of a senior officer of the Service. *And* a close friend of Major Bonner's. Of course, I cannot pretend surprise at such opinions, or indeed of your manner of expressing them, seeing the sort of company you appear to prefer ... but really, I am not used to such a way of speaking!'

'My opinions, Mrs Bonner, and my manners, are very much my own, though allow me to inform you that this particular set of opinions is shared pretty generally by everyone in the garrison!'

'Well!' She drew herself up, bridling, her flaccid chins wobbling with wrath, while Minerva cringed visibly and Kate smiled approval at me.

Unable to endure the mindless haverings of the woman any longer or my acute impatience to see Oliver again, without any excuse for my departure I grabbed my shawl and set off for the hospital.

A scene of chaos met my eyes as I walked into the open air. Every clear space, every lane and roadway of the entrenchment was thronged with a moving mass of carts, carriages, guns, horses, bullocks, camels, soldiers, coolies and families, all in the throes of preparation for the evacuation. So dense was the crowd I had sometimes to force a way for myself along the familiar path to the Banqueting Hall, and over all the hurried comings and goings, the loading of coolies and packing of carts, surged the deafening noise that inevitably accompanies any form of common effort in India.

As I struggled through the crowd I kept a sharp eye open for Toddy-Bob or Ishmial. Oliver, I knew, would have no reason to make part of this hysterical scene, but the other two might well have been impressed into duty on behalf of the families. The last of my pride had dissipated in the graveyard the night before, and I was determined now somehow to send a message to Oliver to come and see me.

Arrived at last at the hospital, I found the two Birch girls still faithfully at their duties, but none of the other ladies. Dr Partridge was on the verandah talking to two strange officers; he nodded to me as I went in.

The long room was oddly silent. An air of desolation pervaded it already, and I formed a vivid mental image of how it would appear in twenty-four hours' time, when the last of the sick had followed us to the Dilkusha. Empty and quiet, the light from windows no one had thought to shut would fall directly on the dirty floor, littered with discarded pallets, blankets too threadbare for further use and, finally, abandoned piles of filthy bandages. There would be battered tin cups and plates lying around—I remembered the men throwing them to the ceiling in their joy at the first relief—leech trays still abominable with regurgitated blood, and a tattered shirt or two taken from the dead in more evil days. At the far end of the room, under the hanging brass lamp that had never shed sufficient light, the zinc-topped table on which so many had died so terribly would still preside from its fear-filled shadows over the strangely unpeopled space.

Things. Merely things. Only things would be left behind.

Yet could that room ever know true silence? Would not the shot-holed bricks and crumbling plaster hold for ever some ethereal echo of the groans, screams and curses of all the men who had lived and died in mortal agony within its walls? Would not the empty air, perhaps, in some far day of peace, when doves called in the neem trees and the shadows of quisqualis vines again stirred gently on the polished tiles of the verandah, would not that empty air give back to some yet unborn visitor, curious and concerned, a true intimation of the suffering and unmarked heroism with which it vibrated now for me? There would be voices always in this long room, waiting only the plucked chord of sympathy to be evoked in ghostly tones for those who had ears to hear.

Melancholy invaded me, and I forgot, for the moment, my anxiety to see Oliver. I was saying forewell to more than the sick men lying so comfortlessly around me; I was taking leave of the girl I once had been and had grown out of in this room. Quietly, heavily, I moved among the figures, shaking hands, fetching a last drink of water, easing a final dressing.

'Goodbye, miss.' 'God bless ye, ma'am.' 'God be with you, lady.' 'Thank ye, miss.' 'Thank you.' 'Thank you.'

They spoke in low voices, pressing my hand, some lifting their heads from their pallets to make their sincerity apparent. A hard lump formed in my throat. I hastened my goodbyes to waves and smiles and worked my way towards the door to escape from this useless grief. In a few hours they would start a further and more cruel purgatory, scores of broken bodies, wracked with pain and fever, thrust hastily on to bullock-wagons, litters and gun carriages; yet, many of them, most of them indeed, were unfit to travel in the most luxurious ease.

I had almost gained the door when I was summoned by a hoarse and unexpected call of 'Miss! Miss Hewitt … please …!' The men seldom knew my name, nor bothered to discover it.

I approached closer and looked down into a face I knew but could not place.

'Dines, miss. 'Member? Me and Mr Miles … were with you … relief … after Cawnpore.'

I knelt down swiftly to hear the gasped, disjointed words, remembering our guests of the night of the first relief and the account of the *Bibighar* in Cawnpore given us by this same young soldier.

'Of course! Have you just come in? Is there something I can do for you?'

He nodded his head, then lay still, gathering strength before continuing. He was very weak and badly injured, I surmised. 'Mr Billy … Miles?' It was a query, and I nodded to signify that I remembered the young officer. 'Dead … yesterday … We was … together. Shell … him … me too.'

'I'm so sorry, so very sorry,' I said sincerely. I had often encountered the two young men, always in a hurry and always together.

'Letter? My mother … please?'

'Of course.' I fumbled in my pocket for a small tablet and a stub of pencil that I usually carried with me to the hospital, though it was a long time since I had been requested to write a letter.

763

Slowly Dines spelled out his mother's address. While he was doing so, Apothecary Saunders came and stood beside us, looking down at the stricken white face of the boy with the resigned anxiety common to our medical men. Dines shut his eyes, and I thought he had slipped into unconsciousness. Saunders bent and felt his pulse.

'Going fast,' he whispered to me. 'Stomach wound. Internal bleeding.'

'Any chance?' I asked softly.

He shook his head. 'Best that he goes before they try to move him, poor young devil.' And he straightened up and moved away.

'Tell them ...' The exhausted eyes were open again. 'Tell them Albert ... done what ... 'e could, miss.' His tongue moved over his cracked lips; I knew how much he wanted water but I knew that for injuries such as his I could give him none. 'Say ... say ... I never ... forgot Lucy ... the baby, Eddie. Say ... I made ... the bastards ... 'member Lucy too!' The effort was too much for him. He closed his eyes and was silent for a long time, his face contorted in pain. I watched him, noting the almost imperceptible movement of the blanket over his chest, and the sweat that started in beads on his forehead as he clenched his teeth over his lips and shuddered. After some time I saw the taut limbs relax, and was sure that he had lost consciousness. Saunders hovered in the vicinity, and I was about to get up and leave, when the lad began to speak again with closed eyes.

'Say ... to mother ... she'll tell Mr Billy's people.' He paused, seemed to discover within himself some little excess of energy and went on in words clearer and more fluent.

'Say, I made ... sixteen of 'em remember our Lucy and the baby. Sixteen ... There was seven pandies at different times, and ... and two *bunnias* in a shop with a woman. An old man. 'E 'id be'ind 'is woman's skirts, so I got 'er too ... There were a boy ... and then 'is dad come out to see, so I made 'im eat a "Cawnpore Dinner" as well. Then ... then there was two others ... at a well. Outside the Shah Najaf, just yesterday. I was glad it were near a well. I threw 'em in afore Mr Billy seen what I done, but one wasn't ... dead, and screamed, and then Mr Billy took on at me 'bout it an' all.'

Horrified by what I heard, my pencil froze in my fingers. The bruised eyes opened and looked at me without seeing me. His voice, when he spoke again, had changed, and was the whine of a fretful child that finds itself in trouble.

'We quarrelled, Ma. Imagine. Me and Billy. We ain't never quarrelled afore. 'E said ... 'e said 'e'd 'ave to put me on a charge! Ma, I told 'im ... I told 'im—it were only right, for what they'd done to Lucy an' all. Oh, Ma! Won't I never forget that? Never? Only when I seen one of 'em dead and known I done it, then I forget awhile, but then I see them little shoes again, with the feet in, and the hair and ... But, Ma, Billy 'ad no right to quarrel with me, 'ad 'e? I was only doin' what was right. But 'e ... then, Ma, 'e said 'e'd 'ave no more to do with me, just like that, like I was someone 'e 'adn't knowed all 'is days. 'E ... 'e said I was a bleedin' murderer, not a soldier, an' 'e went away on 'is own. 'E shouldn't of done that, Ma. I caught up with 'im after a while, though, and I were just goin' to speak to 'im, when ... when the shell got 'im. An' me, Ma—it got me too. I didn't even 'ear it ... just ... just sees Mr Billy lyin' on the ground and bloody, and then ... then I sees me own guts, Ma ... my own guts beginnin' to ooze out of my belly ...'

Pain, or perhaps the horror of that shocking recollection, cut off his words in a high shrill scream. Saunders moved swiftly to Dines's pallet and motioned me to move away as he pulled back the blanket. Sickened, I rose and walked quickly from the ward, the agonized screams echoing after me.

When I could no longer hear them, I stopped and wiped away the tears of pity and repugnance I could not keep back as the boy talked. He had been killed, ruined and crazed by his own hatred. What was it Oliver had said once, when we had been talking of just this 'Cawnpore Fever' that had destroyed young Dines? 'Hatred has a way of destroying the hater more surely than the hated.' Trite, but true in a most terrible way.

'What's this now—not weeping surely? Come now, Miss Laura, no tears from you. This is a great moment!'

Dr Partridge had walked round the corner and caught me blinking away my tears.

'Not really weeping ... just being foolish. That young boy, Dines ... ?'

'Yes? Stomach wound.'

'He ... he has killed sixteen people, because of what he saw in the *Bibighar* in Cawnpore. Sixteen people! I don't think he can be twenty years old.'

'Not the only one, either, my dear. Unfortunately. They've gone mad, some of them—out of control. But he'll not last the day, you know.'

'I know. A fresh-faced country boy, and he's killed sixteen other human beings, very deliberately, and will be dead before nightfall. Doctor Partridge, what has been the point of it all? Is survival really so important?'

'God only knows, lass; I certainly don't. All I can do is my job— when they give me the tools to do it with—and all I can hope is that some day we will understand enough of what has happened to learn something from it. I don't mind telling you, though, that when I think of what's to come for those poor devils inside, the conditions we have to make 'em travel under, I wish I could pack up and join you ladies when you leave, abandon my responsibilities here for ever.'

He fumbled for a stub of cheroot in his pocket. 'Got to thank you,' he said as he puffed it to a glow. 'Good work you've done, and Mrs Barry and the Birch girls. Didn't much like the idea of women around this place, but things would have been even worse without you. Got to admit that.'

'I wish we could have done more.'

'So do I, Miss Laura. Not much any of us could do. That's the trouble with being a doctor; know what's wrong, can't put it right most often. At least, not here. But thank you for what you did.'

We strolled together around the corner of the Banqueting Hall and looked out to the rough rectangle between ourselves, Dr Fayrer's house and the Resident's House, where the women and children were gathered and waiting to make their way down to the Baillie Guard.

About five hundred of us were expected to move out that day. I had envisaged an orderly line of well-conducted females, something like a school 'crocodile', walking or, if they were lucky, riding or being carried, away from the entrenchment in a decorous and mournful procession.

The reality of the evacuation bore no relation whatever to my polite imaginings.

What I saw before me in the dusty morning sunlight was a tumultuous, milling confusion of natives, animals and vehicles, in the midst of which the women themselves were almost invisible. A 'modicum of personal baggage' was what we had been told we could take with us, and I had to laugh, despite my recent tears, at the ladies' interpretation of the term.

Here were bullock-carts piled feet high with boxes, bales, uniform chests and bulbous-topped sea-trunks; dilapidated carts and carriages stuffed to the windows with possessions; palanquins and litters, curtains bulging, their bearers groaning under the weight of packed and unpacked effects, while the ladies, for whom the conveyances had been procured with such effort, walked gaily beside them. *Doolie* men strained under the weight of whole families; and donkeys, horses, mules and even bullocks swayed by under double panniers loaded with bundles, a woman or child perched precariously atop each load. In amongst the wheels and hooves, spindle-shanked coolies threaded their way with mounds of boxes and bundles on their heads and crates of china, mirrors and ornaments of all sorts—spoils from the palaces—strapped to their sweating backs.

Axles squeaked, donkeys brayed, horses whinnied and reared; children cried and women called to each other through the dust, now fast becoming a cloud, while distraught husbands, running alongside the cavalcade, shouted last-minute instructions, or thrust a final package on to an already swaying pile on some coolie's bobbing head.

'Well, they are really off at last, it seems,' said Dr Partridge when we had watched the *mêlée* together for a few minutes, smiling at the pandemonium. 'Don't want to be left behind, do you? Better cut along now, missie.'

'Do you know, Doctor,' I answered slowly, my mind crowded with memories. 'I don't think I'd mind if I were left behind. So much of me will always be here.'

'So it is with most of us, child. But you're young. You'll learn to forget whatever lad it was you gave your heart to here and in time you'll find another.'

He was wrong, but I shook his hand and wished him luck.

'I'll see you in Cawnpore, if not before. I'll come looking for you—when we collect.'

'God willing, missie. God willing.'

Dr Darby, bluff, brusque Dr Darby, whose wife had borne a child to him behind a gun in Wheeler's entrenchment in Cawnpore and then succumbed, with her baby, to a pandy bayonet at the river, Dr Darby had been wounded the day before. I would have liked to see him, but when I enquired, Dr Partridge shook his head. 'He's going, and he'll be glad to go, Miss Laura. Don't fret him with farewells.' We shook hands again and went our different ways.

'Don't fret him with farewells.' Was that what kept Oliver away from me, I wondered, as I walked back to the Gaol by a circuitous route in order to miss the crowds. Could it be that, feeling he had lost me to Charles, he preferred not to re-open old wounds? Did he really intend to keep away from me altogether? I had to find him before we left; I had to explain and, if that was what he wanted, apologize, give in. I had to make things right between us before we left, for what if the pandies, enraged by our safe departure, really launched the great attack against the Residency that had been threatened for days past?

The breaching guns at the Kaiser Bagh, which were to cover our retreat, had been thundering all morning, but we had become so used to the sound of gunfire that I had not noticed them until Kate drew my attention to the noise.

'Well, sure and I'm glad to see you! We thought you'd gone for good; wherever have you been? Those guns are driving me mad! Everything's ready but I don't seem able to collect myself at all. Now what are you doing in that calm way, just sitting down as though you've all of time before you? We must be up and moving. See, Jessie and I have everything prepared.'

'There is no point in hurrying,' I told them. 'You should see the press trying to get out of the Baillie Guard. We are to move off in small groups, it seems, a delay between each; so it will be hours before everyone is through.'

'Och, but they're away already!' Kate nodded her head in the direction of the Bonners' deserted rooms. 'Such a to-do. The *ayah*, the sweeper and poor little Minnie all hung about with boxes and bundles, and herself seated in a *doolie* almost invisible among her possessions, and grumbling all the time, she was, at Sir Colin and his ill-bred lack of consideration for the necessities of the "genteel". I'll tell you and truly, woman dear, that ould besom has been more of a trial to me than all the pandies in Oudh put together!'

'I saw them,' I laughed, 'and many others even more loaded down with worldly goods. Where has all the stuff come from? Maria Germon had to be helped on to her horse by two strong men; she has put on so many layers of clothing, every layer lined with pockets full of her treasures, that she is completely spherical, and on top of everything else she is wearing a worsted hat tied on with a woollen scarf. Such a sketch! Even her horse is alarmed by the sight she makes. But it will be hours before we can get away, so we might as well wait here as in the dust and the crowd.'

'And we're to be the last?' Kate's sharp eyes took in my anxious face.

'No—not the last. But a little longer, Kate, please? A little longer?'

'He'll come by, your man, Miss Laura. We'll bide a whiles and he'll come by.'

'I've never managed to hide anything from you two, have I?' I smiled.

'Not much, woman dear, not much. He'll be no more happy at your going than you are. He'll come, I'm sure of it.'

So, contrary to our expectations, we ate one more meal in that small, dark room so full of associations. Kate produced some salt biscuits and a packet of dates given her by one of the 'Shannons', and for the last time we poured ourselves tepid water from the earthenware jar in the corner, fishing out the mosquito larvae before we drank.

The guns of the *Shannon*, battering the great red walls of the Kaiser Bagh, increased in power and frequency, and idly I wondered if it were true that a party of English prisoners were still held fast in some room of that vast palace. Poor creatures: to run the risk of death from their own guns after so many months in the pandies' hands! I hoped that if the story were true, the unfortunate sufferers were already dead.

We were dusting the crumbs from our laps, when Toddy-Bob appeared on the verandah, grinning from ear to ear.

'Tod! Where have you been all these days? We've seen nor hide nor hair of you for ages,' cried Kate.

My heart in my eyes, I looked beyond Toddy's small form, but his master had not come with him.

'Busy,' Tod said shortly. 'A mite busy the last days 'ave bin, what with one thing and another. But now, we've a nag for you!' he announced with pride and backed on to the verandah, beckoning us to follow. 'A rotten ol' bag o' bones and an insult to the name of 'orse—but yours!' He flourished a hand and we were rewarded with the sight of an extremely tall, extremely thin piebald mare, tied to a post by cracked reins.

'Toddy! It's a miracle!' I exclaimed in delight. 'How on earth did you manage it? ... No, I'm not going to scold.'

'Well now, miss, and I don't know as 'ow the Guv'nor would care for me to answer that question, but what I can say is 'ow we been after that there animal for two nights and a day, neglectin' all our duties into the bargain.'

'God bless you all for it,' said Kate fervently. 'And tell your Guv'nor we don't care a damn how he came by it. We thank him heartily.'

'Yes'm,' responded Toddy demurely with downcast eyes.

'We ... we will see Mr Erskine won't we, Tod? Later?' I enquired timorously.

'Can't say, miss—things being what you might call uncertain like.'

'But surely he will see us before we leave for the Dilkusha?'

'P'raps,' he said doubtfully.

'Toddy, how is he? I have been thinking he might have been injured, we haven't seen him for days.'

'Not injured, no, miss. But in a filthy black temper like I never seen 'im in afore, and more longer lastin', too!' He looked at me with undisguised accusation.

'He is?'

'Yes, miss. Fit to be tied 'e is. Cussin' and swearin' at nothin' at all, nearly took 'is fist to me yesterday and 'e even yelled at Ishmial, and y'know, miss, 'e never yells at no blackie what can't answer back. Says it ain't proper.'

'Aye! That would be his arm,' Jessie said consolingly to me. 'He's the sort o' man who's unco' set on doin' all for himself, and when he finds himself hampered, nae doubt he's like to be a wee bit thrawn.'

'Maybe,' allowed Toddy with scepticism. 'But I'm thinkin' 'is trouble is otherwhere.'

My cheeks flushed under the direct gaze of the black eyes, and I walked away to pat the horse, which stood with its nose in a nosebag and regarded me mildly as it chewed.

'Now look here, Tod!' Kate was peremptory. 'We must see Mr Erskine before we go. We want to thank him for his kindness in sending us that ... that creature. And we must make arrangements for when we meet in the Dilkusha. Nip along smartly now and ask him to come up here before we leave. Miss Laura says it will be some time before we move, but hurry. I suppose you are accompanying us, as we have no *syce*?'

'No, sorry, ma'am. You'll have to manage by yourselves. We've all to wait where we are until word is given us to move. Can't come with you. Orders!'

Orders had never yet kept Toddy in line. I knew he was only putting his master's needs before ours, and loved him for it.

'Well, that's a pity. We could have done with your company, Tod. But never mind, hurry back and ask Mr Oliver to come and speak to me. Please?' Kate almost pleaded.

'I'll do me best, ma'am, but I ain't promisin' nothin'. Like I say, 'e's that difficult, and me askin' 'im to do somethin' don't mean 'e'll do it.'

'We understand, but do try.'

'Right!' and Toddy was away without a word of farewell.

He had not been gone five minutes when we were discovered by an officer whose duty it was to see that the Thug Gaol was vacated. He ordered us to prepare for departure.

'But we are waiting for someone, to say goodbye!' I protested frantically.

'Can't help that, young lady. You should be with the other families now, should have been an hour ago, matter of fact. You might get left behind.'

'Oh, nonsense! I've seen what it is like up there. We'll be ages waiting, and the noise and the dust will be bad for the baby.'

'Come along now, miss. I've no time to waste. Your friend can find you on the parade ground. Mount up now, and a safe journey to you all.'

We had already drawn straws to determine which of us would be the first to ride the horse and hold the baby, and Jessie had won.

We pushed her up on to the saddle, tied our bundles to the pommel with string and bootlaces, and then handed her the child. It was the first time Jessie had been on a horse, but once up she sat as imperturbably as a figure on an equestrian statue, only her face, frozen into immobility by her novel situation, betraying her nervousness.

I led the beast by the bridle. Kate, carrying her umbrella, brought up the rear. Slowly we walked down the alley away from the long low building.

At first glance it seemed that none of the women could yet have left the entrenchment, so many of them still crowded the space before the Resident's House, with their children, servants, possessions and conveyances. On looking down the slope through the Baillie Guard, however, I could see a long, interrupted straggle of carriages, litters and small parties on foot, making towards the far end of the extended perimeter.

For more than an hour we waited in the midday sun, Jessie aloft, still as a statue, or as much so as the querulous baby would allow her to be, Kate and I losing energy by the moment as we tried to keep our positions near the horse, while the jostling throng pushed and heaved around us. How I wished I had drawn the shortest straw and sat where Jessie now sat, in a position to search the faces of the crowd. It was not hot; but anxiety, glare, dust and noise soon had me longing for the dim little kitchen in the Gaol, or if not that, then just to be moving at last. I knew that had Toddy managed to persuade Oliver to come to us, they would have found us on the parade ground without much difficulty. The fact that neither of them had appeared after this considerable length of time served only to heighten my disquiet.

When Charles joined us, full of last-minute instructions and advice, I nodded dutifully, not really listening, my eyes scanning the restless crowd.

We were to keep together, he said, whatever happened, to do exactly as we were told by the officers in charge of the route, and he would see us in the Dilkusha in a couple of days' time.

At last our names were called and we moved into line, Pearl crying, Jessie clutching the child with one hand, the pommel with the other, while I tugged the reins to make the horse move. Then, having gained our place in the motley procession, there was another long wait while the parties ahead of us moved down the slope, through the Baillie Guard and over the broken ground to the palaces, with a considerable pause between the departure of each.

The last thing I remember, oddly enough, of the siege of Lucknow, is laughter.

Inching our way forward in that dull forced patience which long expectation brings, I heard Kate's youthful laughter as she stood, her arms akimbo, in the dusty sunlight and said in the intervals of her mirth, 'Don Quixote! It's pure Cervantes! You, Laura, in your big straw hat are Sancho Panza to the life, Jess in her frozen, frightened dignity could well be the Crazy Knight, and the nag ... but of course, the nag is the very ghost of Rosinante!'

'Barry ... Hewitt ... MacGregor ... Flood, infant. Forward!'

We had reached the head of the column.

'Jessie! It's us. Kate, come on ... come on ... it's us!' Caught almost unawares, I was suddenly panic-stricken that we should not get away. I grabbed Rosinante's bridle and hauled her forward at a trot, while Jessie screamed and clutched the pommel, and Kate ran after us, still laughing, and waving her umbrella in farewell.

This time, at all events, and whatever might happen in the coming days, this time, for us, the Siege of Lucknow was over.

CHAPTER 7

There was no time for nostalgic farewells as we moved for the last time down the slope to the gate.

Laughing at my anxiety, Charles ran up and took the reins from me, leading Rosinante through the Baillie Guard as I fell into step beside Kate, hurrying to keep up with the ungainly stride of the mare. A carriage pulled by two bare-ribbed hacks was so close behind us that I could feel their breath upon my neck if I slowed. While we had been waiting to move, a lucky pandy shell had ignited a ramp of earth-covered firewood forming part of the old defences, and billowing smoke mingled with the dust to dim the sunlight as we went. For a couple of seconds, passing beneath the arch of the gateway, we were in deep shadow; then, once again, we found ourselves in the yellow afternoon light, the dust, the smoke and the Baillie Guard behind us. A moment of darkness; a name we would never forget—a gateway that had led me to a life within my life. I remembered that as we had entered the entrenchment nearly five months before, Ishmial had knelt in the shadow of that arch and laid his forehead to the ground in prayer.

Now the noise of the guns, both our own and those of the enemy, was thunderous, and we needed no urging to make haste. We moved over the stretch of torn ground that had once been no-man's land between the pandies and ourselves, and veered to the left, skirting the high walls of the riverside palaces until the Tehri Kothi was behind us. Halfway along the wall of the Farhat Baksh, we entered a gateway, and then continued eastwards through a maze of alleys, courts and cloistered gardens. The Farhat Baksh had held the throne-room of the Nawabs of Oudh, but now the huge halls of the palace, visible through lofty, shattered windows, were a scene of utter ruin, and at every window and balcony our own armed and curious soldiery stood guard over our progress. A breach in tile-coped wall led us into the park of the

Chathar Manzil, through more gardens, across wide lawns running down to the river, past pretty enclosures full of defaced statuary and marble pavilions picked out with jade, jasper and lapis lazuli.

Progress was slow, for we were stopped often by mishaps suffered by those before us. A sudden thought occurred to me as we waited.

'Charles, why isn't Oliver with us? I mean, why hasn't he left the entrenchment now, as others have? Oliver didn't need to stay; he can't even shoot a rifle, after all. Are you sure he hasn't already set off?'

'Quite sure. How can you doubt it? He wouldn't be caught dead with the women and children, even if he'd lost both arms. Besides, he's done pretty well with his pistol in the last few days. Toddy-Bob has been finding him ammo to practise with (illegally, naturally) and his aim is almost as good as it was. Last I saw of him, yesterday, he was sitting on a balcony near the Mess House, having a great time picking off pandies unwary enough to show themselves below him.'

'Oh, Charles, no! I had no idea he was … he was fighting. I thought he was only in the mines.'

'He's all right, Laura.' Charles showed his impatience at my concern by tugging Rosinante's bridle so sharply that he nearly unseated Jessie. 'He's all right. By heavens, he's managed to take care of himself pretty adequately so far; he'll come to no harm now.'

'If you see him, will you tell him I was disappointed at having to leave without speaking to him, and ask him to come to us directly he reaches the Dilkusha. Please?'

'Very well. *If* I see him.'

'Do try to, Charles, for my sake. And keep an eye on him. He is not yet himself.'

'Very well. Now look, we are moving again, and I can only come as far as the perimeter with you. They are going to move the sick tonight, and there'll be a lot for every man-jack of us to do. You'll be receiving precise orders soon, and for heaven's sake obey them—exactly! Above all, you are to be quiet, absolutely quiet. It's imperative. Not a word or a laugh or a cry, and keep Pearl still, Jessie. Feed her again if it is necessary. Everything depends on your silence, not only for each of you but for all the others. Understand?'

We promised in some bewilderment to do as he said. Why on earth should we be quiet? Who could hope to move such a disorganized body as we were in silence?

'It will only be a couple of days before I join you,' he went on. 'You'll be taken good care of, I'm sure, but if you should want for anything, enquire for Colonel Tucker. I have asked him to have a care for you. There's no need to worry; the country is thick with our fellows now, but do be quiet until you reach the Sikander Bagh, where, by the way, you are to be fed.'

Our way through the palace gardens had taken us through several breached walls, and now we approached another. The delays we encountered had generally been due to the gaps being too narrow for a loaded cart or carriage, and once again we saw a bullock-cart before us being unloaded so that it could be passed through the breach on its side, while soldiers hastily attacked the wall with picks and bayonets to widen the opening for those yet to follow.

'This is as far as I may come,' said Charles as we halted. He was obviously nervous despite his reassuring words, so I felt my nervousness grow in response. What were we about to encounter in the hostile world beyond the wall? Behind us the column had stopped and, though we had set out with considerable intervals between each party, now the long, interrupted line had been concertinaed by the frequent delays, and had become a heaving *mêlée* of animals, carriages and people. Everyone grumbled, of course. Irate heads were poked out of carriage windows to protest, anxious mothers tried surreptitiously to edge themselves and their offspring further forward in the line, while harassed soldiers tried to keep the column from disintegrating, by insisting that drivers stay in their seats and coolies not dispose of their loads while waiting. No one paid much attention to the politely impatient commands; very soon the spreading lawns were peopled with skinny coolies pulling imperturbably on their *biris* as they took their ease, while horses edged their vehicles in all directions to take a nibble at camellia hedges and flowerbeds, their drivers having joined the coolies.

Finally the cart was manhandled through the gap in the wall, and we were ordered to move on. Charles kissed me on the cheek, clutched the baby's hand in his for a moment, then stepped back to allow Rosinante to proceed.

On the far side of the wall, a small group of officers awaited us, stopping each party in turn to issue instructions. We were told that our route would now take us through the outskirts of the city, following the river for a considerable portion of the way, to the Sikander Bagh. There we would be fed and would rest until nightfall, and then move on to the Dilkusha Palace under cover of darkness. We would be covered every inch of the way as we went, but were to remember that the enemy would always be within a very short distance of us as we walked. The guns of the Residency, the *Shannon's* guns at the Kaiser Bagh, and other artillery brought up by Sir Colin Campbell, were harrying the pandies at every point possible to deflect their attention from what was taking place under their noses, but we were never to forget that, though out of the Residency, we were still under fire—constantly. So far the pandies had no idea of the evacuation, and it was imperative that they remain in ignorance of it until our escape was complete—a matter of several hours at least. To this end, we were to be as silent as possible, obey all further instructions immediately and implicitly, and endeavour to keep with our own parties and in our proper place in the column. We would encounter several points on the route which were especially hazardous. At these, we must wait until signalled to proceed, dismounting, stooping or crawling as instructed. The officers wished us luck.

I was still bewildered. A straggling circus of excited women and overwrought children, coolies, animals, soldiers and conveyances could hardly remain hidden from the pandies in broad daylight for very long, particularly since the dust rising above us must indicate that some considerable body was in movement.

However, we fell into position and set off, I prodding Rosinante with Kate's green-lined umbrella, for she was more than a little reluctant to put one foot before the other.

From the final breach in the perimeter onwards we continued our way, guarded by an extended picket of soldiers, weapons ready bayoneted, who stood within a few yards of each other in an unbroken line for the length of our route. On the flat roofs crowning the tall, blank-faced houses, crouched behind balustrades and chimneystacks, further uniformed figures glanced down at us briefly as we passed, while officers on horseback patrolled the road, motioning us forward, halting us, directing us and exhorting us to silence. Brightly plaided Highlanders, blue-smocked 'Shannons', tall, bearded Sikhs, stocky pug-nosed Irishmen, all alike in their tense alertness, as eyes moved watchfully over the rooftops, windows and balconies, and flicked only briefly over the bedraggled cavalcade they guarded.

We had entered a network of narrow roads and laneways cutting through the usual agglomeration of high native houses, walled courtyards and open-fronted shops, all cleared in the battles of the previous two days, but still ground of contention between the pandies and our own men. Rifle and musket fire was continuous and heavy, sometimes from only the breadth of a house away, while from over the river the enemy's heavy guns belched their cargoes of death high over our heads towards the entrenchment. Often the high buildings petered out in low, thatched slum shacks, or were interrupted by the paved and guttered square of a deserted bazaar, leaving our route open to the river or the city. In such places screens of bamboo and sacking had been erected to foil hostile eyes, while in other sections trenches had been dug, along which we were required to walk or crawl, while baggage carts and animals took their chances above us.

It was an eerie sensation that beset us as we padded through those dusty streets deserted by all save ourselves and the soldiery. No sacred bulls nuzzled the choked gutters; no beggars cried for *baksheesh* at the corners; no poverty-marked crowds of tattered men and veiled women thronged and jostled; no naked children played among the heaps of refuse; only here and there a ring-tailed, yellow-eyed pi-dog sniffed suspiciously as we passed, then returned to the undisputed largesse of the garbage.

It was not hot, but in these enclosed lanes stinking of urine and excrement, the base of whose buildings were stained waist high with the vermilion saliva of betel-chewers, we were soon perspiring. The noise unnerved us. Musket and rifle fired so close that we could smell the cordite above the filth; shells burst noisily just out of sight and sometimes, more alarmingly, in the air above us, and heavy shot and ball cannonaded into buildings, filling the air with lime dust and particles of shattered masonry. Beyond the buildings that hedged our passage from the pandies' sight, we could hear the enemy shouting directions and calling to each other, and once I clapped my hands over my ears to shut out the terrified shrieks of a wounded man.

Delays were constant and hazardous, each narrow section of street causing a bottleneck that rapidly backed up vehicles, animals and humans, all fretting with impatience and fear, but none daring to utter a word of protest. Baggage tumbled off carts and out of panniers and had to be replaced under the frenzied eyes of the owners, giving vent to their wrath in dumb-show. Once, a half-starved horse, pulling a landaulet just ahead of us, lay down with a grunt and died; coolies had to be found to take over the poor beast's task. On three occasions, everyone was held up when Mrs Polehampton's harmonium tumbled off the back of the camel that carried it. The harmonium had belonged to the Reverend Mr Polehampton, and his widow would not move a step until it was safely resecured atop the beast.

The tension of the humans communicated itself to the animals, who became difficult to control. Horses reared suddenly, pawing the air, always with some *syce* or soldier clinging to their muzzles to prevent them neighing. Bullocks grunted and stopped stock-still, heads low between their knobbled knees, red eyes rolling with terror; no amount of belabouring could move them. Only our Rosinante, imperturbable if lethargic, and the blinkered mules tightly muzzled with rope, seemed too foolish to catch the infection of fear and plodded quietly on through the noise.

Time and again a man of the picket line would leap from his place to fire at a head or an arm visible on a rooftop, and time and again I closed my eyes and held my breath, waiting for the shout that would reveal our escaping presence and draw the enemy fire. But our luck held. We continued on our way, slowly, with many stumblings, delays and grumblings, but steadily.

The troops lining our way had yet to set foot in the Residency they had fought to free, having been moved up that day from the Martinière or Dilkusha where Sir Colin had left them on his final surge towards us. I noticed that they eyed us with frank curiosity, not untinged, I also noticed, with distaste, and smiled to myself when I realized what disappointment they must feel on finally coming face to face with the 'Dear Creatures' (as Sir Colin insisted on calling us) whom they had delivered. I could only guess the visions they had concocted of the frail and delicate females it had been their privilege to liberate. Frail most of us certainly were from lack of food, but those of us who had survived those 142 days and nights in Lucknow would never again be considered delicate.

What the wondering eyes of those stolid stalwarts beheld was a straggle of scrawny women and pale, big-eyed children, doggedly putting one foot before the other with total concentration on proceeding as fast as broken shoes and blisters would allow. Dressed in a wonderful assortment of shabby garments, usually bonnetless, generally cloakless, wrapped in finest Kashmir shawls from the palaces or in quilted cotton from the servants of the palaces, not a face was entirely clean, nor was there one that did not bear the marks of more years than its owner counted. There were, of course, a lucky few, like the Gubbinses and the Bonners, still adequately dressed and accoutred with the symbols of their state in life. But I speak of the majority of us: the wives of the soldiers of the 32nd, of the officers of mutinous native regiments, or widows and 'unprotected females' like Kate and myself. It was we whom the soldiers had the opportunity to examine, and tired, frightened and bedraggled as we were, we must have looked a graceless lot.

Once, having halted for some delay ahead, I heard a blue-uniformed 'Shannon' mutter to his mate, 'Not what you'd call a likely bunch o' lookers!'

His mate shrugged and replied, 'Can't even thank a fellow for 'elpin' 'em over a wall, let alone out o' Lucknow!' Thereafter Kate and I were voluble in our whispered thanks for any proffered arm, and we were often in need of assistance.

Several times we were ordered to run, when the firing was particularly heavy; several times, too, Jessie was made to dismount and keep under cover of Rosinante when the bullets flew too close. We stooped as we walked; we ran; we crawled through muddy ditches and clambered over broken walls. We sheltered in a ruined house, holding our breath, while a party of pandies hauled a gun over the cobbles just on the other side of the flimsy wall, and halted again, and as nervously, while a battle on the roofs above us moved to a safer distance. We hauled Rosinante over yards of hoof-cutting debris; and pushed her through feet of evil-smelling water; we pulled her through humble courtyards still littered with the domestic remains of small lives; and puffed after her, waving the umbrella, when once a shell burst too close for the comfort of even her stolid mind.

So long unused to lengthy walking, our feet were soon sore, and I was nearly through the thin soles of my old shoes when, at about five in the evening, we at last reached the Sikander Bagh.

The buildings had been thinning out, giving way to orchards, groves and high-walled gardens, when, of a sudden, we found ourselves in the country. Rosinante came to a stop, and I looked up to see fields of sugar cane where partridge called, a jarmin avenue loud with monkeys quarrelling, and mango *topes* glistening in the late and slanting sun. I smelled the fresh and forgotten scent of green things growing in damp soil.

Jessie handed the baby down to Kate and slid wearily from the saddle, rubbing her rear. Kate held Pearl up to see the monkeys, and I bent down and pulled a handful of young grey-green gram leaves from the roadside and sniffed the tangy fragrance with closed eyes.

This was freedom. This was what life had been—before.

Quiet, gentle things; trees and birds, crops springing in the tended earth, and a wide horizon.

Unmindful of our wondering eyes, as we stood silently and watched them, a young boy in a loincloth and dirty muslin shirt, accompanied by a skinny yellow pi-dog, drove his family's milch cow home through the sugar cane, playing a bamboo flute as he went. Further off, a couple of women walked towards the setting sun, tall earthen pots on their padded heads, full cotton skirts swinging rhythmically to their straight-backed graceful stride. An old man with another ring-tailed dog precisely like the first, paused and watched us, chewing betel-nut with toothless jaws. Beyond the cane fields, a smudge of grey smoke against the flushing sunset sky indicated some small hamlet pursuing its ancient humble ways within sound of the guns that had battered us for five gruesome months.

But behind us the cannonade continued, and around us, everywhere, armed men were watchful. We were still within range of the enemy.

In a meadow studded with huge mango trees, within sight of the shattered walls of the Sikander Bagh, families were taking their ease. It was the battle for these very walls that I had glimpsed from the roof of the hospital three days before, when a neighbour had loaned me his fieldglass and I had caught the glint of morning sunshine on massed bayonets. I had turned away, escaping the sight. But here the rebels had been cut to pieces by the Highlanders in a final frenzied blood-letting before they stormed on to the Residency, and here 1,857 bodies had been counted after the carnage. Some of those bodies, we were told, still lay unburied in the fly-infested, stinking space that had once been the flowery, fountain-flowing Garden of Alexander.

Sir Colin's staff had prepared well for us. Under the trees, food was set out: bread, butter and jam, biscuits and platters of fresh fruit. Huge 'dixies' of tea steamed on the usual cook-stoves of three bricks and a few smouldering dungpats. Kate, Jess and I loaded ourselves shamelessly with all that was offered, then retired to a eucalyptus grove where we had tethered Rosinante and partook of our feast with concentration, never uttering a word until the last crumb was picked from our skirts and consumed, and the last drop of tea drained from the mugs. Then Jessie looked at Kate and myself, rose, collected the mugs and set off to have them refilled with wine, while Kate and I lay back and laughed at the picture of our stern Covenanter departing in search of strong liquor.

We drank the wine with even more appreciation than the tea, but not as silently; then watched the alarms and excitements around us with admirable detachment.

Children lost their parents, women mislaid their possessions, servants got separated from their mistresses, and distraught officers scampered through the crowd, trying to find the woman who had requested the cheese or the parent of a loudly objecting child summarily rescued from a tree. Tired infants bellowed for their beds; exhausted mothers smacked and scolded, and the grass was thick with discarded boots and shoes, their owners trying tenderly to restore their feet in the cool evening air. A subdued hubbub filled the area, growing at times to an appreciable roar, as new parties arrived and were screamed at in welcome by their friends.

A strange large soldier, bearded and grim, stood for five solid minutes looking down at Pearl, innocently and sweetly asleep in Jessie's ample lap. Now and then he shook his head. At last he said, 'That babe was born there?'

'Not quite,' I answered. 'She was about two months old when we entered the entrenchment.'

'And she lived!'

He bent down and laid one large finger along the baby's thin cheek. 'She lived!' He shook his head, saluted and went away.

Closing my eyes, my back against a tree, I surrendered myself to this strange experience of liberty. The evening was closing in; to the west, behind the angry city we had left, the sky was rose and red, but to the east it was washed in that pellucid duck-egg green, lined with light, seen nowhere but in India. The copse of long-leaved eucalyptus trees stirred in the evening breeze with the sound of crumpling paper, showering us with lemony fragrance. Flights of emerald, ring-necked parrots shot screaming through the trees, and the mynas, unmindful of war, flight or fear, squabbled for their night-time perches in disregard of the human horde invading their dormitory.

Oliver! Oliver ... I thought, and fell asleep with his name in my mind.

When I woke, darkness was upon us and I was cold on the cold dewy ground. Kate, who had drawn the second longest straw, was already mounted on Rosinante with Pearl in her arms. Cursing my sore feet and broken shoes, I joined Jessie behind her. No lights were allowed us and the night was like pitch.

Soon after we had taken our place in the column and left the hospitable meadow behind us, the disorganized cavalcade degenerated into chaos. The rough road, swept over during these past days by thousands of feet, hooves and wheels, was now a morass of sticky sand, scarred with shellholes and shallow trenches.

Carriages stuck axle-deep in the mire. Horses stumbled, spilling their loads into the confusion and unseating their riders. Bullock-carts sank to their flooring and were abandoned. *Doolie* bearers lost their way and carried frightened women far out into strange fields. The extended picket of the earlier hours of our journey had been replaced by an escort of troops, who, with great goodwill, slung their weapons on their shoulders to heave at carriages full of grumbling, tearful women, whip bullocks into motion, round up riderless horses, carry sleeping children, or thrash coolies attempting to desert with their loads.

Our party kept together by the simple expedient of my holding the reins and Jessie clutching the tail of Rosinante. I lost a shoe in sand, fell more than once, and had my bare foot trodden on by a passing infantryman, but I hung on to those reins as though they grew from my fingers.

For two and a half dreadful hours, confusion reigned in the unrelieved darkness, a heaving turmoil of seemingly directionless movement, during which we somehow covered the miles to the Dilkusha. At last, after a halt due to some mishap further up the column, we learned that we had arrived. At once there was pandemonium, everyone abandoning their places in the line to search for friends, quarters and food. The earliest arrivals had been lucky and were already settled for the night, but the arrangements made for our reception proved entirely inadequate for the numbers. What few tents had been erected were already occupied, we were told by a harassed officer, as also was that part of the Dilkusha Palace not already occupied by Sir Colin's staff.

The night resounded with complaints, grumbles and querulous pleas for help, while embarrassed officers and bewildered men tried to cope with a couple of hundred exhausted, ill-tempered women, children and their cohort of attendants.

'Oh for Toddy-Bob!' I sighed, as we looked around wondering which direction might lead us to shelter and a bed. 'He'd have us housed and fed in a trice whatever the circumstances.'

'We must look for an officer's mess,' Kate rallied herself to decide. 'There's bound to be someone I know. This is the sort of occasion when a man is indispensable.'

So Jessie took the sleeping Pearl, Kate dismounted, and still all holding firmly to some part of Rosinante or her saddlery, we set off.

The darkness of the vast park was almost impenetrable as we threaded our way through tents and carriages, *doolies* and limbers, mounds of baggage and supplies, bells of arms and stacked cases of ammunition, and over lines of weary soldiers sleeping imperturbably on the ground. Here was a corral of horses, fine well-fed ones of the relief, there bullocks dozed heavily, recumbent in a cloud of gnats; camels belched in rude surprise as we disturbed them, and elephants flapped huge ears in curiosity. Small cow-dung fires glimmered under the trees as servants smacked out *chapattis* between their palms, swinging easily on their haunches in the firelight. Above them, hanging upside down among the mango leaves, fruit bats squeaked like mice, red eyes reflecting the flame.

The palace itself was lighted and alive with officers, but so many families had gathered on the wide verandah waiting for help that we decided we would be quicker served elsewhere, even if by chance. But we wandered to the very outskirts of the park and found nothing in the way of a mess tent. At the end of our endurance, beginning to feel that we could sleep standing up if necessary, we were hailed by a mounted officer.

'Ladies ... please! Would any of you know a Mrs Barry? Mrs George Barry?' he called out of the gloom.

'Glory be to God! We're saved and just in time!' groaned Kate, then called out that she was Mrs Barry.

The officer cantered up to us and dismounted.

'Mrs Barry?' He held out a neatly gloved hand, peering towards Kate.

'It is, and you, if I'm not very much mistaken, are Johnny James!'

'Mrs Barry! I …'

'Yes, I know! You never would have recognized me. But it's me all the same. Laura, Jessie—this young man used to be one of my boys, and not so long ago either. Lieutenant James.'

'Why, Mrs B, when I heard that you had been in Lucknow all through, I swore I'd find you out and see you comfortable. I'd heard … about your husband!'

'There you are, you see,' Kate said triumphantly. 'My boys never forget me.'

'But this is wonderful, Mrs B. I was beginning to think …'

'Ah, well, no, I've not succumbed yet! But if I don't soon find some place to lie down and sleep, I probably will, and so will my friends.'

'Come along with me. I've cleared my tent for you and we can squeeze the other ladies in somehow. Oh, and I see you have a dear little baby with you!'

This is no time for sentimentality, I thought to myself ungratefully, and why will a man gush over a baby who can get along quite well without a bed, when he has three exhausted females on his hands?

Lieutenant James was not the Army's most intelligent officer, but he was kind. Soon we were seated on groundsheets before a fine fire, drinking more wine while a meal was prepared for us. The tent would just take the three of us packed like sardines, with Pearl squeezed somewhere between us. None of us, I am afraid, gave a thought to where Lieutenant James himself would sleep that night.

The meal appeared. Ham, bread and butter, cheese and a pitcher of milk. But the day had been too much for me. I ate two mouthfuls of ham, excused myself, crawled into the tent and was asleep before I had closed my eyes.

They tell me that dire confusion continued all that night. Soon after the last of the families were in, the sick began to arrive, and the great treed park resounded with noise and bustle until morning. I heard none of it, and it was nearly noon the next day before I awoke.

Lieutenant James's servant brought me hot water to wash in, and later a meal to which, this time, I did full justice. There were eggs, I remember. Two boiled eggs and toasted bread.

Rested and refreshed, I only then realized how painful my right foot was from having been walked on for some considerable distance without a shoe. The sole showed several cuts and gashes, the toes were bruised and swollen, and blisters, formed during the first part of the journey, had burst and were suppurating. I cleaned it as best I could, and later in the day, on a visit to the quarters of the sick, Kate managed to procure some salve, lint and a bandage for me.

The fearful suffering of the wounded as they were borne away from the Residency had caused many deaths, including that of dear, dour Dr Darby. Those who had survived described to Kate something of the horrors of the journey they had made. Packed one on top of the other into ambulances and litters, jogged, pushed, pulled and dropped along the length of the hazardous and obstructed route we too had followed, wounds burst open afresh, fevers soared, splints on fractured limbs worked loose, dressings were torn off by the struggling limbs of companions, and they were the luckiest who had lapsed into unconsciousness. Now every doctor was hard at work trying to undo the damage of the march, but within a few days the sick would have to endure yet further torment as they were moved on to Cawnpore.

For the next two days we continued quietly recouping our strength, while the troops brought order into the camp, throwing up streets of tents in orderly rows under the trees, digging latrines, providing cookhouses and fuel, removing the various animals to a distance, and cosseting the children with pots of jam from their own ration, and rides on elephants and camels. The women sat in the dappled sunshine in peaceful idleness, or read and reread the letters that had awaited them at the Dilkusha. The children revived in the bright, clean air of the park, and were seldom seen without a crust of the long-coveted white bread or a paper squill full of the even more longed-for sugar. Even without Toddy-Bob, we managed to procure soap and the services of a *dhobi* to wash and iron our clothes.

Always in the distance, however, we could hear the muted cannonade from the city, where the men of the Old Garrison and the first relief made ready to withdraw. Those of us capable of thinking of something other than our new wellbeing were dismayed at the news that General

Havelock, just created Sir Henry Havelock, was said to be on the verge of death.

Despite the salve and bandage, my foot remained painful and swollen, and I was happy enough to remain in a canvas chair placed outside Lieutenant James's tent, relying on Kate and Jessie to bring me whatever news they garnered in their wanderings around the camp. On the second day Jessie, wise in the ways of regimental bazaars, brought me a pair of scarlet slippers to replace my single outworn shoe. They were pretty things, with pointed, curly toes ending in a bobble of scarlet and gold and embroidered in gold thread, but my foot forbade me trying them on. So I placed them near me and spent much time admiring them, the first finery that had come my way in many months.

At sundown on the 22nd November, as I sat alone by the fire waiting for the others to return to the tent for supper, Ungud appeared out of the gathering shadows, leading a fine mare.

'*Salaam!*' he said, touching his forehead as he bowed his head, then continued without preamble, cutting into my exclamations of pleasure and surprise. 'I have brought him a horse, see! A good one. He will need it.'

I knew it was for Oliver, and my heart leapt.

'It is a good horse,' Ungud reiterated, in case I was too foolish to realize the fact, 'and many cast covetous eyes at it. I will take it to the lines and remain to watch it until he comes.'

I agreed with alacrity.

The small brown man, dressed as scantily as usual, with his staff, untidy turban and string-soled sandals, edged closer to me.

'They come ... tonight!' he whispered.

I nodded silently. If Ungud said so, then it was so, but I could guess that this was information neither of us should have had.

'I left three nights ago,' he continued, 'when the sick left. Since then I have scoured the villages for this animal. That the *Lat-sahib* should have no horse of his own is a thing of shame, but more ... I could not remain because I did not wish to see the *Paltan-log* and the *Sahib-log* walk out and leave the place that was theirs in the night. In the darkness—like cowards or thieves. *Lat-sahib* Lawrence must be shamed in his grave, and no man can think it right that it should happen thus.'

'What else can be done?' My answer was purely rhetorical, but Ungud treated it otherwise.

'They are soldiers. They have fought well for many weeks. They could fight on for a few more. They *should* fight on!' And he spat disgustedly into the fire.

'When *Lat-sahib* Lawrence called out that the *Raj* was in need of its servants, what did I do?'

'You went to him at once.'

'Yes! I, and many more like me—more than he thought he needed, because many he sent back to their villages. And they that went back, told all in their villages that the *Raj* would conquer. We that remained and fought, we also said to ourselves that the *Raj* must conquer, for had we not ourselves given merit to the *Raj* in keeping our salt? And now … those are only boys that sling their pellets at the *Raj*, and ruffians from the bazaars, no more. It is not fitting that the *Raj* should leave its own place.'

'Many of us feel the same,' I told him, for his seamed face was bitter. 'Do you return to Hassanganj now?'

'No! Never until the *Raj* is once again the *Raj*. I will not be laughed at by the boys who tend the village herd, and the old women who paint the lucky patterns on the doorsteps. I will go where he goes.'

'With Erskine *Sahib*?'

'With the *Lat-sahib*. My *sirkar*!'

'We all go to Cawnpore, then from Allahabad downriver to Calcutta.'

'Perhaps,' he said non-commitally, glancing at me sideways. 'Who can be sure where any of us will end? But now I will wait for him until he comes. Tonight he will surely come.'

'Stay then,' I said. 'Wait until he comes. Here is money for the horse's food and for you also, for the *Lat-sahib* would not wish you to want for anything in his service.'

The previous day I had sold a pearl from the garter to a *bunnia* for a hundred rupees, and now I gave five of them to Ungud. I knew that the payment he had received for his three dangerous journeys to Cawnpore during the siege had made him considerably richer than I would ever be, but I guessed that he was probably as short of ready cash as most of us. He thanked me, salaamed again and moved away, with the mare following behind him.

CHAPTER 8

As Ungud had said, that night the final withdrawal of the troops from the Residency took place, and next morning found Charles, weary and famished as we had been, sitting down to partake of Lieutenant James's expanding hospitality. While he ate, wolfing the white bread and quaffing the hot tea in great draughts, he described for us the final withdrawal.

'Such fools!' he exclaimed, shaking his head as though he still could not believe what he had experienced. 'Four thousand men, women and children brought out from under their very noses, and they haven't tumbled to it yet! Listen! They are still firing into the old place, and there's not been a soul left in it for hours. Not a solitary soul!'

He paused and we listened for a moment to the far-off dull roar of the cannon firing into the abandoned entrenchment, clearly audible over the myriad noises of the camp.

I shivered slightly, imagining how the Residency must look and feel now: the ruins deserted, silent, littered with the forsaken remnants of five months of troubled living and hard dying.

The same light wind that flicked the feathery neem leaves above me would be blowing down the desolate alleys of the enclave, stirring fitfully through torn books and old papers, fragments of clothing and broken toys, all the relinquished trivia of so many lives. Moving over the space of beaten yellow earth before the Resident's House, it would perhaps raise dry leaves and twigs into a whirling Dust Devil, that would dance a swirling obeisance to the tattered flag still flying from the tower. This same watery winter sun would cast just such pale shadows from the walls still stained with the blood of our friends, over the once elegant buildings that had seen so much suffering and hidden so many tragedies. Squirrels, I fancied, must still play in the shattered tree in our courtyard, oblivious of our absence; monkeys, grown bold in solitude, would swing through open windows to explore empty rooms; when night fell, mynas and crows would chatter and squawk, never heeding that only their shrill cacophony broke the silence. Ruins, graves, dumb beasts and utter silence despite the guns.

'Go on, *Baba-log*! Go on!' Charles laughed, breaking my reverie as he waved his mug in the direction of the guns. 'The more ball you waste, the better for the rest of us! Oh, it was magnificently done, magnificently, I tell you!' He waited until Kate refilled his mug, then went on.

'We started to pull out, you see, with the furthermost position of the old entrenchment—the garrison from Innes's post. It was midnight, and cold and cloudy, not even a star to light the sky. But we'd left all the lights burning in the empty rooms, and more for good measure than we'd ever used ourselves, so that Pandy'd be deceived into thinking all was as usual, and all the time that we were creeping out, the *Shannon's* guns were battering on like the very devil at the Kaiser Bagh, not only to cover our going but to heighten the illusion that we were staying.

'Well, as soon as the lot from Innes's post had marched through in broken step and reached the Baillie Guard, the men from the Redan followed, then the Slaughter-House post, then from Gubbins's, then Ommaney's and so on, until at last the few from the Treasury and ourselves from Fayrer's post, being the closest to the gate, fell in and marched quietly down the slope behind them. All fourteen posts were abandoned, each retiring through its own supports, and at the last Outram and Bluff Jack, after jockeying around for a bit to see who would be the very last out, exited together arm in arm.

'I can't tell you how ... how weird it was, watching the other garrisons softfoot it down the slope, leaving the old buildings all in silence, with their lights glowing. It was ... eerie. Yes, that's the word I want—eerie! And, well, somehow downright sad. There wasn't a man among us who wanted to leave, of course, so we were a pretty glum collection as we went. Even the sepoys were down in the mouth and miserable. There'd been a party or two to finish off the liquor we'd found when we were clearing out the buildings for useful supplies, and some of the men were blubbering like babies. But most were just quiet ... and, as I say, sad.

'Well then, as soon as all the posts from the old entrenchment were out, the fellows from the extended perimeter fell in behind them: first the Tehri Kothi, then the Ferret Box, the Chathar and so on, right through to the newest positions at the Moti Mahal and the Mess House. It was like … well, like pulling out a pocket to empty it, d'you see? The deepest in were the first out.

'When we got to the Sikander Bagh—and it took the devil's own time to get there, believe me—Sir Colin was waiting for us, very anxiously, with infantry and artillery ready drawn up and portfires glowing like fireflies under the trees, ready to open up if the retreat was discovered. I still don't know why it wasn't. You know how we came; you've been over the same route. Of course we were damned quiet. But when you recollect that there were all the guns, and the mule trains of ammunition, and the wheat we discovered last week, all being fetched out on carts, as well as three thousand men …

'We had a bad scare for a while, though. A sudden burst of firing; we all thought we'd been discovered and froze into the shadows or made for buildings; not that that would have been much good, seeing we had to leave the guns, carts and whatnots in the middle of those stinking alleys for anyone to see. Fortunately Peel and his "Shannons" were still pretty well in position, and they sent a few rockets into the Kaiser Bagh to dampen the *Baba-log's* curiosity, and we got through. But all it needed was one pair of sharp eyes looking in the right direction and a shout, and it would have been all up with us.'

'And no one was lost … no one?' Kate asked.

Charles shook his head as he drank yet another mug of tea.

'Not from enemy action! I believe many of the sick died on the way, but that had been expected, I suppose.' He put down his mug and wiped his mouth with the back of his hand.

'Will everyone have left the Sikander Bagh by now?' I asked carefully.

'Oh, must have. Some time ago, in fact. We made pretty smart going once past there, and the rest wouldn't be long in following us, take it from me.'

'Then Oliver should be here any minute. Did you see anything of him in these last few days, Charles?'

'Not much; too busy. But if anything had happened to him, Toddy knew where to find me. He's all right, Laura.'

He was trying to reassure me, and I appreciated his generosity, for the eyes that held mine betrayed hurt momentarily as clearly as his tone betrayed irritation.

Very soon I would see Oliver. There was no way, now, he could escape coming to us, and by nightfall, so I promised myself, I would have made everything right between us. Ungud would be searching the arriving throng with eagle eyes, waiting to lead him to us. If my foot had not been so painful, I would have wandered through the noisy crowds myself until I found him, but the least pressure on the sole made me wince, and I remained reluctantly seated when Charles, having finished his meal, crawled into Lieutenant James's tent to sleep.

All round us the great park stirred like a hive of disturbed bees each time a fresh contingent from the Residency marched wearily in, as wives sought husbands, and relieved fathers clutched up the children they had not seen for three anxious days. Everywhere tired men, the dust and mud of the march still on them, sat under the trees, while the women vied with the servants in bringing them food and drink.

Morning became afternoon and afternoon waned to evening. When sunset merged the shadows of the trees to one continuous dusk, the lines of tents had grown far out into the countryside in the direction of the Alum Bagh and the camp had settled down into a tired, contented quiet of accomplishment. Night fell and exhaustion soon extinguished the campfires and the lanterns in the tents. But still Oliver had not come.

'Well, woman dear,' Kate said, as we prepared for sleep, 'I always told you he was a contrary divil, but by all that's holy, I only guessed the half of it! There is more here than meets my old eye, is there not? No orders now to keep him from you, nor any distance either. So it is disinclination—and you have quarrelled! Is it really such a bad quarrel?'

I shook my head hopelessly.

'It is no quarrel. Only a misunderstanding. A silly, stupid, pointless misunderstanding. I could explain everything in a couple of minutes, if he'd let me. But what am I to do, if he won't give me the opportunity?'

'Well now, lass,' Jessie said, peering at her well-darned stockings for new holes in the light of the lantern, 'if opportunity is nae for the takin', it is always for the makin', is it no'?'

'Hm!' was Kate's comment as she pulled her blanket over her. ''Tis difficult to handle that man, once his mind's made up to anything. Rightly or wrongly; and being male, it will be wrongly as often as rightly. Sleep on it, Laura. Maybe something will occur to you in the night, and morning makes everything look brighter.'

We now occupied a more spacious tent pitched next to Lieutenant James's, and were provided with canvas cots. I tossed and turned, arguing with Oliver in my thoughts, scolding him, explaining to him, and complaining of his heartlessness towards me. And then, suddenly recalling Jessie's words, I realized a way was open to me to 'mak" an opportunity. I fell into sleep like a snuffed candle.

The schoolboys of the Martinière were united in considering their new circumstances one joyous protracted picnic. Still in their tattered clothes, often barefoot, they were everywhere, examining the wonders of Sir Colin's heavy artillery, riding the elephants, grooming the horses, pestering the cooks, and stealing sweetmeats from the vendors who, thanking all their gods for the fortunate chances of war, had flocked in from nearby villages to turn an honest penny. Accustomed to the ragged condition of the officers of the Old Garrison, the boys delighted in derisively mimicking the precise gait of a gloved and spurred cavalry officer, or the smartly-booted stride of an officer of the staff, tucking imaginary gauntlets into imaginary belts, adjusting non-existent helmets on their shaggy heads, or handing a figmentary female over the trodden grass.

They were the first at the tables at meals, and the last to leave, and in between harried the servants for tidbits until the next time they could sit down and stuff themselves legitimately. Young Llewellyn had very soon discovered where we were, and knowing I was bound to my chair, often left his younger brother Sonny with me, while he went off on some private gainful foray.

When the two of them arrived for a visit the following morning, I asked Llew whether he remembered my friend, Mr Erskine. He frowned doubtfully for a moment. Already there was colour in his sallow cheeks and his eyes were assuming a more normal size.

'Erskine?' He screwed up his face in concentration. 'Oh, yes! I remember now. His friend was the very small man who walked like this ...' He hopped up and did a very fair imitation of Toddy's bowlegged rolling gait.

'That's right, Mr Erskine. Have you seen him around? He got in yesterday. He's probably with the men from the Ferret Box; do you know whereabouts they are camped?'

No, he had not seen Mr Erskine, nor the small man who was his friend.

'Do you think you could find him for me? I want to send him a chit, and you are the only person I can think of to take it; these servants would not know what he looked like.'

'Only one arm?' He crossed his right arm, limp-wristed, across his chest.

'Yes. Perhaps it is in a sling still, but I'm not sure.'

'If you want him, then I can find him. If he is here, then there is only this place to look, isn't it? But, it might take a very long time, and I might miss my *tiffin* …!'

'I don't mind how long it takes, but you mustn't on any account miss your *tiffin*. If you do find him, and bring me back a reply to my chit, I will give you a rupee … and many, many thanks.'

'No need for money, miss! But biscuits for Sonny while I'm gone?'

'Lots of them … and for you, Llew. Take some now and there'll be more when you get back. I'll take good care of Sonny.'

'Sonny's not very clever yet, miss. Too small. If he goes off, he'll get lost, and then what?'

'He won't get lost, Llew. I won't let him. We'll play games and I'll tell him a long story. I'll make quite sure he does not stray too far.'

'All right! I'll go then.'

The Colonel Tucker with whom Charles was acquainted had kindly provided us with an assortment of unfamiliar goodies, among them the biscuits with which I was so lavish, and a box of notepaper that included the new ready-folded letter covers called envelopes. Hastily I wrote a note:

> O.
> *I must speak to you, see you.*
> *Please come. Something to explain.*
>   L.

I had neither wafer nor wax, but I tucked the sheet inside the neat little paper packet under Llew's interested eyes, and sent him off with it. Even if curiosity proved too much for the boy and he read what I had written, I had committed no great indiscretion.

Rather sooner than I had schooled myself to expect, Llewellyn was back.

'Oh, man!' (This was an expletive among the boys, not a form of address.) 'Man! He's way out in the new lines, near the 9th Cavalry.

Miles and miles and miles away. But I found him, and, miss, he gave me a rupee for bringing you this.'

Llew thrust a paw into a pocket and produced the same envelope I had entrusted to him earlier; it now enclosed another sheet of paper. I drew it out with hasty fingers as the boy watched.

Explanations are only less embarrassing than apologies.

The writing was unfamiliar and, for a moment, I feared my note had been delivered to the wrong party. Then I remembered that Oliver now wrote with his left hand, and his calligraphy was necessarily less than well-formed.

'Are you very tired, Llew?'

'Now! But maybe after *tiffin* I won't be.'

'Will you come back after you have eaten and take another note for me? Please? It's very important.'

'Man! Again? Oh, all right then, miss. This time I'll take Sonny; we will pass the elephant lines and he will like that.'

Thus, usually through Llewellyn, occasionally through Toddy-Bob, once or twice by Ungud, I managed to institute a private mail service between Oliver and myself.

I have the letters still. Mine on the fine deckle-edged sheets from Colonel Tucker's box, Oliver's scrawled on the coarse absorbent native paper, on leaves torn from old ledgers or later on the monogrammed sheets from some officer's brass-bound military chest, all now almost split where they were folded and bearing still the marks of their frequent anguished handling. I have them all.

On that first afternoon, I replied to Oliver's curt, dismissive words with frank importunity. I could not afford to allow myself to be put off by the tone of his note.

Perhaps. But sometimes quite necessary. Thank you for the mare. She is named Rosinante—more excellent a beast than Bucephalus. Please come to me. Please! L.

I think it better not to for the moment. Unravelled emotions are tedious things to knit together again. Allow me time. I am glad the mare was useful to you all. O.

795

You are being childish, Oliver. Obstinate. Nursing your quite mistaken jealousy. Sulking like a pettish girl. I have an injured foot. Were I whole I would seek you out. To shake you. L.

Have you not already shaken me enough? I trusted you to know your own mind—at last. O.

I do, I do. More so now than when we spoke together on Germon's roof. The rest is so easily explained. Do let me? L.

Perhaps your ability to explain is not matched by my ability to understand. Have we not understood each other without words sometimes—before? O.

Often and so sweetly. But now there are certain facts of which you are unaware. L.

Facts are largely what one makes of them, are they not? Time, Laura. Time. O.

But we have so little time left. I am very lonely and rather frightened. My foot is most painful. Can you not tell me at least why you will not come to me? L.

Because of the loneliness, the sense of unaccustomed isolation to which you have introduced me. I have known little real loneliness until now. I find, with some annoyance, as you may guess, that in overthrowing my heart, you have invaded my mind. With you I found, for a time, a degree of companionship that I have seldom known with a man, never hoped for in a woman. I will not write like a romance-ridden stripling. I know I can find the comforts necessary to my sex and nature in other arms. But never the ease of mind that I have known with you. Yet, you have told me you cannot share my life in the way in which I must live it.

I understand something of your revulsion for this country and its people; I can sympathize with your desire

*for the quiet familiarity of England; I can even believe
that Charles will prove an adequate husband to you in the
circumstances you seem to desire.*

*Forgive me, if, having come to this conclusion, I prefer
not to reopen a wound which needs only continued neglect
to heal. O.*

The length of this note comforted me, despite the brusque dismissal
of its closing.

A couple of days after the evacuation of the Residency, the enormous
camp at the Dilkusha was moved on the few miles to the Alum Bagh
Palace. In the early hours of the day on which we travelled, Sir Henry
Havelock died in the arms of his son, and, so it was said, with a prayer
on his lips. I cannot pretend that the camp was plunged into instant
mourning. Havelock had been too distant and cold a man for his death
to elicit much emotion amongst us. Yet, as we paused in our packing
on hearing the news, I was aware of an unhappy irony in his demise at
that particular moment—the ultimate failure, as it were, for a man to
whom failure, for all his Christian mouthings, was synonymous with
shame. His body was carried to the Alum Bagh and late that night
buried in secrecy beneath a tree, without headstone or marker, so that
whatever force might overrun the park in battles yet to come Sir Henry's
mortal remains might rest undisturbed.

Assembled in the Alum Bagh once again, the camp was re-erected
and, for a further four days of cool November sunshine we waited for
the order to march onward to Cawnpore. The women were sufficiently
recovered in spirits to grumble vocally at the long delay, but Sir Colin,
'Old Crawling Camel' as his troops called him, would not be hurried
by complaints. The Alum Bagh must first be secured against the enemy,
while General Outram, with four thousand men of all arms, deployed
his force over a three-mile front to keep the rebels of Lucknow at bay
until we women had been safely escorted to Cawnpore and Sir Colin
could return and make battle for the city.

My foot was healing, but I still spent much time in a canvas chair.
Through long afternoons, when doves called in the neems to remind me
of Hassanganj, when hoopoes pecked at the earth at my very skirt, and
the odd shabby peacock dragged its dusty tail across the scarred grass
in safety only because we were now sufficiently fed, the great pink

palace of the Alum Bagh stood bathed in golden light, dappled with the shifting shadows of its tall surrounding trees. Around me the myriad noises of the vast camp would hush to a languorous murmur, only the schoolboys and myself eschewing our cots and the afternoon sleep; and I would sit with my box of paper on my knee and remember and think and carefully choose the words and tone that I guessed must dictate the future course of my life.

It was on the first of these peaceful afternoons that Llew brought me Oliver's first communicative note. Promising to return for my answer in an hour, he had run off, jumping over the guy ropes of tents, whooping rudely like a baboon at smaller children he encountered on the way, pausing to kick a speculative toe at some gleaming object in the dust, or leaping suddenly upwards to snatch a clump of leaves from a low-hanging branch. Every line, every muscle in his small tawny body was informed with a singing zest in living that could be expressed only in exuberant movement. I smiled as I remembered the quiet, forlorn waif who had helped me so often in the hospital. He seemed to have forgotten all the terrible things he had seen so short a time before; even the memory of his lost father had receded from his mind.

I read Oliver's letter once again, then set about composing my reply:

> *Very well then. Do not come yet. Perhaps for all my desire to speak to you, it is better so. But let me continue, at least, to reach you through these notes; do not put an end to them.*
>
> *Why are you still so mistrustful of my feeling for Charles? I have told you there is nothing between us and there isn't, despite what you think you saw on the Gaol verandah. Here is what happened that night when you found us embracing. Make of it what you will.*
>
> *We had all been out to view the beacon lit here, on this Alum Bagh palace. I strayed away from the others— following the walls, enjoying the night and the strange scene of the entrenchment in darkness. Well, the long and the short of it is that I was attacked ... assaulted, I believe is the technical term, by a wretched man with whom I had some unpleasant dealings in the hospital. Fortunately, Charles had come in search of me, and I was rescued with*

nothing more than my pride injured. Afterwards, we talked. Of you and of me, of the fact that I loved you. At the end, in a sort of sentimental gratitude, and because I know that Charles does love me in his way and I was sorry to have to hurt him, I reached up and kissed him on the cheek. That is what you found me doing. That is all that I was doing. But you strode off in a jealous rage and for two wretched weeks have been nursing your misconceptions and brooding over a wrong I never did you.

I had come to the end of the page. I scrawled 'PTO' at the edge of the paper and turned it.

My heart and intentions did change once, and an uphill struggle it was for them to do so. It took months, literally months, for me to concede that you had good qualities, let alone that they were those I wished for in a husband. Perhaps it will not take as long for me to be persuaded I was mistaken. L.

Almost before I had time to hope for Llew's return I found myself opening Oliver's reply.

As to Charles, I am sorry if I have been mistaken all along, but allow me to point out that it was a justifiable mistake. I have tried to explain to you why I feared your feelings for him. I had said, once, that the only thing that would prevent me from pursuing my suit would be your own admission that you preferred Charles. What I saw that night on the Gaol verandah (and interpreted wrongly, as you assure me) appeared admittance enough of your preference. So I kept my word and bothered you no further. Now, well, now we have discovered that it is not alone Charles, your feeling for him, my mistake regarding that feeling, that stands in our way, have we not?

By the by, Toddy tells me of your scarlet slippers. He does not think it proper for you to be wearing them. O.

Let there be peace between us now. There is no time for quarrelling. Tomorrow we march for Cawnpore. In a week or so we will be in Allahabad; then the steamers down to Calcutta and the ship home. Remember how few steps we have left. We still have obstacles to surmount, but if they are to be surmounted, let it be by these notes and soon, and not by the tardy Overland Mail. I have spent such aeons of my life waiting for news of you, news from you. Waiting for you. I could not do it again. No, I will not do it again!

You do not care for apologies and neither do I. Let me, however, ask your forgiveness now for any hurt I have done you, and believe it was unwitting. I am so fatally good at giving the wrong impression. On the Gaol verandah you got the impression from my actions that I cared for Charles too much; and on Germon's roof you gained the impression that I cared for you too little. The first, I hope, is cured and finished with; but the second ...? I shudder when I realize how little understanding I had that evening of what you wanted to give me, of how callow was my response to your gift. Yet, believe me, I have learned something, a good deal, of life and you and of myself, even in the few weeks since that long conversation.

Let me have a line before we set off. They say it will be 11 o'clock by the time we make a move, and that means 2 in the afternoon at the earliest; so let it be many lines. Did you know that Charles is not coming home with us? He is accompanying us as far as Allahabad to see us safely on our way and then returns to fight with Major Barrow's Volunteer Cavalry. Laura.

My dear,
It is I that should ask your forgiveness. Yet, woman dear, is not all this beating of the breast between two humans a little unfastidious? Let us forget the wrongs, real or imaginary, we have done each other and start afresh. For you are right; we have little time to squander.

My dear, if you but knew the joy with which I read that first note from you, or the effort it cost me to respond as brusquely as I did. My confidence was badly shaken, you see; I had to be sure you wanted to see me for more than some silly feminine desire for seemliness or to smooth out your own rumpled self-esteem. Day by day, as you have persisted in your dogged way to chip away at my carapace of misunderstanding, anger and hurt, you have displayed yourself to me thoroughly. I know you love me, Laura, but what are we to do about it?

For a time (you may find it difficult to believe) I even tried to see myself living the sort of life you could share with a husband in England. I tried to persuade myself I could do it. I envisioned a decorous and comfortable villa, with elms, clipped hedges and neat lawns; an office somewhere, perhaps, to which I would repair each day, returning at evening to the embraces of suburban domesticity. Or better yet, a farm where I could at least have my horses and a day uncabined by the clock. I tried to convince myself I could learn to make do with a life lacking all those things that have made my life out here worthwhile. It was very hard on Tod and Ishmial, who felt the edge of my tongue every time I spoke to them.

At last I realized I could not do it. I will never make a responsible English business man, nor yet a comfortable English squire.

Laura, I have been as I am now, have lived in the same way for too long to adjust to English life. I will not try. Were I to do so, to try and fit your mould, your idea or vision of what makes for happiness, I would not succeed in subduing my own preferences or inclinations; only in perverting them. We would end in hatred, and I would by far sooner lose you than learn to loathe you. Memory is an inadequate comforter at best, but at least it can be sweet memory. Oliver.

CHAPTER 9

Toddy-Bob arrived with this last epistle on the next morning, just as Kate, Jessie and I were admiring a carriage, shabby but roadworthy, that had been placed at our disposal by the authorities to take us to Cawnpore.

'Well ... it's better'n a *doolie*, there's no gainsayin' that!' Tod agreed dubiously, as we asked him to examine the new conveyance. 'I'll just cast my blinkers over the axles and springin' and that ... make sure that it'll 'old together for you.' And he disappeared under the sagging body of the equipage.

Two horses had also been provided, country animals, shaggy, wild of eye and badly matched in size. These, too, were carefully examined by our friend, with many sniffs of disdain and impolite reflections on their ancestry, but eventually passed as 'prob'ly' capable of getting us to our destination. He then had a few words with the native driver, compounded about equally of threats and promises, and finished with a brief *resumé* of the power, importance and wealth of the *Lat-Sahib* of Hassanganj, whose women we were declared to be and to whom the unhappy driver was now directly responsible for our welfare.

'Doesn't do to let 'em think you ain't got no gentleman to look out for you,' he explained. 'They got no respec' for females on their own, like. I'll make it my business to keep an eye on you, drop by now and then, and remind 'im generally of 'is proper place.'

Contrary to the pessimistic expectation expressed in my note to Oliver of the previous day, the march to Cawnpore began on time that morning. The families and the sick occupied the mid-section of the column but, even so, it was not too long after midday when we began to move out of the Alum Bagh park. There had been rain during the night, which had left the world fresh and sparkling, but which had also softened the ground on either side of the narrow, unmetalled roadway we were to follow, and our driver was exhorted sternly to drive in the very middle of the track or risk losing his vehicle for ever. He salaamed his compliance to this excellent suggestion to the officer giving it; then, with a great cracking of his whip over the unmindful ears of his lethargic steeds, shouted us into motion.

On the slow drive out of the park and down the first mile or so of the open road, our way was lined by the officers and men who were to remain at the Alum Bagh until Sir Colin's return. Time after time, strange hands were thrust into the carriage windows to wish us good luck and God speed; there were donations of fruit, of chocolate and a whisky bottle full of milk stoppered with grass, and a bundle of very out-of-date newspapers. 'Good luck!' 'God be with you, ladies!' 'Safe home now and no harm to yez!' 'Tell 'em at home we're still fighting, ma'am!' 'The best of good fortune to all you ladies!' Thus, each in his own way, the men bade us farewell, and suddenly, above the creak of cartwheels, the tramp of feet, the yells of bullock-drivers and the thud of hooves on soft earth, the eerie note of the pipes was borne to us from a distance. As we came to a halt in the first of a long series of delays, the shrill notes grew louder, until the pipeband of the 93rd, kilts a-swing, spats twinkling, bonnet plumes waving, marched in fine order past us to take their place in the column.

'Aye, 'tis a braw fine sight the laddies make!' Jessie smiled with national pride, holding Pearl up to the window to watch them pass.

Trying to find a comfortable corner among the broken springs of the carriage seat, I felt a deadening return of the old fear and anxiety, which I had almost forgotten during the few days of letter-writing and dreaming beneath the trees of the Alum Bagh. We were still a long way from safety. Fighting, so we had been told, had once again broken out in Cawnpore, that sinister city in which we hoped for an incongruous refuge. We knew no details, except that Sir Colin and an advanced detachment were making all speed to the town; but no accurate knowledge was needed to breed alarm in us. Behind us the pandies were now in possession of the Residency. They had destroyed the semaphore and had been seen through fieldglasses capering and dancing jigs of triumph on the roof of the Resident's House. This last piece of information filled us all with sadness; it was a bitter thought that all our endurance and suffering had found its termination in the derision of an enemy that had never managed to subdue us. Fortunately, we did not learn until much later that the first action taken by the invaders of the old entrenchment was the desecration of our graves.

The first day's march was only fifteen miles, and, since the column was almost twelve miles in length, the vanguard had encamped very shortly after the rearguard had begun to march. Two or three hours after our departure, when one of the unexplained halts found our carriage on a sweep of curving road crowning a fair eminence in the flat countryside, we were afforded a view of the progress of the column both before and behind us, and could form an appreciation of what it must have looked like to the vultures hovering hopefully in the cool blue above.

On either side of the road swampy grassland had disintegrated into a morass of mud, through which struggled the infantry: the Scots, with their white spats now as brown as the mud they marched through; the 32nd ('Our Men' as we always considered them) hardly better clothed than when they left the Residency, but no less dogged; the loyal sepoys of the Old Garrison, mingling in their rags with the smartly uniformed natives of the relief; the sailors of the *Shannon*, easily discernible in their blue and white, swinging smartly through the mud, to show themselves more capable of soldierly endurance than any mere soldier. Flanking the infantry on both sides of the road, the cavalry cantered, whirled and trotted in the first energy of a short march, lances gleaming, pennons fluttering, horses frisking.

Thus guarded and guided, the cause of all the martial concern crept along the broken road, mile upon slow mile in an unending stream of carriages, carts, landaus and broughams, of bullock-wagons, ammunition tumbrils and guns, of *doolies*, palanquins and red-curtained ambulances, of oxen and elephants, camels, mules and donkeys, of goats, sheep and pariah dogs and the gaudily curtained litters and carts that housed, so Jessie told me, the compliant females of the bazaar.

Coolies, cooks, grooms, *ayahs* and grass-cutters trotted between the wheels and the hooves; vendors appeared miraculously from the fields with fresh milk, eggs, sweetmeats, embroidered slippers and glass bangles for sale. Whenever the column halted, from the carts of the bazaar artisans came the peaceful, domestic sounds of the tinsmith's hammer, the carpenter's saw or the cobbler's mallet on the last. I gathered that nor war nor tumult could turn the Indian craftsman from his trade.

That night we slept uncomfortably in the carriage, no attempt being made to pitch a camp, and were on the move again by seven the next morning.

The atmosphere in which the column moved that second day, both physical and emotional, was very different to the almost joyous release with which it had progressed on the first day. To begin with, we set out with the disquieting intelligence that we had over forty miles to cover, for Cawnpore must be within sight when we halted.

The cavalry no longer cavorted in the springing fields, nor left the line to take a pot shot at a partridge or a hare. The infantry hugged the road more closely, many of the Old Garrison limping now in unbroken boots, and the grass-cutters, plying their scythes for animal fodder as they moved, kept carefully within range of a dash to the road and safety.

By noon we were again within the sound of gunfire, and the dull far roar, still unexplained, filled us anew with anxiety. During the many protracted halts, we left the carriage and tried to discover what was taking place ahead of us, but were met only with rumours and counter-rumours. There was talk of despatches arriving from Cawnpore, appealing for help as so often not long before we had ourselves appealed for help. The small force left to hold the city until our coming was said to be besieged by Tantia Topee, the Nana Sahib's chief lieutenant; the bridge of boats, our sole approach to the city, was under attack ... had been cut ... been set on fire ... totally destroyed. We would have to turn back; we would have to take another road; we were to be attacked at nightfall ... no, we were to return to the Alum Bagh.

But we did not turn back nor take another route. Neither were we attacked.

Hour after hour through the slow miles, the incredible caravan moved stolidly onward. Now we were choked with the dust of our own passage. Every eye smarted, every voice was hoarse, every throat constricted and raw. Above us a great cloud of sunfilled motes obscured the sky and, for a mile on either side of the road, the green of field, cane-brake and copse was yellowed by the fine dry powder. In the carriage we muffled our faces in scarves and shawls, but nothing kept out the dust. We had prayed that the rain would keep off for the sake of the men marching beside us; now we prayed for its falling—and for the same reason.

I could not be surprised that Toddy-Bob had not managed to find me and deliver Oliver's next letter, and in a way I was glad that he had not done so. I had something to look forward to when we reached Cawnpore; meanwhile, the discomforts and anxieties of the journey were rendered bearable by anticipation.

Very late that night we at last halted, having covered thirty-eight exhausting miles. Cawnpore, so they told us, lay several miles further on. Through the hours of darkness, the guns pounded and thundered in familiar concatenation. Sometimes a rocket soared into the murky heights of the night or for a brief moment a bursting shell would illuminate the strange landscape. Movement and noise, the shuffle and stir of thousands of men and animals continued until dawn. We were too tired, too dry, dusty and uncomfortable to do more than doze for a few moments at a time. Only Pearl, most blessedly imperturbable of children, slept on Jessie's knees, her small face streaked with dust, her hair dark with its dirt.

Morning, when at last it came, was again dulled by the haze of dust, which still hovered above us despite the heavy dew of the night.

We set off again, I ill-tempered through cramp, fatigue and inactivity. I would have walked beside the carriage for a while to exercise my limbs and soothe my mind, but the condition of the roadway and the verges, after the passage of so many animals and men, was foul beyond belief.

The day dragged by, more wearisome than the last, as we again experienced the lengthy halts, the noise, the dust and the flies.

Every bone ached, every muscle protested, and the skin of our backs was raw from the ceaseless rub against the hard leather upholstery. To grumble at our lot would have been a welcome and understandable relief, but that day we travelled in company with a horsedrawn ambulance. The sight of the bloodily bandaged stumps protruding from the curtain, the sound of the groans that met us as we halted, forced us to long-suffering silence. We were too jaded to want to eat and by midday had finished the last of the flasks of water with which we had set out.

'Only a few more miles,' we had been assured, yet the nightmare progression continued until five o'clock that evening. At that hour, suddenly, the Ganges lay before us—a brown stream, wide and slow, spanned by a bridge of wooden boats tied close together and covered by planks joining a rough roadway. Beyond the river, almost invisible for dust, lay Cawnpore. Smoke mingled thickly with the dust above low and clustered buildings, through which now and then a burst of orange flame thrust from some fired house. There was little we could make out with any precision, but there was little we needed to see to know ourselves again in the heart of war.

Shortly after our first sight of the river, we halted again. An officer came to the carriage to tell us that it would be hours before we crossed the bridge, and to snatch what rest we could while we were stationary. Sir Colin, he said, was already within the entrenchment ...

'Entrenchment?' queried Kate in alarm. 'But why? What entrenchment?'

'It's unfortunate, ma'am, but the firing ... that was Tantia Topee and his lads. They attacked General Windham two days ago. Yesterday the General was forced to retire into his entrenchment and the town, or most of it, is now held by the rebels. They tried to cut the bridge of boats, too, but thank God without success. However, we may be fired upon as we cross, so be prepared.'

'But ... do you mean we will not be able to get on? To leave Cawnpore?'

'Not at all, ma'am! No need for alarm. Early this morning our troops crossed over the river and, with the help of our heavy artillery—which is what you are now hearing—have forced the pandies back. They'll soon be cleared out, never fear, and you'll be on your way to safety and Allahabad as soon as it can be arranged.'

'Good loving Lord, deliver us!' groaned Kate, sinking back to her seat as the officer moved on down the line of carriages.

'So near and yet so far,' I murmured, while Jessie unbuttoned her dress for Pearl, which we had learned was her way of indicating some severe but inexpressible emotion.

All in all it required thirty hours for that mammoth column to cross the gently swaying bridge of boats into Cawnpore.

The moon had been up some hours when our wheels rattled carefully across the first rutted boards, and behind us for miles a snake of yellow light—carriage lamps, lanterns, and torches—winked through the dirty darkness, telling us that more than half the column had yet to reach the bridge. The nearby fire of heavy guns accompanied us as we slowly inched our way over the heaving planks. Rockets and shells lit the dark waters with their incandescence and showed us the ominous glower of flaming rafts drifting slowly downstream towards the wooden boats that formed the foundation of our ephemeral highway. Seldom have any prayers of mine been as sincere or as heartfelt as those I prayed during the tremulous half-hour required to cross the bridge. Next morning we were to learn that Dr Brydon had delivered a baby during the crossing, its first infant wails drowned in the crash of exploding grapeshot. Many a man had been wounded and some had died.

There came then, as the hollow reverberations of the bridge under our wheels gave way to the solid crunch of gravel, an eerie drive through a landscape of burned bungalows, shell-torn trees and huge clumps of spiky cactus laced together with spider webs, all bathed in silver moonlight. Nothing was discernible now of the pleasant and conventional Cawnpore of Kate's memories. Gone were the pleasant gardens and gaieties of only twelve months before. What remained were ruins and terrible memories, the scent of cordite and, in the shadows, armed men once again protecting us in an extended picket as we made our way to shelter.

The following days were spent in a battered, whitewashed barrack, and mostly in longed-for sleep, as the battle continued for the town, and Sir Colin and his staff made arrangements for the departure of dependants and the sick to Allahabad.

Late on the afternoon of our arrival in Cawnpore, I awoke to find a letter from Oliver placed beside my head on the canvas cot. On the cover he had scrawled: *'Written on 28th November, but though Toddy has been absent most of the afternoon, he cannot locate you. Sorry, O.'*

I allowed a few moments to myself for the joys of anticipation, then opened the letter.

> *My dearest,*
> *Here I lounge in the comfort of a tent, pitched and prepared long before my arrival, yet they tell me that 'the ladies' are required to spend the night in their conveyances! I am glad to know from Tod that your carriage is at least adequate for your requirements during the day's travel, but wish there were some way I could see you more comfortably settled for the night. What a perversion of human energy and sense a war is, is it not?*

Since I have received no letter from you in answer to mine, I lack a hint of your present mood, a nuance to guide me now. After I had despatched that last note, I fell into a despondency, thinking it too negative, concerned as it was with all those many things I cannot do, cannot be, even for you, Laura.

I spoke only the truth—yet perhaps not enough of it. Were it only my own inclinations I had to put away on your behalf, perhaps I could manage it; I would, at least, be free to try. But there are also my responsibilities, and these, whatever the present state of Oudh and Hassanganj, I cannot dispense with at pleasure. A great many people depend on me in one way or another; when this madness is over, they will look to me for help, for encouragement and advice. The villages of Hassanganj, unlike those of the neighbouring talukhdars, have been untroubled by any serious strife for many years—until now. Rightly or wrongly, they attribute their comparatively peaceful life to the attitude and endeavours of my family and myself. When peace returns, it is to me that they will look for leadership and counsel—not to any government.

I am being tedious, I suppose, in listing my responsibilities but I want to show you why, even for you, I cannot desert them. They did not come to an end when the house was burned.

But after all, all explanations and justifications aside, can you really imagine me sitting behind a desk from 10 to 4 each day, existing only from shooting season to shooting season?

I do not ask your agreement or approval, but read, if you will, between these lines and try to understand.

Lovingly, Oliver

My dearest,

I could not write on the journey—we had no ink! The wretched bottle was broken in the upheaval of our departure, and oh, how much I wanted to fill the many weary hours of delays and waiting with writing to you! I could not expect Toddy, even the ever-resourceful Toddy, to find us in that incredible confusion, which, of course, did not prevent me from hoping that he would.

But now, can you guess how many times I have read and reread your last two letters? Can you begin to imagine the comfort that just holding them in my hands can bring me? To feel that at last we are talking to each other, inadequately but honestly, again?

Oh, my dear, there is so much to say that cannot be said in a letter, and even in a letter—where am I to begin? It is night now, a very dark night, and tomorrow I shall go in search of Llew to deliver this to you, but in the meantime I must find something to say among all the things I want to say. I suppose I am tired, but a strange constraint has hold of me. Will it do, for the moment, if I just say 'Yes! I do understand'?

I have captured a lamp to myself, borrowed some ink and am sitting on my cot trying to think and write, while down the length of the barrack my 'sisters in misfortune' gossip and grumble and smack their children; and the children rush in cohorts through the serried beds, screaming with joy or bawling in well-deserved pain. I realize all at once that I have not spent a single night by myself in all the nights since we left Hassanganj. I have forgotten the sensation of privacy, but not the advantages, and now I wish I were alone, and quiet in a quiet place, and able to tell you something of all that is in my heart. All that comes to mind in this infernal din, however, is an honest answer to the last question in your letter.

No, definitely not! I cannot imagine you spending your days behind a desk in some grimy London office.

I do not want to imagine it, Oliver. I no longer need to imagine it, Oliver. Oliver, do you understand?

Now you must read between these lines; and if you do so correctly, spare me the embarrassment of explicitation. I have schooled myself to honourable surrender.

Lovingly, Laura

Laura,
Am I right? Is India acceptable to you? Are you really learning to forget already? Can you truly forgive what India has done to you?

My God, woman! I begged for a mood to follow, a nuance to guide me. Not a thunderbolt!

For weeks I have tortured my simple masculine mind in an endeavour to understand your loathing of India, until that loathing became almost more real to me than my own affection for the country. Now you have destroyed the work of all my earnest striving by indicating that you no longer hate the country. Yet, you were once so vehement, so certain. Nothing could ever make you live in India.

To say that I am flattered that my suit should be sufficient to overcome your most understandable aversion to this country is to understate the fact. Yet it also frightens me. Have you forgotten the marital doldrums of which we have already spoken? Think well, my dear, think well! Can you be certain that a man such as I, selfish, as you have often pointed out, spoilt, too set in my ways, unable to bend, balky of temperament, and too sure I am right, can you be quite sure that such a man can make up to you for the sins and sufferings of your experience of India?

Have you really begun to forget? Can you ever forgive?

Oliver

To which I replied:

No, Oliver. I have not yet forgotten, cannot yet forgive.

But I am willing to learn, to be taught—by you in your arms.

And if that is not a damnable capitulation you have forced me to, I don't know what is!

Laura

In the evening of the day on which the foregoing exchange took place, I accompanied Kate, Jessie and a party of other ladies from the barrack to General Wheeler's entrenchment.

Wheeler's travesty of an entrenchment was but a walk away from where we were lodged. In the distance, yet still within the town, the inescapable gunfire continued, but within the low-walled enclosure silence was almost palpable. There were many others making the pilgrimage with us: small groups moving in shocked quiet about the ruined rectangle, gazing at the burned-out barrack where so many had died so terribly, wondering that the wreck of the second long building should ever have been considered shelter. Some of those present now knew that this was where their wives or husbands or fathers had died, and hardly an eye was dry.

Returned to our quarters, I again borrowed the ink and wrote my final despatch from Cawnpore. We were to set out for Allahabad on the following day.

Oh Oliver! I have been to Wheeler's entrenchment, and walked, with your living ghost ever present beside me, the entire circumference of those pathetic walls.

I have measured, almost with a hop, skip and jump, the distance between you and the guns of the enemy, and have gazed with horror on the undefended emplacements of your artillery.

You know that I am not by nature pious, but I prayed beside that terrible well, so close and open to the raking pandy guns, a prayer of thanksgiving that somehow you had safely slaked your thirst at it, a prayer for the forgiveness of mistaken foolish Wheeler, who unwittingly sent so many to their death at it.

I am depressed, horrified, disgusted and amazed all at once. I am also awe-struck—not by the evident heroism, but by the magnitude of the stupidity of human beings. Is all history merely the outcome, the artificially hallowed outcome, of a chance concatenation of ignorance and arrogance in some one character?

How did you survive, Oliver? The walls scarce reached my shoulders. How did you survive?

Laura

My dearest,

It is over. I have no answers. I survived. How? you ask. Kismet, Ishmial would say. Luck would be Toddy's answer. And I? Sometimes I refer myself to Providence, which then disquietingly asks the further question 'Why?' I do not know how, nor why. Only that it is finished, in fact and—as far as I can make it so—in my mind.

Needless to say, I did not revisit the scene. In a way I find myself glad that you did, however. Now let us both lay the ghost of the place to rest.

Tomorrow is a new day and a new beginning. In less than a week we will be in Allahabad, and I fear my resolution will carry me no further without a sight of you. Believe, my heart, that it is not a still-distrustful prudence that keeps me from you, but the certainty that a glimpse, a few hurried words, probably in the company of others, will not suffice me now. I would certainly embarrass you with my ardour! Besides, though we have resolved our respective difficulties of Charles and India, much still remains to be said that never has been said between us ... or written. So I shall stay away for these further few days, until I can have you—to keep you.

I caught a sight of you this morning, walking with Kate down a dusty sunny street. Limping slightly, you trudged along in the determined fashion I remember so well, both of you in the dismal garments you have worn so long—you with your mushroom of a hat, Kate in her old black bonnet and carrying her usual large umbrella. You put me in mind of a plucky small Bantam hen.

Oliver.

CHAPTER 10

The column that set out from Cawnpore for Allahabad on that cold fresh morning in December was indeed much shorter than the one that had arrived there. It comprised now only the families, the sick and wounded and non-combatants of the Old Garrison, together with a few doctors and apothecary assistants, and was accompanied by a detachment of fighting men for protection. Most of the men who had effected the first relief under Outram remained in Cawnpore for battles yet to come, but the news that 'Our Men'—the 32nd—were also to be left behind with Sir Colin's force, was greeted with outrage. Bitter were the farewells between husbands and wives, who had blessed Heaven for allowing them to survive Lucknow together; anguished the grief of children parted at this late hour from fathers they realized too well they were lucky to have had so long. As we moved off, men ran beside the conveyances, still clinging to a wife's hand, or a child's, and for long after the last had reluctantly dropped behind, the sound of sobs could be heard, mingled with the more usual cacophony of movement.

When we were a few miles out of Cawnpore, safely threading our way through a flat landscape of fields and frequent villages wrapped in accustomed morning quiet, we heard behind us the great guns of Sir Colin's force start up in earnest against Tantia Topee.

After that, the journey passed without incident. We slept in pitched camps, made good progress each day, ate adequately, found fresh milk awaiting the children when we halted, and heard guns no more. Of course there were delays, inconveniences and irritations, but there was an air of relaxation, almost of cheerfulness, about the column, despite the sorrow of the women of the 32nd. Halting in the early twilight, we found time to stroll through fields and groves; time, too, to exchange plans, which we at last found the courage to make; to seek out friends and discuss, with some assurance, the return to normal living.

On more than one occasion I glimpsed Oliver aloft on his horse in the distance. I looked my fill but made no effort to attract his attention. A pleasant peace had invaded me, and I was content to wait his coming at what would be, for both of us, the proper time.

Once he was riding beside the cart on which Wallace Avery was travelling, seated between his guards. Oliver, I believe, was attempting to make himself known to Wallace, but Wallace, all unaware, played with his fingers, nodding his head and muttering to himself with vacant smiles, like a child in a private fantasy.

For General Outram and Brigadier Inglis had not, after all, been the last men out of the Baillie Guard, as Charles had told us. Nor yet were either of the two young aides who had lurked behind them, then exited simultaneously from the gate in a rugby tackle, so eager had each been to claim the strange distinction of being 'last man out'. On that final night, as each post filed silently out through the gate, alone in some bright room in the Brigade Mess, Wallace, stupefied by drink, had slept in ignorance through the whole withdrawal. Hours later, waking to the terror of finding himself the only man alive in the silent ruins, he had run headlong through the deserted lanes, out of the Baillie Guard, through the maze of the palaces and, by good fortune, alone followed the path of the retreat. On the following morning, stragglers from the rearguard had come across him wandering in the fields and brought him on to the Dilkusha. He had managed to tell them what had befallen him, but by the time he reached safety, fear had crazed him, and ever since he had lived in a private world, where he talked endlessly to Connie and Johnny of his plans for sending them to England and listened, with delighted attention, to their replies. We did not learn of this last of poor Wallace's disasters until we had reached the Alum Bagh. Then Charles had made it his business to see to the comfort of his relative and was often with him. In Charles's presence, Wallace became, if not rational, at least soothed; to the rest of us he turned a bland but blank eye.

As I watched Oliver bend down from his saddle to talk to Wallace, I remembered the vexatious cause of our interview in Henry Cussens's bungalow so long ago. That IOU had been returned to me, but debts, it seemed, have always to be paid one way or another. Even by Wallace.

For each of the four days of our march, the letters came and went. No longer a means of explanation only, now they explored, described and dwelt with delight on the passion we discovered for and in each other. Lovers' letters, truly, they were meant for no other eyes; so I will fold them now and place them again in their box of fruitwood inlaid with mother-of-pearl. But seldom has the world looked more beautiful to me, more full of grace and golden goodness, than in those hard days of travel, my friends safe beside me, a bourne in sight, and in my heart a love confirmed.

Allahabad stands at the confluence of two great rivers of northern India. Built on a promontory, at the very point where the turgid brown waters of the Ganges meet but do not mingle with the limpid blue stream of the Jumna, is the Fort, a massive Mogul structure, adapted and amplified by the British, in which most of us women were housed on our arrival in the town.

It was late afternoon, and the winter sun lay low on the horizon, as we ended our journey. Military bands blared in greeting, banners fluttered, and throngs of troops and civilians lined the roadway, cheering as the convoy entered the great stronghold.

The password for that day, so they told us, was 'Heroine'.

The waters were awash with bronze and gold, and the ancient stonework of the Fort took on a pinkish glow, as, marvelling, we trod the soft, mown grass between banks of sweetpeas and roses, and looked with silent wonder on a scene of peace and domestic comfort. Allahabad, too, had known its time of tragedy, its massacre of Europeans, its burning of bungalows. But that was in the past. The present was, to us at least, a plethora of unbelievable comforts.

Once again Kate managed to 'pull strings' and have us lodged together with old friends. They inhabited fine quarters, whose spreading garden was bounded by the battlements themselves.

I had expected yet another whitewashed barrack, hastily evacuated by its normal occupants for our use. Instead, I was ushered into a spacious bedroom. There was rose-patterned china in the bathroom, and a dressing-room in which a long mirror caught the last of the light and showed me a woman only six months older but a lifetime away from the one who had last surveyed herself in a similar extravagant glass. The brass bed, covered with intricately crocheted cotton, intimidated more than it invited me, and even more frightening was the fact that it stood alone in the room. For the first time in half a year I would be sleeping in a room by myself.

Dinner was to us a lavish meal, but none of us could do justice to it. Mrs Baines clucked and fussed and pressed us to try the various dishes, plying our plates with her own concerned hands. How could she guess that she was the first prettily dressed, assured and tranquil woman we had seen in months? That her gown of ruby silk, and the susurration of her many petticoats, were a greater wonder to us even than the roast duck and lemon tartelettes to which she urged us so insistently? And how could we explain to her the ambivalence of our sensations on finding ourselves at her generous table, holding in our minds the memory of the rickety board on which we had eaten so many unpalatable meals that had become, sometimes, almost sacramental in the sorrow with which we had taken them, or the deep and grateful joy?

Looking at the strained faces of Kate and Jessie, I found in their eyes a reflection of the unease, the oppression that so many unnecessary appurtenances to living produced in my own mind. We shared a sadness and a strange nostalgia for a time, a way of life, even a hardship, that we knew was gone for ever. We were homesick for the Thug Gaol! The comfort in which we so suddenly found ourselves seemed artificial and false.

We had learned how easily one can do without Turkey rugs, curtained lamps and silver spoons. But how could we learn to forgo the companionship, the community of feeling, and the concerted effort that had given such meaning to our lives?

We were encouraged to retire early. Kate, Jess and I kissed each other goodnight quietly and went alone to our strange and solitary rooms. I was not surprised to see tears in Kate's blue eyes and, having gained the privacy of my apartment, I could not contain my own. I went to the long window and looked out over the still night garden. The scent of nicotiana and stock wafted into the room; trees stirred gently in the river breeze and, beyond the Mogul bastions, the river itself soughed and sighed on its journey to the sea.

Far away in the night, to the north of me, the ruins where in some real sense I had lost my life and found another, where I had learned what friendship is, and fear, and the wisdom of forgetting, those haunted shells of brick and plaster stood bathed in the light of the same waning moon that silvered the grass below me. My heart cried out to them, wanting again the terrible days I had spent in them. More frightened now in safety than I had ever been in siege, I called to them to stay with me, be with me for ever in memory—not as mourning but as inspiration.

Nonsense—you will say, reader—homesick for hardship? And you will be right. It was not the hardship that was necessary, but the impulse to endure, to pit oneself consciously against the outrageous accident of our sufferings, to know that how we confronted our trials dictated how we thought of ourselves, as pawns or human beings. I, at last without the prop of that stringent necessity, was frightened by my weakness. So I wept there at the open window in the moonlight and river-rustle, for days and ways and friends gone for ever, and wished myself safe again in the definition of what they had required of me.

I could not wear the frilled and hand-tucked nightgown and cap laid out on the bed, but put upon myself the ragged cotton I was accustomed to. The comfort of the bed prevented me from sleeping; too used to clamorous nights, I was oppressed by the quiet; for the first time in six months I was truly alone, and the knowledge unnerved me. When at length I fell asleep, I was still weeping.

The first day in safety passed more easily than I had expected when I woke, unrested, to an elegant *chota hazri* served on a silver tray.

I longed impatiently for Oliver, but at the same time almost wished he would stay away—at least until I was respectably dressed. I felt a certain shyness at the thought of seeing him again face to face, and felt that a becoming gown would encourage assurance.

Naturally our shabbiness had not escaped the notice of our hostess, and after breakfast we discovered that *derzis* had been called for to take our measurements, and vendors bearing bales of piece goods, buttons, laces and braids had spread their wares on the verandah for our inspection. Mrs Baines produced a pile of *Lady's Magazines*, and we were soon lost in the remembered but unfamiliar delights of choosing patterns and fabrics for new gowns.

Not even an Indian *derzi* could be expected to produce a new garment in less than a couple of days, however, so Mrs Baines insisted that two of her own gowns be hastily altered for Kate and myself, while Jessie, large Jessie, was fitted out in a dress of black merino donated by a neighbour.

'I am so glad I had something suitable—in black,' the neighbour, Mrs Lyndhurst, remarked, as she laid the gown on a chair, Jessie being too engrossed in fashion plates to try it on immediately.

'Black?' Jessie looked her puzzlement. 'Well,' she said at length regretfully, 'the good Lord kens I ha' forgot I am a widow woman now!' and pushed away the blue cotton I had been persuading her to choose.

'Why, so you are—and I!' Kate looked from Jessie to me. 'We are in mourning, Jess and I, and had both quite forgotten it.'

She smiled, no doubt at how inconsequential such conventions now appeared to us, but Mrs Baines and her friend regarded her in stony silence, disapproval of her want of proper feeling evident on their faces. Officially I was also in mourning, for Emily, though not as 'deep' as that of a widow. But I craved colour, and determined that the exact date of Pearl's orphaning would remain a mystery until it was too late for reproaches.

Within an hour, the borrowed gowns had been made over to fit Kate and myself, and with them, on our beds, we found the customary accompaniments of petticoats, camisoles, corset covers, pantaloons and stockings, together with a selection of heeled and buttoned boots, delivered by a bazaar shoemaker, from which to make a choice.

Delighted with our borrowed plumage, it was natural to wish to show it off to our friends, and hearing the strains of a celebratory band concert taking place on the central grassed square of the Fort, Kate announced her intention of attending it.

'But, my dear,' demurred Mrs Baines as Jessie and I joined Kate with alacrity, 'you are so recently widowed! Are you sure it would be quite the thing?'

For a moment Kate hesitated; then she lifted her chin and, looking Mrs Baines in the eye, announced, 'I'm quite sure, and so would George be.'

'Well, of course, if *you* think it proper, and at a time like this I'm sure no one will think the less of you. But you cannot go out without bonnets and gloves. I will see what I have that will do for the present.' With pursed lips she led us to her dressing-room, where Kate and I with unrepentant laughter tried on most of her bonnets before suiting ourselves, and Jessie, subtly made aware of her status as a common soldier's wife, quietly accepted the use of a bandanna to tie over her hair.

It was easy to discern the women of Lucknow among the crowd seated around the wrought-iron bandstand. Almost all had been solemnly clothed in black by their more fortunate sisters.

''Tis as though they do not approve of us being alive,' remarked Kate. 'As though death were a parlour game, and those who have lost their loved ones must be set apart from the rest of the players who have not scored such high points.'

'Or a charade, in which those who have guessed the answer correctly must remain silent so as not to spoil the game for the rest,' I agreed grimly. 'We are not playing the game by their rules, Kate. We are expected to be downcast, pale and pathetic, like mourners in novels.'

'After all that we have seen of death? And all that we need of life?'

'They know nothing of that need,' I pointed out.

Mrs Bonner was seated in splendour with the Gubbinses and other notables of the siege. She bowed frigidly on catching my eye, but Minerva squealed her excitement on seeing us, and pushed through the crowd to kiss us and ask how we liked her new dress.

Llewellyn Cadwallader deserted his schoolboy friends as soon as he spied us, and sat on the grass at my feet, chewing without cessation on a variety of sweetmeats produced from the pocket of his new tweed knickerbockers. Delighted to see him happy, well and clean, I let my hand rest on his shoulder, and was touched when this small mark of affection called forth the answering gesture of a cheek laid for a moment against my hand. 'Miss,' he breathed, looking up at me with his dark spaniel's eyes, 'miss—sometimes I really thought it'd never be like this again. Never!'

'I know, Llew,' I answered, patting the thin shoulder. 'Me too!'

Naturally I scanned the crowd for Oliver, though my better judgement told me that this was not a function to draw him. Probably he too was busy with tailors and bootmakers, but I allowed myself to hope that an At Home, to be held in our honour at the Baines's bungalow that evening, would prove more inviting. When I remembered to look for Charles, I could not find him either.

We were exhorted to rest after *tiffin*, while Mrs Baines, her friends and servants made ready for the At Home. I went to my room, its unaccustomed comforts already taken for granted, and tried to read a novel. But the print swam before my eyes and I could not concentrate. I was aware again of the ill-defined unease I had known the previous night at dinner. Was it only the sight of four glasses and a silver cruet at each place that had struck me as excessive? Were not the forms and fashions by which the ladies of Allahabad lived, and to which they paid such zealous service, equally unnecessary? The fuss about the varying degrees of mourning, of leaving the house bonnetless, of ascertaining whether the guests invited to the *soirée* were all of a rank acceptable to Colonel Baines's rank—were not these preoccupations as absurd?

Yet this was what I had thought I wanted. There was nothing unusually pretentious about the Baines household, nothing unfamiliar to me. On the contrary: it represented all the security and stability that, until a very short time ago, I felt I wanted more than anything in the world—even Oliver. Oh, to have the opportunity, I had thought not long since, to fill my mind and my days with just such essential trivia. But now, experiencing it, I was filled with irritation, almost with disgust.

As I left my room to meet the arriving guests, I was delayed by Mrs Baines, who tied a wide black ribbon round my left arm, explaining that all the Allahabad ladies were doing likewise as a gesture of respect to the dead of Lucknow. She was sure I would not wish to be 'singular'. I submitted, and wondered, as she patted the bow in place with a satisfied air, what good could derive to the memory of Corporal Dines or the sixteen natives he had forced to 'Eat a Cawnpore Dinner' from my sable adornment. But I was a guest, so I followed my hostess meekly and contrived not to laugh when I came upon a knot of ladies and officers arguing as to whether secular music would be appropriate on such an occasion.

'What would *you* say?' earnestly enquired a young woman with trailing black streamers in her hair as well as on her arm.

'I would say,' I replied, 'by all means let us have any music you care to play. What we have most needed, after a full stomach, a hot bath and a good night's rest, has been a jolly party.' They looked shocked, as I had known they would, so I left them and applied myself to ices and almond macaroons in the garden. Very shortly, however, I was led back to the drawing-room like an invalid, placed upon a chair near Kate and instructed not to move a step: a whole phalanx of gallant officers lived only to serve the gustatory requirements of the 'Survivors'!

Seated thus in state, I felt rather as the Queen must feel at a Court Drawing-Room, but wished I enjoyed Her Majesty's privilege of instigating the conversation. Kate and I were surrounded by a changing but ever respectful crowd of men and women, who, in their efforts to be tactful while satisfying their curiosity, posed the most fatuous questions and volunteered the most inane opinions.

'Oliver!' I suddenly cried in my heart. 'Oh, Oliver, take me away. Rescue me from this unreality!'

Jessie had been informed that 'of course' the At Home for the Survivors was intended only for officers and their ladies, but since Pearl, a prized Survivor, was required to be present, she would be welcome to sit on the verandah with the child. She had also, that day, been given her *tiffin* on a tray in her bedroom. The British caste system, that had alternately annoyed and amused me in Lucknow in peace, had survived the agonies of Lucknow in siege.

After nearly an hour of polite platitudes, during which I had been presented with bon-bons, embroidered sachets filled with lavender petals, and an alarming handkerchief in the form of a Union Jack, bearing the word 'Lucknow' at its centre and edged with black braid, I made the excuse of attending to Pearl and escaped to the verandah. Charles had just arrived and was lost in admiration of his daughter, dressed at last in frills and flounces as small girls should be. The few steps I had taken along the verandah had been sufficient to assure me that Oliver was nowhere to be seen and, as Charles began to congratulate me on my appearance, I broke in impatiently, 'But, Charles, where is Oliver? Surely he is coming? You've seen him today, of course?'

'We shared quarters last night. He left very early this morning.'

'He *left*? But where did he go?'

Charles regarded me steadily for a moment, then drew me away to where we could talk in private.

'Laura, am I to presume that you have patched things up? Are matters between you and Oliver now as they were before ... before the night of the Alum Bagh beacon?'

I had not realized that he could know nothing of the sequence of letters by which Oliver and I had made our peace. Kate and Jessie now knew all, and I had taken it for granted, somehow, that Charles would also be in possession of the facts.

I laughed, happily I am sure, and replied, 'Yes, Charles. And better. We have at last reached a real understanding. In a strange way, that night proved a blessing to us both.'

'I see. I did not know ...' His voice was grave and his eyes guarded.

'Dear Charles,' I comforted, taking his hand, 'don't spoil things for me. I am so happy, and I want your happiness too. You must learn to look elsewhere.'

He sighed and laid his other hand over mine for a second; then squared his shoulders and straightened up.

'I only hope you are doing right.'

'Oh, I'm sure I am, as you will be when you think about it. But tell me, where did Oliver go, Charles? And when will he be back?'

'The answer to both questions is "I don't know". He left at dawn, taking Ishmial and Toddy with him—which was deuced inconvenient, since I was depending on one or other of them being around to get me some stuff from the bazaar and so on. All he told me was that he was going to see some family he knows in the district to make arrangements—living arrangements. Said he was going to fix up married quarters, so then, well, then I guessed that you ...'

'Married quarters!' I gasped.

'Yes. Is the wedding to be so soon?'

'Good heavens, I don't know!' But then, thinking rapidly as I spoke, I went on, 'There is no reason, I suppose, why it should be delayed,' and told Charles that Kate had agreed to accompany Jessie and Pearl to Mount Bellew, should I decide to remain in India.

'I see,' he commented stiffly, so that I at once felt guilty at relinquishing my duties to Pearl. 'And you feel now that you could live in Hassanganj again?'

'I cannot live without Oliver. So I must learn to live again in Hassanganj. And,' I added, gesturing around me, 'I don't think it will be as hard as I expected before renewing acquaintance with all this.'

'Well,' he said with a heavy sigh, 'all I can do is wish you happiness then, dear Laura.' Both voice and gaze were laden with emotion that I hoped he was not going to express. To my relief, he then took an envelope from his pocket and handed it to me. 'Oliver asked me to give you this.' He took my hand and pressed it and after a moment's hesitation, stooped and kissed my brow. Then he walked back to Pearl, leaving me alone with my letter. I tore open the seal and hastily unfolded the single sheet of paper. It bore one word: 'TOMORROW'.

Vexation. And delight. Maddening frustration and subdued ecstasy. The familiar irritation and the more recently acknowledged admiration.

All the conflicting emotions that Oliver had always aroused flooded over me again with the knowledge that, though he had not come when I wanted him, yet his coming was imminent.

I have little recollection of how I passed the rest of that evening, except that it was in every variety of impatience. There was music, I remember and, scruples overcome, a young officer with bushy whiskers laid his hand on his heart and sang a sentimental ballad that he first dedicated to my 'noble and heroic' self.

I suppose we ate dinner, and I must have slept for some part of the night, as I awoke refreshed and eager for the 'Tomorrow' that was now today.

At breakfast I found another envelope addressed in the familiarly unfamiliar scrawl of Oliver's left hand. Its presence went unmarked by the others, so I concealed it until I could open it alone. As soon as manners permitted, I excused myself from the table and hurried to my room. This time even the single word was lacking. Instead, wrapped in a screw of tissue paper, was a little ring of rubies and pearls, such as can be bought at any jeweller's booth in the bazaar. Intrinsically worthless, it remains my greatest treasure.

I slipped it on the appropriate finger and ran into the dressing-room to admire it in the mirror. As I moved my hand in the morning light to bring out the fire of the rubies and the glow of the pearls, I remembered my mother telling me that she was particularly fond of the little pearl and ruby pin she had given me and which I had treasured through all our vicissitudes, since the ruby is the token of love and the pearl of fidelity. Not that Oliver Erskine was likely to know that. Maddening man; if it was intended as an engagement present, why hadn't he brought it himself? I could have waited. But then it occurred to me that the trinket was more probably in lieu of an apology for his tardiness—a placatory offering before bearding the lioness in her den!

The ring calmed my impatience as it filled me with tenderness. I would allow him the last word. This time.

Then, suddenly, I was beset with anxiety regarding my appearance, and scanned the glass to make sure my borrowed dress became me. It was a pretty dress, its dusky rose adding some needed colour to my cheeks. As I carefully scrutinized my face, feature by feature, I recalled a pastel likeness of myself made a year or so before Emily's marriage, and that must still hang in the Mount Bellew drawing-room. A young round face, and neat chestnut hair parted demurely over what Oliver had termed my 'candid' brow. The eyes were a little too large, the brows rather too defined, and the chin too settled into determination for beauty, I remembered, as I remembered also the delicious sense of identity I had enjoyed on first seeing a representation of myself other than in a too-subjective mirror.

The face that looked back at me now was heart-shaped and high-cheekboned, and bore shadows that defined new planes and new lines that accentuated shadows. The magnanimous brow? That remained. The eyes were deeper set, though, and looked darker. The nose was finer, the once amply curved mouth was thinner, but the chin still indicated obstinacy. No great beauty there, I thought, but the expression was an improvement on the untried assurance of the girl in the pastel. The face in the mirror was acquainted with self-doubt, the eyes, though more guarded, were also more benign, and the curving mouth, while retaining its hint of humour, also indicated a steadier gentleness. The short hair was brushed into springy curls and shone in the morning sun.

I turned away, resigned, if not wholly satisfied.

Kate and Jessie had taken Pearl out to be admired by acquaintances, and Mrs Baines was busy with the ordering of her household. I picked up Mr Roberts's copy of Marcus Aurelius and went into the garden to wait.

A white bench stood beneath a spreading tree. A pleasant vista of sloping lawns and bright flowerbeds, backed by the ancient crenellations of the Mogul walls, spread before me. Idly flipping through the gilt-edged leaves of my book, I came upon the inscription: 'The perfection of moral character consists in this: in passing every day as the last.'

I had recalled those words with bitterness as I stood at my friend's grave. They had seemed inappropriate to what I had learned of Mr Roberts's character and knew of his despairing end. Yet he had thought so well of that short sentence that he had given it to me, in a special sense, in his own handwriting. I would never know the frame of mind in which he had copied it for me but, recalling the words at his graveside, I had realized that most of my objections to life in India, with Oliver, sprang, not from what I had already experienced, but from fear of an imaginary future. That swift second of illumination had been sufficient to change my mind, conform my stubborn will to my real desires, and ...

A shadow fell across the book. I looked up from my musings to find a servant before me, holding out a salver on which lay a sheet of notepaper halved and correctly cornered. I took it, nodded dismissal to the man, and opened it.

> *Mr Oliver Erskine presents his compliments*
> *and begs leave to call in person upon*
> *Miss Laura Hewitt.*

I sprang up, poor Marcus falling on his well-bound face in the grass.

'Wait!' I cried to the retreating servant. 'Wait, the *sahib* who brought this ... where is he?'

The servant turned in puzzlement, and I repeated my question.

'There, Miss-*sahib*!' he said, pointing to the corner of garden led on to by the verandah steps. 'He but waits your coming.'

I saw him then, standing at the top of the broad white steps, laughing at me. I suppose he wore new clothes and boots as I did, but I did not take them in. A memory invaded me of another day, and another flight of broad steps on which he had stood waiting for us to leave the carriage that had conveyed us to Hassanganj. He had changed as much as I had, I could see—yet remained so much the same.

I walked towards him—quietly—and only when he threw aside his riding crop and leapt down the steps, did I pick up my skirts and run.

Neither memory nor imagination, and both had been much exercised in the time since I last saw him, had prepared me for the vehemence of his embrace, nor the eagerness of my response. It was as though I had never before felt the touch of his lips or the pressure of his single arm around me. We could not let each other go. When we did draw apart it was solely that eyes might query eyes before our lips sought once again the answer that only lips can give.

He released me at last and, cupping my face in his hand, with the old glint in his eye and the familiar sardonic smile, said, 'This time, woman dear, you are sure. No more doubts. And oh, my love, you have no more fears!'

It was, as so often with him, a statement not a question, but I answered nevertheless: 'Yes, I am sure. Very sure. Oh, Oliver! How could either of us ever have doubted?'

'There will be time to discuss the matter—in the future,' he replied, 'but now ...' And grasping my hand he led me to the bench beneath the tree.

There followed then the usual concomitants of such happy occasions. There were promises made and reasons given and explanations proffered, and, as a result, a measure of deep and necessary joy. There were kisses and continued wonder that we should ever have known misunderstanding, and the breathless reiteration of each other's name.

But I knew, beneath the lovers' murmurings and the fervour of eyes and hands and lips so long deprived, that this was no happy ending, no culmination of desire, nor yet the blissful assuagement of hope deferred. It was something much better, much more filled with both promise and content.

I knew, in that sun-filled and water-whispering garden, with the neem shadows flickering on the grass and the butterflies hovering over the flowers, that this was but the first lesson in the long learning of love.

AUTHOR'S NOTE

Any reader familiar with the period and events covered by the foregoing tale will at once discover that certain small liberties have been taken with the known facts—all too well documented for any novelist's comfort—of history.

First, I have given the *cossid* Ungud (otherwise spelt Angad, Ungad and Anghad) a particular background and certain specific emotional responses to the happenings in which he became involved. This might fairly be construed as impertinence, but not, I hope, as inordinate imaginative liberty. All that is known of Ungud, apart from his three brief and dramatic entries into history during the Siege of Lucknow, is the fact that he was a pensioner of the Bengal Army, who, like many others, rallied to Sir Henry Lawrence's call for assistance at the beginning of May 1857, and that he was a tenant of a '*zemindar* of Oudh'. It is unlikely, though not impossible, that this *zemindar* was a European such as I describe. However, the loyalties and emotions I have ascribed to Ungud in relation to that *zemindar* are merely extensions of the loyalties and emotions that were obviously part of his make-up, as the accounts of his prowess and his relations with the officers of Lucknow make plain.

Secondly, there were only four known survivors of the massacre at the river in Cawnpore: Captain Mowbray Thomson, Lieutenant Delafosse and Privates Murphy and Sullivan. Several accounts, however, mention a 'British officer', 'gentleman' or 'white man', encountered by Havelock's troops after they had taken Cawnpore and were marching to Lucknow. This unfortunate, described as 'naked, heavily bearded' and 'almost certainly crazy', had been sheltered or perhaps imprisoned in some native village, and was thought to be a further survivor of the massacre at the river. Unfortunately, before he could be interrogated, he was shot—some accounts have it by the hostile villagers, another by the alarmed British soldiers. It is therefore at least debatable whether only four men survived the terror of the river.

In this connection also, my hero's musings on the cause of the massacre at the river, though unpopular in his own day and discredited in the accounts that appeared soon after the Mutiny, are not without foundation. In a brief note such as this it is not possible to go into detail regarding the many contradictions, anomalies and paradoxes observed by the survivors and stated in the depositions of witnesses when the matter came to be examined by the British authorities. That there was a struggle for precedence in the Court of Bithur was common knowledge at the time, and that the Nana Sahib always fervently protested his, at least, partial innocence, as 'he had never intended things to go so far' is a matter of historical fact. What was actually in the Nana's mind we can never now know, but I think it is at least possible that whatever scheme he set afoot was expanded, or even directly perverted, by one or other of the three men about him who were jockeying for position, power and a share in the dead Peshwa of Poonah's estate. The convoluted corruptions of a native court would have been well within the experience of a man with Oliver Erskine's background. For the rest, he comments on nothing that was not observed, and puzzled over, by the writers of one or other of the many written accounts.

A third point, though trivial in nature, has given me some concern. Most of the diaries and journals mention the 'heroic work' in the Hospital of Mesdames Polehampton, Barber and Galt in the early days of the Siege, but then indicate that, when these ladies were ordered by the authorities to terminate their endeavours, no further help was forthcoming from among the female population of the garrison. However, by way of contradiction and merely to confuse the poor researcher, it is asserted in more than one account that Miss Birch and her sister-in-law, Mrs Birch, continued to lend assistance to the doctors throughout the Siege, and Mr Gubbins, as always expansive but not particularly accurate, extols the 'Angels of Mercy' who had worked so faithfully in such horrible conditions throughout. Since the Birch ladies were at one time in residence in his house, it is possible that they were the angels in question. On this slim evidence, and for the sake of my story, I have allowed two of my fictional characters to swell the ranks of the 'Angels'.

Lastly, one of my fictional characters undergoes the experience of an actual member of the garrison, Captain Waterman, who, on finding himself alone in the deserted enclave on the night of 22nd November 1857, lost his mind, though happily only temporarily.

The reasons for the revolt of the sepoys in 1857 is still a matter for debate. The explanations given by the characters in this story, though not uniformly acceptable after the lapse of a century, are those held in common belief at the time of the uprising.

The life of a European *zemindar*, as sketched in Book II, remained very much the same until the *zemindari* system was abolished by the Indian Government in the early 1960s. The extraordinary mansion described as Hassanganj still stands, and is still occupied, in Uttar Pradesh in Northern India.